In Love and Friendship

HILARY NORMAN

DELACORTE PRESS/NEW YORK

Published by
Delacorte Press
1 Dag Hammarskjold Plaza
New York, N.Y. 10017

This work was first published in Great Britain by Hodder
and Stoughton Limited.

The characters and situations in this book are entirely
imaginary and bear no relation to any real person or actual
happening. If there are actual people bearing the full names
of any of the characters in this work of fiction, they are
unknown to the author and no reference is intended.

Copyright © 1987 by Hilary Norman

All rights reserved. No part of this book may be reproduced
or transmitted in any form or by any means, electronic or
mechanical, including photocopying, recording or by any
information storage and retrieval system, without the written
permission of the Publisher, except where permitted by law.
For information address: Delacorte Press, New York, New
York.

Manufactured in the United States of America

Library of Congress Cataloging in Publication Data

Norman, Hilary.
   In love and friendship.

   I. Title.
PR6064.074315   1987   823'.914
ISBN 0-385-29505-7
Library of Congress Catalog Card Number: 86–2181

For my father, Henry Norman

ACKNOWLEDGMENTS

There are a number of people and organizations to whom I owe thanks for their assistance during the research and writing of this book, but I would especially like to mention the following (in alphabetical order): Mr. Howard Barmad; the staff of the Bibliothek der Israelitischen Kultusgemeinde, Zurich; Mr. Howard D. Deutsch; Mr. Michael Snell, MCHir, FRCS; Mr. Michael Thomas; my editor, Miss Maureen Waller; Miss Rae White; and most of all, for her unfailing encouragement, humor, and invaluable recollections and advice, my mother.

In Love and Friendship

1

Alexandra Craig Alessandro laid down her pen on the blotter and turned over the page, so that the words sank, hazy and blue, through the soft, absorbent paper.

She pushed back her chair, stood and stretched, the muscles in her neck and shoulders taut and weary from effort.

She padded on bare feet to the open window, and gazed out over her dark garden. The soft Normandy breeze, laden with fragrance, fondled her long, black hair and slipped past her to ruffle the letter on her desk.

Beginnings. Beginnings were always the hardest. She had thought that once the decision was made, the die cast, the rest would flow swiftly out of her, like lava from a long-sealed volcano, but it was so painful going back.

Truth. That was the key.

She returned to the desk and looked at the letter, at her handwriting, slender and sloping, each word clearly separated, like her life from her daughter's at this moment. Brave, beautiful, wild Roberta, thousands of miles away in New York City with her father, and on the verge of embarking on a craziness that only her mother could attempt to halt.

Alexandra stared at what she had written so far, trying to see it afresh, to insinuate herself into Bobbi's mind. How would a seventeen-year-old girl, pledged to honesty, torn and twisted by conflicts, interpret this journal, part epitaph, part confession, part entreaty?

Her eyes settled on the second paragraph, and she began to read.

> . . . For many artists, the art is enough, the paintings and sculptures are their whole life, they need nothing more. For your mother, for many years, that was not true. I needed love more than art.
>
> With Andreas, in the beginning, there was perfect love, a complete rounding of the heart and soul, a warmth that seemed to me

strong enough to heat whole cities. And still that was not enough for either of us—we needed more. We needed you.

There is a price for everything in life, Bobbi, and I think the time has come for me to pay the price in full. Perhaps it should have happened years ago when you were still a child, but there was so much at stake, and I lacked the essential courage to tell you the truth. Suddenly, though, I am so deeply afraid for you— so terrified that you are about to make a mistake that may cost you your life—that I must find that courage. The lie has taken root, the stalk has grown thick and strong, and inevitably new leaves are budding. The truth, my love, is not intended to destroy the stalk or the new leaves; who knows, it may even strengthen them, and then I will be left alone with my fears.

I'm about to bring new disquiet into your young life, Bobbi, though God knows you've had your share already, and it is for this that I beg your forgiveness—and for nothing else.

Go into your father's library, Bobbi, and look at the painting "Life Drawing," the one you told me hangs over the fireplace. You may think you know it well enough already, but go look again.

See the five figures. See how the glow of the smallest, central silhouette illuminates the two figures closest to it, the one a woman, the other a man. See another figure, a second man, half in shadow, hovering on the edge of the glow. And see the last, a third man, remote and darkly shaded, but conspicuous nonetheless.

When you were a small girl, we hung that painting together in our old New York apartment, and you asked me to explain it to you. It seemed important to you in some way, but I would not— could not—answer you honestly, and I believe you soon forgot it. Now I shall translate the painting for you.

The central figure is you, Bobbi, and the woman is your mother. The man closest to us is your father, Andreas. The second man, the lonely, peripheral figure, is our good friend Dan Stone. The last is a stranger, mysterious, inviolable, and yet crucial to the painting and, perhaps, to you.

How difficult it is, now that I have begun, to find a way to tell the story clearly, in stark black and white. It is a story of those five people, inextricably bound to one another in a time frame of forty years. Perhaps the way for me to tell it most frankly, if not easily, is for me to imagine that you're sitting at my knee, a child again, listening while I spin old tales haphazardly, handing down your heritage as mothers so often do.

The words swam together, and Alexandra blinked and rubbed her eyes with the back of one hand before continuing. Down by her feet, on the oriental rug, Flic, her old German shepherd, whined softly and stirred in the depths of a dream. It was late, nighttime, and in most of the neighboring houses in the district, families drew together in sleep, and were warmly quiet.

Alexandra stood and switched off the overhead lights, so that only the desk lamp glowed in her study. She sat again. The house was silent with the loneliness of remembrance.

The single most important element in the story, I think, Bobbi, is the friendship between Andreas and Daniel, so perhaps I should begin there, with their first meeting, way back during the war in Europe. Perhaps I should just tell it the way it was . . . the way they told it to me . . .

Part One

2

Until he met Daniel Silberstein, what World War II meant to nine-year-old Andreas Alessandro could have been summed up in a few succinct words. It was a supreme pain in the ass!

It wasn't the food shortage; everyone knew that most wealthy farming families in Switzerland had enough to eat. It wasn't the cold winters without central heating; the Pfister–Alessandro farm in Küssnacht had its own *Holzerei*, where enough wood could easily be burned to fill their fireplaces as well as those of their close neighbors. What really annoyed Andreas was that just when he had been starting to get the hang of the farm tractor—just when his papa had finally promised to teach him to drive the Horch— the government had banned all private automobiles because of the dumb old fuel crisis!

That was what troubled Andreas about the war. How was he ever going to have what he dreamed about—what his papa encouraged him to dream about—if he couldn't even learn to drive? For more than two years, the Horch had stood idle and in disgrace, a German car, in the stables. By the time the war was over, he'd probably have forgotten all his father had ever taught him. And who knew if the war was ever going to end anyway?

It wasn't even *their* war!

Summer was over, autumn on the way, and it was an afternoon of perfect Indian summer, dappled and sweet-smelling, when Andreas closed the front door with a bang, jumped down the five porch steps, and ran toward the stables, Rolf at his heels.

"Gruetzi miteinand!" old Albert Mutschler called from the tack room.

"Gruetzi, Albert." Andreas headed for the end stable as usual, while the black German shepherd skittered in the dirt, trying to rattle the horses.

Albert shuffled over to the low stone wall and took out his pipe. "Never knew a boy like it," he muttered, filling it with tobacco.

"The face and hair of an angel, just like his mama, the black eyes of his papa, but he acts more like a grown man with a secret mistress than a nine-year-old boy."

The object of Andreas's passion, the gleaming black Horch, stood silent in the hay where it had stood since the April decree two years before.

Andreas stroked the hood. "All that power, just waiting to be brought back to life," he said softly.

Rolf padded into the stable and nuzzled his master's hand.

"Impatient for your walk, boy?" Andreas patted the dog, then polished the hood where his hand had left a mark. "Okay, I'm coming."

Outside, Albert puffed contentedly at his pipe. "Homework finished?"

"Would my mother let me out of the house if it wasn't, Albert?"

Albert shook his head and smiled, showing the large black gap between his remaining front teeth. "Where are you going today?"

Andreas shrugged. "Nowhere special."

"Just remember to get back well before dark—"

"And if I see strangers, run!" Andreas finished the familiar caution.

Albert grunted and relit his pipe.

They set off westward at a fair pace. The land in that section of the farm sloped steeply and was planted with apple orchards since during the frosty spring nights the cold, heavy air could drain away to the valley below, saving the young fruit from premature ruin. Rationing had placed the orchards strictly out of bounds to Andreas and Rolf, but since the fruit was just starting to ripen, and since picking wouldn't begin for another few weeks, a little harmless poaching was unlikely to be discovered.

For one moment, as they approached the first orchard, Andreas thought the pickers had beaten them to the crop after all. Through a gap in the thicket of trees outside the orchard, he spotted a bare, brown-skinned arm snaking up to a fruit-laden branch and plucking from it a shiny red apple.

Rolf growled softly. Andreas hushed him and, crouching low, crept closer for a better view.

This was no authorized fruit picker. This was a tall, skinny, dark-haired boy, covered, rather than dressed, in shabby blue trousers and a torn shirt, sleeves rolled up to the elbows.

Sinking to his knees in the long grass, the young thief took a large bite out of the apple, shut his eyes and munched quickly. He looked like a gypsy, his hair overlong and his face dirty. Apparently ravenous, he devoured the apple and core, and got up for more.

Andreas straightened. "Not so fast!"

The trespasser jumped in alarm, pulled down a branch of the tree, snapped off two hard apples and hurled them at Andreas. One of them hit right on target, striking Andreas on the side of his head, and the boy fled, scrambling like a mad thing through the trees toward the fence, where he tripped over a root and fell headlong.

"Stay, Rolf!" Andreas commanded. The boy didn't look much older than himself and was clearly no match for the powerful dog. Cautiously he approached. The stranger lay flat on his stomach, apparently winded.

"Are you all right?" Andreas bent over the inert body, but the boy rolled suddenly over and struck out at him, bringing him down in the mud. Andreas yelled in surprise and anger, and tried to sit up, but the boy punched him in the stomach and they rolled over and over, fists flailing, feet kicking.

"For God's sake!" Andreas gasped. The boy thrust his knee into his groin but missed, and Andreas hit him in the face, his knuckles gashing the thin flesh under his left eye. Blood spurted, splashing them both, and for an instant Andreas sensed his opponent's naked fear and thought he might surrender, but then he seemed to gather strength again, and the fight was on. For what felt like forever they struggled like savages while Rolf quivered on the sidelines, still frustrated by his master's last command, until at last they lay side by side on the muddy earth, totally exhausted and fighting for breath. Logic kept them from each other's throats; they were equally matched, equally bruised and battered except for the bloody gash on the thief's face. The battle was over.

Anxious because his master was no longer moving, Rolf trotted over and licked his forehead. Weakly, Andreas patted his muzzle. Curiosity overcame anger. Still gasping for breath, he turned his head and looked at the stranger.

"Why were you stealing our fruit?"

"Because I was starving." The accent was unfamiliar.

Andreas sat up. "Really starving, or just hungry?"

The other boy lay still, utterly defeated. "I haven't eaten anything for four days."

Andreas's eyes widened. Having eaten solid farm breakfasts, lunches, and suppers every day of his life as far back as he could remember, it was simply not in his frame of comprehension to imagine what starvation was like.

"Are you a German?" he asked.

"I'm a Jew."

"What's your name?"

"Daniel."

"Daniel what?"

The boy hesitated before offering his surname. "Silberstein," he said.

Andreas stood up painfully, brushing some of the mud and grass from his clothes. He walked to the nearest tree, selected the most unblemished apple he could see, and picked it.

"I'm Andreas Alessandro," he said to the boy, and, kneeling down beside him, placed the apple in his hand.

3

Daniel Silberstein had no childhood.

He was four years old when his uncle Leopold was beaten and left for dead by brownshirts because he wanted to marry the pretty Lutheran girl he had known and loved since they were both seventeen. One of Daniel's earliest memories was of his uncle being carried on a stretcher by two strangers into his parents' house on Guntherstrasse in Nuremberg. Daniel remembered it particularly clearly because it was May 6, his birthday. When he had last seen his uncle, he was a laughing, handsome man with a straight body and strong limbs. Now his face resembled a bleached skull, his eyes were full of horror, and he was paralyzed from the chest down. Daniel remembered his mother's weeping and his father's silence, and he remembered that the two strangers had carried his uncle up the staircase to his room, where he stayed for the next three years, a prisoner entombed between clean white sheets, until Daniel's mother helped him to swallow an overdose of morphine.

Daniel had many other memories of that year, 1935, because it was the year when so many things in their lives seemed to change.

It was the year when his sister, Gisela, was born in the Jüdische Krankenhaus, and his mother wept for three days after she and the baby came home, because this was no time to bring a new life into the world.

It was the year when Fräulein Krauss, the manageress of the fine linen department in his father's department store on Karolinenstrasse, stopped giving Daniel the boxes of jellied fruit he loved.

It was the year when his father stopped going to the store and stayed home every day, because the Nazis had robbed him of his business.

It was the year when the flaxen-haired twin daughters of Pastor Fuchs were forbidden to come to the ballet classes his mother held in the basement of their house.

It was the year when Daniel's best friend, Simon Löwenthal, left for America because Simon's father was a doctor, and had an exit visa.

And it was the year when Daniel's parents began arguing because his mother thought they should move to Berlin, because things were better there than in Nuremberg.

Daniel remembered 1936 and 1937 clearly too; they stood out in his memory for their excruciating dullness. Everyone seemed either depressed or afraid. Poor Uncle Leopold just lay upstairs in his bed, too sick to talk to anyone most of the time. His sister, Gisela, though pretty as a picture, was boring in every other respect, and squandered most of his mother's time now that she was up on her feet and always heading for trouble of some sort. Daniel wasn't allowed out of the house unless his mother or father came along, and though they let him invite friends in to play, it wasn't so much fun as being out on the street. The streets always looked safe enough to Daniel.

He escaped the dreariness twice in 1937 by playing truant from the Jüdische Kindergarten.

The first time, he took a tram into the center of town and got off at bustling Karolinenstrasse. It seemed forever since he'd been there last, and he was keen to know what his father's store looked like now that it belonged to Nazis.

It looked exactly as it always had done—except that the sign over the main entrance, which had previously borne the name SILBERSTEIN, now read FRANCKE, and a poster beside it said JUDEN UNERWÜNSCHT.

The second time he played truant was when Adolf Hitler came to Nuremberg for the *Reichsparteitag* festivities. Everyone knew that Hitler was going to make a speech in the Luitpoldhain, not far from where they lived on Guntherstrasse, where the Nazis had flattened the trees and destroyed the great park to build their stadium. Daniel knew it would make his parents mad if he went, but it was time he saw what a Nazi looked like.

He never saw Hitler, but he did see a great many Nazis, thousands of them, men and boys, in black and brown uniforms, marching and singing, grasping banners and standards, and at one time, as Daniel craned his neck and stood on his toes to get a better look, a stout blond woman wearing a green hat with a feather plucked Daniel off the ground and held him high in the air, as if he, too, was a banner.

"Look, boy, look!" she proclaimed. "The Führer is there! Can you see?"

But all Daniel saw was Fräulein Krauss from his father's store. She was standing on a bench with two men, waving crazily with one hand and clutching a photograph of the Führer in the other. Her face was alight with joy, tears streamed down her cheeks, her mouth was a wide, red slash of hysteria as she screamed *"Heil Hitler!"* over and over again, a high-pitched animal sound that bobbed over the general clamor of the mob to Daniel's shocked ears.

Fräulein Krauss scared him more than the rest of the Nazis put together, and he wriggled out of the blond woman's grasp, kicking her accidentally in the stomach so that she gasped in surprise and anger, and he ran home as fast as he could, forgetting that he was supposed to be at school, forgetting that he was bound to be punished, thinking only of the safety of the big, dull house in Guntherstrasse.

Daniel did a lot of thinking after that day. He spent more time thinking than was good for a boy his age, but as 1937 stretched into 1938 there wasn't much else to do.

He thought about dodging school again, but since the *Reichsparteitag* episode, his mother came every day with Gisela to collect him. Daniel thought about how much he hated being a prisoner at home, even if it was a lovely house with beautiful things in it, richly patterned rugs, spice-scented wood, leather books that he liked to hold in his hands even if they were too grown-up for him to understand, and no shortage of toys for him and Gisela to play with.

He wondered how it felt to be Uncle Leopold, trapped in bed upstairs. He thought about how his mother was changing, how thin she was, how her lovely black hair had wisps of gray in it, and he thought his father seemed stranger every month, hardly ever smiling, his hair disappearing instead of growing white, his dark moustache drooping against the pallid skin making him look like a sad walrus most of the time.

Daniel felt sorry for Gisela because she had nothing to look forward to, though she seemed unaware that she was missing anything, and smiled and giggled whenever he played with her, for nothing in the world was better than a game with her big brother.

In September 1938, Daniel received a letter from Simon Löwenthal, written in a place called Kingston, New York, in the United States of America. Simon wrote that his father now worked at the local hospital, that they lived quite near New York City, which was the greatest town in the world, bigger even than Munich, that he had made new friends in Kingston, but that he still missed Daniel a heck of a lot.

Daniel showed his mother the letter, and asked her if they could go to America, but she cried and tore it up—and later she stuck the pieces back together, and told him she was sorry and smiled her gentle smile, and said that they couldn't go to America but that things were bound to get better before long—but Daniel knew she was lying to make him feel good.

"Couldn't we go somewhere else, even if it isn't America?" he asked her later. "Anywhere, so long as there aren't any Nazis?"

His mother turned her back on him, and he knew she was crying again, but when she turned to face him, there was a new, fierce expression in her eyes.

"I'll talk to Papa," she said. "I don't know where we can go, but we must leave this place." She hugged him tightly. "It won't be America because your papa couldn't get a job as easily as Simon's papa—"

"I don't care where we go, Mutti!" Daniel pleaded. "I hate it here!"

She held him even tighter. "Try to be patient, *Liebling.* Your papa loves this house very much. It's hard for him to think of leaving because he worked so hard for a long time so we could be comfortable and happy here—"

"But we're not happy!" Daniel thought he could feel the walls of the house squeezing him, suffocating him. "Talk to Papa, please, Mutti! Make him take us away!"

She tried to soothe him, alarmed by the fierceness in him. "I will, Daniel, I promise."

He pulled away from her, and his eyes were dark with fear. "I'm afraid if we stay here," he said.

"What will it take to convince you, Josef?" Antonia Silberstein asked wearily. "Nuremberg is finished—*our* Nuremberg. We have to leave."

Josef was a good, gentle man, she realized, but too passive for the times. Ever since that terrible morning three years before, when his soft-spoken accountant, Werner Francke, had slid like a smug snake into his office with the single slip of paper authorizing him to "Aryanize the store"—to steal his employer's business on behalf of the state—her husband had become what Antonia now regarded as dangerously fatalistic.

"What will it take?" she repeated.

Josef sat back in his armchair, his eyes vacant behind his spectacles. "You know how I feel, Toni," he shrugged. "Everything we have is here."

"What do we have? Our house? For how much longer?" Her voice was reasonable and low, but her eyes were bitter. "They took the store. What makes you think they won't want the house too?"

Josef's face hardened resentfully. "You forget I'm a German patriot, Antonia. I served my country during the war. They will remember."

Antonia knelt on the rug and took her husband's hands in hers. "Josef, dearest, they made our housemaid leave our home because a pretty young Aryan girl under the same roof as a Jewish man is considered in physical danger." There were tears in her eyes. "Is this the way they treat a patriot?"

His mouth was set defiantly. "What makes Berlin so much better than Nuremberg?"

She shook her head. "Nothing. It's too late for Berlin." She paused. "I think we should go to my cousins in Friedrichshafen."

"To Sigi? His wife isn't even a Jew."

"As good as. She's one of us, Josef." She lowered her voice. "I've already written, and Sigi sent word yesterday. They can help us."

Josef sat forward, suspicious. "How?"

"Constance to Kreuzlingen in Switzerland is the shortest crossing over the Bodensee." Antonia watched him carefully.

For an instant a flash of fear crossed his face—then suddenly he snorted loudly. "You're joking, Toni!" He began to laugh. "My God, Toni, for a moment I thought you were serious."

Slowly she stood, went to the sideboard, took a cigarette and lit it, then turned to face him. "I am serious."

The laughter left his face. "You're mad," he said flatly. "The pressure's getting to you." His mouth worked. "We have no passports. All our possessions—all we have is here, in this house, in Nuremberg. We have two young children—"

"Daniel is desperate to leave. He begs me every day to persuade you, Josef."

"In case you've forgotten, Antonia, you have a crippled brother upstairs who can't go to the bathroom, let alone take a boat ride across the Bodensee . . ."

There was silence in the room.

"I'll take care of Leopold," Antonia said quietly at last.

He stared at her.

"Don't worry about Leopold." Her voice was steady as a rock. "He and I have worked this out together."

Josef stood up suddenly, his forehead beaded with sweat, his fists clenched. "Listen to me, Toni, and listen well. Your idea is insane. *Insane!* I've told you, I am a German patriot. I have a drawerful of medals. I love my country. The Nazis will go so far and no farther, believe me. The German people will not stand for more. When things settle down, they will drop these restrictions. No one is really being hurt."

"What about Leo? Didn't they hurt him?"

"Your brother was a fool. Wanting to marry a shiksa. I didn't need Hitler to tell me that was a sin."

Contempt blazed quickly into Antonia's eyes. She stubbed out her cigarette so vehemently that the ashtray spun like a top on the sideboard. And then, just as suddenly, her anger dissolved.

"You're the fool, Josef Silberstein," she said wearily. "I can forgive you only because I know that in normal times you would never have said such a thing to me, and because, in spite of everything, I love you."

He stood in the middle of the room, his arms hanging limply by his sides, shame in his eyes, saying nothing.

"But you mark my words, Josef," she went on. "Things will get worse, much worse, before long. I listen to people, I keep my eyes and my ears open, and I tell you something terrible will happen soon." She came within an inch of him and looked so deeply into his eyes that he flinched. "And you will have to change your mind then, Josef. I only pray it won't be too late."

On November 9, Gisela began to complain of a bad sore throat and headache. That afternoon, and right through the night, while the SS pogrom raged in Nuremberg and throughout Germany, the child vomited and her fever soared, but it was late the next afternoon before their neighbor, Dr. Grünbaum, was able to call.

"Scarlet fever," he diagnosed when he had made his examination. "Can't be positive until the rash has developed, but there's a minor epidemic in the area."

"Take off your coat, Karl, and let me make some tea," Antonia offered. "You look exhausted."

"Coffee would be better. Black, plenty of sugar."

They went into the salon, and Antonia poured from a silver pot.

"Such normality in these homes." The doctor sighed wistfully. "And out there in the streets the world is a festering scab, a filthy sty crawling with swine." His eyes were bleary, his face was unshaven, and there was blood on his coat. "I've seen fifteen patients already today, Toni. Fifteen of our friends. All of them beaten, most of them in shock."

She was appalled. "Can I do anything, Karl? Once Josef gets back, I could help you on your rounds."

"Thank you, Toni, no." Grünbaum smiled. "You must stay with Gisela, she'll need her mama. It's a nasty illness. Where is Josef?"

"With friends." She shrugged. "This sitting around drives him crazy. I encourage him to get out."

"And Daniel?"

She smiled. "Upstairs with Leopold. He reads to his uncle often now after school. He's a good boy."

"Let's hope he doesn't catch this from his sister." He finished his coffee and stood up to leave. "Lock your doors tonight, Toni. And stay clear of the windows, for God's sake. If those vermin come into the suburbs, these are the houses they'll choose as their targets."

She saw him to the front door. Nervously she patted her hair. "Karl—"

"Yes?" Grünbaum buttoned his coat and picked up his hat.

"Can Gisela be moved?"

"Definitely not," he said firmly. "With scarlet fever there can be complications."

"What kind of complications?"

"That depends. Abscesses quite often. Mastoiditis sometimes." He opened the door, anxious to be on his way. "Unlikely, Toni, but bed rest is important."

"I see." Calmly, she kissed him on the cheek. "Thank you for coming, Karl."

At ten minutes past three on the afternoon of November 12, while Antonia was teaching a small class in the basement, and while Daniel was sitting with Gisela up in the nursery, two agents of the Gestapo came for Josef.

Antonia heard the doorbell, and knew instinctively. Briefly she closed her eyes, thanking God with all her heart that once again Josef was not at home.

Quickly she sent the class out through the studio door, scribbled a message of warning for Josef and gave it to Frau Cohn, the pianist. Then she flew upstairs, ordered Daniel to lock himself in with Gisela, and went back down to open the front door.

"Frau Silberstein?"

She nodded.

"Wo ist Ihr Mann?"

"Ich weiss nicht. Er ist gerade nicht hier."

They came in, closing the door firmly behind them.

"Wir werden warten."

For two and a half hours, while the two men waited for Josef to return, Antonia sat opposite them in icy silence, moving only to pour them glass after glass of tea. For two and a half hours, while the men spoke to each other in short, deliberately sinister sentences, moving frequently around the salon, eyeing the Silbersteins' books and works of art, touching with fat, acquisitive fingers the heavy drapes, the Bechstein piano, the gold-edged walnut cabinet, Antonia prayed that Frau Cohn had got to Josef, that he wouldn't come back, that he would have the sense to stay away.

And then, as suddenly as they had come, they grew apparently bored and stood up.

One of them, a plump Berliner with greasy hair and bad teeth, nodded curtly at her. "You will please make sure your husband stays at home tomorrow."

Antonia stared at him.

"Natürlich," she said.

Josef came in through the basement door just after nightfall. Antonia was waiting for him in the salon. Swiftly they embraced. He was ashen-faced and trembling.

"I was afraid they might hurt you, Toni," he whispered, kissing her hair.

She began to weep, the first tears she had shed that day. "Thank God you weren't here . . ."

"I wanted to come straightaway, but the Cohns made me stay with them until Edith Grünbaum telephoned to say they had left."

Antonia pulled out of his arms and wiped her eyes with the back of her hand. "Karl and Edith are good friends, Josef." Tenderly she stroked his cheek. "We have to talk now, *Liebchen.*"

He sat down heavily, suddenly exhausted. He took off his glasses, propped them on the arm of the chair and rubbed the bridge of his nose with his fingertips. Then he saw the suitcases against the wall.

"Antonia." His face grew even paler. "Why are the cases down here?"

She took the silver-rimmed stopper out of the whiskey decanter and poured out two double measures, handing one to her husband. The steadiness of her hands amazed her.

"I asked you a question." Josef's voice was harsh and frightened. "Why are the suitcases in the salon?"

Antonia sat down beside his chair on the rug and took hold of his right hand. "You and Daniel are leaving here tonight, Josef."

"I beg your pardon?" Josef asked politely, his eyes opaque with shock.

She smiled at him brightly, her voice calm, as if she were organizing a family picnic. "I've packed warm clothes, books, and there's a hamper of food in the kitchen." She squeezed his hand. "I've sewn twenty thousand marks into the lining of one case, and my diamond ring, the brooch and earrings into the other. There's more than enough gas in the car—"

"What car?" Josef spoke starkly. "We sold the car."

"Karl has lent us Edith's father's Hispano. It hasn't been driven any distance for two years, but Karl starts it regularly—"

"Toni."

"—and there's enough gas to get you to the Swiss border, but you won't need that much; I've bought train tickets for you both from Augsburg to Friedrichshafen, and Karl will collect the car from—"

"Antonia!" Josef snatched his hand away and put his glasses back on his nose, his fingers trembling violently, his eyes growing large beneath the thick lenses. "Are you insane, woman! Have you lost your senses? What are you talking about? I'm not going anywhere, and certainly not alone."

"Not alone, no," she soothed him. "With Daniel." A small, dark pain, which had started in her head after the Gestapo officers had left, was growing now, beginning to spread through her like a great inkblot, chilling her, threatening to weaken her resolve. With a great effort she pushed it back. "Now please, Josef, let me finish. There's so little time—"

"Shut up, Toni!" He leapt to his feet and dragged her roughly up from the floor. His hands clamped around her forearms like steel cuffs, her frightened face bobbed within inches of his own as he shook her as he would an animal. "For the love of God, what are you saying? You must be crazy! What's got into you?"

"What's got into me?" Gathering all her strength, Antonia shoved Josef back down into the chair. "The *Nazis,* that's what! Adolf Hitler! Heinrich Himmler and his goddamned SS!" Half hysterical now, she panted, "What's got into me, Josef? The two sadists who sat here in this room all afternoon, so politely, waiting for almost three hours to take my husband away!"

"Toni, please . . ."

Again she fought the pain, desperate to have the hideousness over and done with. "Josef, they'll come back for you tomorrow, and they'll never bring you back!"

"But why do you keep talking about *me,* Toni?" Josef pleaded, rage gone, confusion in its place again. "What about you? What about Gisela?"

"We can't come. Not tonight." She found the calm place again, the safe spot in the center of her agony that allowed her to speak normally. "She's too sick to be moved. Karl said so. He said she could develop an abscess which might lead to mastoiditis—that can turn to meningitis. My cousin died of meningitis, Josef, remember?" Gently she tried to comfort him. "In a few days, when the worst is over, we'll follow you, my love. You mustn't worry about us, the Gestapo aren't taking women and babies, just men." She paused. "And boys."

"Boys? Young boys?"

"Not today, perhaps, but soon."

Josef shook his head, trying to clear the tangle of thought that was like a thick mist behind his eyes. "Daniel? You think they'd take Daniel?"

"He's a male Jew. Why not?"

"But that would be inhuman."

Again Antonia knelt on the rug, and this time she reached up and took his face between her hands. "Josef, they are not human. These people are insane. They are monsters."

The room was silent, apart from the ticking of the clock and their breathing.

"We won't go," he said presently.

She kissed the bald part of his head and felt the tears pricking her eyes again as she selected her next weapon and plunged it into him.

"If you don't, Josef, our son may never reach his bar mitzvah."

His sigh was a shudder.

"We'll wait until Gisela is better."

"No."

"It's unthinkable." He shuddered again. "I can't leave my wife and baby."

Again there was silence.

"How long—?" Josef hesitated. "How long before you could follow us?"

"Karl says Gisela should be out of danger before the end of the week." She held her breath.

Very slowly, like a sleepwalker, Josef took her hands away from his face and kissed each of them, palm upward. The lenses of his glasses were misted, hiding his expression.

"Come upstairs, Toni," he said softly.

"Josef, you can't forget this by going to bed."

"I'm forgetting nothing," he said fiercely, brokenly. "We have a few hours, don't we? Let's not waste them, for pity's sake."

She took the glasses from his face then, with great gentleness, and she saw the pain and tears in his eyes, and she saw that she had won, and that she had lost.

It was four in the morning when they woke Daniel. The boy lay on his back, his dark hair curling over his forehead, his lips slightly parted, and when Antonia kissed him, he smiled up at her and murmured, his voice still fuzzy and sweet with sleep: "I dreamed we were all in America, Mutti. . . . And Gisela was well, and . . ." His voice faded and he sat up. "What's the matter?" He saw his father in the doorway. "Why are you dressed, Papa? Where are you going?"

Josef could not speak. His face was hidden in the dark shadows.

His mother took his hand. "You have to get up now, Daniel. It's time to leave."

The moonlight from the window caught Daniel's face—his eyes were bright and suddenly alert, half hopeful, half fearful. "Are we going to America, Mutti?"

She shook her head. "Not to America, but on a long journey. Do you remember I promised you would leave here?"

"Away from the Nazis?"

She knelt and took him in her arms. "I hope so, *Liebling,* I hope so. You're going to Onkel Sigi and Tante Gretchen." She stroked his hair and looked deep into his eyes. "They live very near Switzerland, and I hope they will help you to go there."

Daniel frowned, his eyes suddenly suspicious. "What about you and Papa?"

Antonia bit her lip, and her voice quivered a little. "Papa is taking you on the first part of the journey, Daniel, but Gisela and I will join you very soon."

"No!" he shrieked suddenly, piercingly. "I won't leave you!"

"Hush," she whispered. "You'll wake your sister."

He pulled away angrily. "I don't care. I'm not going."

"She needs her sleep, Daniel, you know that. She must get well very quickly, so that we can come and join you and Papa."

"But I told you, I'm not going without you," he said stubbornly. "Why do we have to go now anyway?" His eyes narrowed. "Is it because of those men who came?"

"They came to take your papa away from us, Daniel." She took him by the arms. "And they're going to come back for him later today. That's why he has to go."

She looked over her shoulder at Josef, who stood still as a statue, afraid to move in case he broke into pieces, and then she looked back at her son. Only seven years old, and being exposed to torments she'd never dreamed could exist when she was his age.

"But why do I have to go?" His voice shook. "Do they want to take me away, too?"

"Oh, no, of course not, *Liebling.*" She kept her voice very low so that Josef couldn't hear. "But Papa needs you. He can't go on this journey alone—he isn't strong like some fathers, and he's very unhappy about leaving your sister and me, even for a few days."

Daniel looked her in the eye. "Is it really for a few days, Mutti?"

Unnerved by his directness, Antonia swallowed hard, and when she answered her voice was throaty. "I hope so, Daniel."

He knew then that she was lying to him again, just as she'd lied when she'd told him things would get better one day. They wouldn't get better. And maybe she and Gisela wouldn't come at all. He thought if he screamed, perhaps, and cried, that maybe his parents might change their minds . . . but something deep inside him said they would not.

"I'll go," he said.

An hour later, after the three had stood together, their arms around each other, in Gisela's room, looking down at her flushed face, and after they had all stood together in the salon, looking at the suitcases, weeping, Daniel took his mother's hand and led her out into the hall.

"What about Onkel Leo?" he said, looking up at her.

Antonia froze. "What about him, Daniel?"

"How will he come? Who will carry him?"

Her mind raced. This was one truth she would keep from him with her last breath. "Onkel Karl will come with us," she lied.

"And Tante Edith?" he asked quickly.

"Of course," she answered briskly. "They don't want to stay in Nuremberg either."

"May I go and say good-bye to Onkel Leo, please?"

"You'll see him soon. It's a pity to wake him."

"Just the same, I'd like to see him." His small face was determined, and Antonia realized with a shock of terror that he hadn't believed a word she'd said.

"All right. But don't be long."

When he came downstairs again, Daniel's cheeks were marked with dried tears, but there was no protest.

"Onkel Leo said he'd like to talk to you when Papa and I have gone."

"All right." She turned to Josef and was alarmed by the pallor of his face and the rigidity of his body. He seemed too shocked to speak, as if a single word might crack his resolve. "Josef, are you all right? Can you drive the car?"

He nodded, but still did not speak.

Daniel went to his father and, looking up into his face, took his hand. "Papa? Do you think we should go now?"

Josef stared, unblinking, ahead of him for another moment. And then, like a man waking from a deep sleep, he stirred and looked down at his son.

"Yes. Yes, Daniel, we must go."

Antonia opened a drawer in the secretary and took out the envelope, which she handed to her husband.

"The tickets. If there's any trouble, you're committing no crimes, remember, just going to visit family. If you have no choice, mention Gretchen's name, that should help—but try to keep them out of it. They're helping others, too."

Turning to Daniel, she took the fine gold chain with the small six-pointed Magen David that hung around her throat and, kneeling, refastened it at the nape of his neck. Her hands were icy as she tucked it inside his sweater, but he didn't murmur.

"Keep it for me, Daniel."

He came into her arms and nuzzled against her, his eyes gleaming with unshed tears. "I'll give it back to you when you come, Mutti."

Josef cleared his throat. "I'm going to load the car, Toni. Will you help me, please?" He looked at Daniel gravely. "You stay in the house and listen for your sister."

The night was clear, the stars fairly littering the sky with uneven, untidy bunches of light. When the cases were in the trunk, Antonia turned toward the house, but Josef caught at her.

"Wait, Toni."

Her face was very pale, her dark eyes luminous in the moonlight. "Oh, Josef," she whispered despairingly, "I didn't mean it to happen like this."

"I know," he said fiercely. "Do you think I don't know that, Toni?" Gently he drew her close and kissed her forehead, stroking away the heavy hair. "Neither of us wanted it."

And then she was weeping, the tears streaming down her

cheeks. "Oh, God!" she burst out wretchedly. "I didn't mean to cry! I wanted to be so strong—"

"You *are* strong—the strongest woman I ever met." Josef's eyes glittered.

"I know you'd rather have stayed, whatever the consequences," Antonia whispered tearfully, "but Daniel needs his father with him, and—"

"And Daniel must have his chance to live," he finished quietly. He paused. "What will they do when they find we've gone?"

She stepped back, and her tears dried. "They will be glad," she said lightly, "that there are two less Jewish males in Nuremberg."

Josef looked at the house and saw Daniel standing silhouetted in the doorway, a small and lonely figure.

"You lied to him about Leopold, didn't you?"

She said nothing.

"What will happen to him when you and Gisela leave?"

"Whatever Leo wants, that will happen."

Josef shook his head, his eyes full of compassion.

Antonia kissed him once more, hard on the mouth. "You must go now," she said. "It's important you catch the first train from Augsburg, and you must drive normally, carefully, so you are not noticed."

He walked ahead of her up the path to the house. Swiftly he kissed the tip of his right index finger and touched the mezuzah on the doorpost.

"Perhaps none of us will ever see this house again once you and Gisela have left," he said, his voice strangled in his chest. He took her in his arms and held her. "Go upstairs and look after our little girl," he whispered, his own tears starting to fall onto her dark hair. "I don't want to see you standing here when we drive away." He kissed her again. "Come soon, my love," he said abruptly, and released her.

Quickly, her heart bursting, Antonia knelt and hugged Daniel to her. "Look after your papa," she said, and then, with her mouth so close to his ear that Josef wouldn't hear, "and if Onkel Sigi says it's time to take the boat to Switzerland before Gisela and I arrive, make sure you do as your uncle says."

He pulled away, "But Mutti—"

"Promise me!" she said sharply. Her eyes were ablaze with love. "I give you my solemn word, Daniel, we will come as soon as Gisela is well, but you must promise me you will get away from the Nazis. *Promise* me!"

Daniel swallowed the lump in his throat, fighting against the tears that burned behind his eyes. He nodded dully. "I promise, Mutti."

Josef took him by the hand and led him back down the path, and put him into the car. And he looked back, just once, as Antonia closed the front door, and was gone.

Inside, Antonia climbed the stairs and walked into the nursery.

Gisela was still sleeping. Antonia touched her forehead with the palm of her hand . . . still feverish, but at least she was no worse. "By morning, my little love," she whispered, "we'll be all alone." She bent and kissed the damp curls. "Get well quickly, my sweetheart, so we can follow Papa and Daniel."

She straightened, and left the room.

At Leopold's door, she paused, and tapped lightly.

"Come in."

Her brother's waxy face smiled wearily at her. "Have they gone?"

She nodded.

"How's the little one?"

"Not bad. She'll get over it."

He coughed, the hollow, painful sound from his chest that was always followed by agonized wheezing. "And you, Toni?" he asked, when he could breathe again. "Are you still strong enough? To cope alone?"

Again she nodded, not trusting herself to words.

Leopold sighed, but it was a blissful sound, a long exhalation of contentment. "Thank you, Toni," he said.

Antonia's hands were behind her back where he couldn't see them, clenched in tight fists. "Are you sure, Leo? Are you really ready?"

Bitterly he laughed, and his eyes were wet with tears. "Antonia, I have been ready for three years."

Silently she went to the medicine cupboard fastened to the wall opposite the window, and opened it. Her fingers closed on a glass bottle, and she turned around.

"Are you really sure, Leo?" Her eyes were pleading. "Won't you let me look after you? We can manage, Leo—they might not separate—"

"Antonia." His voice was a rebuke, and there was a cutting note of anger in it. "Life is agony for me. I will never let them touch me again." He grew gentle again. "I want to die, Toni."

Quickly she mixed the fluid in the bottle with water from the tap in the corner basin, and poured the mixture into a small medicine glass.

She brought him the glass and sat on the edge of the bed. Her voice was even now, as calm as when she had told her husband and son to leave. "Do you want to pray, Leo?"

His answer was scornful. "For what?" Again he grew kinder, aware of her pain. "If you want, Toni, say the Shema for me. But later . . . when it's over."

Antonia bent, kissed him once, and then, propping his head and shoulders as she had done a thousand times for a thousand pathetic meals, she placed the glass against his lips and watched while he drained the morphine to the last drop. Then she gave him some water to take away the bitterness from his mouth, and wiped his lips.

"I want you to go to bed now, Antonia," he said softly. "I'm going to go to sleep. Simply go to sleep." He smiled, and his eyes were as youthful as they had been in the days before his life had been kicked out of him. "Take care of Gisela . . . and don't worry about Daniel, he'll look after himself. . . ." For a second he closed his eyes, and then he opened them, and stared intently up at her. "Kiss me good night, Toni."

She sat on the bed, and laid her cheek against his forehead. Then she kissed him, once on each closed eyelid, and on his mouth. Then she stood.

"Thank you, Toni," he said. "With all my heart."

"Are you comfortable, Leo?" she asked.

"Yes. Thank you."

Antonia turned, walked to the door, and opened it.

"Good night, Leo," she said quietly. And then, even more softly, "Shalom."

4

The train was almost an hour out of Augsburg when Daniel, suddenly aware of some new, as yet unidentifiable loss, put his fingers to his neck and discovered that his mother's gold chain was missing.

"It must have broken when we were loading the cases," he said miserably when they had abandoned their search in the compartment.

Josef sat back and sighed. He didn't want to think about the chain. The loss of it, so soon after their departure, seemed too much of an evil omen.

"We could ask the guard to call the station at Augsburg, Papa, couldn't we? They might find it on the platform."

"Certainly not," Josef said hurriedly. "We mustn't bother anyone." He picked up his copy of the *Berliner Tageblatt* and stared unseeingly at the front page. "Just sit there, Daniel, and don't draw attention."

"There's no one here but us," Daniel grumbled. It was the first train of the morning, and they'd been the only first-class passengers boarding at Augsburg.

"Even so," Josef said, glaring, "we want no questions asked. If the guard does come, you speak only when spoken to." He thrust the newspaper back up again like a shield.

Daniel sat, stiff and chilled, watching the gray morning landscape skimming past. He looked at his father's shiny bald patch over the top of the paper, and he wished, more than ever, that his mother had come with him instead of his father.

The rain drummed on the roof of the carriage, and Daniel counted the splashy streaks on the window until they grew too many and began to merge into gloomy vertical pools of water, clinging precariously to the glass before being thrust by the wind back into the void, and then he fell asleep, his head flopping uncomfortably onto his chest, thinking vaguely about the little gold Magen David lying abandoned on the wet station platform at Augsburg. . . .

At Friedrichshafen they were met at the station by a tall rugged man with fair hair and Slavic cheekbones.

"I am Klaus," he said simply, shaking Josef's hand in an iron grip. "Into the truck, please."

Josef looked into the back of the truck and saw crates of fruit and vegetables. "Where is my wife's cousin? I thought he would come to meet us."

Klaus shrugged. "Gretchen is waiting at the house." He gestured impatiently. "Please."

They emerged into watery sunlight outside a white stone house surrounded by neatly mowed grass and well-clipped bushes. The front door opened, and Gretchen Meier appeared, all smiles. Klaus disappeared quickly into the house with the suitcases. Gretchen kissed them both warmly and exclaimed about Daniel's height and likeness to his mother.

"You must be hungry." She folded an arm about Daniel's shoulders. "Come into the kitchen."

Daniel liked his cousin straight off. She had steely gray curls but a young, pretty face with bright, gleaming squirrel's eyes. Her figure was more angular than his mother's, and she sprang from task to task in the kitchen with bustling energy. Quickly she brought two bowls of hot bouillon to the table and sliced a loaf of bread and some big hunks of cheese.

"You probably would have preferred to freshen up before eating," she said to Josef, "but food comes first, and we never know when we may be interrupted."

They fell to drinking the soup, Josef with slow, languid dips of his spoon into his bowl, Daniel as rapidly as the hot liquid would allow, looking around between spoonfuls at the white stone walls and the heavy pine dresser loaded with blue and white china.

Before they got to the bread and cheese, Gretchen cocked her head to one side, listening to the distant sound of an engine.

"Company," she announced suddenly, getting to her feet and clearing the table.

Klaus reappeared in the doorway. "Come."

Daniel eyed the food hungrily. "Couldn't we take it?"

Quickly Gretchen wrapped the bread and cheese in a napkin. "Don't drop it on the stairs," she warned.

They followed Klaus up the stairs. On the first-floor landing, he opened what at first glance seemed to be a closet, pulled down a wooden shelf inside, and opened a second door, behind which stood a ladder.

"Up, please."

Daniel went ahead, his father puffing laboriously behind him. They heard Klaus shutting both doors, and then there was silence.

They stared at their new surroundings. They were in a small attic room measuring no more than nine feet square, with plain whitewashed walls and ceiling, and a wood-planked floor. On their left were two camp beds, freshly made up with white sheets and blue quilts. On their right was a makeshift washstand with a porcelain bowl, enamel jug, and two white towels. Against the wall beside the washstand stood their two suitcases.

Daniel sat on one of the beds and bounced experimentally. The mattress felt hard, but the quilt was soft and warm.

"Is this where we're going to stay until Mutti comes?"

Josef sat on the other bed. His mouth was slightly open beneath his moustache, and he was breathing heavily.

"Papa?" Daniel stood up and then sat beside his father. He took his hand and squeezed it. "It's okay, Papa," he said. "I'm sure Tante Gretchen will come up for us soon."

It was more than two hours before anyone came, and then it was Gretchen's husband, Sigmund.

"Welcome, both!" He shook Josef's hand firmly and then Daniel's. His skin felt callused, he smelled of the apples and oranges he sold in his fruit and vegetable store, and he was the most unusual-looking man Daniel had ever seen. His hair was flame-red, his eyes were bright green, he had a long, pointed nose and broad mouth, and he was even taller than Klaus.

"Sigi, thank God!" Josef was profoundly relieved. "Why did Gretchen bundle us up here? Was it the Gestapo?"

Sigmund shook his head. "Just a precaution. It's best no one knows you're here." He ruffled Daniel's hair and grinned. "Exciting, huh? Bet you never slept in a secret room before, did you?"

Josef was worried. "How dangerous is it for you to keep us here? What's the situation in this area? Are they picking up the men here too?"

"Gretchen has family connections," Sigmund said. "It's a protection that should last a while yet."

By nightfall, Josef and Daniel understood their situation. Sigmund and Gretchen were running an underground ferry service across the lake from nearby Constance to Kreuzlingen in Switzerland with the help of friends, one of them Klaus, who owned two fishing boats. All passengers were refugees, mostly Jews, without exit visas.

"You understand, Sigi," Josef said, "we shan't leave without Toni and Gisela."

Gretchen nodded vigorously. "Of course not, Josef. You know you're welcome to stay with us as long as is necessary."

"But you cannot go outside, and you will have to spend most of each day in the attic," Sigmund reminded them. "And Josef, *you* must understand that crossings are limited by circumstances. There may come a day when—"

"We don't have to think about that yet," Gretchen put in hastily, thinking of Daniel.

Sigmund ignored her. "There may come a day when you and the boy may have to make the crossing whether or not they have arrived."

Daniel was white-faced. "They'll come," he said, fists clenched. "Onkel Karl said Gisela will be better in a few days, and then they can leave Nuremberg."

"And they will." Gretchen looked accusingly at her husband. "They'll be here in plenty of time. Now how about some sleep? You must be very tired."

Daniel nodded. "Papa?"

Gretchen rose and took his hand. "I'll help you with the doors, Daniel. Sigi and your Papa want to talk awhile."

The door closed behind them and Josef looked at Sigmund. "May I telephone?" His face was pinched with strain.

"Go ahead."

Josef asked the operator to put him through to the number in Nuremberg and then waited. He waited a long time. When he replaced the receiver, his hands were trembling.

"No answer?"

Josef shook his head, unable to speak.

"Gretchen tried earlier," Sigmund said. "She wanted to let Toni know you were safe." He reached for his briar pipe and lit it. "We thought there was no point in worrying you unnecessarily—after all, she might just have gone shopping."

"Maybe she's taken Gisela to the hospital." Josef's legs felt gelatinous and he sat down again. "Or Leopold."

"Perhaps." Sigmund puffed at his pipe.

"God." Josef felt tears starting to his eyes. "Oh, my God, what have I left her to?"

Sigmund laid a hand on his shoulder. Smoke lifted from his pipe in a gentle swirl. "You did what you had to, my friend." He stretched out for a bottle of schnapps and poured. "Drink some of this. It's good and strong."

Josef took the glass. "She'll answer tomorrow." His eyes behind the thick lenses were scared. "I won't leave without her, Sigi."

"Sure," Sigmund said.

There was no answer the next day either, and it was three more days and nights before they received a call from Edith Grünbaum, their neighbor in Guntherstrasse.

Leopold was dead, she reported. He had died in his sleep the night Josef and Daniel had left Nuremberg, and the Gestapo had arrived next morning, had brought Gisela next door to Edith and taken Antonia away for questioning. The next day they had come for Karl, her husband, and since then Edith had heard nothing from either of them.

"I'm coming back," Josef said, sweat on his brow.

"That would achieve nothing, Josef. You want to orphan Daniel and Gisela?"

Josef held the receiver so tightly that his knuckles bleached white. "I have to come," he said. "I can't abandon Toni."

"Listen to me, Josef," Edith said harshly. "You must not come back. You have to get away for Daniel's sake."

"And my wife and daughter? Do I just forget them? Is that what you suggest?"

Edith ignored the reproach. "Listen," she said again firmly. "I shall wait here for Antonia." She paused. "I shall wait seven days. If she doesn't come, then I'll bring Gisela to you myself."

Josef was ashamed. "Edith?"

"Yes?"

"Thank you. You're a good friend."

"It's no more than I'd expect from you and Toni."

Josef hesitated. "I'm sorry about Karl."

"Yes."

"May I call you tomorrow?"

"No, Josef, wait till I get in touch. It's best that way."

"All right." He paused. "Look after our little girl, Edith."

He could hear the tears in her voice, but she answered him warmly. "With all my might, Josef."

Later, when Josef had lain wearily down on the camp bed in the attic, and when the only light in the room was the dull glow from the skylight, Daniel stirred in the other bed.

"Did you speak to Mutti, Papa?"

Josef swallowed. "Yes, Daniel."

"You didn't tell her I lost her chain, did you?"

"No, Daniel."

"How's Gisela? Is she well yet?"

Again, tears stung Josef's eyes. "A little better."

There was a short silence. Then Daniel said, "You didn't really talk to Mutti, did you?"

"No, Daniel."

The child's bed creaked. "We're still going to wait for them, aren't we, Papa?"

Josef's voice was husky. "Of course we will." He stifled his weeping until his bones and muscles ached with pain, and he turned over and buried his face in his pillow.

They did not hear from Edith again. The seven days of waiting passed them by, and then another seven, and Josef grew haggard with grief and Daniel thin and silent.

At the end of their third week in Friedrichshafen, Sigmund took Josef aside after a desolate supper, and suggested they should be prepared to leave at short notice, but Josef refused to consider it.

"They will come."

Sigmund shook his head, but said nothing.

Another week, and Sigmund spoke to Josef again. "It's becoming dangerous."

"For you and Gretchen?"

"For you and the boy."

For a moment Josef appeared to ponder, but then slowly he raised his head. "No."

"Daniel is pale with lack of fresh air and exercise. He never laughs, hardly even smiles."

"Why should he smile? Has he reason to be happy?"

"So give him a reason, Josef. Give him freedom. You have the power."

"I can't. I must wait."

"They may not come."

Josef's mouth quivered. "They will."

Sigmund sighed. "You'll have to spend more time in the attic. The risk is too great."

Josef shrugged. "So be it."

The attic became a prison; a nine-foot whitewashed cell in which a seven-year-old and his fast declining father lived and breathed and mourned side by side. Day after day they sat or lay on their sea-blue quilts and stared up at the skylight. The weather wafted and shifted and rumbled overhead; they saw rain clouds and snow-flakes and lightning and sunshine, and the last was hardest to bear.

At Chanukah, Gretchen brought them a silver menorah and found small, attractive gifts for Daniel most nights of the festival; at Christmas, as they listened to the church bells heralding mid-night mass all over Friedrichshafen, she sat with them and listened to Daniel's hazy, fretful memories of his first and only *Christkindles Markt* in Nuremberg, until the aroma of spiced lebkuchen, bratwurst, and gluhwein seemed to swirl about their heads in the chill, barren room.

After New Year's, Gretchen came less and less to the attic. In late January, Hitler pledged publicly the annihilation of the Jewish race in Europe; names that had until now been spoken in hushed whispers, rang out in horrified cries, ugly pestilent worms writhing just beneath the surface of the land breaking free and stretching, expanding, standing to be counted—Buchenwald, Ravensbrück, Dachau, on and on, more and more. Sigmund and Gretchen and their colleagues worked night and day, as did others like them all over Germany, wanting to help, needing to help some of those who fled from Munich and Berlin and Stuttgart and Hamburg, from the homes that were no longer secure or comfortable.

Winter melted into spring, and Josef, stubborn as a mule, re-fused to budge. He hardly spoke to his son, finding nothing to say, and Daniel began to turn in upon himself, remembering with longing his mother and sister, and the trap he had thought was Nuremberg.

One evening in June, Sigmund summoned Josef down into the living room and Gretchen climbed the ladder into the attic just after Daniel had gone to bed.

"Are you sleeping?" she asked softly.

Daniel sat up. "No."

She sat on the edge of the bed. "Can we talk?"

"Of course." His voice was tense.

Gretchen saw his expression and her heart thudded inside her. "Daniel," she began carefully, "I want to talk to you as I would to a grown man. What I have to say may sound wicked, but believe me, I speak as your friend."

There was a short silence.

"I know what you're going to say." His voice was low and flat. "You want us to leave without Mutti and Gisela."

God help us all, Gretchen thought. "That's right, Daniel."

He lay back. "Is my mother dead, Tante Gretchen?"

"No, I don't think so." She spoke firmly and clearly. "She isn't dead, but I feel sure she will not be allowed to follow you and your papa for a long time."

"Why can't we wait until they do allow her?"

"Because very soon I am afraid they may come and find you here, Daniel."

"Would they take us to join them?"

Gretchen's throat ached. "No, I don't think they would."

He considered for a moment and then asked, "If they took Papa and me, would they lock us up, do you think?"

She paused before answering. "Yes."

"Oh." And then, "I hate to be locked up."

Oh, my Lord, Gretchen thought, *the child's hardly known freedom, and he's only eight years old.*

"What is Switzerland like, Tante Gretchen?"

"It's beautiful. Greener than Germany and very clean, with wonderful high mountains."

"And Nazis?"

"No, Daniel. No Nazis."

Daniel sat up again and Gretchen saw the sparkle of tears in his eyes as the light from the roof caught his face. "Do you want me to ask Papa to go without Mutti and Gisela?"

She swallowed. "I think he may go if you ask him."

He put out his hand and touched her arm, and she caught his fingers and held them tightly.

"Shall I tell Papa that they will follow us to Switzerland when the Nazis let them?"

Gretchen gritted her teeth. "You could tell him that they'll come to you if they can."

Daniel was considering. "Will you and Onkel Sigi come with us?"

She pulled him to her then, and cuddled him close, feeling the warm, thin wiriness of his body. "No, Daniel, *Liebling,* we can't come with you. We have to stay here in case there are others who need help."

"Like my mother and sister," Daniel whispered into her ear, his fingers pinching the flesh of her arms.

Gretchen kissed him. "Yes, Daniel," she said.

Downstairs, in the kitchen, Sigmund said to Josef: "Dachau."

The flesh on Josef's face went gray, then waxlike, and Sigmund told Gretchen later that he felt he'd seen a living death.

"Who told you?"

Sigmund's stomach shrank inside him, but his face remained impassive. "My information is good."

"Both?"

Sigmund nodded. "Yes."

When Josef hit the floor, his right shoulder struck one of the silver Sabbath candles that had just been lit by Gretchen, and the flame went out.

5

From the night Josef and Daniel finally left Germany without Antonia and Gisela, to the night four years later when Daniel joined the escape bid from the internment camp, Josef deteriorated steadily into an advanced state of premature senility, and Daniel grew up into a twelve-year-old man.

It was late August before Josef was strong enough to attempt the journey, and more than another month passed before they neared the head of the ever-growing line of refugees waiting for help. By that time, the situation had considerably worsened.

On September 1, Switzerland's new commander-in-chief, Henri Guisan, asked the federal government to mobilize the army. On the third, the United Kingdom declared war on the German Reich, and World War II began. On the fifth, it became compulsory for anyone entering Switzerland to have a visa; on the seventeenth of October, Swiss police were ordered to expel anyone trying to cross into their territory without such papers. Refugees and émigrés who contrived to bypass the frontier guards were often interned and, with little accommodation ready for them, were sometimes even held in local jails. The Swiss nation, united in its resolve to remain neutral whatever the cost, were dismayed by the harsh decree and the obvious plight of the refugees, but the government, supported by the trade unions, were fearful that if the trickle were permitted to turn into a flood, it might prove hazardous to the country's security and, secondarily, to Swiss jobs.

When they made the crossing from Constance to Kreuzlingen, stuffed into roughly woven sacks at the bottom of Klaus's boat, covered with crates of stinking fish and nets, Josef and Daniel expected to find freedom on the other side of the lake. Switzerland —green and pleasant land. Instead, when they were hauled out of their sacks onto the Swiss wharf, they were met by uniformed police.

"Nazis? Papa!" Daniel clung to Josef, terrified.

"No, little one," Klaus reassured. "Police, that's all. Count yourselves lucky," he said to Josef. "You might have been turned back." He shrugged. "They don't know what to do with so many of you, it's hard on them too."

"And now? Won't they send us back?"

Klaus lowered his voice. "I have made an arrangement for you."

In the back of the police truck, Daniel asked one of the guards —a young man with a sympathetic face—"What will happen to us?"

The guard smiled kindly at him. "A safe cell for a few nights till they find somewhere, then a camp probably."

"Camp?" Josef whispered, aghast. "Concentration camp?"

"Of course not, Herr Silberstein. Just a place for you and the boy to stay while housing is arranged."

They were in the jail of a small town near Kreuzlingen for two weeks. Two weeks of hell for them both. The cells were damp and cold, and Josef quickly contracted a chill. He could not tolerate the prison food and drank only water and soup, and soon he was coughing in a way that frightened Daniel, who watched him like a hawk, fighting to keep up his spirits and coaxing him to take some nourishment. At night Daniel suffered his own torments. In the attic he had longed for freedom; now he yearned for the attic and Tante Gretchen. He found it almost impossible to sleep, kept awake by his father's hacking cough and the other haunting prison sounds, and when he did sleep his mind conjured up hideous nightmares, so that he woke more drained than before.

On the fifteenth day they were summoned for an interview.

"This was unfortunate," they were told, "but in the circumstances it was the best that could be arranged."

"And now?" Josef croaked, shivering.

"Now you can join others in your situation in the *Auffanglager*," came the reply.

The most positive aspect of the *Auffanglager* to which they were sent, not too far from Frauenfeld, was that they were among comrades-in-suffering. The Swiss, it was evident, had little idea of what to do with them. They were lucky to be there at all, the internees agreed among themselves; clearly it was only the humanitarianism of the Swiss people that was preventing their government from keeping all foreigners out. Anyway, they reasoned, they would not be kept in this place long, and in the meantime they could take comfort from the knowledge that they had their lives and their freedom.

Freedom of a sort. They were with German, French, and Austrian refugees, mostly Jews, interned in a derelict factory, living in cold, dark, barnlike rooms, sleeping on hard wooden boards strewn sparsely with straw. They lived lives as strictly regulated as the lowest army ranks at war; up at seven, lights out at nine-thirty. Occasional attempts were made to see to their needs—some of the older men complained of the chill in their bones; pullovers were promised, but they never arrived.

Months passed. Some were transferred to the *Arbeitslager* to work, but the Silbersteins remained in the factory because Josef was not fit for work and Daniel was too young. They became accustomed to the rituals of their new lives; they made friends, only to lose them again as they were moved away, like pawns on a chessboard; they learned to barter for necessities and their marks began to dwindle away in the face of inflated prices at the camp "shop." After several months, Josef sewed what remained of the money into his new straw-filled mattress when it arrived, a gift from the Red Cross.

In time, there were signs that conditions might improve; their *Hauptmann,* a warmhearted man from Zurich, gave permission for short, tightly supervised excursions to Frauenfeld and even farther afield to Winterthur. Daniel's hopes soared, but within two months the intake of refugees and émigrés rocketed, making excursions impractical, and the *Hauptmann* was replaced by a stricter disciplinarian.

"How much longer will we have to stay here?" Daniel asked camp officials weekly.

"Until suitable arrangements can be made for you," came the regular reply.

"Unless you get an entry visa for the United States or Palestine, or the war ends and you can go home again, they will never let you out," one of the Frenchmen told Josef. "You're under retirement age, and there's unemployment in Switzerland. They're afraid you'll steal a job from a Swiss citizen."

"But they won't even let me work in the *Arbeitslager,*" Josef protested.

"Because you'd have to do heavy labor, and you might have a heart attack and blame them. Outside it would be different." The man drew Josef aside. "You have funds, don't you, Silberstein? Why not ask for a lawyer to help you and the boy with a visa?"

"I don't want to leave Switzerland," Josef said. "My wife and daughter might not find us."

"I thought they were in Dachau. What makes you think they'll ever get out?"

For an instant, Josef longed to smash his fists into the Frenchman's insensitive face—but then he began to cough, and the now familiar lethargy overwhelmed him again, and he felt his spirits slump.

Conditions were worsening, with fifty to sixty people sleeping in each room. They ate their meals in the "dining room" elbow to elbow with their neighbors, so cramped that a latecomer was forced to climb over the tables to get to his place. Two toilets were shared between three hundred men, women, and children, with distressing and unhygienic results. There were regular examinations by camp physicians, but only in cases of fever could they go to the "infirmary," a third-story room with a ceiling so low, a man could easily touch it; the moment the fever went down, the patient was returned to the overcrowding below. The official policy of the camp was "confinement without cruelty"; the internees knew they were safe, and most understood the difficulties faced by the authorities, but many were becoming increasingly depressed. For Josef, a man accustomed to privacy and luxury, it was an unbearably lonely and humiliating experience. For Daniel, it was yet another form of imprisonment.

There were two things that made life tolerable for Daniel.

The first was the knowledge that he was keeping faith with his mother by taking care of his father.

The second was his new friend, Ben Kemelman.

Ben was a snub-nosed, freckle-faced, husky boy of ten, who had come to the camp from the Austrian border, which he had crossed with his parents three weeks after leaving Vienna, where they had lived in a huge, rambling house on the outskirts of the city. His mother and father were easygoing academics with definite tastes in classical music and art, and they, having each other for basic creature comforts, soon found kindred spirits in the camp and spent most days in the company of their friends, making what music they could, and discussing every composer from Bartók to Strauss. Bored to death, Ben daydreamed about becoming a soccer player, and every day, after their compulsory walk around the small compound, he and Daniel sat by the tall wire-mesh fence and made wild, fantastic plans about how they would escape one day and run away to America to make their fortunes.

It was on the first day of Passover in 1941 that Ben got sick the first time. He got stomach cramps while he was kicking a ball around outside, and fell to the ground doubled over with pain. Daniel was inside at the time, reading a book that one of the refugee-aid people had brought him, and only heard about Ben's illness later.

"Is Ben okay?" he asked Mr. Kemelman that evening after supper.

Mr. Kemelman smiled vaguely. "Sure. He ate too much at Seder, that's all."

"Will he be up tomorrow?"

"If he's better."

"Has he seen a doctor?"

"For overeating? In this place?"

It was a week before Ben got sick again. This time it began with a bad nosebleed and ended with his passing out. When Daniel visited him in the infirmary, he thought Ben looked pale and thin.

"What did the doctor say?"

Ben shrugged. "Nothing."

Daniel looked at his arm. A great black bruise had wrapped itself around Ben's forearm. "Where'd you get that?"

"Don't know. Must have knocked it."

Next day, Ben was removed from the infirmary and taken to the hospital in Frauenfeld for tests.

"Can I see him?" Daniel asked the *Hauptmann*.

"Only his parents may visit. In any case, he will be back here tomorrow."

Daniel went next day to meet Ben as usual by the fence. His friend was sitting up against it, legs splayed out in front of him, looking troubled.

"We're going to have to think up a new plan, Danny."

Daniel sat beside him. "Why?"

"I don't think I could climb the fence anymore."

Daniel looked at him. There was another of those dull, dark bruises on him, this time on his wrist and hand. "Don't worry," he said, "we'll find another way."

"I couldn't tunnel either, Danny."

"There are plenty of other ways, Ben. Brains instead of brawn."

Ben smiled. "That's more your department." Then he frowned. "Better make it soon. This medicine the doctor gave me makes me feel so tired."

He was back in the hospital less than a month later. Word filtered back that Ben had lymphatic leukemia, and that he was going to die.

"You have to let me see him," Daniel protested when an official told him again that only close relatives were permitted to visit.

"I'm sorry, Daniel," the man said sympathetically. "Besides, the hospital doesn't allow children under twelve in as visitors."

Daniel looked at him bitterly. "Only if they're dying."

The next day, Daniel went on a hunger strike. He refused to eat, and refused to walk, and when Josef heard about it he was furious, but nothing anyone said changed Daniel's mind. They waited until he had fainted three times before they relented.

Ben looked like a ghost, hardly Ben at all, but his eyes gleamed when he saw Daniel.

"How did you manage it, Danny?"

Daniel shrugged and sat on the bed. "Said I wouldn't eat till they let me in." He looked at the tubing attached to his friend, and the portrait of Christ on the cross that was the only thing Ben had to look at in the room, and at the charts suspended at the foot of the bed.

"So when will they let you out?"

"You know I'm never getting out of here." Ben stared at the bag of blood hanging next to him. "You'd better start planning life in America without me, Danny."

Daniel ignored him, and concentrated on curling his toes inward until they hurt, to stop himself from crying. "Summer's coming, Ben. Whole days outside."

There was a silence. Ben shifted a little with pain.

"Do you need something? Shall I fetch a nurse?"

"No," Ben said. "It comes and goes." His mouth trembled. "Heard any more news about your mother and sister?"

"Nothing." Daniel paused. "I think they're dead." It was one way of reaching the subject he felt Ben needed to talk about. "My father won't admit it, but I'm sure he knows it too."

"How old was Gisela when you last saw her?"

"Three."

Ben shut his eyes for a moment, and when he opened them again there were tears shining in them. "When my father first told me I was going to die, I kept thinking, why me? What did *I* do? But what did your poor baby sister do to anyone, for God's sake!" He shrugged. "I think I'm getting used to the idea now."

"Are you really?" Daniel's voice was husky.

Ben shook his head. "No." He smiled. "But at least I don't have to worry about escaping anymore."

"That's true." Daniel swallowed, reached for Ben's hand and held it tightly, and then he lost the battle, and the tears brimmed over onto his face. "Oh, God, Ben, it isn't fair. It just isn't *fair!*"

"Poor Danny," Ben murmured. "Losing everyone that matters to you. . . ."

Because of Daniel's protest, they let him see his friend once a week after that, but at the end of June, just before Daniel's Sunday afternoon visit, Ben Kemelman died.

Daniel was in the dark. Since leaving Nuremberg, he had nurtured hazy memories of his early days, days of normality and prosperity when his father, the businessman, had seemed the strength of their family, had lifted him proudly into the air and chucked him under the chin, and waltzed his mother around their salon and laughed, before the Nazis had taken away his pride. Now it seemed to Daniel that any lingering spirit and individuality remaining in Josef Silberstein had crumbled away like stale cheese. His promise to his mother that he would look after his father became more and more difficult to keep.

The next year filtered away for everyone in the camp, the formula for living unchanged. Outside, the world went about its way, smoldering and dangerous but, it seemed sometimes to Daniel, tantalizingly unpredictable.

At the end of August 1942, that uncertainty was dangled temptingly before him by two of the older boys in the camp. Bernhard Segal and Erich Mazinski were going to get out, they told Daniel, and they were willing to take a third person with them.

"We're sick of being pushed around, sick of watching our parents being grateful for being locked up like animals in a cage! What hope do children our age have in this godforsaken hole?" spat Erich vehemently. A sallow, narrow-eyed boy who had been bar mitzvahed in the camp two weeks earlier, he reminded Daniel of a weasel, always slinking furtively about.

"Who knows how long the war will go on?" the older boy, Bernhard, reasoned. "Our parents are past fighting. They think the Swiss will let us all out of here one day and say, 'Here's a nice job and a house for you.' "

"You don't believe shit like that, do you, Daniel?" asked Erich.

Daniel shook his head and looked at Bernhard curiously. "What's your plan?"

"Don't tell him anything unless he's with us," Erich said.

"What do you say, Danny?"

Daniel looked from one to the other. He liked Bernhard better than Erich. He was the last person in the world you would associate with wild escape plans; a scholarly looking boy with vague hazel-colored eyes and neat brown hair, quite grave and nondescript. But Daniel felt he could be trusted.

"I can't leave," he said wistfully. "I'd like to, but it's impossible."

"I told you he was a waste of time," Erich said.

"Why not?" Bernhard asked, ignoring Erich.

"My father."

Bernhard nodded. "It's difficult, I know. Our parents would have each other if Erich and I left. Your father would be alone."

"But he could stay here forever," Erich hissed, looking around to make sure no one was within earshot. "He might as well bury himself with his pal, Kemelman."

"He's right, you know, Danny. You're going to have to think about yourself sometime. You have rights too."

Daniel's lips tightened. "There's nothing to think about."

"Don't say we didn't ask you." Erich departed contemptuously.

"I'm sorry," Bernhard said.

Daniel shrugged. "Not your fault." He looked at him curiously again. "Why do *you* want to leave the camp? It's safe here, isn't it? What would you do if you got out?"

Bernhard smiled, a soft, faraway, wistful twitch of his lips. "Erich wants to fight," he said, and there was a touch of envy in his voice. "He thinks he could get to England and join up. He thinks they would let him. Erich is a little crazy sometimes, Danny, but he's not a bad boy."

"And you?"

Bernhard shook his head. "I can't stand to be cooped up like this. If I thought maybe there was a chance it might all be over in a few months, even a year—that they would let us out—I'd probably give up the idea and stay put." He sighed. "But I don't believe it, so I'll go with Erich."

"It's the same for me," Daniel said quietly. "It seems like I've been shut up in one cage or other almost my whole life." He closed his eyes. "Sometimes I think I can't stand it anymore."

They fell silent for a time, and then Bernhard asked: "Would your papa come with us?"

Daniel laughed shortly. "Not a chance. Papa hated it more than I did at the beginning, but now I think he almost likes it. All he ever does is wait to be told what to do. Someone wakes him in the morning, tells him when it's time to take his cold shower, reminds him when it's time to eat lunch. And if there's nothing else to do, he just lies on his bed and stares up at the ceiling."

"I expect he misses your mother."

Daniel nodded, and tears pricked behind his eyelids. "So do I."

Bernhard took his hand and squeezed it. "Do me a favor, Danny. Don't make any decisions now about coming with us." He grinned ruefully. "We'll be here a long time yet. Erich talks big, but we have no real plans yet. Think about it."

Daniel shook his head. "It's no good. My mother made me promise to look after my father, and he would never have left her if it wasn't for me." He forced a smile. "It's not really so bad."

But Daniel did think about it in spite of everything. He couldn't help it. Freedom, even with its implicit dangers, seemed like a great glowing light beckoning him, but then there was guilt, like a black, stifling blanket, and the awareness that he was perhaps luckier than many to have a responsibility to his father.

Winter that year was cold and bleak, and Josef suffered chill after chill, with fevers and bronchitis. Like many others, he would find himself up in the infirmary one minute, then back down again the next, when his fever was down.

At the supper table one evening in February 1943, Daniel saw that his father's cabbage and potatoes lay untouched on his dish.

"Papa? Not eating?"

His father's face was flushed. He stared vacantly down at the dish.

Daniel touched his hand. It was hot. He felt his forehead. "Papa, you have another fever."

The man on Josef's left, Saul Petzer, put his hand on Josef's dish, ready to claim it. No one in the camp let food go to waste while they had their health and strength. He continued to shovel his own cabbage leaves into his mouth while holding on to the spare portion.

"Papa," Daniel said again. "Let's get you out of here."

Josef turned, seeming to notice Daniel for the first time. He shook his head, his flabby jowls trembling. "Not the infirmary," he whispered, and his face crumpled, as if he were a child about to weep.

With difficulty Daniel stood up, in the process elbowing the man beside him, who merely grunted and continued to eat. "Come on, Papa." He put one arm protectively around his shoulders and his other hand supportively under Josef's arm. The heat seemed almost to sizzle through his father's thin shirt into Daniel's flesh.

Daniel climbed up onto the table, the only way to make an exit from the room while the other internees sat eating. He helped Josef up and pushed him gently ahead, trying to steer him clear of the food and soup bowls.

"*Scheisse!*" A dish went spinning, caught just in time.

"*Blöder Ochs!*" Thomas Meier, a surly German with a violent temper, seized Josef by the ankle, then let him go. "Get out of here, you clumsy old goat!"

Daniel felt his father trembling, and caught him just in time before he fell. "*Schwein!*" he hissed under his breath at Meier, deliberately grinding his heel into the man's cabbage. Meier leapt up, trying to grab Daniel, but the boy was too fast, maneuvering his father agilely out of reach, farther down the table.

"Sit down, Meier, you fool," came a tired voice from behind them. "Can't you see the old man's sick?"

"It's okay for you—it wasn't your dinner," snarled Meier.

"Dinner you call this?"

"Better than nothing," a third, more patient voice reminded them.

"Better than a gas chamber anyway."

And the voices hushed.

Josef went to the hospital in Frauenfeld, where Ben had died. Since he was the only blood relative, this time there was no protest about Daniel visiting once a week, but the visits were frustrating, one-way affairs. At first, Josef, who had double pneumonia, was in a delirium, but when the fever was brought down, he seemed hardly more lucid. Daniel would sit on the edge of his bed, holding his hand and talking, trying to rouse his father's interest in something, anything, but Josef responded less and less; instead of talking to his son, he began to hold conversations with an imaginary Antonia, while Daniel sat there, bewildered and anxious.

Physically, Josef recovered, but mentally he regressed steadily. In April he returned to the camp and became the first permanent patient in the infirmary. Daniel spoke to the doctor one day, asking why his father couldn't sleep downstairs with him.

"I'd look after him," he said.

"Your father is better off in the infirmary," the doctor replied. "He needs nursing."

"But his chest is better, isn't it?"

The doctor sized up Daniel. An intelligent boy, he thought, and like many in these camps, wise far above his years. He decided on the truth. Josef was suffering from premature senility, he told him, brought on by his general physical condition and an inability to come to terms with the reality of his situation.

"It might," he added gently, "have happened under any circumstances."

Daniel looked him straight in the eye. "Will he get better?"

"It's possible. There have been such cases," the doctor answered, "but it's unlikely that your father will ever improve significantly." He patted the boy's arm. "I'm sorry, Daniel, but he is, at least, quite happy in this state most of the time."

When Daniel left the doctor, he went directly to the infirmary to find Josef. He was warmly dressed for the first time in years, seated in a straight-backed chair, looking out of the window; his sparse hair was combed neatly down to the nape of his neck, and his thick spectacles perched on his nose. He looked very frail to Daniel, and very old.

"Papa," Daniel said clearly, "are you happy here?" He tried to penetrate the thick lenses to fathom his father's expression.

"Happy?" said Josef. He seemed surprised. "Sure I'm happy. Oma is coming to visit me soon, you know." He smiled at Daniel. "Are you staying here, too?"

Daniel stared. His grandmother had been dead for more than twenty years, and Papa believed she was coming to see him. "Papa," he tried again, speaking even more distinctly.

Josef frowned. "No need to shout."

"I want to know if you're happy, Papa." Daniel could hear his own voice trembling. "I have to know. Because if you are not, then we must tell them so that they will let you out of the infirmary."

Josef shook his head vehemently. "Happy?" he said angrily. "I'm very happy." His mouth quivered. "Don't you go making trouble for us again, Leo."

Daniel studied him anxiously. A nurse entering the room looked disapprovingly at him. Quickly, his legs shaking, Daniel kissed his father on the cheek and left.

Downstairs the day room was crowded as usual, and Daniel, needing solitude, went outside. The air was freezing, and it was starting to snow. He took a few deep gulps of air, and went back inside, going to the sleeping quarters.

He sat down on his mattress and stared at the floor. Physically his father had looked in better shape than he had since Nuremberg. And he had seemed placid enough. But he hadn't known his own son.

Daniel stood up and walked over to his father's bed. He picked up the small, hard pillow and saw that the photograph he knew Josef kept hidden there had not been removed with the rest of his things to the infirmary; a photograph of his father and mother standing in front of their house in Guntherstrasse with himself in the foreground in a stroller.

He went back to his own mattress and sat down again. He stared at the photograph. In Nuremberg, it had stood in a small silver frame on his mother's dressing table, and it still smelled faintly of her fragrance. Daniel raised it to his nostrils and breathed in deeply. Then he placed it under his own pillow, lay facedown on his bed, and wept until he fell asleep from sheer exhaustion.

The next afternoon he sought out Bernhard and Erich.

"Well?" said Erich.

"I want to ask you two questions."

"Go ahead."

"Has anyone escaped from here before?"

"No one has tried." Bernhard shrugged. "People feel safe. Better in than out."

"Fools," Erich said.

"What's your second question, Danny?"

"Why are you still here?"

"We're waiting for summer," Erich answered.

"Why summer?"

"Because there are more children on the streets then," Bernhard said quietly. "School ends at lunchtime and the days are long, and we can move about more safely without being noticed."

"So?" Erich asked impatiently. "Are you with us?"

Daniel looked at him evenly. "I'll think about it."

In the last week of June, two things occurred that finally made up his mind.

The first was a dream—short, but exquisite in its simplicity. Daniel dreamed that he was standing in a meadow, holding the string of a kite. It was beautiful, designed for perfect flight, but Daniel felt heavy, his feet leaden, so that he could hardly move, and the kite tugged on the string, its full potential thwarted, like a bird with clipped wings.

Suddenly, out of nowhere, his mother appeared. She walked

slowly toward him, and as she came closer Daniel saw with a rush of joy that he was now as tall as she. Half a meter away from him she stopped, reached out with one hand, and lightly brushed his cheek with her fingers. He tried to catch her hand to kiss it and hold her, but she took it away, smiling her sweet, warm smile— and then she caught the kite string and, with a tiny pair of silver scissors, cut the string. The kite bobbed for a moment and then floated away on the breeze, and Daniel realized suddenly that he, too, was lighter than air, and that the weight that had pinned him to the ground had vanished.

He woke then, on his straw mattress, but though the coughing and moaning was all around him as always, he felt that the peace in his dream remained with him and he knew, irrationally, that his mother had given him her blessing for his escape.

The second thing happened two days later. Bernhard and Erich summoned him urgently to a meeting at the fence, and when they met, both boys looked grim.

"What's wrong?" Daniel asked.

"Something you should know," Bernhard said, and glanced uncomfortably at Erich, who, for once, seemed lost for words.

"What is it?" Daniel felt suddenly afraid.

"They're going to put you into care, Danny," Bernhard said. "Because your father is sick."

Daniel's eyes widened. "What does that mean?"

"It probably means some kind of orphanage," Bernhard answered.

"With even less freedom than you have here," added Erich. "And you'd be stuck then till you're eighteen. You couldn't be adopted by a family because your father's still alive, and anyway, who would want to adopt a twelve-year-old Jewish boy these days!"

Daniel thought hard and fast. He felt no need to question their sources; he knew instinctively that what they said was logical and true.

"If you get taken away and locked up in some stinking orphanage," Erich said, "you'll never get out."

"Well?" said Bernhard.

6

The day before Daniel left, he cut the stitches his father had sewn in his mattress, and took out the Reichsmarks that were left, and his mother's diamond jewelry. He took two thousand marks and tucked them into the waistband of his underpants, and put the rest of the money and jewelry in a bag and took it to the *Hauptmann*.

"My father's," he explained. "He was keeping it hidden, but I'm afraid someone may steal it while he's sick."

Gravely the *Hauptmann* accepted it. "He should have handed it over long ago." He wrote a receipt and gave it to Daniel. "It will be kept safely for him."

Daniel longed to write a letter to his father, but it was a risk he dared not take.

Escape was comparatively easy. The inmates of the camp were not guarded like prisoners, because they were not considered prisoners. There were high fences, but no alarm systems and not an inch of electrified wire; there were no tracking spotlights either, because there was a mandatory blackout all over Switzerland in case of bombing raids, and also because no one in the camp really wanted to escape.

Except Bernhard Segal, Erich Mazinski, and Daniel Silberstein.

They got out through a small hole made with wire cutters stolen from the camp workshop, and when they were through, they took the time to fix the hole so that it would take longer before anyone noticed it.

They wore dark clothing, and each had a small flashlight, a little money, food purloined from the canteen kitchen, and a sleeping bag, made in secrecy by Erich.

They felt bold enough until they were about a hundred meters from the fence, until the blackness of night slapped down before their faces and the sounds began, the spooky sounds of night; and then they joined hands for safety and comfort, and jogged gently forward like a bobbing, dark, linked chain.

"Daniel," whispered Bernhard, when they had stopped for breath about a half-hour later. "Are you okay?"

"Fine," whispered Daniel.

"Last chance to go back. Are you still game?"

A trickle of perspiration ran down Daniel's back. "Yes."

"You too, Erich?"

"I wouldn't go back if they threatened to cut off both my legs." Erich's voice was hoarse and too loud in the night. "What about you, Bernie?"

"Just let's get to the other side of the city by morning, and I'll start breathing again."

From the beginning, Daniel knew he couldn't stay with them indefinitely. Erich's streak of wildness worried him. Somehow, somewhere, Erich was going to get into trouble, and Daniel did not intend to be there when it happened, however much he liked and respected Bernhard.

There were advantages to being a threesome, though; a sense of physical security, especially at night, a feeling that three heads, three separate sets of skills, were better than one; the fact that Erich seemed to know how to steal food, and that Bernhard knew how to make it last.

Erich showed signs, in fact, of having the potential to become a first-class thief. Daniel and Bernhard abhorred the notion of stealing, even though for the time being they had no choice, but Erich enjoyed it. On the outskirts of Winterthur one night, without warning, he cut out the lock in the door of a small general store, and came out with new batteries for their flashlights, three bars of soap, and a change of clothing for each of them.

Daniel was furious. "We don't need clothes," he hissed at Erich. "You're nothing but a lousy thief!"

Erich was unmoved. "If you had half a brain in your head, you would know they must be after us by now. Different clothes will make us a little harder to find."

Daniel held up the blue jeans and shirt Erich had given him. "They probably won't fit."

Erich looked contemptuous. "They'll fit." He turned to Bernhard. "You're very quiet. Do you think I'm just a lousy thief too?"

Bernhard hated unpleasantness. "Of course not, Erich. I just wish you'd be more careful."

"Let's get out of here," Daniel whispered. They were standing in a cobbled alley, and in the distance they could hear the purring engine of a car coming closer.

"All right," Erich said. "But next time I'm going to get cash. That way we can start living."

On the fifteenth night after their escape, when they were sleeping in a barn near Kloten, just outside Zurich, Daniel crawled out of his sleeping bag and woke Bernhard.

"Ssh!" he hissed. "I don't want to wake Erich."

Bernhard pulled himself half out of his bag and blinked as Daniel's flashlight struck his face. "What's up?"

"I'm leaving."

"*What?*" Bernhard rubbed his eyes, as if he thought he might be dreaming. "What are you talking about?"

"Don't wake Erich." An owl screeched outside the barn. Daniel turned off the flashlight and crouched low on the straw. "I'm sorry," he whispered, "but I don't like the things he's planning. I don't want to spoil everything for you, but I'm not a criminal, and I don't want to get caught and put back in the camp."

"For God's sake, Danny, none of us does! Erich says wild things sometimes, you know that."

"He does them too."

The straw rustled as Bernhard tried to sit up properly. "Don't go, Danny, please. Stay with us. We'll tell Erich not to steal anymore."

"He won't listen, and you know it. Besides," Daniel said quietly, "they must be searching for us. They'll expect us to stay together, so if I leave maybe we'll all stand a better chance."

"What will you do? How will you live? I hate stealing as much as you, but for the time being I can't see an alternative."

Daniel touched the wad of money in his waistband. "I have a little cash I didn't tell you about." He flushed in the dark at his own conspiracy. "I'm sorry, but I guessed I might need it one day."

"You were right." Bernhard reached for his hand and squeezed it firmly. "Don't worry about it, Danny. Do what you feel you have to."

"Would you come with me?"

"I won't leave Erich. He wouldn't make it alone. He'd be in trouble and get picked up the first week."

Slowly, Daniel got to his feet. He turned the flashlight back on and put one hand over the bulb to dim the glare. "I'll move at first light."

"If you get caught, Danny—"

"I won't say anything about you or Erich," Daniel said quickly.

"That's not what I meant," Bernhard sighed. "I just wanted to say that it might not be the end of everything if any of us *were* caught."

Daniel crouched down again. "Are you having second thoughts, Bernie?"

The older boy chuckled quietly. "More like twenty-second. Haven't you?"

"Of course." But then he added: "But I'm not going to get caught. And neither are you."

Switzerland was a formidable country in which to vanish without trace. Physically, Daniel was unsuited to making the mountains his allies; even in summer conditions they were often treacherous, and Daniel was a city boy, incapable of catching even the smallest rabbit or even of spotting poisonous berries. In the flat, rural areas, all strangers were quickly noted and reported, particularly because it was wartime. Daniel read in discarded newspapers about spy rings being uncovered in Berne; though he was just a boy, and a Jew, he was afraid that the Swiss would never trust a German.

He spent two weeks in and around Zurich, sleeping rough in barns and outbuildings. Once, during the first week, he walked down the main street in Rüschlikon, a suburb close to the lake, and went into a bank, five hundred of his Reichsmarks in his hand.

The bank smelled of floor polish, flowers, and civilization, and Daniel noticed a woman, writing on a slip of paper near the entrance, wrinkle her nose in distaste as she saw him.

There was no line, and he went up to the first teller, a young woman with clean fair hair and glasses. Daniel pushed his bank notes over the counter.

"I would like to change these into Swiss francs, if you please," he said carefully. A man in a business suit came into the bank and stood in line behind him.

The teller spoke to him, but her Swiss-German was so fast, Daniel was unable to understand. His palms began to sweat.

"Change, please," he said again, and smiled at her.

"I asked, where did you get this money?" the teller said, this time in German, frowning and taking off her glasses to examine the notes more closely.

"Can't you change them?" *What was wrong with them?*

"I think you could change them at our chief branch in Zurich, but I will check." She picked up the notes and left the counter.

The man behind Daniel grunted, irritated by the delay. Daniel watched, panic-stricken, as the teller spoke to someone in another room behind a glass partition, an older woman who stared at Daniel for a moment, and then picked up a telephone.

As slowly and calmly as he could, Daniel left the counter, pretending to examine the leaflets displayed near the street door. He felt the businessman's cold stare at his scruffy clothes and greasy hair, and the instant his gaze lifted, Daniel turned and darted out of the door.

"Your money!" he heard someone call after him, but he ran for his life, kept on running, not stopping until he was right out of Rüschlikon and almost a kilometer out into the countryside, where he could hide until nightfall.

After that day, he didn't dare to try changing any more money, and now it was he who had to steal food, but found he could not bring himself to break into a shop. He learned to hover around the back doors of restaurants and cafés in the evenings, and when the opportunity arose, he would run into a deserted kitchen, look around quickly for the most easily transportable food, grab what he could, and dash out again before he was noticed. He became nimbler than he would have believed possible and, he told himself, at least he would not starve to death.

It wasn't too bad moving around in the city at first, because the schools were closed for summer vacation and there were dozens of children on the streets, but then the schools reopened and Daniel's age became his greatest handicap. In spite of his hard-earned maturity, Daniel still looked like a child, and too often in Zurich he found himself being stared at by policemen or well-meaning ladies, troubled by the shabbiness of his appearance.

On the third day of September, Daniel gave up the city and struck out again for the countryside. A few kilometers from Zurich he spotted a truck bearing a Lucerne license plate standing in a parking area while the driver took a nap at the wheel. The back of the truck was open, protected by a tarpaulin. Quickly looking around, Daniel padded over to the back, heaved himself over the side, and tucked himself under the tarpaulin with the load, which turned out to be steel piping and not the fresh vegetables Daniel had hoped for.

The driver slept on for more than an hour, and Daniel dozed too, to be woken by the noise of crashing gears and bumping steel pipes as they slipped back onto the highway south in the direction of Lucerne. Daniel pulled the tarpaulin clear of his face, and enjoyed the fresh air and blue sky, but less than an hour later the truck ground to a sudden halt, and he heard the driver cursing loudly. Quickly, Daniel yanked the tarpaulin back over himself and listened as footsteps approached.

"*Grüss Gott,*" he heard a voice say from the road. Another vehicle pulled up behind them.

"*Salut,*" the driver answered. "*Was ist los?*"

Daniel froze. Police.

"*Ihre Papiere, bitte.*" And then: "*Danke.*"

There was a long pause, presumably while the driver's papers were checked.

"What's your load?"

"Building materials."

"Going where?"

"Emmenbrücke. Want to see the stuff?"

Daniel's heart stopped beating.

"That's all right," the policeman's voice said, and Daniel felt sweat break out all over him.

"What are you looking for?" the driver asked.

"Just making spot checks." The driver's cab door banged. "You can get on your way. Drive safely."

The gears groaned, the motor whined, and the truck moved off again, but it was fifteen minutes before Daniel risked moving the tarpaulin, still shaking with fright.

On the outskirts of Lucerne, Daniel realized it was time to get out. He was not sure where Emmenbrücke was, but it might not be far away, and if the driver began unloading, he would be in trouble.

His chance came quickly. The truck pulled off the road again into another parking area, and the driver jumped down from the cab and walked off into the trees to relieve himself.

Daniel sat up, took a quick look around, saw no one, and jumped over the side, twisting his foot as he landed on the hard tarmac. Hurriedly he grabbed his bedroll and ran into a cluster of trees in the opposite direction. When the truck moved off, Daniel began to limp along the edge of the road under cover of the trees, but his foot hurt and his progress was slow.

He didn't dare enter any town or village that evening—he couldn't be sure of running fast enough, and he wouldn't be nimble enough to steal food from a restaurant. He found a stream, bathed his foot, washed himself as well as he could, and then settled down in his sleeping bag in a small forest close to a lake. He was hungry and miserable.

It was another two days before his foot was comfortable enough for him to walk with any speed, and by then he was weak with hunger. He made his way in what he thought was a southerly direction, but soon realized he was going around in circles and was only a few kilometers away from where the truck had stopped.

He left the highway and began to roam the fields. It seemed like good, rich farmland; maybe he could find something to eat on the land.

It was impossible, wheatfields everywhere, and when he tasted the wheat, it was so dry and prickly, he was forced to spit it out. And cows—useless, bad-tempered beasts. He tried one evening, after dark, to milk one, but the animal kicked him in the stomach and he gave up, weeping with frustration.

For four days and nights Daniel ate nothing at all, and he was close to desperation. The bleakness of his past and present rose up in his mind, and the future was blotted out. He began to yearn for the cabbage-and-potato diet he had so despised in the camp.

And then, on the fifth day, wandering aimlessly through the fields, he found the apple orchard.

7

"That's quite a story."

"Don't you believe me?"

"Of course. No one would invent such things."

Andreas and Daniel sat propped against the sun-toasted bark of two apple trees, the cores of at least a dozen apples littering the long grass around them and Rolf, the dog, making easy work of the cores one at a time, holding them between his paws while he nibbled away at them with a delicacy belying his size.

"You'll get a bellyache," Andreas said lazily, brushing a fly off his mud-spattered trousers.

Daniel smiled. He was experiencing a most unfamiliar sense of well-being, sitting there on the earth beside this stranger; a boy with the most striking face he'd ever seen, a boy who just an hour earlier had been fighting with him in the mud, but to whom he had just unburdened himself as if he had known him all his life.

"You need some real food," Andreas was saying. "You'll come home with me, and my mother and grandmother will look after you."

Daniel blinked, the contentment dissolving. "No," he said, stiffening, ready to run.

"Why not?" Andreas asked, surprised.

"They might not want me around," Daniel said cautiously. "I'm a stranger, they know nothing about me."

"So I'll tell them." Andreas got to his feet and Rolf dropped the apple core he was eating and ran to him, tail wagging. "Come on."

Daniel stayed put. "No," he said. "Thank you, but no."

"You're not scared, are you? There's no need to be, honestly."

"I'm not scared of you."

"You can't be scared of my family!" Andreas knelt beside him. "They're *good* people, not monsters like the Nazis. If I tell them what's happened to you, they'll want to help."

Daniel said nothing.

"For goodness' sake." Andreas was exasperated. "What choice

do you have? From what you've told me, it's lucky you found me instead of a farmer—and you've nowhere else to go, have you?" Irritation left his eyes, and they began to shine with adventure. Life had been dull for so long, but now suddenly here was a real, live victim of the war, and he, Andreas Alessandro, was in a position to help. "My mother and father are quite important around here, you know," he said proudly. "They'll do something for you —maybe even get your papa out of the camp."

"No!" Daniel grabbed him by the wrist, his eyes wild. "They'll send me back, and I won't go! I'd rather die than go back!"

"All right!" Andreas pulled away from him and rubbed his wrist. "No need to get crazy. I won't let them send you back."

"Don't tell them anything about the camp."

"If I don't tell them, how will they understand what you're doing here?" Andreas asked reasonably, and waited for a response, but none came. "Will you come?"

Daniel's eyes were dull. "I don't know."

"Daniel, my papa's always complaining because they wouldn't let him be a soldier. He's Italian, you see; he only came here to marry my mother, and if you're not Swiss-born, you can't join the army. But he hates the Nazis, I know, so when he hears about you, he'll never let anyone take you back."

For a few moments more Daniel sat still, his head down, his chin touching his chest. Andreas was right—he had no choice, none at all. He had to trust someone sometime. "All right," he said, and was surprised that the words seemed to relieve him of a great load.

"Good." Andreas stood up again. "Come on, then, it's getting late, and it's a fair walk back to the house."

Daniel heaved himself to his feet with an effort. Every bone and muscle in his body ached, his ankle still throbbed, and his face, where Andreas had punched him, stung.

"You look bad. Can you walk?"

Daniel nodded. "I'm stiff from resting. I'll be better in a minute."

"My mother will probably throw you right in a hot bath," Andreas said cheerfully. Maybe she would ask him to stay with them until the end of the war, he thought happily. That would be fun, almost like having a brother.

Daniel swung his arms, trying to get the circulation going again. Somewhere at the back of his mind, hope twinged remotely.

"Let's go." Andreas started to walk, his muddied blond hair blowing over his forehead and shimmying in front of his eyes in the breeze.

When Anna, Andreas's mother, saw her son walking into the forecourt, muddy and bloodied, with a dirty young gypsy in tow, she screamed in fright for her husband.

"Roberto, *komm schnell!*"

She ran out onto the porch just as Roberto emerged from the barn.

"Andi, what happened?" She pulled him close and examined him carefully, thankful there seemed no real injury in spite of the blood. She glared accusingly at Daniel. "Who's this?"

Roberto took the porch steps two at a time and towered above them, hands on hips. "What's going on? What happened to you, Andreas?"

Andreas pulled away from his mother. "I'm fine, Papi, it's only dirt." He made a gesture toward Daniel and grinned proudly. "This is Daniel Silberstein."

Daniel stood awkwardly, his hands sticky with mud, apple juice, and sweat, his heart pounding. Any second, Andreas's mother would disappear into the house and call the police, he was sure. He wondered whether to run or stand his ground.

Andreas's father stooped and put out his hand. He sensed the boy's fear as he might be aware of a young calf's alarm when first approached by humans. "Roberto Alessandro," he introduced himself gently. "Would you like to tell me what has been going on, since my son doesn't seem able to?"

Anna's lips tightened with suspicion. "They have been fighting," she said. "Are you sure you're not hurt, Andreas?"

"*Ja, ja,* Mutti." He took a deep breath. "Daniel's a refugee. From Germany." He looked up at his father, and his eyes gleamed. "He's Jewish, and he needs our help."

His mother made a small gasping sound and took two steps back closer to the house. Her flaxen hair was tied neatly at the back of her head in a knot, and she patted it nervously.

"Andreas," Roberto said quietly. "Go upstairs to the bathroom and ask your grandmother to see to you."

"But Papi, I need to tell you about Daniel," Andreas protested.

"Daniel is quite capable of telling us about himself, I'm sure," Roberto said firmly.

"I promised that we would help him—"

"Do as your father says!" Anna snapped.

Andreas took a quick backward glance at Daniel and saw that he was very pale. "Don't worry, Daniel. It'll be all right."

"Get out of here, Andreas! *Subito!*" his father thundered. Andreas ran into the house, and Roberto turned to Daniel. "Now you come into the kitchen."

"The scullery, Roberto," Anna ordered. "His clothes are filthy."

Daniel turned from pale to pure white, swayed, and caught the porch rail with both hands to stop himself falling. Roberto grabbed his arms and was shocked by their thinness. "For God's sake, Anna, get some food. Heat some soup or something, this boy is half starved!"

"But we don't know who he is."

"He's very hungry, we know that much." Roberto guided Daniel through the front door and propelled him through the kitchen into the scullery. Anna laid a cloth quickly over her clean chair before Daniel could sit down.

"You stay there, boy," she said, not unkindly. "Since you're so hungry you can clean up later." She busied herself next door in the kitchen.

"Are you sick, Daniel, or just hungry?" Roberto asked. "Shall I call a doctor?"

"No! No doctor, please." He clutched the arms of the chair. "I'm fine."

Roberto smiled. "Then just do as my wife said and sit quietly. We can talk when you have some food inside you."

"How did you know I was starving?" Daniel asked, his voice flat but curious. "I didn't say anything."

Roberto grinned wryly. "I come from one of the poorest parts of Naples, boy. I remember hunger."

Anna came in with three slices of freshly baked bread and a large cup of milk.

"Start with that," Roberto said, "and eat slowly. No one will take it away from you."

He looked at his wife. She was staring down at the boy as he wolfed the bread and gulped the milk, and her expression was one of profound alarm.

8

Later on in life, Andreas looked back on the twenty-four hours that followed as the time when he became aware of the fundamental differences between his parents, and when he began to grow apart from his mother.

It was nine o'clock in the evening when he crept out of his bedroom to listen to their argument from the top of the stairs. Their voices were stiff and heated. He knelt down and hung onto the banister rail for comfort.

"I refuse to place my family at risk," he heard his mother say. "It is insane to help a boy who has had every kindness offered him by our country, and who has simply turned his back—"

"He's a child, Anna, for Christ's sake!"

"Don't swear, Roberto."

"I don't understand you, Anna. You've listened to what that madman has to say, you've heard the stories from Germany; you *wept*, for God's sake, when our frontier guards turned back the French refugees and they committed suicide, and yet now, when you have the opportunity of helping a Jewish child, you want to send him back!" Andreas had never heard his father so angry, his voice so choked.

"Not to Germany, Roberto." Now his mother's voice was reasonable. "To a camp here in Switzerland, where they will look after him, where they know how to look after these people."

"These people," his father echoed, "are no different from us. They have feelings too. Daniel told us how he felt, didn't he? He's a very articulate boy. He couldn't stand being locked up anymore, he said. He would rather die."

"Of course he says such things, Roberto, he's a child, he doesn't know what they mean. If he had stayed in Germany, maybe he *would* be dead. He's a lucky boy, in many ways."

"*Lucky?*" Andreas heard his father hammer the table. "Don't you feel for him, Anna?"

"Of course I feel. I'm a mother, aren't I?" Her voice softened, and Andreas had to lean forward to hear, ready to run back to his room if the door opened suddenly. "But it's because I have a son of my own that I have to think of him first. It would be a crime, you know, to keep that boy here. I will not become a criminal for a stranger."

Andreas clenched his fists. Daniel was right after all. He could hardly believe it.

"What if he stayed on as a farm worker?" his father asked, trying again. "He could work for his keep until the war ends."

"Don't be a fool." His mother's tone was acid. "He is a child, and far too weak to be of the slightest use." She paused. "And anyway, how could we trust a thief?"

"What in heaven's name do we care about a few apples, Anna? He had no choice, he was forced to steal because he was starving." There was another silence, and Andreas could hear his parents' angry breathing. "If you won't let him stay here, I shall give him money to help him find people who will."

"Give him money?" Anna laughed harshly. "What you have, Roberto, is my family's. It is not yours to give away."

Something inside the room moved, a chair banged loudly. Andreas stood, poised for flight.

"The Nazis say the Jews are cowards, don't they, Roberto," Anna said heatedly. "If they are so wrong, let this boy prove it— let him fight his own battles!"

The door handle moved, and Andreas ran.

It was another two hours before all the lights in the house were turned out and both his parents were in their bedroom. His father had gone to his study after the argument and had stayed there long after Anna had gone to bed, and all that time Andreas had lain like a statue in his own bed, his soft quilt pulled up to his chin, Rolf vigilant beside him, tail twitching. He could not sleep, *would* not sleep. He knew what he had to do now, and nothing was going to stop him.

When the grandfather clock in the hall struck half past eleven, Andreas left Rolf in his room and padded on bare feet up the uncarpeted stairs to the story where the housekeeper slept, and where Daniel had been given a room for the night. He pushed the door ajar.

"Daniel?" he hissed into the dark. He crept over to the bed and prodded the sleeping shape. Daniel stirred with a groan.

"It's only me," Andreas said. "Keep quiet." He went to the window and opened the wooden shutters to let in the moonlight. Daniel sat up.

"Don't make any noise," Andreas whispered. "Just listen to me." He sat down on the edge of the bed and stooped to rub his cold feet.

"What's the matter?"

"You have to leave."

Daniel lay back against the pillow. In the half-light his eyes were two hollows in his thin, pale face. "I know," he said, his voice dull. "I didn't expect to stay." He shifted closer to the wall and patted the mattress with his hand. "If you're cold, get in and warm yourself."

Andreas shook his head. "I mean you have to leave tonight."

Daniel jerked to a sitting position. "What happened?"

"Nothing—don't be scared. I heard my parents talking, that's all." The words were hard to get out, the truth difficult to face. "My mother is worried, I think, about having you here."

In a flash, Daniel's feet were on the floor, his eyes hard with suspicion. "Have they called the police?"

"Of course not." Andreas put a hand on his shoulder. "Don't get so excited. Please. My father wants you to stay, and—"

"Your mother thinks I'm a criminal, I suppose."

"Don't be so touchy!" Andreas protested, not knowing why he bothered, since it was the truth. "The point is, you need to get out of here."

Daniel pushed the long hair off his forehead and stood up. "I'll get dressed."

"No, not yet. Lie back down, try to sleep if you can—but be ready to leave in two hours." He tiptoed to the door. "I'll be back before then."

"What for?"

"I'm going to help you," Andreas said.

"You're only nine, you're just a child." Daniel was taller than Andreas, and now he drew himself to his full height and looked down at him. "How can you help? Go back to bed. Forget about me. Don't worry, by morning I'll be gone."

Andreas glared at him. "Wait here." He slipped out through the door.

Daniel sank back onto the bed and covered his face with his hands. The thought of having to run again so soon, alone, was almost more than he could bear. And then the weariness returned, and he lay down again, sinking into the warmth, hardly caring if Andreas ever came back or not.

It was almost an hour and a half before he did return, convinced by now that everyone in the house was sound asleep.

Daniel was dressed, standing by the window, staring out into the night. Andreas put down the bag he was carrying and handed over an armful of clothes.

"Change into these. I know I'm younger than you, but you're so skinny they'll probably fit."

Daniel shook his head. "I don't want to take your clothes."

"Do you want to escape or not? You'll have a much better chance if you look respectable. Put on the boots too. That way, if the trousers are short it won't show." He opened the bag. "There's enough food here to last you a few days—longer if you're careful. And there's a change of clothes, too. And here . . . I brought a little money."

Daniel stared as Andreas fished in his pockets for a handful of loose coins and a thin wad of notes.

"What makes you think I would take your money?" He eyed the notes suspiciously. "Where did you get all this, anyway? It's not yours, is it?"

Andreas grinned. "I took it out of the housekeeper's cupboard —it's only a bit of the shopping money. Don't make a fuss, it isn't much, but it should get you quite a way."

"I don't want to steal," Daniel said softly. "Don't ask me to, please. I took your fruit because I had no choice, you know that. I'm not a thief."

Andreas put the money roughly into his hands. "Do you want to go to prison? You said you couldn't stand being cooped up. Do I have to explain *everything* to you? Why don't you understand? By morning my mother may have convinced my father that it's their duty to give you up." He shrugged, but the truth hurt. "She sounded very strong. I think she'll have it her way."

Daniel walked over to the window. He stared out into the night. "My mother was stronger than my father too, Andreas." He paused. "Maybe you should do what she wants."

"*No!*" Andreas's voice rang out fiercely in the darkness, and he lowered it to a whisper again. "Not if I know she's wrong. Now hurry and put on these clothes." He went to the door. "I'm going to fetch Rolf."

When they left the house, the moon was just disappearing behind a bank of thick, scudding clouds, and the first drops of rain were beginning to fall.

"Good," Andreas said. "Too much light would be risky." He

led the way, confident in the pitch darkness, Rolf at his heels, the soft jangling from his neck chain the only sound; Daniel followed, the blood pumping fast through his body, fear hard in his chest.

They skirted the back of the house and slipped between two outbuildings, the earth under their boots squelching and stinking of cow dung. Andreas stopped and pointed out a shadowy building some hundred meters away. "Behind that shed is a tractor," he said. "The only one working in the canton. We'll go on in that."

"What? We can't—"

"I can drive," Andreas said with pride. "I'd take my father's car, but it's too close to the house and someone might hear. Anyway, if we took the Horch onto the roads, we would be stopped by the police."

"Where can we go in a tractor?"

"It will get us from farm to farm without touching a single road. I know this land like the back of my hand. No one will see us. Now come on."

Some cows lowed nearby, and Rolf growled softly. Daniel followed Andreas to the back of the shed, and there was the tractor. Andreas pulled a small flashlight from his jacket pocket and shone a beam of light at it. "Isn't she a beauty?" he said triumphantly. "Let's hope she starts."

He pulled himself up into the driver's seat, took the bag from Daniel and helped him up. The older boy's shoulders were shaking.

"Cold?"

Daniel smiled. "Just scared."

Andreas unzipped his parka and took out some folded sheets of notepaper. "I almost forgot." He shone the torch on them. "They have the stamp of our company on them. Pfister–Alessandro. You never know, they might be useful one day." He grinned, as if daring Daniel to protest again. "I got them from my father's desk. He wouldn't mind."

Daniel took them, leaned his head back, and smiled into the dark. "I don't believe you are younger than me, after all," he said. "Is there anything you haven't thought of?"

Andreas zipped up his parka and leaned forward, and in a second the tractor's motor fired and they were rumbling along, the sound as deafening to Daniel's ears as a hundred caged lions.

It was almost four in the morning when Andreas stopped near the road outside Emmenbrücke, far away enough from the farm for Daniel to continue safely alone.

He pulled up the hand brake and looked at him, his face grave. "I wish you could have stayed."

Daniel picked up the bag from the floor and climbed awkwardly down into the mud.

"Look after yourself on the way home," he said. He patted Rolf, who thumped his tail and whined. "Watch your master."

Andreas leaned over the side and touched the wound under Daniel's left eye. "Does that hurt much?" he asked. "You're going to have a scar."

Daniel blinked back the sudden tears in his eyes. "I hope so, Andreas Alessandro. It was your first gift to me." He stepped back, away from the tractor. "Tell your mother and father that I stole the money and the food," he said. "Don't make more trouble for yourself than you have to."

He turned without another word, and slipped away into the night.

The whole house was up when Andreas got home at six o'clock, the lights inside and on the porch ablaze in the predawn gloom in spite of the blackout.

When he opened the front door and stepped inside, the first things he saw were the frightened faces of his mother and grandmother as they sat huddled together near the telephone, wearing nightclothes. His mother looked as if she'd been crying; there were streaks on her cheeks and her eyes were red.

She saw him and flew to take him in her arms.

"Andi!" She hugged him so hard, he thought his ribs would crack. "We were so frightened! We thought you had run away! We thought—"

His father and grandfather came down the stairs, his father fully dressed, and Andreas pulled away from his mother. "Papi, I'm sorry."

"What happened, Andreas?" His father stood over him, his face taut with anxiety, staring down at his son who was filthy and smelled of cow dung, but who had the brightest flushed cheeks and shining eyes he had ever seen.

"It was that boy, wasn't it?" his mother said fiercely. "He made you go with him, didn't he?"

"Well?" asked his father.

"No," Andreas said clearly, though his stomach was clenched in a knot of panic. "It was my idea. He was against it."

"But why?" Anna demanded, still half hysterical. "And where have you been? It's after six!"

"I heard you talking last night. I thought he would be safer away from here."

"Where did you go, Andreas?" Roberto asked.

Andreas looked at them defiantly. "I took him away. Far away," he said, gritting his teeth. "You won't find him."

"You're a bad, crazy boy," his grandfather said, still at the foot of the stairs. "You scared your mother and father half to death. If I were your father, I would put you over my knee and give you—"

"Johannes, stop it," his wife, Mathilde, scolded him, though she, too, was pale with fright.

Andreas stared at the telephone. "Did you call anyone? You didn't call the police, did you?"

"I would have done if your father had let me," his mother said, anger heating now that fear had quieted. "He called the neighbors to ask them to watch for you. Hardworking people woken in the dead of night—"

"We must tell them he's back." His father went to close the front door.

"No, Papi, Rolf's still out there."

The big dog sat on the mat outside the door, ears folded back as they always did when the family argued, fur matted with mud. His tail thumped twice tentatively, and he put one paw over the threshold.

"No, Rolf!" Mathilde shooed him back outside. "You're filthy." She looked at Anna, glad of a chance to escape unpleasantness. "I'll go around the back and clean him up."

"No, Mama, that's Andreas's job," Roberto ordered. "It's the least he can do."

Andreas stood his ground. "I took some food for Daniel, Papi, I thought you should know." Better to get it all out now, he thought. "And a little money—"

"I don't believe it!" His mother was horrified. "You stole for that boy?"

"I didn't steal it." He was still so angry with her, he couldn't look her in the eye. "I borrowed it from the shopping money in the kitchen." He decided against mentioning the tractor; he might never be allowed out again if he did.

"Borrowed it?" Roberto said quietly. "And how will you pay it back?"

"From my pocket money." He looked from his father to his mother, and then at his grandparents, standing together in the background, their faces unreadable. He felt the first weariness creep up through him, from his legs up his back and into his mind.

The lights in the hall were too bright, they hurt his eyes. "Can I go and bathe Rolf now, please?"

Slowly his mother shook her head. "You'd better go on up to bed, Andreas. You need your sleep." She looked odd, somehow, sad and deflated, like a pricked balloon.

"Don't you want me to get cleaned up first?" he asked, surprised.

She shrugged. "Just your face and hands and go to bed." Still that sad note in her voice, as if she had lost something. Andreas wished he could feel sorry that he had scared her, but for the first time in his life he didn't really care. If only he hadn't heard them fighting last night—but then Daniel would have been sent back to the camp.

His grandfather picked up the telephone. "I will call the neighbors. You go back to bed, Mathilde."

"I'll take the boy," his wife said.

"No, Mama," Roberto said quickly. "I'll see to him. You get some rest." He looked at Anna. "Are you all right?"

Anna nodded wearily. "I'll just wait with Papa until he's finished."

Andreas went upstairs, his father behind him. In his bedroom he took off the parka and sweater and trousers in silence, laying them unusually neatly over the back of a chair. The sheets on the bed were still rumpled from the night before.

"Well?" his father said as he washed his face and hands at the basin. "Aren't you ashamed?"

Andreas dried himself and looked at his father. He felt as if he might cry and hoped he wouldn't.

"No, Papi."

Roberto frowned, lines appearing between his eyes. Andreas realized how rarely his father looked so serious. "You scared us all very badly, you know. Your grandparents are too old to be given a shock like that."

"I'm sorry I frightened them. And you, Papi. But I'm not ashamed I helped Daniel." He shivered. "I hope they never catch him."

"Get into bed." His father tucked him in, smoothing the sheets with his big hands.

"Thank you, Papi."

Roberto sat on the bed. "How much did you hear last night?"

"Enough."

"I don't have to tell you that you should never have listened, do I?" He paused. "Are you very angry with your mother?"

Andreas nodded, not trusting himself to speak.

"You shouldn't be." His father's face was sad, his voice low. "She cares very much about us, about her family. That's why she—"

"But she would have let them send Daniel back to that terrible place!" The tears sprang to his eyes at last.

"You know, Andi, that might not have been the worst thing for him. He was safe there, at least."

"But he *hated* it! He was unhappy there, Papi."

Roberto nodded. "Well, he's away from it now." He held out his arms, and Andreas came into them. His father's warmth and solidness were like soothing balm and he felt the tension in him beginning to ebb away.

"Don't be angry with your mother anymore, Andi."

Andreas clung to him, and whispered against his neck, "But she was mean to you, Papi."

"That was just grown-up fighting. Sometimes we say things we don't mean, Andi." He held him at arm's length and looked at him sternly. "That's one reason you shouldn't have been listening. You should have come downstairs and told us you were awake, and then we could have talked the whole thing out."

Andreas sniffed, and wiped his eyes with the back of his hand. "But Mutti would still have sent Daniel back."

"Maybe," his father murmured. "Maybe not." He kissed the top of his head, a lingering, warm kiss. "Get some sleep now. And when you wake up, I want you to do a little thinking about your mother's reasons for acting as she did."

"All right." Andreas lay back.

Roberto stood up and went to the door.

"Papi." Andreas stopped him before sleep claimed him completely. "Will you make sure Rolf is all right, please?"

His father smiled. "Of course. Good night, Andi."

"Good night, Papi."

9

Roberto Alessandro understood better than his wife what such tragic, sweeping circumstances must do to a boy like Daniel. In his own case there had, thank the Lord, been no such catastrophes, and he had been several years older than Daniel when he traveled alone across Europe in order to recast himself in a new mold. But he had known poverty, he had known hunger, and he had known sorrow.

He had also known great happiness. It was true that he was born in one of the most impoverished districts of Naples, but Roberto was a dreamy, contented child who grew into a skinny, irrepressible, absentminded boy about whom his father, Paolo, a fisherman with a great leonine head and a hot temper, complained loudly and often. Roberto would never amount to anything, he grumbled, so long as he was happy lounging in the stern of a boat, letting catch after catch slip through the nets that swung in the warm Tyrrhenian waters. Paolo believed that the world began and ended in the hot Neapolitan sunshine, and that any son of his must grow up wanting no more from life than a good day's fishing, a carafe or two of cheap red Chianti, and a hardworking, full-breasted woman to warm his bed at the end of the day.

Roberto's mother, Marina, had different ideas for her firstborn. She had given Paolo two more sons besides Roberto to fulfill his expectations, and she believed that Roberto must look elsewhere in the world to find his destiny.

By the time he was seventeen Roberto had grown into a gentle, handsome giant with dancing brown eyes, a strong chin deeply cleft by a dimple, a voice that seemed to sing every spoken word, and a generous, idealistic nature. The girls adored him; even during siesta in the roads near the big fish market in the Via Carmignano, when shops closed and houses slept, the girls would materialize suddenly from behind closed shutters and beaded curtains when Roberto passed by, waving their greetings or beckoning with seductive smiles.

Roberto understood that by working hard for his father he was making his mother's life a little easier, so he hauled, tugged, and heaved cheerfully with the other fishermen, and found that life drifted painlessly by. Yet all the time, in his head, he was spinning dreams about the true *grande passione* of his life—the world of auto racing.

The images conjured up by everything he heard or read about the sport and about the flamboyant, courageous drivers were more real to Roberto than Naples. Since the age of twelve, in the port, he had listened to the old men's tales of the legendary French driver Boillot and of their own countryman, the great Nazzaro; by the time he was sixteen he had his own heroes to follow, as Nuvolari and Varzi formed the Bugatti team and hurtled from victory to victory. While it was the stench of fish that entered every pore of his skin, in Roberto's nostrils was the smell of gasoline. . . . While the men shouted and sang around him, in his ears he heard the roar of the engines. . . . While his large, capable hands sorted fish and hauled in nets, in his imagination those fingers gripped the wheel of a Ferrari or a Bugatti. . . .

Marina slaved over dressmaking and alterations late into each night while Paolo snored in the next room, and she indulged her son to the limit of her resources, her pride in him as intense as her desire to see him escape the confines of their world. Unlike her husband, Marina was unafraid to venture out into the more prosperous areas of Naples. The clothes she made for herself were practical; they covered her decently, kept her warm in winter and cool in summer, and were generally of printed fabrics in order to disguise their wear and tear. But on a rail at the back of her workroom she kept what she called her *raffineria*—one well-cut dress of plain cotton, and a coat of pure black wool that she had spied in a flea market years earlier and that she now kept for her forays into the shops and workrooms of the *zone eleganti*. The men and women for whom she worked considered her a craftswoman, and during the bad times when the fishing hauls were meager she often earned more money than Paolo. What was not handed over to him and was not spent on essentials, Marina tucked away carefully in a hiding place at the back of the small alcove which housed the figures of the Blessed Virgin and the saints.

"*Vieni*, Roberto," she would whisper once every few months, beckoning him into the workroom. "I have a little gift for you," she would say, and then from her apron she would take a small bundle of notes and push them into his hands. "For the race in Milano."

"Mamma!" Roberto's face would crease in wonder. "How do you know?"

Marina would reach up to her tall son, and take his face in both hands. "You know I always find out. And I always help when I can, *piccolo gigante.*"

"It's too much, Mamma. I cannot take it. What if there is an emergency? What if Papa needs it?"

Then Marina would fold her arms sternly across her chest and speak fiercely to him. "You go to Milano, you see the race, and then you walk around. You visit the Duomo, you go to see La Scala, you look at the galleries and museums, and then you watch the businessmen and the doctors and lawyers."

Roberto laughed. *"Sì, Mamma."*

"You must travel, Roberto, you must see the world. There is more than Naples—more than the port and the Via Carmignano!"

In May 1931, when Roberto was nineteen, Marina bought him a third-class train ticket to Brescia in the north of Italy. It had taken her months to save the price of the ticket, but this race was special —the Mille Miglia, the classic thousand-mile road race, won every year by Italians.

For the first time Italy was defeated. Their man, Campari, finished just eleven minutes behind the German, Caracciola, and Roberto howled along with the rest of the home crowd.

His hands plunged deep into his pockets, his cap pulled low over his eyes, Roberto left the Piazza Vittoria staring down at the path, looking neither left nor right. He didn't notice the young woman until it was too late. Their collision knocked the bags out of her arms.

"Trottel!"

"Mille scuse, signorina!" He retrieved her scattered possessions and dumped them into her large straw basket. "I was not looking, I did not see you—" He pressed the basket and a brown paper parcel tied with string into her hands. "Are you hurt? Did I—?"

He stopped. In all his life, he had never seen such a girl. In Naples the girls were almost all dark and olive-skinned, and though they were often luscious, they were either openly seductive, willing to whore for the price of dinner, or else forbiddingly virginal and never out of the glare of their chaperones.

This girl was tiny and golden, dressed like the women he had seen in photographs in glossy magazines dropped in the waiting room at Naples station. Her skin was marble white, her flaxen hair was tied beneath her hat in a soft knot at the back of her neck, her

eyes were blue and bright, her lips deliciously pursed, her cheeks
flushed with vexation—Roberto had never seen a creature so
sweet and soft . . . and neat!

"Must you stare?" She spoke Italian well, but he could tell it
was not her native tongue.

"Forgive me, signorina." He stepped back. "Allow me to make
amends."

"There is no need."

"At least let me carry your bags." He spoke hastily, confused by
her loveliness. For the first time in his life, he was ashamed of his
shabbiness, of his gaucheness. "Could I offer you something to
drink?"

Impatiently, she straightened her hat.

"A cappuccino," he added urgently, "to revive you." He
thought he would die on the spot if she refused.

For the rest of her life, Anna Pfister was never quite sure why
she said yes.

She was born in 1915 on her parents' farm in Küssnacht in
Switzerland in a wooden four-poster bed in a large bedroom with
oak beams and a great window. It was early morning, and her
father, Johannes, who was in the room at the moment of her birth,
claimed afterward that the seven-pound infant had blinked her
blue eyes several times in surprise at the sunlight, and had smiled
at the sound of cowbells in the meadow outside, before rendering
the obligatory first yell of her life.

By her first birthday Anna looked like Mathilde, her mother, a
dainty, pretty, flaxen-haired beauty. By her fourth birthday, it was
plain that she had inherited Mathilde's common sense and her
father's strength of will and reserved nature. By the time she was
ten, she was as wedded to the land as any good Swiss farmer. By
fourteen, Anna was considered the "catch" of the district, for not
only was she uncommonly pretty and bright, but the Pfisters were
prosperous landowning farmers, and any future bridegroom could
look forward to a handsome dowry.

Anna's nature was self-contained; her priorities as well ordered
as her life. She saw the land as past, present, and future, and her
role in life as dutiful daughter to her beloved mother and father
until the time would come for her to leave them for a husband,
who would cherish the land as much as the Pfisters always had.

The unchaperoned journey she took in the spring of 1931 from
Küssnacht to Brescia was an unprecedented adventure for a six-
teen-year-old girl of Anna's status, but she was sensible and confi-

dent for her years, and her aunt and uncle in Brescia had looked
forward to her visit for many months, so her parents agreed.

The young Italian who had run into her seemed so genuinely
upset that she decided it was only courtesy to permit him to accompany her to the *bar-ristorante* in the station. She was shaken,
after all—and he *was* extraordinarily handsome, with his gentle
brown eyes, and the gleaming black hair that reminded Anna of
the young stallion kept tethered apart from the other horses at the
neighboring farm in Küssnacht.

"Just one cappuccino, please," she said firmly, checking the time
on the restaurant clock and trying to ignore the bustling crowd
around them. "My train will be boarding very soon."

Roberto ordered from the waiter and turned to stare at her,
making her blush. "What is your name, signorina?"

"I am Fräulein Anna Pfister," she said haughtily. "And your
name, signore?"

He introduced himself, and his gaze intensified. She was an
angel—he was utterly enchanted. "Where did you come from,
Fräulein Anna Pfister? And where will your train take you when it
comes?"

Anna cast her eyes downward. If her parents knew that she was
sitting in a public place with a stranger—and a foreigner, at that—
they would be appalled, and she would be rushed to the local
priest for immediate confession.

"You are not Italian," Roberto observed. "Are you German?"

She tossed her head. "No." A flicker of pride flashed in her
eyes. "I'm Swiss."

The waiter brought their drinks, and Roberto studied Anna as
she sipped from her cup and then delicately dabbed the white
froth from her lips with a fragile embroidered handkerchief. *Santa
Maria!* She was exquisite.

"Are you feeling better, Fräulein?" he asked after a minute.

"Much better, thank you." Her confidence increased a little.
"Do you live here?"

"No, I am from Naples." He smiled. "I came to see the end of
the race."

"Oh." Under cover of her eyelashes, Anna watched him. He
had the body of an athlete, she decided, his face was burnished
bronze, and his hands were large and strong. "Are you a driver?"

He laughed deeply. "No, I am a fisherman."

For a moment Anna fought to conceal her disappointment—but
then disdain melted before a vision of Roberto Alessandro stand-

ing tall in the stern of his fishing boat, the hot sun beating down on his dark head, the muscles of his shoulders and arms rippling as he hauled in the nets.

"It's a long way to come, just to see a race," she said uncertainly.

"I would have come a thousand kilometers to see the Mille Miglia."

Anna drank a little more coffee and glanced again at the clock. She began to pull on her white gloves. "I must go. My train is boarding."

Roberto tossed some coins on the table and leaped to his feet. "May I see you to the train?"

Anna shook her head. "That's not necessary. You have been most kind." She gathered up her belongings and rose.

"At least let me carry your bags."

For a second, her resolve weakened. But then, with a firm gesture, she extended her right hand. There was no point in drawing out the departure. They were from different worlds, and however handsome and charming he was, her parents were much too conventional to consider—it was hopeless. "I shall manage alone, Signor Alessandro," she said. "I hope you enjoy the rest of your stay in Brescia." She turned and walked away.

Roberto stared down at his scuffed boots, depression descending in a great wave of self-pity. He heard the door closing. She was gone. Soon her train would glide up over the alps into Switzerland, and he would never see her again.

"Trottel!"

It came from outside, from the platform. A clear, ringing cry of indignation.

Hope surging, Roberto rushed from the dining room.

Anna Pfister stood not thirty yards away, white-gloved hands on hips, bags and packages strewn again on the paving stones around her.

Roberto ran to her.

"A boy," she gasped. "Ran into me."

He picked up the paper parcel and smiled at her. "I hope there is nothing fragile in here."

"Nothing."

Roberto pointed to the clock and gathered up the rest of her things. "We must hurry."

Anna's cheeks were crimson and her heart was pounding, but she kept her head. "Platform six," she declared, and began to run, one hand steadying her hat.

The conductor held open the door of the first-class carriage. Roberto clutched at one remaining, fluttering straw. "Fräulein, I would like very much to write to you."

She gazed up at him. "You haven't my address."

He snatched at the label on her bag and stared hard at it. "I will remember," he said triumphantly. "Will you write back to me?"

Anna smiled in spite of herself. She pushed a stray wisp of hair from her face and stepped up into the carriage. "I may," she said, "if my parents do not object."

A whistle blew piercingly and Roberto jumped up onto the platform of the train. The conductor laid a hand on his arm. "Do you have a ticket, signore?"

Anna looked down at him as he retreated in defeat. Her eyes were very bright. "I'll watch the mail for an Italian postmark," she said very quickly, and turned away.

It took Marina nine months to save the money for her son's ticket to Switzerland. She had Paolo's fury to contend with, and the struggle to sustain and feed four grown men, but the constant flow of letters back and forth between Küssnacht and Naples were filled with such burgeoning romance that she thought her heart would break if she failed her son now. In March 1932 the target was reached, and the precious ticket bought.

She walked to the bus station with Roberto. She wore her special black coat and Sunday hat, and though she had sworn on her knees before the Blessed Virgin that she would not weep, her eyes were full of tears.

"You look beautiful, Mamma," Roberto said huskily, his own throat choked with love.

"And you are very handsome." She handed him a paper parcel. "What is it?"

"A wedding gift," she said simply. "If your young lady accepts you, she can use it on Sundays and feast days. It is my grandmother's best lace cloth."

Roberto held the parcel tightly against his cheek. He felt suddenly afraid. He was abandoning his mother to a harsh life, throwing himself at the mercy of strangers in a foreign land.

Perceiving his fear, Marina reached up and touched his cheek. "Don't be afraid, Roberto. Anyone who knows you cannot fail to love you. Just be yourself. Do not change too much, even for Anna Pfister." She smiled through her tears. "Work hard, my son, but never lose your dreams."

"I will work hard, Mamma, and earn enough money to send you a ticket."

She bit her lip. "If you are unhappy, come home." In her heart she began to pray that he would hate Switzerland, that Anna Pfister would not love him.

"*Roma!*" bellowed a uniformed official, and passengers began to board the bus.

Roberto bent and took Marina in his arms, realizing with a fierce pang of love how tiny and fragile she was, and yet what a profound force she was in his life.

"How can I ever thank you, Mamma?"

She held his face between both her hands and kissed him hard on the mouth. "There is nothing to thank me for, *piccolo gigante.*" She felt the first sob welling up in her breast and pulled away. "Catch your bus, Roberto."

He picked up his bag and clutched the paper parcel to his chest. "Be safe, Mamma. Tell Papa and my brothers that I love them." His voice was choked. "Make them take care of you." Quickly he turned and walked to the bus, half stumbling on the steps, not daring to look back in case he broke down and wept openly.

Marina watched until he was inside the bus. "God bless you," she whispered, and crossed herself. And then she, too, turned, and began to walk back through the crowds toward home.

Johannes and Mathilde Pfister were perplexed. The correspondence between Anna and the young Italian had at first seemed harmless enough, but before long the arrival of each thick letter from Naples had taken on such significance for Anna that even her unquestionable dedication to the farm had suffered while she sat in her bedroom, reading avidly the Italian words of love over and over again. Now, suddenly, Roberto Alessandro, handsome young Neapolitan fisherman, stood before them on their doorstep, undeniably eager, suitably humble, with black eyes that shone as they fell on their daughter's pretty face.

Anna pleaded with Johannes to allow him to stay. "After all, Papa," she cajoled her father in the kitchen, while Roberto shifted anxiously in the hallway, "he is a visitor to our country, and quite dependent on our hospitality."

"But he is in love with you."

Anna blushed and lowered her eyes.

Johannes was unconvinced but, as always, helpless before the charm and will of his only child. Times were troubled in Italy now, he fretted, as they were becoming all over Europe. It was all too easy, he feared, for an attractive fortune hunter to use an impressionable girl to gain safety and comfort in a neutral country.

"I intend, of course, to work for my keep, Herr Pfister," Roberto said on the first evening, using Anna as interpreter, and passing his first test of integrity.

"And what would you like to do, Alessandro?" asked Johannes skeptically.

"I would like to learn about farming, sir. From the bottom, of course," he added, passing the second test of humility.

And on the second evening, after a grueling day's work shoveling cow dung: "I think I should learn German, don't you, Herr Pfister?"

Johannes lit his pipe, looked across at Mathilde, who paused in her embroidery to smile, and grunted grudging approval.

"I shall teach him," Anna said firmly—and the third and fourth tests of intelligence and willingness to adapt were passed.

Anna was in love for the first time. There was a part of her that rejoiced at the sight of Roberto, and sighed with pleasure at his kisses; but that part lay beneath layers of an entirely different joy born out of common sense. She saw Roberto as an exciting yet malleable personality, a tender, passionate lover who, though he stemmed from a different background, would work hard on the land, be pleasing to live with, and who would give her sturdy, beautiful babies to carry on the Pfister tradition. In return, Anna intended to take the name of Alessandro, and to be a strong, attractive, useful wife.

The wedding took place one year to the day after Roberto's arrival in Switzerland, and the marriage of opposites thrived, partly because it was the difference in their natures that so attracted them, partly because neither tried fundamentally to change the other. Roberto remained romantic and impulsive; Anna, self-contained and levelheaded. Sometimes Roberto dreamed at night of an Anna softly curved and naked, crying out with passion; yet he adored the real Anna, the proud, sweet wife who lay waiting for him in her white batiste nightgowns, who never failed to satisfy him, though she found it almost impossible to express her feelings or her own needs while he made love to her.

Gradually, Roberto learned to understand his wife's private nature, to read the meaning of her subtle signals . . . the tiny, glowing light that flickered in her eyes when she was aroused . . . the way her lips curved when she was especially happy . . .

He never saw her more sublimely happy than on the night in

October when she whispered to him with exquisite shyness that she was pregnant.

"Are you sure?" Roberto asked, hardly able to take it in.

She nodded, her dimpled cheeks flushed dark with pride and joy. "I was certain even before the test," she said, "but I wanted to hear Dr. Angelis say the words before I told you."

He did not know which way to turn—he felt he would explode into a thousand exultant fragments at any second. The thought of a child—the prospect of his Anna, swollen and ripe with new life growing strong inside her . . .

"Who is this doctor?" he demanded anxiously. "Is he the best?"

Anna laughed with pleasure. "His name is Stefan Angelis, he is the most sought-after obstetrician in Lucerne, he works only at the Geiger Klinik, which is a most favorable place"—she kissed his cheek—"and I love you."

Roberto put his arms about her and cradled her, his eyes shining in the half-light from the window. "I hope for a girl, *mi'amore,* a tiny *bella ragazza* with angel's hair like her mother, another Anna for me to cuddle."

"It will be a boy," Anna said confidently. "A son, to grow strong and help you and my father—"

Roberto placed his large hand on her flat stomach. "Are you listening, *piccolo bambino?* Do you hear what your mamma tells you?"

Shy again, Anna pulled out of his grasp.

Roberto reached over and switched on the bedside lamp. "Anna, this is no time for modesty." He sat up and looked at her. "What does this doctor say about lovemaking? Is it dangerous?"

She laughed. "Of course not."

Again, with reverence, Roberto placed his hand on her stomach. "This baby will make you even more beautiful," he whispered. And slowly he untied the white satin ribbon of her nightgown and began to kiss her breasts, until she shivered with desire and her eyes gleamed. . . .

During the months of her pregnancy, Anna found her Italian husband more than ever the man of her dreams, responding with natural instinct to each and every need, spoken or tacit. She suffered no morning sickness and permitted herself none of the foolish whims or cravings that were often associated with pregnancy, but still Roberto contrived to spoil her as extravagantly as he could. He bought a book on pregnancy and childbirth, and pored over it at night, reading from it to Anna until she groaned with impatience. He told her when their child had developed fingers after two months, fingernails in the third month, and at six months, when the book said that eyebrows and lashes ought now to be present, Roberto was beside himself with excitement. Each week he bought red and pink roses, red for Anna, pink for Mathilde, teasing her about becoming a grandmother; each night he stood in the future nursery, eyes closed, praying as never before for a healthy child.

Anna's pains began during the evening of the last day of May. Their son, Andreas Peter, was born ten hours later. There were no complications, the baby was pronounced perfect in every way from the top of his delicate head to his tiny, plump feet, and he and his mother were home from the clinic in less than a week.

"I knew it," Anna proclaimed jubilantly. "A boy! And so simple. I could have given birth at home. Such a waste of money."

"How can you say that? Look at our child!"

She gazed down at the bundle in her arms. "He's quite fine, isn't he."

"Fine? He's exquisite!"

Roberto was even more triumphant over the baby than he had been over Anna's swollen belly. If Andreas so much as gurgled, he would crow with rapture. One might have thought that no more special child had ever been born in the length and breadth of Switzerland!

Andreas was indeed spectacular—a soft, peachy-skinned baby with his mother's white-gold hair and his father's dark, almost black eyes. It was as if a playful sorcerer had waved his hand and duplicated the most striking physical characteristics of both parents, and to great effect.

At last, persuaded to abandon Paolo and Roberto's brothers for a week, Marina arrived in Lucerne for the baptism. Roberto stood on the platform waiting, and was surprised to see his mother alighting from a third-class carriage at the far end of the train.

"But Mamma," he said, after they had embraced and wept a little, "I sent you a first-class ticket."

"I changed it," she said, feeling in her purse for an envelope, which she handed to Roberto. "I couldn't let you waste such extravagance on an old woman."

"But I wanted you to travel in comfort," he protested. "It's such a long journey."

Marina's face was bright with joy. "I knew I was coming to you, and to your wife and son. Why should I care what my seat is made from?"

Roberto tried to press the envelope back into her hand. "At least keep the money—buy something for yourself—or use it for another visit."

She made a face. "Who knows when I will come again? I want you to save it for little Andreas."

"Andreas won't need it, Mamma. The farm is prosperous, and I am learning to run it well. Your son is quite a good farmer, you know—a better farmer than he was a fisherman."

Marina smiled, pride glowing in her cheeks. "Just the same, save the money for my grandson. It is good for a grandmother to feel she can give something."

"I'm sure it's not the only thing you have brought, Mamma," Roberto replied, eyeing her heavy bags.

She gestured dismissively. "A few things for the *bambino.*" She reached up and stroked his cheek. "Surely you would not spoil your mother's happiness, Roberto?"

He bent and took her in his arms again. "Of course not, Mamma."

The Pfisters warmed quickly to Marina, drawn and impressed by her natural elegance and kindness, and finding a common bond through her devout Catholicism, but it was the first and last visit Marina made to Küssnacht. The following winter, after a short illness, she developed pneumonia and died suddenly. In her secret place, at the back of the alcove housing the Virgin Mary and the saints, Paolo discovered a little bundle of lire in a tin marked clearly in Marina's tidy handwriting: *Per le visioni*—"For the dreams."

Roberto buried his grief in his new family and his work. Farming interested him more and more, and almost daily, new ideas for increasing efficiency and productivity came to him. Because of his imagination, their farm was the first in the district to have a motorized tractor, and it was Roberto's suggestion that they open their own *Molkerei* and *Käserei*—until then, like all their neighbors, they had sent their milk for pasteurizing and cheesemaking to the bigger centers like Weggis and Emmenbrücke, but now, with new modern facilities on their own land, they were fast becoming the largest employers in the region.

Roberto began flexing muscles he might never have known he possessed had he remained in Naples. The love of the land, like an infectious fever, captivated him, as did the brand-new thrill of ownership and success. When his father-in-law named the new plant Pfister–Alessandro, Roberto was overjoyed and proud. This was solid and true, he thought, unlike the sea from which his own family had scratched their precarious living; something worthwhile to build on and give to his son.

Andreas, it appeared, had inherited more than a mix of his parents' physical characteristics. He was like them in other conflicting ways, too, and the blending of Roberto's impulsive nature and Anna's veiled reserve in one small soul was often confusing to others. One minute he might hurtle into a room and hug his parents and grandparents until their ribs ached—the next, if pressed for an open display of affection, he might retreat, politely but firmly, like a disdainful turtle.

Roberto never wearied of playing with him. The years when automobiles were all that he had dreamed about were behind him now, but Andreas was clearly a rough-and-tumble child and already showing signs of sharing his love of speed, and Roberto was swift to respond. Every Sunday afternoon he would strap Andreas safely into the back seat of his Lancia convertible, and drive along the wide valley roads with little Andreas shrieking with joy as the wind lashed his face.

Anna was furious. "How can you endanger your child?"

"There's no danger, Anna," he replied, laughing at her. "I never drive really fast."

"A two-year-old has no place in cars. And on a Sunday too. You should be ashamed."

"But he loves the car, and the fresh air is good for him."

She raised her eyes heavenward. "For a clever man you can be so stupid, Roberto. How can a draft be good for a small child? Take him for walks—he will get all the air he needs and he will like that just as much."

"*Si, cara,*" he sighed.

She looked at him sharply. "Don't humor me. I mean it, Roberto. I don't want him in the car. It frightens me."

But the next time Andreas put his little hand into his father's and said imploringly, "Car, Papi, car!" Anna's words were forgotten, and they would climb back into the Lancia, the lake and the reflected mountains flashing past as if on some heavenly, wildly accelerated film.

When Anna became angry with him, Roberto tried to sweeten her with lovemaking, hopeful that soon she would be pregnant again, with more important things to worry about—but that wish did not come true. Andreas's third and fourth birthdays passed, and still the longed-for second baby remained a pipe dream. Dr. Angelis was abandoned, and then another specialist from Zurich, but when Anna and Roberto returned from a visit to Berne, having seen one of the finest gynecologists in Switzerland, they knew there was nothing left to do but pray for another child, and to be grateful for the one they had.

Andreas was an only child, everything to Anna and Roberto. The contrasts between them became more marked than before. Anna lavished ceaseless love and tenderness on Andreas, believing that her care was the gentle yoke that would bind her son to the land; Roberto remembered the meaning of love as taught to him by Marina. Love meant freedom to choose. To dream.

10

For three days after Andreas put him down from the tractor near the road to Emmenbrücke, Daniel walked by day, slept in barns and haystacks by night, and ate sparingly of the food Andreas had given him. His ankle still ached, the new clothes looked respectable but felt uncomfortably tight, and he was anxious that someone might steal the money that burned a hole in his pocket.

On the fourth day, he hid outside a *Rasthaus* patronized by long-distance truck drivers, and waited for an opportunity to present itself. At last it did, in the shape of a large truck carrying electrical equipment to Berne, the capital, so Daniel overheard the driver telling a colleague as they went into the restaurant. Daniel waited until the door closed behind them, and then he ran to the truck, slipped the bolts on the tailgate, and settled down for another long wait.

At Berne he made straight for the railway station, and by stealing free rides in freight compartments, he traveled via Fribourg to Lausanne on Lake Geneva.

The thought of Lausanne was daunting because the spoken language was French, and Daniel had only a slender knowledge gleaned from the French Jews in the camp, but at the same time it was a comforting complication—he was far away from the camp and Küssnacht.

At Lausanne railway station he purchased a pair of scissors, some shampoo, and a bar of soap in a drugstore, and spent almost an hour in the men's room washing, trimming, and combing his hair into an acceptable style. When he was done, he looked at his reflection in the mirror for the first time since his escape. It was like seeing a stranger. When he had got out of the camp he had still looked like a twelve-year-old child, skinny, scared, and too young to be away from his mother. Today, just over two months later, he was taller, lanky rather than skinny, tentative rather than scared, and older.

He dropped into the attendant's saucer the coins he had got back in change at the drugstore and ventured out of the station into the Rue de la Gare, into a world of swift-tongued elegance, stores, office workers, and noisy traffic. He turned left into the Rue de la Grotte and wandered into a large square with a great, beautiful church in its center. He felt dazed but serene; this was a new beginning. No more running, no more hiding, no more petty thieving. Thanks to Andreas Alessandro, he had a chance, and nothing would stop him taking it. Tonight, a bed he could pay for. Tomorrow, a new plan of action. He was free.

He found a place to stay in the Avenue de Milan after spotting a sign in the front window of a dusty house: CHAMBRES A LOUER.

The concierge was a woman in her fifties with a lugubrious face and spindly legs. She seemed satisfied with Daniel.

"Combien, madame?"

Her answer came too rapidly for him, but when he took out his thin wad of notes, she peeled a couple from the top and beamed at him. *"Vous voulez manger?"*

His stomach lurched with longing, but he held on tightly to his money and asked again: *"Combien?"*

"C'est tout compris." She smiled, and pushed his money back toward his pocket. *"Rien à payer."*

The room was at the top of the house, up three flights of narrow stairs, and so reminiscent of the attic in Friedrichshafen that for a moment despair struck Daniel like an arrow through his heart. The image of his father on the first night away from his mother, standing in loneliness and disbelief, imprinted itself again on his brain.

"Le dîner est servi!" came the call from below, and Daniel came back to the present with a jerk of ravenous hunger.

At breakfast next morning *Madame la Concierge* asked him where he had come from.

"Zurich," he answered lightly, taking another sip of coffee from the huge cup and spreading peach jelly on one of the delicious flaky croissants she had served him.

"Et vos parents?" She beamed, but he had a sense that there was a sly curiosity behind the question.

"En route," he said, hoping she would stop there.

"Ah." She smiled. "You will meet them?"

"Oui, madame." He thought for a moment, and then asked her in slow German, "Do you have a typewriter, madame?" He

mimed the act of rolling paper into the machine and then striking the keys.

She had.

The letter, on one of the sheets of paper bearing the Pfister–Alessandro stamp, declared that Daniel Silberstein, age sixteen years, was a hard worker, and that, though young, was honest and strong. It was signed with a scarcely legible flourish.

My last crime, he thought.

He was away from the Avenue de Milan by ten o'clock, and by eleven he was seated on a bench in the botanical gardens nearby, armed with a local newspaper, a dictionary, and a map of the area.

He struggled through the classified advertisements, muddled by the profusion of jobs and the language. It seemed there was nothing suitable for him in Lausanne, but in the town of Vevey, at the Restaurant Lemans, there was an opening for a kitchen boy.

He looked at the map. Vevey was to the east of Lausanne, on the shores of Lake Geneva, on the way to Montreux. Just a bus ride away.

The Restaurant Lemans was a bustling little place with whitewashed walls and blue wooden shutters framing each window. It stood on the Rue de Lavaux one kilometer outside Vevey.

When Daniel arrived, it was two in the afternoon, and lunch was still being served to a few stragglers. It was warm and sunny, and so the guests sat outside in the garden. The solitary waiter, serving both inside and outside, was rapping cups of coffee down on the tables and mopping his forehead in a mood of apparent irritation.

"Qu'est-ce que vous voulez?" he demanded of Daniel, daring him to ask for food.

Daniel held out the newspaper and pointed to the advertisement.

"Vous voulez le patron, Monsieur Bresson," the waiter said, and jerked his chin toward the building.

Daniel went inside. It was shady and cool, and except for two corner tables, all the diners had left. There was a pleasing aroma in the air, a blend of onion, coffee, and stale cigarette smoke. The walls were painted stark white, the only decoration a collection of empty wine bottles strung together with green twine just over the bar.

Behind the bar stood a tall, heavyset man, wearing a striped blue and white apron.

"Monsieur Bresson?" Daniel asked tentatively.

The man turned around. He was more than heavyset, Daniel saw. He was fat; his apron strained at the waist, and three chins wobbled as he smiled. *"C'est moi."*

Daniel showed him the advertisement and pointed to himself.

"Vous ne parlez pas français?" Bresson pursed his lips. "No French?"

Daniel shook his head. *"Allemand,"* he said, but took the dictionary from his bag. "I am learning."

Bresson shrugged twice, very quickly, and then smiled. *"Eh bien.* At least you try." His German was halting but adequate.

"Oui, monsieur."

Bresson untied the apron and slung it over the top of the bar. "Come. I show you the kitchen."

Daniel followed him. The kitchen was not exactly dirty, but it was far from clean. Potato peelings littered the stone floor, meat juice still covered a chopping board on one of the work counters, and the man standing over the sink washing dishes smelled sour.

Bresson grimaced in the man's direction and shook his head. "I need a boy to scrub the kitchen, clean the restaurant, and help my chef."

Daniel waited politely.

"Are you strong?" Bresson eyed him doubtfully.

Daniel bent and took the letter of recommendation from his bag. He handed it to Bresson.

"A reference," Bresson said, amused, but reading it nevertheless. *"Une ferme,"* he murmured. "No experience in restaurants?"

"No, monsieur. But I love food."

Bresson laughed. There was something about the boy that troubled him, but in spite of that he found himself liking him.

"The wages are small," he said. "Do you have a place to live?"

"Not yet, monsieur."

Bresson shrugged again, the same rapid movement. "You may stay here if you wish. There is a room above the restaurant. It would cost you nothing." It suited him to have staff on the premises—at least they were around when he needed them.

Daniel tried to suppress his excitement. "I should like that very much, monsieur."

Bresson glanced at the letter. "You are sixteen?" He was certain the boy was no more than fourteen.

"Oui, monsieur." The palms of Daniel's hands grew sticky with

sweat. A twelve-year-old could never pass for sixteen, especially not before a man with eyes as penetrating as Michel Bresson's.

Bresson mused. A young Jewish boy all alone, and German-born, not Swiss, he was sure . . . Still, there were refugees everywhere these days. The government forbade private individuals to help them, but then he had no proof, did he? And besides, he needed help as much as Daniel Silberstein needed food, work, and a roof over his head. The kitchen staff to whom he paid good wages were scum these days, filthy and uncaring.

"You have no papers?"

Daniel's heart sank like a rock in a pool. "No, monsieur."

Bresson's eyes pierced him. "Are you in trouble with the police?"

"No, monsieur." The answer was definite.

For twenty years Bresson had owned restaurants, first in Paris, where he had shared a café-restaurant with his brother Gilles, until Gilles had married his bitch of a wife, and then here in Vevey. Twenty years, and he'd kept to the letter of the law more scrupulously than most policemen he knew. And now here was this Jewish boy with his sad, bold eyes, with no legal papers and certainly underage, and yet Bresson knew without a doubt that he was going to take him in.

Daniel was staring at him, his face gaunt with strain, the wound under his eye raw in the pale skin. Bresson wondered where he'd got such a cut.

"*Eh bien*," he said suddenly, making Daniel jump, "we'll try. One month, and then we'll see. Work hard and be honest with me, and we'll get along." He waited. "What do you say?"

Daniel wiped his hands on Andreas's trousers and held out his right hand. "I say thank you." The gratitude was naked in his eyes. "I will work very hard, monsieur. I give you my word."

Bresson gave a sharp, satisfied nod. "*Bon.*"

11

"Set menu twice—extra *petits pois* instead of *pommes frites* with one! And hurry it up!"

"One *potage de légumes*—one *crudités*—one pâté—one *soupe de poissons!* And the boss says take special care, they're old friends of his!"

"Daniel! What happened to my order of *glace panachée?* You don't have to cook ice cream, you know!"

Daniel whirled, and whipped, and sliced, and chopped, and slammed the refrigerator door, and lit the gas for the tenth time that night.

"Merde!" he swore. "Do you think I'm an octopus? I'm a man, with two hands!" He ladled soup into a bowl and tossed raw vegetables into a glass jug for the *crudités.*

Michel Bresson appeared at the kitchen door, his round face scarlet. "All right, Daniel? Need help?"

Daniel took time to grin at his boss. "No, I'm fine," he shouted. "No problems."

"Good boy!" Bresson beamed with pleasure. "A cognac later."

"If I'm on my feet!" He dipped a spoon into the simmering *soupe de poissons* and tasted it. *"Parfait!"* he said out loud, and smiled. A year ago he would have used German.

For eighteen months he had been at the restaurant. For the first six months he'd washed dishes, scrubbed potatoes, floors, and lavatories, transported and burned garbage. Michel Bresson was well pleased—his kitchen and restaurant had never shone so brightly—and he had been fair to Daniel in return, making sure the rest of his staff didn't take advantage of the boy because he was young and spoke little French, and increasing his wages as proof of satisfaction. Daniel had loved every moment of it—he was free, so who the hell cared what he was asked to do!

In March 1944, the second chef was laid flat on his back with a slipped disc, and Daniel had been commandeered to help with the cooking. He was in seventh heaven—there were food shortages because of rationing, but it only made him more creative. People came to a restaurant, he reasoned, because they didn't want to stay home, or have a sandwich in their office or store. It was up to them to give them something worth eating. The head chef, Felix Galle, a Genevan who had worked for Bresson for ten years, had originally been a good worker but in recent years had begun to slack off. Daniel, with his natural flair for food, was a wonderful addition to his kitchen, and Galle sensed he had something to hide. What better way to get his work done for him—after all, a boy with a guilty secret was not likely to complain.

When Daniel first realized that Galle was pilfering food and drink, he was anxious and uncomfortable. If anyone were likely to be blamed for shortages, it would be he, not Galle, the senior man. And he could not simply report the head chef to their boss— Bresson was not the type of man to take kindly to an informer.

He found Galle's cache by accident, in a recess in the storeroom wall behind a mountain of empty cartons, while he was searching for a clean box. He looked at the good bottles of wine, at the excellent cuts of meat and loaves of bread, and he burned with anger. Galle was responsible for stocktaking, and Bresson trusted him. Things were tough these days for most restaurateurs in Switzerland. Unlike the French, who worshiped food against all odds, the Swiss were prudent and frugal, determined to make ends meet in trying times. Michel Bresson could not afford these losses.

That afternoon, after a lunch rush, Daniel confronted Galle in the storeroom just as he was adding a shoulder of lamb to his hoard.

"Why do you do that?" His voice rang out.

Galle dropped the meat, unnerved. His face turned the color of cooked beetroot. "Do what?"

"Steal from Monsieur Bresson."

The older man's eyes narrowed. "I beg your pardon?" His voice was harsh.

Daniel stood his ground. "You heard. I asked why you steal from our boss when he's so good to us."

Galle came closer, his shoulders hunched, his figure swaggering. "Been poking that long nose into things that don't concern you, Silberstein?"

Daniel flexed his fingers into fists. He had never hit anyone, with the exception of Andreas Alessandro, and that had been for survival, or so he had thought. He wanted to hit Felix Galle.

"I discovered it by accident."

Galle's eyes were icy cold. "And what do you propose to do about it?"

"Nothing," Daniel said pleasantly. "If you replace what you've stolen, and guarantee that it will stop."

Galle's face was within an inch of his, and Daniel could smell garlic and cognac on his breath. "Is your record all that clean, Silberstein?" he jeered. "Is that why a bourgeois little Jew's been hiding here in the dirt with us for more than a year? Stinking Jewish pig!"

Daniel punched him as hard as he could, catching him on the nose, feeling the jarring impact from his clenched fist right through to his shoulder. Galle crumpled to the floor, groaning, the blood spraying from his nostrils.

"Get up."

Daniel spun around. Michel Bresson stood in the doorway, a knife in his hand, his eyes like gimlets.

Galle moaned and wiped the blood from his face. "He hit me, Michel!" he cried, astonishment in his tone. "I caught him stealing food and he went berserk!"

"Get up." Bresson's voice was cold steel. "Pack your things and get out."

Daniel gaped. He looked down at his right hand, streaked with Galle's blood, and wiped it urgently off onto his overalls. Red smeared clean white. He felt sick.

"What's the matter with you, Michel?" Galle protested, climbing to his feet, eyes wounded. "This boy, this stranger"—he searched for words, feigning outrage—"this *viper!* He steals from you, tries to kill me, and you tell *me* to get out! It's unbelievable!"

"You are right, Felix, it is." Bresson's voice was still calm and cold; only the deep flush rising up his neck and over the first of his chins betrayed his emotion. "That you have taken advantage of my kindness after all these years—"

"Michel, you're mad!"

"Stop your lies, they disgust me!" Bresson snapped. "How long have you been thieving?" He gestured angrily with the knife. "Tell me!"

Galle's bravado disintegrated. He shuffled to the table and sank into a chair, the swagger replaced by abject penitence. "Just the past few months, Michel, I swear to you!" His eyes filled with tears. "You must believe me, Michel!"

Daniel shifted uneasily, watching the performance with something akin to admiration, wondering if Bresson was going to relent.

"I believe you."

Galle looked up hopefully. A tear ran from one eye and mingled with the blood and snot from his nose. He wiped his face with his sleeve. "By God, Michel, if you give me another chance, you won't regret it—"

"I wouldn't give you another chance if you got down on your knees and crawled from here to Zurich."

Galle's expression changed again, his face distorting with anger. "You can't do this to me."

"Can't I?" Bresson marched over to him, grabbed the back of his collar, and yanked him to his feet. "Now get out of here!"

"What about my pay?" Galle choked.

"Pay? Count yourself lucky I don't call the police. Pilfering food during rationing! What in hell do you think they would do with a turd like you?"

Galle tore free and turned venomously on them both. "The little Jew and the pig Jew-lover—or maybe that's what you are, lovers! Does he climb into your bed at night, Michel?"

Enraged, Bresson bellowed and charged at Galle, the knife flying from his hand and clattering to the floor, his fingers grasping at Galle's throat. For a moment, Daniel stood frozen watching, then he flung himself between them, trying desperately to prise Bresson's iron hands away.

"Stop it! You'll kill him!"

With a roar of disgust, Bresson let go, and Galle escaped. In the doorway he looked back, eyes still popping. "You're crazy, Bresson! A maniac! You should be locked up!"

"You'll be locked up," Daniel snapped, "if you don't leave!"

The door slammed so hard that the bottles on the racks quivered and jangled.

Daniel looked at his boss. Always a fastidious man, he hardly ever seemed to perspire, but now a thin cord of sweat shimmered above his brow, and Daniel could almost see the hot anger about him.

"Sit down," he said softly, pressing him into a chair. He left the room and came back with a glass of cognac. "Drink this."

Bresson shook his head. "I'm fine, Daniel. Don't worry about me." He sipped the cognac anyway. In a moment he smiled wryly. "It seems you're in for a promotion, Daniel." He took a deep breath to steady himself. "A little sooner than expected, but I'm not sorry about it."

Daniel stared at him. "But I *am* sorry. I should never have started it."

"Of course you should. I heard the whole conversation from outside the door." Again he smiled. "If you had reported Galle to me, I might have had doubts about you, but as it is . . . ." He drank the rest of the cognac. "Go change your clothes, then come back and have a drink with me. We have arrangements to make, *n'est-ce pas?*"

Daniel smiled.

It was March 1945. Daniel Silberstein was master of the kitchen at Restaurant Lemans; he ran it single-handed, had done since the departure of Galle, and he was content.

Not happy. How could he ever be happy, with those wounds burned into the flesh of his brain? On and on and on, life passed. Vegetable markets at five in the morning—composing menus with Bresson—preparing food—cooking, roasting, baking, grilling—patience, tantrums, humor—cleaning up—and the same all over again for the evening.

With his second week's chef's wages he bought a radio. The BBC's World Service broadened his horizons, opened the whole world to him. News, music, plays in English: he listened avidly, his English dictionary at his side. He listened to dance bands and saw in his mind's eye his parents dancing close together in the salon at Guntherstrasse, the way they had long ago, when he had sat in his highchair, eyes round with wonder, and watched them.

He found a bookshop close to the local colleges on the Rue du Simplon, and began buying English books. One at a time, novels by Arthur Conan Doyle, Agatha Christie, and John Galsworthy. He wrote himself, too, filling whole exercise books with recipes he had created since taking over the kitchen.

And he thought. About Bernhard Segal and Erich Mazinski, where they were, if they were as free as he was. About Andreas Alessandro, if they would ever meet again. And he thought about his father. Alive? Dead? Aware that his son had abandoned him?

He did not think about his mother or his sister, and he did not think about Dachau. And if voices on the radio talked about Adolf Hitler or Heinrich Himmler or their concentration camps, he turned the switch to "off." He could not think about them because it was unbearable. Better to cut them out of his mind.

He thought, sometimes, that with the drudgery of the work he might tire, lose balance, shed the fine skin of quietude. But he did not. Life was good to him. He had no cause to steal or to run. He had respect. The war might be drawing finally to an end, but half the world still drowned in fire. He could hardly ask for more.

12

"My niece is coming to Vevey next week, Daniel."

"How nice. Will she be staying here?"

"Regrettably, yes."

Daniel glanced up from the menu he was writing. "Don't you care for your niece, Michel?"

Bresson folded his letter and replaced it in its envelope. "No," he said.

"So why is she coming?"

"Because her dear mother, my sister-in-law, decided it might be a pleasant change for her." His tone was ironical. "Natalie's first vacation since the war ended."

"How old is she?"

"Seventeen."

Daniel returned to the menu.

"Daniel."

"Yes?"

"Strange, I know, from an uncle." Bresson sighed softly. "Steer clear of her while she is here, Daniel."

Daniel looked curiously at him, then shrugged. "Whatever you say." He smiled. "You're the boss."

Natalie Bresson had come into the world, six pounds and five ounces of artfulness, spite, and acting ability. Her mother, Marie, had despised her own pregnancy, been repelled by her misshapen body, cursed her way through labor; but at the last, Natalie had sprung her first surprise and had slid and tumbled past Marie's thighs as easily as soft, ripe fruit falling from a branch.

She was exquisite; not a blotch of red, not a wrinkle. But she did not breathe. The obstetrician was compelled to turn her upside down by her round heels, to slap her tiny rump, to clear her airways, and finally to blow his own oxygen into her lungs before Natalie took her own first breath and, instead of wailing, curved her rosebud mouth and offered him her minute hands with their sharp, perfect fingernails. Enchanted, aware as a man of science

that newborn infants had no power to smile, the doctor was nonetheless captivated and had plucked her from the table and held her
close—whereupon the baby had plunged her needle-nails into his
cheeks, drawing first blood.

Thus initiated in enticement, Natalie had alternately purred and
hissed her way through infancy into childhood. Her father doted
on her passionately, blindly; her mother knew her from the first.
They were exactly alike.

By the age of five, Natalie was a consummate woman, possessed
of feminine wiles. She kept her papa and all his male friends in the
tender palm of her round little hand. If she was naughty or disobe-
dient, Marie would become angry and summon Gilles to administer a punishment, but the little girl would turn up her innocent,
imploring face, and rub her soft cheek against her father's face
with such sensuality that paternal discipline never exceeded the
mildest chastisement.

Only her uncle saw through her. So far as Michel was concerned, his brother had made a grievous error in marrying Marie
Jourdan. The beautiful Parisian fascist had been consistently unfaithful to her husband throughout their marriage, as Bresson had
predicted, but Gilles remained wildly in love with her. Marie was
a deeply erotic woman with an iron will and a streak of malice. She
had turned Gilles Bresson into mush. Michel recognized the stamp
of the mother on the delicate features of the child, and dreaded
the grown woman who would inevitably follow.

As he dreaded her visit.

It was impossible to ignore Natalie Bresson. Half girl, half
woman, all feline, like the small kitchen cat that lurked in alcoves
and rubbed itself seductively against your ankles when you least
expected it, as if it knew that its sensual twining might cause you to
drop the dish you were carrying and provide it with an extra meal.
Natalie was sharp and neat, with light brown, doe-shaped eyes and
mascaraed lashes, and red lips that drew right back when she
smiled or spoke, exposing tiny white teeth. Her hair was brown
and shoulder-length, permed by a Parisian hairdresser into soft
waves; her breasts were already amply curved and still growing;
her skin was smooth and white, and she brought a whiff of the city
into the gentle bustle of the Restaurant Lemans.

To begin with, Daniel knew her only by what she ordered from
the kitchen. Escargots—filet mignon, *bleu!*—*salade niçoise* with extra anchovies—never dessert, only cheese—no wine, just mineral
water. Daniel observed the different ways she ate; first, with Mi-

chel, demure and tidy, legs folded elegantly at a slight angle, and then, alone at the table, chin resting on the palm of her left hand, cigarette burning in the other, a fine, careless sophistication about her.

Once, as he watched, she caught his eye through the glass and stared coldly, so that he ducked down, face burning with embarrassment, and didn't go near the doors again all evening. She was a dreadful snob, he decided. Michel was right in warning him to stay away from her.

The summons came on the third day of her stay.

"Daniel, my niece insists on thanking you personally for the excellent dinner last night." Bresson looked around the door into the kitchen.

"Two minutes," Daniel said. "Let me finish this."

He chopped the rest of the onions he was preparing, turned them into a pan, switched off the gas, and plunged his hands into cold water.

"If Mohammed won't come to the mountain . . ."

He swung around to see Natalie Bresson in the doorway, one hand flat on the door, the other on her hip. She looked amused.

"I'm sorry, mademoiselle." He wiped his hands on a cloth. "There were things to complete for this evening." He gave her his hand and she accepted it briefly, her fingers warm against his chilly skin. "I'm sorry," he said again. "I used cold water to kill the smell of the onions."

She sniffed delicately at her hand and pulled a slight face. She lowered her arm carefully, clearly trying not to touch her skirt.

Daniel stood awkwardly, not knowing what was expected of him. She was shorter than he was; he had grown so tall in the last two years. And there was a curiously delicious scent about her that made him want to shut his eyes to savor it, better even than the smell of a perfectly seasoned duckling roasting in the oven, which until that very second he had always considered the finest smell in the world. He was aware suddenly of his eyes being drawn like magnets to her face, then to her body, to the secret curves beneath her white blouse—it was an effort not to stare.

"I wanted to congratulate you," she said. Her voice was clear and quite high, with an imperious note. "Your *sauce béarnaise* was really quite good."

"You're very kind."

"I've had better, of course, in Paris," she added, "but I wanted to show my appreciation."

She pushed something into his hand. Daniel looked down and saw three coins.

"No!" he said loudly.

"I beg your pardon?"

"It's out of the question, mademoiselle." He gave the coins back to her firmly. "Your thanks are sufficient," he said stiffly.

Natalie shrugged. *"Tant pis."* She turned, tossing her hair. "We are ready for coffee," she said haughtily. "Bring it, please."

"The waiter will bring it," he answered coolly, but as the door swung closed behind her his heart sank. He had offended her, and now Michel would be angry.

He took down a new bag of coffee beans and poured them into the grinder.

"Daniel." It was Bresson again.

"Just making a fresh pot."

"No hurry. Join us when it's ready."

Daniel looked up in surprise. "But—"

"No customers left, and Jacques and Félicité want to go off now. My niece wishes you to join us, so don't make difficulties, there's a good boy." Bresson smiled briefly and disappeared.

Jacques, the waiter, came into the kitchen, untying his apron. "I'm off," he said. "The boss said you'd see to the coffee."

"Okay, Jacques. See you tonight."

Jacques grinned. "Pretty girl, don't you think?"

Daniel reddened and busied himself with the coffee. He poured into three small cups, placed them on a tray with cream and sugar and picked it up. Then he set it down again and took off his own apron. If he was going to drink coffee with them, let it be as an equal, not as a kitchen hand.

"Ah, bon." Bresson beamed a welcome. "Off duty." He patted the chair beside him. "Sit down, take the weight off your feet."

"Mademoiselle." Daniel nodded politely at Natalie and sat down. "Cream and sugar?"

"Let me," Bresson said. "This place has been crazy the last few days. Relax."

"Business is good, Uncle?" Natalie asked.

He shrugged. "Not bad. Much of it due to Daniel here. He has changed our image—quality is popular and important these days in Vevey."

"As it is everywhere in France," she said.

"Ah, but in France it's different. If a Frenchman dislikes his meal, he lets you know quickly, passionately. In this country, it's more subtle, it takes longer to detect your mistakes." He smiled. "Thanks to Daniel, we seem to be on the right track."

Natalie examined Daniel with interest. "So he is more than just an ordinary employee, Uncle?"

"Certainly not!" Daniel protested, flushing with embarrassment.

The telephone rang, and Bresson went to answer it at the bar.

"I'm sorry," Natalie said quickly, "about the money. I should have realized it was an error." She smiled at him charmingly.

Daniel unbent a little. "Not at all, mademoiselle. I understand that some people might be—"

"But not you," she said. He could not tell if she was mocking him gently or not. "Shall we forget it happened? And begin again?" Her doe eyes were innocent. "Please?"

Daniel blushed again, disarmed. "Of course."

There was a pause.

"Do you work all the time?" Natalie asked.

"Of course not."

"What do you do in your spare time?"

He smiled. "More work."

Her laugh was high-pitched and fluting. "In your time off? At what, for heaven's sake?"

"I study languages, and I read and write."

"What do you write about?"

"I invent new recipes, and write them down."

"How clever," she said dryly. "But all work and no play—you know what they say, don't you, Daniel?"

He swallowed. She was flirting with him, he realized. He didn't know if he liked it or not. "I know," he said.

"Well, then, maybe you would like to spend a little time with me."

Bresson finished his call and sat down between them again. *"Enfin."*

Natalie smiled at her uncle. "I think you work Daniel too hard."

"That's not true!" Daniel flashed her an angry look.

Bresson looked from one to the other. "He works hard," he said steadily, "but I think he enjoys it, *n'est-ce pas,* Daniel?"

"You know I do."

"I was just suggesting that he might like to show me a little of the area, but he said he was too busy."

"I said nothing of the kind." Daniel's eyes pleaded with Bresson to stop the conversation.

Again Natalie smiled. "Well, you implied it." She leaned closer to Bresson and took his hand. "You would give him time off for that, wouldn't you, Uncle?"

Bresson removed his hand. "That would be up to Daniel, I'd say, wouldn't you?"

Daniel stayed out of Natalie's way as much as possible for the next week, but her presence in the restaurant was a constant pressure on him. Like a butterfly she kept after him, one minute fluttering down to flirt, the next soaring away out of reach. Daniel was uncertain whether she irritated him or flattered him. No, on reflection, she confused him.

Monday was his day off from the restaurant, the day when, if he wasn't writing or reading or visiting the bookshop on the Rue du Simplon, he allowed himself the luxury of switching on his radio and drifting away on a cloud of thought and memory.

The second Monday of Natalie's visit was such a day. He woke late, bathed, saw it was a beautiful day, and then lay down again on his bed, exhausted, and went back to sleep.

It might have been minutes or as much as an hour later when the knock came. He stood up, put on his robe, and opened the door.

"*Bonjour,* Daniel." Natalie was dressed in a fluffy beige wool dress, her hair tied back off her face so that the sharp edges of her features showed more prominently, set off by the softer curve of her cheeks. "If you have nothing else to do," she said politely, "I would be happy if you would join me for a picnic."

There was silence. Natalie contemplated him with more interest than ever. He really was a most arresting boy—not handsome, she thought, but the body was lean and strong and the face was a combination of softness and angles, the eyes a sensitive brown, the broken-looking, almost Greek nose and the scar under the left eye completing the image of the youthful pirate.

"Well?" she said softly. "Will you come?"

Daniel looked over his shoulder into his room, and then back at Natalie. No contest.

"Yes," he said. "Would you prefer the beach or the park? The beach is closer."

"Which is more private?"

"The park."

"Well then," she said.

They went to the Parc de l'Arabie and sat under a tree not far from the water. The leaves rustled, the sun shone, birds sang, they ate legs of roast chicken, tomato salad, and freshly baked bread, and they drank the bottle of red wine Natalie had brought with her.

"I thought you didn't drink wine," Daniel said.

"Sometimes I do, sometimes I don't," she answered elusively.

Daniel thought that something strange was happening to him. The wine, he thought, and the sun and air, and Natalie, fluffy and curvaceous in her soft wool and silk stockings, was making his blood flow faster through his veins, making his pulse weaken and then stir. It was an uncommon feeling, he decided, uncommon and excellent.

"How old do you think I am?" she asked suddenly, when they had finished their food and only the cups of wine remained.

"Seventeen," he said.

"And you?"

"Eighteen," Daniel answered steadily. *She can see through me,* he thought. *She knows.*

"Really?" she said, raising an eyebrow skeptically. *Sixteen,* she guessed, *no more.*

She moved closer so that they were no more than a foot away. Daniel felt his heart beat faster. She reached out with one hand and ruffled his hair. A simple, friendly gesture. Neutral, sexless. *Fourteen, just a child. Yes, she knows.* The hand left his hair and touched his face. His chin, the fine stubble that he had only recently begun to shave.

"Have you ever kissed a girl?" she asked, her voice quiet, surrounded by birdsong. But before he could answer, the hand left his face and was at his throat, the index finger with its long scarlet nail stroking down to the top of his chest. Horrified, Daniel felt his penis grow hard inside his trousers. *Christ!* he thought, *she'll see!* And Natalie slipped her hand a little farther inside Daniel's white shirt until she found one of his nipples and began to touch it, playing with it gently with two fingers until she felt him shiver with excitement.

"Would you like to kiss me, Daniel?" Without waiting for an answer she moved closer and placed her lips gently over his. His mouth was dry, his lips rough. She drew slightly away, moistened her own lips with the tip of her tongue, and then came closer again and licked his lips. They parted for her, and she kissed him hard, darting her tongue quickly around the inside of his lips and then drawing away again. Daniel put out one arm and pulled her back. More, he wanted more of this deliciousness . . .

"No." Natalie pulled away and lay back on her elbows, smiling at him. "Bad boy. You have to let *me*, you know. You must lie still."

Daniel was frantically aware of his penis, still rigid, and he felt perspiration on his forehead. "I'm sorry," he said in a low, ashamed voice.

"Good boy," she said, and rolled over so that she was right beside him. "Now lie down—on your back, that's right."

He felt a surge of panic. "What if someone comes? It's a public park—"

"No one will bother us." She looked around. "Look over there."

Daniel looked. A few hundred yards away lay a couple, tangled in embrace in the grass, oblivious of the rest of the world. Daniel was hot with embarrassment.

"Would you like to stop now, Daniel?" Natalie asked earnestly, her hand resting on his chest lightly, tantalizingly.

He shook his head, unable to speak. She slid closer, so that their hips touched and burned, and she bent her head and kissed his earlobe, fondling it with her tongue. He groaned, unable to help himself, and Natalie smiled, her eyes darker than before. Her hand slid inside his shirt again, farther down, gliding across his chest, stroking the fine hairs there, and drawing a straight, lingering line down toward his navel. He moved involuntarily—it was impossible not to—his penis felt like a rock, he felt that anyone passing within a hundred yards must see it! Suddenly, swiftly, Natalie's other hand moved over him and began to unbuckle his belt. His excitement was unbearable, he tried to help her, but she pushed his hand away.

"Don't move," she threatened, "or I'll stop."

She unbuttoned his fly and grasped him through his shorts, gently but firmly. He moaned and clenched his fists, pounding them into the ground.

"That's it," she whispered in his ear. "That's it, my boy, you're learning. Don't you dare to move . . ."

He longed to punish her then—the feeling came over him in waves, like a torrent. He wanted to take her practiced little hands and pin her down and kiss her as she had kissed him. She was taunting him, teasing him, trying to break him—well, he would show her, he'd wait, bide his time, and then he'd show her how quickly he could learn. . . .

Once more she squeezed him, and then, without a moment's warning, she took her hand away, leaving him exposed and vulnerable, drew her other hand out of his shirt, and rolled away from him.

"There," she said lightly, like a mother who has kissed a scratched knee better. "That's all for the first lesson."

He was dumbfounded. How could she do this to him! It was impossible, unbearable! Had she, after all, decided he wasn't ready, that he was too young? He couldn't stand it. . . .

"Don't worry, *chéri,*" she said, smiling sweetly at him, her lips a little swollen, giving her a pouting look that belied her eyes. "The next lesson takes place in an hour. In your room."

There was no doubt about it. It was the most glorious, the most excruciatingly exciting thing that had ever happened to him.

"Take off your clothes," she commanded him as soon as they got to his room. She sat on his bed, straight-backed, the teacher staring coolly at her pupil; and he, shy as he was, felt there was little point in removing his clothes since her eyes seemed capable of undressing him without any assistance.

He obeyed, though, in perfect silence, and his erection, which he had lost on the way back from the park, and which he had been afraid he might never achieve again, returned in an instant as he trembled under her gaze.

And then it began in earnest.

"Sit on the bed," she ordered, "and look at me."

She undressed, slowly and deliberately, and Daniel was riveted by her movements and by her body. It was all so graceful, so indescribably voluptuous—she flowed out of her clothes until she stood naked before him, her flesh creamy beige, her breasts commanding his eyes, their nipples rosy and pointed.

"Now lie down." She knelt on the bed beside him. "Move over a little."

He obeyed without question. All the aggression he had felt earlier in the park had vanished, only admiration remained.

"Now keep still. If you move, Daniel, or try to touch me unless I tell you to, I swear I will stop and never come near you again!"

Perish the thought!

She bent over him and began to kiss him, first on his lips, lingeringly, almost fondly, then back up over his hair and down on his eyelids. When she kissed his earlobes again he shivered as he had done before, and she whispered, "Remember, nothing unless I tell you." She moved farther down, blowing on each of his nipples and licking them, and Daniel lay motionless as commanded, using self-control he could never have imagined possible. Farther she slid down the bed, down and down, using her hands, her mouth, her feet, her whole body, tickling, licking, flicking, rubbing, slithering, until Daniel burned and moaned in terrible desire, and then she crouched over him and took him in her hands and guided him into her—

"Wait," she warned. "Not yet, wait."

And she moved over him, sliding up and down, then off him altogether so that he cried out in genuine distress, and then she was on him again—

"Yes!" she hissed. "Now! Yes!"

Daniel exploded into her, his orgasm agonizing and powerful as a rocket, and he reached out in the midst of it and took hold of Natalie's arms and turned her over so that she was beneath him, and he watched her face as he climaxed and was aware that, as hard as her slanting doe eyes were, she, too, was riding the wind with him.

Later, after the third time, they lay sated and exhausted on the crumpled sheets.

"You're a strong boy, Daniel," Natalie murmured. "You must let me teach you many things."

"Later, Natalie," Daniel replied, recovering again. He began to suck on one of her nipples until it grew hard, and he came quickly to the happy conclusion that there were some things in life for which one did not require much tuition.

A few minutes later, fondling his penis, Natalie whispered: "Daniel?"

"Mmm?"

"You are a Jew, aren't you."

He stiffened slightly. "Yes." He rubbed his fingers idly over her soft belly. "How do you know?"

"Your cock." She kissed it, then inspected it curiously, as if it were a rare species of animal. "I never had a circumcized cock inside me before."

He flushed, but asked steadily, "Was it good?"

She smiled. "Would you like to do it again, Daniel?"

"Of course."

Unexpectedly she squeezed him hard, hurting him, and then, as she felt his new erection grow large in her hand, she laughed out loud. "Beg me, Daniel."

"That's painful, Natalie," he gasped.

"Beg me, boy!" Her eyes glittered. "If you're a Jew, you must beg for it!"

Daniel froze, not believing his ears.

"Come on, Jew-boy," she taunted, and then, too quickly for him to struggle free, she moved on top again and thrust him into her, grinding herself up and down like an automaton, brutally, mannishly, bringing him swiftly, against his will, to another orgasm.

She rolled off him, breathing hard. "I wanted to do it again so I'd be sure to remember what it felt like."

Wordless, Daniel lay still, staring at her, trying to gather his thoughts, but his mind felt as blasted as his body.

Natalie smiled. "I thought they had killed you all," she said. "In Germany now, you could be put into a museum."

Daniel thought he was going to be sick. She was no better than a Nazi, and he'd just made love to her, put his body inside her.

He scrambled off the bed and began to search for his clothes, trying to collect his thoughts, to buy time. He was trembling violently—he felt guilt-racked and appalled and full of loathing.

"How long have you worked for my uncle?" Natalie asked, the prurient fascination still on her face.

He ignored the question.

"Are you Swiss?"

He found his shorts and climbed into them, relieved at concealing his nakedness from her. "Of course," he answered curtly.

"Where were you born?"

"Is this an inquisition?"

She appeared repentant. "Don't be angry with me, Daniel," she said coyly, curling herself into a small ball on his sheets. "You mustn't blame a girl for showing interest in the men she sleeps with."

Men! he thought with revulsion. "I was born in a place called Emmenbrücke," he said, putting on his trousers and buttoning the fly. "You wouldn't know it, it's a small town near Lucerne." He finished dressing, his fingers still shaking. How much could she know about Swiss dialects, he wondered? "I have work to do." He picked up her dress, leaving her underwear on the rug, and tossed it at her.

Lightly, with her fingertips, she touched her breasts to tease him, and her nipples sprang out again, rosy and luscious. Daniel felt himself hardening, and cursed his lack of self-control in silent fury.

"Get dressed, Natalie. I told you I have to work."

"On your day off?" She seemed amused by his impoliteness and discomfort.

"I make it a rule to study and write each day."

"To improve yourself?"

"That's right."

"Okay." She sprang lithely from the bed and pulled on the dress. "Button me up please, *chéri.*" Quickly she stooped, picked up her lacy brassiere and panties and stuffed them into her purse.

"I'm going, then," she said airily.

"Yes."

She stared down at his trousers and grinned. "Enjoy your work."

Again the maddening blush rose into his cheeks. "I shall."

"Aren't you going to thank me for your lesson, Daniel?"

He closed his eyes for a second, praying for her to go. "Thank you."

She shrugged. "Not very gracious." She opened the door and looked at him. "But don't worry, Daniel," she added, "I won't tell my uncle what happened here."

Just to let you know that she could.

Hatred expanded in him. "Thank you," he said again.

"Do you realize, Uncle, that you have a refugee in your restaurant?"

Bresson eyed his niece with distaste, the bar between them. "If that were true, which it is not, is there some law against it, Natalie?"

"Not if the refugee has permission to work in this country." She smiled. "Does he?"

"Who?"

"You know very well who."

"If you mean Daniel, he doesn't need permission. He was born in Switzerland."

"Ah, yes, he told me. In Emmenbrücke, wasn't it?"

"That's right."

"Does he have papers to prove it?"

Bresson stared coldly at her. "Is that your concern?"

She shrugged. "Not really, since I'm a citizen of France, but I was thinking of you, Uncle. I know the laws here are strictly upheld, and it might mean serious trouble for you if you were aware—" She broke off and smiled. "But of course, Uncle, you are a loyal Swiss, aren't you, so there is no cause for me to worry for you."

"None at all." Bresson uncorked a bottle of red wine. "Have you made any plans to return to Paris, Natalie?"

She grinned. "Do you want so badly to be rid of me, Uncle?"

"Of course not."

"I'm glad," she said, "because I am enjoying my stay here so much." She walked toward the door and then turned back. "How old is your little Jew, by the way, Uncle? Did you tell me? I can't remember."

Bresson poured himself a glass of wine. "I did not."

On Wednesday night, at one in the morning, Natalie came to Daniel's room. She tried the handle, but the door was locked. Lightly, with the tips of her fingernails, she tapped on the wood. There was no response. She tried again, more firmly.

The key turned on the other side, and the door opened a crack. Daniel looked out at her, his face questioning. He was naked to the waist.

"Why do you lock your door, *chéri?*" She pushed against the handle, but Daniel held it fast.

"Because I don't want anyone coming into my room." He was unsmiling, pointedly ignoring her white satin nightgown. "Good night, Natalie." He began to close the door.

"Not even me?" she purred, stopping him, her expression seducing him.

"Particularly not you."

The smile on her face tightened. "If I were you, Daniel Silberstein, I would be more prudent in the way you speak to me." Without warning she shoved hard against the door and thrust her way into the room.

Sitting up in Daniel's bed, the sheets pulled up to her crimson cheeks, sat Félicité, the pretty young waitress from the restaurant.

Natalie's eyes widened and she twisted around, her lips white with fury. "How dare you!" She gathered saliva in her mouth and spat in his face. "You filthy, fornicating little Jew!"

Daniel was stupefied. He had dreamed over the years scores of nightmares where he had come face-to-face with a Nazi. In those dreams, images of his mother and sister had flashed before his eyes, pictures of them with shaved heads being led to their deaths . . . he had seen his Onkel Leo again, reduced and pitiful in his bed, and his father's defeated face . . . and in the dreams his hands had fastened around the throat of his own personal brown-shirted devil. And yet now, a young girl, too young to be a part of the horrors, but still a fragment, severed by age and geography

from the torso, stood before him—spat in his face and abused him
—and he could do nothing except this paltry, impotent thing, this
tiny insult, this rejection of her power.

He looked briefly, pityingly at Félicité, then back at Natalie.
And he forced a laugh, quick and sharp.

"You taught well, Natalie, and I learned well. And I even
learned to select my own company—and I learned that I don't like
Nazi whores!"

Her hand flew into the air, but he was swifter—he grasped it by
the wrist and slammed it against the wall. "Don't even think of it!"

She shrieked in pain and he let her go. She ran to the door and
turned back to face him, and Daniel realized with shock that the
small humiliation had been enough—that Natalie Bresson was un-
stable, and that her own petty brand of viciousness was built on
hysteria and egoism.

Like a serpent's, her breath hissed irrational hatred: "I don't
need to tell you that I will make you regret this, do I, Daniel
Silberstein? You must know it already."

The crash of the door shook the room.

13

"But why, Daniel? Why in the name of God did you have to involve yourself with her? I *warned* you, didn't I! I told you to stay away from her before she even arrived!"

They were in Bresson's private salon. It was ten in the morning, a couple of hours before the midday rush, and Daniel had nothing to say. What could he say that would make any difference? She was Bresson's niece, in his care while she stayed with him. He stared down at his shoes and shook his head miserably.

"She claims you attacked her, forced yourself on her."

Daniel looked up. "And when am I supposed to have done that?"

"Late on Monday night. After your picnic in the Parc de l'Arabie." He stressed the word *picnic* with distaste.

"And why did she wait until today, Thursday, to tell you?"

"She says she was too shocked, too upset to speak out earlier."

Daniel gave a snort of disgust.

"Oh, Daniel, you fool." Bresson threw both hands in the air and paced the salon, ten long strides each way to the window and back again to the bookcase. "What can I do?"

"I didn't do it, Michel," Daniel said quietly.

Bresson sighed. "I know you didn't." He stopped pacing and sank down in the armchair facing Daniel. "But something must have occurred between you. Even Natalie would not invent this without some inspiration." He raised his hands as if fending off a blow. "Never mind, don't tell me—I don't want to know. If you insulted her in some way, I expect you had your reasons."

"Michel, you were there. All last week you must have seen how she baited me, teased me—how I tried to avoid her—but you did nothing to help me!" Daniel's voice was a plea.

Bresson's mouth twisted ironically. "I gave you more credit for instinct, Daniel. My judgment was impaired. For that I am sorry."

Downstairs, in the restaurant, doors banged and someone dropped a tray.

"What happens now, Michel?"

Bresson shook his head sadly. "When Natalie is bent on destruction she is like a dog with a rat. I have seen her at work before." He shrugged. "Her mother is similarly endowed, but I think the young one is more dangerous. Marie, at least, always had self-control, but I fear Natalie is not always quite right in the head. She wants revenge, Daniel." It hurt him deeply to say the words. "She wants me to fire you. She says she will make trouble for you if you stay."

Daniel stared at him. Trouble? Trouble would be leaving this place, this haven, without working papers, with nowhere to go— trouble would be having to leave his only friends. His mind spun, he felt sick.

"Daniel."

He felt a hand on his arm.

"Are you all right? You look ill."

Daniel shook his head. "Yes, I'm all right." And then he laughed, abruptly, bitterly.

"Want a drink? Cognac?"

"No. Nothing. Thank you."

"Well, I do." He took a bottle from the shelf and poured the liquid into a glass. "My God, Daniel! I have to repeat myself, you are a fool. To spoil everything you have achieved here." He drank some of the amber liquid and set the glass down so hard on the table that it splashed up the sides and over the edge. "It's been so good for me having you here. I'm not a young man anymore. I thought—I hoped—"

"I'm sorry, Michel."

Bresson sat down again, heavily. "Natalie was terribly convincing. She wept bitterly, the tears streamed down her cheeks. The innocent victim. A jury would crumble before such wronged purity."

Daniel was shocked. "A jury?"

"No, I don't mean it would come to that. At least not if I do as she demands and get rid of you. She senses how happy you are here, and she sees this as the finest way to punish us both because she and I have never seen eye to eye."

"I see." Daniel felt the trembling begin, saw the old specter of flight, of insecurity, raising its hideous head again, like an unremitting game of hide-and-seek, but in the dark, never in the light.

"Isn't it time, Daniel, that I knew the truth about you?" Bresson asked gently.

Daniel raised his head. He looked into his friend's eyes.

"You do trust me, Daniel, don't you? How can I help you if you don't tell me everything?"

"You can't."

"Well, then."

Daniel shuddered. "I think I will have that cognac after all."

"So my chef is a fourteen-year-old boy." Bresson was white-faced. It was perhaps the least important aspect of the story he had just heard, and yet it shook him deeply.

"Not anymore," Daniel said quietly.

"No," Bresson agreed. He was still trying to absorb it. "Have you written to the Red Cross? Have you tried to trace your family?"

"How could I without giving myself away?"

They fell silent.

"We'll write now," Bresson said.

"My mother and sister are dead."

"You can't be sure."

Daniel shrugged. "I am." He glanced at his watch. "We're late. I should be in the kitchen." He was numb, had felt that way all through the telling of the story. A protective mechanism, he supposed. He had expected relief.

"We'll go soon," Bresson said. "I'll help you."

Daniel swallowed. "Does Natalie expect me to leave right away?"

Bresson's eyes glittered. "If she does, to blazes with her. My guests must eat, no?"

Daniel forced a smile. His face felt wooden. "Let me go down, Michel."

"Daniel—"

"Yes?"

"If you were to discover that there was nothing you could do for your father—if, indeed, you are right about your mother and sister—where would you choose to go?" He paused, and then added, "If you had the choice."

Daniel shut his eyes and thought.

"America," he said at last. An image, a vision, burst suddenly into his mind. Open spaces, tall buildings, thousands of people, joyous music and sounds. Freedom. Where the vision had come from he wasn't sure—from his mother—from his old friend Simon, who had gone there so long ago—from books he read— from the voices on his radio?

"America," he repeated, and there was wonder in his tone.

Bresson leaned forward and touched his hand. "I shall do my best for you," he said.

Natalie returned to Paris the next day, but not before she had extricated a promise from her uncle that Daniel would be out on the street as soon as a replacement could be found.

She looked pale and exhausted as Bresson put her on the train, almost as if she was such a consummate actress that she could think herself physically as well as mentally into the role of her choice. A truly brilliant performance, Bresson thought.

"Remember, Uncle," she said in a low voice before he slammed the door of her carriage. "Maman will check to make sure that he is gone." Her lips trembled. "Such a brute—he should be in prison. . . ."

Bresson shook his head. "Natalie, how like your mother you are."

Her eyes and voice sharpened. "Don't cross us, Uncle. Get the Jew out, for your own sake as well as his. And very soon."

Bresson returned to the restaurant and telephoned his lawyer, a friend of many years' standing, and a Jew.

"Maurice," he said. "I have a favor to ask of you."

"Go ahead. I owe you two."

Bresson smiled. "One is enough."

"Then it must be a big one."

"It is."

"So? Spit it out."

"I would like you to make inquiries into the fate of three friends, two last heard of in Dachau, one in an internment camp here in Switzerland."

"Why not go through the Red Cross, Michel, and save yourself my fees? The ICRC are doing magnificent work in tracing missing persons with the help of IBM."

"Because these inquiries must be made discreetly and as quickly as possible."

"Is that all?"

"No." Bresson took a breath. "I want you to help another friend to get a visa, for the United States of America."

Antonia, Gisela, and Josef Silberstein were all dead. Less than two months after Daniel's escape from the camp, Josef had died of pneumonia and ensuing complications. After further inquiries had been made, it transpired that Daniel's cousins, Sigi and Gretchen

Meier, had been caught and shot by the Nazis at the beginning of
1940.

Daniel had hardly expected to feel such sorrow; he had believed
himself drained, no longer able to feel such a profound sense of
loss. But he did. He grieved deeply, attended the synagogue in
Vevey every day for two weeks, as arranged for him by Maurice
Weinberg, Bresson's lawyer; he sat Shiva in his room over the
restaurant, all alone, and wept late into each night.

"It's good that you're letting some of it out," Bresson said one
evening, "but you have to start thinking about the future. About
your own life."

Daniel turned to him with tear-stained eyes. "I feel so damned
guilty, Michel."

"For God's sake, Daniel, why?"

"Because when I heard that my father had died so soon after I
left the camp, I was *relieved!* So relieved that he couldn't have
known he had been abandoned by his only son—relieved that I
don't have to consider him now—that I can go to America if I get
the papers!" His face was agonized.

"Ah, Daniel, my boy—" Bresson put his arms about him and
felt him shaking with silent sobs. "How could you possibly feel
any other way? You're not a saint, you're a human being! You left
him there because you knew it couldn't matter to him anymore—
you would never have gone otherwise."

"I wish I could be sure," Daniel said bitterly against his shoulder.

"Be sure." Bresson held him at arm's length, and his own expression was fierce. "Be very sure! Stop torturing yourself. You
have mourned enough, though God alone knows you may carry
on grieving for many months yet, it's only natural. But grief and
mourning are two separate things. You have to look ahead—you
must leave the guilt behind you." He paused. "Daniel, do you
think I look forward to losing you? I hate it." He smiled gently.
"Don't make it worse for me by dragging your pain with you into
your new life."

For a few moments there was silence in the room, broken only
by the murmur of traffic outside on the Rue de Lavaux.

"Alors," Bresson said softly. "Will you come downstairs now?
Have dinner with me, drink a little wine? Though the good Lord
knows the food this temporary chef serves needs something
stronger than wine to make it palatable."

Daniel tried to smile, but his lips still quivered. "All right, Michel." He looked ashamed. "I feel like a child again."

"But how good that is, Daniel, don't you see? When did you ever have a chance to be a child? And there won't be much time for that once you get to America." He smiled. "Now come with me."

"On one condition."

"Which is?"

"You let me back into my kitchen to give this man a hand with our dinner."

It took Maurice Weinberg several months to secure a visa for Daniel, and during that time threats flowed menacingly out of Paris from Natalie and her mother. Bresson gritted his teeth and rode out the storm as diplomatically as possible; he hoped that his brother, Gilles, was perhaps discouraging the women from bringing assault charges against Daniel—which, in the event, might leave a stain on his beloved child's reputation—and that, before much longer, Daniel would be safely out of the country.

On the fifth day of May in 1946, Daniel sailed from Marseille. He had in the breast pocket of his new suit official papers, a letter of introduction to a restaurant in Yorkville, New York City, which had promised to employ him as a junior chef, and enough money to see him through until his first week's pay. In a side pocket of his suitcase, to which he clung tightly, was his mother's diamond jewelry, kept in good faith by the *Hauptmann* of the camp, and returned to Daniel via Weinberg.

He was legal, and he was free. The only lie he would continue to live was his claim to be one day away from his nineteenth birthday. Had he admitted his true age, he would have been required by law to attend school in America, and probably have been sent to an orphanage. As it was, his birth certificate was lost forever, and there was no one alive who would argue the point. Daniel was nineteen tomorrow, a young man. Those four years were yet another casualty of the war.

14

Alexandra, shivering, rose quickly from her desk and went to the window to close it. The night sounds, together with the cooling air, disappeared. Over on the rug, Flic stretched and opened one eye to check on her mistress, who stood motionless, staring out through the stained glass into the dark garden.

"It's hard, Flic." Alexandra spoke softly, sensing the dog's watchfulness. "Remembering all the important details, getting down just enough to make it clear for her." She turned from the window and leaned against the wall. Her shoulders and right hand ached, but she realized her task was barely begun. *Not even my memories yet,* she thought; *other people's history. But she has to know it all, if she's to try to understand.*

She wandered over to the baby Steinway, seldom played, laden with family photographs framed in leather and silver. She rested her elbows on the edge of the piano and cupped her chin in her hands.

The entire cast, almost, of the story, all present and correct and immortal here in her study. If only she had found the courage to do this long ago, when Bobbi was still safe here in Honfleur, how much easier life would be now!

Alexandra smiled at the yellowing photograph of John Craig, her father, bent over his easel in the studio in Boston, and at her mother, Lucy, black-haired and windswept in her tiny Cornish backyard. Her eyes roamed over them all, lingering warmly on Roberto Alessandro, undisputed patriarch, resting thoughtfully on Dan Stone, pictured with Andreas outside the Park Avenue Alessandro's. And lastly on Bobbi herself, in the last snapshot mailed by her from Manhattan, standing on the sidewalk outside Andreas's town house, slender and tall, hair scraped back in a ponytail from her tender young face.

Alexandra forced herself back to the desk, rubbed her eyes and dragged her mind back again. In order to go forward into the future and survive, it was necessary first to go back into the past. However much it hurt.

. . . You have written to me, Bobbi, of blood ties. Of the great new bond with your father; something which, I know, has brought Andreas immeasurable joy and relief, for he thought he had lost you forever. But while I can never begrudge him happiness, I am filled with dread at the consequences.

When I first met him, first loved him, I realized immediately that for Andreas there had never been any other route. I think he was born with his appetite for driving, a hunger provoked by his father in spite of his mother. Andreas never had a choice and I saw that. So you see, Bobbi, although you are my only beloved child, if I could believe—truly believe—that you need this thing as much as Andreas did, I would not stand in your way. But I do not believe it.

I never knew Andreas's mother, Anna; only now can I begin to pity her. She loathed and feared everything connected with automobiles, but Roberto could not help himself. He pumped his own unfulfilled obsession into Andreas's veins, thrust that love of steel and speed and danger into him like a pusher feeding drugs into a new addict. Andreas was only nine when he drove Daniel to safety in the farm tractor; thirteen when Roberto built a miniature racetrack on Pfister–Alessandro land so that Andreas could become not only the best, but the safest driver in the land! In 1948, Roberto took Andreas, against Anna's wishes, to see the Swiss Grand Prix, his first big race. Three men died that weekend in Berne—Andreas seemed so shocked that his father felt Anna might, unwittingly, have won. But Andreas went right back to practice when they got home. "They weren't good enough," he told Roberto in innocent arrogance, "or they would not have crashed." Anna had lost.

Andreas did have moments of doubt. It cost him a great deal to inflict such pain on his mother, I am sure. But however much he may have wavered, he did not change his mind. In 1952, when he was on the point of submitting to three years at the University of Geneva, for Anna's sake, he accompanied both his parents on a business trip to Milan. Roberto bought three tickets for the Italian Grand Prix at Monza—Anna, naturally, refused to go, so father and son went alone.

It was the final hook.

Part Two

15

He touched his father's arm, closed his eyes, and tuned into the sounds. Monza. Tens of thousands of voices, yelling, laughing, cursing, chattering in a gaggle of discordant languages and dialects. Down in the pits, the racket of jacks, spanners, wrenches—steel, rubber, crashing, grinding, tapping. And the engines, turning over, revving, throbbing, like the tuning-up noises of a monstrous orchestra, trembling first from every angle in the 180-degree spectrum from his seat—and now gradually coming together, converging, focusing into one mighty whine. Twenty-four of the fastest, most powerful cars and drivers in the world on the starting grid, poised for the start of the twenty-third Italian Grand Prix, the Gran Premio d'Italia, the most famous racetrack in Europe.

Monza! His promised land, his magnet, his Jerusalem!

Andreas opened his eyes. His father, beside him, was watching him, his own dark eyes dancing.

"Va bene?"

Andreas smiled. *"Molto bene, Papi."*

Roberto raised his field glasses, surveyed the grid, and passed them to Andreas. "Look! Ascari! And Farina!" he said excitedly, pointing out the two Ferrari drivers.

"And Villoresi!" Andreas squinted through the glasses. "Where's Fischer?" he asked, searching for the Swiss contender.

"Fourth row, next to Bonetto."

The minutes ticked down, the fumes hung suffocatingly low in the hot air. An American with bare fleshy arms and sweating forehead leaned across Andreas and spoke to Roberto.

"What do you think, signore? Ascari again?"

Roberto laughed, "Who can say? Maybe the Argentinian."

The American snorted. "Gonzales? Never! I'm betting on Ascari—he wins today, he gets the championship." He hauled himself back into his seat and wiped his face with a large red handkerchief. "This heat is terrible. How those guys can concentrate beats the hell out of me."

"They don't feel it," Andreas said quietly.

Roberto took out his stopwatch and sat forward, his face intent. When he spoke, his voice was hushed. "Five. Four. Three. Two. One."

The ferocious blast of the engines hit Andreas like a massive, clenched fist in his stomach. He grinned swiftly, once, at Roberto, and then his head whipped around, his eyes zigzagging with the leaders off into the first lap.

"Gonzales!" Roberto yelled. "Look at him go!" He held Andreas's arm in a vicelike grip as the Maserati shot away from the other cars in the second row and took the lead, surprising everyone. A huge roar went up from the crowd and flashed around the circuit like a human thunder roll.

An hour later, Gonzales was still ahead, though with the handicap of a fuel stop yet to come, and the attention of the crowd transferred from the second-, third-, and fourth-place Ferraris, from which the eventual winner was most likely to spring.

"Son of a gun, he's lost it!" screamed the American somewhere around the fortieth lap as Gonzales went into the Maserati pit. He slapped Andreas on the shoulder. "Your man's out of it! Now watch Ascari go!"

Andreas barely noticed. He was lost, immersed in the race. He felt he was down on the track in the burning heat, consumed by his own adrenaline, the roaring of the crowd a million miles away like an inkblot on the horizon, nothing counting but his brain, cold and calculating, his eyes, all-seeing, his hands and feet and body in perfect command of the power . . .

Roberto took up the glasses again, focused on the Maserati pit for an instant, moved away, and froze.

In the stand below them a figure caught his eye. A woman, on her feet, a white scarf covering her hair, wearing a blue sleeveless dress. She seemed to be staring, like everyone else, down at the track, but then suddenly she thrust both her hands, clenched in tight fists, over her mouth, and began to push her way through the bunched spectators, running wildly, trying to get out.

His shock transmitted itself to Andreas, who glanced at him. "Papa?"

Roberto dropped the glasses in his lap.

"Papa, are you all right?"

"Your mother."

"What?"

"I saw her." He pointed to the spot. "There. She was watching the race."

Andreas took the glasses and searched for her. "I don't see her. Are you sure?"

"She went out."

"Did you leave her the third ticket?"

"I left it in the suite—she didn't want it."

"But if she changed her mind, why didn't she come and sit with us?"

"Perhaps she couldn't find us." Roberto stood up, his face anxious. "I'm going after her."

"But the race—"

"You stay. Enjoy it." He pushed his way through to the aisle and shouted back over the din, "Don't worry if we don't come back—we'll see you at the hotel."

Outside the Autodromo, Roberto made for the cabstand, checking every doorway and entrance as he ran. There were a handful of taxis waiting in line. The drivers stood in a huddle, smoking and chatting. Roberto stopped, breathing heavily.

"Did you see a woman just now—about forty, blond?"

And then he saw her, walking very slowly away from the stadium, chin tucked down almost against her chest, head scarf in her left hand, trailing on the ground.

He ran to her side.

"Anna, *Liebchen*. What are you doing here?" He bent to kiss her, but she continued walking and his lips brushed the air.

"Anna?" He caught at her arm and held it firmly, stopping her. "I asked you what you're doing here?"

"I came to see the race."

"Why?" he asked, worried by her distant, morose expression. "You didn't want to come—you said you would never come."

"May I not change my mind?" she said abruptly, defensively. "Or have I no rights at all anymore?"

"Anna!" he said, perplexed. "Don't say such things."

She looked up at him. There was perspiration on her forehead, and over her top lip, and her eyes were bright. "You asked me to come, Roberto. Why aren't you happy now I'm here?"

"Because I don't understand *why* you came," he said in exasperation. "Why you came alone. Why you ran out like a frightened child! Why, Anna?"

Quickly she turned and walked to the first cab in the line. The driver detached himself from his colleagues and opened the back door for her. She got in, and when Roberto followed she made no protest but moved as far as possible to the other side.

"Hotel Principee Savoia," Roberto told the driver, and looked at Anna. "I want an answer."

The car moved forward.

"I wanted to see for myself, Roberto," she said quietly, and took a shaky breath. "I guessed—no, I *knew*—how I would feel, but I thought, 'Be fair, Anna, be fair to them. You must not condemn what you've never seen, never experienced—you must see for yourself.'" Her lips trembled.

"And now?"

"Now I've seen."

"And?"

Her eyes filled, and she wiped them with the back of her hand with childish fierceness. "And I shall never see another race. Nor change my mind about our son."

Roberto slid across the seat and tried to get her to look at him. "Anna, what in God's name was so terrible? The race was smooth, there were no accidents, no injuries—"

She jerked away from him, her eyes wide. "What was so terrible? It was evil, Roberto! Profane! Can't you see that? Machines built to kill and maim! Madmen who drive them without respect or gratitude for the life God gave them!" She clenched her fists tightly in her lap so that the nails cut into the flesh of her palms. "And the spectators! Screaming like a godforsaken mob in a Roman arena!" She paused briefly, panting for breath. "And you expect me to permit my only son to enter that arena to be slain, Roberto!" She challenged him. "You, his father." She shook her head. "I am ashamed to be your wife."

She turned and faced the window, her back stony. Roberto, saddened and defeated, moved back to the far side of the car, and for the rest of the journey back to the hotel the only sounds in the taxi were the creaking of springs, the purring of the engine, and the happy humming of the driver.

Today was mine, Andreas mused as he sat at the dinner table with his parents that evening in the grill room of their hotel. *That's my world, that will be my life.* He looked at his mother and father through the glowing crystal of his wineglass. They'd had a fight before dinner, he guessed, though like many disciplined families in a public place, they gave an outward impression of civility and calm.

"Just coffee, please," his mother was replying to the waiter.

"For me too, please," Roberto echoed quietly.

She had taken more trouble than usual with her appearance,

Andreas noticed. Her hair was pinned up into a French twist that suited her better than the *Hausfrau* braids she wound around her head each morning at home, and her black dress made her pale thinness appear fragile and almost sexy. It surprised Andreas to think of his mother as sexually attractive.

"All right, Andreas?" his father asked. "You seem far away."

He smiled. "Fine, Papa. Just remembering this afternoon."

Papa was a different story altogether, he reflected. He managed to retain the same look of king-size masculinity whether he wore a work shirt or a dinner jacket. The Neapolitan fisherman and the successful farmer and businessman blended together perfectly.

Andreas caught the eye of the young girl at the next table, dining with her parents and older sister, and she smiled at him shyly. Not bad at all, he thought, that gold-streaked hair curling around her forehead, and that peachy skin. Her mother patted her hand gently, rebukingly, and the girl colored slightly and turned away.

The waiter brought tiny cups of espresso, and Andreas noticed his own reflection in one of the stained antique mirrors on the wall. There was a new air about him, a visible, tangible aura of exhilaration. *It was the race,* he realized. *I feel like one of them now. I even look like one of them.*

"Andreas," his mother said suddenly, curling her thumb and forefinger around the handle of her coffee cup. "What did you think of the race?"

Andreas glanced at his father for inspiration, but received none. "I loved every second of it, Mother." He hesitated. "What about you?"

Anna patted her hair. "I detested it," she answered softly.

"Oh."

"Don't you want to know why?"

"I suppose so, yes."

Roberto made a gesture of appeal with his hands. "Anna—"

"Papa, it's all right." Andreas sat forward. "If Mother made the effort to see something we both know she disapproves of, I suppose I want to know what she felt about it."

"How reasonable." Anna was aloof, isolating herself from them.

"Well?"

"It was the first race I have ever seen," she said, "but I'm afraid it was just as I expected it to be."

A waiter passed by, fussed for a moment with the ashtrays, and wafted away. Anna sipped her espresso. When she spoke again, her tone was quiet but clear. "Ugly, unsportsmanlike—a blood sport participated in by godless masochists and relished by a Philistine mob."

Andreas sat still, astonished.

"I was deeply ashamed," she continued, "to think that you and your father were part of that mob, Andreas, and find only the smallest comfort in the knowledge that, at least today, you were not one of those on the track."

"Anna, stop this, it isn't like you," Roberto said, reaching for her hand, but she withdrew sharply.

"I have another question, Andreas."

He stared at her.

"And I hope for an honest answer."

"Of course, Mother," he replied stiffly.

"In one week," she said, "you leave home to go to Geneva to university. To study for even greater success on the land—our land."

"Yes, Mother."

"Tell me—do you intend to waste all that by becoming an auto-racing driver after you leave university? Is that what you and your father have been plotting behind—"

"Plotting?" Andreas's calm snapped. "Papa never does anything behind your back and you damn well know it!"

"Andreas, that's enough," Roberto broke in sharply. "Do not speak that way to your mother."

"For Christ's sake, Papa, she's accusing you—"

"Enough, I said!" Roberto signaled a waiter for the check, his face dark with anger. "Both of you will kindly wait until we are out of here before you start a scene."

"Andreas," Anna continued unperturbed, as if nothing had interrupted her flow. "I would like to know. Do you mean to drive or to farm when you leave university?"

Andreas stood up and flung his napkin on the table. "Neither, Mother." His fists were clenched tightly by his sides. "As of this moment, I have not the slightest intention of going to university at all."

Without another word, he turned on his heel and stalked out of the restaurant.

The bedroom was pitch black when Roberto woke out of a deep sleep to feel Anna's lips brushing the hair on his chest, and the top of his silk pajamas unbuttoned to the waist. For a few moments, the only emotion that came to him was one of purest delight, and he lay unmoving, his eyes wide open in the dark, feeling himself growing quickly erect and saying nothing.

Anna rubbed her cheek against his nipples and he stirred in new surprise. She so seldom initiated lovemaking, and never had she deliberately seduced him from sleep; her nature was far too modest for such impetuousness.

"Anna?" he murmured at last. "Are you all right?"

She laughed softly against his chest, and he thought how young her voice sounded in the dark. "Of course." She tugged at his pajama trousers and reached for him with one hand, and he gasped with the unexpectedness of her touch. His thoughts whirled. She had been stonily silent when they'd gone to bed; perhaps she was feeling guilty for her attack on him—that outburst in the restaurant was so unlike her.

Anna leaned over him, kissed his eyelids and held his penis, fondling it uncertainly, squeezing him lightly and then, with a quick sigh, letting him go. Immediately he rolled over and put his arm around her, hugging her tightly, feeling her relax against him. He knew what it cost Anna to break the ice after any battle, while for him an apology was such a simple gift.

"Anna, *mi'amore* . . . *Grazie*, Anna . . ." He burrowed his face in her soft hair, then kissed her and felt a searing joy as she parted her lips and gave herself up to him passionately.

"Love me, Roberto," she whispered, breaking away from the kiss just long enough to speak. "Make love to me, please."

"Always, Anna." He slipped the straps of her nightgown down over her shoulders and felt her nipples hard against the palms of his hands as he began to stroke her lightly. "I'm always here for you, my love, whenever you want me." For a moment he stopped his caresses, turned on his side, and lay his head in the soft curve of her shoulder.

"Don't stop, Roberto!" she cried quickly.

He placed a finger against her lips. "Never—I just want to feel you against me for one moment, gently, to savor you . . ."

Anna moaned quietly, and he began again, his hands moving quickly over her body, touching her where he knew from long experience she loved it the most, kissing her first gently, then more roughly, and then, because he sensed that she wanted him so urgently, he moved swiftly over her and took her, face-to-face, gazing into her eyes, a part of him surprised again because Anna, who for almost twenty years had closed her eyes at the moment of penetration, tonight kept them open and gazed back at him.

Later, when it was over and Roberto lay exhausted but contented, his mind and flesh still throbbing and filled with the memory of her, Anna stirred slightly and sat up.

"Anna," he murmured, "lie down. Sleep."

Through his half-closed eyes he saw her reach for her nightgown at the foot of the bed and pull it slowly over her head. Then, with a swift and deliberate movement, she stretched out her hand and switched on the bedside lamp, dazzling him.

"What is it? Are you ill?"

"Roberto?"

"Yes?"

"Did you enjoy making love to me?"

He sat up, bewildered. "Of course I did. What a question! You know I always do."

She sighed. "That's good," she said softly. "Because I wanted you to enjoy it very much."

"Of course," he said, confused. "Anna, what's wrong?"

"I'm truly sorry," she said, "because I loved it just as much as you, Roberto. But it cannot continue." Her face seemed composed.

"What are you talking about?"

"It's very simple," she replied. "You have a strong influence over our son, haven't you?"

Roberto ran his right hand through his hair in frustration. "Anna, if this is about what went on earlier, stop now. Andreas didn't mean what he said—I'm sure he spoke in anger, which is what I am trying very hard not to do now."

Anna looked at him with detached compassion. "I can't blame you for being angry. I wouldn't even blame you if you struck me—"

"Anna! For Christ's sake, when have I ever done such a thing? What's the matter with you?"

She patted her hair and smiled. "Roberto, please do try to listen. I have told you, it's perfectly simple. If Andreas goes to Geneva, and studies agriculture as we all planned and agreed, then for the time being things can continue as always between us."

"Damn you, Anna," Roberto said suddenly, swearing, "for the sake of our marriage, don't go on with this! You have no idea what you're doing—"

"But I have," she soothed. "For the third time, I tell you it's very simple and quite reasonable." Her eyes were innocent. "You will agree, Roberto, surely, that our son was enticed by *your* dreams—that they have always been *your* dreams, not his own. So you will agree, too, that you are the one who should pay the price." She shook her head pityingly. "And I am sorry, my dear, but I cannot think of a better way. Perhaps you will decide that it doesn't matter to you, that you won't miss me—"

"Are you saying that you'll leave me if Andreas doesn't go to Geneva?"

"Of course not. I would never leave you, Roberto, you're my husband." She slid her legs over the side of the bed and stood up, looking down at him. "I just won't sleep with you anymore."

The bubble that for twenty years Roberto had thought protected his ideals and his love for Anna against trouble and adversity, seemed suddenly to burst inside him, and he felt ice-cold. His Anna was standing there—Anna whom he loved with all his heart —on the verge of smashing everything he cared about because she wasn't strong enough to face her son's desires and ambition.

"Anna," he said unsteadily. He got out of bed and laid a hand on her arm. "I understand that you're very upset—that you think you mean this now—"

"Oh, *believe* it," she said vehemently. "Please believe it."

Reason dissolved and he felt sudden fury. "Anna, God damn you to hell for this! Are you so incapable of handling the fact that we have brought up a son with a mind and will of his own? Where's your womanhood, for Christ's sake? You're his mother! I could understand if you collapsed and wept, and told me you were terrified for his life, that you would do *anything* to stop him—I could understand it if you begged me to help you!" He felt the tears springing to his eyes. "Do you think I don't fear for him, Anna? Do you think I'm so sure what I'm doing is right? I *love* my son, he's my own flesh!"

The sound that came from Anna was half moan, half hiss. "How can you *say* that? How can you claim to love him while you lure him to his death! When he was a baby, you spoon-fed him with engine oil!"

"But he's a man now, Anna, not a baby! And he has an ambition burning in him, and maybe I helped set it alight, but I couldn't help it!" He grasped her other arm and shook her. "You could have stopped it, Anna, with warmth and reason, but *no*, you had to withdraw from it, from us, to stand away from us out in the cold—"

"Let me go, Roberto—"

"No!" He trembled violently. "You're like a stone, not a woman! And it isn't enough to rob me of your heart, but now you make threats to steal away your body, too!"

"You could always rape me!"

With a roar he threw her from him, and she fell onto the bed, sprawling, her eyes wide with shock.

"You fool, Anna, you sanctimonious fool! You can say that to me, after all our years together. When have I ever hurt you?" Like a wounded bear he strode back and forth across the room, his tears wet on his face. "You were my virgin bride—I loved you, I worshiped your modesty, your sweetness, I understood that it was terribly hard for you to be demonstrative—but, sweet Jesus, can it still be necessary after *twenty years?"*

She wailed—suddenly, appallingly, shockingly—a deep, keening wail from the heart, and Roberto was beside her in an instant, kneeling by the bed, pity sweeping away the rage. "That's right, *mi'amore,* cry, shout, scream if you want to—"

"I can't, Roberto—"

"You *can!"* He tried to turn her face toward him, but she buried it in the quilt. "You must, Anna, it's the only way. Believe me," he pleaded. "We'll forget tonight, forget what you said—we'll talk together, you can tell Andreas how you feel, listen to what he has to say—"

"No!"

"What?"

Anna raised her head from the quilt, and her expression was tormented. "No, Roberto." Her mouth twisted. "I did mean it—I can't forget it. I love you, you must believe that, but I did mean what I said. If you cannot convince Andreas that going to Geneva is the right thing to do, then I—"

"Anna! Why do you torture me?"

"Do I, Roberto?" Slowly, painfully, she pulled herself back up to a sitting position. "Do I?" she repeated softly, her eyes sad. "I thought it was only myself I was torturing." Helplessly she shrugged. "I'm not asking so much, Roberto. Just that our son goes to university, as he promised he would." Again, wearily, she shrugged. "It's up to you—not to me."

In his single bedroom on the floor above, Andreas poured another glass of champagne for the young girl with the gold-streaked hair.

"Do your parents know where you are?" he asked, stroking her shoulder.

She tossed her hair. "Of course not. They think I'm with Lucia in our room."

"What about her?"

"She'll cover for me, don't worry." She chuckled. "My sister and I always look out for each other."

"Have some more champagne?"

Her eyes sparkled. "I don't need drink to find you attractive, you know." She put down her glass, moved closer to him on the couch, and took his face in her hands. "You're quite handsome." She laid her lips on his, a long, teasing kiss, just brushing his mouth.

"Wait." Andreas put down his own glass, dipped his fingers into the champagne and stroked the cold liquid onto her lips. "Better than drinking it," he said, and licked it away. Her lips parted, and her mouth enveloped his, her tongue tiny and darting and hard. He reached behind her back and fumbled with her zipper.

"Let me help you," she murmured dreamily. "That's it, peel me . . . like a banana . . ." She giggled, and her brown eyes glittered. "There. You like?"

She wore no brassiere, just a satin slip, and her body was tanned and supple, the skin tight as a drum stretched over her small round breasts and belly, rolling into her gold-streaked pubic hair.

"I like," he said, his voice husky.

She pulled away, stood up and kicked away the dress and slip. Then, one at a time, she lifted her legs, toes pointed, undid her garters, and rolled down her stockings.

"Now you," she said. "I want to see you naked."

Quickly, eagerly, he undressed, dropping his clothes on the carpet beside hers.

"You are beautiful," she whispered. "I knew you would be. I watched you all through dinner."

"I thought you looked shy." He laughed and made an awkward grab for her.

She slithered away. "Don't be so impatient."

He reached for her again and kissed her long and hard, feeling new power surging through him. He had never felt so aroused, and yet he knew he was more in control than ever before—he felt he could make love to her for hours and still not come unless he wanted to. And it was more than this girl, who was luscious and lovely as could be—it was the race, the Gran Premio and Monza that had really done it. And the fight at the dinner table. He had hated confronting his mother, it upset him to see the hurt, closed expression on her face, but it had needed saying, and once the words were out he had felt lighter than for months.

"Come on," he said, pulling her to the bed, his fingers already buried in the golden fur between her thighs.

Afterward, she smiled at him. "Very good."

"Really?"

She nodded, and her hair tumbled over her eyes. "A star."

He grinned, pleased.

She sighed and rolled over onto her belly. "What do you plan to do with your life? Or don't you know yet?"

Andreas stretched, feeling all his muscles tighten in perfect control. "Oh, I know," he said, and he shut his eyes, seeing the vision again of the presentation at the Autodromo that afternoon, the sunlight glinting on Ascari's hair and on the trophy, the garlands, the champagne exploding through the air, the laughter of the women . . .

"I am going," he said, "to be the auto-racing champion of the world."

16

On a Wednesday afternoon in May 1952, seven days after what was officially his twenty-fifth birthday but was actually his twenty-first, Daniel Silberstein was granted full citizenship in the United States of America.

He had not thought it an event that would affect him vastly; after all, why should he be affected by mere documentation when it was *living* in America that had transformed his life? But he discovered on his way to meet Leon, Sarah, and Roly for a celebration at Leon's, that it made him feel good, very good indeed!

Bowling across town on West 44th Street, he came upon the Algonquin Hotel, and decided on a drink, a private, commemorative toast before seeing the others—for who else could truly understand how he felt when even *he* had not fully understood until this very moment? And what better place to float into on his personal cloud of jubilation than this bastion of New York civilization?

He strode over the threshold into the lobby, and directly into the tiny Blue Bar.

"A table, sir?"

"Certainly."

He sat in the corner, at one of the most desirable tables. An auspicious omen, he decided. He rang the small bell.

"Sir?" A waiter stood before him.

"A glass of champagne, if you please." The lingering vestiges of his accent troubled him less than usual.

"Thank you, sir."

Daniel relaxed into his seat and warmed to the strangers about him. The Algonquin was one of those places where one could sit alone for hours and not mind a bit. God, how he loved New York! Its crazy opulence, its appalling poverty, the way those two things merged; the way its inhabitants, if they had the spunk and good fortune, could fling rope ladders of optimism across the city from the slums to Fifth Avenue and haul themselves over, just as he had done. New York City was concrete, glass, and steel, but it was a living, breathing animal also, aware of its self-importance and uniqueness, and it stirred Daniel to the core.

The waiter brought olives, potato chips, nuts, and his champagne, the glass misty cold. Daniel sipped at it, glanced at his watch, and sank into memory.

He had not exactly started out in the slums, that was overstating it. With his mother's jewelry secure in a safe-deposit box at the Chase Bank (where he had opened an account with his first twenty-five dollars, determined that his savings, however paltry, should rest beneath the most solid roof he could find), Daniel had lived at first in a damp, cockroach-infested one-room apartment in Yorkville, close to the restaurant where he worked. He hadn't minded at all, because at least he had arrived in America, and because he was free.

He remembered his first impressions of Yorkville as if it were yesterday. He recalled the dull thud of foreboding when he saw store after store covered in German writing. To many refugees "Germantown" was a comfort; not to Daniel, who wanted to speak English, to learn new customs, to belong.

His fears, however, were quickly dispelled when he met Leon and Sarah Gottesman, proprietors of his restaurant. Leon was a Hungarian Jew who had lived in Berlin before Hitler, working as a highly successful chef in Weiss Czarda on Kurfürstendamm. One of the luckier ones, Leon had escaped with money to America and, during his first year in New York, had grabbed his chance to open his own place, serving a mixture of Hungarian and German-Jewish specialties. Sarah Levy had come to work at Leon's as a cashier in 1941, and within a week they had known they were made for each other. Sarah joined him in wedlock and in business partnership, and Leon's flourished. Whenever possible they employed young Jews, aware of the hardships many of their people were enduring, even in New York City, and when Leon read the advertisement placed in the *Jewish Journal* by Michel Bresson's lawyer, he was swift to reply.

"But we have no vacancies," Sarah protested, worried that her husband was overstretching his generosity. "The boy will arrive from Switzerland and we'll have no job for him. You must write again and say you made a mistake."

"I'll do no such thing. The boy's a chef, not just a waiter or a busboy."

"In case you've forgotten, schlemiel, we have a chef—you!"

Leon wagged his finger at her. "Watch your tongue, Mrs. Wise

Guy. Maybe you've forgotten how often you tell me I work too hard." He mimicked her, " 'Ah Leon, you look old before your time! Leon, *mein Schatz,* I'm worried sick about you, you look so tired! Leon, you must learn to delegate!' " He put his arm about her. "So here's my chance to delegate, Sarah. I want this boy for my assistant. *Das Geschäft geht gut*—we can afford it."

So Daniel came to them with his books of recipes and his radio and his English dictionary, and, like Bresson before him, Gottesman became fond of his hardworking assistant and taught him all he could, while his wife made motherly overtures and filled Daniel with plentiful *Lockschen,* blintzes, *gulyasz,* and *palachinken.*

In the first week of 1947, Daniel received a disturbing letter from Switzerland.

My dear friend,

First, I send you warmest greetings for this New Year and, as always, the heartiest hopes for the success and happiness of your future. Alas, however, that is not my sole reason for writing.

My niece Natalie and her dear mother learned some time ago that, instead of dismissing you, I assisted your entry into the United States. As you can imagine, they were far from pleased, and have since been engaged in trying to persuade the authorities that I was aware of your illegal status when I first employed you. These days I seem to receive regular visits from officials investigating "anonymous" complaints about my safety precautions or my hygiene standards—even my tax affairs are under close scrutiny. Daniel, I am, and have nearly always been, a prudent man, so you need not worry about this mischief-making.

I feel, however, that you should worry a little on your own account. I never asked to know what happened between you and Natalie, but it has only recently become quite clear how very passionately she hates you. What did you do to her, I wonder? Or rather, what does her fertile, hysterical little brain believe you to be guilty of? Perhaps she will forget in time—perhaps she will leave you in peace altogether—perhaps her rage will burn itself out. But I think it wise for you to be on your guard and never entirely to forget *her.* Try not to do anything in the future which could be used against you (a sensible maxim, anyway, in life, Daniel). A young woman who can try so imaginatively (with her mother's help) to wreck her uncle's life would probably have few scruples about damaging yours.

I shall weather this little storm, be assured. Do not allow Natalie Bresson to obsess you, but it is wise to know one's enemies.

Write soon with your news, and send my warm regards to the
Gottesmans—how good they have been to you.

With great affection, your friend

Michel

Distressed, Daniel wrote back quickly, offering to intercede with
the authorities. A reply came two weeks later, cheerful and brief;
there was no need for Daniel to worry. He wrote again, repeating
his offer, but this time there was no reply, and in March, concerned by the silence, Daniel telephoned Switzerland from the
Gottesmans' apartment.

The number in Vevey rang several times.

"Allo, j'écoute."

"Restaurant Lemans?"

"The restaurant is closed."

"Closed?" Daniel frowned. In Switzerland it was almost eight in
the evening. "Closed for dinner?"

"Permanently closed."

Daniel's mind raced. "Where is Monsieur Bresson? *Le patron?*"

"I have no idea, monsieur."

It was May before the letter from Maurice Weinberg arrived. Michel was dead, Weinberg reported tersely, and Daniel was now the
beneficiary of eighty thousand Swiss francs.

Overwhelmed, Daniel called Weinberg. "What happened?"

"Michel died three weeks ago."

"But how? He wasn't sick."

"He died from a badly neglected bleeding ulcer."

Daniel was distraught. *"Why?* How could it happen?"

Weinberg paused, and the line crackled. "I'm afraid he became
careless with his health, Daniel. He was, as I think you know,
preoccupied with many problems during his last months."

When Daniel replaced the receiver he was trembling and his
skin burned. *"Preoccupied with many problems . . ."* Just one problem—Natalie Bresson. The doe eyes and sharp white teeth flashed
before his eyes, and he longed to smash his fists into her face. He
wanted to fly to Paris. He wanted to challenge that bitch and her
mother, for he knew with chill certainty that they were as good as
responsible for Michel's death. He wanted to fly to Vevey. He
wanted to stand by his friend. But it was all too late.

The money was another matter, a staggering and unexpected piece of generosity that brought tears to Daniel's eyes. Weinberg wrote again, more sympathetically, offering financial counsel, but Daniel declined. He had the funds transferred to his account at Chase Bank, and looked forward to seeing a glimmer of respect on the phlegmatic face of the manager.

Weinberg reported too, off the record, that the Bressons in Paris were outraged and furious about the bequest.

"But there is no possible action they can take," he said on the telephone when Daniel called him. "They cannot discredit you, cannot challenge Michel's will. Forget them. It's in the past."

Poor revenge, Daniel thought, but better than nothing.

By 1948 Daniel spoke, thought, and sometimes even dreamed in softly accented English, dated thoroughly American girls, and received frequent job offers from American citizens opening delicatessens and coffee shops, all of which he turned down.

In the early fall that year, however, following a steamy Manhattan summer that had left him sick of the smells of goulash and red cabbage, he knew it was time to think about moving on.

As always, Leon and Sarah were staunch friends.

"Don't think about us!" Leon flashed angrily when Daniel expressed worries about leaving them in the lurch.

"You think you're indispensable?" Sarah teased. "Such notions."

"You're crazy to stay here. You have money in the bank, you could open your own place."

"That's not what I want, Leon, at least not yet," Daniel said in frustration. "You say I'm crazy to stay, but sometimes I think I must be crazy to think of leaving. For the first time in my life I have security, a good job, wonderful friends. It's a cocoon, I'm safe here."

"So what's safe?" Sarah's warm eyes were accusing. "A mole is safe, burrowing in the ground, hiding in the dark! You're not a mole, you're a young man—you have gifts, talents, ambitions."

Leon hugged his wife. "This job was never meant to be your life's work, Daniel. Sarah's right, you have to get out or you'll never know what you're missing—you'll stay in the dark for the rest of your life."

He made his move to the Edwardian Room kitchen at the Plaza, but was quickly convinced that he was still on the wrong track. Dollars, furs, and diamonds oozed tantalizingly under the swinging kitchen doors, and Daniel felt trapped. For the first time he grew resentful, then turned his resentment into self-condemnation and began critically to examine his life. Each morning, he observed, he woke in the cell-like apartment, went to work, took orders, had a little late-night fun with his girlfriends, and collapsed exhausted onto his bed. Had he thwarted the Nazis and lost his family in order to sweat at someone else's stove for the rest of his days?

He changed his routine, began to go straight home after his shift, determined to resolve his problems. Back in Yorkville, he closed his front door, brewed pot after pot of coffee and sat in his armchair, sifting through ideas, hopes, and feelings. Most nights he simply fell asleep where he sat, but one night in early December, several ideas collided in his weary brain like express trains.

On the first day of 1949, Daniel moved from Yorkville to Amsterdam Avenue on the West Side. The rent was higher than the place deserved, but the apartment was tailor-made for his needs. Who cared if the living room was narrow and dark, and if the bedroom was no bigger than a shoe box? The kitchen was what mattered, and that was large, bright and well equipped.

He placed advertisements in *The New York Times* and the *Daily News:*

SWISS MASTER CHEF will consider requests
from suitable clients to cater and
supervise private parties and business
functions.

The advertisements were placed for three weeks before Daniel's telephone began to ring. The first call came from a lady in Central Park South who needed five waitresses for her daughter's birthday party, the second from a fish restaurant on Second Avenue looking for a new chef. The third call brought Daniel his first booking: a newly married girl fresh from Wisconsin, daunted by the prospect of dinner for her husband's boss and board of directors. When Daniel arrived at her apartment for their first consultation, she was pale and flustered—when he left in the early hours after the dinner party, she was glowing and triumphant.

Word spread quickly, and as the blossoms sprawled over the parks and down the avenues, the pages of Daniel's appointment book filled with names and dates. By his sixth month of operation he had a small staff of handpicked experts to help him, led by one Roland Steinbeck, a myopic, rotund, unambitious twenty-five-

year-old who was a prodigy with food and accounts. Roland's father was a stock market genius, and his mother a Long Island
socialite, and Roland had never needed to work for his living. He
met Daniel at four o'clock one morning at the Fulton Fish Market,
where they were both buying lobsters, Daniel for a client's dinner
party, Roland for his own lunch. They liked each other on sight
and adjourned to Roland's three-story house near Washington
Square for a hearty breakfast; by nine o'clock Daniel had an ally.

"My mother may die when she hears I'm going to serve dinner
to her friends!"

"Maybe you shouldn't?"

Roland beamed, his round cheeks flushed with pleasure. "Dear
boy, what better reason for wanting to?"

Daniel chose not to renew the lease on his apartment the following January. Instead, he moved into a brownstone on Riverside
Drive and 73rd Street, where he rented a duplex, living on one
level and running his business from the other.

He loved the duplex, and the success it represented. The ceilings were high, the walls were dry, the views of the Hudson were
panoramic from living room and office. Sometimes, on quiet days,
he sat on his terrace sipping wine and gazing at the ferries and
tugboats; was there any sight more impressive, he wondered, than
the *Queen Mary* slipping away down the river, passengers crowding
her decks?

The proximity of his bedroom to his office provided an unexpected fillip to his sex life. Many of the wives whose names
adorned his appointment books were happy to occupy Daniel's
bed too. He adored women—all kinds of women, and it was unfortunate, he realized, that so many of them had husbands. It was
not that he deliberately sought out married women, but they were
sometimes so tantalizingly available that it was impossible for him
to reject them.

"Roly," he said one morning when they were buying vegetables
at Hunter's Point Market, "I'm so happy I could burst!"

"I'm glad." Roland inspected his list. "Asparagus," he said, bustling on.

"The diary's full for the next three months, we have money in
the bank, I have friends—"

"Beans."

"Do you think it could all collapse?"

Roland stopped and peered at him. "Is this an anxiety attack or
Jewish pessimism?"

"I mean it, Roly. It seems too good to last."

"Well, that's up to you, dear boy." Roland patted him on the shoulder. "You give them value for money. The product's good, and you're even better. You do realize it's *you* they pay for, don't you?"

"That's not true."

"You know it is. You're a charming young European with fine social graces, three languages, and talent. You give them what they want, even when they're not sure what that is, and they trust you. Keep on doing all that, and I see no reason why it shouldn't last."

Daniel grinned. "From your mouth to God's ear."

17

Everything in New York seemed to grow. It was like a garden fed constantly with rich fertilizer—it was impossible for anything, animal, vegetable, or mineral, to stand still. So it was in Daniel's life. He had never felt fitter or stronger. The years slipped by—the 1953 appointment book for Silberstein Inc. grew fat and dog-eared and was laid to rest in the bottom drawer of a filing cabinet, and the 1954 book began to swell.

The Silberstein client list now included more than a dozen "star" customers who used his services frequently, and who demanded excellence at any price. One of his very best clients was Bernardi Liquor, Inc., a chain of liquor stores in New York City and Chicago.

At the outset of his business dealings with the liquor group, Daniel had been warned off by a colleague.

"Joe Bernardi's a psycho, Silberstein. If you're straight with him, he may be okay, but if he gets it in his head you're letting him down, even if it ain't true, he can be vicious. He's put guys in the hospital just for reneging on payments."

"Why haven't the police stopped him?"

"Bernardi has friends. In the gutter and in heaven. You remember that politician, Wilbur Johnson?"

Daniel remembered. A young southerner, well respected for his moral integrity, Johnson had made national headlines when his car had plunged from a bridge in Virginia, killing him. When the police had pulled him out of the river, his body and clothes had reeked of whiskey and perfume.

"What did Johnson have to do with Bernardi?"

"Not a damned thing, except Johnson opposed changes to the Virginia liquor laws, so Bernardi hated him."

"Why?"

"Because unless the laws change, Bernardi can't do the business he wants there." He chewed on a cigar and spat. "He's a dangerous man."

"You're saying he killed Johnson?"

"I'm saying nothing, Silberstein. I'm just warning you."

"I've already signed a contract."

The man shrugged. "Then you better make sure you don't poison any of his pals."

The business relationship had proved fruitful and straightforward. Daniel never met Bernardi, dealing only with his subordinates. But he did meet his wife.

Rosa Bernardi was forty-two, tall, elegant, and seductive. Born in Rome, she had met Joe Bernardi on her first visit to New York twenty-one years before. They had married after three months, and within five years Rosa had given Joe two sons and a daughter.

Rosa was Joe's single soft spot, the only person he tenderly indulged, and Rosa cherished him in return. In his view, the marriage was idyllic. In Rosa's, sadly, it was not. Joe could be a fine lover when he had time, but over the years business had absorbed so much of his time and energy that his sex drive had flagged, and their lovemaking had become discouragingly infrequent. Rosa's own appetite was robust, her physical and emotional tension acute when she was sexually deprived for long periods. She never blamed Joe, never accused him of neglect, aware of his devotion, but she had to go elsewhere—as much, she told herself, for the sake of their marriage as for any other reason. She knew Joe's temper, knew he must never find out. She chose her partners with care.

Daniel's first meeting with Rosa was in his office on a dark, wet Monday afternoon in November 1953.

"I want to surprise my husband with a small dinner party."

Rosa was not beautiful in a traditional sense, Daniel thought, though her figure seemed trim and mature. Her hair was thick and wiry and her nose was curved and small, but her wide mouth seemed to be inextricably and expressively linked to her soft brown eyes. Daniel found it hard to look away.

"A special occasion, Mrs. Bernardi?"

"His fiftieth birthday." She smiled.

"And when is that?"

"Tomorrow."

He looked up in surprise. "Tomorrow?"

"Am I too late?" she asked anxiously. "Until this morning, I believed he was leaving for Italy tonight, but now he is to stay in New York. I would so like to please him."

Daniel frowned. "It's difficult." He watched her face fall and checked the calendar. "But not impossible." Her mouth and eyes brightened. "I'm afraid I won't be there to supervise in person, though, but my colleague Mr. Steinbeck will see to it that nothing is less than perfect."

She smiled in obvious relief. "I'm sure that will be fine."

Daniel took up his pen. "And now, dinner. Had you something in mind?"

"Nothing."

"Normally," he began, "I would ask for a list of your husband's favorite delicacies, his dislikes and allergies, if any, and I would take time to prepare several possible menus, but in this case—" He tuned his mind to his Italian repertoire. "Does he eat shell-fish?"

"He adores it."

"Good. *Aragosta Siciliana*—lobster grilled with Parmesan and a touch of Sambuca."

Rosa clapped her hands. "Wonderful!"

"And to begin—"

"Joe likes salad very much. He's very American for a Sicilian."

"Very well." He wrote on the pad. *"Insalata mista."*

"Nothing between the salad and main course," she said, her brown eyes alight and resting on Daniel's face. "And for dessert, my husband enjoys anything with *Amaretti*. If you have trouble finding them, please try at Balducci's."

He shook his head. "No trouble." He smiled. "But I am devoted to Balducci's." He scribbled again. *"Amaretti,"* he mused. "That will require a little creative thought. Will you trust me, Mrs. Bernardi?"

Rosa waited. She looked around the office, took in the stripped pine, the rust-colored wall-to-wall carpeting, the bookshelves laden with Conan Doyle, Galsworthy, Twain, and Cronin, and then, deliberately slowly, she looked back at Daniel.

"I will trust you."

A prickle of excitement disturbed the back of Daniel's neck. He looked away from her, and scratched a few superfluous notes on the pad.

"I think that's all I need from you now, Mrs. Bernardi." He rose. "Shall I cost this for you? I could telephone you at the end of the afternoon."

"If you like," she said lightly, standing too and picking up her purse and gloves. "But I do trust you." She smiled again. "And my husband seems pleased with your work so far."

"I'm glad to hear it. Though this will be the first private party we've arranged for Mr. Bernardi."

She drew on her left glove and extended her right hand. "I'm sure it won't be the last."

Daniel took care to avoid personal confrontations with Rosa Bernardi for several months. If she came to his office, either Roly saw her or else Daniel made certain his secretary was present. If she had been the wife of another man, he might have been less circumspect, but she belonged to Joe Bernardi, and there was something about her that sent an erotic shiver down his spine. One afternoon in June, however, Rosa almost slipped her net over his head.

Daniel had been asked to arrange a party to celebrate the confirmation of Bernardi's niece at his brother's home in Great Neck. The day was warm and sunny, and by four o'clock one hundred and fifty guests were scattered over the lawns, in the pool and summerhouse. Daniel was in the main house, en route from the kitchen to one of the reception rooms, to check that luncheon had been cleared away to his satisfaction.

In the corridor, materializing suddenly before him, wraithlike in silk chiffon, Rosa Bernardi held out her hand. "Daniel, come with me." Swiftly, she darted over and opened a door. "Please," she said softly, and tugged at him to follow.

They were in a library, a shadowy room deprived of sunlight for the sake of the leather-covered books by heavy drapes at the windows. As Daniel became used to the dark he made out a broad mahogany desk with a leather chair behind it, and a small pair of library steps. There was no other furniture in the room.

Rosa chuckled huskily. "I chose the wrong room. I thought we might sit peacefully for a while." Daniel said nothing, so by way of further explanation she added: "I don't know this house well. Joe's brother only recently moved in."

Daniel swallowed. "It's a beautiful house."

Rosa moved over to the window and slipped her hand through the gap in the drapes, letting in a little light. "You've been avoiding me, Daniel," she said, still facing the window.

"I don't know what you mean."

"You've made sure we've never been alone, is what I mean."

"That's not true, Mrs. Bernardi."

She turned, letting the drapes fall back, her movement light and girlish. "Won't you call me Rosa?" She smiled. "Please?"

"Sure."

She came closer. Even in the gloom he could tell her skin was flushed. "Why do you avoid me, Daniel?"

"I don't, Rosa." He kept his tone light. "I was just on my way to check the dining room."

"Are you worried that someone may come in? Don't be, they're all outside." She was so close that he could feel her body heat through his shirt. "You deserve a break—the meal was exquisite, everyone's asking for your number." She placed her right hand against his chest. The pulses in his temples began to throb. . . .

"This is not a good idea, Rosa."

She smiled. "I think it's a fine idea." She kept her hand pressed against him. "You're a discreet man, Daniel. I can trust you."

"Your husband," Daniel said.

"Don't discuss my husband, please. This has nothing to do with my marriage." Her eyes were large and dark. "Don't you find me attractive, Daniel?"

He hesitated, half delighted, half nervous. "Of course I—"

Footsteps rapped sharply on the parquet floor outside the room and Rosa moved quickly away. She touched the door handle. "Let me go first." Her manner was regretful but calm. "You follow in a few minutes." Unexpectedly, she leaned forward and kissed his cheek. "Don't hate me," she said softly, her eyes suddenly sad. "Use me—but don't hate me."

And she was gone.

On September 5, at nine in the morning, Daniel's answering service called him in his apartment.

"Message from Mr. Bernardi. He wants to see you at ten o'clock in his suite at the Carlyle."

"Did he say why?"

"No, but the message was that it's urgent."

Daniel showered, shaved, dressed, and caught a cab on West End Avenue. Traffic was bad as usual, but the driver was spirited, dodging the snarls skillfully and getting him to the hotel with three minutes to spare.

On his way upstairs Daniel grew tense. He'd had no direct dealings with Bernardi, met him only briefly in a roomful of guests. Why did he want to see him now? He straightened his tie and knocked on the door.

"Come in, it's open!"

A woman's voice. Rosa? Daniel's mind twisted. He could turn around, take the elevator back to the lobby. Or was Bernardi with her?

"Come in," she called again.

He opened the door. Sunlight struck him in the face, blinding him. He smelled polish and scent, and blinked. The room was lovely, all the furnishings, right down to the wastebasket beside the writing desk, coordinated in cream.

Rosa sat on the settee in the corner. Alone. *Perhaps Bernardi's in the bedroom? Or taking a shower?* She sat like a businesswoman, aloof and lovely in a navy linen suit and cream silk blouse, ruffled demurely at the neck.

"Good morning, Daniel." She gave him her hand and crossed her legs neatly. Her skirt was slit at the side; four inches of sleek, honey-colored thigh came into view.

"Your husband sent a message. Isn't he here?" He felt foolish, like a schoolboy with the headmaster's wife.

"I sent the message." Rosa patted the cushions beside her. "Sit down, Daniel. Have some coffee."

He sat, leaving a foot of clear space between them. She leaned forward and poured from a silver pot on the tray before her. "Cream and sugar?"

"No," he said. "Thank you."

She passed him a cup, and her scent swirled lightly past his nostrils. The coffee was tepid. Daniel wondered how long she had been waiting.

"What is it you want to discuss, Rosa?"

She took a cigarette from her purse, and Daniel felt that her calmness was a sham. *Why is she doing this when she's nervous as hell?* She picked up the lighter from the table and Daniel moved automatically to take it from her, then stopped. She caught the halted gesture, her lips and eyes twitched in a rueful half-smile, and she lit her own cigarette.

"I could tell you, Daniel, that I wish to discuss a dinner party." She placed the cigarette between her lips and inhaled deeply.

"Yes."

She leaned back and watched him, her eyes half shut. Her lashes were thick and not false, and gave her eyes an enigmatic slant. "Or I could say it's another birthday surprise for my husband."

Daniel looked away from her eyes and watched her hands. Thin and long, one pinched the cigarette tightly, like the hand of a novice smoker, the other played with a gold chain around her neck.

"But we both know the truth." She took another nervous drag from the cigarette and bit suddenly on her lower lip, as if she felt it would tremble.

She's scared of herself, he thought. *She's out of control.*

"You don't have to explain anything to me, Rosa—"

"Of course not. You know." Her voice grew brittle. "I got you up here so that we could fuck."

The words seemed to reverberate in the room, and abruptly Rosa's eyes gleamed with the light of challenge.

Daniel stood up uneasily. "I think I should leave."

She grabbed at his hand, her skin scalding, pulled him close and stroked him through his trousers.

"Rosa, for God's sake!"

She looked up, her eyes beseeching, and he weakened. Leaning forward, she pressed her cheek to his cock.

"Rosa, please."

She kissed him through the fabric.

"Christ, Rosa, I'm only flesh and blood!"

She moaned softly, and Daniel was lost.

He sat down. Slowly, deliberately, he slid the skirt up over her legs, felt the silkiness of her stockings and the firmness of her flesh, kissed her mouth. Rosa closed her eyes, blotting him out, and Daniel felt that she was trying to nullify him as an individual, perhaps to lessen her betrayal of Joe. The thought was oddly stirring. He shifted around to face her. The settee creaked under their weight. He unfastened the top buttons of her blouse and slipped his hand inside—her breasts were warm and full, their nipples hard against his palm.

She pulled away. "Lock the door. Hurry!" She was breathing very quickly; her face was flushed, her lips a little swollen and parted. *"Hurry!"*

Daniel hung the DO NOT DISTURB sign on the door and turned the key in the lock. Rosa was already through to the bedroom. He followed, pulled her close, kissed her again—she tugged urgently at his hands. He undid the remaining buttons of her blouse.

"No—my stockings! Just my stockings. *Please!"*

She kicked away her high-heeled shoes and swayed back against the edge of the bed, her shaking fingers pushing up her skirt and unfastening the clips on her garter belt. She wore no panties. It was the most exciting thing Daniel had ever seen any woman do. Unbearably inflamed, he rolled down the stockings and tossed them away. Her hands were on him, pulling at him, unzipping him, squeezing him . . . and then she lay on the bed, skirt up around her waist, legs spread wide.

"Now, Daniel!"

It was the worst and the best sex Daniel had ever experienced.

Rosa seemed half animal, half woman—she needed it desperately, insanely, and she despised herself at the same time. She came almost before he entered her, panting wildly, her face contorted. Daniel, rock-hard inside her, forced himself to pause while she calmed, then began to move, to rock back and forth, then to thrust.

Rosa moaned. He thrust deeper, as deep as he could. She gasped fiercely, cried out, "Joey!" and then, half sobbing, *"Voglio morire!"*—and her whole body went into spasm as Daniel climaxed.

For a moment he lay on her, his eyes closing, waiting for the pounding of his heart to lessen, for her to relax with him. But Rosa still gasped, her spine still arched as though in mid-orgasm. Daniel opened his eyes. Her face was twisted in apparent agony.

"Rosa, what is it?" Carefully he moved off her and knelt on the bedspread. "What's wrong?"

She couldn't speak. She couldn't seem to catch her breath. She began to twist her head to and fro, her arms thrashing wildly—and then the flesh of her face turned a ghastly white and a blue tinge appeared around her lips.

Horrified, Daniel snatched up the telephone. Rosa moaned again, a fearful groaning sound from deep inside her chest, and then her eyes flew open, staring, and her body went rigid.

Daniel slammed down the receiver and looked down at her in horror.

"Rosa?"

He stared at her.

"Rosa!"

He grasped her wrist and tried in vain to find a pulse. Nothing, not even the faintest flutter. He pressed his face against her breasts, listening for her heartbeat.

Nothing.

Rosa Bernardi was dead.

Daniel stumbled into the bathroom and threw up until he was empty. His head exploded with pain. He ran the cold-water tap, splashed his face and neck and hands. His skin was blazing hot. He wanted to scream—to run. His face, mirrored in the cabinet, was almost as white as Rosa's, his dark eyes huge with panic. He shut his eyes and tried to control his breathing. His limbs trembled as if he was in the throes of a fever. He couldn't run. He had to stay, had to think.

He pitched into the drawing room and sank into an armchair. One of the coffee cups, with Rosa's pink lipstick on the rim, reproached him. *Christ, what do I do?* Call a doctor—an ambulance. They could do nothing for her. *Wait. Wait and think!*

He stood up and fumbled for a cigarette in Rosa's pack. He rarely smoked, but he had to do something with his hands. He lit it, inhaled, choked . . . put it out again. *Think.*

He couldn't run. He had been seen by hotel staff—they might identify him. And he couldn't, *wouldn't* leave Rosa lying there all alone.

What was the last thing she'd sobbed while he was inside her? He ground his knuckles of his hands into his eyes. *"Voglio morire!"* it had sounded like. "I want to die." Hadn't the Victorians called orgasm death? Why had she said that? Had she known what she was doing? Had she had some heart condition? Was she hoping, in some bizarre way, to punish herself for what she was doing to Joe?

The thought of Bernardi was like a sock on the jaw. His mind cleared a little, and the shaking lessened. Had Rosa called herself that morning, or a secretary? Surely she would not have involved a third party. Unless she wanted to be found out? He couldn't believe that. She must have been careful—she would never have wanted to hurt Joe.

Daniel walked, slowly, back through the bedroom, averting his eyes from the bed, and into the bathroom. Again he splashed his face and neck, dried his hands carefully and walked back to the bed.

He forced himself to look at her. He touched her bare ankle. Still warm. Soft. Tears stabbed at his eyes and he felt the shaking beginning again. No! *Stop that!* He had to act.

A heart attack could happen any time, any place. If he could get Rosa back into the drawing room, onto the settee . . . His answering service would confirm that he had been summoned to a business meeting.

He looked around for her shoes. One lay a few feet away, the other near the door to the drawing room. By the window, on the pale rug, lay the lacy garter belt and both silk stockings. He picked everything up, smoothed them out and lay them, one at a time, at the foot of the bed.

He took one stocking and rolled it carefully so as not to make a run, the way he'd seen girlfriends roll their stockings before putting them on. *No, that's wrong—garter belt first.* He put down the stocking and picked up the belt. He put his hand under the heel of her right foot and raised it. His stomach lurched. The nail polish on her toes was pale rose pink, matching her fingernails and lips.

Her perfume wafted in the room; stronger than before, clinging to his nostrils . . . and something else, too . . . sweetish, yet salty. "Oh, my God!"

He dropped her foot, and it flopped limply onto the bedspread. He smelled semen.

He ran to the bathroom, found tissues and towels, dampened the tissues with warm water. Back in the bedroom he eased the towels under Rosa and very gently, very carefully, set about washing her thighs, washing the sticky, curled dark hair. . . .

He stopped, and a great, dark ripple of unbidden, crazy laughter surged up in his chest, so that he could hardly control it. What in God's name was he doing? Any person found dead in a hotel suite would surely be subject to an autopsy—there was no way he could wash himself out of her body!

He began to tremble again. After the autopsy, Bernardi would know. Even if he knew all about Rosa, about her weakness, a man of his reputation and power, a Sicilian, a man passionately in love with his wife, the mother of his children—Bernardi would get to Daniel somehow. And then what? He might kill him—cripple him. An image, half forgotten, of his uncle, trapped in his bed in Nuremberg, flashed through his mind, and he shuddered. And yet violence wasn't what terrified him most. There were other forms of revenge, inside the law. Had he actually committed a crime? An outrage against Bernardi, yes—but a crime? A good lawyer might twist it to manslaughter, which could mean . . . Imprisonment was the unendurable thought. *Never!* Never again.

He'd wasted enough time. Touching her as lightly as he could, Daniel dried Rosa and slid the towels from under her. He flushed away the tissues and hung the towels over the heated rail; they were damp with water, nothing more. He came back to Rosa. The garter belt hooked easily round her slim waist, but when he raised one foot again and guided it into the first stocking, hot tears brimmed over, stinging his cheeks, and again his stomach heaved in revulsion. . . .

At last it was done. Daniel checked the time—just three minutes after half past eleven. A woman dead, his whole life wrecked again in less than two hours! He wiped his perspiring face and bent again. Clumsily, painfully, he lifted her, holding her under his arms. For a moment he propped her against the headboard so that he could straighten the suit and blouse. He stooped to lift her again—her eyes stared into his.

At fifteen minutes to twelve, Rosa Bernardi was in the drawing room, slumped on the settee where she had sat earlier. Everything was as it had been—coffee cups, cigarette stubs. No point moving anything, cleaning anything up in here.

He took his diary from his briefcase, racking his brains. In the notes section for the first week of November, he wrote, *J. Bernardi. Surprise birthday dinner. 50 guests. Carlyle?* He laid the diary, closed, on the coffee table, clipped his pen back in the inside pocket of his jacket, then checked one last time over the bedroom and bathroom to make sure all was in order.

Slowly, he walked back into the drawing room, wiped the palms of his hands with his handkerchief, and picked up the telephone.

"Whatever it is, it can't be so bad that you have to destroy *everything!*" Roland stared at Daniel's suitcases open on the bed and on the floor, and watched as suits, shirts, pullovers, and jackets were snatched from the closets and laid flat in the cases. "Daniel, my dear friend, you must stop and think!"

"There's nothing to think about, Roly. I have no choice. Believe me."

"Can't you tell me about it?"

"No."

"Don't you trust me, dear boy?"

Daniel looked up. His face was sheet-white, his eyes hollow. "Of course I trust you, Roly, you know better than that. But I'm not going to tell you."

"For *my* sake, I suppose?"

"That's right."

Roland marched over to the telephone and picked up the receiver. "I'm going to call Leon and Sarah."

Daniel twisted around, seized the receiver and slammed it down. "Don't you dare! I'll break your arm if you touch that phone again!"

Roland shrugged, defeated. He sat on the chair in the corner of the bedroom.

"I'm asking you again," Daniel said, sweeping socks and underpants into a case. "Don't you want the business? I'm giving you full power of attorney. You can wind everything up, cancel the bookings, pay everyone off—whatever you think's right, Roly, and be generous, they deserve it, God knows. Or you just run it instead of me."

"I don't need your fucking business."

Daniel looked up, startled. Roland never swore. "Of course you don't need it, I know that, but you've enjoyed it, haven't you?"

Roland's eyes behind his glasses were hurt and angry. "I enjoyed it because we were in it together, you bloody fool. I don't need to work, Daniel. I could live in my house for the next thirty years and never lift a finger to wipe my ass. It was kind of a game for me, but I took it seriously because it was so damned good watching it work for you, watching you make it." He shook his head. "And now you're tossing it all out of the window."

Daniel closed the lid of one case. "Do me a favor, Roly—sit on this, will you?"

Roland sat on the case and it sank in submission. "Do you want your stuff put in storage, or shall I keep them at my place?"

"Put them in storage."

"Someone may want to know where you are, and you don't want me involved. Right?"

Daniel ignored the sarcasm. "Right." The locks on the suitcase clicked. "Thanks."

"I don't want the company, Daniel."

"Okay."

"I'll take care of this week's bookings, and I'll do as you ask and wind everything up, but I don't want anything to do with it after that."

"Okay, Roly, I don't blame you."

Roland threw up his hands in despair. "Daniel, for the last time, let me get my lawyer over here. What could you have done that's so terrible?"

"Leave it, Roly, *please!*"

Roland sighed. "Where are you going?"

"I'm not sure."

"Not sure, or not saying?"

"Both."

"For my sake again, I suppose?"

"If you like."

"I don't like."

"I know, Roly. I'm sorry."

At about five o'clock that afternoon, Daniel sat alone in the back of a Yellow cab threading its way toward the 59th Street Bridge and out of the city. If he'd had more time to think things through, Daniel knew he would still have arrived at the same conclusion. How could he, with the memories of the years of confinement still so clearly burned into his mind, risk imprisonment? The hotel manager and doctor had accepted his account of Rosa's heart attack at face value. The police coroner would not. Nor would Joe

Bernardi. It was not the first time he'd left an old life for a new one.

Just inside the Idlewild perimeter, the terminal buildings ahead, the driver craned his head to look at Daniel.

"Going where, bud?"

Daniel rested the back of his head for a moment against the hard cab seat.

"Paris," he said.

18

The black-coated waiter at the Römische Stube served the *Salzburger Nockerl* with a flourish, and vanished behind the red velvet screen that separated the alcove from the other diners in the restaurant.

Hermann Rudesheim, the man Andreas had driven four hundred convoluted kilometers to see, poked his fork hungrily into the fluffy dessert. "The only *Nockerl* in Bonn worth eating!" he said with a beam, anticipation lighting up his broad, flat-featured face.

Andreas tasted his. "Delicious."

For a few moments Rudesheim ate concentratedly. Then he leaned back in his wheelchair, surveying Andreas critically. "So!" he said theatrically. "I guess we can assume that you consider yourself the boldest, bravest, most talented young man in Europe. But are you fit enough?"

"I'm fit."

"I didn't ask you that, I asked you if you're fit *enough.*"

"I exercise every day."

"What kind of exercise?"

"I run, play tennis, lift weights."

"Good. Weights are important. You need a neck and shoulders as strong as a bull's. How are your eyes?"

Andreas shrugged. "Twenty-twenty, I think. I've never had a problem—"

"Not good enough. They must be perfect, better than perfect. Have you tested your peripheral vision?"

"No, but—"

"Train it." Rudesheim paused to fill his mouth with *Nockerl*. "And shoot clay pigeons—the finest exercise for coordination. You must teach your eyes and hands to work in exact unison, Alessandro, and, of course, your feet. How often do you practice?"

"Every day."

"Not enough." The German shifted impatiently in the wheelchair. Even after nineteen years, his huge, muscular upper half looked insanely out of place, trapped by the paralysis below his waist. "You must practice each time you sit in *any* car, *anywhere.* Even in Zurich, in the Bahnhofstrasse, you must study concentration, never let up!"

Until the German Grand Prix of 1935, Rudesheim had raced with as much arrogance and nerve as von Brauchitsch the Prussian, but after his crash in that memorable race, he had sat out the war years in a sanitarium in Baden-Baden, praying daily for an enemy bomb to finish him off. After 1945, however, he had come to live in Bonn, solely because of its proximity to his beloved Nürburgring, pulling the shattered pieces of his life together with a magnificent obstinacy that every doctor and nurse he had ever raged at was forced to admire. Rudesheim still lived and breathed his sport in 1954, still exercised exhaustively every day, still spent thousands of marks every year maintaining his fleet of cars, still waited for a miracle to pluck him out of his despised wheelchair.

"Use every minute, Alessandro," he said fiercely. "Drive more smoothly than any other driver. Use everything—even a traffic holdup—choose the spot you want your wheels to be when you next stop, and make damned sure that's where they are, not a centimeter out."

Andreas stared at Rudesheim in awe.

"How are your nerves?"

"I'm not afraid, sir."

Rudesheim leaned back his head and laughed, the veins in his great neck standing out. "Not afraid?" he mocked. "You should be scared shitless you're such a greenhorn!"

"Surely a nervous driver is a danger to himself and others on the track?" Andreas, wounded, defended himself.

"That's only partly true, Alessandro. You are proud of your courage, aren't you?" He swept on. "Don't be. No driver worth a pig's fart will ever expose himself to danger. A good driver does everything to avoid unnecessary risks—"

"But how can you win if you don't take chances?"

"I said *unnecessary* risks. You must listen, Alessandro. I have no time to waste on a *Lausejunge* with no patience to listen to the voice of experience."

Andreas reddened. "I'm sorry."

"Don't be," Rudesheim said, relenting. "It's not wrong to ask questions or to disagree with me, so long as you're sure of your facts."

A girl with flaming red hair swung saucily past their table and Andreas swiveled quickly to watch her exit.

"Your reflexes are not too bad." The German grinned.

Andreas laughed. "No, sir."

"Your papa believes you have a future in racing."

"He hopes so, sir. That's why he wrote to you on my behalf."

"Tell me, are you a warm Latin like him, or a cool Swiss like your mother?"

"A mixture, I'm afraid."

"Don't be. There have been some great drivers with high-strung emotions, though I think it is easier to achieve success if one can learn control."

Andreas sat straighter. "Racing is everything to me."

"Don't you like girls?" Rudesheim teased. "But yes, of course, you just demonstrated that, didn't you. Anyone special?"

"No time."

The German shrugged. "You're young. Each man is different. Maybe it will be better for you to be alone, who can say? It depends more on the woman. If you find the right one, you can have both things." For a moment, the old warrior softened. "Take me, for instance. Without my Mara, I would be a lonely man today."

The waiter reappeared to clear the dishes, and Rudesheim ordered coffee and schnapps.

"Herr Rudesheim," Andreas began, ready at last to ask the questions that had burned in his brain since they'd sat down at the table. "What do I do now? How do I get a start? I mean a real start. I've rallied, I've hill-climbed, but I need a real race. What about funds? What do I need?"

"Enough!" Rudesheim held up both hands as if parrying a blow. "Only the last questions are pertinent. Money. You can't think of racing without it."

"That's going to be one of my problems, sir."

"I thought your father was financing you."

"He is, for the moment. But I can't rely on that for long."

"Why not?"

Andreas flushed. "It's a family problem."

"You mean your mother?"

Andreas looked startled.

"Yours is not a unique situation, Alessandro," the German said gently. "There cannot have been many, if any, women born on this earth who would let their only son seek death without a battle."

"The battle is over, sir."

"And who has won?"

"I don't think anyone has won. She'll never change her mind. Since last year, when both my grandparents died, she has been even more rigidly against it."

"And that's why you're living in Zurich?"

"Yes, sir." He flushed and added, "It's better for all of us this way."

"Do you have a job?"

"I saw a garage owner two days ago. There may be news when I get back."

Coffee arrived and was poured. Rudesheim helped himself to cream, Andreas to three sugar lumps.

"Watch your diet, Alessandro. If you need sugar, take glucose, not this white *Scheiss.*"

Andreas smiled. "Yes, sir."

"Back to finances. You have no qualifications as an engineer, have you?"

"No."

"So if this garage owner takes you on, it will be as a trainee?"

Andreas nodded. "But with the money I have in the bank, I should be able to survive some time." He grinned. "I'm not exactly living in luxury."

"Good. Not only will you have to buy a car, you have to be able to maintain it. Even if the officials don't spot a slightly worn tire immediately, you're crazy if you don't replace it right away."

Andreas leaned forward. "If you were beginning now, Herr Rudesheim, in '54, what car would you go for? With limited funds," he added keenly.

Rudesheim picked up the slender bottle the waiter had left, and poured schnapps into both glasses. "Can you stay in Bonn another day?"

"Sure."

"Before I answer, I need to see you drive, and you have drunk too much today to be safe in a car."

"Where can I drive around here?"

Rudesheim raised his glass and took a large shot of schnapps. His eyes glittered as he watched Andreas.

"At the 'Ring, of course."

The Nürburgring, Germany's most famous circuit and arguably the most arduous in the world, was looped around the Eifel mountains just south of Bonn. The setting for countless Grand Prix and Grande Epreuve races, on this wet, windy afternoon, the circuit was deserted with the exception of the mechanic Rudesheim had brought with him.

"I have a little treat for you, Alessandro," Rudesheim said, raising his voice over the strong wind. "As you may know, I am something of a collector of cars."

"My father told me, yes."

"I bought, last year, at an insane price, one of Juan Fangio's cars, the Tipo 159 he drove and won with all through the 1951 season."

Out of the corner of his eye, Andreas noticed the gleaming Alfa Romeo sliding onto the track a hundred yards away.

Rudesheim fixed Andreas with a beady gaze. "Would you like to drive her?"

Andreas stared at him.

"Just today, you understand," Rudesheim added. "She is, and will always remain, *my* car. But I should like to see you drive her."

Andreas turned to watch as the car reached the start line. It was a dream. Involuntarily he pinched himself on the thigh.

Rudesheim laughed. "Believe it, Alessandro." He maneuvered his chair a few yards. "Manfred!" he yelled to the mechanic just climbing out of the 159. "Take Alessandro around once, then let him take her!" He looked back at Andreas. "The 'Ring is more than twenty-two kilometers, and full of dangers. When Manfred drives, watch his hands, listen to the changing sounds of the track, feel the surface characteristics with your body. He will point them out anyway, but watch out for Bergwerk and Karussel, and be ready for the first curve, it's a devil!"

Andreas's heart began to pound, and sweat coated his palms. "It's only a one-seater," he said.

"We've adjusted the seating, so there's room to squeeze in. Manfred will drive slowly, like an old woman on a shopping expedition." Rudesheim's eyes danced with amusement. "Are you chicken, Alessandro?"

In response, Andreas marched down to the starting line and took his position, as directed by Manfred.

"This is the boss's idea," the mechanic said, disapproval plain in his rough Berlin voice. "Hold tight, for Christ's sake! I won't go faster than sixty, and this baby can do around one-ninety, but if you fall out and break your neck we're both going to look fucking stupid."

"I'm not arguing," Andreas murmured, his voice lost as Manfred began revving.

It was one thing to drive a beaten-up old Opel or Volkswagen in a hill-climbing competition or a local auto club rally, when you could hurl your machine into corners and bends at wild angles and escape back into the straight with your foot hard down. You had no one to answer to, if you smashed up your car, but your pulse rate and the bank manager. It was something cosmically, galactically different to take the wheel of the great Juan Fangio's Alfa Romeo and, glory of glories, be entrusted with her on a circuit like the Nürburgring!

"The boss must be nuts to let you take her out in this *Scheisswetter*," Manfred grumbled as he handed Andreas a pair of goggles and climbed out. "Don't start playing champion, and if you crash her," he warned menacingly, "make sure you kill yourself in the bargain, or Rudesheim will have you for breakfast, lunch, and dinner!"

"*Holy shit!*" Andreas screamed to the hills in ecstasy as any lingering fear dissipated and shot away in the roaring backwash of the exhaust, as he left the first treacherous curve far behind him and gathered momentum—as he began to feel, just as Rudesheim had said he should, the changing personality of the track's surface through the molding of his spine and his buttocks against the leather seat. It was all there, all in his eyes and in his hands, and his feet just followed through, took commands in total obedience. Nothing in the world, nothing in his life had ever felt so fucking wonderful! *Nothing,* not even sex, could come remotely close to the joy of guiding this great steel beast over this soaked, endless black road!

"Bloody little maniac!" seethed Manfred after Andreas brought the Alfa screeching to a halt just ten feet from where the mechanic stood. "I saw what happened at Schwalbenschwanz, don't think I didn't!" he shouted. "You damn near lost her, didn't you?"

"*So? Wie war's?*" bellowed Rudesheim, his face scarlet with excitement, propelling himself back and forth in his chair as Andreas wove his way back on legs that still shook beneath him. "How was it, Alessandro?" he demanded again, his voice roaring and imperious.

Andreas stopped in front of the wheelchair and stared down into the great man's face, his own eyes still masked by the goggles. *Unbe-fucking-lievable!* he wanted to yell to Rudesheim and the Eifel mountains—but instead, hands thrust deep into his pockets, in a voice so calm, it sounded almost nonchalant, he replied, "Not bad. She may be past it for the big stuff, but she's not bad at all."

Rudesheim's face turned white with rage. Of all the ungrateful
—the consummate insolence of the young Swiss! Yesterday he had
been all humility, and now, given one crack of the whip, the
young greenhorn sounded as cool as if he'd asked him about the
weather! He took a deep breath, ready to give him the tongue-
lashing of his life—and then he stopped as Andreas took off the
goggles. There was a flame in his eyes, a fire from the brain licking
away at all that Latin blackness, that betrayed Alessandro's appearance of calmness. Rudesheim knew that look, recognized it, remembered seeing it in the wing mirrors of his own cars after every
race he had ever driven.

He swallowed his anger and looked intently at the young man,
who seemed taller and stronger than before—and then he put
back his head, opened his mouth, and roared with laughter.

"Oh, Alessandro!" He wiped his eyes and looked up at the
astonished Andreas. "You don't fool me for a minute! I see it in
your eyes!" He jabbed an excited finger toward his own. "You
forget, I was there too! I know how it feels! You never lose that
feeling, even after twenty years!"

"I guess not." Andreas smiled, flushing.

Manfred stalked toward them, scowling. "She's all right."

"Of course she is," Rudesheim said rudely.

"He took her up too quickly," Manfred complained. "He's
lucky she didn't blow."

"Sure he took her up too quickly," Rudesheim agreed. "He
made many mistakes, but I didn't expect anything else." He
winked at Andreas. "Manfred is a mechanic. An engineer with an
engineer's soul. He cares nothing for us drivers, his only passion is
for the car. If you injure her, you wound him." He wagged a
finger in the air. "Remember that always, Alessandro. You need
the Manfreds of this world a damned sight more than they need
you."

Grudgingly, Manfred slapped Andreas on the back. "The boss
is right, pretty boy," he said, "and don't you forget it."

Later that evening, in the grand salon of Rudesheim's nineteenth-
century retreat on the outskirts of the Venusberg forest, the
"boss" took a cigar from the humidor close to his elbow.

"Havana, Alessandro?"

"I don't smoke, thank you."

"And a good thing." Mara Rudesheim, a handsome, broad-
shouldered blonde with forceful features and gentle eyes, rose
from her chair. "You smoke too much and you know it," she

chided her husband. She bent and kissed him on the forehead. "I'm going to bed. I'm sure you two want to talk shop, and I've had enough of cars today."

Rudesheim chuckled fondly. "She gets mad if she has to sit in traffic for more than a minute."

Andreas stood up. "That was a wonderful dinner."

Mara smiled. "Don't keep Rudy up too late."

Rudesheim noted Andreas's empty glass. "You need a refill. Help yourself and give me another too."

Andreas went to the bar and poured cognac for them both. "This afternoon meant a great deal to me, sir. I hope you know that."

"Of course. I told you, it was in your eyes. We're both drivers, Alessandro, even if I fester in this chair. What no one else can ever comprehend, we share through instinct, like animals of the same species."

Andreas handed his host a glass and returned to his armchair.

"So," said Rudesheim, "what will you do now?"

"Start looking for the right car, I guess. Then for the right competitions."

The German was poker-faced. "Do you want some help?"

"What kind of help?"

"Sponsorship."

"What do you mean?"

"You're not a fool, Alessandro, you know what I mean. You need help, financially and every other way." He sipped his cognac and his eyes grew beady and sharp. "I am prepared to give you that help, under certain conditions."

"What conditions?"

Rudesheim snorted. "Full of shit you are! What do you care about conditions? I'm offering you the chance of a lifetime, and under your mother's Swiss nonchalance, your black Italian heart is pumping blood so fast you're probably getting a hard-on!"

Andreas laughed. "One more question?"

"Yes," he grunted impatiently.

"Why?"

Rudesheim shrugged. "Hard to answer."

"Is it because of my father?"

"Don't insult my intelligence."

"I don't mean to." Andreas's forehead creased in genuine puzzlement. "Why then? You've never seen me race."

"I've seen you drive Fangio's car."

"With the track to myself, and at speeds even your wife would approve of."

"Don't underestimate Mara—on the open road she's a demon. Are you trying to discourage me, Alessandro? Trying to talk me out of sponsoring you?"

"I doubt you could be talked out of anything, Herr Rudesheim."

Rudesheim bellowed with laughter and slapped the arm of his chair. *"Lausebengel!* You're right, of course." Again he boomed, and the chandelier overhead shivered tiny crystal bells. "All right, then. This is what I propose."

Andreas leaned forward intently.

"Most people would declare me incompetent. They would say, 'Let the boy prove himself first,' 'Make him go the slow way, the traditional way,' and perhaps they are right, those people." He shrugged. "But I am not most people." He drank more cognac. "How do you feel about driving German cars? Any notions left from the war, or are you too young to give a damn?"

"If I reject German cars, I reject some of the finest machines in the world."

"Correct. The new Mercedes-Benz will soon wipe the smiles off their faces at Maserati and Ferrari." He paused for effect. "I may own a W-196 before very long."

Andreas was silent, wondering why Mercedes-Benz would let their new star model go to a collector like Rudesheim. Such machines were created to be driven, to fly with the wind, not to be consigned to a museum, however loving the daily greasing and polishing!

"When I do get her," Rudesheim continued, "I shall need the services of a driver-mechanic."

For a second Andreas's heart seemed to stop, then thudded furiously into action again.

"There are many young drivers who would, I think, be eager to take the job."

You bet there are, Andreas thought feverishly.

"But I think you might work very well, Alessandro. What do you think?"

He couldn't speak—he opened his mouth, but no words came out.

"In the meantime," Rudesheim continued, aware that he had confounded the young man, "before I take delivery of the W-196, I have a little car you might care to enter in some sports car events. If, that is, you are interested."

Andreas again had the urge to take the flesh of his arm between thumb and fingers and pinch it to convince himself this was really happening. This man was some kind of sorcerer, a mad wizard, aware of the folly he might be committing by giving such an opportunity to a beginner!

"Well?" barked Rudesheim, growing impatient. "Are you interested or not?"

"*Interested?*" Andreas shouted suddenly, his voice hoarse with excitement as he jumped to his feet. "How could I not be?" He wanted to embrace Rudesheim, he could have wept with triumph, but good sense and masculine pride prevailed, and he compromised with a handshake, pumping the German's arm up and down until the older man withdrew it in protest.

"Sit down, for pity's sake," he growled. "We have business to discuss. And pour me another drink before you do."

Andreas picked up the decanter again and poured amber liquid into his host's glass. "I don't know what to say."

"Say nothing, just pour the damned cognac and listen." His hands restless, he moved the red-and-blue-checked rug that covered his useless legs. "I shall require you to sign a contract, Alessandro."

"Of course," Andreas said, returning to his chair.

"Don't agree so quickly. I shall get my lawyer to draw it up, and I advise you to let your own check over the small print. And talk it over with your father, he's a clever man."

"I will." Andreas was trying to concentrate, but his mind kept returning to the Nürburgring, reliving the afternoon, and then flashing in wild fantasy to the future, to the image of an Alessandro at the wheel of the W-196, accelerating away from the start at the 'Ring, or Monza or Bremgarten—

"You will have to agree that until further notice you drive only for me, Alessandro."

"Naturally."

"And if I feel you're not shaping up, I shall have the power to terminate our contract without argument."

Cold reality jolted Andreas back into the present. There was no denying it, he was being offered a chance of a lifetime. From here on, from this moment, from this beautiful, antique-filled salon, he could make it, could fulfill his dreams and those of his father. But it was up to him, to grueling work—exercise, technique, study, until he understood as much as the Manfreds of the racing world about the cars he drove—practice, practice, and more of the same.

"While we're getting fixed up, and as long as the driver-me-

chanic tag applies to you, you will have to live in Bonn. Shall you
mind leaving Switzerland?"

"I've always expected to travel."

Rudesheim grimaced. "Bonn is a dreary place, though much
improved since it became the capital. Now, at least, the restaurants
are better, but the roads are too crowded."

"And it's close to the 'Ring."

The German smiled. "Quite so." He patted the rug over his
thighs, regarding his lower half with distaste. "Even with these, I
make sure I'm never far from a big track. My sanitarium in Baden-
Baden is near Hockenheim, so when I return once a year for their
tortures, it's almost bearable."

"I don't know how—" Andreas stopped.

"What?"

"Nothing."

"You don't know how I live like this? Without my legs, without
the cars?"

"Yes," Andreas said awkwardly.

"I thought for many months, Alessandro, many *years,* that I
could *not* live, not bear another day. Without Mara I would have
shot myself through the head; it would have been easier. Maybe
one day I still shall." He twisted in the chair and pointed to the
writing desk. "The revolver is in there, in a locked drawer. Mara
knows it's there, but only I have the key." Suddenly he smiled.
"But you see, I still have the cars, don't I! And perhaps one day,
my friend, who knows, through you I may relive the driving."

The grandfather clock chimed midnight. Simultaneously, both
men drained their glasses.

"I should go," Andreas said quietly.

Rudesheim nodded. "Yes. Mara will have your head if you
overtire me. If I behave myself, she treats me like a stud; if not,
like a naughty child." He chuckled. "I prefer the former."

He propelled himself toward the double doors. Andreas was
there before him, opening them wide to allow the chair through
on its way to the oak-camouflaged elevator. Rudesheim pushed a
button, and the doors slid open. Quickly he spun the chair around
so that he faced Andreas again. "Can you see yourself out, Alessandro? I have a man, but he retires earlier than I."

Andreas gave his hand, and the German gripped it tightly.
"Don't start thanking me," he said gruffly. "Get back to Zurich,
wait for the contract, and then, if you sign, we'll see about giving

those Italians your papa is so crazy about, something to worry them."

"I'll sign."

Rudesheim reversed into the elevator. "I know you will."

19

The call came as he was reading a clipping from the *Neue Zürcher Zeitung.*

> With the Dutch and Belgian Grand Prix both canceled, and
> Rouen his first race since Indianapolis, it will be interesting to see
> how Alessandro fares this season. I suggested midway through the
> '56 season that Alessandro should consider terminating his con-
> tract with friend and mentor Hermann Rudesheim, who has suf-
> fered major setbacks lately, first with the withdrawal of Mercedes-
> Benz from competition and then with the loss of his wife in a
> plane crash, and who is no longer the force he once was. Alessan-
> dro had been labeled a playboy by the popular press, but he is
> also a talent to reckon with—now that he has made an amicable
> split with Rudesheim, his Swiss fans must hope that, with his new
> Maserati, in which he will be racing as a private competitor, he
> will now find the discipline he has until now seemed to lack.
>
> The British star Moss is sick and unlikely to race at Rouen, but
> Fangio and Behra are fit and——

Andreas picked up the telephone. "Yes?"

"Andreas?"

"Papa, how are you?"

"Andreas——"

A tremor of premonition snapped through him. "What's wrong?"

"You must come home."

"What's happened? Is it Mother?"

"Come home." His father's voice was dull. "She's sick."

"How sick?"

There was a short pause. "She's dying. Come home, Andi."

The house smelled of cancer in spite of the brave alpine flowers arranged in each room by Anna's grimly optimistic nurse. The wooden shutters at every window were thrown back, as if those inside the house dared the angel of death to invade such an undimmed place.

In the drawing room, Roberto avoided his son's eyes.

"How long have you known, Papa?"

"Six months."

"*Jesu Maria*, Papa! What am I, a distant cousin? Why didn't you tell me?"

"She wanted it this way. Just as she refused to leave the house. I wanted her to go to a sanitarium in Davos—"

"Would it have helped?"

Roberto shrugged wearily. "Who knows? Probably not, according to the doctors in Lucerne and Zurich. But anyway, she wouldn't go."

Andreas stared at his father. "Did she ask you to send for me?"

Roberto didn't answer.

"I see." He sank into an armchair, his voice bitter. "Let me guess, Papa—she said I should not bother to come home unless I'm prepared to stay and give up racing. Am I right?"

Still Roberto was silent.

Andreas nodded. "I have the picture."

Her dying, less than two weeks later, was not peaceful. Within moments of seeing Andreas, Anna knew he had come to say farewell, not to stay. With her husband she became softer and kinder, but with Andreas she was unrelenting.

"Why, Papa? Why is she doing this?" Andreas appealed to his father one night after another long vigil. "She lets me sit there for hours on end, but she gives *nothing!*"

Roberto's features were gnawed by grief, and he stooped, unable to contemplate life without Anna. "She's punishing herself, Andreas," he said quietly. "Can't you see that?"

"But why? Does she hate me so much? All she repeats, over and over, is 'Have you thought, Andreas?'—meaning will I give it up for her?"

"She's a woman, Andi, a mother; you must try to understand."

"Why doesn't she try to understand me? Why can't she see that driving's in my blood, that I inherited a dream from you, just the way she inherited the farm from her parents?"

Roberto raked his fingers through his still thick but whitening hair. "I think she does see it, Andi, but she can't accept it."

"Won't accept it."

Roberto sighed. "Does it make a difference?"

Toward the end, Anna seemed to crumble away. She was so weak, she could hardly move, too feeble even to weep properly over the indignities she suffered; the tears would simply leak out of her unblinking eyes and trickle down the parchment face.

One night, late, when the rest of the house lay sleeping, she reached for Roberto's hand with a great effort, and held it weakly. Her lips trembled. "Would you touch me, Roberto, please."

Roberto bent closer. "Of course, my love."

"For so long," she whispered, "I wouldn't let you near me."

"I have forgotten that, Anna, and so must you."

"I never could show you, Roberto, how much I loved you . . . I tried—I meant to, but it was so hard for me." She made an attempt to sit up, then sank back.

"I know, *mia cara,* don't torment yourself."

"Time went so fast . . ." Breath rasped in her throat, but her grip tightened. "And I was so crazy, because of Andreas . . ."

"Please, Anna, try to rest."

"I can't, Roberto, I want you to forgive me. Please, can you try?"

"There's nothing to forgive, Anna." He knelt very close to her, kissing her damp forehead, stroking the thin gray hair that had once been so rich and gleaming. "About Andi, *Liebchen*—won't you help him a little now? He feels so cut off from you, he's so lost. You could ease his pain with a few words."

Behind him, the nurse had entered the room, rustling starch. "The priest is downstairs, Herr Alessandro."

Roberto rose to his feet and looked down at Anna. She had closed her eyes again and her expression was perfectly composed, as if she had not just wept, not begged his forgiveness, not heard his own plea.

She died three hours later, Roberto holding her hand and the priest on her other side—Andreas in the doorway with the nurse.

20

It was exactly one year later, Bobbi, to the very day, that I met Andreas.

Twenty-five years. Could it be?

Alexandra examined her hands for signs of age, and ran her finger over the eternity ring Andreas had given her at the time of Roberta's birth. Why did she wear it still, she wondered? Were her emotions, after all, as vividly scarred as her memories? And how could she put away the ring as long as her feelings on that day, more than two decades past, still returned to her with such dazzling clarity?

Everything she had written up to now in the letter was only background, like a canvas covered with light, preliminary backwash, subjects tentatively outlined in base color, all substance and meaning yet to be added. For the hundredth time she asked herself if she was right to continue. Could she truly justify this?

She picked up the pen. No more hesitation, she was quite resolved. She laid a fresh sheet of paper on the blotter.

> I was back in England after a short stay in Reims, snatching sketches of the Vanwall team preparing for the French Grand Prix, in the hope of consolidating enough material for the triptych I planned as the centerpiece for my next exhibition. My fascination with auto racing was still an infant preoccupation; it had begun that May, with the much publicized Monaco race—

The past collided with the present in her brain, pain and joy exploding like catherine wheels, making it impossible to write.

Again she put down her pen, and leaning back, her whole body trembling, she closed her eyes and gave herself up to the memories.

Part Three

21

"Did someone give you permission to draw me?"

She frowned in irritation but continued to sketch, her right hand flying back and forth across the paper.

"Maybe you didn't hear me." His shadow spread itself over the drawing.

The stick of charcoal in her hand snapped in two, and she slammed the sketch pad down on her knees.

"You're blocking my light!"

He glowered at her, the sweat on his naked chest shimmering in the sunshine, his oil-covered hands on his hips.

And then the sketch caught his eye.

She was drawing his car.

Alexandra had come to Silverstone to observe Alessandro at close quarters. It was one of her rules never to select a subject from photographs alone, and certainly the press shots she'd seen of this particular man had not prepared her at all.

She'd seen handsome men before, great flocks of them during her years in America and at art school, but this was quite the most startlingly attractive man she'd ever come across. Those eyes, which in photographs merely sat, black and opaque, on the glossy paper, were in reality two pieces of molten coal, spitting fire at her; the ludicrous, incongruous white-blond hair that she had dismissed as bottle-reared, was actually natural, purest sterling silver. He moved extraordinarily well, too, for a stockily built man, his steps light and loping, his gestures fluid and relaxed.

He was certainly handsome. He was also damned arrogant.

He stared at the sketch, perplexed.

"Your car suits you," she said truthfully, not intending to flatter.

His eyes flicked from the drawing back to her face.

"Are you going to have me thrown out?" she asked.

"Why should I?"

"I am a trespasser," she said. "No one gave me permission to paint you or your car, Alessandro, so I guess you have every right to kick me and my sketch pad out of your pit."

"It isn't my pit."

"No," she agreed.

"What's your name? You seem to have the advantage."

She slid down off the fence on which she'd been perching, and gave him her hand.

"I'm Alexandra Craig." In her sandaled feet, she was almost his height.

"Are you a famous artist?"

She shrugged. "Not yet."

For a moment they watched each other, eyes meeting evenly, and then abruptly he said, "Wait here."

He strode back to the red Maserati on which he'd been working with Salvadori and three other mechanics. "Can you manage without me for the rest of the day?"

Salvadori looked up, surprised. "I thought you were so worried about the transmission." Alessandro never allowed anything to interfere with work.

"I want to talk to the lady."

The Italian grinned. This he understood. "Go," he said magnanimously. "We can fix this little one so she purrs like a pussycat."

Andreas picked his shirt up from the ground.

"She's a beauty," Salvadori commented. "Who is she?"

"I have no idea." Andreas looked back at Alexandra. "But she paints cars."

Salvadori stuck out his lower lip. *"Va bene."* He ducked his head down again over the motor.

Andreas strolled back to where she stood by the fence, his shirt slung over his shoulder. "Will you have dinner with me tonight, Miss Craig?"

"No." She bent down to pick up the broken pieces of charcoal and the large wicker basket she carried with her everywhere, which was filled with the tools of her craft.

"Why not?"

"I don't know you."

"I don't know you, either, but I still want to have dinner with you." He took her sketch pad from the basket and regarded it.

"By all means," she said dryly. "Help yourself."

His silver brows beetled in concentration. "It's excellent," he said in surprise. "Inaccurate but powerful."

"Thank you," she said coldly.

"Why?"

"Why what?"

"Why were you drawing my car?"

"An exercise. I'm planning a work revolving around auto racing."

He looked at her curiously. "Are you an American?"

"I am."

"I get confused by accents." He smiled. "Irish and American sound almost the same to me."

She took the pad out of his hand and returned it to the basket.

Andreas continued to stare at her. There was something about her that was oddly affecting. Salvadori was right, she was beautiful. But she was more than that. His eyes raked over her, taking in her absurdly unsuitable white cotton sundress and sandals, admiring her fine lines. She reminded him of a brilliantly reared Arabian filly—every part of her was long and sweeping, yet softly curving at the same time. Her hair was ebony, swinging from a perfect parting to her shoulders, her nose was narrow and perhaps longer than perfection, but it swept down her face between her sparkling eyes and clear-cut cheekbones to her tightly closed, slightly piqued mouth.

"Are your eyes gray or green?" he asked suddenly, peering at them.

"Both," she answered. "Either."

"Sneaky. What makes them change?"

"My state of mind."

He laughed. "That's good. You can't hide your feelings."

She raised her right eyebrow. "What color are they now?"

He looked. "Gray. Smoky."

She smirked imperiously. "Exactly."

The mechanics, twenty yards away, started the Maserati's engine, and it roared, beastlike, into life.

"Let's go." Andreas took her arm.

"I don't mind the noise."

"Maybe not, but they don't like spectators."

Alexandra looked at her watch. "I have to leave anyway."

"Do you have an appointment?"

She raised her chin. "No."

Still he held her arm. "Have dinner with me."

"I told you, Alessandro, I have to leave."

He stepped closer. Ordinarily he would be impatient by now; there were women enough who would jump at his invitation. "A drink, then."

Disconcerted, she stepped away, and his arm dropped to his side. "I don't enjoy liquor without food."

Andreas smiled. "So it's dinner?" He paused briefly. "Good. Eight o'clock. Shall I come to your home, or do you prefer to come to my hotel? I'm staying at the Dorchester."

"Make it eight-thirty, and I'll meet you there." She glanced over at the car. "You can run along back to your friends now, Alessandro."

He grinned. "Your voice is delicious. Like Katharine Hepburn's."

"Luckily," she said, "I adore Katharine Hepburn."

For the second time she gave him her hand, but this time Andreas gripped it tightly. Alexandra became aware of his bare skin, sunburned and damp with sweat, just inches from her own body. She withdrew her hand, and escaped.

She stalked into the marbled lobby of the Dorchester three hours later, wearing a strapless dress of gray silk chiffon caught at the waist with a narrow silken rope, with shoes and a tiny clutch purse to match. Her hair was swept up in a low chignon that accentuated the curves of her neck and shoulders.

Andreas was kicking his heels in the main hall. "You're late."

She smiled. "I know."

"Aren't you sorry?"

"I'm not that late." She surveyed him. "You look splendid."

It was his turn to smile. "Thank you. Would you like a cocktail here, or shall we go directly to the restaurant?"

"I told you, I don't enjoy liquor without food."

"Okay."

"Where are we going?"

"Do you know a place called A l'Ecu de France?"

"I've heard of it but never eaten there."

"I'm told that it's excellent."

They took a taxi to the restaurant. It was a Monday night and the streets were quite empty, the theater crowds already in their seats, and many Londoners preferring to sit out the sunny evening on their terraces or in their gardens. The drive to Jermyn Street took less than five minutes.

They went to their table right away and ordered simply but sumptuously from the impeccable menu. As they scooped *Cavaillon* melon out of their ice-frosted dishes, Andreas found out that Alexandra was an orphan and an Anglo-American. As they dipped slices of filet mignon into béarnaise sauce, he discovered that her friends called her Ali, and that she had made quite a name in the London art world with her darkly romantic portraits of the theatrical community; as they sipped from the huge goblets of Château Margaux, he found that his throat tightened whenever he looked into her eyes, that his fingers itched to touch her—and that he hadn't a scrap of concern for the transmission on his Maserati!

"I thought drivers had to keep to strict regimens," Alexandra said, watching as Andreas devoured another spoonful of wild strawberries and crème Chantilly.

Andreas laid down the spoon. "Don't talk about driving tonight." He raised his wineglass, and the chilled dessert wine swirled. "This evening is special."

She laughed. "Should we send our glasses crashing to the floor as a grand gesture?"

He leaned closer. "There's no fireplace. There has to be a fireplace if you want to smash glasses."

There was a brief, warm silence. Then Alexandra sat back and looked at him. "Will you let me paint you?"

"Why in God's name would you want to do that?" he asked, bemused.

"Because you're quite beautiful," she said without a second's hesitation. "Artistically speaking, that is."

Andreas looked startled.

"I'm sorry, I've embarrassed you." She sat forward, her face earnest. "But you must know how attractive you are. Why else do you suppose you've made the covers of *Newsweek* and magazines like *McCall's* when you're not even in line for the championship?" She bit her lip, regretting the words the moment they were out.

"I thought I had invited a woman for dinner," Andreas snapped, "not a Fleet Street reporter with a paintbrush instead of a camera!"

"I'm sorry, truly," she said again. "That was tactless." Her eyes were serious. "I'm here because of *you,* not because of painting, or not entirely anyhow. But my work isn't anything like snapping away for a quick profit. If I see something or someone I want to paint, it becomes an ache." She shrugged. "I'd be lying if I said that selling my paintings isn't marvelous. If I hadn't achieved some success over the past few years, I'd probably be slaving in some office and miserable as hell." She smiled softly. "I certainly wouldn't be here, in this wonderful place, asking to paint you."

Andreas's eyes narrowed. "If I agree, will you do me a favor?"

"It depends on the favor."

"Let me dedicate my next race to you."

She laughed in delight. "I thought you were a driver, not a toreador."

He leaned over, took her right hand and kissed it. "It's much the same thing," he said. "Yes or no?"

A tremor of excitement rushed through her and she stared at him.

"Well?"

"All right, then. Why not? Yes."

"Good." He turned her hand over and kissed it again, palm up this time, his lips brushing and lingering. For a moment, she closed her eyes. Then her lashes flicked up and her irises glittered.

"There!" Andreas said so suddenly that she jumped. "They've changed!" He leaned closer, searching her face so thoroughly that she blushed. "And they're not just ordinary green, they're too brilliant—they're more like malachite, polished malachite!"

She tugged her hand free and laid it in her lap out of his reach. "My, you're poetic for a racing driver," she said huskily, and changed the subject! "When's the race?"

"The main event? On Sunday. Will you come?"

She laughed. "How can I stay away from a race that's going to be dedicated to me?"

"You can't," he answered. "It would be unspeakably rude."

"And will you sit for me?"

"Where?"

"I have a studio in Highgate."

"Where's that, out of London?"

She smiled. "Not at all. Fifteen minutes usually, thirty in the rush hour. Shall we make arrangements now?"

"I'll call you."

"You won't forget?"

"If I do, you won't come to the race, will you?"

She tossed her head mischievously. "Of course not."

"Well, then."

It was three in the morning when the telephone woke her.

"I've worked out my schedule," he said, without apology or explanation. "How is tomorrow?"

"Andreas, it's the middle of the night!"

"I couldn't sleep. Is tomorrow good?"

She rubbed her eyes. "I guess so."

"Good. Four o'clock?"

"Anything you say."

"Do I get English tea?"

"If you keep still."

"Go to sleep. It's very late."

Alexandra felt comfortable with cavalier attitudes; they reminded her of her father. John Craig had been an artist, too, though a less than successful one. Her parents, who had married and tried to settle in New York City, had divorced when Alexandra was five years old. John Craig had moved back to his hometown, Boston, to resume his old bohemian life, and Lucy, Alexandra's British-born mother, had applied for a teaching post at a girls' school in Cornwall, where her sister lived.

Mother and daughter had arrived in England just three months before the outbreak of war, and set up housekeeping in the comparative safety of Polperro. But in June 1944, Lucy, in London to spend a day with her RAF officer boyfriend, was killed by a V-1 flying bomb. Alexandra remained in Cornwall with her aunt until it was safe enough for her to cross the Atlantic to rejoin her father.

For the next six years she went to school in Boston and lived joyously with Craig, keeping house for him and discovering in herself an inherited love of art. In spite of his haphazard lifestyle, Alexandra adored her father, who drank too much, made less money than he might have from his work, and who brought home a steady flow of "unsuitable" women to their ramshackle house on Huntington Avenue, positioned just far enough away from the Craig family mansion on Beacon Hill to be out of spitting distance.

Alexandra found him, one morning in 1952, slumped on the paint-splattered rug in front of his easel, stone dead. Gathering up all her strength and resources, she arranged the funeral, sold the house and, now eighteen, headed for Europe, as determined as Craig had been that his Brahmin family should have no opportunity to exert its influence on her. For a year she lived like an urchin, in Italy, letting the glories of Florence, Rome, and Venice wash over her and eking out a Spartan living by painting street portraits of tourists; the next year she spent in France, reveling in the unconventional extravaganza that was Montparnasse, and the balmy, soothing, artistic haven that was the south.

By 1955, however, she began to see that a measure of discipline was necessary if she was to build any kind of security for herself; the proceeds from the house sale had been greatly diminished by the bills that Craig had run up in his last days, and it was impossible these days to make money from art unless one learned how to satisfy the demands of the art-buying public. She said a painful farewell to Paris, squeezed her belongings, now reduced to the bare necessities, into one trunk, strode onto the cross-Channel ferry at Calais, came to London, and marched without an appointment into the secretary's office at the Slade School of Fine Art.

"It is simply not possible to walk into the Slade, Miss Craig. Applications must be made in the correct manner, and in any case, there are no places available for overseas students for at least two years," she was told by the secretary to the secretary, a stalk-thin woman dressed in sweater set and pearls, with a sternly set mouth but encouragingly warm eyes.

"But I can't wait!" Alexandra heaved open her large portfolio and began to pull out pastels and watercolors until the office floor was carpeted with the vivid vermilions of the Latin Quarter, the titians and russets and olives of autumnal Vence and Eze, and the hueless, anemic tones of the toiling American tourists blending with glowing, nut-brown Neapolitans.

"Miss Craig, please!" begged the secretary. "There's nothing I can do for you."

"All I need is a year—"

"Miss Craig, please listen to reason. Our courses are normally of four years' duration—"

"Normally," Alexandra leapt in.

"There are schemes for nondegree students for one year—"

"That's all I need!" Alexandra picked up one of her favorite works, a lightning pastel study she'd made of a young French boy in the Accademia in Florence gazing up at Michelangelo's *David.* "Please—show these to someone! I've come thousands of miles just for this—I need to be taught self-control and humility and technique!" She detected a glimmer of a twinkle in the Englishwoman's eyes and pounced, laying the pastel sheet in her lap. "You must try and help me, *please.*" Exhausted, tears threatening, she knelt on the floor and, suddenly fearing the worst because of her impassioned eruption, began collecting up the fruits of her labors.

The secretary sank back in her chair. "My goodness," she murmured, half to herself, half to Alexandra. "You're right, you certainly do need to learn moderation, and perhaps a touch more humility might not come amiss."

Alexandra, still down on the floor, sighed. "Oh, boy, I fouled up, didn't I?"

The Englishwoman leaned forward, elbows on her desk, her

eyes alert and amused. "Did you really come all that way just because of the Slade?"

"Yes, indeed," Alexandra answered ruefully. "I've come here today straight from Dover."

"Have you somewhere to stay?"

Alexandra shook her head, abruptly lost for words. Suddenly her actions seemed like folly of the worst kind. She should have stayed in Paris—at least there she had friends, there was always somewhere to lay her head and grab a meal.

The secretary rose, her manner brisk and kindly. "Well, then, clear up that mess, Miss Craig, and we'll go and take a look at the notice board. There's usually a student somewhere looking for a kindred spirit to share lodgings." She eyed Alexandra curiously. "Do you have any money?"

"Yes, I have savings. That's why I knew I had to act now, before they're all gone."

"Fees here are high, you know. No grants are available for overseas students."

"I do have quite a bit in the bank," Alexandra said hastily, "and I could always get a night job." She stopped, and her eyes widened. "You mean there's a chance?"

The other woman held up her hand. "Not so fast! It's very unlikely, you must understand that. But . . ." She hesitated, choosing her words cautiously. "I'm quite impressed by your work. That does not mean it will find favor with anyone else here, and even if it does, there are the regulations. You have to realize, Miss Craig—"

"Yes, I do, I do! Just as long as I get a chance!" Suddenly her weariness vanished again. She was ready to tackle this whole daunting city single-handed if need be.

The secretary smiled. "You'll have to part with your portfolio, my dear."

Alexandra hesitated.

"You can trust me."

She blushed. "Of course I can. It's just that I hate the feeling that I'm abandoning it."

"I do understand. I always feel that way about my own work."

Alexandra flashed a startled look at her impeccable exterior. "Are you an artist?"

The other woman laughed, an unexpectedly round sound emerging from her narrow chest. "It isn't compulsory for all artists to wear sloppy sweaters and black stockings, you know."

For the second time, Alexandra's cheeks reddened. "I'm sorry, I didn't mean—"

"No, of course you didn't." She gathered up a notebook and pencil from her desk top and swept around the desk to the door. "Now let's investigate that notice board, shall we. That way, perhaps you'll have an address at which we can reach you when there's a decision one way or the other." She turned on her heel and looked again into Alexandra's face. "Have you ever modeled?"

"No."

"You could consider it, you know; a little extra pocket money when you need it most."

"Could I model at the Slade?"

The secretary smiled. "We'll see. You do have a most unusual face. Our students would find your eyes absolute hell."

It was the key to everything. Alexandra studied at the Slade for the year she'd begged for. She was taught restraint and order, she was shown how to master her natural gifts for color and structure; she was harangued, tamed, drilled, enlightened, and emboldened. She came away finally with a feeling of relief—she was free again, if she wished, to lose herself in utopia, but now she could also, when necessary, capitulate sufficiently to work on projects that thrilled her less but brought in funds.

It was while she was still at the Slade that her first commercial opportunity struck. At London's Phoenix Theatre to see a play starring Sybil Thorndike, Alexandra was so devastated by the actress's fragile beauty that she waited at the stage door until she emerged and, while others pleaded for autographs, expressed her own urgent desire to paint her portrait. Dame Sybil had already been painted by a number of reputable, established artists, but thankfully she took a liking to the young American girl, sat for her before curtain time one evening each week until the painting was completed, and finally insisted on buying it at a very generous price. It was an auspicious beginning. By the end of 1956, Alexandra had painted William Squire as Captain Cat in *Under Milk Wood* and, in Stratford-upon-Avon, Patrick Wymark in *Toad of Toad Hall.*

Through 1957 she worked on twelve more theatrical canvases, enough for a small exhibition at a Mayfair gallery, where, to her delight, her work actually sold! Then, shifting focus, she visited Badgastein for the 1958 World Alpine Skiing championships, and was artistically drawn to the athletic body. Quickly she spread her range from skiers to gymnasts and divers, and then to the dramatic world of auto racing.

Here, surprisingly, she found the cars as fascinating as their drivers. To Alexandra they were not inanimate; they were living extensions of the men who drove them, men whose personalities, on the whole, tended to elude her paintbrush until they were seated behind the wheel.

She had assumed that would be the case with Alessandro, had wondered what he would be like away from the track, away from his cars. But she had not intended to paint him in her studio. Now, at three o'clock in the morning, after his offhanded call, Alexandra lay on her back staring into the dark, unable to sleep. Painting Alessandro would be difficult, she fretted. A circuit Casanova was all she needed!

She closed her eyes and tried to relax. His face danced before her, those flickering coal-black eyes taunting her. She sighed, and felt her heart miss a beat.

22

They were settled in her studio by five next afternoon. It was another hot day, with the windows flung wide, and while Andreas lounged comfortably on a paint-stained couch at one end of the room, Alexandra, dressed for work in a short-sleeved gray cotton smock, feet bare, her hair tied back off her face with ribbon, perched on a stool several feet away, working on her preliminary sketches.

Andreas stretched. "It's peaceful here. I haven't had much peace since I left Switzerland."

Alexandra ripped a sheet of paper from her pad, and started a fresh sketch. "Are you ready for the race?"

"No. Official practice starts on Thursday, but the car still needs work. I left the boys to get on with it."

She stopped drawing for a moment. "Should you be here?"

He shrugged. "Why not? It's unusual, perhaps, for me to take time before a race, but nothing for you to worry about."

She smiled. "Then I won't."

Later, she stood up and brought her pad to him. "Want to see?"

He looked at the strong, sparing strokes and was startled. There was the confident image that cameras tended to catch, but there, too, in the eyes, was a vulnerability he had thought well concealed.

"You *are* very good," he said after a moment. "I thought so when I saw the sketch of my car, but this is quite different." He nodded emphatically. "Better."

She took the sketches back. "Will you stay for dinner, Alessandro?"

"No more work?"

"Not today," she said firmly. "Dinner?"

"Sure, but first I need a favor."

She looked suspicious. "What?"

"A shower before we eat. I came straight from the pit."

"Be my guest," she said.

While Alexandra pottered in her kitchen, seasoning meat and chopping salad, and Andreas stood under the shower in Alexandra's bathroom, needles of hot spray stinging his flesh as he soaped himself with her Chanel soap, their thoughts were running on a single level.

Andreas thought he had never wanted any woman as much as he wanted Alexandra Craig, and yet he was glad she was in the kitchen instead of with him under the shower. It was safer to think about her from a distance; any involvement was unwise.

Alexandra, peeling onions, felt weak with the knowledge that Alessandro was in her bathroom. All afternoon they'd eyed each other, she under cover of art, and Andreas with the conviction many men had that they were entitled to inspect any woman from head to toe.

"Who am I kidding?" she muttered. "We *both* inspected— Christ, we practically devoured each other, didn't we."

She diced an onion and dropped the knife into the sink with a clatter. "This," she said decisively, "is no time to be conventional."

After all, she convinced herself as she ran up the narrow staircase and locked herself into the second bathroom, there was a special rival to consider in Alessandro's life. Just because she'd drawn him away from his precious car for one afternoon, perhaps even created a precedent, there was no reason to assume it might ever happen again. There was a strong element of will-o'-the-wisp about Alessandro. If she didn't act quickly, he might just elude her.

Furiously she scrubbed at her hands with cold water and soap, damning the onions, until she'd removed every trace of their smell. Then she slipped out of the bathroom and into her dressing room and sat down in front of the mirror. Her fingers trembled as she untied the hair ribbon, dabbed Madame Rochas perfume behind each ear and on her wrists, and brushed her hair with a bristle brush until it shone like ebony and sparked with electricity.

She had just stepped out of the gray smock, and was slipping into a pale blue silk robe, when the door opened and Andreas walked in from the bathroom, a white turkish towel knotted around his waist.

"Jesu Maria!" he murmured.

Alexandra's courage deserted her. Her fingers sought the belt of her robe, fumbling to conceal her nakedness from the stranger who stood directly before her, his black eyes seeking and holding the clearly defined contours of her body.

He closed the door behind him and turned back to her. "Don't hide, Alexandra, for God's sake don't hide yourself from me!" His voice sounded maddened, strangled.

She dropped her hands to her sides, and the blue silk parted again, revealing the long lines of gleaming, curving flesh and the tiny, contrasting mound of black, curling hair. With a small sigh she took two steps toward him, standing tall, her eyes clear green now and gazing directly into his.

Andreas angled his head slightly to kiss the sweetest curve of her cheek, first on one side, then on the other. Slowly he unknotted the towel about his waist and let it drop to the floor. They were standing very close, not touching, each feeling the heat from the other's body.

Alexandra placed the fingertips of her right hand against Andreas's lips, then slipped the robe from her shoulders. She felt the silk brush against her back and legs as it fell to the carpet. Andreas moved at last and folded her into his arms, clasping her close to his chest, kissing first her eyes, then her throat, his mouth brushing, nibbling, tasting the skin of her shoulders and then her breasts and her belly and the perfume of that delicate, tightly curled hair.

She moaned suddenly with a new, joyous impatience. She pulled out of his arms, grasped his hands, and drew him into the bedroom. Andreas lifted her in his arms and laid her on the bed. He ran his fingers over her lips, then down into the dark, flowery moisture of her body, then out again, up through the soft tangle, now finding her hands and guiding her fingers over his own body —until they became, of their own accord, inquisitive, nimble, and finally demanding. . . .

When he could bear it no longer, Andreas lifted her chin and looked deep into her eyes.

"Ali?"

It was the first time he'd spoken, and the single word was at once gentle and ferocious. Her answering expression was glowing and rapturous—he needed no further confirmation. As tenderly as his urgency allowed, he rolled her over onto her back and parted her thighs. She threw back her head in anticipation—"Yes, Alessandro, yes!"—and when he entered her, huge, and fierce, the sensation that took over her entire essence was so piercingly pleasurable that she thought she might scream, but instead, without a sound, she was moving with him, two figures locked together on a speeding carousel, and his violence was gentling as she yielded, her body inviting him farther and farther . . .

Four days later Alexandra stood in the pit at Silverstone, her loneliness, like an invisible shroud, blocking off the world around her.

Since Tuesday night Andreas had ignored her right through the civilized hours of daylight, and then telephoned her at two or three o'clock in the morning, his voice husky with desire. Now she stared about, wishing him beside her.

Earlier that morning he had kissed her warmly on the cheek in the lobby of the Dorchester, handed her a pit pass, and headed off to a waiting car with two swarthy Italians, leaving her to find her own way to the track. She understood that kind of preoccupation very well. But all the same, at this moment, surrounded as she was on all sides by sweating, bellowing madmen and purposeful-looking young women bearing stopwatches and clipboards—right now she cursed him profoundly.

Later that night, relaxing in a steamy perfumed bath, Alexandra found it hard to remember what had troubled her most that day: her sudden conviction that she would never see Andreas Alessandro in one piece again—or the noise. It was *deafening,* beyond any human or mechanical clamor she'd ever heard, shaking the very earth she stood on, sending violent tremors through her spine, agonizing her eardrums. For an instant, before the race, she saw Andreas, eyes already masked by his goggles, silvery hair hidden by his helmet; shutting her eyes, she imagined his gleaming scarlet machine hurtling through the air, steel crumpling like eggshell . . .

Once the race began, she felt better. They were committed to the track now, spinning like manic tops around and around, lap after lap, slamming into view with a great explosion once every circuit and then vanishing again. It became impossible to tell the cars apart—who was leading, who was trailing, who was out of the race. Once she thought she spotted Andreas, and a burst of adrenaline made her yell his name with all her strength as she saw he was in the lead.

A tiny blond girl standing nearby lowered her clipboard and snapped a button on her stopwatch. She smiled at Alexandra. "He isn't leading, you know, honey. He was just lapped by Collins."

"Where is he placed?" Alexandra shouted.

The girl thrust out her hand, thumb down. Piqued, Alexandra turned her back. If only she could hear the commentary; when she'd been to other races, she'd been able to follow with the rest of the crowd, but in the pit it was impossible to catch more than a word at a time.

Time passed. Fear and discomfort began to give way to numbing boredom, and she shuffled her feet, digging small holes in the earth with the toes of her shoes, and then smoothing them over again with the soles.

Suddenly there was a localized swirl of agitation, an extravagant waving of flags on the pit wall, then a flurry of activity by the mechanics, and a moment or two later, after the two leaders had pounded by, the scarlet Maserati rolled into the pit.

Andreas climbed out, ripped off his goggles, and unbuckled his helmet. He was out of the race. Alexandra watched from a distance, studying him in defeat. Relief that he was out of danger flowed like salve over her fractured nerve endings; she felt guilty and treacherous.

"Gasolio!" yelled a mechanic, but Andreas threw up his hands in disgust. She swung around and saw the blonde scribbling rapidly on her clipboard.

"What went wrong?" Alexandra asked.

"The engine bearings are ruined."

"Can't they fix them?"

The girl glanced up briefly in amusement. "You must be joking. He's out."

It was painful watching him but not going to him, not holding him in her arms as she wanted to do. But this was his territory, as her studio was hers, and the rules were unfamiliar. She waited quietly, patiently, until Andreas was ready to come to her.

"I'm sorry," he said, when he did come.

"What for?"

"It was your race. I should have won."

She touched his cheek tentatively. "Another time."

A pattern was established. Andreas, enjoying the first completely self-indulgent period he could recall since his childhood, threw himself into a holiday spirit. For one third of each day they were in the studio, for another third they made love in Alexandra's bed or on the studio floor, and for the last third they ate and drank.

Ever since leaving Küssnacht, Andreas had enjoyed what he thought of as "playing" with food. If he hadn't wanted to drive so much, he sometimes thought he might have made a fine chef—but never before had he met a woman for whom he wanted to prepare soups and mousses and wildly extravagant, experimental dishes. While Alexandra worked on her canvas, Andreas raided the best delicatessens, butchers, and bakers in the neighborhood. "We'll both contribute what we do best," he said when Alexandra protested. "You paint, I'll cook."

The next Grand Prix was three weeks away at the Nürburgring, but Andreas hardly considered it. For the first time in his life he had found a woman with whom he wanted to spend more than one night at a time.

"Ali," he said suddenly one evening in bed after oysters and sex, "are we in love?"

Alexandra wriggled a little way down the bed, hiding her face, kissing the pale golden hairs on his chest. Then she shut her eyes tightly and clenched her fists. Love was almost a physical pain inside her, bursting to get out, but she felt sure that Andreas needed more time to accept his own feelings before coping with hers.

"Ali, did you hear me?" His voice was reproachful. "I asked if you think we're in love?"

Her face still buried in his chest, she muttered, her voice muffled, "I don't know."

"Why don't you know?" He sat up abruptly. "Dammit, woman, talk to me!"

Alexandra rolled over onto her back and giggled. "You're pouting, Alessandro."

"Don't call me that."

"It's your name, isn't it?"

He reached for her. *"Piccola diavola."*

"What's that mean?"

"Little demon."

She laid her head in his lap and sprawled across the bed so that her long legs draped over the edge. He stroked her hair as tenderly as if he were caressing a small creature. Her eyes filled with sudden tears. "You touch me," she whispered.

His eyes gleamed. "You still didn't answer my question."

Alexandra craned her head so that she could see into his face. His expression was uncharacteristically grave, and her heart clenched.

"No, I didn't," she said softly, and squeezed his hand.

In the last week of July, Andreas flew to Germany to begin practice for the 'Ring. Three days later, when Alexandra answered a buzz at her front door, she found him standing on the mat.

"Take off that smock and come with me."

"Jesus, Alessandro, what are you doing here?"

He stepped over the threshold and gripped her by the arms. "Aren't you pleased to see me?"

"Oh, you fool!" With a cry of joy, she flung herself at him and covered his face with kisses. "But you're not here—you're in Germany, driving your little red car around and around in great dizzy circles!"

"That's correct," he said, and pushed her away. "I'm a mirage —but I'm a big, strong mirage, and I order you to get undressed, or dressed, or whatever you like, and come with me!"

She smiled, and wiped the back of her hands across her eyes, scrubbing at the tears that threatened.

"Yes, Alessandro."

He drove her car, like a crazy person, through miles of wet London streets, then parked, just off Baker Street. He slammed and locked his door, came around, opened hers, and took her arm.

"Close your eyes, Alexandra."

She obeyed. "Sometimes you're a real Teut, Alessandro."

"What's that?"

"Teutonic." She opened her eyes and grinned.

"Shut them, and don't dare open them until I tell you."

He led her firmly along the street and into a shop. Alexandra wrinkled her nose and heard whispers exchanged.

"I smell animals," she said loudly.

"Quiet!"

"Yes, Alessandro."

"Now," he said.

She opened her eyes—and stared down at a perfect golden retriever puppy, standing, or rather sprawling, on the shop counter. A salesman in a brown coat, with sprigs of straw engagingly twined in his hair, stood behind the counter smiling.

"Pick him up," Andreas said.

Alexandra held the wriggling creature in her arms, marveling at his velvet softness. "He's beautiful," she breathed. "Oh, Andreas!"

"Right," he said sternly, "now put him down again and listen to me." He took her arm and drew her gently away from the counter. "You have a choice. Either I give you that puppy to remember me by—"

The light went out of Alexandra's face. The realization that he was going again, and perhaps for good, hit her more resoundingly than she'd dreamed it might.

"Or you can go home now, pack enough things to last you the

rest of the summer, and fly with me tonight to Bonn. We can pick up the pup some other time."

Alexandra was dazed. "He'll be sold by then," she murmured.

"Quite probably," the salesman interjected, looking bemused.

"Then we'll find another one."

She shook her head. "It may not be as perfect."

"Darling, darling Ali, please be serious."

"All right," she said slowly, thoughtfully. "I'll be serious." She tugged at the sleeve of his raincoat. "Come outside."

"A moment, please," Andreas said to the salesman, and followed Alexandra out onto the sodden sidewalk. The rain, which had begun almost a week before, poured in torrents along the narrow gutters and into the drains.

She stood at arm's length. Large raindrops fell on her eyelashes, then tumbled down her face, streaking her mascara. "All right," she said again. "Honesty time." She took a deep breath and looked directly into his eyes. "The puppy's adorable, Andreas. You're adorable, too. But if I have to choose between you, I would like to know something."

"Anything, Ali."

"Are you talking about a summer fling? A fun, steady round of driving, cooking, and fucking?"

He blinked, startled.

"I'd appreciate the truth, Andreas."

The truth, just like that! He couldn't think straight; those damnable glorious eyes, now cool gray, threw him completely, as did her absolute, infuriating unpredictability. One second she was soft as marshmallow, the next she was impulsive and crazy; and sometimes, as right now, she was so goddamned challenging that she unnerved him utterly!

"You're getting soaked, Ali," he said, reaching out to touch her drenched head. She stepped back, and he sighed. "Isn't it enough to know I want you with me, Ali?"

"No."

He glanced back inside the shop; the salesman was stroking the small animal and staring at them curiously. Vexation at being cornered spilled into his voice. "I can't answer something like that so quickly, Ali."

"Then I guess I'd better take the dog," she said softly.

"I guess so."

They stood still, two figures frozen in the London rain. Andreas felt as if a huge, multicolored balloon had been burst, jabbed maliciously with a pin, and all his warmth and optimism and newfound peace was draining out of him onto the sidewalk like blood.

"Well?" she said. "Shall we tell the man?"

He stared at her. She was immobile, waiting for him, tall and apparently undaunted. He experienced a sudden kick of shock deep in his gut. Was this what Hermann Rudesheim had meant when he'd talked about the *right* woman?

"Andreas, it's all right," she said gently, but he held up his hand commandingly, silencing her. He was beginning to see what a fool, what a complete horse's *ass* he'd be if he threw her away. Okay, he had meant to give *her* a choice, an amusing ultimatum, and she *had* managed to turn the whole thing on its head and lay the ball in his court, but even so . . .

He took her hands, one at a time, from the pockets of her too thin jacket, kissed them tenderly, warming them with his breath, and then lifted his eyes to hers.

"I didn't know," he said simply. "I didn't know I wanted to live with you. Not for always. So I took the easy way and said, hey, let's grab the summer and see what happens—"

"Andreas," she interrupted, bewildered.

"No, let me tell you, Ali. Let me find the right words." He dropped her hands and ran his fingers through his wet hair. "I can't lose you, Ali. I can't and I don't intend to, and if that's what it takes, then I'd sooner put up with you full-time than not have you at all." He saw her eyes fill with tears. "I'm not the most romantic man in the world, but it's the best I can manage at such short notice."

She began to tremble, partly from cold, partly from the enormity of what was happening to them both. "I didn't mean to demand commitment, Andreas, truly. Please, oh, *please,* for both our sakes, don't say something you don't really mean!"

He put his hands on her cheeks, his long fingers framing her face. *"Gänschen,"* he murmured, shaking his head. *"Kleines Gänschen."*

"What does *that* mean?" she asked frustratedly.

He laughed. "Little goose. Don't you know I would never say anything like that unless I was sure?" He wrapped his arms around her and folded her close, trying to stop the quivering, wanting to shelter her from the rain. For a few moments she let herself go and sobbed against his chest from sheer relief, and then she raised her head, and he marveled to see that the gray irises had again blazed into that extraordinary malachite color.

"Let's go home, Andreas," she said shakily. "I feel like a

drowned rat standing here." She smiled through her tears. "And it takes me forever to pack."

Inside the shop, the salesman shook his head, stroked the top of the puppy's head, and put him back in the cage.

23

The summer and fall of 1958 passed as a bright patchwork of rich experience for Andreas and Alexandra. Andreas's racing was dogged by bad luck and technical difficulties, but Alexandra filled his life away from the track with warming tenderness offered with such an intelligent lightness of touch that he was able to overcome his disappointments.

Roberto Alessandro adored her on sight. He was enchanted by her beauty, her humor, her easygoing adaptability and boundless energy. Three days after their first meeting at his new city apartment in Zurich, right after the German Grand Prix, Alexandra sketched Roberto and captured, in seconds, the quixotic, dreamy aspect of his nature that he had believed lost.

"So, Papa, what do you think?" Andreas asked his father as the three of them sat down to dinner one evening.

"I think you should watch out, Andi, or I may have her kidnapped and kept in Switzerland!"

"Bellissima, no?"

"Si!" Roberto's eyes danced, watching her devour *tagliatelle* with gusto. "I think she is secretly a green-eyed Italian, the way she eats pasta! And her name"—he nudged Andreas playfully—"is perfect, is it not? Alexandra Alessandro!"

Alexandra laid down her fork. "If you two don't stop discussing me as if I'm a stick of new furniture that pleases you, I shall abandon you both!"

Andreas poured more Chianti into her glass. "You're correct in your assumption that we find you pleasing, Ali, but I think it only fair to say that neither my papa nor I have found any similarity to a stick of furniture."

She giggled and hit him with her own napkin, tilting the wine bottle and splashing the carpet. Quickly she leapt to her feet. "Signor Alessandro, I'm so sorry. Where's the kitchen? I'll get a cloth."

"Sit down, *cara,"* Roberto soothed. "Leave it as it is, please. It will wash out, don't fret. Believe me, it's more than worthwhile for me to feel such vitality in my home. Often I have to check my reflection in a mirror to be sure there is anyone still alive in the apartment."

Impulsively, Alexandra took hold of his hand and squeezed it tightly. "Andreas," she said, "where's the next race? Portugal, isn't it?"

Andreas nodded. "Oporto. Just over three weeks away."

Alexandra turned back to Roberto. "Won't you come with us, Signor Alessandro? It would be such fun for me to have company while Andreas is practicing!"

"It's a good idea, Papa," Andreas agreed. "You haven't seen me race for months, and it would do you good."

Roberto smiled. "I think you are both charming, but as it happens, it is out of the question. This is always a busy time of year for us, if you remember, Andi."

"Do you drive to Küssnacht every day, Papa?"

"Sure I do. You think I enjoy driving any less than I ever did? Sometimes I stay at the farm, but I prefer it here."

"Fewer memories?"

Roberto nodded, his eyes dark with introspection. "It's strange, you know, Andreas. I always knew Anna was no saint—who is, after all?—but now I seem to forget any disillusionment, any sorrow, and all I remember is the pretty young girl I met so long ago in Brescia, and the sweet, contented mother you once had . . ." His voice trailed away, but he was smiling.

"That's good, Papa," Andreas said softly. "I try, too, to remember the better times."

There was a short silence.

"If you can't make Oporto," Alexandra said, breaking the mood, "maybe you could join us at Monza?"

Roberto patted her hand. "My son is fortunate." He raised his glass. "To Monza."

Later that night, in the guest room, Andreas squeezed Alexandra's hand.

"It was kind, *Herzchen*, what you said about Papa joining us in Portugal."

"It wasn't meant as kindness. I'd have loved having him along."

"You like him, then?"

She sat up. "How could anyone fail to like him? He's a sexy bear of a man."

Andreas stroked her breast. "You find him sexy, do you?"

She laughed huskily. "Like son, like father." She pressed her own fingers against his hand, and the nipples of both breasts sprang out, hard and full of desire.

"You're an insatiable woman, thank God." He pulled her down on top of him and kissed her.

"Of course," she whispered. "I have the future champion of the world in my bed."

They did not marry until the winter. They had traveled together from August right through to December, like a blissful pair of soaring, exotic birds, drawn initially by the schedule of the big races to Portugal, Italy, and then, for the last Grand Prix of the 1958 season, to Morocco; and finally, wanting to explore new terrain together, to Acapulco and California, and to New York, a city Andreas had never visited.

It ensnared him, Manhattan, spread its dramatic, sensuous tentacles around him and squeezed hard, trapping Andreas as surely as it had millions of other travelers through the years. It was the city of champions, a city of winners and men and women of ambition. It was also a city for lovers. Andreas and Alexandra took joy rides in Central Park, skated in Rockefeller Center, stood at the summit of the Empire State Building, dined at Sardi's, and took the subway from one end of Manhattan to the other.

"I could live here," Andreas said on their seventh morning as they drank coffee in their bedroom at the Plaza and gazed out over the park.

Alexandra smiled. "I knew you'd love it."

"How could you know? I'm a country boy, remember? I thought I would hate it."

She shook her head. "No, darling, you're a New Yorker. Being born in Switzerland was just an accident—this is where you belong."

"What about you?"

She adjusted the belt of her white satin robe. "What about me?"

"Would you want to come back? I know your childhood wasn't all that happy; would it worry you?"

"My childhood was just fine! For goodness' sake, I left New York when I was five, and I suppose when my father died and I left Boston, I never really thought about coming here, I just dived straight over the Atlantic."

Andreas stood up and began pacing the rug. "Would it suit you artistically?"

"Hard to tell."

"I mean, do you need grass and trees around you to paint successfully? Might all this glass and concrete and steel not block your creativity?"

She smiled. "It might sometimes, I guess, but the city's surrounded by thousands of acres of countryside. Most of New York State's heavenly and close." She paused. "Why, darling? What are you plotting?"

He shook his head. "I'm not sure. We have to go in a couple of days, and I find I'm reluctant to leave." He grinned. "I just wanted to know your feelings."

It was winter itself that called a halt, gently but firmly bringing the lovers back down to earth. The need for a home—with a studio, the single thing Alexandra had lacked during their nomadic months. And if they were to have a home, why not marriage?

The wedding took place in Zermatt, the little town that nestled at the foot of the Matterhorn. It was a compromise arrangement; not a Catholic, Alexandra was nevertheless keen to please her future father-in-law by marrying in Switzerland. Roberto, it seemed, cared only that they should be joined in the sight of God; the denomination of church didn't matter. So when Alexandra remembered the tiny, picturesque Anglican church in the village all three of them loved, he was content to agree.

The locals had never seen a wedding like it in their tranquil corner of the Valais. The bride and groom attracted a curious mixture of guests, and days before the ceremony the Mont Cervin hotel trembled with the sounds of festivity, as international auto racing stars and Italian mechanics fraternized with surprising ease with stuffy Swiss industrialists and the conservative British contingent.

When the newlyweds emerged after the service and made their way down the steps from the small graveyard where so many fallen British mountaineers lay buried, it was snowing hard, and even the hard-bitten press yelled approval as Alexandra settled the white fur hood of her cloak over her dark hair, smiling radiantly before Andreas lifted her up onto the horse-drawn sleigh decorated with pink rose petals, the horses' manes threaded with white carnations and showered with snowflakes.

They honeymooned for seven days in Zermatt, a week in Paris, and another seven days in London, enabling Alexandra to say her farewells and pack her belongings before they boarded their ocean liner at Southampton, bound for New York City and their new home.

In Manhattan they took a suite at the Plaza while they hunted for, and found, a perfect duplex on Central Park West. Soon Alexandra was in heaven, thriving on the city's abundant decorator stores and auction rooms.

"Look what I found!" she cried to Andreas one afternoon, returning to the hotel with armfuls of sample fabrics and wallpaper cuttings. "That place was a treasure trove! I don't know how I restrained myself—I could have filled suitcases with things for you to see!"

"For heaven's sake, Ali, you know I have no patience for this," Andreas complained, not for the first time. "Just decide what you want, it'll be fine with me."

"But I want to be certain you *love* what we choose, Alessandro. It's all very well your saying now that I should do anything I want, but in six months you may be sick at the sight of it, and then it'll be *my* fault, won't it!"

He held up his hands in a gesture of surrender, and spent five minutes pretending to sift through the samples. "This!" he said, jabbing at random at a piece of vermilion silk.

"Oh?" she raised an eyebrow. "And the paper to go with it?"

"I don't know, Ali, and I don't have the time right now to look."

"You see! I only put that one in as a blind, it's far too aggressive! You haven't really looked, Andreas, you just get bored and pick anything for a bit of peace and quiet!" She sank into an armchair and feigned anger until, contrite, he came up behind her and planted soothing kisses on her neck.

"Ah, baby," she sighed, pulling him down onto the chair, "this is all you ever think about. You're such a Latin."

"I think about cars, too," he added, nibbling her ear.

"Blue," she breathed softly, "robin's-egg blue for peace and space."

"Great."

"Creamy linens, I think, don't you?"

He maneuvered her out of her jacket, "Absolutely right."

"Andreas, you're not paying attention."

"I am. Take off your blouse."

If Andreas chose to let Alexandra take charge of furnishing and decorating her home, as far as her studio went he had no choice at all.

She chose the brightest room, the broad area that had previously been the master bedroom, overlooking Central Park on the

upper floor, and she had the parquet flooring treated for hard
wear and easy cleaning. Beyond that she required nothing except
a great expanse of pure white wall, windows that opened in summer and sealed tight in winter, and the twin luxuries of peace and
quiet when she wanted them.

The new lawfulness of their commitment suited them both as
well as the months of unfettered play had. As long as she could
escape regularly to her studio, Alexandra was content to accompany her husband from one Grande Épreuve to another. If her
heart and stomach churned uncontrollably each time Andreas
climbed into the cockpit of the Maserati, the idea of staying away
when she might be needed was even more intolerable.

There was only one area of real controversy between them during their first year of marriage. Andreas was impatient for babies;
why else had they married? He adored his wife, ergo he wanted
their child. Alexandra wanted, needed, to wait; she had married
Andreas to be his wife first, the mother of his children second.

The matter was raised frequently, whether they were at home or
traveling, and more often than not it was raised in bed. Andreas
would run his hands over her full breasts and down over her hips,
shake his head and exclaim: "Perfect! *So gut gebaut!* One hundred
percent guaranteed satisfactory baby-making equipment going to
waste!"

"Must you be such an Italian, Alessandro?" she would answer.
"I promise you we will make babies . . ." She would plant fluttering, teasing kisses on his face and chest, and stomach. "Only the
best, most handsome babies, darling . . . but all in good time."

It was not always possible, of course, to distract him with sex.
She tried hard to make him understand how precious this time was
to them both—the only time for many years, perhaps, during
which they would have each other to themselves. Andreas listened
with half an ear, but the memory of a conversation with his father,
shortly after his eleventh birthday, was louder in his mind than all
Alexandra's arguments. In that conversation his father had described the time when Anna was pregnant with him, her excitement, the way she had grown with him—*Like a ripening, luscious
apple,* Roberto had said.

He wanted that.

Following on the heels of his professional disappointments in the
last two years, Andreas's early successes in the 1960 season were
intoxicating. He came third at Sebring, in a heat wave so fierce
that driver after driver fell by the wayside; at Monsanto he won

second place, narrowly missing the first—and then, at Montreal, in Canada, on June 3, his Grand Prix ghost seemed finally laid to rest when he roared home to a flamboyant victory!

There were few other new stars on the horizon, Andreas was ballyhooed by the media as the great Swiss hope for the championship. He was savagely content with his lot; even if Ali had not yet surrendered on the subject of children, he was bound to win in the end—and so, in the middle of 1960, creeping steadily higher on the World Points Table, it seemed to Andreas Alessandro that fatherhood and the world championship were at last open to him, and that the future held no shadows. He was unstoppable.

24

Daniel might just as well have been in Frankfurt, or even Detroit, as in Paris, for everything in that most resplendent of cities seemed to him to be covered with gray mesh.

For the first two weeks after he walked into an anonymous and gracelessly modern hotel on the Rue de Clichy, he stayed in his room, emerging only once a day around dusk in search of a meal, dining in the same austere restaurant each time, drinking little and eating less. He was entirely indifferent to his surroundings. He was a failure. He had as good as killed Rosa Bernardi, and he had fled, was on the run again. Only this time it was almost worse than before because he had run out of cowardice, and because, whereas in the past escape had always turned quickly into the pursuit of a goal, this time he could see nothing ahead.

One morning, however, at the beginning of the third week, he woke with a violent start to see a man staring at him from the other side of the room.

He sat bolt upright, clutching the sheets, heart beating wildly. The other man did the same. Only then did Daniel realize that it was his own reflection that stared madly back at him from the mirror over the chipped hand basin.

He swore, and slumped back onto the mattress. His mouth was stale and his eyes prickled.

The telephone was ringing. Tentatively he picked up the receiver and listened.

"Monsieur Silberstein?"

"Oui."

It was the front-desk clerk asking him to settle the *note de semaine,* which had been pushed under his door the previous afternoon and which Daniel had ignored, not because he was short of funds but because it seemed too great an effort to go to the hotel safe to fetch cash.

He replaced the receiver and got out of bed languidly; the cheap carpet prickled the soles of his feet. He went into the bathroom and ran the shower. He had never grown accustomed to the American habit of showering, still preferred the luxury of a long European soak in a hot bath, and now he got under the spray and washed rapidly, wishing for the first time since his arrival that he'd asked for a room with a bath.

Turning off the water, he grabbed the skimpy towel and dried himself. Again he caught sight of himself in the mirror. Unshaven, hair in need of cutting, dark shadows under his eyes. A nonentity.

"Silberstein," he said aloud, rubbing his stubbled chin, "you should be ashamed."

He remembered another time when he'd stared at his reflection and taken stock. Lausanne, 1943, on the run from the Swiss authorities, when he'd bought scissors and soap at the railway station, and taken the first steps to put his life in order.

He sighed. "Shit, Silberstein," he accused the mirror, "are you going to be the original wandering Jew all your life?"

He dropped the towel on the floor and walked naked back into the bedroom. What the hell was he doing in this dump when he could easily afford a top-class hotel? For the first time since he'd checked in, he pulled up the wooden blinds and blinked at the sunlight.

"Ici Paris," he said. And then he turned, went into the bathroom again, and began to shave.

Within three hours he had packed, paid his bill, breakfasted at Kardomah, and checked into the Crillon in the Place de la Concorde. From there, he called his bank manager at Chase Bank in New York to arrange a large transfer to the Crédit Lyonnais, and then he dialed Roland Steinbeck's number.

"Roly?"

"Dear, dear boy! Where are you?"

"France, Roly, and I'm fine. I just wanted you to know."

"You took your time. Where in France?"

"I'm sorry, I haven't been quite myself. Doing some sorting out."

"You're all right now?" Roland sounded doubtful.

"Absolutely." The line began crackling and he raised his voice. "I'm okay."

"You haven't told me where you are."

"In France, I told you."

"And you won't say where, is that it?"

"Not won't, Roly, can't. No point anyway. I'll be moving on

shortly, and don't know where I'll be. I just wanted to check in with you, let you know my plane didn't go down in the ocean."

"I'd have heard the splash, dear boy."

Daniel smiled. "How about you? Are things good?"

"Of course." The line sounded dangerously like breaking up, and Roland shouted anxiously, "Stay in touch, for Christ's sake! Don't just disappear, will you!"

"I won't, Roly, I swear. And Roly—"

"*Yes!*" he yelled.

"Don't tell anyone you heard from me."

With even a remote chance that Joe Bernardi might be looking for him, it was only common sense to make sure that Daniel Silberstein was nowhere to be found. The morning after he moved into the Crillon, Daniel located an American attorney and discovered that the process of changing one's name was comparatively simple. It took a little less than three weeks, and in that time Daniel became a tourist. Joining the throng, he strolled through the Tuileries, saw the Madeleine, window-shopped along the Rue du Faubourg St.-Honoré, pausing for an hour at the Galerie Charpentier; he took a bus to Montmartre, the metro to the Sorbonne, and one evening, the *bateau mouche* from the Pont de l'Alma along the Seine as far as the Pont d'Austerlitz. And he dined—*le canard pressé* at Tour d'Argent, *poulet Docteur* at La Pérouse, and a bowlful of *gratinée* at Les Halles near dawn.

Once, at noon in the Rue de Castiglione, Daniel thought he saw Natalie Bresson through a store window, buying a long-handled lacy umbrella. The skin on the back of his neck prickled, he stood poised like an animal ready for an attack—she stepped out of the store and looked into his face, merry blue eyes smiling, and she was not Natalie. Daniel remained motionless for several minutes. He had almost forgotten her, but now, abruptly, Michel's letter of warning sprang into his mind: *Try not to do anything in the future which could be used against you.* The elegant street receded in a haze; Daniel felt sickened.

The man who boarded the Train Bleu at the Gare de Lyon three days later bore the name of Dan Stone, and he was bound for Lyon itself, the gourmet capital of France.

He took rooms in a small but charming pension on the right bank of the River Saône in Vieux Lyon, the old section of the city. The *propriétaire,* Jean de Luc, and his wife Gabrielle, were a couple of indeterminate age, prosaic but honest French people who made snap evaluations of strangers and were seldom wrong. Gabrielle de Luc liked Dan Stone. She liked his strong, sensitive face, his manners, his intelligent air, and most of all his open smile. But he perplexed her, because although he was undoubtedly *un homme sympathique,* he was also entirely alone.

For as long as she could bear it, Gabrielle studied their guest from a polite distance, but one morning she could control her curiosity no more.

"Mistaire Stone," she called out as he was walking out into the street after breakfast.

"Madame?" Daniel stepped back into the house and approached the desk behind which Gabrielle perched for several hours each day on a high stool, working on the accounts of the pension.

"Another beautiful day, Mistaire Stone." Gabrielle had learned English as a child, and enjoyed any opportunity to make use of her limited knowledge.

"Every day is beautiful here, madame."

"True." She smiled. "But I did not call you in order to discuss the weather. My husband and I should be happy if you could join us this evening for a glass of calvados."

"I'd be delighted, madame."

"*Très bien.* Ten o'clock? By then we are over the dinner and in need of relaxing and conversation." She picked up her pencil again. "Will you want your table this evening, or do you go outside?"

"I believe I shall stay here, thank you."

"*Bien,*" she said again, and bent her head over the accounts. "*A ce soir.*"

"Tell me, Mistaire Stone—"

"Dan, please, madame."

"And I am Gaby. Tell me, Dan," she began again as her husband poured their fifth refill of calvados, "is there trouble for you in America?"

Daniel waited a beat. "What do you mean?"

Gabrielle shrugged. "What I say. You have described much of your life; your severance from your family, your time in Switzerland, your success in New York—but you do not say why you left America and are here in Lyon."

"Please, Dan, do not be offended," Jean de Luc interjected. "My wife does not mean to be curious."

"A *little* curious, *peut-être,*" Gabrielle said smiling. "No, Dan, I do not wish to hear about your personal affairs, but I have a good reason to ask if you have trouble." She eyed him candidly. "With the police, perhaps?"

Daniel looked straight back at her. "No."

She nodded, satisfied, and leaned back in her armchair, waiting for her husband to speak.

"You have," Jean said, "no intention of returning to New York at present?"

"None."

"We can assume, however, since you were successful in the United States, that you hope to continue that success?"

"Of course."

The de Lucs looked at one another, then nodded simultaneously. Gabrielle sat forward, her eyes bright. "You must visit Madame Edouard."

"Who is she?"

"Madame Edouard," Jean said, "is the widow of Alain Edouard. Surely you know of him, Dan? He was a legend in his own lifetime."

"I'm afraid not."

"He was one of the great geniuses of *la cuisine française.*"

Jean told Daniel that it was said people had crossed the earth in the thirties just to sample one dish prepared by Edouard at his restaurant in Givors, near Lyon. Edouard, as well as being the winner of three Michelin stars, was also a fine human being. During the war, he and Jeannette, his wife, had aided the Resistance on numerous occasions, displaying courage for which they were decorated after the war.

"He died three years ago, but Jeannette is a remarkable and strong woman. She controls Maison Edouard with an iron fist, and some say the food is better than ever."

Gabrielle's eyes sparkled. "You must meet her, Dan. If anyone can show you the right direction, it is she."

It was three weeks before he was granted an audience. The meeting was brief, but it proved to be the turning point of Daniel's career.

"You are no true chef, monsieur," Madame Edouard said calmly. "But neither are you simply a businessman." Plainly, she required no response; these were declarations. She continued briskly. "You may love to cook, and you may even cook more than passably, but you don't have it in your blood."

"I'm sure you are right, madame."

She fell silent, apparently wrapped intently in thought. Jeannette Edouard was a woman of perfect grace and contentment, dressed in clothes of timeless elegance, subtly and deliciously perfumed, and wonderfully framed by her salon, a room out of Daniel's dreams, filled with photographs (mostly, he guessed, of her late husband), fresh flowers, and delicate antique silver.

"Have you ever eaten at Maison Edouard?" she asked abruptly.

"No, madame, alas."

"*Bon,*" she said decisively. "You will take luncheon with us, and then we shall speak again."

It was almost three hours before Daniel sat again in the salon, but now his nervousness and awe had dissolved, and he relaxed blissfully into the deep armchair, still half immersed in the delirious pleasure a feast of near perfect refinement could evoke in him.

Madame Edouard was beaming. "Did you enjoy the *queues d'écrevisses,* Monsieur Stone?"

"Enjoy is hardly the right word for such ecstasy, madame," he lyricized. "I must thank you, with all my heart."

She raised an elegant, narrow-fingered hand, the gesture almost regal. "*De rien,* monsieur."

"It was most kind of you to invite me. I shall never forget my first meal at Maison Edouard." He spoke in French, pleased by the easy fluency that was returning to him despite the years in America.

"It was the least I could do for my friends," she responded. "Jean and Gaby tell me you are seeking new avenues. They have explained something of your history, and ask me to advise you. I am, unfortunately, not a prophet."

"Of course not, madame."

"However, I do have one suggestion for you. Gaby tells me that you are fond of writing, and," she said, smiling, "you are evidently fortunate enough to have a refined palate."

Daniel laughed. "Food has become my life, Madame Edouard, and yes, I have a love of books and also of writing."

She paused slightly. "If food is your life, Monsieur Stone, then why not try to write about it?"

"For publication?" he asked, taken aback.

"Why not?"

"I'm not sure I have the talent."

"It is a suggestion, nothing more."

The art of gourmet writing, Madame Edouard explained, had been practiced in France since the eighteenth century, but there were not many writers nowadays who justified their existence. That, at least, was the opinion of the Toque Blanche, a group of about seventy Lyonnais chefs who met regularly to discuss their trade and art.

"My husband always wanted to have the time to teach others his skills," she went on, "and he also longed to write on the subject, but one cannot do everything." She shrugged. "I'm sure you realize, monsieur, that nothing truly worthwhile in life is acquired without hard work."

"But how to begin?"

She folded her hands neatly in her lap. "Perhaps you would like to write about what you have just enjoyed in our restaurant?"

"That would be a pleasure."

"*Voilà.*" She rose. "If you consider that your words express adequately what your senses have enjoyed, then I am sure we can meet again."

What Daniel experienced during the next few months was the closest thing to an expert education he was ever likely to acquire. Once he had presented her with his humble, but clearly expressed, critique of that first luncheon, Madame Edouard seemed to warm to him. She intended, she declared, to be his teacher. She was firmly convinced that no one whose whole working life had taken place outside France could even begin to comprehend what *grande cuisine* was about. The first step for Daniel, she decided, was to study within the walls of Maison Edouard.

"You will rise before six o'clock and accompany Louis Fernand, our *chef de cuisine,* to the markets in Lyon, and watch and listen while he orders our produce. By half past eight all the staff will have arrived in the restaurant, and you will be allowed to watch as Fernand instructs the *chefs de partie,* although I must warn you, Dan, that if you do not blend silently and perfectly into the background, Fernand may send your head to the *garde-manger!*"

Daniel looked anxious. "Surely I'll be able to help in some way."

"Heaven forbid! The kitchen here is like the headquarters of an army, and Louis Fernand is the most disciplined of men. But he is also kindhearted and quite prepared to teach you all he knows, on the single condition that under no circumstance will you touch one clove of garlic or even the cloth that will polish the Baccarat glasses." Madame Edouard chuckled. "Don't look so discouraged, Dan."

"It's only that I will find it very difficult to exist in a kitchen without working, madame."

"*Pouf!*" she said dismissively. "Believe me, my friend, once you have seen the *plongeurs* scrubbing the floors for the seventh time and have paid close attention to the *rotisseur*, the *poissonier*, and the *pâtissier* all through the morning, afternoon and evening—when you have leapt out of the way of the madly racing waiters, melted from the heat of the ovens and dodged the blows of our passionate *saucier* at the *commis-saucier*—I think you will begin to feel that you have indeed worked, or at least endured."

Daniel swallowed the obvious retort, that he had, in his time, acted out the roles of everyone from floor washer to *chef de cuisine.* "And when the restaurant is closed at night, madame," he said keenly, "I will sit in my bedroom at the pension and write detailed accounts of the day, *n'est-ce pas?*"

Jeannette Edouard nodded approvingly. *"Exactement."*

The learning of a new craft brought an extra dimension to Daniel's life, and he began to drive himself furiously. Once his strange apprenticeship at Maison Edouard was at an end, he kept on his rooms at the de Lucs' pension while he traveled, like a culinary pilgrim, from restaurant to *auberge* in the Lyon area, and then farther afield in Provence. After every meal he made careful notes in a journal, and each night he compiled meticulous reports on quality, service, atmosphere, scrupulousness, and price. And he read into the small hours as many of the great gourmet writers as he could, from Brillat-Savarin and Careme to Monselet and Curnonsky.

In the spring of 1955, he was able to repay some of the de Lucs' kindness by offering to run the pension for one month, so that they could take their first vacation in six years, and it was during that period, once the guests were all finally asleep and the house prepared for the new day, that he wrote his first articles.

He began to think of himself as Dan Stone, to assemble the parts that would make up his new identity. It was Daniel Silberstein, the refugee, who had been a magnet for disaster, and who had been abandoned in that hotel room on the Rue de Clichy in Paris. It was Dan Stone who sent his first article to *Paris-Match* and who received, by return, a check in payment together with a letter inviting him to submit further pieces for consideration. It was Dan Stone who scribbled late into the night, working harder on each successive item until he was sufficiently pleased with the results to press on with the next, and it was for Dan Stone's articles that a market quickly opened up, so that by the summer of 1956 he was writing specially commissioned pieces in English for *Punch* and *Vogue,* in French for *Paris-Match* and *France Dimanche,* and in German for the Swiss newspaper *Neue Zürcher Zeitung.*

Dan Stone was a rambler, a nomad without a permanent home. He lived either in hotels or with the de Lucs, traveling from place to place with one suitcase and a portable typewriter. He grew a beard, which he kept well trimmed, small, and neat; he bought new clothes, let his thick hair grow slightly longer, having it cut only when he was in Paris by the barber in the George V, and he watched his face mature and his manner become cosmopolitan as he shed the informality of New York life.

In December 1956, *Paris-Match* contracted him to write a series of critiques on Parisian nightspots. The evening before publication of the first edition, the magazine threw a party for Daniel and two other new contributors at a restaurant on the Avenue de l'Opéra. It was a Sunday, the restaurant was closed to the public, the food was less than excellent, and, apart from his editor, Félice Delmar, Daniel knew no one in the close-knit crowd. He felt lonely, and planned an early visit to Gaby and Jean in Lyon.

Leaving the party just after midnight, he heard a woman calling his name as he strolled in the direction of his hotel. He turned around.

"Well, thank heaven for small mercies!" she said in English with a strong American accent. "You've been in another world; I called your name five times before you stopped."

Daniel peered at her in the lamplight. "Do I know you?"

She was tall and reed thin, but tough-looking, with unruly red hair, and she wore low-heeled crocodile-skin shoes and a dark mink coat.

"Fanny Harper," she said, and gave him her hand. Her skin was cold, her grasp strong. "I was at the party, but there were too many people bending my ear for me to get a chance to meet you."

"Glad to know you," Daniel said politely. The north wind blew harshly, and she pulled her coat more tightly around her. "Which way are you heading?"

"I live on Avenue Kléber. Mind if we walk together?"

"Why not?" He felt the first drops of rain. "Or we could find a cab."

"I prefer walking." She began to stride purposefully beside him. Her voice was husky, almost abrasive.

"With that cold," Daniel said, "you shouldn't get wet."

"Okay." She stepped quickly off the curb and hailed a taxi.

"Actually," she said, once they were dry and inside the car, "I have no cold. I always sound like a lousy case of laryngitis; it comes from a lot of neighborhood bawling when I was a kid in Chicago."

"How long have you lived in Paris?"

"About five years, but only part of the time. I have places in Berlin and New York as well."

Daniel looked at her curiously. She was, he estimated, in her mid-forties, and though she was certainly not beautiful, she was handsome, with creamy, transparent skin and remarkable pointed ears. The diamond pear-shaped drops that fell from those ears were chunky and blue, and as his eyes flicked automatically to see what jewelry she wore on her fingers, he saw that her hands were strong and sinewy, her fingers square at the tips, like a workman's.

A police car stormed past, sirens screeching, and vanished in a rain cloud into the Champs-Elysées.

"I'll drop you at the Plaza Athénée first, and take the cab on to my place," she said.

"How do you know where I'm staying?" Daniel asked. "I told the driver Avenue Kléber."

She smiled. "I know a great deal about you."

He raised an eyebrow. "How's that?"

"Fanny Harper knows all, sees all," she said lightly. "Has Félice mentioned me to you?"

"No," he said.

The cab slid to a halt, and one of the doormen from the Plaza Athénée ran forward, umbrella unfurled.

"Would you lunch with me tomorrow, Mr. Stone?"

He took some notes from his wallet, but she shook her head. "This is my ride."

"Why do you want to lunch with me?"

"Because I have a business proposition to put to you. Are you free?"

The rain, unleashed by the wind, blew sideways into the cab, and Daniel got out hurriedly before she was soaked. "Where and when?"

"You like oysters?"

"Sure."

"Prunier. Twelve-thirty suit you?"

He nodded. The doorman banged the door, and Daniel walked into the light and the warmth.

He could not remember when he had enjoyed himself more. Fanny Harper was a brilliant lunch companion. They swallowed a dozen oysters each, drank Dom Pérignon, and Fanny spoke in light, amusing anecdotes, tickling his sense of humor and warming him gently with episodes of her career.

Daniel had not arrived at Prunier unarmed. He had telephoned Félice at ten that morning to ask about Fanny Harper. The answers had flowed easily; everyone, it seemed, knew about Fanny, but Félice Delmar, an avid gossipmonger, knew more than most. Fanny, she told Daniel, was a powerhouse; a dollar millionairess in America alone, and a lesbian. She'd lived in almost every country in Western Europe as well as in the States, and had amassed a considerable fortune, with bank accounts in so many cities that the IRS appointed one person for several days each spring to deal with her tax affairs.

"She's a PR genius, Dan, and a backer."

"Of what?"

"People and projects she believes in specially." Félice hesitated. "Or rather, *believed* in. Fanny is, I gather, in a self-imposed early retirement. She certainly doesn't have to raise a finger for the rest of her life." Her voice grew curious. "Has she contacted you, Dan?"

"In a manner of speaking."

"Then, *voilà*, you are made!"

"You said you had a proposition to put to me," Daniel said after the meal as they sipped cognac.

"Yes." Fanny sat back in her chair. "Dan, do you have the slightest idea where you're going? Do you have a strategy?"

"What do you mean?"

"Ye gods, you answer questions with more questions!" She fished for a cigarette in her purse and leaned forward, and Daniel lit it for her. "It's simple," she said. "I know your work, and I gather from my sources that potentially you may just be the most exciting gourmet writer since Prince Curnonsky, but buzzing around Europe like a blue-assed fly with no plan of campaign isn't going to get you where you ought to be."

Daniel smiled. "And where's that?"

"Where would you like to be?"

"I'm not sure."

"Darling, you must surely realize that magazine work is a dead end."

"It's keeping me quite occupied for the moment."

"But you're not a hack, you're a gourmet writer. Where does a gourmet writer's work belong?"

"Not in magazines?" Daniel fenced.

"In books, darling. Hard-cover books for the collectors, paperbacks for the rest. People who love good food frequently love books too—it's a proven fact."

Daniel stroked his small beard, which, together with his thick dark hair and the old scar beneath his eye, gave him a roguish, piratical appearance. "Why are you telling me this, Fanny? What's your interest?"

"Order more coffee and I'll tell you."

He signaled the waiter.

"In the first place," Fanny said, her brown eyes dancing and her wiry red curls gleaming, "I'm bored to death and I need amusing. In the second place, I've had half an eye on you for some time, and I've a sneaking hunch that you have it in you to become a considerable success." She smiled. "And in the third place, I think we might get along."

Daniel raised his glass. "I'll agree with the third."

"Don't be so irritatingly tentative, Dan! There's nothing duller than false modesty. You know quite well that you have talent, and you're bright enough to realize that you don't have the know-how or instinct to handle your career alone." She took a long, hard look at him. "What are you doing here anyway?"

"Writing for *Paris-Match,* you know that."

"I mean, what are you doing in Europe, living out of suitcases in hotels? There's a good measure of American in that fascinating accent. You've spent time there. Why did you come back?"

Daniel stiffened. "Reasons."

"None of my business, right?"

"Right." The waiter poured fresh coffee into clean cups, then melted away. Daniel relaxed again. "You still haven't explained your proposition."

Fanny stirred sugar into black coffee. "As I said before, Dan, I'm bored."

"So what does that make me, a hobby?"

She looked impatient. "Hobbies are for desperate housewives or retired senior citizens."

"I've heard that you're retired, if not exactly pensionable," he countered.

"From Félice Delmar?" Fanny smirked. "She's a fount of information, but not all of it meticulous." She sipped some coffee. "I think the French word *divertissements* has much more style than *hobbies,* don't you?"

Daniel chuckled. "And what exactly is the *divertissement* you have in mind that might involve me?"

"Okay, Dan." She flicked ash off her cigarette. "What is your opinion of restaurant guides today?"

He blinked, but answered steadily enough. "With the exception of Michelin, low."

"And the Michelin, of course, is in a position of unique power."

"Absolutely." He shifted in his chair. "Why?"

"I'll explain." Fanny stubbed out the cigarette. "Michelin is a highly competent and complex organization, Dan, as you probably know. They're impartial, conscientious, and accurate, and they'd be damned hard to beat as far as they go. Part of their strength lies in their compactness—the symbols were an ingenious idea, let's face it—but I believe there are wide-open spaces available for one more top-quality guide of a different character."

"There are others."

"You said yourself that your opinion of them is low, and in any case, what I have in mind is something rather special."

"In what way?" Daniel asked quietly.

Fanny's eyes were fixed on his face. "Your writing, Dan, has the qualities of richness and economy. It strikes me that you have sound judgment, good taste, and an ability to write mouth-watering prose." She paused, still watching him closely. "I've researched the market to within an inch of its life, and I've concluded that it would be entertaining and profitable to try to whip up a little competition with that old tire company and the others." She smiled. "Feel like helping me create a best seller?"

Daniel sat back, confused. "My God, Fanny, it's a hell of an idea."

"So what do you say?"

"I need—" He tried to gather his rapidly moving thoughts. "I need a little time to think about it."

"Good grief, man, did you think I wanted you to sign a contract here and now? Sure you have to think about it—do you imagine I'd do business with a fool?" She took out another cigarette and Daniel lit it mechanically. "Just try and dispense with that damned caution, or fear, or whatever it is that's wrong with you, and give me your gut reaction."

Daniel stared across at the extraordinary woman and abruptly remembered exactly how he'd felt years ago, sitting in his little Yorkville apartment, when he'd first had his idea for the catering business. The same sensations were beginning to flood through him now . . . it was like turning on a tap of hot, bubbling excitement. . . .

"Well?" Fanny prodded him more gently.

He stirred and sat up straighter. His eyes gleamed and his mouth was set firm. "I have just one thing to say, Fanny." He picked up his glass of cognac, and the amber liquid tilted and glowed.

"You've made up your mind," she said softly.

Daniel smiled into her eyes.

"Yes."

25

Daniel lifted the book out of the white tissue wrapping paper and felt its weight in his hands. It was a special edition, ordered as a gift for him by Fanny, hand-bound in beige calf printed with gold lettering on the front cover and down the spine.

Slowly he raised the volume to his face and inhaled the unique, leathery aroma, and then, with an unfamiliar prickle of excitement, he opened it, turned the first blank page, and stared at the title.

THE STONE GOURMET GUIDE
TO PARIS

Was it true, after all, what they said about books and immortality? For this moment, at least, he believed them. And if so, then it was Dan Stone who was immortalized, edging Daniel Silberstein still farther back into the dark recesses of his memory. He wondered, fleetingly, how his parents would have felt about that.

"Dan?" Fanny's voice nudged him gently.

He blinked and looked at her.

"Well?"

"I don't know what to say, Fanny." He shook his head. "It's better than perfect, so I'm stumped for words."

She looked over his shoulder. "The frontispiece works well, don't you think?"

"You know it does." He smiled proudly, a new father surveying his infant. "I still can't believe you got him to do this, Fanny."

The frontispiece was a reprint of an illustration painted especially for the book by Salvador Dali as a personal favor to Fanny. It was, fundamentally, a still life: a rosy lobster, a succulent slice of rare chateaubriand, an onion so meticulous its scent flew off the paper, and two glasses, one misty with chilled white wine, the other aglow with red. The only Daliesque aberration was that these delicacies were pictured inside a human stomach, a grotesque fancy but, under the master's hands, astonishingly charming and appetizing. The original work, lavishly signed, hung in the kitchen of Fanny's Paris apartment.

The first *Stone Gourmet Guide,* little more than an expansion of Daniel's *Paris-Match* articles, thanks to Fanny's prepublication exposure was already creating a stir at the foot of the nonfiction bestseller list. Stone's style, the critics said, was refreshing; he wrote informally, addressing his readers briskly, wittily, and truthfully. In less than two hundred clearly arranged pages, Daniel had plucked from obscurity a number of excellent but unknown restaurants, some of them little more than brasseries situated off the beaten track, and had shaken the reputations of three notable and pretentious establishments. Laurent-Fournay, the publishers, were delighted, and Fanny knew her hunch was going to be vindicated.

Daniel and Fanny made a formidable team. They complemented each other and Daniel, increasingly in his element, recognized his great fortune in having been sought out by her. All he was expected to contribute to the new partnership of Harper and Stone, now officially launched, were his taste buds and his penmanship—Fanny took care of everything else.

Fanny's private life was apparently as well ordered as her business activities. When in Paris, she shared the apartment on Avenue Kléber with Céline du Pont, the wife of a wealthy misogynist banker, from whose house Céline escaped whenever possible. When in New York, she lived in a Murray Hill town house with Robin Fielding, a brilliant rising young film editor. When in Berlin, Fanny slept alone, in her permanent suite at the Kempinski. Céline and Robin were aware of each other; it was a tribute to Fanny's honesty and tact that neither objected.

Daniel felt surprisingly close to her. It was a source of amusement to them both that their frequent outings aroused gossip, and he found it both novel and pleasant to enjoy a warm relationship with a woman without sexual pressure. His own libido had only narrowly survived the Rosa Bernardi episode, and for months after his flight from New York he had avoided sex altogether; even once he was over the worst, he had found himself guilty of "fucking gently" and inadvertently wrecking numerous promising relationships.

After one such disaster he had decided to take Fanny into his confidence. She had listened carefully to the tale of Rosa's death and sympathetically to his account of his ensuing escape to Europe, but his description of his greatly altered sex life had produced a different reaction.

"Oh, Dan! My poor baby!" She had looked at his startled face and burst into gales of laughter. "What do you want to do? Get an ECG reading for every woman before you get her in the sack? It was a tragic, million-to-one accident!" She stopped suddenly. "So, your real name is Daniel Silberstein?"

"It was."

She grinned. "That's one good thing to come out of the mess, anyway. 'Dan Stone' will certainly be easier to fit on a jacket cover!"

The second book was to be a vacation guide, designed to lead first-time vacationers gently by the hand through the capitals and nooks and crannies of Europe, acquainting them with excellence, charm, and value. For several months at the end of 1958 and the first half of 1959, Daniel traveled through France and Italy, some of Spain, all of Luxembourg, and a little of Belgium, and, avoiding Germany, came finally to rest in Switzerland. He was exhausted by food and travel, suddenly unhappy with the lack of permanence in his life, and, in this small, exquisite country he had last seen in 1946, disquietingly haunted by the past.

At the beginning of September, Fanny arrived from Berlin and joined him in Vitznau, a picturesque village fifteen minutes from Lucerne, at the Park Hotel.

She came across him late one afternoon, sitting on the thick white carpet of his suite, an unopened magazine beside him, staring into space.

"What's up, Dan?" She kicked off her high-heeled shoes, hitched up her skirt, and sat beside him on the floor.

"Nothing."

"Don't try and fox me, Dan Stone!" She fixed him with a stare. "You look shitty."

"Thanks."

"So? What's your problem?"

Daniel scratched the dark stubble on his cheek. He hadn't trimmed his beard for a couple of days, and there were shadows under his eyes. "I saw a photograph of someone I once knew, and it took me back, that's all."

"In the magazine?" Fanny picked it up.

"The cover."

A strikingly beautiful young couple laughed at Fanny from the glossy cover of the automobile magazine. They were standing outside the front entrance of the Palace Hotel in St. Moritz, arms linked. She recognized the man right away.

"You knew Alessandro, the driver?" she asked. "Or his wife?"

"The driver." Daniel's eyes were hazy with memory. "He saved my life."

Fanny's eyes widened. "When? What happened?"

He smiled vaguely. "He was only nine years old at the time, and actually he didn't quite save my life, but he gave me a chance to live it when no one else would have."

"Same difference." Fanny looked back at the photograph. "Handsome son of a bitch, isn't he?" She waited a moment, but Daniel said nothing. "You *are* going to tell me about it, aren't you? I get little snatches of Daniel Silberstein every now and again, but it's like pulling teeth."

"I'm sorry."

"Sorry my ass!" she declared, exasperated. "You can't just sit there on the floor and tell me that one of the most charismatic drivers on the racing circuit today was your own personal savior when he was nine years old, and then clam up!"

Daniel smiled again. "Okay." He felt the tug of the past—of Daniel, of the Nazis, and of Andreas, the boy—reaching out for him with long, cold fingers, wrapping him in confusion and fear. "I try not to remember things most of the time, Fanny. It's long ago, and it's full of ghosts."

"Alessandro's not a ghost, he's very much alive!" She paused. "Maybe you'd feel better if you let some of it out for a change."

"Maybe I would," Daniel said softly.

Afterward, Fanny said in genuine surprise, "Why have you never been in touch with him? He'd be thrilled to know how you made out."

Daniel shrugged. "I thought about it, but it didn't seem right."

"Why not? You owe him that, surely?"

"Yes, I owe him," Daniel agreed almost angrily. "Maybe I owe him not to embarrass him."

"How the hell could that embarrass anyone?"

Daniel laughed harshly. "Fanny, Alessandro was a kid when all that happened, a child without politics or prejudices. But I remember his mother, and you know as well as I do that a lot of kids grow up just like their parents."

"It seems to me that he took after his father, the Italian." Fanny sat forward. "I think you're afraid of embarrassing yourself, not him. You're still thinking of yourself as a half-starved refugee, when you're actually a highly successful individual. Your self-image is all wrong, Dan."

He got to his feet and sat down again on the white linen-covered settee. "He probably doesn't even remember."

"No one forgets something like that, it's too exciting." She, too, stood up, groaning at her stiffening joints. "Look at this man," she commanded, thrusting the magazine at him. "An ego the size of the Empire State Building, and you think he'll have forgotten an act of heroism, particularly when it involved his precious driving!"

Daniel looked again at the cover. Two strangers, clearly enchanted with each other, belonging together. He shook his head. "It doesn't matter, Fanny. It's too late. He's married now—"

"What does that have to do with anything? I'm suggesting a reunion, not an affair!"

He took no notice. "He's married, he's famous, and he must have a thousand friends. He doesn't need me to materialize out of the blue." He stood again, took her hand, and planted an affectionate kiss on her forehead. "Forget it, Fanny. It really isn't that important."

She tossed her head impatiently.

"Please."

"I think you're wrong. It is important."

"I don't agree."

Her eyes narrowed. "You've been in a filthy frame of mind since I got here, long before you saw that magazine. Are you going to tell me why?"

He shrugged. "I don't know."

"I do. I see what you feel, Dan Stone. You have so much, you think, yet you lack more, and it spoils what you *do* have; isn't that right? It's blunting the edges of your pleasure."

Daniel looked admiringly at her. "That's exactly how I feel, Fanny. How is it you can see through me?"

"Friendship."

"But I don't think it's right. I should be feeling great, surely."

"It's fatigue, Dan, that's all. You've been living out of suitcases for too long, and it's wrong for you. You need a home; you're not a gypsy."

He sighed. "That's true, but I don't know where I'd want to live."

Again her eyes raked him perceptively. "And we both know why that is, though you won't admit it. It's because you wish you could live in New York again, and you kid yourself that you can't."

"*Kid* myself?" Daniel turned away, vexed. "You don't know

what you're saying, Fanny. You have no idea what I'd be dealing with if I went back."

"You'd be dealing with your fear, Dan," she said more gently, "and I guess you're not ready to handle that yet." She laid a hand on his arm. "Just as you're not ready to go down the road to Küssnacht to check out the driver's old home."

"You just don't understand," he said through gritted teeth. "That was no garden party." He shook her off and went out onto the balcony. He stared out over the vast lake, so hazy it was impossible to tell where sky or land ended and water began. "I was a kid, there was no place to hide—I was running for my life, and I was hungry and scared enough to shit in my pants a thousand times over." He turned back to face her, tears in his eyes. "There are places I'd like to see again, and people. I would love to have gone back to Vevey—I was happy there. But Michel's gone, and if that bitch, his niece, was anywhere around, I'm not sure how I'd react."

They fell silent for a few minutes. Fanny stepped out onto the balcony and stood beside him.

"Do you trust me, Dan?"

"Of course."

"I mean, do you trust me to do what's right for you?"

He smiled wryly. "Within reason. Why?"

She lifted a hand, silencing him. "Just leave things to me."

"If it's anything to do with Alessandro—"

"Shame on you," she said. "I thought you said you trusted me."

He winced. "I'm sorry. I didn't mean—"

"It's all right, I'm not offended." She swept suddenly back into the room. "Where's my purse? Dammit, Stone, you hide everything!" She found it, slipped her feet back into her shoes and grew two inches. "Right, Dan, I'm leaving," she called. "I won't be back for a few days."

He came inside. "Where are you going?"

"Away." She opened the door. "Try enjoying yourself for a change, Dan—climb a mountain, find yourself a nice Swiss *Fräulein*, go skiing—"

"It's summer."

"So go swimming."

"Fanny, will you tell me where you're going—"

The door closed.

26

"So? Do you like it?"

Daniel and Fanny stood in the narrow, pale cream entrance hall of a tiny three-story house in Montpelier Walk, London SW7.

Daniel's eyes passed over the carved umbrella stand, up at the exquisite pure white cornices, and through the dainty archway that led into the drawing room. He closed his eyes and breathed in. "It smells wonderful."

Fanny pursed her lips. "That's me."

"No." He continued to sniff the air. "No food. Not a whiff."

Fanny took his arm. "The only food in this house is in the ice-box, and you don't ever have to look at it unless you choose to. There are more than enough restaurants and cafés in the area, and there's Elsie, the maid, who's prepared to come in anytime you like in the mornings to give you breakfast."

"I don't want to even think about food."

"You will soon enough." She tucked her arm more firmly through his. "Come see the drawing room." She led him into a room of surprising size, painted the same soft creamy color as the hall, with charming chintz drapes at the windows and a three-piece suite to match. The only other items of furniture in the room were an antique mahogany writing desk, topped with a Georgian silver ink-stand, a matching, beautifully carved sideboard with glass doors, and a pair of formal, straight-backed chairs on either side of the fireplace.

"Genuine Adam, so I'm assured. And most of the figurines in the sideboard are Dresden and old Meissen—oh, yes, and the sideboard itself and the desk are Sheraton."

"I hope it's all well insured."

Fanny laughed. "I think a third of the rent must be going to the insurers. Look at the paintings—Stubbs, every one in this room. Not my taste, or yours, I think, Dan, but not something you could complain about in London."

Daniel picked up a bronze poker and ran a finger down it. "I guess no one's ever lit a fire in here, it's all too clean."

"That's Elsie. She's 'done' for the tenants of this house for about fifteen years, I gather. She considers herself its guardian and custodian."

"Sounds formidable."

"Not at all; a dear Cockney charmer," Fanny reassured him. "And she's going to take one look at that tired, sexy face, and decide you need looking after."

"I hope not," Daniel said in alarm. "I've come here to be alone."

"If you choose," she answered noncommittally. "But Elsie claims to know all about 'young gentlemen' wanting their privacy, so you should have no problems with her."

Daniel turned with a rush of energy and strode over the oatmeal Wilton carpet toward a closed door. "Let's see the rest."

There were few surprises, but the library was a gem, a room only twelve feet square, squeezed in between the master bedroom and guest bathroom up on the second floor. But it was loaded with reading for most tastes, from children's adventure thrillers, science fiction, and horror, to a set of leather-bound *Encyclopedia Britannica*, another of *Americana*, and a whole shelf of political biographies.

"And not a single cookery book," Fanny said triumphantly. "I had them removed and boxed in the attic, though I left a couple in the kitchen, one of them an original Mrs. Beeton I thought you might like. That's yours to keep, incidentally," she added. "I bought it in Harrods, which is less than five minutes away in Brompton Road; you *will* want to go there, Dan, however reclusive you feel today."

Fanny saw to it that Daniel was acquainted with Elsie, stocked with sufficient logs to keep a fire crackling in the hearth for at least three months, and equipped with enough liquor, street maps, and club memberships to keep contentment in easy reach and boredom at arm's length. Then she flew to Paris to see Céline, and to reassure Laurent-Fournay that work on the guide would begin as soon as Daniel had rested.

She returned to London on Christmas Eve, to a city aglow with illuminations and bonhomie. The narrow cobbled streets behind Knightsbridge, and Montpelier Walk, in particular, were as peaceful as ever, and with Elsie's help, Daniel had turned the house into an enticingly welcoming sanctuary, scented with balsam wood and alight with stacks of candles in every room.

"Joyeux Noël, darling," Fanny said, husky with sentiment, after

they had embraced in front of the blazing fire. "I've missed you, you obstinate man."

"Not as much as I've missed you," Daniel replied, a lump in his throat, only realizing at that moment how lonely he'd been without her. "I'm glad you made it."

Fanny threw her suede gloves onto the sofa and slipped out of her brand-new sable coat.

"That's very fetching." Daniel smiled. "A little gift to yourself?"

She shook her head, and her red curls glinted in the firelight. "From Céline. She has to spend the holidays with her husband, poor baby. She sends her warm wishes, by the way, and commands you to look after me for a few days."

"When do you go back?" He tried to mask his disappointment.

"Not for weeks—but I've sworn to Robin that I'll be in New York for New Year's Eve. For the last three years we've hired a limo with a bar and fur rugs, and we've been driven around Central Park, ending up in Times Square to drink champagne at midnight. It's a heavenly custom—the two of us, snug and safely locked in the limo with all those insane, happy people shoulder to shoulder outside."

"Sounds like fun. It seems I'm lucky to have you at all."

Fanny looked at him askance. "You don't have to stay shut in your cloister, you know, Dan. You could always come with me. It's a great season in New York, you must remember."

There was a short, awkward silence, which Daniel filled by picking up her coat and gloves. "I'll put these in the closet, and if you want a rest before dinner, now would be the time." He smiled. "Elsie was sorry to miss you. She was here till six o'clock, but I sent her home to her family."

"I gather you've overcome your dislike of food."

"With Elsie's help. Her 'good plain cooking' drove me back into the kitchen, and I've even ventured into a few of the restaurants you recommended. By the way," he said as an afterthought, "Elsie insists we leave the clearing-up for her to do in the morning."

"Oh, surely not! We can't let her work on Christmas Day—she'll want to go to church."

"Elsie is not religious. She was most firm about that when I asked; said she never goes all year, and she wouldn't be such a hypocrite as to start on Christmas morning."

Fanny grinned. "You and she certainly seem to have hit it off."

"Couldn't have got by without her. You were right, as always."

He threw a fresh log on the fire. "Just as you were about this place. It was what I needed, having a home for a while."

"Don't you need it anymore?"

"A while longer would be good."

"Have you managed to get any work done?"

"A little," he answered lightly. "Not as much as I'd hoped, but it's a start."

After dinner they sat in candlelight over the remains of the wine, casting shadows on the wall.

"You haven't lost your touch, Dan."

He traced the outline of his glass with a fingertip. "It's good to share it with you."

Fanny gave him a long, penetrating look. Then abruptly she rose. "Wait here."

She slipped out of the dining room and Daniel heard her on the staircase, moving quickly up one flight, stirring briefly on the floor above, then returning to his level.

"Voilà." She sat again at the table, cheeks a little flushed, and pushed a small, gift-wrapped packet toward him.

"What's this?"

"An offering."

His eyes lit up. "Now I really know it's Christmas!" Eagerly he ripped away the paper, found a little box and opened it. Inside, on a bed of cotton wool, lay a solid gold key, the end still uncut.

He looked at Fanny curiously. "What's it for?"

She opened her mouth to answer, then stopped. "Finish your wine."

"What's the key for, Fanny? Don't go mysterious on me—you wouldn't have given it to me if you hadn't expected me to ask."

Fanny sat back in her chair. "Dan," she said softly, "how long has it been since you left New York?"

He paused. "Five years last September," he answered steadily.

"And you would like to go back, but you still feel it's too risky. Right?"

He sighed. "Fanny, darling, it's Christmas Eve, and I really don't want to have this discussion again."

"You wanted to know what the key was for, didn't you?"

He nodded, silent.

"It's for the front door of the offices that Harper and Stone would open on Madison Avenue, if you would allow it to happen."

His eyes widened. "You haven't rented space, Fanny?"

"No, of course I haven't," she said to calm him. "How could I, without your agreement? That's why the key isn't cut." She paused. "But it is what I'd like to see happen, and it's what I think would be right for you."

"Maybe so. But it's not a practical possibility."

"Why not, Dan?" she said more sharply. "It's madness, sheer madness for you to be anxious about Joe Bernardi. Five years dampen anyone's rage, even a Sicilian's. You've changed your name, you're older, and I'm sure you look different—I've seen changes in your appearance even since *we* met—and you said yourself you hardly ever saw the man face-to-face."

"I dealt with his staff regularly. They might know me again."

"Employees leave. I'm your friend as well as your partner, Dan, and I know that you and Manhattan are meant for each other."

"You've never seen me in Manhattan."

"Don't be pedantic. The proof is in your history and in the way you tell it."

Daniel picked up the golden key, felt its weight in his palm, struggled against half-buried temptations. He remembered the city, its towers and turrets hazy in the polluted sky, recalled the feeling of being Daniel, new citizen of the United States of America, striding across the town on strong, infallible legs; he thought about the Hudson River, and about Leon and Sarah and Roly . . .

"Dan?"

Biting his lips, he put the key back on the cotton wool and closed the box. "Do something for me, Fanny."

"Anything." Her face was alight with warmth.

"Stop this. Let it go for now."

"For now?"

He nodded. "It's Christmas. There's a brand-new decade just around the corner."

"All the more reasons for making decisions."

"I'm happy here, Fanny."

"You're not happy, Dan. You're not actively sad, but you're far from happy." She sighed. "Keep the key, Dan. When and if you're ready, let me know. I won't mention it again. I just hope you change your mind before it's too late."

"You make me sound like an old man."

Fanny smiled. "You have great potential, Dan, but you'll never realize it in Europe. You were born on this continent, yes, and you may always be drawn back from time to time, but America is where you'll achieve your major goals."

Daniel laughed thinly. "You overestimate me, Fanny. Why

should I need more than this? What's so bad about the success we've had so far?"

Angrily she pushed back her chair and stood up. "Why do you need to be dragged through life by the roots of your hair?" She paced back and forth over the parquet floor. "You have courage, Dan, but you've always needed other people to haul you to your feet! The boys who got you out of the camp—Alessandro, who seems to have stopped you giving up once you were out—your friend Michel, who got you to the States in the first place—and now me, to shove you back there again!"

Daniel flushed, stung by truth. "I thought you'd finished on that subject."

"I have." She marched to the door and yanked it open. "I won't mention it again, Dan. I'll just leave you to stew in your safe little pressure cooker until the lid finally blows off and the fact penetrates your thick skull that all the juices that go to make up Dan Stone, or Daniel Silberstein, or whoever you really are, have evaporated with you in the pan!"

"Fanny!" He jumped up. "Fanny, don't go."

She shook her head. "I'm going to bed. I don't think this conversation has any farther to run."

He threw up his hands helplessly. "You may be right, Fanny. About everything. Just try to understand that for the first time in a long while I feel a little security, and I don't want to let that go."

"I understand, Dan. I really do understand more than you think." She smiled sadly. "But you're wrong to believe you're any safer, any more secure, here than anywhere else. Our troubles, our mistakes, follow us, track us down wherever we are."

It was another three months before the impact of Fanny's words struck home.

He'd begun writing again, more successfully, after Christmas, and well enough to satisfy Laurent-Fournay, but Daniel still realized that the words and mood of his writing lacked sparkle. Still, with the rented house in Montpelier Walk a cocoon around him, he convinced himself that London was the place for him to be.

Until, one morning in the first week of April, he saw Natalie Bresson.

He was strolling comfortably in Old Bond Street, early for a luncheon appointment at the Westbury Hotel. The weather was pleasant for early April, mild and dry, and he was glancing idly at an ivory chess set in one of Asprey's tall windows when a taxi rattled to a halt behind him. He glanced over his shoulder and saw Natalie step out onto the curb. She paid the driver, turned, and looked straight at Daniel.

His immediate impression was of tense, crystalline beauty, exactly the kind of loveliness one might have expected Natalie to develop. Fifteen years had added elegance to the feline prettiness that had briefly tempted him from boyhood; she wore a black cloche hat with a gray ostrich feather, a black chalk-striped cashmere suit, gray silk stockings, and black patent shoes. Her face was still pert, the features still sharp and neat, but the brown eyes were now more vixen than doe.

The taxi drew away, but Natalie remained less than four feet away, motionless. For a brief moment she seemed not quite able to place him. Then, in the space of a few seconds, darkness gathered savagely in her eyes, like storm clouds blown suddenly together by hurricane winds. She stared right into his face, and her thin red lips drew back from her perfect, tiny white teeth in a snarl.

Daniel felt lashed by the power of her hatred. Involuntarily he stepped back, as if anticipating a violent slap. He thought she would spit in his face, gather saliva in her mouth and spew it at him as she had done all those years ago—but instead, with devastating reversal, she smiled. Not at him, but to herself.

She stepped forward, eyes still clamped on his. The Asprey doorman opened the double door for her; she swept past him, and was gone.

For a few moments Daniel remained rooted to the spot. He felt nauseated, shaken to the core. And then suddenly a need came over him to escape the narrow, claustrophobic street, and, moving one foot before the other, mechanically, he made his way toward Piccadilly, lunch appointment forgotten—everything forgotten—in his need to get away from Natalie.

At the corner of Albemarle Street he hailed an empty taxi and directed the driver to take him back to Montpelier Walk. He sat still, confused and unaccountably disturbed. Such hatred, such loathing! After so many years.

The driver's voice jolted him. They were outside the small white house. He paid, overtipped, and unlocked the front door, relieved beyond measure to find himself inside the cool, narrow hall.

Quickly he poured himself a large shot of whiskey and sat down on the chintz-covered sofa. He took a sip of his drink and felt himself relax.

"That woman," he said aloud, "could sour honey."

The sound of his own voice in the quiet of the drawing room brought back reality. Daniel checked his watch, called the Westbury Hotel, and made his excuses for his nonappearance.

The greatest shock, he decided, after a second whiskey, was his own reaction. He realized now that as he and Natalie had faced each other across the sidewalk, the words of Michel Bresson's warning letter had come back to him again. He had known in those brief seconds, without a shadow of doubt, that Michel had been right about her; that Natalie had cold-bloodedly set about her own uncle's ruin, and that Natalie was still dangerous.

"Ridiculous," he said. To fear her now was foolishness. Fifteen years ago he had been Daniel Silberstein, an illegal immigrant and a scared boy; today he was Dan Stone, a successful writer with the strength of money, friends, and a legal status. His eyes hardened and his mouth quirked. Let Natalie try to make trouble for him if she could find him—he would see that she was punished for what she had done to Michel!

Fanny's words to him at Christmas flashed through his mind. "You're wrong to believe you're any safer here than anywhere else," she had told him. "Our troubles, our mistakes, follow us, track us down wherever we are."

Daniel wandered around the room, looking at the paintings and porcelain. Valuable, all of it, beautiful, some of it, but none of it his. He poured a third drink and took it upstairs to the library, his favorite room.

He took down one of his best-loved books, the leather-bound thesaurus of quotations, and sat down. He took a sip of the whiskey, felt wariness take a swift and decisive back-flip, and turned to the category marked *Timidity*.

He who is afraid of every nettle should not piss in the grass, he read, and smiled.

What is more mortifying than to feel that you have missed the plum for want of courage to shake the tree?

He reached for the white telephone on the small desk in the middle of the room. For a moment he paused, checking over the number in his mind. Then he dialed Fanny's apartment in Berlin.

It rang three times before he heard the familiar hoarse voice.

"Fanny," he said, and felt the first pangs of joy welling up in his throat, "I've been thinking about New York."

27

"Why must you be so obstinate about this?"

"Why must *you?*"

"Because it matters! Because being with you—together with you—in the same place as you matters more than anything else in the world! Isn't that enough reason?"

"No, Ali, not anymore."

Andreas slapped his hands on the marble mantelpiece and leaned his weight against the great stone fireplace that was the main attraction of the Veneto Suite in Milan's Grand Hotel Medici. Stylistically, the fireplace was an architectural aberration, standing stoic as a slice of Yorkshire amid soaring, delicately flowered walls and ornately carved cornices. But the sheer daring of the designers, who had blown tradition to the wind and mixed some of the best aspects of as many as five different decorative styles, had for more than thirty years drawn the wealthy and fastidious from all over Western Europe and the Americas.

Alexandra fought to keep her rising temper down. Her nerves were frayed after nearly two hours discussing the same subject—the only subject she knew of that could bring the consistent gladness of their marriage to a grinding halt.

"Andreas, darling, we've been through this a thousand times. If we had a baby now, I'd be at home in New York, not here with you."

Andreas gripped the mantelpiece tightly. "Nurses," he said through gritted teeth. "One can hire nurses. We could *all* be here. A real family."

"That isn't right and you know it," she flared at him. "It wouldn't be fair to drag a small baby back and forth across the Atlantic and all over Europe. A child needs a routine—"

"And we need a child!"

Andreas strode out of the salon and snatched up his jacket from the hall chair.

"Where are you going?" Alexandra followed him, her silk robe crackling against her legs.

"To Monza."

"But it's too early—I'm not ready." She stared at her husband, nonplussed by his bitterness. They often argued over babies, but never during the buildup to a race.

"You can come on later," he said sullenly.

"Andreas—"

He jerked his chin and challenged her. "Yes?"

She came close, tentatively touched his cheek with her fingers. It felt rough, stubbled; he hadn't shaved yet.

"It's early," she said again, softly. "You don't have to go yet. We could—"

"What?" He jerked away from her. "Go to bed? Make wild oh-so-spontaneous love? Just you, me, and your diaphragm!" He sat heavily down on the antique chair and covered his eyes with one hand.

Alexandra felt completely at a loss. Despair from her controlled, hard-to-read husband was something alien to her.

His hand dropped down by his side and he stared up at her. His eyes were brilliant black. "Ali?" His voice was low.

She stayed where she was. Later—much later—she would remember this moment, recall that she had stood apart from him. "Yes?"

He stood up. "Perhaps you should stay here today, Ali, and do some thinking. About us."

He turned and opened the door to the corridor. Then abruptly he swung round and kissed her quickly on the mouth. The last thing Alexandra saw before the door banged shut behind him was how pale his skin seemed under its top layer of sunburn, and how haunted his expression.

For a while she stood in the small hall, waiting, hoping he might change his mind and come back, but knowing that would be out of character for him; at times, Andreas could be as stubborn as a whole pack of mules.

She turned her head slightly and was confronted by her reflection in the mirror. Her face, too, was unhappy, the corners of her mouth tight, her eyes gray and anxious, verging on tears.

"This is craziness," she said out loud.

The decision came to her with such clarity and conviction that she wondered why she had taken so long to come round to it. What had made her so obdurate, so rigid?

She flew to the front door of the suite and flung it open. A young room waiter, passing, looked up and then politely averted his gaze. She ignored him, her eyes raking the long corridor toward the elevators, but there was no sign of Andreas.

She closed the door. Act now and tell him later. She leaned against the wall, her heart pounding, a new smile on her lips. Tonight, she'd tell him tonight. . . . They'd have dinner in the room first; she'd order his favorites, nothing too heavy because of the race tomorrow, and no wine . . . but they wouldn't need wine because they'd be so happy . . .

Tightening the belt of her robe, she ran through the bedroom into the bathroom.

The mirrored cabinet swung open at her touch. The little plastic case was there on the shelf. She took it down and stared at it with distaste. Such madness, such folly to let this destroy their marriage! What had happened to compromise?

With a clear, sure movement she lifted the offending diaphragm high into the air and let it drop into the toilet bowl.

"I never liked you anyway," she said, and flushed it into oblivion.

The telephone call came three minutes after she saw it on the black-and-white television set in the salon of their suite.

She was lying on her side, fully naked, on the carpet, exercising as she did most days. Her right leg, supporting her, was straight, while her left leg knifed up and down through the air, toes pointed, muscles stretched. The local station was playing *The Untouchables,* Robert Stack's voice badly dubbed in Italian, but she stayed with it because she found that her own limited knowledge of the language benefited from television, and she enjoyed surprising Andreas with new phrases now and again.

She didn't notice that the commercial break had switched to a news flash until she saw the photograph.

It was the shot that hung, framed, in a place of honor in their Manhattan home—Andreas, victorious at Montreal in June—silvery hair wet with sweat, champion's cup in right hand, the left raised high in a clenched fist of triumph.

Alexandra froze, her ears tuned in frustrated agony to the jumbled, rapid voice of the newsreader.

Nothing! She understood *nothing*—just "Monza . . . von Trips e Ginther . . . And then: *"Alessandro—"* Just names! And then they were back to *The Untouchables,* and Alexandra was on her feet, naked in the middle of the room, turning knobs on the television set, frantically switching channels, eyes dry and burning, getting nowhere . . .

Until the telephone rang.

The nurse was middle-aged, with prematurely withered skin and a gentle expression. Tactfully she stood away from the bed while Alexandra stood helpless, staring down at the stricken body of her husband.

"When will they operate?" She felt the pulses beating thick and strong in her temples, striving to keep time with the erratic high-pitched sound of the machine beside Andreas's bed, marking his heartbeats.

"It's not certain yet. He must take more blood first to be strong."

He lay unconscious beneath a single white sheet supported by a frame to prevent it from touching any part of his body. Aside from a long scratch on his forehead, stained purple-red with antiseptic, and the ugly tube coming from his mouth and taped to his cheek, there was no evidence of injury—he might have been asleep.

"Where is the doctor?"

The nurse stepped forward and touched her gently on the arm. "The *dottore* is awaiting you, signora. In the office."

Andreas had misjudged a curve during a practice run and had somersaulted off the high bank just before the long home straight. Miraculously there had been no fire, and so they had been able to cut him with slow tenderness from the wreckage of the scarlet Maserati; but both legs and his pelvis were badly fractured, and the extent of his internal injuries was not yet known.

After the transfusions, the operations began.

The corridors in the hospital were endless and all exactly alike: disinfected linoleum floors, gleaming white walls and ceilings, with crucifixes at almost every turning. People passed Alexandra by as she glided on her interminable, aimless route around and around the seventh floor, oblivious of the hours ticking by on the clocks at the nurses' stations, careless of the fact that her feet throbbed, that neither food nor drink had passed her lips since breakfast the previous day.

She had telephoned Roberto earlier, and was comforted to know that he would soon be with her. She felt like a ghost, a wraith afloat on a sea of sickness and pain and suffering. From time to time, a woman in flowing white nurse's headdress would come

and pat her kindly on the shoulder and offer her a place to rest—
she need not fear that they would not call her if there was news—
but she refused. She had the sensation that if she stopped walking,
ended her vigil even for a few minutes, Andreas would surrender,
would disappear from her life forever, as if he had never existed,
and there would be nothing left of him except the photographs of
victorious Montreal on their wall in New York. Nothing. No part
of him. No child.

"Will he live?"

She stood before the surgeon who sat, exhausted, on the hard
visitors' bench, his hands, exquisite, long-fingered, brilliant hands,
limp on his knees. Alexandra still refused to sit. It was twenty-
three hours since she had arrived in the hospital.

The surgeon looked up, and she thought his red-rimmed, weary
eyes the most beautiful she had ever seen.

"Yes, Signora Alessandro, he will live."

Alexandra sat.

Andreas had experienced comparatively little suffering in his life
until the accident. Physical and mental pain come in variable packages, from the paltry and easily forgotten to the outsize and irre-
trievable lacerations. If torment could be better organized,
stepped up by gentle degrees, perhaps some people might know
what to anticipate and be better able to bear it. But it seemed to
Andreas that what he endured during the months that followed
the Monza crash was so intense that the very strain of opening his
eyes and finding himself still alive was intolerable—so after a time,
in spite of the efforts of his wife and father, he simply gave up
fighting and lay, for hours on end, in a state of self-imposed tor-
por.

"Try to think of this as his personal form of analgesia, Ali," Theodor Salko, the orthopedic surgeon who had assumed care of Andreas after his return to Manhattan, reassured Alexandra one afternoon in early December after a cry for help had summoned him to
the Alessandro apartment.

She accepted his outstretched hand and allowed herself to be
led from the darkened room that had once been their bedroom
but was now exclusively Andreas's sickroom.

"I try," she said outside in the hallway. "I really do." Her lower
lip quivered with the effort of not weeping. "But sometimes it's
just too much."

They walked down the narrow spiral staircase that split the two levels of the duplex, and went into the small den where Alexandra spent most of her time nowadays. The other rooms in the apartment were bright, big, and unbearably desolate without Andreas, and this tiny sanctuary, clad in gentle fall colors, brought her a degree of peace.

"A drink, Theo?"

Salko loosened his tie and removed his jacket. "I'd slay a battalion for a cup of coffee, Ali."

She smiled weakly. "You don't have to go that far. Just join me in the kitchen while I switch on the percolator."

The kitchen was the only room in the Alessandro home in which Andreas had taken a personal hand. Up until the crash, whenever they were in New York he had continued to play the role of chef within their marriage, and the layout of the units and appliances reflected his matter-of-fact attitude to cooking: square, cool, and workmanlike, with long, scrubbable surfaces and plenty of stainless steel.

Alexandra filled the pot with cold water, spooned ground coffee into the container, and flicked the switch. Salko sat at the breakfast counter and patted the stool beside him.

"Take the weight off those lovely feet."

She sat next to him. Salko's well-shod toes dangled six inches from the floor, while her own sandals brushed the tiles easily.

"I hear what you tell me about Andreas," she said quietly. "I hear you say that he's getting better. I know that the physiotherapist thinks he should really be back on his feet before long."

Salko nodded. "That's right."

"But I also hear him report that Andreas has no willpower . . ." Her lips quivered. "That he doesn't try hard enough. That he's known people with far more serious injuries to be walking at this stage."

"That's also true."

"How long, Theo? How long can this go on?"

"Which part of it?"

"All of it! How long before Andreas gets out of bed to do his exercises because he *wants* to?"

Salko shrugged lightly. "They're tough to do. Painful."

"I know they're painful, goddammit, Theo! But we both know that pain isn't the reason my husband is lying upstairs with his eyes sealed shut!" She grasped his arm. "How long till he gets over it? Till he wants to help himself? And what do *I* do, meanwhile, to help him? Tell me, Theo, for God's sake!"

He smiled wryly. "You can start by letting go of my arm. I might need it for surgery this week."

She flushed and relaxed her grip. "I'm sorry. Forgive me. I'm not myself today."

"There's nothing to forgive, Ali."

"Yes, there is. I have no right to make demands of you."

"Sure you have." Salko grinned. "I think we're friends after all this time, don't you? And I'm supposed to have all the answers."

"But you don't, do you," she said in a small voice.

He looked at her compassionately. "I'm not a shrink."

"Is that what he needs?"

"In time, perhaps."

"When he knows for sure he can't drive anymore?"

"He will be able to drive."

Alexandra laughed bitterly. "Like Mr. Average."

"Better than that, I expect."

"That won't be good enough, Theo."

Salko shrugged again. "He's a very lucky man. He might have been killed or forced to spend the rest of his life in a chair."

"Like Rudy."

"Who?"

"A friend. A great driver until he was paralyzed." She shook her head. "Andreas never understood how he could live that way. He was unable to see what a miracle it was that he had—still has—so much power and thrust."

"I told you, Andreas has been lucky. But you can't expect him to see how lucky he is—not for a while. It's you who has to understand that."

"I'm not the one we have to worry about, Theo. Unless he can be a real contender for the championship again, I don't believe Andreas will ever understand. He wouldn't accept being 'Mr. Average' in anything. He wouldn't be happy just competing in low-level competitions. He did that on the way up; he's not ready to go down."

"He may have no choice. You have to be almost physically perfect, I suspect, to be a top driver. Hell, you need to be very flexible just to climb in and out of those machines. I had to give up a beautiful little British sports job a few years ago because my back played up."

"But his back wasn't injured—"

"No it wasn't, but his fractures were severe, with dislocations. And with his internal injuries, that combined to keep him immobile for a long time. The chances of permanent stiffness or even disability are always greater in such cases."

"Then his cooperation with the physiotherapist is all the more important, isn't it." Alexandra looked at him searchingly. "I sometimes wonder if we should lie a little, tell him he *will* be able to drive again so long as he fights hard."

"And if it doesn't work? If he never races again? Will he forgive the lies?"

They fell silent. The red light flashed on the percolator.

"Coffee's ready," she said with an attempt at brightness. "Let's take it through to the den." She loaded a tray with cups and a dish of cookies, and led the way.

Salko eased himself into a large, soft-cushioned chair and stirred three spoonfuls of sugar into his cup, his brow deeply furrowed. On Central Park West, a police car, trapped in traffic, blared its siren continuously, the wailing sound rising clearly over the honking of irritable horns.

Alexandra fingered a cookie but left it on the dish. "Theo," she began again cautiously, "what should I do for him?"

"You could try making it with him."

The air vibrated with her shock.

He smiled. "Don't look so stunned. You're married. It's legal."

She put down her cup, outraged. "Theo, he can hardly move! He barely acknowledges me half the time—"

"And the rest of the time?"

"He resents me."

"How do you know that? Has he told you?"

"No, of course not, but—"

"But what? You sense it?" Salko's tone was suddenly mocking. "Bullshit, Ali! You've expected him to resent you from the start. You told me so when you first got back from Milan."

"And I was right."

"You do nothing all day but create your own images of how the patient feels. I think you've stopped thinking of Andreas as an individual, as a man."

"That's not true, Theo! You're being unfair." Her voice shook with injustice. "I spend hours with him when he's awake and when he's asleep, or pretending to be. I hold his hand, I read to him—I try to keep his interests alive—I don't avoid the sports pages in the newspapers. I make sure he knows what the weather's like, even when he insists on having the drapes closed—I tell him what our friends are doing—"

"In other words," Salko interrupted sharply, "you're his single link with normality. And yet you maintain he resents you. Without you, Ali, the man might as well be dead. Get a grip—stop feeling sorry for yourself. Your husband will get better. The extent of his recovery is, of course, mainly up to him, but you have an important role to play."

He scrambled out of the armchair and planted himself on the rug at her feet, grabbing one of her hands. "Sex, Ali!" His eyes sparkled. "Screw the drugs! Screw the exercises! Screw the shrinks! They may be necessary and fine, but I'll wager you that one single roll in the hay with you will do more to get Andreas up on his feet again than anything!"

Alexandra chuckled in spite of herself. "What do you suggest, Theo? Rape?"

"If that's what it takes. But I doubt that'll be necessary. One of these days—it may take weeks, but it *will* happen—you'll be sitting beside him and you'll notice a spark, a tiny hint that there's still something there, some need, some longing. And then, my dear lady, it will be up to you to turn that sickroom back into a bedroom!"

"I wish it could be that easy, Theo."

He looked sternly at her. "I never said it would be easy." He glanced at his watch. "I have to get back to the office."

In the hallway she said: "Andreas's father is due for another visit next week. He hasn't been here since the last operation."

"That should do some good. They get on well, don't they?"

Alexandra smiled, thinking of Roberto. "His father is a remarkable man. They have a marvelous relationship." Her eyes became wistful. "I just wish Andreas was in better shape for Roberto's sake. He's been through so much."

Salko took his jacket from her and opened the front door. "Signor Alessandro looked like quite a tough old guy when I saw him. Don't worry so much, Ali. You've forgotten what bad shape Andreas was in two months back; his father will find him much improved by comparison." He patted her shoulder. "I do have to leave." He looked at her piercingly. "Are you okay now?"

She nodded. "Much better, thanks to you, Theo." She kissed him on the cheek. "I'm so grateful. I needed you."

"Any time," he said softly.

Alexandra closed the door and leaned against it. Her cheek felt hot against the cool wood. The farewell smile faded on her lips.

The door to her studio, on the opposite side of the entrance hall, was closed. It had been that way for months. She could not work, felt she would never work again unless Andreas got well, unless they were happy again.

She looked up at the grandfather clock. Almost five. Time to take Andreas a cool drink.

The guilt was the worst of it, the very worst. Wondering if he would still have crashed if they hadn't fought that morning; knowing he would not. Both of them aware, but not speaking of it. She felt it standing between them—silent, accusing, a vast, unbreachable rift.

She shut her eyes for a moment. Then, one hand resting lightly on the rail, she started up the spiral staircase.

28

The spark of which Theo Salko had spoken that December afternoon ignited twelve days later, one hour after Roberto departed for Zurich and home.

Alexandra kissed Roberto farewell under the canopy of their building as Joseph, the doorman, whistled down a cab and stacked suitcases in the trunk.

"He'll be better soon, Papa." She touched his cheek, still distressed by the lines that seemed to have etched deeper into his skin each day since his arrival in New York.

He patted her hand and smiled wanly. "I know, *cara,* I know. But it's—"

"No buts!" Her eyes were fiercely green. "He will be better, and that's all that counts. The doctors say he's getting stronger every day."

"Yes, in his body, but his spirit is weak, Alexandra." He shook his shaggy head sadly. "I've tried to talk to him, to make him voice his fears, but he's burying them deep inside."

She gripped his hand hard. "It's still shock, Papa. One day soon he'll be ready to face things. That's when he'll really need us. The two of us." She kissed him and pushed him toward the waiting cab. "I'll miss you."

"I'll miss you too—both of you." He tilted her chin and looked deep into her eyes. "When Andi is well, *mia cara,*" he said confidentially, out of earshot of Joseph, "you must have babies. My son will maybe never be able to drive again, but children will help him to forget." He stopped as a new thought struck him. "You do want babies, don't you, Alexandra?"

Her eyes swam with sudden tears. "Of course, Papa."

He smiled with satisfaction and kissed her on the forehead, like a benediction, and she could see that for Roberto, at least, the future was almost resolved.

"Go on, Papa, or you'll miss your plane."

Joseph opened the cab door, taking off his cap as Roberto

slipped some bills into his hand before climbing heavily into the back.

"*Ciao*, Papa," Alexandra said, fighting back the tears. "Safe landing."

He blew her a last kiss. "Be brave." And as the grimy Yellow cab pulled out into the traffic and horns blared, he gave her a quick thumbs-up and was gone.

Up on the eleventh floor, when Alexandra shut the front door of the apartment behind her, all was cool and a little eerie. Most of the doors to the sunny rooms facing the park were closed, and the entrance hall resembled a forest glade, dapples of sunshine smearing the deep shadows.

After a week of Roberto's strength and warmth, she had a sudden feeling that she was the only living being in the apartment— that only she breathed, watched, listened, ate, drank and longed. The thought struck her abruptly that if she no longer visited Andreas upstairs in the sickroom, if she abandoned him utterly, that he might not notice, might not call out, might simply drift away into oblivion without a fight.

She sat on the bottom step of the staircase and lowered her weary head onto her knees, felt the hot skin of her forehead against the silk of her stockings, and stared into the dark.

The sound was so slight that she almost missed it altogether.

Alexandra raised her head from her knees and tilted her face, like an animal, to listen.

Again. From above. Faint and low, just stirring the silence, and so unfamiliar that for three or four seconds she failed to recognize it as her husband's voice.

"Ali."

Andreas had not called for her since they had carried him back into the apartment. In hospital, soon after the accident, when the first strong sedation had begun to wear off, she remembered he had cried for her suddenly, his voice full of terror, but never in their home had he spoken to her above a quiet tone, never had he summoned her, as if the thought of being a bother to her was intolerable.

"Ali!"

She tore up the stairs, taking them three at a time, and threw open the door to his room.

He was at the edge of the bed, half sitting, his fingers groping around the blankets, his eyes wide in the dim light, his chest heaving.

"Darling, what is it?" She flew to his side and covered his hands with her own. "What's wrong? Are you in pain?"

The despair in his face was so clear that her heart clenched in pity. He released the blankets and grasped her fingers.

"I couldn't hear you. . . ." His voice was torn with fear. "I thought you'd gone—with Papa."

He was like a child, a small boy with a nightmare or afraid of the dark. Alexandra pushed him gently back onto the pillows and stroked his hair.

"I was just downstairs," she soothed. "I was here. Of course I was here. Don't worry, my love. I won't leave you."

She started to stand up, but he stopped her, pulling at her hand. "No," he said, his voice a little less weak.

"I was only going to open the curtains. It's too dark in here."

"No. That's not it, Ali."

"What then?" she asked, confused.

He shook his head, his hair tousled and overlong against the pillows. "I don't know," he murmured, as if he, too, were puzzled at himself.

And suddenly she knew, with certainty, what it was.

Quickly she rose again, firmly disengaging her hand, ignoring his protest, and left the room.

In her bathroom, on the other side of the hall, she undressed completely, laying her clothes in a neat heap. She piled her hair onto the top of her head, pinned it into place, and stepped under the shower. After a few minutes she turned off the water, dried herself carefully with a large fluffy towel, sprinkled talcum powder, dabbed a touch of perfume, and brushed her hair so that it hung, heavy and dark, around her shoulders.

Her movements were calm but her heart pounded wildly, as if she were in the throes of panic. She reached out her hand to take her robe from its hook, then changed her mind.

Her brain raced madly. She was like a last-ditch gambler, pulses galloping uncontrollably, throwing everything into one heart-wrenching hunch.

Abruptly she turned and looked in the mirror. It was months since she had studied her body this way, appraisingly, checking that she passed muster. She felt like a virgin bride with an unwilling groom, jittery and unblooded.

If Theodor Salko was wrong about this, she'd kill him!

Silently she opened the bathroom door and passed, nude and wraithlike, through the hall and back into the bedroom.

Andreas was supine again, eyes closed, mouth more taut than

usual. Alexandra shut the door, deliberately causing the latch to click so that he glanced in her direction.

The light was so dim, she could not see his expression, but she felt tension spring up in him, and fear.

She drew closer, not near enough for him to touch, just so that he could see the rise and fall of her breasts, smell the new-washed scent of her.

Still he lay rigid, eyes black and impenetrable, and for a moment, heart sinking, she believed she had failed. And then she saw that his mouth was trembling.

Very slowly, gliding, terrified of doing anything to break the atmosphere, Alexandra moved to the far side of the big bed, pushed back the sheets, and got in beside him.

His body was stiff, unyielding; his limbs seemed welded to the mattress, but his skin was surprisingly hot to her touch. Gently she wriggled closer to him, until she felt the whole length of him with her body—and then she, too, lay perfectly still.

Time passed, an eternity of suspended agony for her. And then she began to move. Slowly, her fingers no more than a whisper of movement, she let her hands travel over Andreas; a long, languorous, interminable voyage, seeking out the hidden places, rediscovering the flesh and bone and muscle, much reduced but still exquisitely recognizable to her loving fingers.

At first, she made her own body remain still, merely touching, not moving, but then, as she felt Andreas starting to quiver, sensed his heart beating faster and faster with the suppressed tension of an unexploded, ticking bomb, she moved over him and knelt, legs on either side of him. And then, joy of joys, she felt his erection, was aware of his growing strength, saw in his face the shock and sheer delight and life of it, and realized how greatly he had feared that this moment might never come again.

"Don't move," she hissed, longing for him to reach for her, to take her with the old fierceness, but knowing it was too soon, that he was too physically weak, that he might fail at the crucial moment and everything might be destroyed. "Not an inch, darling. Just let me . . ."

He gasped as her right hand encircled him, squeezing lightly and then rubbing and caressing, and as she stared into his face, she saw his eyes darken even more and fill with tears, a wall of painful tears rising up out of him, dammed up by the months of anguish.

She took his own right hand then, and guided it over her skin, pausing fleetingly over her breasts, letting him feel their heat and fullness, and then pulling his fingers down to her own moisture, so that she teased herself unbearably—and something in his face, in his expression, seemed to burst, and he threw out his arms and wrapped them around her and drew her close, wordlessly, kissing her face, her mouth, her eyes, her hair. For a few minutes she allowed herself to luxuriate in the warmth, but then she forbade him again and continued her own caresses, insinuating herself against him, over him, around him, catlike, and all the time her fingers rubbed and squeezed, her lips kissed, tongue flashed and flickered, until Andreas exploded with a low scream that was not just physical release but a rediscovery of love and life itself.

It was several moments before she realized that something was missing.

Much later that day, or perhaps it was night, when they lay together in their bed, arms and bodies still entwined, Andreas took Alexandra's left hand and touched the gold wedding band on her finger.

"I don't know where my ring is," he said. "They took it off after the accident and never brought it back."

"It doesn't matter," she murmured. "We'll get another."

He sighed, a deep, trembling sigh. "I'm sorry."

"How can it matter now?"

"Not about the ring. Everything. The way I've been the last weeks, months. . . ." He covered his eyes with one hand, trying to suppress this new damnable urge to weep, shrugging bitterly. "I don't know how long I've been in this room. Everything just seemed to stop. I wanted to stop."

She leaned closer, kissed his lips, took his hand from his eyes. "How could you have felt differently? You went through so much."

"I made it worse for you." He stirred as a memory struck him. "My father was here."

Alexandra smiled. "He left this afternoon."

"I hardly spoke to him. He sat here for hours, and I never said a word."

"We'll call him first thing tomorrow. He'll be so happy to hear you."

Andreas tightened his arms about her. "The doctors, too, Salko and whoever else it takes." He twisted to face her, and gasped as a spasm of pain hit him. "I'm going to drive again, Ali."

"Of course, darling."

His eyes glittered. "I'll get back. Whatever they say, whatever I have to do."

Her heart began to pound again with new fear. "I hope so, Andreas. Oh, God, I hope so. But you took quite a beating—"

"Moss broke both legs *and* crushed a vertebra, and he only missed two races."

"All injuries are different, darling. You can't rush things—it's bound to take time."

He sat up gingerly, wincing. "What month is this? How many races have I missed?"

"Just one."

"Riverside."

"Not to mention Monza."

He smiled wryly. "Who won?"

"Andreas, I told you. I sat right here and read you the reports. Don't you remember?"

"I guess I didn't listen much. I'm sorry." He stroked her hair. "Humor me, please, Ali. Tell me."

She sighed. "Phil Hill won at Monza, Moss at Riverside."

"And today's date?"

"Eighteenth of December."

He relaxed slightly. "So I have until May."

She rubbed her cheek against his back. "You have the rest of your life, darling."

The room was very quiet. Husband and wife lay back against the pillows, alone with their thoughts. Then at last, unable to bear it any longer, Alexandra shut her eyes and asked, "Why did it happen?"

"What?"

"Why did you crash?" She held her breath.

"I lost concentration."

"Why?"

"The dog."

Alexandra sat up. "What dog?"

He shrugged slightly. "Damned little mongrel. Ran across the track. One second's lapse and here I am."

A shudder of relief went through Alexandra and she lay back again, feeling herself tremble.

"What is it, *Herzchen?*"

"I thought—"

"What?"

"That it might have been my fault."

"*Your* fault?" Andreas said in astonishment. "How could it have been your fault?"

"We had a fight. Before you left for the track."

He remembered. "So?"

"I thought your mind might have been on that—instead of on your driving." She bit her lower lip.

Andreas took her right hand and kissed the fingertips. "And you've been worrying about that ever since?"

"Of course." She turned her face to him, her eyes filled with tears. "Tell me it isn't true."

"I just told you." He laughed, but his expression was tender and loving. "It was the dog, nothing to do with you at all. Poor baby, carrying that load on top of everything else." He took her in his arms. "I can hardly remember what our fight was about."

"I can," she said huskily. "It was about babies. And when you'd gone, I went into the bathroom and flushed my diaphragm down the john."

Andreas held her away from him. His eyes were brilliant. "Why did you do that, Ali?"

She swallowed. "Why do you think?"

A look of almost unprecedented happiness came over Andreas's face—and was replaced by another expression, far less readable.

"What is it, darling?" Something inside her twinged in alarm.

It was a long moment before he spoke. "Did you notice?"

"Notice what?"

His voice was flat. "When we made love."

She hesitated infinitesimally. "It was beautiful."

"You did notice, didn't you?"

"Yes," she said calmly.

"Why do you suppose it happened?"

"I don't know." She kept her tone light. "Could be any number of reasons, I guess."

"To do with the accident? With the operations."

"Maybe." She snuggled back against him. "I'm sure it's nothing to worry about, sweetheart."

"Should we—try again, do you think?"

Alexandra chuckled. "I think perhaps we should wait at least a day. We don't want to shock your whole system."

His eyes darkened. "You're afraid in case the same thing happens again, aren't you?"

"No, of course not!"

He tried to make himself relax. "Maybe you're right. It's probably hoping for too much to expect everything to be normal right away."

Alexandra stared into the dark. "Let's give it time."

*

"Retrograde ejaculation. That's what the urologist told him."

"And do you understand what that means, Ali?"

"Yes. Instead of ejaculating sperm in the normal way, it's ejaculated backward into the bladder."

"Do you understand what that means to you?"

Alexandra's voice was low. "Probable infertility."

It was January, and Alexandra was seated in Theodor Salko's Park Avenue office. Once again, she had gone to him out of sheer despair.

"I need help, Theo."

Salko shook his head. "I'm not the one to help you with this problem, Ali. I'm an orthopedic surgeon."

"Maybe you can help by talking some sense into Andreas."

"In what way?"

She ran a hand through her hair in frustration. "He refuses to do anything about the situation. Ever since the urologist told him what the problem is, he's gone back into his shell. He isn't even considering treatment."

"I very much doubt if there is any treatment that would help him, Ali."

"There must be!" she argued fiercely.

Salko shrugged. "When Andreas was first admitted to the hospital in Monza, they found that his urethra had been ruptured. That often happens when the pelvis is fractured; the prostate gland and the—"

"Theo, I know what happened," she interrupted. "I want to know what we can do about it now."

"Probably nothing at all."

Alexandra's eyes were wide with dismay. "But surely another operation . . ."

"They operated in Italy, and quite successfully."

"Successfully?"

"Absolutely. Ali, you must understand—in a way, once again, Andreas has been very lucky." He held up his hand. "No, don't yell at me, just listen." He got up from behind his desk and came to sit beside her on the leather sofa. "Andreas might not have been able to urinate. He might also have been impotent. But there's no problem of that nature, is there?"

"No, thank God, but—"

"But nothing."

The knife that had been embedded in Alexandra's chest since

Andreas had come home from the urologist's office twisted and plunged, more brutally than ever.

"It's my fault," she said.

"How can it be *your* fault, Ali. Be sensible."

"He wanted a child," she said softly. "He had so much . . . his driving . . . our marriage . . ." Her eyes were rimmed with tears. "He's an Italian, Theo."

"Half Swiss."

"More Italian. He wanted a child. And I deprived him of that."

"Not you, the accident."

"Me!" The wildness rose into her throat, into her voice. She clenched her fists tightly, the nails tearing into her skin. "He wanted babies, but I wanted time alone with him. He begged me, but I was so stubborn, I wouldn't listen!"

"You couldn't know what would happen." Salko tried to comfort her. "It was because you loved him that you wanted—"

"And now he's got to endure the next few months with the pain, fighting an impossible, crazy battle to get back on the Grand Prix circuit—and I'll be there, every single damnable day, to remind him."

"That's exactly what's going to help him, don't you see? Having you there with him."

"To *remind* him!" Suddenly she covered her face with her hands. "He'll see me walking easily in and out of the apartment while he limps about on crutches. He'll watch me painting, doing what I love best. I'll bring him his meals on trays, like a child. He'll look at races on television. And he'll sit out on our terrace and see the mothers and fathers wheeling their baby carriages into Central Park! And I tell you he'll hate me."

Salko took her hands gently away from her face. "He won't hate you, Ali."

The first tear rolled freely down her cheek, but her voice was steady as she returned his gaze.

"Yes, he will," she said. "He'll despise me."

Later that evening, when Andreas was already asleep, just before she turned out the lights in the hall, Alexandra opened the door to her studio and slipped inside.

The easel stood, angular and orphaned, in the center of the floor, awash in moonlight. All around the room, against the walls, her canvases, covered with sheets, waited. The air felt lonely.

"Soon," she whispered.

Ghosts of unfinished paintings, of unstarted sketches, whirled suddenly through her mind, tiny phantoms of unfulfillment.

Alexandra touched her belly. She felt hollow.

"Soon," she said again, and went out into the hall and up the stairs.

29

Daniel was home.

He felt it in more ways than he'd ever imagined possible. When he looked in a mirror, he saw it in his eyes; when he walked, his step was springy; even when he was lying down, he was conscious of the blood singing in his arteries. His mouth smiled more often, he noticed that women took second and usually third glances at him—when he dined out with them he knew he was more fun to be with than he'd been in years, and when he made love to them he no longer had the terrifying apprehension that they might twist beneath him in sudden agony, the terror that had dogged him since Rosa.

New York was the place he wanted to hang his hat, the place he felt most comfortable in, the place where he belonged.

He was home.

Fanny, as always, had come up trumps. The moment she'd learned of his change of heart in April 1960, she'd sprung into action, flying straight from Berlin to London armed with the latest Sunday edition of The *New York Times,* property bulletins from three of the top Manhattan real estate brokers, and her big, pigskin Gucci address book.

She stalked into the creamy little house in Montpelier Walk, withdrew just those items from the smallest of her five matching Mädler suitcases, and laid them on the dining table.

"Changed your mind again?"

Daniel looked her in the eye and smiled. "No."

"To business, then." There was no hint in her voice of the pleasure she felt, but her eyes glittered.

"Two things. A home for you, and a suite of offices for Harper and Stone." She jabbed the papers on the table. "Start looking."

"Shouldn't we get there first—check into a hotel maybe and then look?" Daniel asked mildly.

"Absolutely not."

He shrugged, amused. "Fanny knows best."

"If you don't know that by now, my darling, you never will."
She reached for his hand and squeezed it hard. "Where's the
key?"

He stood up. "I'll get it."

Slowly he unlocked the mahogany writing desk, opened a small
inner drawer, and withdrew the tiny box that Fanny had given him
for Christmas a few months earlier.

He brought it over to the table and placed it, unopened, before
her. *"Voilà."*

"Take it out, Dan."

He obeyed and found to his surprise that his fingers trembled
slightly. The uncut, solid gold key was cool and heavy in his palm.

"Now," Fanny said huskily, "let's you and I find our suite of
offices—and then I will fly straight to New York with the key, and
I will have it cut to fit the door of your personal office."

"No, Fanny. That key should open the front door of the suite.
That's *our* key—our offices, our future."

Fanny glowed. This was one human being—one of the very few
in her life—who had never given her grounds for regret. She'd
always known she could spot the good ones, people with that
indefinable spark, and Dan Stone was a good one—he had spirit,
spunk, and sex appeal, but he also had soul.

Her gaze became critical. "You shaved off your beard."

"Yes."

"And decided to grow it again?"

He touched his stubbly chin.

"Camouflage for the jungle?" she asked perceptively.

He felt defensive. "Perhaps."

"You won't need it, Dan."

"Probably not."

She studied him seriously. "You do trust me, don't you, Dan?"

"With my life."

"Then believe what I tell you. I know it's going to be okay for
you back in New York. I feel it *here.*" She struck her heart with her
right hand. "I'm not sure why you changed your mind about going back, and I'm not going to ask. But your timing is perfect.
You've left it long enough. Remember the old cliché. Time does
heal all wounds, and that applies to the Joe Bernardis of this world
as much as anyone. You have a new name. You've changed since
you were last in the States; God knows you've altered since *we* met
—and maybe you should keep the beard, by the way. It suits you
wonderfully. Blends with the scar, gives you an image the TV
people will adore—"

"Hey, slow down! What TV people?"

"Don't you worry about that side of things," she said, dismissing the subject. "You just concentrate on where you want to live."

Not for the first time, and not for the last, Daniel stared at Fanny in wonder. She was more than a marvel where he was concerned, she was almost a life force.

He smiled. "Yes, Fanny."

They found him an apartment on 11th Street in the West Village and he was in by June. It was in a well-run building with courteous uniformed doormen on duty night and day, and maintenance staff permanently on call, prepared to change a light bulb or ease a stiff faucet at four in the morning. Daniel delighted in small things—the way the team of doormen all knew him by name, the way all the neighborhood stores quickly laid in stocks of his favorite wines and cheeses, even the brands of soap and socks he liked best. It all combined to signify one elemental fact: He belonged again. He was home.

Fanny had been so right, except in one respect. He had emerged from the shadows, but on occasion fear and guilt still stalked him. Whenever he came anywhere near 34th Street and Seventh Avenue, where Joe Bernardi's head office had been situated, he gave it a wide berth; each time he passed a branch of Bernardi Liquor, a sharp twist of discomfort jarred him and he crossed the street; and almost nothing on earth could have persuaded him to enter the Carlyle Hotel, however excellent the food or entertainment. His intellect condemned his instinct—if Bernardi had wanted to locate him, he probably would have done so years before. And, as Fanny had often pointed out, he had changed in many more ways than his name—but fear was a stubborn master.

"So when did you start writing, Daniel?"

"What's Paris like these days?"

"Is there any decent food to be had in London, or do you still have to be a millionaire to afford it?"

"Tell us, Daniel! Don't be so stingy!"

"That's something you can't say about Daniel Silberstein—he's never been stingy."

"And he's not Silberstein anymore either!"

"So he has a new name—name, schmame! He can call himself Czar Nicholas and he still won't be stingy!"

"Don't be so touchy, Sarah. I only meant he's very slow with his answers."

"Perhaps he'd like to eat something, Leon. Is this a press conference or dinner?"

"Children, children! We mustn't squabble or the poor man will never get a word in."

Daniel looked across the remains of the *boeuf en croûte* at his friends, and his eyes glowed.

"Thank you, Roly. I'd forgotten what these two are like once they get their motors started!" He grinned lovingly at Leon and Sarah Gottesman. "They never could let anyone else speak for long, let alone each other."

"A common enough trait, I've observed," Roland Steinbeck remarked dryly.

"*You* should talk, Steinbeck," said Fanny.

Daniel warmed with the sheer joy of having his four best friends around his table together for the first time. The Gottesmans and Roly had met only briefly on a few occasions before he fled the country in 1954, but from the second round of martinis (though Sarah had stuck to sherry) until this moment, they and Fanny had taken to one another like olives to vermouth.

The four had a single trait in common—a faculty (or a failing) for making snap assessments of their fellow humans. By the time Daniel had served the fish course, each had decided. Fanny observed that the Gottesmans were two of a kind—earthy, warm as toast, and staunch—and she found Roland slightly erratic, fundamentally misguided but kind-natured. Roland thought Fanny sublime—better even than Diana Vreeland, and *she* was his goddess! —and the Gottesmans quaintly Yorkville. Sarah found Roly outlandish but charming, and to her Fanny Harper was the most alarming woman since her headmistress back in Dresden, though *she* had been an anti-Semite, and no one who loved Daniel could possibly be that! Leon had slight doubts about Roly; no one with a name like Steinbeck, he felt, should be quite so un-Jewish in type —and as for Miss Harper, if it wasn't for his Sarah he thought he might have fallen in love with her. Formidable she might pretend to be, but he, Leon Gottesman, knew a pussycat when he met one!

"I made *palachinken*, Sarah," Daniel said, "with cherries and sour cream."

"*Palachinken?*" Sarah echoed. "After vichyssoise, red snapper and beef Wellington? Does that go together?"

"Did any of it?" murmured Fanny weakly. "Not that it didn't taste great, Dan."

Daniel stood up. His limbs felt warm and a little heavy from the food and wine, and from delight.

"The food tonight," he said, " 'goes together' as well as the company." He turned to Roland. "The soup, old friend, was for you, because I remembered how much you used to like it."

Roland raised his glass appreciatively to Daniel. "Still do."

"Snapper *is* still one of your top five fish, Fanny?"

She smiled and nodded.

"Beef Wellington was always your favorite when I was at Leon's, Mr. Gottesman, sir—and you, Sarah, never once resisted the temptation to steal from the customers' plates when they ordered *palachinken* with cherries and sour cream!"

Sarah wiped away a tear, beaming. "I just hope you made enough, so I won't have to poach from my neighbor's plate tonight."

"I made for eight." He lifted his wineglass. "And now I want to drink a toast."

"Good idea," said Roland.

"To friendship in New York."

"Anywhere," Fanny corrected.

Daniel smiled at her. "Anywhere."

A few minutes later, as he added the finishing touches to dessert in the kitchen, Fanny came to join him.

"No help needed," he said. "Just enjoy yourself."

"I haven't come to offer help."

"Oh?"

"I have a question."

"Go ahead."

"When are you going to contact your other friend?"

"Who?" he asked vaguely, busy with the sour cream.

"Alessandro."

Daniel looked up in surprise. "Why bring him up now?"

"Because you're so obviously happy putting down roots, seeing old friends, and it comes to mind."

He spooned the cream into a cut-glass bowl. "Not to mine."

"Why not?"

"Why should it? You can't compare a stranger to real friends, Fanny. I was a kid when we met—oceans under the bridge for us both since then." He reached across the counter to kiss her on the cheek. "Drop it, darling."

She shook her head. "I don't think I can."

"Why not?"

"Because I feel he's still important to you. Because I think knowing him again might help close the circle."

It wasn't necessary for Daniel to ask her what she meant. Gently he moved the crystal bowl to a tray.

"I'm not ready, Fanny." He sighed. "You may be right. I probably will know him again, and"—he spoke slowly, feeling his way—"and my memory of him is important. But not yet."

"Is there, by chance," she asked obdurately, "some old ethnic ritual I may not be familiar with that says if someone gives you something precious, you may not see them again unless you can give like for like?"

Daniel shifted awkwardly. As usual Fanny was uncomfortably near the mark. "No ritual," he said.

"But you do think, don't you, that because Alessandro saved your bacon when you were children, you need something extra special to offer him in return? Well, don't you?"

"I guess so."

Sudden anger flared in her. "Don't you realize that in saving you, he gave himself a gift too? He became a hero, goddammit! What nine-year-old boy hasn't relished that in his fantasies? And what grown man, even a racing driver at the peak of his career, wouldn't like to be reminded of it?"

"Damn you, Fanny!" He startled her by banging his fist hard on the table. "You can't know that! We don't know what happened to that nine-year-old when he got home that night. They didn't give medals in Switzerland in 1943 to people who aided and abetted Jewish criminals!"

"Don't be idiotic, Dan. You were never a criminal."

"No?" He was flushed and his neck prickled with old resentment. "I broke more than one law, Fanny, before Michel Bresson made me legitimate, had me sanitized!"

"Calm down, Dan, for heaven's sake. The others will hear."

"I am calm!" He sank onto a chair. "I'm just pointing out to you that Alessandro might be more embarrassed than happy to hear from me."

"And my theory? About repaying the debt?"

Daniel's shoulders sagged slightly. "There may be something in that," he admitted, "but I still wish you'd leave it alone."

"A dog with a bone."

"I beg your pardon?"

"That's what my mother used to say about me when I pestered the hell out of her." She bent her thin, elegant body and brushed his cheek with her own. "Forgive me?"

He shrugged. "Nothing to forgive."

The door opened and Roland came in. "We couldn't figure out what a former catering wizard could find so difficult about a precooked dessert. Waiting for the cream to sour?"

"Right first time." Fanny passed him on her way back to the table.

"Are you all right, dear boy?" asked Roland.

"Perfectly," Daniel answered, getting up. "Help me serve the *palachinken.*"

The heat in Manhattan that summer was as intolerable as it was every year, the humidity driving the inhabitants unfortunate enough to have to stay in the city into the chilly, air-conditioned buildings at every opportunity. Daniel hardly noticed it.

Fanny had finalized the deal with their new publishers before Daniel had even arrived back in New York, winning them a handsome advance on the royalties that were certain to follow when *The Stone Gourmet Guide for the Sensualist* was eventually printed. Eating would not commence in earnest until late fall, when the bite in the wind would tilt Daniel's appetite to full potential, but in the meantime research was under way to select suitable candidates for inspection. "Restaurants of any classification with a proven *raison d'être* of enhancing romance" was the criterion. Standards would be as high as before—an oyster bar with the most charming service, softest lighting, and bedrooms upstairs would not stand a ghost of a chance unless kitchen hygiene was up to snuff.

"You're going to need help, aren't you?" Roland asked Daniel one day on a visit to Harper and Stone's Madison Avenue offices in early September.

"I thought you'd never volunteer."

"Why didn't you ask me?"

"After the way I ran out on you last time?" Daniel swiveled his chair and gazed out of the window.

"I forgave you long, long ago. And besides, life without Silberstein has been dull."

"I wish you'd forget that name, Roly."

Roland shrugged. "A Silberstein by any other name . . ."

Daniel swung back to face him, grinning. "What do you want to help with? Just the eating, or *real* work? And what about a salary? We both know you don't need money, but—"

"Won't Fanny object?"

"She's already suggested it. We have no staff—only Kate, my

secretary. Fanny, of course, has people littered all over the world, but they aren't going to work for Harper and Stone."

"Where is she, by the way? Still in Paris?"

"No, she's in town. So"—Daniel reached for the telephone—"Shall I call my lawyers and have them draw up a contract, or . . ."

Roland winced. "Do you think we could remain a tad more flexible? Contracts make me uneasy, and I can never remember whether I'm officially contracted to my papa's corporation or not."

"No problem." Daniel picked up a fountain pen. "Title?"

"Manager. I'd adore to be called a manager. The last time I really upset my mother was when I told her I was waiting on tables with you. The very idea of her firstborn being called 'manager' should make her bust a gut at least!"

"Manager it is." The intercom buzzed. "Yes, Kate."

"Miss Harper's on line one."

"Put her through." He waited. "Fanny?"

"Have you seen the evening paper?"

"Not yet."

There was a pause. "Alessandro crashed yesterday in practice for the Italian Grand Prix."

Daniel didn't answer. A curious unreality had swamped him. He felt cut off from his surroundings.

"Dan?" Fanny said. "He wasn't killed, but he's critical."

Still he didn't speak.

"Dan, are you all right?"

"Yes. Yes, of course." He stirred himself. "Thank you for letting me know. I'll—buy a newspaper."

"Sure."

"You coming in today?"

"Too busy. I'll be home tonight if you want me."

"Fine." He remembered Roland sitting opposite. "By the way, Roly's with me. He wants to be our manager."

"Does he, by George." She hesitated. "Sorry to give you bad news, Dan."

"Don't worry about it."

"So long."

He put the receiver down slowly. Roland regarded him quizzically. "Why do you have to buy a newspaper?"

The strange, bloodless feeling was still with him. With an effort he shook it off. "Something happened to someone I once knew. Not that important, really."

"I'd hate to see you when you get really bad news. You're white as a ghost." Roland stood up. "Let's go to the St. Regis and celebrate my promotion from waiter to manager. And you can dirty your fingers on the evening paper."

He waited until three in the morning before he called the overseas operator and found the telephone number of the hospital in Monza. It took twenty-five minutes to get through, and another eight minutes before he reached the right floor of the hospital.

"*Pronto,*" said a female voice.

"I'm calling from the United States for information about a friend," Daniel shouted over the poor connection in halting Italian. "Signor Alessandro."

"Alessandro?"

"Yes. How is he?"

"Who is calling, please?"

"A friend!"

"Name, please."

Daniel hesitated. "Silberstein," he said.

"Are you related to the patient?"

"No, I told you, I'm a good friend! Do you have some news? I'm calling from America!" he yelled.

There was a pause, filled with crackling. "They are still operating on Signor Alessandro."

"Is he badly injured?"

"I have no more information, signor. Do you wish to leave a message?"

"No. Thank you. No message." He hung up.

At eleven the next day, after a restless night and a listless early morning, Daniel shut the door of his office and called the hospital again.

"Signor Alessandro is as well as can be expected."

"But is he all right?" Daniel asked.

"I am permitted only to give information to close family relations, signor."

"I'm a very good friend," Daniel said in frustration. "Can you at least tell me if his life is still in danger?"

The voice relented. "Signor Alessandro is expected to live." The line went dead.

"Is he okay?" Fanny stood in the doorway.

"I'm not sure." Daniel passed a hand over his eyes. "They said he's expected to live. I don't know what shape he's in."

"Why didn't you leave a message, Dan?"

"Come in, Fanny, and close the door."

She came toward the desk, hands raised as if surrendering. "I know, I know," she said, "I had no business listening, and it's none of my damned business—"

"Shut up, Fanny. Please."

"Right."

"Drink?"

"Scotch."

"Coming up." He rose and walked over to the wall cabinet and poured slowly, playing for time, steadying himself. He brought them back to the desk.

"Okay," he said, and took a swallow. "This is how it is. The news threw me, shocked me, yes. It knocked me back seventeen years, yes. I didn't sleep last night, and until I heard them say that he's going to survive, I didn't do a stroke of work. But he is out of danger."

"Darling, listen—"

"No, you hear me through. I didn't leave a message because, in the first place, he's almost certainly unconscious or sedated to the hilt, and in the second place"—he looked at Fanny intently—"if I didn't think Alessandro wanted to hear from me before this, I certainly don't think that now would be the best time to rise from the ashes." He took another swallow of Scotch. "Okay?"

Fanny smiled very gently. "Understood," she said, and downed her drink in one.

Daniel returned to his chair. "Now," he said clearly, "Kate's found us five more possibles. Shall we do a little work?"

30

For Andreas and Alexandra the spring and summer months of 1961 were months of tedium, strain, and depression, with only just enough splashes of optimism thrown into the deep murky pool of New York dog days, when they arrived, to make life bearable.

June was best, or, rather, least bad. The air was still fit for human consumption and the temperatures tolerable, and Andreas was at his most determined. He struggled, fought, even managed an occasional joke. When July entered the apartment like a steaming monster, piercing the double windows and defeating the air-conditioners, Andreas matched it. The first flush of real disappointment was upon him. He worked out doggedly every day with Jan, his physiotherapist, and swam ten lengths of his club pool, refusing to admit that he wearied after three lengths and was fit to sink after five, but though his muscles were stronger than before, progress was painfully slow. The Grand Prix at Monaco, Zandvoort, Spa, Rheims, and Aintree passed him by, and he could see the rest of the season lying ahead, unchallenged.

August was the pits, the nadir. On the tenth day of the month, Jan stormed out of the apartment, never to return. On the twentieth, Andreas rented an MG sports car, forced his stiff body into the driver's seat, bulleted out of the city, ripped up a storm on the New Jersey Turnpike, and ended up slap-bang in the rear end of a new Cadillac convertible, lucky to be in one piece, with pain and frustration singing in his ears.

On the twenty-first day of August, Alexandra decided that enough was enough.

"You're acting like a pig," she said one evening as she tossed a casserole into the oven and turned on the timer. "I love you, but you act like a boor sometimes and I hate it."

"You have blue paint on your cheek."

"So? If I had more time to myself there'd be paint all over me.

As it is, I've hardly had time to touch anything in my studio for weeks."

"I don't ask you to spend every day with me," Andreas said sullenly.

"I don't see I have much choice."

He hunched over the sink and stared disconsolately out at the sky. "What would you have me do?"

"How about fixing us both a drink? I'll have a small Scotch, please."

Alexandra sat at the breakfast bar while Andreas left the kitchen and came back a few minutes later with two glasses. He handed the one with less liquor to her.

"Is that part of your fitness program?" she inquired disagreeably. "That's a good two fingers in there, you know."

"Yes, I know, and no, it's not part of the program. I don't have a program."

"Of course you do. Jan listed—"

"Jan isn't here anymore."

"I can't say that I blame him. How long did you expect him to put up with your abuse?"

"Until I'm well."

"Oh, Andreas, play another tune! There are a thousand people out there on the streets who would like to be as fit as you are." She relented. "What do you say we do something together tomorrow? I mean really *do* something, not just molder at home like two old crocks?"

"Like what?"

She shrugged. "Something different. We could forget problems for a day and enjoy ourselves for a change."

He put his glass down on the counter. "Don't I have an appointment with Salko tomorrow?"

"Not till Thursday."

"What do you have in mind?"

"I thought," she said tentatively, "it might be fun to take a helicopter ride to Rhode Island."

"Why Rhode Island, for Christ's sake? And why do you want to fly? You're nervous of helicopters."

"I am not," she retorted, "and there's supposed to be a really terrific new restaurant in Newport. I just think it would be different—do us both good." She shrugged. "But if you don't want to, that's okay."

His eyes narrowed. "Oh, I get it. You know your driving makes me crazy—"

"I drive very well!"

"You drive like a painter," he dismissed. "And you know riding in trains reminds me I can't drive myself, so you found the only other option open to us."

"That's nonsense," she protested.

"No, it isn't, and you know I'm right." For the first time in weeks he smiled at her, really smiling with his eyes as well as his mouth. "Thank you," he said.

Relief flooded through her. "Can I make reservations, then?"

"You mean you haven't already made them?"

She laughed. "Of course not. I have the number upstairs. I'll go call them now."

In their bedroom, she fumbled in her purse until she found the cutting. Andreas was quite correct, she had already organized their flight, but she'd been looking for an excuse to make another, more important call.

She smoothed out the crumpled piece of paper, took a deep breath, and dialed the number.

"Herr Rudesheim? This is Ali Alessandro." She paused. "It's all right. He's agreed to come. We'll be there at noon."

Rudesheim waited for the right moment. Andreas and Alexandra had made their way through tourists and sailors to the anonymously fronted restaurant, identifiable only by a tiny brass plaque reading NUMBER THIRTY-FOUR, and had taken their seats in a plush booth. They had declined first courses, still a little queasy after a bumpy ride from Manhattan, but the broiled crayfish they'd ordered for their main course had been superb.

Andreas shut his eyes in appreciation. "I haven't eaten crayfish that good since I don't know when." He opened his eyes, still trying to identify a memory sparked off by his taste buds.

A waitress approached, menus in hand.

"We'll wait awhile," Andreas said.

"A gentleman has recommended that you order the second item on the dessert menu, sir."

Irritated, Andreas regarded the list. His eyes widened. *"Salzburger Nockerl?"* He looked up in surprise. "In Newport?"

With an electric whir, a wheelchair emerged from the back of the restaurant, and a familiar voice boomed, "The only *Nockerl* in the United States worth eating!"

Andreas twisted around on the banquette, winced with pain, and instantly forgot it as he saw Rudesheim's face.

"I don't believe it! Rudy! What the hell are you doing here, of all places?" He slid out of the booth, grinning with delight and astonishment, and grabbed his hand. "Ali, you remember Rudy, don't you?"

Alexandra regarded the man in the chair with quiet pleasure. "We only met once at the Nürburgring, and yes, I remember Herr Rudesheim very well."

Rudesheim steered his wheelchair expertly around to make a third place at the table, and promptly a waitress appeared with a glass of schnapps.

"Thank you, *Liebchen.*"

"You're welcome, Mr. Rudesheim."

Andreas looked surprised. The big German reached out and patted his hand. "Sit down, Andreas." He looked at Alexandra and winked.

Andreas slid back to his place. "So," he said accusingly, "a terrific new restaurant, just a helicopter ride away." He stabbed at the menu. *"Nockerl* on a Newport menu! What's going on? When did you two cook this up?"

Alexandra smiled. "Just think of it as a belated birthday present."

Andreas shook his head. "How long has it been, Rudy?"

"Too long." Rudesheim signaled the waitress, who was still hovering politely nearby. *"Nockerl* for three, *Liebchen.* And tell Karl to make it special."

"I sure will." She beamed.

"Do you own this place or something?" Andreas was still puzzled.

Rudesheim nodded. "A partnership."

"But why here? Don't you live in Bonn anymore?"

"Not for some time." The big face, with its flat features and more lines than Andreas remembered, grew somber. "I didn't like it any more without Mara. I sold the house."

"Where are you now? Not in Newport, surely?"

Rudesheim shrugged. "Some of the time, yes, but I live most of the year near Baden-Baden. I need to be close to the sanitarium these days, you know."

"But you always said you couldn't live away from the 'Ring."

Rudesheim smiled. "I think at last I grew out of the 'Ring, Andreas." He paused. "You cannot imagine such a thing, can you?"

Alexandra reached across the table for her husband's hand, squeezed it quickly, and released it again. She felt suddenly intrusive and ill at ease; having brought the two men together, she felt perhaps they should be alone.

Rudesheim seemed to read her mind. "You're a lucky man, Andreas. She's a part of you, just like Mara and me."

"Yes."

The German chuckled. "I came to Newport the first time because of the cup."

"The America's Cup? Why? Since when are you interested in boats?"

Rudesheim's great laugh rattled the crystal on the table. "How can a driver be interested in anything but cars?" He explained: "Since a good friend, a competitive yachtsman, took me out with him on the Elbe. That's a river near Hamburg," he explained to Alexandra. "They chained my chair safely onto the deck and strapped me in like a baby so I should not fall in the water and waste their time. And I fell in love all over again." He looked seriously at the younger man. "Such things do happen, Andreas."

For a moment Andreas stared at him. Then he flushed dark. "If the two of you are trying to talk me out of driving, you'll have to think again." His voice was harsh. "It's different for you, Rudy, as you should know. After your crash you had no choice, but I can walk—I can work out better and longer in a gym than most men I know." He glared at them both. "I can, and I will, drive again."

Rudesheim was unruffled. "Perhaps. If it's God's will. But I hear the doctors are less optimistic."

Andreas turned on Alexandra. "You had no right to go behind my back!"

"Don't be a fool," Rudesheim rapped, seeing Alexandra's dismay. "She's your wife; she's afraid for you. She had every right." He paused. "In any case, I made the contact."

"When?"

"Last week."

"Why then? Why not before?"

"After your accident," the German explained, "I waited for word from you. I wanted to come to Monza—then I was ready to fly to New York after they brought you back, but I wasn't certain it would be right."

"Why not?"

"Every case is different, my friend. I was worried that seeing me might remove all hope."

"That's crazy."

"Not really. You might have suspected the motives of your doctors, allowing a cripple to visit you. You might have accused them of putting rehabilitation before cure."

"I doubt it." Andreas shrugged. "Maybe."

The dessert arrived, served with a flourish by the cheerful waitress, and for a few moments they ate in silence.

"So"—Rudesheim gestured with his spoon—"what are your plans, Andreas?"

"No plans. Just work."

"What work?"

"Strengthening exercises—swimming, weights . . ."

"That's not enough to fill a life. What other plans do you have?"

"What do you think I should do, Rudy?" Andreas challenged.

"I'm asking you."

"I wish you'd understand that it's different for me. When you crashed, you'd already been German champion three times. You had the respect of everyone in the sport—you'd been in the public eye for five seasons. You had time."

Rudesheim shook his head. "Not enough."

"Of course not. But at least you were equipped to find another foothold connected with racing. You wrote articles, your book. If I had made world champion—if I'd even got close—I might have gone into journalism, and the television networks would have chased me to do commentaries—"

"These things are still open to you. After all," Rudesheim said, smiling wryly, "there's always a shortage of living ex-drivers."

"I don't agree. I'm not, and never have been, a household name. Not here in America—not even in Switzerland."

Alexandra was unable to stay out of the discussion any longer. "How many drivers have been on the covers of *Newsweek* and *Time,* may I ask? How many have a fan club?"

"That isn't real, Ali. It's not the same as being established. By next season I'll be forgotten." He paused. "Unless I come back."

Rudesheim's sharp focus on him made a mockery of his next smiling words. "In which case they'll fete you like a young Viking and hang garlands around your neck."

"Only if I win."

The German shrugged. "If you lose, they will pat you on the back and nod respectfully, perhaps compassionately. And then they will forget you."

"And if he dies," Alexandra added, "he'll get a page to himself in some racing book—maybe even the whole book. But he'll still be dead."

"There's nothing new in that, Ali," Andreas said, sounding aggrieved. "You've always known the risks. You've never complained."

"No, I'm the perfect driver's wife, and if you have your way, maybe I'll be the perfect driver's widow one day." Her voice was quite bitter. "I'm just stating facts. Reminding you that you are alive, and that I, for one, am glad of that, even if you don't give a damn." Her eyes were wide and gray. "Life and death, Andreas. Worth thinking about, don't you think?"

Her words hung in the air.

"I asked you a question, Rudy." Andreas broke the silence. "What do you think I should do? Given that you, at least, accept my determination to come back."

Rudesheim looked him in the eye. "Come sailing."

"What?"

"Come sailing with me, my friend. Stand beside me on the deck when they strap my chair to the boards, and let the wind and the salt scrape your skin and sting your eyes!"

"And what would that achieve, except lose me valuable training time?"

Rudesheim snorted rudely. "You could work out on board as much as you like, Alessandro. The air would brace you, improve your appetite; and a little time off dry land might help broaden your mind."

Alexandra looked hopeful. "It's a wonderful idea, don't you think, Andreas?"

"What about you?"

"Don't worry about me. I have plenty to do. I'm supposed to finish a portrait of Theo Salko's daughter in time for her birthday at the beginning of October, and we've only managed a single sitting to date."

"So, will you come?"

"Last time I sailed I got sick for two days."

"Last time you sailed was with me on the Hudson," Alexandra retorted, "and your stomach was as tranquil as the Mona Lisa's smile."

"Well, Alessandro?"

"Have I a choice?"

"Bravo!" Rudesheim thumped the table. "The man has some sense."

31

Alexandra had not been so positive about anything since the day Andreas had returned from Germany for her and she had decided, standing in the pouring rain outside the pet store, that their life together had to be all or nothing!

It was Andreas himself who had unwittingly planted the seed in her head, and once it had taken root, it seemed as if it had always been there. She simply could not fathom why she hadn't thought of it before.

The two weeks Andreas spent at sea with his mentor—fourteen matchless, briny days and nights surrounded by ocean and elements in all their capriciousness—were exactly the tonic they had been intended to be. Andreas came home to Manhattan tougher, almost jocular, as determined as ever to make a comeback in time, but with a more rational approach than before. For hours he described to Alexandra the stormy days when Rudesheim had bellowed good-humoredly over the noise of the waves, and the tranquillity of lying stretched out on the blazing deck, his flesh scorching almost as dark as his eyes. His hair, too, longer and even more strikingly white-gold than usual, made him ludicrously handsome, and for an entire day and a half after his return from the high seas, the new sailor and his willing mate rose to new heights in their king-size bed.

"What was the best time, darling?" Alexandra murmured in his ear, exhausted but still exultant at his rediscovered indefatigability. "I mean, what did you enjoy most?"

"Five o'clock this morning," Andreas answered without hesitation, tightening his grasp on her narrow waist.

She laughed and nibbled him lightly on the ear. "Not with me, silly, with Rudy."

"Ah, I see, with Rudy. Let me see . . ." He lay back on the pillow, his eyelids heavy and his mouth relaxed. "I think, perhaps, *Herzchen,* the very best time was the last dinner."

"What did you eat?"

"It wasn't so much what we ate, Ali, as the evening itself. We had a large crew—three just in the galley—and I wasn't permitted to lay a finger on the food itself, but"—he smiled at the memory—"on that last evening I took charge. Ordered their every move. It was fun, sweetheart. It reminded me of the early days in London when you painted my portrait and I cooked for you, and yet it was even better."

"What made it such fun?"

He hesitated before answering. "Perhaps just being in control again, of something I enjoy."

"What did you eat?" she asked a second time.

"Lobster, naturally. Brought aboard still fighting."

"How cruel!" Alexandra dug her nails lightly into his skin as punishment, chuckling inwardly at her own hypocrisy, knowing how she, too, adored the sweet flavor of lobster meat.

"Not at all. He had a nice, peaceful death, poor beast. We laid him in a comfortable basin of fresh water, where he simply slept himself to death in a couple of hours, and then glorified him with calvados under the broiler."

"In the broiler," she corrected.

"Don't be pedantic. My command of American is admirable, as is my instinct for excellent cuisine."

Alexandra sat bolt upright, her pulses pounding. "That's it!"

"What?"

"That's the first time in I don't know how long—maybe ever—I've heard you completely and utterly passionate, bumptious even, about anything except driving."

Andreas tugged at her. "I don't know what you're talking about. I think you've had too much sex. It's affected your brain, *Herzchen.*"

"And you're calling me *Herzchen* again," she said excitedly. "You've hardly called me that since the accident."

He smiled, his expression soft. "I haven't felt this good since the accident, Ali."

She pulled away, sitting up again. "Don't change the subject. I was talking about food."

"Why? Are you hungry again?"

"No, fool—"

"You shouldn't call your husband names. You're meant to have respect. We Italians—"

"Tell my husband to stop interrupting me while I'm in the middle of a brain wave, then, and I'll respect him."

He released her. "Is this a brain wave he's going to like?"

She considered. "Perhaps not at first. But after a while, if—*when* he gives it a chance, he'll come to realize that, second to marrying him, it's the finest idea I've ever had."

The idea, the brain wave—Alexandra's masterstroke—was "Alessandro's." It took her nearly four weeks of argument, reasoning, sophistry, and downright wheedling to get Andreas even to acknowledge that it was an idea worth discussing, and another two months before he finally agreed to give it a shot.

With a little help from their new partner Rudesheim, Alessandro's was going to be Andreas's new life, his alternative world. Not a substitute for auto racing, never that. At best, it might be a spirit-saving stopgap until such time as he might beat his injuries. At worst, it might at least be second best.

New York City is, and was then, crammed almost to bursting point with eating places. Restaurants, bars and cafés opened every week of the year—a handful to acclaim, some to mild success, most to instant disaster. But occasionally, of course, one of these places struck it really lucky, and from then on in Manhattan it was rich pickings all the way. Restaurants rescued from the abyss of bankruptcy and jerked back up to street level by new owners, sometimes perked up for a while in a kind of brief resurrection, but nine times out of ten the kiss of life failed, and then it was back down into the bottomless pit.

Was there a sure recipe for success? If there was, no one was telling. In the same week that Andreas and Alexandra threw open the doors of Alessandro's, with Rudesheim biting his nails anxiously in the wings, a pair of likable young gay gourmets opened an authentic brasserie on Second Avenue. They had decorated and furnished it in style, they rose before dawn every morning to heap their kitchen with fresh, fine ingredients, they baked their own bread and personally charbroiled their meat and fish—and they failed.

Alessandro's, tucked away behind an imposing but discreet oak door at the corner of Park Avenue and 63rd Street, was a winner from the start. It was small, seating no more than fifty in comfort at any one time, and it had a menu and *carte des vins* with prices that could bring tears to the eyes of some of the wealthiest diners in the city, but New York adored it—took it, along with its glamorous proprietors, to its heart. The rich were prepared to stand in line to get a table (after word got around that slipping fifty or even a hundred dollars into the hand of Stephen del Rey, the maître d', would not help them get a table any quicker), the medium-salaried pleaded for reservations six weeks ahead of special family celebrations, and the low-paid drooled and saved so that some day they, too, could join in the fun.

It was, of course, partly because dinner at Alessandro's was almost always a feast—but mainly it was because Andreas and Alexandra were modern American heroes in the grand style. Andreas, golden boy of the racetrack, career in tatters but body only indiscernibly damaged, prepared to start from scratch; and Alexandra, devoted and beautiful, ready to abandon her own talents in order to stand beside her husband, helping him to battle injuries and disappointments, and laying new foundations. In America, a woman of proven gifts and independent status generous enough to surrender everything, even temporarily, for the greater good of wifehood, was tantamount to Joan of Arc!

In truth, until Jerry Murray, the doorman, opened the doors and saluted the first clients, the bulk of work that went into launching the new venture was undertaken by Alexandra. Andreas sat back and watched her with a mixture of pleasure, amazement, and respect. He had married a beautiful woman, soft, gentle if not pliable, and gifted, but suddenly it seemed he was wedded to a positive Titan. Alexandra had decided to collaborate with Zizi Markheim and Frank Jasper, two of Manhattan's top interior designers, on the decor for Alessandro's; but she still retained the final say, in spite of their expertise in the technique of "client-bullying," a feat almost unprecedented in New York society. During the first five months of 1962, Alexandra found time to enter her own studio no more than a dozen times; instead she spent hours on end sitting on the bare floorboards of their newly gutted restaurant-to-be, buried in brilliant, vivid silks, finding it more satisfactory to examine potential drapes in situ than in showrooms; with Zizi and Frank in tow, she trudged from furniture design houses to every retail outlet in the state in a quest for the impossible—an irreproachable dining chair. In the end, she found what she was looking for on a short trip to Florence, where a brilliant young Italian had indeed constructed perfection—a chair that, although it appeared at first to be an elegant, traditional Carver, at the touch of a concealed button metamorphosed into a luxurious recliner, enabling a diner to enjoy a digestif in complete relaxation without moving from the table.

Alessandro's was ready for its launch at the beginning of November, but they all agreed that early December was the right time, when waistlines were beginning to relax again after Thanksgiving, and the general bonhomie of Christmas was already under way.

They chose the fifth of December.

"They're going to want a party," Alexandra said for the eighth time as she, Andreas, and Rudesheim sat in their apartment checking the first-night menus they had just collected from Tiffany's.

"Then they'll be disappointed."

"Why are you so set against a party, Andreas?" asked Rudy, leaning forward in his chair.

"Because they expect it, and the unexpected is often more successful," Andreas replied slowly. "And . . ." He paused. "And because I dislike being gawped at as an object of pity."

"Hardly pity," Alexandra argued. "In their eyes, a man defeated by fate, who succeeds a second time around, whether at the same thing or another, is not to be pitied but envied. Isn't that so, Rudy?"

Rudesheim shrugged. "He knows that, Ali. But I think he may be right about the surprise element. So long as the first guests have the dinner of their lives, they won't feel cheated. They will have hoped for a party, one of their ritual Manhattan festivals, so at least they will leave still wanting more, and that's always good."

Alexandra, knowing she was beaten, got up and kissed Andreas on the cheek.

"By two to one," she said, surrendering. "No party."

They had counted without their clientele. New York restaurant society are accustomed to having their own way. They *wanted* an event—a gala night, at least—and that was what they intended to have!

"If you don't want the chore of organizing it," Zizi Markheim cajoled Andreas one afternoon, three weeks after the first night, "then let your friends take care of it. We won't let you down, you know. Just let us do things *our* way."

"Their way" meant a guest list of current Manhattan celebrities (Zizi and Frank had both intended from the first that the right people were going to have the right kind of opportunity to see their latest achievement in all its glory) including Lee Radziwill, Rudolf Nureyev, Jim Clark, Harold Robbins, astronaut John Glenn, and . . .

When the guests arrived, Alessandro's was resplendent. The walls, part oak-paneled, part mirrored, glowed with warmth, reflecting the huge, rich silks that tightly draped the ceiling, and the gleaming Christofle cutlery. The morning after, however, once the lobster mousse had been scraped off the Chinese rugs and the champagne-drenched ceiling had been ruefully surveyed, it became clear to Alexandra that all the fabrics were ruined. Thank God, she thought, the designer had attended the party and witnessed the mayhem at first hand. Otherwise he might have blamed the Alessandros and thrown a temper tantrum, refusing a second run of the precious silks that he had, after all, designed exclusively for Alexandra.

Alessandro's flourished easily for almost three months. From the moment business had actually begun, Andreas had gone into action. Alexandra had been right; here was something else he excelled at and which fulfilled him. His quality control could not be bettered. When the chef Andreas had imported from the Paris Ritz became savagely homesick in his sixth week, Andreas bought him a first-class ticket back to France, rolled up his shirt-sleeves and, with the enthusiastic aid of their staff and with a chef on temporary loan from Rudesheim's Newport restaurant, took command until the new chef arrived.

At the beginning of March, however, they hit a major snag. Through a drastic error, the inspector for the most influential restaurant guide in the city was served the first mediocre meal to come from the kitchen since the opening, and there was nothing to be done to heal the wound until the next printing of the guide.

"Shit!" said Alexandra.

"Scheisse!" echoed Andreas.

"Verfluchte Scheisse!" bellowed Rudy, stubbing out his cigar.

Alexandra eyed him with interest. "What does that mean?"

"Just more of the same." He smiled at her.

"Well, now we all know how we feel," Alexandra said, more calmly than she felt, "but what exactly are we going to *do* about it?" It was all well and good being the favorite spot with the "in" people, but New Yorkers were fickle; rumors of failure spread like the plague, and without the support of tourists and regular out-of-town diners, their goose might, before long, be well and truly cooked. That, she was sure, would spell disaster to her husband's morale.

He walked over to the corner bar. "Have a drink."

Rudesheim glanced at his watch. "You only have time for one, Andreas. You should be at the restaurant already."

Andreas poured three good glasses of Chivas Regal, frowning.

"Perhaps we need a press agent. A real ballsy New York–type agent, I mean."

"You mean sensationalism," Alexandra said. "Snappy articles about who sat in the corner booth with who at Alessandro's last night."

"We don't have booths."

"You know what I mean, though, don't you. I thought we wanted Alessandro's to be classy. You were the one who said it— that what Manhattan needed was a truly top Zurich-style restaurant. They seem to exist forever without a word of scandal, let alone advertising." She spoke the last word with distaste.

"But we're not in Zurich, Ali." Andreas knocked back his drink and went to pour himself another.

"Have you given up training?" Rudesheim asked disapprovingly.

"Of course not. I'm just concerned."

"Chivas won't solve anything."

"It helps me think. Stop acting like my conscience, Rudy."

"The two of you stop it, please." Alexandra looked worried. "Bickering between ourselves isn't going to help at all. What we need to do is to think for a while. We'll come up with something. It isn't as if we aren't fully booked for the next two weeks."

"No, but we were booked up for six weeks a month or so back."

"Well, I know what I'm going to do," she said, getting up determinedly. "I'm going in my studio to paint. And don't come and interrupt me either. And I'll stay there until I come up with either a decent piece of work or a good idea, or preferably both!"

"Good," Rudesheim said emphatically. With one hand he slipped his chair into gear, finishing his drink with the other. "Will you be so kind, Andreas, as to help me to the elevator. I'm going back to Newport. Maybe a little sea air will clear my mind, send me a brilliant solution to our small problems."

"Small?" Andreas queried wryly.

Rudesheim gave him a cool stare. "We are all three of us living, are we not? We have our eyes, our ears, and our taste buds, do we not? We none of us need the funds, do we?" He smiled. "Yes, my friend, our problems are very small. And what is more, they will be overcome."

Alexandra came to him and kissed him warmly on the cheek. "Is the car outside?"

"Sure. My driver is a good, patient man." He patted her hand.

"Tell this impatient boy not to worry so much. It's bad for him, and bad for you."

She laughed. "I will, don't *you* worry, Rudy." She walked alongside as Andreas pushed the wheelchair toward the front door. "Go find us a fairy godfather or something. After all, Newport's where we found you again."

The "fairy godfather" they sought was not in Rhode Island, however. He was, surprisingly, much closer at hand.

32

Daniel, Roland, and Kate worked like dervishes for two years. The *Sensualist* guide was on the bookshelves in time for Thanksgiving of 1961, and reassessments already needed for the paperback publication timed to follow the subsequent spring. While Daniel and Roland neglected the office, eating and drinking their way through the city, Fanny hovered close by, never flying farther than Chicago, in case Kate needed an urgent executive decision. Once Daniel was ensconced in his apartment, writing and interviewing illustrators, Roland assumed his official role as manager of Harper and Stone, and Fanny was at liberty to retreat to Europe, only returning to New York to organize the hard-sell promotions.

In the weeks preceding hardback publication, interviews with Dan Stone—photographed by Milton Greene on the flat roof of his apartment building wearing a bath towel, tasting beluga caviar from a silver cocaine spoon and looking every inch the tender brigand, his gentle brown eyes belying the semicircular scar and sharp beard—were printed in *Vogue, Cosmopolitan, Good Housekeeping,* and *Time* magazine. He was invited onto the *Today* show, and took part in a pre-Thanksgiving audience phone-in show on WOR radio. When the first copies of the book came into Doubleday on Fifth Avenue, Daniel was on display for six hours, signing each purchased book with a warm smile and a handshake.

Just after the paperback was published in May 1962, when the Milton Greene photographs were strung through every bookstore in the city, NBC came forward with an amazing offer—his own show! To be called simply *The Gourmets,* the project was aimed at a midmorning audience and designed to blend gourmet cooking with star names. In August, on a hellish set with a defective air-conditioning system, they taped the pilot show, with Lucille Ball showing Daniel how to make her favorite sauces and Jerry Lewis creating chaos with desserts. The show culminated in the three of them serving up the results to a specially invited clientèle at "21." The pilot was a runaway—the NBC switchboard was jammed with calls for over an hour after the show went on air, and Daniel was signed for a series of six to be networked coast-to-coast the following season.

Preparation for the next guide got under way. The first American book, with its undertones of sexuality, had brought Dan Stone to the public's attention; now Fanny and Daniel, employing more inspectors because of Daniel's decreasing anonymity, set their sights on respectability and the establishment. That was the way, they realized, that the soft beige–covered guides would in time become *the* ones that visitors to the city, and even the natives themselves, would reach for when they wanted dinner.

On December 6, Daniel had read the review in the *Times* for the newly opened Park Avenue restaurant, Alessandro's. *Gourmet* had followed promptly with raves.

Five months later, Fanny stood before his desk, holding up an open book, quiet triumph in her eyes.

"They bombed." She smiled. "He needs you."

That evening, Daniel went into his library and reached for his faithful thesaurus of quotations. He flicked through the pages—*I hate it in friends when they come too late to help.*

He chose an evening when Kate discovered that Alessandro would be out of town. Nevertheless, when he and Roland were ushered to their corner table by Stephen del Rey, Daniel's pulses were throbbing painfully. Although Daniel had insisted on conducting this critique personally, he had insisted to Fanny that they would play the game to the last degree, without favoritism, but now he found himself praying that the new chef Alessandro had brought in was tonight at the peak of his powers.

His prayers were answered. He ordered *potage crème de faisan* for his first course while Roland consumed a *terrine aux trois poissons; turbot au champagne rose* for his entrée, *canard sauvage aux cerises* for Roland's; for dessert they shared *soufflé Alessandro* and a *tarte chaude aux pommes.* They drank very dry Pouilly Fuissé, Daniel consumed a half bottle of Veuve Clicquot and Roland the same of Pomerol, and they declined the wide selection of dessert wines offered by the sommelier. When they left the restaurant, Roland's round face was rosy and cherubic, his eyes more myopic than ever; and Daniel was afloat, his senses sailing aloft high over Manhattan as he hurried home, his fingers itching to start writing his critique.

The day after copy had been mailed by the publishers to the forty restaurants included in *The Stone Gourmet Guide for the Sensualist,* Kate buzzed Daniel in his office.

"Andreas Alessandro on line one." She sounded excited.

Daniel paused. "Take a message, please."

A moment later she buzzed again. "Mr. Alessandro said he understands how busy you must be, but that he and Mrs. Alessandro would appreciate an opportunity to meet you."

"Did he make a suggestion?"

"Lunch or dinner at your convenience any day this week."

Daniel took a minute. "Call him back, Kate, when you have time, and say that tomorrow evening is best for me."

He stood up, for no reason in particular other than that it seemed impossible to remain seated. His office was quite silent, sealed off from the frenetic world outside as only a top-rental Manhattan high-rise executive office can be. His own breathing had all but ceased.

He looked down at his diary, open on the desk. Tomorrow would be September 4, 1963. He did not remember the exact date that other September, twenty years before, when Andreas Alessandro had saved not only his future but also his faith in humanity, but it was close enough.

He wondered if Alessandro would remember.

It was a quarter past nine when Jerry Murray, the doorman, ushered Daniel from beneath the royal blue canopy into Alessandro's.

Inside, under the newly designed fresh, warmly autumnal silk ceiling, the patrons already seated at tables and bar stirred slightly, like the smallest ripple on a quiet pond, but not a lacquered hair was turned; the Park Avenue set knew a celebrity when they saw one, but were disciplined like no other coterie in the art of polite nonchalance.

"Mr. Stone." Stephen del Rey materialized elegantly. "Mr. and Mrs. Alessandro are awaiting you."

He led the way to a table tucked in the farthest corner of the small room—as in every well-run restaurant, there was a table comfortable enough, but discreetly enough placed, to seat a proprietor who wished to dine "at home" but in peace.

"Mr. Stone, welcome."

Andreas Alessandro rose in greeting, held out his right hand, and grasped Daniel's firmly. Their eyes met. In Andreas's there was no hint of recognition.

"May I present my wife, Alexandra."

Ali Alessandro sat in half shadow, so that the gray-green eyes, made so much of by society writers, were dimmed, but there was no mistaking the beautifully drawn bone structure and clear skin, accentuated more than ever by her new and fashionable hairstyle, the heavy ebony strands cut in a jaw-length casual bob, with the forehead partly concealed by a soft fringe.

"How do you do." Daniel made a slight bow and they, too, shook hands.

"I'm so very glad to meet you," Alexandra said in her quiet, low voice, watching him keenly. "Please sit down. We had two places laid, as we weren't sure if you might bring a friend."

The maître d'hotel removed the fourth setting, and the men sat down simultaneously.

Daniel touched the fabric on the arm of his Carver. "I have to compliment you on these chairs."

"Glad you like them," Andreas said.

"It's no good!" Alexandra burst out unexpectedly. "I am going to tell Mr. Stone right away that his three red hearts may well have hauled Alessandro's from the brink of the chasm, and that we're eternally grateful." She heaved a sigh of relief and grinned. "Thank God that's said. Now we can simply enjoy the rest of the evening."

"Ali," Andreas scolded, "you've embarrassed Mr. Stone. It may not be etiquette to say such things in public."

"Rot!" she said amiably. "He knows perfectly well that's why we begged him to come for dinner—or at least one of the reasons," she added.

Daniel laughed, relieved. "Fortunately the Stone guides haven't existed long enough to demand such rigid etiquette. And please," he said, warming to the strangers beside him, "my name is Dan."

"So what brought you to New York, Dan, when you could have stayed in Paris?" Andreas asked almost two hours later. "In my case, it was my American wife. What's your excuse?"

"I think Dan must have spent time here in the past. His English is too good to be the result of school—or have you lived in Britain?" Alexandra swung her head to face Daniel.

"Shall we say that—there's something of the gypsy in me," Daniel prevaricated, smiling at his hostess. Ali Alessandro was not the static, queenly beauty he'd thought at first; she was highly mobile, a rhythmic delight. Not in a restless way—her hands, unless employing a knife, fork, spoon, or glass, reposed easily in her lap—

but her face, her head, those eyes, darted back and forth as she turned her attention from her husband to her guest to her food, the black hair constantly falling forward and being pushed impatiently back behind the ears to reveal, involuntarily, her pear-shaped diamond earclips.

"We're being shamefully inquisitive," she said suddenly. "Forgive us, Dan. It's simply that you are, as you must realize, a most interesting man."

"And a very successful one," Andreas added curiously. "And apparently, almost without a past."

Daniel shrugged lightly. "Believe me, my past, unlike your own, is not comparable with my present."

Andreas darkened slightly, and Daniel saw that the nerves severed in his accident were still too raw to touch carelessly. He made a mental note.

"Coffee, everyone?" Alexandra asked, lifting the atmosphere. A waiter began to pour from a *cafetière* almost before she finished speaking.

"May I change the topic, Ali," Daniel suggested, "and ask about your career? I've heard rumors of new and exciting commissions. Is it true about Washington?"

Alexandra nodded, blushing. It was a fortnight since she had first heard from the White House, but the weight of the honor bestowed in that invitation, and the impressive future potential implied, still staggered her. The mantle of responsibility for Alessandro's had slipped from her shoulders to Andreas's once the restaurant had opened, although she still took a lively interest and sat in on all major discussions with him and Rudesheim. But since the early spring she had restarted work in earnest. There was a new sense of calm in her life. Her husband's calamity had, in a way, restored him to her, whole and out of danger, and the three years of trauma had taught her priorities; her concentration was more intense, her eyes more observant, her fingers stronger and defter than before. And for Ali Alessandro, modern Manhattan heroine, there was no shortage of commissions.

"They're selecting from a group of artists," she said modestly. "Nothing is decided."

"And you're not saying who the subject is?" Daniel probed. "Is it the President?"

She laughed. "No."

"The First Lady?"

"I wouldn't tell you if it was," she insisted. "Now stop prodding, please."

Daniel grinned and looked at Andreas. "What about you? Where will the next Alessandro's be opening?"

Andreas raised an eyebrow. "Isn't one enough?"

"Of course not. Not for a man of energy." Just in time he prevented himself from saying "man of speed," but the implication was there. "Fanny and I—by the way, I do hope you will meet her soon—have been hovering between downtown and Washington. Are we close?"

"As locations for a new restaurant?"

Daniel nodded.

"Isn't it sensible to cement the success of one before branching out?"

"Without being egotistical, I hope that three red hearts will be enough to cement anything."

"Not if standards are allowed to drop."

"Obviously. What about it, then? Are we to be restricted to a single Alessandro's?"

"Maybe." Andreas shrugged. "Maybe not."

"Another enigma," Alexandra joked. "The three of us do have two things in common—healthy curiosity and an overdose of discretion."

"Perhaps we all enjoy mystery," Daniel suggested.

"That sounds too furtive. As if we had secrets to hide."

"Maybe Dan does have secrets."

Alexandra shot Andreas a warning glance. "There's nothing sinister in keeping one's counsel. It's good European reserve. You should know—you have plenty of it when it suits your convenience." Her eyes glinted. "I think Dan may be right. One restaurant doesn't seem enough to occupy you, or certainly not your imagination. I'm sorry," she said to Daniel.

"For what?" He smiled. "All this mutual interest only signifies that we'd like to know more about each other. Is that so bad?" He looked at his watch. "I should say good night. It's late, I have a breakfast meeting, and you probably want to check up on things behind the scenes."

"No time for a cognac?" Andreas made a slight gesture with one hand, and del Rey appeared.

"Thanks, but no," Daniel refused politely. "A perfect lily requires no gilding."

"Do you need a cab? Jerry will get one for you. Is it still raining, Stephen?"

"It let up a while ago, Mr. Alessandro."

Daniel rose. "I'd like to walk a little." He leaned forward, took

Alexandra's hand and raised it to his lips. "I hope we meet again
soon."

She smiled. "I'm sure we will."

Andreas got up. "I'll see you out."

The sidewalk smelled fresher after the heavy rainfall. The cabs,
which half an hour earlier must have been rare as gold dust, now
rolled slowly up and down Park Avenue hunting custom.

Andreas shook Daniel's hand strongly. "It was good of you to
accept the invitation, Dan. I know these things can sometimes be
awkward, but—"

"A man has to eat somewhere."

"Next time, let's make it neutral territory, okay? Alessandro's is
excellent, I know, but I enjoy ringing the changes."

Daniel stared at him. "I'm sure you do."

Andreas returned the look thoughtfully.

"I'll be in touch," Daniel said, and walked away.

After about a hundred yards he stopped on the corner of 62nd
Street and stole a backward glance. Alessandro still stood where
they'd parted, under the canopy of his restaurant. Breath escaped
his lips like a narrow ribbon of steam, and he was motionless,
watching Daniel.

"You didn't tell him?" Fanny, exasperated, stubbed out one of the
long, thin cigars she'd recently taken to smoking.

"Of course not." Dan gave an ironical laugh. "Just like that?
You thought I'd tell the man right there and then, in front of his
wife?"

"Why not?"

"It wasn't suitable."

They were in the bar at the Sherry Netherland, sitting at a small
corner table, their privacy protected by the loud buzz of lunchtime
gossip.

"Dan, sweetheart." Fanny leaned closer, her expression earnest.
"I don't understand this at all. It isn't as if you were going to give
him bad news."

"I know that. But—"

"It's a reunion, that's all. Oh, don't look like that, I'm not un-
derplaying the importance of this for you, far from it."

"Then you ought to understand that I need to time it properly."

"But what are you waiting for? It isn't a love affair, Dan. You're
not a young girl who has to tell her boyfriend she's pregnant but
longs to hear him declare love before she confesses the awful
truth."

He glared at her.

"You're overreacting, Dan . . . I'm sorry," she said helplessly. "I do want to understand." She chewed at a finger of one of her long black suede gloves. "Maybe if we shift the emphasis. Let's forget that you decided, for whatever reason, not to expose yourself to Alessandro. What's he like? How did you feel?"

"When I first saw him?"

"Uh huh. Start there."

"Like I was meeting a stranger for the very first time."

"So you were."

"That's not true, Fanny. What is true is that it was perfectly logical that I should feel that way. Adults seldom resemble their childhood photographs, after all." A champagne cork popped at a nearby table. "I had hoped, I think, for instant recognition."

"On both sides?"

"Of course not. No, I'd hoped to see something in his face that I could grab on to right away, but when that didn't happen, in a weird way I think I actually began to relax. It was as if we stood a better chance of—of developing a friendship. A genuine friendship, not something based solely on a thing that happened twenty years ago." He took a sip of his martini. "Do you begin to understand?"

She softened. "I do."

"That doesn't mean I didn't keep on searching for a point of identification. All through dinner, I found myself staring at the man, trying to locate the nine-year-old who stole, who broke God only knows how many laws, who drove a giant tractor through the blackout, for me."

"But you didn't find him?"

"The boy?" Daniel shrugged. "Brief flashes. In the eyes, of course, when he laughed. Strange how age drops away when people are happy. And I remembered the shock of the contrast between that dazzling hair and those coal-black eyes—he's a striking man."

"What about Ali?"

"Everything a man could dream of. More beautiful even, or perhaps just more interesting, than her press shots. Highly intelligent. We know she's very talented." He grinned suddenly. "And I liked her."

"So I gather," Fanny said dryly.

"Alessandro's hard to read. His racing days aren't behind him yet. I don't know what his physical condition is like—there are no obvious scars, but he's stiff. In his head I'm sure he's still out there on the track, or planning to be. The restaurant has surprised him. It suits him, being *le patron.*" He chuckled. "I told him he should open more."

"I trust you didn't promise him red hearts for everything he decides to dabble in?"

"I did not. But I doubt, somehow, that he 'dabbles' in anything."

Fanny lit another cigar. "I had this pegged three different ways, you know. One, you'd get cold feet, back off completely. Two, you'd come straight out with it, and there'd have been drinks and strong masculine hugs all round, and you'd both have come away with warm glows and probably have exchanged Christmas cards for the next ten or twenty years."

"And three?"

"The man would make as much of an impression as the boy did, which would make life more complicated." She blew smoke over his head. "Both Alessandros seem to have made an impression, in fact, don't they?"

"They do," he agreed.

"You look smug about it."

"Smug?"

"Mildly." She signaled a waiter to bring the check to sign. "I have to run. I'm meeting Robin at Bergdorf's."

"How is she?"

"Busy. Have you made plans to meet Alessandro again?"

"Not yet. I said I'd be in touch."

She initialed the check and rose. Two waiters hurried over to pull out the table for her. She planted a kiss on his cheek. "Don't wait too long."

Daniel called Alessandro's ten days later and left a message asking Andreas to telephone him. It was forty-eight hours before his call was returned.

"I was in Europe."

"No problem." Daniel suggested dinner, this time at Sardi's. There were few places he enjoyed in the city that would raise enough hubbub to cover the conversation he hoped to keep private, and though Sardi's was always populated by celebrity watchers, heads that might turn when Alessandro and Stone sat down together were bound to refocus attention the moment an actor or movie star arrived.

Alessandro was tentative. "This may be a tough week to orga-

nize. My wife's flying down to Washington in the morning, and
I'm—"

"Just the two of us, then?" He sensed Alessandro's surprise at
his casual but implicit pressure. "Or we could leave it—"

"No, let's aim for Thursday. If that's good for you."

Just for an instant Daniel wondered if plain business sense was
causing the other man to juggle his schedule, but as if reading his
thoughts, Andreas added, "I enjoyed our meeting. I'll look forward to Thursday."

Sardi's was at low ebb when Daniel arrived just before ten o'clock
that Thursday night, though as soon as the theaters emptied, it
would become a mob scene. Andreas had not yet arrived, but
Daniel elected to go directly to their table rather than wait at the
bar on the upper level.

He was ordering his second martini twenty minutes later when
he noticed his guest at the entrance. He was not alone.

With a flash of instant recall, Daniel recognized the other man
immediately.

Automatically, he rose in welcome. Roberto Alessandro was still
the gentle giant of his memories, the rolled-up shirt sleeves of the
gentleman farmer replaced by a superbly tailored suit, the dark
hair half snow-white, the features craggier and lined, but otherwise apparently unchanged.

"I tried to reach you, Dan, but I was too late," Andreas was
saying. "I had no idea Papa was flying in today. He likes to surprise us." He stopped. "I'm sorry. This is my father, Roberto
Alessandro. He arrived from Zurich two hours ago without warning and called me from the airport." He touched his father's arm.
"Papa, this is Dan Stone."

"I am very glad to meet you, sir," Daniel said clearly, his mind
in turmoil.

"Delighted," Roberto responded. His black eyes, so like his
son's, but warmer, less veiled, pierced Daniel's, and his great right
hand pumped Daniel's suddenly nerveless fingers. "Will you forgive this imposition?" he pleaded with great charm. "I told my
son I could easily dine alone or with friends, but he insisted I join
you. I said you might wish to discuss business or personal matters,
but—"

"I shouldn't dream of it, sir," Daniel said more calmly than he
felt. "Please sit down." He summoned a waiter for a third place
setting. "What would you both like to drink?"

A fresh bottle of Chivas Regal was opened at the table and

another martini brought for Daniel. Polite small talk began—the weather in Zurich, the rate of exchange between the U.S. dollar and the Swiss franc, Alexandra's excitement in her burgeoning career, Roberto's recent visit to Britain to purchase new equipment. . . .

"Have you been to England, Mr. Stone?"

"I lived in London for a few months, Herr Alessandro. A most enjoyable experience."

"Yes," Roberto said, beaming, "but damp." His gaze was penetrating. "It's curious, but you seem familiar somehow to me, Mr. Stone."

Andreas laughed. "Dan's a celebrity, Papa. You'll have seen his face in magazines, or on television."

Roberto nodded slowly. "That must be it, and yet . . ." He shrugged. "My mind must be slipping. Old age creeps up on us."

But he was not an old man. Daniel was gripped by a cold, unpleasant sensation. His plans were in shreds, the informality he'd hoped for was ruled out. The evening would, he had postulated, if the new friendship had unfolded cordially, have been topped by his revelation—no drama or embarrassment, just an unlocking of memories with gentle warmth and enduring gratitude. But now that was impossible. Alessandro's father had, he knew, been a helpless bystander twenty years ago, a kind, fundamentally generous man dominated by his wife; but Daniel remembered Anna Alessandro's iciness, her distaste for his Jewishness, and her fear of involvement, and her shadow cast a gloom over his dinner table.

The captain took their orders, and Daniel was aware that he spoke normally and with confidence. He selected the right wines mechanically, but he had no memory of what he ordered, and all the time his mind twisted and turned, seeking escape . . .

He rose suddenly. Andreas and Roberto glanced up in surprise as the table jolted and their drinks spilled.

"I'm sorry. I—I must—" Daniel's hands clenched into two fists that he thrust into his pockets. "Please excuse me." He strode from the table, walked through the din and clutter of the ever-filling restaurant, ignoring the polite inquiry of the captain, sweeping past the doorman, through the doors, and out into the street.

The night was chilly for September, but dry and still. Cars whipped past swiftly, tires whirring, the traffic light now that the theater crowds had poured into restaurants and bars. Two couples strolled side by side, arms linked, taking up the whole width of the sidewalk, laughing, their voices low and happy. On the opposite side of the street a vagrant searched a trash can and came up with nothing.

A small sound by his feet roused Daniel. He looked down and saw a little black street cat regarding him with interest. He crouched down and held out a hand. The cat sniffed and began to rub its hard small head against his arm.

"So what do you think, cat?" The animal miaowed and twined its scrawny body against his legs. "Why am I out here on the sidewalk, instead of sitting in that nice warm place being honest with one of the best friends a man ever had?" He shifted his position slightly, and the cat skittered away, eyes yellowing suspiciously. "No, don't run off, cat. That won't help any, you running onto the street that way, it'll just get you knocked down by some car." Soothed by his voice, the animal relented and returned.

The doors behind him opened, and a couple came out of Sardi's, casting a curious glance at Daniel as he squatted there with the stray.

"Let's make a deal," Daniel whispered. "You tell me if I should go back in there and straighten things out before they get out of hand, and I'll get you a piece of fish." The cat sat silently and gazed up at him. Daniel chuckled. "You prefer crab? Or lobster maybe? I don't know if they have lobster in there tonight, but I'll try and swing soft-shell crab for you. How about it?"

The cat remained silent as the grave.

"Right, this is it, cat. Do I leave right now, get in a cab—run away?" He held his breath. The cat was still speechless. "Or do I go back and spill the beans?" He closed his eyes.

The cat craned its head, licked his hand with its rough tongue, and miaowed.

Daniel opened his eyes and smiled. Relief swamped him like balm. "Thanks, cat. I won't forget you for this." He scratched the top of its head and straightened. The doors opened again, and he put out a hand quickly to stop them closing.

He looked down. "Crab if there's no lobster." Then he went back inside.

Roberto and Andreas had begun their starters, uncertain whether or not their host intended returning. They looked vaguely apologetic.

"I'm sorry," Daniel said, sitting down.

Andreas looked at him. "You okay?"

Roberto nodded. "He's okay."

Daniel took a sip of the white wine that had been poured into his glass. "I have something to say," he began, "but first I must speak to the captain." He looked around and signaled him over.

"Are you ready for your hors d'oeuvre now, Mr. Stone?"

"Thank you, yes. But I wondered, do you have any lobster tonight?"

"Not that I would recommend to you, sir, to be frank. Only lobster tails, and very small."

"That's fine."

"Is that to replace your starter, Mr. Stone, or your entrée?" He looked perturbed. "They really are very small."

"They're not for me." Daniel smiled. "There's a small black cat sitting outside the restaurant. They're for him."

"Oh, I *see!*" The captain appeared relieved, as if guests at Sardi's often tethered cats, like horses before Henry Ford's day, outside the restaurant. The idiosyncrasies of celebrities, within reason, were to be humored, it was a house rule. "Is it *your* cat, sir?" he asked confidentially. "We could have him brought inside. The attendant in the ladies' lounge would probably take care of him."

Daniel grinned. "I don't think that this cat would take kindly to being hauled off the street, though it's a generous suggestion. No, just have someone take some lobster tails—out of their shells, of course—in a napkin, and put them down on the sidewalk. And add them to my check, naturally."

"Naturally. However, Mr. Stone, you may not be aware of it, but there are city ordinances forbidding—"

"Would you prefer me to do it myself?"

"No, of course not." The man swallowed. "Lobster tails. For the cat. Right away." He escaped.

Both Alessandros seemed equal to the situation.

"If the regular man had been on duty," Andreas said, "there'd have been no fuss at all."

"*Is* it your cat?" Roberto was enchanted. "Imagine, Andi!" He pounded a fist on the table. "If the cats in Napoli were only fortunate enough to have Dan Stone as their protector—lobster for every meal!" He roared with laughter.

"You said you have something to say, Dan?" Andreas prompted curiously.

"That's right." Daniel took another sip of wine. The alcohol content began to blend encouragingly with the five parts gin contributed by the bartender to the martinis he'd drunk before his walk in the cool air.

He kept his tone low and even. "Herr Alessandro," he began,

"a little while ago you mentioned that you thought my face familiar."

Roberto nodded.

"You were right."

"You mean you two have met before?" Andreas broke in.

Daniel waited a moment. He was no longer in the least afraid. "Not just your father and I, Andreas." His skin began to burn a little; he was suddenly impatient for the truth to be out. "Do you remember 1943?"

Andreas looked confused. He began to say that he didn't remember, why should he? And then he stopped. "In 1943? I was— eight, no, nine years old, and the war was four."

His father gave a sharp, involuntary breath. Andreas looked at him. "Papa? Do you know what he's talking about?"

Roberto sat very still, his face impassive. "Don't you remember, Andi?" His voice was so deep it rumbled. "Think harder."

"My face, Andreas. Look at it." Daniel's heart pounded. "Under my left eye." The other man looked, leaning closer. "Now do you remember '43? A certain September night?"

"I don't believe it," Andreas whispered. For an instant he turned pale, and then he flushed with excitement. "I can't believe it! Daniel? Daniel *Silberstein?*" He half rose from his chair, then sank back down. "Papa, it's him—our hero of '43, our own refugee!"

"Hero?" Daniel laughed harshly, incredulously.

"Of course!" Andreas turned to his father and clutched his arm. "Papa, you remember how for months we used to whisper about him, wondering what happened to him after that night?"

Roberto nodded. "And now we know." His eyes spoke volumes. "Dan Stone."

"Why did you change your name?"

"Lots of people changed their names when they came to America."

"I didn't."

"You're not a Jew."

The evasion seemed to satisfy Andreas. "My God, I still don't believe this. And you recognized him, Papa?"

"No, no. Not in a thousand years. Your hero was a starving ragamuffin, all brown eyes and fear, and the cut you gave him— which he still carries. But I never recognized him. He just felt familiar."

Daniel shook his head. "That's the second time you used the word *hero* about me."

"Why not? After Ascari and Caracciola—but you were real, alive."

"I was a refugee. I was running, afraid—"

"You were terrified! And you let me help you." Andreas's eyes glazed suddenly, his consciousness digging deeply into the past. "I haven't thought about Daniel Silberstein—about you—for a long, long time; but whenever I used to remember, to wonder, and rejoice over that night, it was *that* which stuck out. You let me help. You trusted me. *Me*—the first time ever that I had an identity of my own, I wasn't just the child of my parents—" He broke off and looked hard at his father. "You understood that, didn't you, Papa?"

"I did."

"My mother didn't. She couldn't. To expose her family to any threat, to any disgrace, was unthinkable," Andreas explained to Daniel. "I thought, for a long while, that I hated her for it."

"But you didn't," Daniel said quickly.

"Of course not. They say that hate and love are related, but I don't believe it. I didn't always like my mother, but I loved her."

Roberto stirred suddenly. "At the risk of giving the unfortunate captain the impression that we are *all* crazy, I am going to leave."

"But Papa, your dinner—"

"Herr Alessandro, there's no need—"

"Yes, there is." Roberto looked intently at Daniel. "This is a reunion."

"For all three of us," Daniel protested.

"For the two of you," Roberto insisted. "I guess that is what you had in mind for tonight, and I walked in on your subtlety clumsily."

"You were hardly to know, sir."

"That's true. But now that I do know the truth, I think the least I can do is to make a graceful exit." He smiled. "Please don't feel that I'm not happy to see you. The very fact that you are here in New York, and such a great success, fills me with joy. I hope very much to have an opportunity to meet you again, Mr. Stone." Roberto rose to his feet. "But not tonight."

The two younger men stood too. "Do you have your keys to the apartment, Papa?" Andreas asked. Roberto nodded and they embraced quickly.

"Good night, Daniel," Roberto said softly. *"Auf wiedersehen."*

Daniel took his hand. "I hope so."

They sat again, and in a few moments the captain, together with the waiter bringing Daniel's starter, approached, his expression apprehensive.

"Is everything satisfactory, Mr. Stone?"

"Without doubt." Daniel smiled. "Unfortunately, one of my guests had to leave, so we are, as originally planned, à deux."

"Very good, sir."

Andreas chuckled as the captain slid smoothly away. "In the past," he said, "I might have felt bad, but at my place, almost every night, guests arrive and depart with as much consistency as the weather. One grows accustomed to it." He stared suddenly at Daniel. "We have a great deal to talk about. My father was right to leave."

Daniel eyed him curiously. "You aren't offended by my deviousness?"

"Why should I be?" Andreas shrugged. "You acted cautiously, not dishonestly. We might have disliked each other on sight, and then this would have been a sour reunion."

"A woman would not understand so easily."

Andreas laughed. "Certainly not. But then, isn't that the great thing about masculine friendship? Understanding without the constant need for explanation. Better eat your prosciutto," he said lightly. "The management, however long-suffering, can only stand so much."

Daniel's knife slit a long sliver of the pale raw ham. "Who goes first?" he asked. "I mean, twenty years—how do we go about it? And how much do we want to know?"

"Prosciutto first. Then you." Andreas leaned closer, black eyes glittering. "I last saw you, Daniel Silberstein, or Dan Stone, or whoever you are, in a dark, muddy field near Emmenbrücke, in 1943. For months I think I thought about you almost every day, wondering if you were free or in prison, or even if you were still alive." He picked up his wineglass and drank some of the crisp, cold Antinori. "You go first."

It was after two in the morning when they were ready to leave the restaurant, and both men, having drunk, talked, and listened exhaustively, were a little unsteady on their feet.

"No cab, Mr. Stone?" the doorman asked.

"We'll walk a little way, and then pick one up," Daniel told him, and put a ten-dollar bill in his hand.

They had gone a few yards up the street in companionable silence when they heard the miaowing behind them.

"Your cat?" Andreas laughed. The small black animal curved itself around Daniel's left leg in response.

Daniel bent down. "Hello again, cat," he said softly. "Enjoy your supper?"

"I trust your lobster tails weren't too small," Andreas murmured.

"I owe you one," Daniel told the cat. "You were right."

"You already gave him supper. That not enough?"

Daniel straightened. "Apparently not. This is a bright cat—above average."

Andreas nodded gravely. "Good night, smart puss."

When they reached Broadway, however, the little animal was still at Daniel's heels, its purring penetrating even the late-night traffic hum.

"He seems to think he's a dog," Andreas said, "and he certainly doesn't have a home to go to, judging by the state of him. What are you going to do?"

Daniel chewed his lip. "Get in a cab?"

"And dump him? You won't do that. He might get knocked down or picked up by the cops."

"For what? Loitering with intent?"

Andreas nodded soberly again. "Happens all the time in New York."

"But I live in an apartment. This is a street cat."

"I have a feeling you'll work that out between you."

On impulse, Daniel bent down and scooped the creature into his arms. "I'll bet he has fleas. I'll have to find a veterinarian."

Andreas scanned the street. "Better find a cab first. You can drop me off, and then you two can get properly acquainted." He sighted a cab and waved it down, then turned and looked at Daniel. "It's incredible, you know. I keep staring at you, trying to find the ragamuffin my father described, and I see you, Dan Stone, instead. And my only genuine point of recognition is *that*—" He reached out and touched the old scar tissue under Daniel's left eye.

Daniel smiled. "Your first gift."

"That's right." Andreas yanked open the cab door abruptly, his eyes unexpectedly moist. "Let's the three of us get in the cab, Dan."

33

"Why won't you invite him to dinner?" Alexandra stood barefoot in the middle of her studio floor, pummeling a large lump of clay into submission.

"I'm not surprised they loved you in Washington," Andreas said from the corner where he perched awkwardly on a wooden stool, the only place he was allowed to sit while his wife worked, and there only under sufferance. "You're not a bad artist, and you're much sexier than Picasso."

"That," said Alexandra, "is a matter of opinion."

"I didn't know you liked bald men."

"Adore them." She rubbed at her cheek with the back of one hand, and several tendrils of hair worked their way loose from the green ribbon she'd tied them back with. "I've always said your hair is an exaggeration," she said critically.

"It's not long."

"The color, fool. It's what the French call *outré*—over the top." She smiled angelically and slapped the clay again. "And don't dare come near me," she added as the stool tilted. "I asked you a question, and I'd like an answer."

"To what?"

"Why haven't you, or rather why haven't we, invited Dan Stone to dinner?"

Andreas shrugged. "I already told you. He eats for a living. It'd be like inviting the attorney general to do jury duty for fun. Dan has more edible masterpieces served to him any one month than I do, and I own one of the best restaurants in Manhattan, for Christ's sake."

"So if *we* cook, it'll make a change." She made a face at him. "I don't know, Andreas—invite him for cocktails—or for nothing, I don't care. He'll start thinking I don't like him."

"Of course he won't."

Something occurred to her. "Or maybe he doesn't much care for me? Has he said that?"

"You're crazy. He loved you—you know he did—just like everyone else."

"The man's only met me twice, Andreas. He can't really have formed an opinion, can he?"

Andreas slid off the stool, groaning, and rubbed his backside. "I'm going to buy you a chair, Ali. This is an insult to human flesh."

"You will not, or I'll throw it out," she threatened. "This is a place of work, not a salon for layabouts."

"I have comfortable chairs in my office," he grumbled.

"That's different. You work in a restaurant. Stop grouching."

"Okay." He came closer and stroked her hair. "Do you remember London?" He kissed her neck and tried to undo the knot in her ribbon.

"Leave that alone, you sex maniac. I have to get this stuff covered or it'll spoil."

He ignored her. "You had a wonderful couch in your studio there, so old and battered the horsehair lanced your skin when we laid down on it. You weren't such a hotshot on concentration in those days, I seem to recall. . . ."

"I'm a married woman now," Alexandra argued vainly, but some of the clay fell from her fingers onto the floor and she wiped her hands on the old silk shirt of his that had become her favorite working outfit. "I've made it a rule," she said faintly. "No love in the studio."

"You make too many rules, *Herzchen*." He unfastened the top button of the shirt, nibbled her right ear, then pulled away a little, peering at her eyes. "Good," he said smugly. "They're green." His fingers found one of her nipples beneath the silk and caressed it, shutting his own eyes almost reverently as he began the sweet business of taking precedence over his wife's beloved work.

"They're not green, they're still gray, I can feel them."

"Oh, God, but you taste good," he murmured, licking the skin of her left breast with the tip of his tongue.

With a last halfhearted attempt, she tried to push him away. "You've changed the subject again. I wanted to talk about Dan Stone."

"Will you shut the fuck up about Dan," he ordered. He tugged a large white sheet from a pile of canvases and threw it on the floor, pulling her down with him on top of it. He raised himself up on one elbow, and with hands that were at once so tender and yet so commandingly firm that she envied them as sculptor's hands, began to trace the long curving contour of her right side, pushing the silk shirt away. "You know," he said wickedly, "I could go and fetch a mirror for you."

She clutched at his arm. "Don't you dare leave me now!" she frowned. "What do you want a mirror for, for heaven's sake?"

He rolled over on top of her and laughed into her face. "For you to get your facts straight, darling. Your eyes are as green as I've ever seen them." He kissed her open mouth hard, then drew away again in mock alarm. "The clay!" he whispered. "It'll spoil."

"Fuck the clay," she said.

"It's a pity Ali couldn't come this evening," Daniel said two weeks later, handing Andreas a coffee cup and lighting Fanny's thin cigar for her.

"Thank you." Andreas put the cup and saucer on the small table beside his armchair. "It is a pity, but when Ali gets really hooked on something, she's unmovable."

"What's she working on now?" Daniel asked, sitting on the sofa beside Fanny.

"I'm not permitted to say. She'd kill me if I did."

Fanny raised an eyebrow. "The sanctity of commissions?"

"Something like that, yes."

"So it must be someone who's in town?" she fished.

"As a matter of fact, no. That much I'll tell you. Ali's working from photographs—she often begins that way."

"She'll be traveling again, then, soon?" Daniel entered the game. "Out of the country?"

"Yes. Europe." Andreas threw up his hands. "And that's my last word."

"Okay, but I still say it was a shame she couldn't take a few hours off. Everyone has to relax sometime." There was a small scuffling from the hallway and Daniel stood up again to open the door. "You sinful creature," he scolded the cat fondly, "staying out so late again."

"How does he get in?" asked Fanny. "This is the fifth floor, for Christ's sake—what is he, Supercat?"

"Through my bedroom window."

"Impossible."

Daniel laughed. "You'd be surprised what's possible for this one. Most apartment cats in this city believe they have no choice but to stay home, but not Cat."

"You're forgetting he was a street cat, Fanny," Andreas said.

"And no cat learns quicker than a street cat how to work new territory," Daniel added. "Cat knows the streets were dangerous, and the food came in scraps. But all these apartments have terraces, and they're set just close enough for him to take a gamble and jump.''

"What does he find on the terraces? Birds?" Andreas tapped the edge of his armchair with one hand, and the black animal streaked silently across the room and sat down neatly, watching Daniel.

"Cat? Eat birds? Cat loves birds—I think he talks to them." Daniel paced the rug, and the feline eyes followed his every move. "No, Cat has made friends. Not next door—they hate him, so he cuts his visits short—but two apartments down there's Mrs. Levy, who's rich and all alone."

"What does she give him? Lobster tails, I suppose."

Daniel shrugged his shoulders. "Probably. But he does even better in the corner apartment at the other end. I've watched him come back from there, and I tell you, that creature always has cream on his fur, and I'd swear one time I saw caviar on his whiskers."

"I thought he was getting plumper." Andreas scratched the top of the animal's head. "Really fell on your feet, didn't you, Cat."

Fanny sighed. "I just wish you'd call it something intelligent, Dan. 'Cat' will look so hopeless in your memoirs, you know."

Daniel snorted with laughter. "Memoirs!" He watched as his companion began an elaborate flirtation with Andreas. "No, Cat he is, and Cat he'll stay. I couldn't confuse him now by changing his name. Look at him now—I wish Ali could see him. She might sketch him for me."

"At least that way we might get to see her." Fanny blew a smoke ring. "This is the third time, isn't it, Dan, that your invitations have clashed with Alexandra's commissions? Doesn't she enjoy eating anymore, Andreas? Too much of a good thing at Alessandro's?"

Andreas's eyes grew darker.

"Next time, Dan," she went on regardless, "you'll have to get your wires uncrossed and discover Ali's slack season, if she ever has one."

"Shut up, Fanny," Daniel said shortly.

She watched Andreas, still tickling Cat's fur, and she leaned her chin on one hand, wondering.

"Why so sharp, Fanny?" Daniel asked, pouring himself another Armagnac. "It isn't like you."

"It's exactly like me."

"Not with my friends. You're reading too much into this."

"I'm not so sure. Maybe Alessandro doesn't pass on your invitations to his wife. You haven't spoken directly to her, have you?"

"Fanny!" He shook his head, more irritated than before and wishing she'd go home. It was over an hour since Andreas had left, and Daniel was more than ready to go to bed.

"Well, who can tell? Perhaps it's his Italian blood. Leaving the signora safely at home."

"You really are being ridiculous. Andreas is Swiss, and Ali is American, and if you met his father, you wouldn't make such ludicrous remarks about Italians."

"Not so touchy, Dan." She grinned at him. "You must at least admit he's a little reluctant about her—a shade too much mystery, I thought. Are you sure they have such a good marriage?"

"So far as I can tell, it's perfect. I think they're mad about each other."

Fanny fingered the emerald drop on one pointed ear. "Then he's jealous."

"Of what?"

"I mean in the possessive sense. Does he have many close male friends, do you know?"

"He's very fond of Rudesheim, his partner."

"Father figure. Doesn't count. I would guess, Dan, that Alessandro doesn't like sharing. I think he wants both you and her to himself."

"You should have been a shrink," he said sarcastically.

"Andreas probably compartmentalizes everything in his life. Take his driving—I expect he still intends to make a comeback. You said as much yourself after your first dinner at Alessandro's. I doubt he discusses that much with his wife. We both know he won't talk about her any more than he has to. I wonder if he's even told her everything about your first meeting."

"Sure he has."

"And what it meant to you, and to him?"

Daniel rapped his glass sharply down on the glass-topped bar. "Of course he has!"

Fanny nibbled on a fingernail, her eyes shrewd. "Wanna bet?"

Alexandra was still awake, snuggled warmly under the sheets. "Turn on the light, darling, I don't mind."

Andreas snapped on the light in the dressing room and opened the door. "Did I wake you? I'm sorry." He tossed his tie onto a chair, came over to her side of the bed, and leaned over to kiss her on the mouth.

"It's okay, I couldn't sleep anyhow. Nice evening?"

"Mmm, not bad."

"Good men's talk? How is Dan?"

Andreas slipped off his shoes and put them in the closet. "He's fine. Sends his regards." He strolled into the dressing room and through into the bathroom.

"Did you ask him to dinner?" she called, but he didn't answer, and in a moment she heard water running in the shower. When he came out, a towel wrapped round his waist, he was grinning. "What they say about cold showers is bull. I'm horny as hell. How do you feel, *Herzchen,* or did you work too hard?"

"I told you I'm not starting till next week." She pulled a grimace. "Tell you the truth, Alessandro, I'm nervous as a kitten about this job. If only she wasn't quite so beautiful."

"You've painted dozens of beautiful women."

"Not like Audrey Hepburn." Alexandra sat up and opened a drawer of her bedside table. "Look at these!" She waved a sheaf of photographs at him. "It's going to be difficult not ending up with something hackneyed."

He took the photographs from her firmly and put them back in the drawer. "It'll be fine once you meet her. You always say you need the flesh-and-blood person before you really start to function." He looked at her shrewdly. "You are too tired, aren't you?"

"Too edgy."

He smiled. "That I can cure." He sat down on the edge of the bed and took her hand.

"Did you invite Dan?"

He snapped his fingers and swore softly. "I forgot. I'm sorry, sweetheart, I meant to. I promise I'll call him soon."

"Okay," she said, and lay down, pulling the sheet up to her chin. Andreas put his hand out again and leaned over to kiss her, but she drew away. "You're still wet," she murmured, and closed her eyes. "Good night."

For a minute or two he stood looking down at his wife, his expression tender. Then he went back into the dressing room and shut the door.

34

. . . We all prospered.

Andreas took Dan's advice and opened a second restaurant in
Washington, and we began plotting two more Alessandro's, one in
Paris and the other in Zurich, by the middle of 1964.

Your mother had three glorious weeks in late October and
early November with Audrey Hepburn and Mel Ferrer in Bel Air,
while Hepburn was filming *My Fair Lady,* and right after that I
flew to London to set the seal on my first royal commission.

Harper and Stone flourished too. While Fanny jetted between
her different worlds, Dan took on more staff and made forays to
the West Coast to formulate their first Californian guide, leaving
Roly and Kate at home to mind the store. New York continued
weaving its magic wand, binding us all tighter to its Jacob's ladder
to success. Up and up we all went, on our own separate routes,
each prodded and motivated by different forces. "The trick,"
Fanny told Dan one day, "is to remember to get off the ladder
now and again. There's no fun in going higher and higher unless
you reach the occasional plateau, take a few good deep breaths,
and enjoy it."

Toward the end of November that year we all, together with
half the world, reached a plateau and stood deathly still as the
President went to Dallas and Lee Harvey Oswald turned the an-
them into a requiem.

Dan stayed home, took down his book of quotations, read Eu-
ripides, Omar Khayyám and F. Scott Fitzgerald, and found nothing to comfort him. Andreas drove up to Watkins Glen, borrowed
a Lotus-Climax and raced it round the circuit that would, in another fortnight, see the sixth United States Grand Prix, and suc-
ceeded only in putting his spine and legs into spasm. Fanny
opened up the office, even though it was a weekend, and sat for
ten hours, reading files, checking paperwork and hatching new
ideas. When she emerged at three in the morning, the Sunday
papers were on the streets along with many of the people of New

York, gray faces still or again stained with tears as they scanned newsprint and stared at photographs.

I wrote a letter to Jacqueline Kennedy, and then I went to my studio and locked the door. I didn't know what time it was, hardly knew what day it was, had a fair idea of what my husband was doing, and found myself incapable of work.

It wasn't just the President's death that had rendered me so disorientated, my darling Bobbi, nor the fact that Andreas might be risking his neck on a racetrack. I wanted, needed, to sit quietly and alone to mull over the realization I had come to over the last few weeks and that, increasingly, threatened to swamp me body and soul.

I had reached a plateau, had thought it sweet, then suddenly, unexpectedly, found it barren, and had come to a decision.

I wanted a child.

Part Four

Part Four

35

"Adopt! You're out of your mind!"

"Why not?" She fought to keep her tone reasonable. "People like us do it all the time."

"Like us? What the hell does that mean?"

"Like you and me." She touched her heart. "A man and a woman who want children, but who can't."

"Wanted." Andreas's voice was chilly.

"You still do, darling, I know you do. We both do."

"Not anymore, Ali. I got over that, just as I had to get over driving."

"But it's not the same! How can you compare them?" Alexandra heard her voice growing wilder and forced it down. "Won't you at least talk about it? Give it some time, think about it."

"I told you, I'm over it."

"But I'm not!" She took his hand and squeezed it, appealing to him. "Please don't punish me, Andreas. I know it was my fault we didn't have babies before the accident, and I've cursed myself for it often enough, but now—"

"Now is too late." He removed his hand, not unkindly. "I'm not punishing you, don't think that. But I've learned there are things we just can't have, no matter how we want them. You may think my racing wasn't so important—"

"But you're not over your racing, you know you're not! Given the slightest improvement you'd be out there again scaring me to death! And you're not over this either." She grasped his hand again and pulled it over her flat stomach. "We can't have this, you're right—and that is something I've had to accept, but there are hundreds of babies out there who need parents. We have so much to offer—" She broke off, startled, as he snatched his hand away.

"Finished?" he asked acidly. "Good. Then maybe you're ready to listen to what I have to say. I am, and have always been, repelled by the thought of adoption. It has always been an incomprehensible process to me. The urologist and your friend Salko mentioned it to me more than once, and I told them it was out of the question—I'm surprised Salko didn't pass it on to you."

"Why would he?"

Andreas shrugged. "You were so close for so long, I just assumed he reported back to you." His mouth twisted. "Or perhaps you were too immersed in each other."

"Andreas!" she cried. "This isn't like you. Just because we've hit a sensitive subject, don't start inventing sins to hurl at me."

"I apologize," he said coldly. "Forgive me."

"Of course I forgive you, darling." She felt confused, part of her wounded, part of her wanting to take him in her arms.

"Good." He walked away, then turned back. "But get this clear, Alexandra. No more talk of adoption, *ever*. I forbid it."

He left the room. Alexandra had the feeling she had been slapped in the face.

"And you haven't mentioned it since?" Theodor Salko asked quizzically. "Not a word?"

Alexandra threw up her hands in despair. "How could I, Theo, after that. It's his right, after all, to refuse. Something like this has to be wanted equally by both partners, doesn't it?"

"Of course, Ali. But it ought to be discussed at considerable length before it's either agreed on or rejected." He looked around the den appreciatively. "It's been some time since I was here. It's such a lovely apartment."

She smiled. "It's home. Another cup, Theo? You know I drown myself in coffee whenever there's a crisis."

"You shouldn't. Caffeine makes tension worse. No more for me either, thanks." He leaned forward in his armchair. "Do you want me to talk to Andreas?"

"God, no! That would really light a fuse under us. He's jealous of you already, you know."

Salko grinned. "You're kidding."

"I wish I was. We spent a lot of time together while he was sick, and he still resents everything about that period. I don't think he really believes it, but it makes him feel better to have something to throw at me when the going gets rough."

Salko whistled. "I had no idea. I guess you're on your own, then. I'm sorry, Ali. You're probably right to give him time to calm down before you try again."

"And if I fail?"

He looked her frankly in the eye. "Then you'll just have to learn to survive without motherhood. You're a strong woman.

And you have creative work to help you. Lean on that for a while." Salko smiled gently. "And who knows, you may even change his mind."

For five months Alexandra painted furiously, churning out onto canvas what she felt in her heart. But the desire for a child lodged deep in her gut, unyielding and disturbingly potent, permeating her whole body and mind like an uncontrollable virus. Just once during that time she brought up the subject of adoption again, with the result that Andreas refused to speak to her for over a week. Then, one morning in early June, while standing in the kitchen writing a shopping list and listening to the radio, she heard the words that were to change her life.

"Sometimes," a male voice said, "it takes three to make a baby."

She'd hardly been paying attention, but now she focused intently on the program. It was a phone-in for childless couples, and the caller on the air was a woman whose husband had been diagnosed as sterile.

"Have you and your husband discussed AID?" the radio doctor asked.

The caller replied that she had heard of it, but was reluctant to talk about it to her husband until she knew more. "AID," the doctor explained, "stands for artificial insemination by a donor. Male semen, belonging to a donor, and often kept frozen in a sperm bank, can be placed into a woman by a method other than intercourse." If a baby was so conceived, he went on, careful counseling prior to and during the pregnancy should lead to that baby's being raised as the natural-born child of both husband and wife.

Alexandra switched off the radio and dialed Theodor Salko's office number.

"Theo, I need your help. Can you come over?"

"Trouble?" Salko sounded concerned.

"No, not at all. But I do need your wisdom."

"I have two more patients this morning, Ali, but I can be there in my lunch hour if you'll make me a sandwich."

"I'll go shop for a hero," she laughed. "See you later. And thanks."

"Frankly," Salko said two hours later, halfway through his hero sandwich, "I think you're crazy."

"Why?" Alexandra demanded.

"You know why, Ali. With *your* husband? If he was revolted by the thought of adoption, which is a natural and all-round beneficence—" He picked up a napkin and wiped his mouth, his eyes wide behind his spectacles. "I mean, Ali, adopting does everyone concerned a favor. That's why I thought there might be an outside chance of persuading Andreas to go through with it. You'd have your child; he'd be able to do his Italian papa act; and some unwanted kid would have a great home. If Andreas is turned off by that—and don't get me wrong, there are many men who can't stomach the idea—then you're nuts to even contemplate AID." He shook his head. "I'm truly sorry, Ali, but there it is."

"Not necessarily."

"How so?"

She waved her hand. "Before we go any farther, I'd like to know how you feel about artificial insemination."

Salko frowned. "As a doctor or as a man."

"Both."

"Remember I'm in orthopedics, Ali, not gynecology."

"I do."

He pursed his lips and exhaled through his nose. "Okay. From the professional point of view, I'm not convinced that AID shouldn't be a jailable offense—though not AIH. That's where sperm is provided by the husband, by the way."

"I know that. Go on."

"It's a minefield, Ali. Morally and legally." He shuddered. "Genetic engineering—enough to freeze the blood, let alone the sperm."

"But you must believe there's a good side."

"Of course there is. The brilliant achievement of enabling a faithful wife of an infertile husband to give birth to a child by natural means."

"There you are!" Alexandra cried. She was flushed with excitement. "If we can persuade Andreas at least to consider this—"

"Hold on just one minute! You can forget the 'we,' Ali. You're on your own. You asked me a moment ago for my opinion as a man. Well, I'll give it to you. I think it's one of the most selfish things ever invented. I believe it may work in some marriages, but only where the husband either has such a strong ego nothing can shake it, or where he has a deep-rooted aspiration to be a saint."

"You forget one thing!" she broke in, her voice breaking with disappointment. "You're not a married man, Theo. I don't believe you know anything about that kind of love. Andreas and I have been through a lot together. When he went through that awful black depression, I was there all the time—"

"You want a medal? You think he owes you?"

"No, of course not!"

"It sounds like it to me."

"I can't help the way it sounds to you," she said angrily. "What I'm talking about is love. Sharing, and giving. I'm perfectly aware that Andreas will be against the idea at the start."

"Forgive me, Ali, but I think that's the understatement of the decade."

"But if I fight him, just enough to get him to listen—maybe to come with me for some counseling. I wouldn't ask him for any promises, Theo."

"I should hope not, for Christ's sake!" he yelled, and then looked on, distraught, as she buried her head in her hands and began to sob uncontrollably. "Oh, God, Ali, I'm sorry. I'm being insensitive. Forgive me, sweetheart, please." Alexandra just wept harder and he threw down his napkin and went to her, putting both arms around her. "That's it, you let it go, let it out. That's the wisest thing you've done since I got here."

She pressed her face into his lapel, and he felt the fabric of his suit getting damp with her tears, as her whole body shook with sobs.

"Maybe I'm a dumb old man with no imagination. If you feel you can talk Andreas around, or even if your desire for a baby is so strong that you feel you have to *try*, whatever the outcome, then of course you must."

"But that's it," she said, still weeping, but able to draw away from his security. "That's it exactly, Theo. If I don't try everything, I don't think I'll be able to live with myself."

Salko pulled a handkerchief from his pocket and wiped her wet, tearstained face gently. "I honestly didn't realize your maternal instincts were this strong, Ali."

"Nor did I until last year. I always knew I wanted to have children, and after Andreas's crash I wanted to beat myself black and blue for being so stubborn about waiting. But I thought I was right to do that, Theo," she said, the tears starting again, brimming over her lashes. "I thought we should have some years alone together—that a baby would be all the more welcomed if it was a while in coming. I didn't know—" She grabbed the handkerchief out of his fingers and pressed it over her mouth, trying to suppress her sobs.

"Of course you didn't. How could anyone have guessed that

would happen? Now stop crying," he said gently. "Maybe I can help a little."

She emerged from behind the handkerchief, biting her lip. "How?"

He raised a restraining hand. "Oh, nothing very much, I'm afraid. As I said, you're on your own so far as getting the dialogue under way with Andreas, but I could do some research for you—get names of specialists in the field, and the appropriate counselors to help you."

"You'd do that for me?"

"Of course I'd do it."

Alexandra hugged him gratefully. "What would I do without you, Theo? You're the best friend I have in the world, next to Andreas."

Salko reddened, and looked soberly at her.

"Let's hope that's true," he said.

Her first attempt at "dialogue" with Andreas was a complete disaster. To begin with, when she mentioned artificial insemination, he pretended not to have heard her. Then when she tried to continue, he turned on her, eyes blank with unspeakable anger, and said, with far more violence, the very words that Theodor Salko had used: "I think you must be crazy."

He left the apartment right after that, and did not return until the following night, when he acted as if the incident had never taken place.

Alexandra found she could not leave it. She called the first on the list of professors of obstetrics and gynecology that Salko had given her, as promised, and was told that she could not be seen without her husband. The next two said much the same. To the fourth doctor Alexandra lied outright, saying that she and her husband would be attending together.

The first available time was three weeks away, and the tension of guarding her precious secret gnawed at her nerves, making her bad-tempered and guilty. She didn't even dare tell Salko, aware that he'd only agreed to help her if she could persuade Andreas to take counsel.

She had never felt more alone.

"And you say that your husband agrees in principle with AID?" Dr. Manetti asked gravely. He was a serious man in his mid-forties with dark, slightly tousled curly hair and narrow, piercing eyes set close together. He had seemed taken aback when Alexandra had arrived alone, and had taken some convincing to talk to her at all.

"Absolutely," she lied with sincerity. "It's just that he's had so many disappointments we both felt it best to discover first if I'm physically suited for the process."

"I see." Dr. Manetti tapped his pen against his blotter. "Well, you seem to be in perfect health. You're thirty, which is perhaps slightly older than ideal for a first child, but if tests prove you're fertile that's no more of a problem with AID than with any other pregnancy."

"My periods have always been regular."

He smiled. "We have all that information now, Mrs. Alessandro. There's no reason to assume that you are not physically suitable, and in cases such as yours we can boast a fairly high success rate, particularly with fresh sperm, though the rate of achievement using frozen is somewhere between fifty and sixty percent."

"And if it works, it usually happens within the first six months?"

Dr. Manetti nodded. "That's right. But there's not much more to be added, is there, until your husband is ready to join you here." He frowned. "If you're looking for guarantees, I'm afraid you're out of luck."

Alexandra looked him clearly in the eye. "Of course I'm not, Doctor. I just want to have a baby."

Dr. Manetti closed her file. "Well, I think I've told you all I can about the methods and preparation. You might like to know that, on the whole, AID does not seem to affect marriages adversely. On the contrary, research shows a lower divorce rate among couples having children this way, probably because so much more thought and planning has to go into the conception. It's the husband, obviously, who has the greater load to bear, and it's your husband, Mrs. Alessandro, who has to sit there beside you and convince me and your counselor that AID is what he truly wants."

Alexandra had never seen Andreas so livid. He stared at her as if he were seeing a stranger for the first time, so alien was the suggestion she was making.

"You *are* insane."

She struggled to keep her voice calm. She had known it would be like this, she rationalized. Andreas was too proud, too unreasonably ashamed of his infertility—it was bound to take time.

"I don't think so. I just want us to talk about it, to have a conversation."

"There is nothing to talk about."

"Yes, there is!" she cried, and then quietened, knowing it was vital she didn't lose her temper or break down. "There's a great deal to talk about, Andreas—because if we don't, our marriage may be at stake."

He looked disgusted. "Don't do that, Alexandra. I've had too much experience of the emotional blackmail of women. My mother was a mistress of the skill, but she never won with me."

"I'm not blackmailing you!" she protested. "I'm not asking you to accept AID, just to let me tell you the facts."

He stood up and strode to the door of the sitting room. "I have not the slightest intention of listening to anything so unnatural, so . . . . so immoral!"

Alexandra leapt to her feet and blocked the doorway. "No, Andreas! This time you're going to hear me out. Whether you like it or not, this is the most important thing in the world to me at the moment!" She was panting with emotion. "I'm tired of repenting because I wasn't ready to have a child before the accident—because that's what it was, an accident!"

"Get out of my way!" he thundered.

"Not until you listen!" She felt her whole body trembling. "I didn't plan on feeling this way, Andreas. I thought I could handle not having a baby. I thought our love would be enough—our love and my work. But it isn't any more." She made a fist of one hand and struck at her stomach. "I feel this emptiness every hour of every day! I feel hollow and barren and useless—all the hackneyed old clichés I've read in bad fiction and never truly understood."

For an instant she thought she had gotten through to him. There was something, a flicker of compassion, in those black, angry eyes.

"You need help, Alexandra. You need a shrink."

She grabbed his arm. "No! I just need you to come with me to the counselor so that he can explain it to you, so perhaps you'll understand. It's normal for you to feel repelled by the idea of my having another man's sperm inside me—it must sound horrible, like infidelity, but that's just what it isn't!" She knew she was babbling, but it was impossible to stop. "No one else would ever know it wasn't your baby—it's quite anonymous, especially when they use the sperm banks—"

She saw his free hand swinging at her when it was too late to duck, and it struck her cheek with all the force of his rage. She leaned against the door and stared at him in disbelief, feeling the burning of her flesh where his fingers had collided. She felt a great sob rising up in her chest but knew that her eyes were dry.

Andreas was aghast. In all his life he had never hit a woman, and now, of all people . . . He wanted to reach for her, to take her in his arms and beg her forgiveness, but the terrible insensitivity of her words still rang in his ears.

They stood very still, like two wild animals on the verge of mortal combat, keeping a safe distance between them, aware that any movement, however slight, could send them hurtling over the brink.

Alexandra was first to recover. "I'm sorry," she said, her voice sounding hoarse with shock. "This isn't the way I wanted it to be."

He raised his hand and gently brushed her flaming cheek, distraught as she flinched at his touch. He swallowed hard. "It's I who should apologize," he said painfully. "I wouldn't hurt you for the world. I don't know what came over me. I was just suddenly so angry—"

"Don't say any more," she said, stopping him. "Not now, there's no point. Maybe I should never have told you, but I figured that's what marriage was about—speaking our minds, telling each other what's in our hearts."

"Ali," he pleaded. He'd never seen her look so sad, and it wounded him more than he'd believed possible.

She shook her head, tossing her hair. "No, Andreas, not now." She forced a half smile to her lips. "It's all right. I forgive you for hitting me. In a way that's the least of it, isn't it? Just a small explosion, a letting-out of steam." The tears came suddenly into her eyes. "It's just that I love you so very much, and I see a way for us to have the child we both want." She bit her lip. "But I can also see how that might be impossible for you, and so I'm going to try my damnedest to forget all about it."

"Ali, *Herzchen,* come and sit down." He put an arm about her shoulders, but she drew away.

"No, not now. Later maybe." Her voice was quiet and defeated, and she felt as if all the energy and courage she'd started with had drained out of her. "Right now, I think I just need to be alone for a while." She touched his face with kind fingers. "Let's both try to forget this, shall we?"

"Do you think you can?"

Alexandra hesitated, her hand on the doorknob.

"I don't know."

36

"How about a few days on the Côte d'Azur?" Andreas asked Alexandra in the middle of August.

"Too busy this time of year," she said, dabbing moisturizer onto her skin and regarding herself critically in her dressing table mirror. "A zillion people and almost as hot as here. Manhattan stinks, but at least we have our lovely cool home."

"I don't mean right now. I thought perhaps September."

She smiled. "Now you're talking. Anywhere special in mind? Any particular reason?"

"Do I have to have a motive?"

"Of course not. But we haven't had a real vacation, just for the sake of it, for a while."

"Then it's time we did. Anyway, someone suggested we might open a place in Cannes or Nice."

Alexandra laughed. "I thought so. Do you think that's such a great idea?"

He shrugged. "Probably not, but it's an excuse for me to take you away. We used to travel so much together in the old days, before—" He turned away.

"Well, I think it's a fine idea," she said brightly.

"Good. I'll make reservations." Andreas studied her for a moment, taking in the few fine lines on her forehead and the darkish circles under her eyes that hadn't been there before the summer.

"You look tired, Ali."

She sighed and turned back to the mirror. No point talking about her feelings. There were so many words left unsaid these days. Since that bleak June evening she'd forced her needs as far back in her mind as possible, and had tried to get on with the business of living, making the best of things. She had to face it, things weren't exactly bad, but silence seemed to imply a kind of dishonesty, however well-intentioned, and it was beginning to take a toll on them both.

"I'm all right." She smiled. "Roll on September."

*

Nice seemed a little tarnished, her streets and sidewalks trampled into dusty exhaustion by the August hordes, and yet there was a kind of relief in the air, as if the town realized it had survived yet another season and could breathe again.

The Negresco stood tall and creamily imposing on the Promenade des Anglais, its cool, high-ceilinged lobby welcoming the Alessandros and other new arrivals. It was early evening when they checked into their suite, and they elected to order dinner from room service and get an early night.

Next morning dawned clear and dry, with the fine blue sky and soft glow that fortunate autumn travelers could look forward to. Andreas went for an early stroll round the harbor, leaving Alexandra to a lazy breakfast in bed. While he gazed at crisply painted yachts and fishing nets, clearing his brain of business problems, she lay back on snowy pillows and sorted artistic inspirations as they poured suddenly and freely through her consciousness for the first time in months. *This is a fresh start,* she promised herself. No more maudlin self-pity, no more fretting about things that were not to be. The breakfast tray collected, she ran a scented bath, shampooed her hair, and slipped back between the sheets to wait for her husband.

Two days passed blissfully. Then, on the third evening of their stay, as they were strolling hand in hand from the grillroom, a man in a pale blue suit rose from his table and called Alexandra's name.

"I thought it was you when you came in," John Manetti said, smiling, "but I didn't like to intrude before dinner."

A flush of embarrassment rose in her cheeks as Alexandra introduced them. Manetti shook Andreas firmly by the hand.

"Glad to meet you."

Alexandra took Andreas's arm firmly, hoping to steer him away. "It was good seeing you again, Dr. Manetti."

A waiter came forward to draw the doctor's table out from the banquette.

"I've just finished too," he said, "so we can walk out together." He smiled at Alexandra. "How have you been?"

"Just fine, thank you," she replied, her skin scorching. Surely ethics would prevent Manetti from mentioning their professional encounter, but why didn't the man walk away to save her this agony? Out in the hall she glared at him, but Andreas tightened the noose by inviting Manetti to join them for a digestif.

"How do you two know each other?" he asked when they were seated in the lounge.

Manetti glanced briefly at Alexandra, noting her discomfort. "We met through a mutual friend, Theodor Salko," he said noncommittally.

Andreas signaled a waiter. "I thought perhaps my wife had consulted you," he said casually. Manetti said nothing, and Alexandra played nervously with her hair, twisting a long strand between her fingers. "Are you a general practitioner, Doctor, or do you have a specialty?"

"I'm an obstetrician," Manetti answered easily.

"I'm sure Dr. Manetti doesn't want to talk about his work," Alexandra said quickly. "He's on vacation, aren't you?"

"Actually I'm attending a symposium here, but I flew over a couple of days early so I could get some R and R before the hordes arrive." He grimaced. "After the opening sessions of these things, you get no time to breathe. I'm usually happy to get home to my family."

Andreas ordered a bottle of Rémy Martin. "You have children, Doctor?"

"Two. A girl and a boy."

"You carry photos?"

Alexandra bristled. In all the years she'd known him, she'd never heard her husband asking to see snapshots of children. With a jolt, she wondered if Andreas had guessed who Manetti was. When the waiter poured her cognac, she clutched her glass tightly, a feeling of foreboding sweeping her.

Manetti took a wallet from an inside pocket of his jacket. "Typical father," he beamed, "willing to bore the pants off anyone who's polite enough to encourage me." He showed them a pair of photographs of a fresh-faced, dark-haired boy and girl.

"They look just like you," Andreas said. "You're a lucky man."

"They're charming," Alexandra offered.

Andreas swallowed down his cognac and refilled his glass. "What's the subject of your symposium?" He stressed the last word unpleasantly.

Manetti took only the briefest of pauses. "Infertility," he said, and flashed Alexandra a look of pity.

"Strange subject for an obstetrician. I thought you dealt only with the birth of children."

"I'm a gynecologist also," Manetti responded coolly. "Most men don't understand the difference."

"I've made a small study of the area," Andreas countered. "And so has my wife. Or maybe you know that already."

For a moment Manetti sat still. Then he pushed back his chair and rose. "I'm rather tired, so if you don't mind I think I'll go up to my room."

"Not at all," said Andreas, not getting up.

"Good night, Mrs. Alessandro. I hope your stay is enjoyable."

Alexandra nodded silently.

Andreas waited until Manetti had vanished in the direction of the elevators. "Quite a coincidence."

"Wasn't it."

"I can't quite figure out if it was contrived or not."

She stared at him. "What do you mean?"

"That *is* the doctor you visited in New York, isn't it? The one who filled your head with all the stuff about—" He stopped, anger rising and stifling his words.

"Artificial insemination?" she finished for him. "Yes, it was Manetti. And no, it was not contrived, if by that you meant did we arrange to meet here. If you recollect, coming to Nice was your idea."

"Something tells me you visited him more than once."

"I did not."

Andreas drank more cognac and his eyes darkened. "Whatever you say. I'm the sucker, after all—I'm the failure in this marriage."

"Andreas, please."

"It's true, isn't it?" he railed, so forcefully that the couple at the nearest table looked up startled. "And to think this was meant to be some kind of second honeymoon. . . ."

"Andreas," she begged, reaching for his hand, distressed as he pulled away. "You have to stop feeling this way." She tried to speak quietly in spite of her urgency. "I do understand how you feel about this. I made up my mind long before we came here that I'd give up the idea. If you hate it so much, after all, there'd be no point."

"Did you see him more than once?"

"What difference would it make if I did? So long as I can understand your point of view—"

"My point of view!" he echoed. "Is that what you call my sense of inadequacy, my abhorrence for what you and he suggested?"

"For God's sake, Andreas," she whispered, "get the check so we can continue this upstairs."

He sat back, and for a second he looked at her with such violence that she felt quite shaken. Then, suddenly, he clicked his fingers to summon a waiter, and scrawled his initials against their room number. "Let's go," he said tersely and, taking her hand roughly, strode toward the elevator.

In the suite he turned the key in the lock and switched on all the lights.

"Now, Alexandra," he said harshly, "let's see just how understanding you really are. Prove how generous a wife you can be!" He threw his jacket onto the rug and unbuckled his belt.

"You must be drunk," she said in alarm.

"So now I can't hold my liquor?" His eyes flashed. "It isn't enough that I'm sterile—isn't that the right term?" he demanded sarcastically.

"Don't keep talking as if it's a crime," she begged, "or some kind of failure. You know it isn't, and you know *I* don't think that way—I've been the one to feel guilty for the last—"

"Prove it!" He unzipped his fly. She walked away, but he gripped her shoulder and swung her around. "Don't turn away from your husband, Alexandra. You're such a fabulous wife, the least you can do is fuck me!"

"Andreas, what's the matter with you?"

Still holding her tightly with one hand, he stripped quickly with the other. She sucked in her breath, her mouth dry as she gaped at him—her husband, often a tiger between the sheets but always loving and tender at the same time, stood before her like a raging bull, his erection huge and glaring.

"Look at me," he snarled. "I can't give you sperm, so you want to shop for them, but I can still fuck you till your head blows off!"

"For Christ's sake!" she hissed at him, and wrenched her shoulder from his grasp, but he was too quick for her and seized her around the waist.

"I said look at me! Big enough for you? Or do you want to go find Manetti—he can give you kids, can't he!"

Alexandra panicked, realizing he was completely out of control. "What about this morning, Andreas? We made love then, didn't we? It was wonderful, wasn't it? Don't you remember? You were—"

"It stank! You always make love to me like I'm still a patient."

"How can you say such things? I love you! Andreas, let me go before you regret it!"

"Is that a threat?"

"Don't be ridiculous!" He strengthened his grip on her waist.

"You're hurting me!"

"And haven't you hurt me? How many months have you plotted with Salko, and now with that bastard Manetti?" He shoved her down onto the floor and she began to fight, punching his chest and kicking at his legs, but his strength defeated her.

"My wife the wildcat!" He laughed harshly. He yanked at her skirt, and she heard the fabric ripping and felt small pain as his fingers tore roughly at her panties. His hands moved to her shoulders, pushing them down so violently that her head banged against the floor, and he kneed her legs apart.

Suddenly, all the fight seemed to go out of her. She stared into his face in disbelief. "Don't do this, Andreas. I'm begging you." Her voice sounded flat. "If you rape me," she said, "how will I ever forgive you?"

"Why not?" he yelled, his breath half sobbing in his throat. "After all, you can't get pregnant, can you!" And still holding her down, he stabbed into her, shutting his eyes, losing himself in wild blackness, pouring all his pent-up fury and hurt into her—but at the end of it there was nothing, none of the tenderness and quiet of their usual lovemaking. Alexandra lay limply on the rug, not troubling to move, unable to weep. Her lips were bruised where he had forced his mouth over hers, and her eyes were open and sad as death.

Alexandra checked out of the hotel next morning, took a cab to Nice Airport, and sat with her bags in the narrow departure lounge, waiting for the next flight to Paris, where she could catch a connection to New York. The sensation of numbness that had invaded her as Andreas had forced himself inside her was still with her like a protective shield. She sheltered beneath it, wrapped it around her, praying it would remain with her all the way home, for once it was gone there would be decisions to make, and she could not, just could not, bear to think about that.

Andreas sat in the suite. For a long time—was it one hour or two, perhaps longer?—he did not move at all, was quite inert. Occasionally, a thought filtered through to the surface—always the same thought, repeating over and over like the intermittent but insistent tick of a broken clock: *What have I done? What have I done?* But there was never an answer.

From time to time there came a quiet rapping at the door as a chambermaid tried to gain entry, but he ignored every knock. Some time during the afternoon, he went into the bathroom, pissed into the bowl, and shaved, mechanically, with his cutthroat razor. He looked at his reflection, saw blood where he'd nicked himself, and returned to the armchair near the window in the sitting room.

At seven in the evening the telephone rang and he leapt to his feet, thinking it might be her, but it was only the housekeeper asking if he wanted his rooms cleaned. "Why not?" he said, and next time the maid knocked, he opened the door, dressed quickly in the bathroom, and went downstairs to the lobby.

"Book me on the next flight to New York," he told the concierge.

"It's not so easy." The man shrugged. "The planes are mostly full."

Andreas gave him a heavy tip. "The next flight," he repeated, and turned away toward the revolving door, needing fresh air.

Manetti stood before him.

"Mr. Alessandro, a word?"

"I'm busy." Andreas continued walking, but Manetti laid a hand on his arm.

"Forgive me, but this is very important."

Andreas stopped. "Take your hand off my arm."

The American doctor ran a hand through his already tousled hair. "Could we please sit down somewhere?" he asked quietly. "Just a few minutes of your time."

"Why should I?"

"Because I ask it."

Andreas snapped back the sleeve of his jacket and glanced at his watch. "You have ten minutes."

Manetti led the way into the bar and sat down at a corner table. "Scotch all right?"

Andreas shrugged. "Okay." He needed a drink badly; why not now.

The waiter brought the glasses quickly. Andreas took a first sip urgently. Manetti watched him.

"So?" Andreas said testily. "Time's running out."

The doctor hesitated for a second, then plunged right in. "I heard you book a flight back home?"

"That's right."

"One seat."

"My wife left this morning," Andreas snapped. "But maybe you know that?"

Manetti nodded. "I saw her leave." He paused. "You had a fight last night. Because of me—"

"Don't flatter yourself."

Manetti smiled. "Hardly. Because of AID." He raised one hand. "No, please, let me go on."

Andreas's finger tightened around his glass.

"Your wife consulted me some months ago, on one occasion. I gave her the basic information she sought, and reminded her that it was not possible to continue unless you were present and in full accord. I gather you disliked the suggestion."

Andreas gave a short laugh.

"You think the idea sucks, am I right?"

"You got it."

There was another short pause. "I felt the same way."

Andreas looked up, surprised.

"When Maureen, my wife, first brought up the subject, I was repelled."

"But your—the children in the photographs?"

Manetti nodded. "Our boy and girl by artificial insemination."

"I don't believe you."

Manetti was not offended. "Why should I lie? We wanted children. I am infertile. Like your wife, Maureen longed for a baby. It's the truth, Mr. Alessandro."

"But they look like you."

Manetti smiled. "A small bonus that can often be arranged for fathers with AID—"

"Fathers!"

"Oh, yes, I am the father of those two kids, make no mistake. Most couples who elect to have children by this method hope the baby will resemble the father. And the majority also want the whole procedure kept secret and completely anonymous."

Andreas gritted his teeth. "It's immoral."

"Many people would agree with you," Manetti answered calmly. "Personally, I find it one hundred percent moral and humane."

Andreas looked at him cautiously. "You're an Italian by descent. Are you a Catholic?"

"My papa, God rest his soul, was a good Catholic until the day he died. In my case"—he spread his hands expressively—"it's never been that simple. I'm what you might call a believer, I guess, but the God I believe in didn't raise one single objection when I put the question to him. And I did, believe me." He waited a moment. "Are you a churchgoer?"

Andreas shook his head. "My father still goes regularly, but I—"

"Have you discussed this with him?"

"He lives in Switzerland. He knows nothing about my . . . problem."

"Doesn't he wonder why you haven't had children?"

"Possibly. I don't know."

"Do you have brothers or sisters?"

"No."

Manetti looked at the clock on the wall. "Time's up."

Andreas met his eyes. "I guess I can spare a few more minutes."

"Good. Another drink?"

Andreas signaled the bartender. "I'll get these."

For the first time Manetti relaxed. "Funny," he said.

"What?"

"I thought you might throw a punch at me."

Andreas shut his eyes for a second.

"You're not generally a violent man, are you?" Manetti asked with gentle perception, not expecting an answer. "Mind if I make a suggestion, Mr. Alessandro?"

"Go ahead."

"Don't rush home. Stay a few days. Give yourself a chance to straighten things out in your head."

"I think I should straighten things out with my wife first," Andreas disagreed shakily, curiously grateful to talk to this stranger.

"Does she love you?"

"Yes."

"She'll probably forgive you."

Involuntarily, Andreas shuddered.

"That bad?"

"Worse."

The fresh drinks arrived. Manetti sat forward again, his close-set eyes urgent. "Don't go back yet. You both need time to let the anger cool. Look . . ." He hesitated. "I'm not for a moment advocating a positive decision. I know nothing about you, Mr. Alessandro, except that you used to drive fast cars, and I know little about your wife except that she's a talented artist and wants a child. Ultimately, it has to be what you both want. AID is strong medicine, strictly for believers. For anyone else, it's pure poison."

Andreas took a drink. "Show me those snapshots again, would you mind?"

Manetti smiled. "My pleasure." He took out his wallet and extracted the photographs. Andreas took them from him and studied them closely. Manetti remained silent. Andreas gave them back.

"They're beautiful kids."

"I agree." Manetti returned the wallet to his inside pocket.

For several moments they sat in almost companionable silence, then Andreas said slowly, "Don't you ever wonder about him? Aren't you jealous?"

"Of the man who made those two babies possible?" Manetti shook his head. "Never."

"You're a better man than I, Doctor."

"Let me ask you something. When you had your accident, did you lose a lot of blood?"

"Sure."

"And they probably gave you a transfusion, right?" He went on. "Did it ever enter your head to think about the blood donor who made the transfusion possible? Of course not. The man whose sperm fertilized my wife's eggs was a third-year medical student with dark curly hair, narrow eyes, and a similar build to mine. That much I know about him, and not a single thing more. He walked into a laboratory someplace because he cared about people like you and me. Just like your blood donor in Italy."

"It's not the same."

"No, of course not. Babies ought to be made by two people who love each other hitting the sack together and fucking till they get the bull's-eye—in an ideal world, that is. But it isn't an ideal world."

In spite of himself, Andreas smiled. "Do you talk to all your patients this way, Doctor?"

"I'm not your doctor, Mr. Alessandro," Manetti said gravely. "But I want you to understand, you and your wife can still do most of those things—it's just some invisible hand that's going to try and hit dead center." He picked up his glass. "No, I'm not jealous of that medical student. My wife didn't bed him any more than your blood donor poured his or her sap directly into your veins."

"That's some analogy."

"You're right. It's lousy. It's too flippant by far. No one, male or female, should contemplate trying the method without months of careful thought, open discussion, and professional counseling. But I'd consider it a tragedy if a couple with a secure, loving marriage and a mutual, intense longing for children, threw away a chance, however remote, of their own flesh-and-blood infant without even giving AID a hearing." He shrugged. "I rest my case."

Andreas gave a low whistle. "An effective case."

"Effective enough?"

"Not to turn me into a believer."

"I didn't plan to." Manetti studied him. "Will you give some thought to talking to your wife about it?"

Andreas hesitated. "She may not feel much like talking to me about anything."

Manetti leaned back. "Take my advice," he said. "Give her time."

Andreas stayed in Nice another forty-eight hours, until he could stand it no longer. Next morning he flew to London and caught the lunchtime plane to New York.

He called the apartment from a booth at the airport. Alexandra answered.

"May I come home?" he asked.

There was a brief hesitation.

"Yes," she whispered.

She was in the hall when he opened the front door with his key, standing motionless, and Andreas had the sensation that she had stood there waiting since his call. She wore a black silk shift, quite plain. She was very thin, and very beautiful. She said nothing.

"May I come in?"

She stepped back a couple of feet in answer, giving him room to pass with his suitcase. He closed the door quietly and looked at her.

"More than anything in the world"—he tried to swallow the lump in his throat—"I wish I could blot out what happened."

Alexandra stood immobile. She had no makeup on her face, and her skin was white and translucent, but her lips were as steady as her eyes, inner strength defeating her fragility.

"I was crazy." Andreas fumbled for words. "The talk about babies, and"—he forced himself on—"artificial insemination. I felt you were attacking me, conspiring against me. That I wasn't necessary anymore. . . ." Sweat broke out on his forehead. He realized he was more afraid than he had ever been about anything. To lose her . . .

"I understand." Her voice was like cool rain.

"After you left, I spoke to Manetti."

Alexandra raised her eyebrows but didn't speak.

"He explained some things to me. I did a little thinking—no, that's not true, I did a lot of thinking."

"There's no need," she said, and her mouth quivered suddenly. "I knew the way you felt about things. I told you I'd given up the idea."

"But not the longing!" he exclaimed. "You can't have stopped wanting a child."

"No, of course not," she answered quietly. "But, like you, I've come to terms. There are things we both wanted that we can't have."

"But we can!" he pleaded. "I see that now. I was blind and selfish."

She raised her eyes to him. "What are you saying, Andreas?"

A shiver passed down his spine. He wanted like hell to take her in his arms, but he didn't dare touch her. "I'm saying I want us to try."

"Try what, Andreas?" she asked evenly.

"To have a child."

She blinked, and now there were tears of yearning in her eyes that were impossible to control. "You mean that?" she whispered.

"I do." His voice was husky.

"Oh, my God," she murmured. She began to tremble, her lips, her arms and hands, her knees so weak she thought she'd fall. "Oh, my God! You really, really mean it?"

"I wouldn't say it if I didn't."

She stumbled, like a grateful child, into his arms, and he held her, his heart pounding with his own gratitude, burying his head in her softness and warmth.

"We mustn't go ahead blindly," she said against his cheek. "We have to talk about it, to think about all the good and bad sides of it—"

"No! There's nothing to talk about. I've made up my mind."

"But it isn't that simple. You have to want it as much as I do, darling, not just for my sake."

"I do want it! I always wanted us to have babies, you know that!"

Her tears of joy mingled with his own, wetting their faces and their hair. "It doesn't always work—sometimes people try for months and—"

"It'll work for us, Ali, I know it will. Don't talk like that."

She pulled her face away a little. "We have to be realistic—"

"No! The only reality is us," he said fiercely. "Our marriage and our child." He kissed her hair. "You go and see Manetti tomorrow."

"He's probably still in France."

"Then find another doctor."

"No." She laughed through her tears. "I'll wait for him to come back. He's a good man. I trust him."

"All right, wait for him. And then you go see him right away."

"We'll both go, Andreas."

He said nothing.

"Andreas?" She looked hard at him. "We'll both go."

He nodded. "Of course, *Herzchen*, of course. Whatever it takes."

37

On the first Monday in October the Alessandros had their first session in John Manetti's office.

"The next step is for you both to meet with a counselor."

"That's unnecessary," Andreas said.

Manetti raised an eyebrow. "How so?"

"I've talked all I need to about this. It's what we both want."

The doctor looked concerned. "Who have you discussed it with?"

"With my physician," Andreas lied tersely, "and I've done some reading." He ignored Alexandra's look of surprise. "I don't want to wait any longer."

"Darling, if Dr. Manetti thinks we should see someone, surely we—"

"Alexandra," he interrupted, laying his hand over hers. "Dr. Manetti has enough experience to understand that everyone reacts differently to something as personal as this." He smiled at Manetti. "You don't have to worry on my account. I know that fathers sometimes have psychological problems with AID"—the words fell convincingly from his lips—"but I had my reactions before. I believe I am ready."

For a few moments Manetti studied him in silence. Then he turned to Alexandra. "How ready are you, Mrs. Alessandro?"

Her eyes glowed with anticipation. "I've never been more ready for anything, Doctor."

There was another short hiatus while Manetti considered. "Well, then." He opened a drawer in his desk and withdrew a buff-colored envelope. "This contains papers I want you to read, and consent forms that must be signed before treatment can commence."

Andreas took a gold pen from his inside pocket, but Manetti held on to the envelope. "Not yet. I want you to take the papers home. You should read them at your leisure, give yourselves a chance to digest their substance and implications. Then"—he looked piercingly at them both in turn—"and only then, if neither of you has any doubts, you may sign them."

Alexandra smiled warmly at him. "Thank you, Doctor. I promise you we'll be careful."

"Good." Manetti turned his attention to Andreas. "If you find, after all, Mr. Alessandro, that you have any questions—whether moral, legal, religious, or social—don't hesitate to call me. I want everything aired before you sign. If insemination is successful, I turn my patients over to their own obstetrician for prenatal care and delivery." He stood up. "And please, both of you, remember —no guarantees."

Outside Alexandra kissed Andreas, her eyes shining. "How can I ever thank you?"

He grinned. "I'm going to have this baby too, you know."

"You bet you are." A tiny frown formed between her eyebrows. "You *are* certain, aren't you? You're not just doing this for me?"

Gently he stroked her cheek with his hand. "I swear it, Ali. I'm doing this for both of us."

Back in the apartment he held out his hand. "Give me the envelope."

"I thought we'd wait, look at the papers together this evening after dinner."

"I don't want to wait."

"Okay," she agreed breathlessly. "I just didn't want to rush you. Let's read them now." She gave him the packet and walked into the den.

"If you don't mind," he said slowly, "I'd sooner do this alone. Manetti said we should concentrate, take everything into account."

"You're right, darling, of course. Take them into your study." She kissed him. "I'll brew some coffee."

"Better make it something stronger." He smiled. "How about champagne?"

"Well all right!"

In his study, Andreas closed the door, sat behind his desk, and opened the envelope, slitting it cleanly with a paper knife. He pushed aside the small leaflets, and went directly to the consent form.

We, husband and wife, he read, *having considered the alternatives of continuing to try to have children by sexual intercourse . . .*

He skipped ahead to the next paragraph.

We understand that this procedure will involve the collecting of sperm from a donor and the introduction of that sperm, by Dr. John Manetti or his designated associate, into the cervix of the wife either . . .

Andreas stopped reading. With a hand that trembled slightly he took out his pen and signed his name at the bottom of the form, and dated it.

He replaced the papers in the packet and went to find Alexandra. She was in the kitchen, cheeks flushed, gingerly working on the cork of a bottle of Veuve Clicquot. Andreas handed her the envelope.

"Please excuse me," he said faintly, and then he climbed the spiral staircase, went directly to the bathroom, and threw up.

"Still no luck?"

Theo Salko looked at Alexandra as she joined him at their booth in the Russian Tea Room after her latest appointment with Manetti.

She shook her head, biting her lip.

"Never mind, kid," Salko said comfortingly. "It often takes couples years to crack it."

"Not with AID, Theo, you know that. Manetti told us six months is usually the limit. After that you may as well give up." Nervously she twisted some hair around her index finger. "We're more than halfway there already."

"So what's halfway? Complain when it's happened, Ali, not now. Right now you need to be positive, and you have to try to relax."

"How easy that sounds." She laughed wryly.

"What are you drinking?"

"Nothing. Grapefruit juice, maybe."

"You're not even pregnant yet. You're still allowed a drink or two even then."

"Andreas is drinking enough for both of us."

Salko shot her a look. "Are you worried he might have had a change of heart, or is he just edgy because of the delay?"

She shrugged. "I wish I knew, Theo. When I try talking to him about it he reassures me, but I can't tell how he really feels anymore." She lowered her voice. "He won't come with me to John's office—never has, not once since we signed the consent paper. And when I come home after the inseminations he looks at me so strangely, I almost feel that I've been unfaithful."

"He needs some therapy, Ali. He should have had sessions with a counselor when Manetti suggested it."

Alexandra groaned. "Do you think I don't know that? Theo, we're supposed to be closer than ever right now, but he spends more time with his friends than with me."

"A man needs friends."

"I know that too. Don't think I want to deprive him of the other side of his life. Meeting Dan Stone again was really important to Andreas, and I've tried to let him know that I do understand—but he sees him almost more than me."

"Do you think perhaps you're too understanding?"

"Oh, no, Theo. This is so tough on him."

"How's your sex life?"

"That's another thing." She chewed at a nail. "We're not supposed to have sex before insemination, but afterward Manetti encourages it—I guess so that if I do become pregnant, my husband will feel even more like the father." She sighed. "Right now we're farther apart than we've ever been."

"Don't you make love at all?"

"Hardly ever."

"Perhaps Andreas is afraid he may damage your chances of conceiving?" Salko offered, aware he was fishing vainly in her troubled waters.

"Maybe. Frankly, I'm scared and I'm lonely. I feel like I don't have a husband sometimes—like I'm a single woman, going out of her way to get pregnant—like I'm crazy."

Alexandra celebrated her thirty-first birthday at the beginning of April alone in the apartment. Earlier in the day Manetti had inseminated her for the twelfth time, and as she'd lain on her back motionless for the recommended half hour afterward, tears of despair had begun trickling down her cheeks.

Manetti had walked into the room and, after handing her a box of Kleenex, had pulled up a stool and questioned her.

"Your husband should be here with you, but he never is. Why is that, Ali?"

"He cares too much," she lied. "I've told you before."

"You've told me, but I don't believe you. I'm not happy about this whole procedure. You have a husband who clearly still dislikes the idea of AID; you're much too tense and unhappy. I feel maybe we should call it a day."

"No! John, please, don't say that!" Distressed, Alexandra sat up and grabbed his hand. "Not yet, please! We have another month at least—you said so yourself!"

"And what if we succeed? Who's to say Andreas is going to feel any better when you're pregnant? Are you sure you can cope?"

Alexandra raised miserable eyes. "I'll just have to, won't I." She wiped at them fiercely. "Because I'm damned if I'll give up."

Tonight she was still alone. Andreas had called from Washington with hollow apologies. In previous years, nothing short of a nuclear attack would have kept him away on her birthday. But things were very different now. She felt their marriage disintegrating, tasted it, inhaled its slow decay, and wondered, helplessly, how to halt it.

"Make love after each insemination," Manetti had instructed on previous occasions. But where was her mate when she needed him?

Huddled on the paint-splattered floor of her studio, Alexandra drank from the champagne glass that had been refilled four times already from the bottle she'd opened in defiance. Such pointless hubris! No one to see the dashing of her small, pathetic pact with her unfertilized eggs. "You get lucky, I'll be good as gold," she'd whispered to her belly back in November. Oh, God, it seemed a hundred years ago! "I won't drink, won't smoke, won't jaywalk, won't drive fast."

The studio was cold and forlorn, the ever-present smells of paint, spirit and varnish suddenly nauseating. All her life, back as far as the cradle, she remembered loving those smells; they reminded her of wild John Craig immortalizing his women while she, faithful daughter, kept house for him; of the times in Europe when her own gifts had flowered; of the precious days and nights in London when those same skills had helped her to ensnare her husband. And tonight they made her sick to her stomach.

Overwhelming, blinding anger flared suddenly up inside her. Rage against Andreas, against the hateful egoism that stopped him realizing her needs. Yes, he loved her! Couldn't bear to think she might leave him—that was true. Why else had he signed that cold-blooded document? She should never have allowed it, should have known he was just paying lip service to their marriage, had never, even for a second, intended to share the experience with her!

Alexandra dropped her glass, and it shattered on the floor in a hundred fragments. Snatching up a new canvas from the pile by the window, she tore off the brown wrapping paper and hurled it up on the easel. Trembling wildly, she stared at the dead white fabric, then strode to the table where her fresh paints were stacked in boxes, ripped open the cardboard, and grasped the new, fat tubes in her hand. Paint it away! Lash her fury onto canvas!

She snapped off the caps from the tubes and they rattled to the floor and rolled into dark corners. She kicked away her shoes and failed to notice as the soles of her feet were pierced by broken glass. Paint it! With thick, broad brushes and with knives and with her hands! She squeezed hard, and long, plump worms of paint, a crescendo of color, splashed onto the canvas. Reds, blues, greens, yellows. No—the colors were all wrong. Vividness like that stood for joy and warmth. She threw more boxes aside on the table, searching for and finding the new tubes of black. With her broadest knife she slashed ebony gloom like thick icing over the rioting primaries. Then, with fresh salt tears stinging her eyes, she slapped both hands, palms down, flat against the canvas, and with a howl of pain that wrenched her stomach and filled the empty studio, her nails ripped right through paint and fabric, and a searing, ugly gash appeared.

She woke with a pounding head, body spread-eagled on top of the quilt on their bed. The pillows were smeared with paint and mascara where she'd buried her face in the night; her fingernails were caked with black, and the soles of her feet throbbed. She groaned as she moved her legs over the side of the bed, then cried out loud as her feet touched the rug.

"Shit!"

She bent and examined the flesh gingerly. At least three quite large glass splinters, coated with dry blood, were visible on the balls of both feet, and her left heel fairly sparkled with fragments ground into dirt. With great care, Alexandra limped into the bathroom and prepared to repair the damage with tweezers and a bottle of antiseptic.

It was an hour later, when she was lying in the bathtub soaking away some of the pain and tension, that she decided she had to get away. Her nerves were shot to shreds, that much was clear. Last night she'd destroyed a canvas, and, Lord knew, to an artist that was tantamount to child beating! Maybe it was as well she wasn't pregnant. . . .

Slowly she dried herself, put more antiseptic on her feet and bandaged them. Staying in New York, in this apartment, while she was in this state, would be an error. Springtime in Manhattan was invigorating if your world was whole and your life rounded, but if you stared out of your window onto the fresh green buds of Central Park and saw only grime and your own misery, you were at risk. She must go, she concluded, immediately. If she waited, like an adolescent, for Andreas to call or return, there was the risk that tempers would again be lost, and rifts spread into ravines.

By noon she had packed two bags, tidied the apartment, locked the studio, too appalled to repair the damage she'd done in there, and written a short note to Andreas.

> Maybe I expect too much. You are everything to me, husband, lover, best friend.
>
> A little time for myself, that's all. Too much sadness at home right now, too many disappointments. I'll pull myself back, I promise, and I pray you'll do the same. We need each other, I think.
>
> France. The south. What's good for Picasso, Matisse, and Chagall must surely be therapy for a mere Alessandro, don't you agree?

She propped the note in an envelope on the hall table, checked her purse again for her passport, checkbook, and driver's license, and buzzed the doorman.

Saint-Paul was cool and peaceful when she arrived late the following afternoon. She had spent the previous night at the Ritz in Paris, hiding unhappily in her room from the blatant romantic harmony that swirled through the corridors and salons of the hotel, and spilled out onto the Place Vendôme. The flight to the south in the small Air Inter jet and arrival itself at the cluttered airport in Nice had also been less than joyous, the memory of her last stay still too fresh in her mind, and for a while Alexandra feared she had made a mistake in coming back. Until she parked her hired yellow Citroën in the narrow approach road to the village, and limped slowly toward the gate of the Colombe d'Or hotel.

It had rained up in the hills earlier in the day, and the sandy path that, later in the year, would bake hard and red, was still damp and soft, and a tangy fresh scent rose from each footfall. Now a sheet of pale apricot spread across the early evening sky, and the old men of the village sat on benches in the square, smoking and arguing contentedly, preparing for yet another game of boules.

Alexandra checked in and went straight to her room. She smiled as she entered; it was stark, but handsome. A hotel manager in the United States would balk at offering such severity at these prices, but in truth there was nothing lacking. The walls and ceiling were freshly painted stone, the structure was simple and pleasing, with beautiful round alcoves and archways and careful soft lighting. The bed was large, the floor polished stone, with just one soft white rug in which to bury's one's toes in the shock of first rising. The dresser was marble, and the only other furniture was a pair of antique tapestry-backed side chairs. The whole room had the effect of calming the senses, rather as one might expect a nun's quarters to appear in a luxury convent, were such a thing to exist.

She unpacked quickly, pushed the simple clothes to which she had restricted herself out of sight, and lay down on the bed to rest. She was exhausted, she realized. The failures of the last few months had sapped her strength and drained her of humor. She murmured a swift prayer for resilience, then closed her eyes. She didn't often pray these days, hadn't been inside a church since the Italian hospital chapel after Andreas's crash. Briefly, she wondered if God was perhaps punishing her, and then sleep overcame her.

In the morning, the room waiter drew the drapes and rested a breakfast tray on her knees. The sun shone, the coffee was strong and good, the rolls were freshly baked, and the *confitures* were homemade. An auspicious beginning, she felt.

Before leaving the room she picked up the bedside telephone and asked the operator to connect her with New York. The ringing went unanswered and she hung up. Five in the morning and Andreas not home. She clenched her fists and fought bitter disappointment.

As she passed the hotel's remarkable little art collection and strolled out into the sunshine, her mood lifted. She visited three galleries, admired honestly the work of a young Spanish painter, and, because it was cooler than she'd first thought, bought a hand-knitted pullover from a tired-looking woman and tugged it over her head. Emerging from pale blue fluff and brushing a few stray strands out of her eyes, she saw a face reflected in a shop window a few yards away. She blinked, and momentarily the face vanished before she saw it again and was sure.

"Dan?" He didn't hear, and she called out more loudly. "Dan Stone!"

Daniel turned and looked at her. For a moment his brow furrowed, then he recognized her and broke into a smile. "Ali!" He shook her hand warmly. "I didn't know you were in Saint-Paul. Andreas never said a word."

"He didn't know. It was a last-minute decision."

"Is he here with you?"

"No."

"Where are you staying?"

"At the Colombe d'Or."

"I have a rented house for a few weeks."

"In Saint-Paul?"

He nodded. "Just up the road." He laughed. "Small world."

"Isn't it."

"I suppose you're here to paint?"

"Not specifically," she said carefully. "And you?"

"I have a book that needs writing, and in New York there are just too many distractions. As usual, Fanny took command and sent me packing."

"Fanny sounds formidable."

"I forgot you haven't met her yet. Too many commissions."

"I beg your pardon?"

"Oh, nothing," Daniel said easily. "Just that you've always been busy when we've invited you to dinner. Our bad fortune." He grinned. "Don't worry, we'll work something out one day."

They stood awkwardly together on the narrow street, neither certain what to say or do next. Alexandra's mind was working fast. To her knowledge she'd never turned down a single invitation from either Dan or Fanny Harper. Which meant, presumably, that Andreas might not have passed on her own invitations to Dan either.

"Would you like some coffee?" Daniel asked suddenly. "We could sit outside if you're warm enough."

She nodded. "I'd love it."

They walked back to the main square. Alexandra was relieved to sit down, for by now her feet were aching badly again. Daniel ordered coffee for them both, and they settled comfortably back in their chairs.

"How long have you been here?" she asked.

"Just short of a week."

"How's it coming?"

"The writing?" He shrugged. "Not bad. It's not exactly Proust, but I guess it's what's needed. At least I hope so."

She watched him as he spooned froth from the top of the hot milk and floated it on his coffee. He was more interesting to look at than she'd first thought. His brown eyes were beautiful, lustrous and compelling, and with that slightly crooked nose and spicy small beard it was easy to see why women across the United States tuned in to his shows.

"Where did you get your scar?" she asked.

He looked surprised. "Don't you know?"

"Should I?"

He paused. "Your husband gave it to me."

It was her turn to be taken aback. "Really?" She peered at it more closely. "It's old, isn't it. When you were boys?"

"That's right."

"He didn't tell me." When he said nothing, she added, "What a reticent pair you are."

"Did he tell you he saved my life?"

"What?" A thought crossed her mind. "Roberto, his father, said something like that to me once, but Andreas denied it."

"It's true."

"What happened?"

Daniel smiled. "Maybe I'll tell you sometime. Just now I don't feel in the mood for old stories."

Silence slipped uncomfortably back between them. All around the square, from open windows, smells of lunch cooking filtered out over them and blended with the scents of budding jasmine and mown grass from the hillside gardens close by.

"Well . . ." Daniel drank his coffee in a single gulp. "I should be getting back to work. That's the only curse of a place like this. It's such a damned temptation just to sit outside and while away the day."

Alexandra sighed softly. "That's exactly why I chose it. A chance to stand and stare."

"New York's like that, isn't it," he sympathized. "Too much of a good thing. Sometimes you just have to get out, however much you love it." He pulled some francs out of a pocket and put them on the table. "Forgive me if I have to leave, Ali." He stood up. "If you're at a loose end one evening, maybe we can have dinner. Friends in far-off places and all that." He looked down at her.

She smiled. "I'd like that."

"Good. I'll call you at the Colombe d'Or when I get the next section of the book cleared away."

At seven that evening, the telephone beside her bed jangled abruptly. It was Daniel.

"Hello," she said. "You surely can't have worked that hard."

"Quite right. I did almost nothing the whole afternoon, so now I have to work on through the evening and some of the night."

"I'll just have to enjoy dinner alone, then."

"If you're staying there, drink the *Cave Maison.* It tastes ordinary, but it has a real sting in its tail."

She laughed. "Maybe I should stick to mineral water."

"I didn't call to advise you on wine. I thought perhaps instead of dinner, I could use a break around lunchtime tomorrow. We could drive out into the hills, maybe take a picnic."

"That sounds fine."

"Good. I'll provide the essentials and come to find you around noon."

She put down the receiver smiling, then looked back at the telephone, wondering if she should try calling home again, but decided against it. For the first time in a long while she felt the beginnings of relaxation come over her, and discovering that Andreas was still not back was hardly the way to prolong that feeling.

In a small whitewashed house up the road, Daniel also stood and looked at the phone. Something about the call troubled him. Was there an element of risk, he wondered, in lunching with the wife of his friend? Because of Andreas's curious behavior, Ali Alessandro was almost a stranger, but she was also stirringly lovely.

He shrugged, impatient at the thought. What could be more innocent, after all, than a picnic lunch? But he remembered another picnic, long ago, in Vevey with Natalie Bresson, and an almost forgotten image of heat and desire passed through his mind and made him shiver.

38

A bee traced a flight path low over the crumbled remains of the picnic lunch and finding nothing sweet, transferred its attentions to Alexandra's hair. Languidly she raised one hand and waved it away.

"Bees in April," she murmured. "Unusual."

Daniel shifted his position slightly against the thin trunk of the pine tree on which he was leaning. "It's warm for April."

"Mmm . . ."

It was uncommonly warm for early spring. They were reclining lazily on the top of a grassy knoll, succulent meadows spread all around; just a few hundred yards from their picnic site the view spun dizzily away over the *moyenne Corniche* and down to the Mediterranean. Alexandra half closed her eyes and watched Daniel, jacket off and shirt sleeves rolled up, and had the feeling that they might almost be part of a painting by Renoir. Idly she glanced at her own bare arms. It was the quality of the light that gave everything that luminous sheen . . . her skin and the sparkling foliage. She was aware that she ought at least to be sketching, but she felt weighed down by lethargy, had not the slightest desire to pick up charcoal.

"More wine?" Daniel offered, picking up the almost empty bottle of Provence *rouge.*

"No, thanks." The sunshine and the young wine had made her head spin a little, and she bent her legs and folded her arms around them, resting her head on her knees.

For comparative strangers, she reflected, they were getting along very well. Earlier, when Daniel had walked into the hotel, she had felt a small prickle of tension about committing herself to an unspecified number of hours in his company, but as soon as they were on the open road she had begun to appreciate his calm, natural charm. Driving with her husband was never relaxed; a hairpin bend was to Andreas just extra practice for a racetrack chicane. Daniel drove like a man with nothing to prove; on the tricky sections of the corniche he took his time and concentrated, and on the straight inland roads he stuck to the right and enjoyed the view.

Driving away from Saint-Paul toward Grasse, they had stopped a number of times, walking and climbing on rocks, and Alexandra had felt emotional strain trickling away. She was still unusually tired, but she'd summoned strength determinedly, blowing away her troubles like dandelion flock on the breeze, and soon they had both run races as if they were city children off the leash the first day at summer camp.

"Feel okay?"

Alexandra raised her head from her knees. "Fine. Just a slight headache."

"What's wrong with your feet?" Daniel asked, looking at them. She'd kicked off her espadrilles so that the bandages showed.

"I stepped on some glass at home." She grinned wryly. "Quite a lot of glass, actually."

"But you should have told me," he said, concerned. "All that running and climbing. Are they painful?"

"They weren't so bad this morning, but now they are a little sore." In truth, they were throbbing badly in time to her head. That was all she needed! She hadn't been sick for years, but suddenly the sunshine was starting to feel unpleasantly hot and sticky. She shivered involuntarily.

"Ali?" Daniel eyed her sharply. "Are you feeling ill?"

She smiled weakly. "Some picnic companion I turned out to be."

He was up on his feet and packing the leftovers and cloth into the straw pannier before she could protest. "Come on," he ordered gently. "Let's get you back to your hotel."

"I am sorry, Dan. It's just the sun and the wine."

"More like a touch of flu, I'd guess." He bent and took her arm, helping her up. "Okay to walk to the car?"

"Of course," she protested, but halfway back to the road, her head swam so fiercely that she staggered. She felt Daniel's arm strongly around her, supporting her and helping her into the passenger seat of his Renault.

Back in Saint-Paul, in front of the Colombe d'Or a crowd had gathered to watch a fight of some kind between two locals, and it was impossible to park close to the hotel. Daniel glanced at Alexandra. She was shivering uncontrollably now, her teeth chattering, and it was clear she was running a high fever.

"Right," he muttered, "back to my place and into bed where

you belong." He took her hand briefly and squeezed it, before reversing back down the road a little way and then turning up toward his house.

Two hours later he was sitting on a chair next to the bed in his spare room, lightly sponging her baking forehead and cursing the unreliability of French doctors. Alexandra was tossing and turning, her black hair soaked with perspiration, her lips moving constantly as she murmured incomprehensible words in breathy whispers.

Daniel unfolded the covers at the end of the bed and took a look at her feet. They were greatly swollen and a dull red color. Damn that doctor! Quickly he left the room and returned a minute or two later with a bowl of fresh warm water, a bottle of antiseptic, and scissors. As gently as he could, though Alexandra seemed quite oblivious, he cut away the bandages and stared in concern at the soles of her feet. He'd bet the proceeds of the next Stone guide that she had blood poisoning, in which case antiseptic alone wasn't going to do any good at all.

Angrily he went back to his own bedroom and dialed the doctor's number again. His wife answered, sounding irritated. No, the doctor was still out on calls. Yes, the second he got back. Now if monsieur would just clear the line in case her husband was trying to contact her—

Alexandra seemed less restless when he went back into the spare room, but when he peered more closely he saw that she was trembling violently and was icy to the touch. He ran to his own room, yanked the blankets from the bed, and covered her gently. Within ten minutes she was baking hot again and muttering hoarsely. Daniel wiped her face, dabbed her lips with cool water, and watched her intently. There was nothing else to do but wait.

It was almost eleven o'clock when the doctor, a balding, spindly man with a red face, rapped at the door. He reeked of garlic and cognac, and Daniel had to control his temper with an effort.

His examination was thorough, however, and when Daniel drew his attention to Alexandra's wounded feet, he uttered a short exclamation and listened again, with even greater care, to her heart and lungs.

"Is it blood poisoning?"

The doctor shrugged. "A bad infection certainly." He bent down at the end of the bed and looked more closely at her feet. "Also, I think there are still splinters of glass in the left heel."

"How bad is she?"

"Her lungs are clear and her heart is strong, but the fever is hectic. I shall have to go to my office and fetch some things I need."

"But don't you have everything with you?" Daniel asked angrily. "I described the symptoms to your wife."

The Frenchman smiled tolerantly. "There are many messages to give me. She cannot remember every detail." He snapped his bag shut. "I will return quickly, don't worry."

True to his word he was back in less than a half hour, administering shots of penicillin and tetanus antitoxin. "And now, *cher monsieur,* you must watch and wait." He rose. "If you can get her to drink something, give her cool water, not too cold, little and often."

Daniel went with him to the front door. "Will you be back later?"

"In the morning. Provided the lady is more herself, she can take the antibiotic in tablet form, and I shall be able to look after those feet." He grimaced. "I would guess that she tried to take care of those splinters herself, without calling in professional help."

"Which, of course, was foolish."

The doctor shook his head. "It was more than foolish. The lady could, in theory, have died."

In the morning, Alexandra was far from being herself, but she was greatly improved. Her fever was down to a more manageable level, and while every bone in her body seemed to ache and her feet still throbbed, she was able to talk lucidly to Daniel and the doctor.

"Why didn't you call your own physician, madame?"

She rubbed her eyes. "I thought I could take care of it myself. I mean, splinters—anyone can take out splinters."

"Apparently not." The Frenchman gave her another shot of penicillin. "And now, would you allow me to administer a little local anesthetic so that I may extract the remaining pieces of glass from your feet." He shook his head. "If I may say so, madame, any physician who performed such an atrocious piece of surgery would be struck off the medical register."

Alexandra smiled weakly. "I'm an artist, not a physician."

The doctor patted her arm benevolently. "Then I would venture to suggest, madame, that you stick to your canvas and your paints."

By dusk Alexandra's fever was down almost to normal and her feet were encased neatly in clean white bandages.

"Dan?" she called. "Where are you?"

"In the kitchen," he yelled back.

"Good!"

He poked his face around the door. "Why? Are you hungry?"

"I think I am. There's a great hollow place inside me that's beginning to complain."

He smiled. "Excellent. I won't be long." He disappeared again.

"What are you making? It smells delicious."

"What does one make when someone's sick?" His face appeared for the second time.

"I don't know," she said.

"Chicken soup. What else?"

At ten o'clock Daniel tucked Alexandra back into the spare bed. The chicken soup with which he'd spoon-fed her had done its work. She'd been strong enough afterward to take a bath, though Daniel had refused adamantly to allow her to wash her hair. By now she was exhausted again and ready for sleep.

He looked down at her. "Do you need anything else?"

She shook her head. "Not a thing." She grinned weakly. "You have it all worked out."

He smiled. "Not quite all."

She took his hand. "You've been so kind. I don't know how to thank you, Dan."

"What's to thank? You gave me a great excuse not to work."

"I wasted your time."

He studied her for a moment. Till now he'd always seen her at her best, wrapped in lovely clothes, makeup perfect, hair freshly done. Tonight she lay in bed wearing one of his shirts, without a scrap of makeup and her hair combed through but still a little damp and stringy—and yet he thought her more beautiful than ever.

"Get some sleep," he said softly, and bending, he kissed her on the forehead.

Her eyes closed. "No trouble at all . . ."

Quietly he let himself out of the room. In the tiny salon he opened the bottle of calvados and poured himself a large drink.

The creaking of pipes woke Alexandra. She stirred in the strange bed and the creaking came again. She sat up, heart pounding, fingers clutching at the sheets.

There were no drapes at the window and the moon, striking through the branches of a tree in the garden, cast shadows across the room, narrow and black, falling like bars over the bedclothes. A small bat, flying low just outside the window, screeched suddenly, and Alexandra cried out in alarm. In a second the door opened and Daniel hurried in, tying the belt of his robe around his waist.

"Ali? What's wrong?" He switched on the overhead lamp and light flooded the room.

"I—I heard—" Her eyes, wide and gray, stared out of the window.

"Do you feel bad?" He sat on the edge of the bed and felt her forehead with the palm of his hand. "Should I call the doctor?"

She shook her head, still wordless from the panic that had grasped her out of sleep.

"Did something scare you?"

"I . . . think so. Out there." She stared into the garden, now inky black in contrast with the brightness in the room.

"Let me take a look." He got up, snapped off the light again and went to the window, peering out. "Can't see anything." He turned to her. "What did you think you saw, Ali?"

"I heard—" Her voice was breathy. "I don't think it was anything really. I just woke up afraid and I don't know why."

Daniel sat on the side of the bed again. "Strange house, strange bed, and you've been very sick. You've had a crazy fever and you probably still have poison running through your body. I'm not surprised you felt frightened."

She sank back against the pillow. "I haven't been scared of the dark since I was a little girl."

"You want the light back on?"

"No," she said quickly. "There aren't any drapes and with the light on I can't see what's outside."

"Okay," he said gently. "But there's nothing in the garden except the trees and grass and maybe a bat or two."

She laughed shakily. "I think that might be what I heard. I'm not too fond of bats."

"They're outside, Ali," he reassured her, "and they're much more scared of you than you are of them."

"Don't bank on it."

"I won't." Sitting so close to her in the half-dark, Daniel became suddenly uncomfortably aware of her near nakedness and the sweet, natural scent of her skin. The buttons of the shirt she was wearing had come adrift as she'd tossed in her sleep, and the soft curve of her breasts gleamed in the moonlight. His mouth was dry. He stood up unsteadily.

"Don't go, Dan."

"You should get back to sleep."

"I don't think I can just yet."

"You want something to drink? Or to eat?"

She smiled. "More chicken soup? No thanks."

"Okay," he said. "Then I'll just stay here and sit quietly, and you talk if you want, or sleep if you can."

"Thank you." Suddenly her lips trembled, and her eyes glittered with tears. "Dan?"

"Yes, baby?"

"Would you mind very much holding me?"

For a moment he sat like a man on the brink, afraid of touching what he knew now, irrevocably, he desired more than anything.

"Please," she whispered. "Just for a while."

Daniel shifted slightly, holding out his arms, and she wriggled closer and came into them. Her body smelled of soap and heat, and her skin felt supple and silken as young flower petals. She quivered in his arms, and Daniel wasn't sure if she wept or sighed, and he pressed himself closer and was lost in her warmth and the long, narrow curving lines of her body.

Her right cheek freed itself from his chest, and she drew back a little, staring at him, and he saw that her face was wet with tears.

"Ali, what is it?" he heard himself murmur, but her wide eyes came closer still and her mouth brushed his unbearably, tantalizingly, and he kissed her back, gently at first, then harder, crushingly, and her hands were at the belt of his robe, tugging and unknotting, and his own hands were under the cotton shirt, cupping her breasts and feeling the hard, small nipples against his palms. *Ali, we mustn't, we shouldn't,* his thoughts pounded in his brain, but he said not a word. And then he was lying on the bed beside her, over her, inside her, and she was unfolding for him languidly, then eagerly, and he felt as if he was riding a dream, hazy but cherished, and the wonderful creature beneath him sighed and wrapped herself around him. And outside, in the night sky, a pair of bats wheeled and screeched and played and made love, and for just a brief second Alexandra opened her eyes—and then they shut tightly, and nothing on earth could have stopped them.

An hour before dawn the weather changed. Dark rain clouds rolled in from the north, the wind lifted and the red tiles on the roof of the little house creaked and groaned, waking Daniel and

Alexandra, who lay clutched in each other's arms in the narrow bed.

Their eyes opened, they gazed at one another, brown on gray, and as gentle sleep escaped their bodies, fear invaded, starting with a vague tingle at the backs of their minds and spreading through heart and soul right to fingertips and toes.

Aware that at any moment she would draw away, that he might never again in his life hold her in his arms, Daniel touched her face with his own, stubble against silk, needing more, yearning for more, but making do with the warmth and feel and scent of her.

And then, as he had anticipated, Alexandra pulled, as tenderly as she was able, away from him. Her heart pounded, her mind throbbed, and she felt him still—thought she would always feel him—between her thighs and inside her eager, empty body, and her guilt was so great, she thought she would shrivel and die, and almost longed to do so.

"Don't look that way," he whispered. It was still quite dark in the room, but the light from her eyes burned through him.

Alexandra got out of bed. The room was freezing and she shivered. Reaching over Daniel, she fumbled in the bedclothes, looking for his shirt, and put it on.

"Don't," Daniel said, getting up too. "You mustn't stand there in the cold. You'll send your fever up again."

"Where did you put my clothes?"

"Get back in bed," he begged gently. "Please, Ali, just get into bed."

She shook her head vehemently, her teeth chattering. "No. I have to leave."

"It's not morning yet. Wait a few hours. I'll go to my room and drive you to the hotel later."

She jerked her head toward the window. The dawn was starting to break, the heavy clouds scudding rapidly through the sky, large drops of rain striking the glass noisily.

"I'll go now."

"The doors will be locked."

"They'll unlock them." She looked at him pleadingly. "Dan, please, where are my clothes?"

"I'll get them."

When she was dressed and ready by the front door, gaunt and foolish-looking in the light spring dress she'd worn for the picnic, Daniel tried to take her hands, but they were cold and limp in his.

"Ali, please. Be angry with me if you must, but not with yourself."

"I'm not angry with you." Her mouth quivered. "You're not to blame at all."

"Of course I am. But I can see that maybe events propelled us into this—"

"Perhaps you, Dan. Not me. I propelled myself." She raised a hand and touched his cheek. "I've done you as much wrong as Andreas."

"No! Don't ever think that, Ali." His eyes burned. "This has been the night of my—"

"Don't say any more," she interrupted. "I feel guilty enough already."

"But you have nothing to feel guilty about! You came here depressed—I don't know what about—and then you got sick. I took advantage of you—"

"Dan, stop that! It isn't true at all. I'm a grown woman and I knew exactly what I was doing last night. But I have a husband."

"And you love him," Daniel added quietly.

"That's right," she whispered painfully. "Take me back to the hotel now, Dan, please."

In the car, outside the Colombe d'Or, as the sun rose, Alexandra turned to him. "I'll go back to New York tomorrow, Dan. I'll give myself another day to rest up." She glanced ruefully down at her bandaged feet. "Give these a chance to heal a little more."

"You stay, Ali. You need a holiday. I'll go back."

She shook her head. "You have work to do here. You said yourself there were too many distractions in New York."

"I think I'd welcome those distractions now," he said softly.

There was a silence, then Alexandra looked at Daniel despairingly. "I have to go home. Before it's too late."

He sighed. "Perhaps you're right."

She glanced at him sharply. "Don't let this come between you. Your friendship is too important. Andreas will never, ever hear what happened from me."

He flashed her a wounded look. "Could you think, even for a second, that I would tell him? He's my best friend, for God's sake!" he said bitterly.

"You've done nothing to hurt him, Dan. You looked after me, that's all. Even last night you were still caring for me—" She broke off, unable to continue.

Was that all it meant to her? he wondered. Maybe it was better that way.

"That's right," he said softly.

"So you'll stay awhile?"

He nodded, not trusting himself to speak. She leaned closer and kissed him on the cheek, her lips cool. "Thank you, Dan. For everything."

"You know," he said abruptly, "suddenly I'm glad Andreas has this thing about keeping us apart. I've never understood it. Fanny thinks it's some kind of two-way jealousy; she says he needs to compartmentalize his life, his emotions."

"Perhaps she's right. Fanny sounds wise."

A sad smile tugged at his mouth. "Anyway, I thank God for it now."

More guilt stabbed her. "I hope," she said, trying to be gentle, "one day we're able to be friends, Dan."

"We already are," he said. "Any time you need me." He reached over her and opened the passenger door, letting the cold early-morning air rush into the car. "I'll watch to see you get in safely. I think it's better I don't come with you."

She nodded.

"Be safe, Ali," he said quickly, wanting her gone. "And be happy."

Swiftly she moved against him and hugged him, animal-like, needing warmth and last-minute reassurance, and then she was out of the car and limping toward the gate.

When she was out of sight, Daniel rested his forehead for a moment against the cold, hard steering wheel. Another of those old, never forgotten memories surged through him: his mother bending and holding him to her that night, long ago in Nuremberg. He had never seen her again, and though he knew that he and this stirring woman would almost certainly meet often in their lives, the same vast sense of loss swamped him again now.

Alexandra telephoned Andreas from Kennedy Airport, just as he had done the previous September.

The line rang dully three times, and she held her breath.

"Hello?"

She shut her eyes. "May I come home?" she whispered.

"Ali? Thank God! Where are you?"

"At Kennedy."

"Wait there, I'll come and get you."

"No," she said. "I'll get a cab, it'll be quicker."

"All right." He paused. "I broke down the door of your studio.
I was frantic."

"It's okay," she said, and tears seeped from between her closed
eyelids. "See you soon." Carefully she put the receiver back on
the hook.

Two weeks later her period had not come. *Maybe it's because I was
sick,* she thought at first. *Or the journey. Women are often late when
they fly.* But she was never late.

John Manetti was cautious. "I'm glad you're not overreacting,
Ali," he said. "I'd hate it if you were too happy and things went
wrong."

She looked directly at him. "I don't feel pregnant. I don't think
I can be."

He smiled. "I'd like a dollar for every time I've heard that. Not
everyone throws up on day one, you know. In fact, not everyone
has morning sickness."

Hers began the very next day. She sat down to breakfast with
Andreas, glanced down at her toast and coffee, and bolted for the
bathroom.

Andreas looked up enquiringly from the *New York Times* when
she came back to the dining room. "Are you okay?"

"I threw up," she answered lightly. "I'm all right now."

His gaze hardly wavered. "Maybe you should fix up an appointment with Manetti."

She picked up her coffee cup. "I already have. I'm seeing him
this afternoon."

Later that night, as they were getting into bed, Alexandra said to
Andreas, "I had a call at six o'clock from John Manetti."

Andreas wound up the alarm clock. "I thought you saw him
today."

"I did." She paused. "I had a pregnancy test this afternoon."

There was a silence. Andreas put the clock back on the bedside
table. "And did you kill the frog?"

Her hands gripped the bedclothes. "Dead as a doornail."

Andreas sat down on the edge of the bed. "Poor son of a
bitch."

Alexandra watched his back. "How do you feel?"

He turned around. His eyes were blank. "Glad for you," he
said.

"Would you hold me, please?"

"Sure." He got under the bedclothes, reached over, and held

her lightly. "Just in the nick of time," he said. "Manetti must have thought he was going to flunk out." He lay down and turned out his bedside light.

Alexandra waited a moment, then moved closer until they were touching. She put out her hand tentatively, but Andreas lay still and her heart sank.

"Actually," she said after a minute, "I don't think they use frogs anymore."

The life inside her fluttered and grew large. The first time it kicked her, Alexandra laughed out loud and took Andreas's hand.

"Feel it," she whispered, her eyes sparkling, but he snatched his hand away and the joy went out of her. *How can I love it?* she wondered. *If it is born with Dan's eyes, then it will destroy all that's left of our marriage.* Andreas was solicitous enough, but she knew he could not bear to touch her with another man's child growing inside her.

Every night and morning, Alexandra locked herself into the bathroom, knelt on the rug, and prayed: *Dear God, let it look like Andreas so that he can love it.* After all, she reasoned, it was still possible that the insemination had worked, and Manetti had sworn to make every effort to match Andreas's physical characteristics. *Oh, God,* she bargained, *I'll do anything, give up painting, give up sex, anything only please let it look like Andreas!* And then the child kicked again, and love assaulted her, scorching her heart and making her breathless.

Her pains began on the morning of the eleventh day of 1966. Andreas had gone to a meeting at the Park Avenue restaurant, and so she took the suitcase that had been packed and ready for a week, and took a cab to New York Hospital. She labored for seven hours before Andreas arrived at her side, white-faced.

"Why didn't you call me?"

She shook her head, wordless from the last pain.

"How could you be so thoughtless?"

"I thought—" She stopped, startled, as Andreas took the cool compress from the nurse who had been attending her, and touched it gently to her forehead. "I didn't think you'd want to—"

"You're my wife," he said quietly. "I love you. If you're going to suffer, I have to be with you."

She grasped gladly at his hand. "And the child?"

"The child has nothing to do with it." He pulled a chair close to the bed and sat down. His eyes were compassionate. "Don't be sad, Ali," he said gently. "I can't help it."

The girl was born at two in the morning. She weighed six pounds and nine ounces and yelled lustily. When the nurse brought her, swaddled in white, for Alexandra to hold, Andreas turned away.

Dear Lord, Alexandra still prayed, knowing it was too late, *let her look like him.* The warm bundle moved in her arms and she opened her eyes. Her heart pounded. The infant had dark hair, and her eyes were clenched tightly shut.

"Mr. Alessandro?" The nurse nudged Andreas. "Wouldn't you like to look at your beautiful girl?"

Slowly, Andreas turned around. His face was ashen, and Alexandra realized he was panic-stricken. Her heart went out to him.

"Come and say hello," she said gently.

The nurse drew up a chair and Andreas sat down heavily. With a sudden urge of curiosity he put out his right hand and touched the baby's tiny curled fingers. The child opened her eyes.

"Look at that!" he exclaimed. "She has your eyes exactly! The same gray-green."

The nurse, on her way out of the room, scoffed. "What nonsense! All new babies have blue or brown eyes!"

"Come and see for yourself," Andreas insisted.

She returned to inspect her. "My Lord, he's right!" She straightened up. "Most unusual."

Alexandra stared into her daughter's face. It was red and wrinkled. "Let Mama see them too, sweetheart," she whispered. Sure enough, a mirror image of her own. *Thank you, dear God!*

The child waved her tiny arms abruptly and clutched at Andreas's hand, one small fist clenching his index finger tightly.

"Jesu Maria," he breathed. "She's holding me." His eyes filled with tears. "It's going to be all right," he said in amazement. "She knows me. It's going to be all right."

"Nurse!" Alexandra called, her voice trembling. "Would you mind taking her for just a minute?" The nurse bustled over and took the infant, cooing sweetly. Alexandra held out her arms. "I want to hold my husband," she said softly.

Andreas hugged her hard. "I was so scared," he said, his eyes streaming and his voice strangled. "I thought she would be a stranger, that she'd be nothing to do with me—that I might hate her."

Alexandra clenched her fists behind his neck in exultation. "That's all over now, darling. We have our daughter."

The nurse came back with the baby. "Just a few more minutes," she said, "and then we'll tuck her up in the nursery and Mama can take a nap."

The small weight lay in her arms again, and Alexandra drank in her smell and committed it to memory.

"I've been thinking," she said after a minute. "Her name. What about Roberta?"

Andreas pulled a handkerchief from his pocket and mopped his eyes. "Papa would be happy. But I thought you might want to call her after your mother."

She smiled. "After you, there's no one I feel closer to than Roberto."

"It's a fine name."

"And Bobbi for short, if it suits her."

A great wave of weakness swept suddenly over her and she lay back against the pillows. The vigilant nurse took the baby quickly from her and made her comfortable. Andreas stood up.

"You have to sleep."

She nodded gratefully. "You too, Papa." She smiled. "See you both later."

As the door closed behind them, the realization struck her.

Now I shall never know whose child she really is.

39

In the spring of 1966, Daniel was not happy.

When he was not at Harper and Stone, he was at his desk at home, writing. When he was not writing, he was at the studios filming the new series of *The Gourmets*. When he had a break from directors, cameramen, or guests for the show, he was being invited to the best restaurants in town. When he was not being openly courted by America's innkeepers, he was being almost as openly pursued by their wives. And that was just in his working time.

When Daniel was not working, he was lonely as hell. He saw as much of Fanny as ever when she was in town, and he saw Roly whenever he was at the office, but fond as he was of him, there was only so much of Roly you could swallow at a single sitting. Sarah and Leon scraped aside a few hours every now and then when their busy restaurant would allow. And, of course, he saw Andreas. That is, he saw him when Andreas wasn't staring dewy-eyed into the eyes of his baby daughter. Ali, thank God, he'd seen only once since Saint-Paul, at Roberta's baptism, and then she'd been almost as immersed in well-wishers as the charming, creamy-skinned, raven-haired infant had been in holy water. Only Cat had limitless time for him.

Daniel was not happy.

At the beginning of May, he went to California to look at office space for the new catering corporation Harper and Stone had formed. He flew into Los Angeles on a Friday afternoon, and that night a party was thrown in his honor at a mansion in Beverly Hills.

It was the kind of affair Daniel had come to detest. The women were stunning, but they flaunted their Saint-Laurent originals and suntans with voluptuous brutality. The men, without relief, were television producers or moviemakers; most wore white silk turtle-necks, Gucci loafers, and fat cigars. Nearly everyone shouted pen-etratingly or murmured conspiratorially. Everyone laughed all the time. Nowhere, except in the food, was subtlety to be found. It

was, Daniel reflected, as if good taste had died and gone to
heaven.

In danger of drowning in Dom Pérignon and Estée Lauder perfume, he went in search of the kitchen, interested to see whose
talent lay behind dinner. In the center of the kitchen he found a
calamity in progress. The chef, a short, stout Frenchman with no
more than twenty hairs on his round head and wild eyes, had just
sliced through most of his right index finger with a chopping
knife. Blood poured from him, spreading like vivid roses on his
white overall. But the pain did not seem to trouble him—what was
driving him to the verge of hysteria was the fact that while the
gâteau aux fraises des bois and chocolate mousse were ready and
waiting to be served, the *omelette norvégienne* had yet to be started.

"It is Monsieur Stone's favorite dessert!" he wailed. "But if I
beat ze eggs, I will bleed into zem!"

A young American, apparently his assistant, tried to calm him,
but he was in no state to be soothed. *"Quelle catastrophe!"* he
moaned.

"You should have that finger looked at right away," the assistant
offered reasonably. "I can beat the eggs."

"Pah!" snapped the chef. "Your hands have ze delicacy of ba-
nanas! You could not beat your wife wiz success, let alone my
eggs!"

Stung, the assistant fell silent and the chef continued to bellow.
No one took the slightest notice of Daniel, who stood as a man
walking in a park might hover, seeing someone struggling in a
river. He could leave, or he could save him. After all, he rationalized, it had nothing to do with him. And yet—this man was in
distress because of *his* dessert.

Decisively he whipped off his jacket, loosened his tie, rolled up
his sleeves, and removed his watch. Still he was ignored.

"Someone take this man to a doctor!" he said loudly, and striding over to the sink, he scrubbed his hands and forearms as if he
were a surgeon. "And find me something to cover these clothes."

All activity ceased. They stared.

Daniel clapped his hands. *"Vite!"*

The chef had gone pink with outrage. "And who ze fuck are
you?"

"I," said Daniel clearly, "am a chef."

"But where did you come from?"

"Down the chimney, like Santa Claus. Now, do you see any
special reason to stand there and bleed to death? Which, inciden-

tally"—Daniel peered closer at the injured hand—"I think you may do, given time."

"Are you a doctor too?" the Frenchman snarled.

"No, just a chef."

"But ze *omelette norvégienne!*"

"It so happens," Daniel said gently, "that I have made this dessert for Mr. Stone on a number of occasions." He whirled around. "So where's my overall? One of your aprons will do." He turned on the waitresses, who stood gaping. "And I hope the eggs aren't in the refrigerator! Room temperature! They are? Excellent! You!" He addressed the assistant. "Show me the serving dishes, I want to see their size. And where's the Grand Marnier? Mr. Stone likes a double dose in his *omelette!*"

For the next thirty minutes Daniel was transported back more than twenty years to the Restaurant Lemans in Vevey. As he folded sugar into the California eggs, he saw himself again as the skinny young apprentice with the kindhearted boss, chopping and paring and grilling and weighing and tasting for Bresson's busy, fussy customers. Those had, he often thought, been the best days of his life, until—

"Sir?" the assistant nudged him politely from his memories. "I think it's ready."

Daniel stared into the oven. The dessert was indeed done to perfection, the peaks of the egg whites exquisitely bronzed.

"Good," he judged, and removed his apron. "Serve it," he ordered.

"Where are you going?" the young man asked in surprise.

Daniel smiled. "Back up the chimney."

He left the kitchen, his jacket slung over his shoulder, fastening the strap of his Cartier watch, just as a stranger from the party barged out of a room, clearly the worse for liquor, brandishing a magnum of Dom Pérignon and struggling with the cork. Daniel realized that the inevitable was about to happen, and tried to step aside, but too late. The cork exploded from the neck of the bottle and Daniel, together with the silk-clad wall behind him, was drenched in champagne. The drunk looked at the bottle in dismay, raised it to his lips, and staggered away.

"Of all the dumb, selfish things—"

Daniel, wet and bemused, looked behind him. In the kitchen doorway stood a waitress, hands on hips, eyes flashing.

"Just because you're hired help he thinks he can dump a bottle of champagne on you and just walk away!"

Daniel's lips twitched.

"I don't know why you're smiling," she said. "You look ridiculous, and your clothes are ruined." She grabbed his arm. "Come on."

"Where are we going?"

"We have a room at the back where they let us change." She tugged at him encouragingly. "Come on. Don't be shy."

In the narrow, poorly lit room, which looked as if it was normally used as a storage closet, she ordered him to remove his suit.

"Don't worry." She grinned. "I won't peek. Anyway, I have three brothers." She examined the soaked fabric. "This is nice. Feels almost like silk." She grimaced. "Well, there's nothing much I can do for it here except sponge it and hang it to dry."

"And what do I wear meantime?"

She opened a locker. "These belong to Joe—Monsieur Gérard's assistant." She held out a pair of denim jeans and a red-and-blue-checked shirt.

"Is Monsieur Gérard the chef?"

"Sure." She was wide-eyed. "You mean you're a chef yourself and you don't know who he is?"

Daniel smiled. "I'm from the East Coast. I'm just here on a visit."

"Really?"

They regarded each other with interest. She was very young, no more than twenty, Daniel guessed, and she was a pale honey blonde with navy-blue eyes that caught the light and sparkled even in the dark closet. She was tall with long, coltish legs, and even in her uniform it was impossible not to notice the swell of her breasts and the narrowness of her waist. Daniel found it hard to look away.

"What are you waiting for?" she prompted shyly. "You'll catch a cold in those wet things."

He took off his white shirt and trousers, glad that in spite of the years of good food he was still in relatively good physical shape.

"Not bad," she said, watching him zip up the jeans with minimal difficulty. "Joe's only twenty-eight, and they're snug on him."

Daniel wondered if banana-fingered Joe was her boyfriend. The thought was distasteful.

"What's your name?" she asked suddenly.

He thought rapidly, reluctant to embarrass her. "Daniel."

"Daniel what?"

"Silberstein."

She tilted her head to one side, and her soft, curly hair tumbled with it, brushing her left shoulder. She started to sponge his trousers.

"And what's your name?" he asked, smiling, as he buttoned up his shirt.

"Barbara Zabrisky," she answered. "How come you were at this party? Do you know this guy Stone?"

"I came with friends," he said noncommittally.

"Would you like me to find them and tell them what happened?"

He shook his head. "I don't think so, thank you. I'd had about enough of the party anyway."

She took his wrist and glanced at his watch. "I should be getting back."

"Do you think Joe would object if I take off in these clothes for a while? I could go change, then come back here a little later."

"Oh, sure," she said easily. "We'll all be tied up here till pretty late anyhow, and your tux might be dry then."

He grinned at her. "I'll leave it here as collateral for the jeans and shirt."

She smiled back. Both cheeks were dimpled. "Let me show you the way out."

"Through the back, I hope."

"Of course through the back. Those snobs in there would bust a gut if you strolled through looking like that."

Daniel took a cab back to the Beverly Hills Hotel, took a shower, and changed into a pair of worn cords and a clean white shirt. Then he took the elevator back down to the lobby, where he tipped the night manager fifty dollars to unlock the flower boutique so that he could buy a huge armful of wildly colored, fragrant spring flowers.

At two in the morning he was still standing outside on the street, waiting for the last guest to leave. There was no point going in search of her yet; he knew the clearing-up operation would continue for a while before the waitresses were finally let off duty. He sat down on the back steps, clutching the bouquet and Joe's clothes, and stared up into the sky. The night was clear, the blackness littered with hundreds of stars and a crescent moon. *New enough to wish on?* he wondered, and did so, crossing his fingers at the same time.

"Daniel?"

Her voice, gentle and sweet, shook him from sleep. He was still clasping the flowers. "I must have dozed off."

Barbara picked Joe's clothes up from the steps and folded them. "I guess so." She hesitated. "I thought you weren't coming. Then one of the girls said there was a guy hanging around outside and I thought it might be you."

He got to his feet and held out the flowers. "These are for you."

She was clearly exhausted, but there was no disguising the pleasure on her face. "How beautiful! Where did you find them at this time of night?" She buried her face in the petals, inhaling their scent.

"It wasn't so difficult," he said, drinking in the picture of her. "Barbara?"

She looked up. "Yes?"

"Are you too tired to let me buy you dinner? Nothing fancy," he said hurriedly, "just something light."

"I don't know," she said uncertainly. "It's awfully late."

"You shouldn't go to sleep on an empty stomach."

"It isn't exactly empty. I had a snack before the party."

"That doesn't count."

"Are you sure?" She made up her mind. "All right. I'll just get these back to Joe and I'll be right back." She ran up the steps, then turned. "Do you have a car? The buses don't run this late."

"There's a cab waiting around the corner."

"But that'll cost you a fortune. How long have you been here?"

"Not long," he lied.

"I'll be right back," she said again, and disappeared into the house.

They found an all-night diner on the highway near Santa Monica. Daniel wanted to ask the driver to wait for them, but Barbara was outraged.

"They always have numbers of cab services in these places."

She ordered Manhattan clam chowder and a hot turkey sandwich on rye bread with gravy, while Daniel stuck to the chowder. She ate with relish, Daniel noticed with pleasure. So many women he took to dinner nibbled cautiously at their dishes, like Siamese cats lapping daintily around their bowls of milk, because their dieticians had warned them against speed and enjoyment. Barbara Zabrisky was hungry, ergo she ate. When her hunger was satisfied, she began to talk.

"How long have you been in L.A.?"

"Since this afternoon. Or rather since yesterday."

"Have you been here before?"

"A few times."

"What do you think?"

"I'm not sure."

"Don't you like it?" Her eyebrows arched.

He didn't want to disappoint her. "I don't think I've seen enough to know."

"Have you been to the beach?"

"Not here. But I've seen a lot of beaches."

"Not the same." She waved airily and dug back into the turkey sandwich, coming away with a forkful of meat, potato, gravy, and bread. "I'll show you, if you like," she offered after she'd swallowed.

"I'd like that. Have you ever been to the East Coast?"

She shook her head. "Never."

"In New York, you can stand out on the street and get to know the city from the outside in."

"I guess I'll have to get there before I'm much older. That's where the work is."

"Do you work with Gérard all the time?"

"God, no! I'm a dancer."

Daniel looked at her. Of course! That explained the perfect posture, the narrow neck, and the graceful long legs.

"Are you working at the moment?"

"I'm teaching eight-year-olds to point their toes and master arabesques and entrechats. That's for two hours every weekday afternoon, sometimes three, and in the evenings, if Gérard needs extra help Joe calls me up. And in between, I drive my agent crazy and check the signs outside the theaters and clubs."

Daniel smiled. "Would you like some dessert?"

She hooted with laughter. "You think I eat like a horse! You're right. I'd adore some apple pie, please. Once I get started, I'm afraid it's like stopping a runaway streetcar!"

"I wouldn't dare try."

The dimples sprang back into her cheeks. "Unless you think it's bad to sleep on a full stomach."

"I wasn't planning on sending you to bed just yet."

"Good. I've nothing to do in the morning except practice anyway."

They went to the beach around five, took off their shoes, and walked barefoot in the sand. It was blissfully quiet, the only definable sounds the gently rolling surf and their own low-pitched voices. Daniel traced her name in the damp sand with his toes and stood back to look at it in the starlight.

"Barbara Zabrisky," he murmured. "Looks great in lights, don't you think?"

She squeezed his hand. "This feels like a movie by Frank Capra. You're Jimmy Stewart and I'm Jean Arthur."

"I'm too old to be Jimmy Stewart and you're much prettier than Jean Arthur."

"I wish I had her voice."

"What's wrong with your own voice? Sweet and low. Do you sing?"

"Not well enough. I take lessons when I can afford them. It's pretty important to be able to act and sing as well as dance these days if you want to get somewhere."

"Where do you want to get to, Barbara?"

"Oh, I don't know." She sighed. "I dance because I have no choice. When I was a kid, if someone switched on music—any kind of music—I'd have to get up and start jumping around. Even on Sundays in church, though my people soon stamped on that and told me I was blasphemous. I don't think I was. I think God wanted me to dance."

"Were you born in Los Angeles?"

"No, I'm from a town called Northfield in Minnesota. It's near the Twin Cities, but there's not much more to be said for it."

"Not much scope for a dancer."

"You'd better believe it. I was raised with my brothers by my aunt and uncle after my parents were killed in a car accident. They're kind people, straight and honest. I should get back to see them more often than I do."

"No wonder you love California," Daniel said. "All I know about Minnesota is that they have spectacularly cold winters."

"And pretty hot summers."

He looked hard at her. "New York's the place for you," he said softly. And almost in the same breath he asked, "Would you dance for me, Barbara Zabrisky?"

"I hope so. Sometime."

"Now?"

Even in the starlight he could see the shyness in her eyes. "Here?"

"Where better?"

Her mouth curved sweetly. "You think this is a movie, too, don't you, Danny?"

He shook his head. "No, this is real life."

But as she moved away across the sand, and the moonbeams caught her hair and he saw the long, gentle sweep of her limbs as she skimmed without music toward the surf, pirouetting lightly, like a nymph in a dream, he thought that perhaps he might be wrong.

Later, on the feather mattress that lay on the floorboards of Barbara's one-room apartment, they made extraordinary love, and Daniel felt another pang of unreality, as if the warmth of her skin and her tiny, perfect apple-like breasts were just too good to be true. After they'd slept awhile, curled tightly together, he woke her and told her the truth about who he was, because he didn't want any lies to come between them.

"Why did you pretend to be a chef?" she asked without rancor, just curiosity.

"I was a chef, once. I knew I could help, and I thought it would be fun. Was it wrong?"

"No, it was kind."

"I don't think I did it to be kind. I did it to take myself back there again."

"Is life so sad for Dan Stone?"

He shook his head. "Not really sad at all. He's been a lucky son of a gun."

"And who's Daniel Silberstein?"

He nuzzled her breasts. "That's someone I'll tell you about sometime."

She took his face between her hands. "Only if you want to, Danny. You don't have to do anything at all you don't feel happy about."

They spent every minute of his stay in Los Angeles together after that. Barbara knew nothing about the Stone guides, and she'd never seen *The Gourmets*. She was incredulous that it was possible for anyone to make that good a living simply from eating good food. She reveled in his suite at the hotel, and accompanied him to the restaurant of his choice every evening, but insisted on two out of five nights that he come back to her apartment to sleep.

"I don't want to forget what I am," she explained.

"You wouldn't."

"I might."

Daniel found himself enjoying her semibohemian life. There was no denying he thoroughly relished the comfortable existence that success had brought him, but something about her barren studio reminded him of his early New York days in the forties, and made him unashamedly sentimental.

Each night they rolled joyfully on the mattress or in the king-size bed at the hotel, and each morning he woke to find her naked before the mirror, doing her routine exercises.

"My mother was a dancer," he said on the second day, watching her with deep contentment.

Barbara unfolded herself and came back to bed, fitting snugly beside him while he told her about his boyhood and his parents, and she wept as he described his separation from his mother and the years in the camp with his father. After a while she left him in bed and disappeared, returning with a paper bag containing warm bagels.

"There's a Jewish deli round the corner. I asked them what was good and they told me bagels, lox, and cream cheese. Were they right?"

"Absolutely."

After breakfast they swept away the crumbs and lay down again.

"Tell me more," Barbara whispered, rubbing her cheek against his chest. "Please, Danny, I need to know."

So he told her about escaping from the camp and roaming Switzerland, and finding Andreas and Michel and security, and losing it again because of Natalie.

"Why did she hate you so much?" she asked in wonder, as if that kind of loathing were as alien to her as child abuse or murder.

"Because I was a Jew, mainly, I think," he answered slowly. "And because I saw through her and made a fool of her. And then, later, of course, there was the money." He shook his head. "It's hard to understand. Her hatred seemed so irrational. That's what made it frightening."

Barbara kissed him on the lips. "Don't ever be scared, Danny."

He sat up suddenly and stared at her.

"Would you come and live with me, Barbara, in New York?"

A dark cloud seemed to flit quickly over her face, and he was deeply afraid that she was going to refuse.

"It won't be the same there, Danny," she said quietly.

He took both her hands and squeezed them in his. "No, it won't be the same. We'll sleep in a big, comfortable bed instead of a mattress on the floor, and you'll work out in a bright airy studio instead of on splinters, and you'll have to let me spend money on you. But we'll love each other just the same."

She took a great, deep breath, and her whole body quivered, and Daniel was reminded of a small, slender fawn he'd once seen in the forests of Switzerland that had watched him out of its great brown eyes for a long moment, and then taken off in alarm. He shut his own eyes quickly and said a silent prayer.

"Okay, Danny," she said softly. "I'll come."

"So, you like her?"

Fanny tipped ash from her cigarette holder into an onyx ashtray on her desk. "You know I do, Dan."

"Why?"

"First, she loves you. Second, she's the antithesis of most women you meet; she's childlike, spontaneous and generous."

"Childlike?" Daniel frowned.

"I don't mean lacking in maturity. But she's young, you can't deny that."

"Too young for me?"

Fanny shook her head. "I've never believed in age barriers, Dan. Stop being concerned about a few gray hairs." She smiled. "She's one of those sun-kissed Californian love children. What does Andreas think of her?"

"I think he loved her on sight. Mind you," he added, "I haven't seen that much of him lately. We often meet, but it's generally brief and even then the conversation usually centers on the baby."

Fanny grinned. "I hear little Roberta is a killer."

"Spitting image of her mother." A small shadow veiled Daniel's eyes. "Though I don't often see them."

"Does Andreas still play that game?"

Daniel shrugged. "He must have his reasons."

"I can't imagine what they are," Fanny said dryly.

Barbara seemed almost to metamorphose during her first months in Manhattan. Carefully and intelligently, she took two thirds of herself in hand so that she could fit more comfortably into Dan Stone's world, but she built a barrier around the remaining third, which she regarded as her soul, and only special friends and her Danny were allowed to enter.

Daniel had given her carte blanche to make whatever changes she liked in his apartment, which he was aware she found elegant but essentially cold. Barbara remained adamant; she would not alter structure or decor. It was his home, and he'd been happy with it until her arrival. Instead she shopped in East Side and Village stores and galleries, bringing home small things—lamps, cushions, rugs, plants, gradually creating new life and color in the apartment.

When Daniel left in the mornings, Barbara telephoned her new agent to check for audition news, and then went to her dance class on University Place, where she stretched herself into a perspiring, aching pulp until lunchtime, and then went with her new friends for something to eat and a cup of coffee, before taking a stroll through the park, checking out more stores, or going to another class. The walks in the park became crucial to her; she was becoming tree-hungry. God knew they had pollution in California, but she'd never experienced anything as stifling and oxygen-starved as Manhattan in summertime.

On the evenings when she and Daniel had dinner plans, she made certain she was home in plenty of time to straighten herself out, take a long, cool bath and dress to kill (she wanted, more than anything, for Danny to be proud of her). But the times she loved most were when he came home just to be with her, and then she would cook simple, basic dishes, and they'd share a bottle of wine before slipping into bed to watch a movie, the air conditioner saving their lives. Danny loved her cooking—he said it wouldn't win rosettes or gold hearts, but that it had purity and strength, and was the kind of food a man wanted when he was really hungry— and besides, he'd never been looked after before.

Honeyed months slipped by. Barbara got a part in an off-off-Broadway show, and in two television commercials, one for shampoo and the other for a new brand of cat food. (She brought a carton of cans home for Cat, but he took one sniff and skipped over a couple of terraces for a quick gourmet snack at Mrs. Levy's place.) Daniel could not recall a time when he'd been happier.

In the spring of 1968, he got home one evening to find Barbara waiting for him, cross-legged on the hall rug, with Cat in one arm and a large envelope in the other.

"For you," she said.

Daniel bent to kiss her hair and took the envelope. Cat climbed out of Barbara's arm and rubbed against his legs, purring. "What is this?" he asked.

"You'll find out if you open it."

Inside were two air tickets.

"New York–Tel Aviv?" He stared at her. "How come?"

She remained cross-legged on the floor. "Because you've never been. Because I've never seen you as worked up as you were last June during the war. Because you're a Jew."

"Did you buy these?"

"Sure I bought them. I have some money now, you know." She uptilted her face and looked anxiously at him. "Don't you want to go to Israel, Danny?"

Love swept through him with such force that he dropped the tickets and knelt down beside her. He felt himself trembling as he wrapped her in his arms.

"Danny?" she whispered. "Why are you crying?"

He felt the wetness on his cheeks and held her tighter against him. "Because you are everything to me now."

"And you to me. Why does that make you sad?"

He shook his head. "It doesn't make me sad, Barbara. It just makes me want to weep. It's too much."

"No," she said fiercely, "not too much. It's what you deserve. You ought to be loved, Danny."

"But you understand so much about me."

She nodded solemnly. "That's true."

They traveled to Israel two days after Bobby Kennedy was murdered at the beginning of June, landing at Lydda Airport with the other pilgrims, overwhelmed by the heat and emotion in the air as they stepped down onto the tarmac from the airplane. Barbara studied Daniel as he watched three old bearded men falling to their knees.

"How does it feel?"

His eyes glittered. "Like my love for you."

"And how is that?"

"Right."

They stayed at the Sheraton Hotel, eating kosher food and resting and arguing with the waiters, and then they hired a car and drove to Jerusalem, passing by foot through the Jaffa Gate into the Old City. For hours they strolled through the bazaars, the eyes of the old Arabs falling obliquely and incuriously onto them, the dark, bearded Jew and the golden gentile girl hand in hand, gazing with fascination at the sights and sounds and smells of the souks.

At the al-Aqsa Mosque, Barbara was turned away because she wore only a short-sleeved blouse, and at the Wailing Wall she stood back as Daniel walked with the other men to touch the ancient sun-baked stones and to stand for a few moments lost in thought.

"How did it feel?" she asked again when he came back to join her.

"Strange," he answered. "I wanted to feel more, to dig deep and locate my Jewishness—to understand it—but I couldn't."

Barbara touched his face with the palm of her hand. "I wonder if there's anything to understand " she said. "I think you just carry it with you anyway."

"Maybe," he said.

At Yad va-Shem, the memorial dedicated to the Jewish victims of the Holocaust, Daniel emerged gray-faced and silent until they climbed back into their waiting car.

"How do *you* feel?" he asked.

"I wanted to know all of you," she said simply.

"And now?"

She smiled. "Now I think I do."

That night, in their Americanized hotel suite back in Tel Aviv, she rubbed her cheek against his.

"Make love to me, Danny."

Willingly he rolled toward her and held out his arms.

"Give me a child," she whispered.

He smiled into the dark. "Now?"

Her face was grave. "Yes, now," she said urgently. "Tonight. Here, while we're still in Israel."

"Why?"

"Because I can never give you a Jewish baby, and because I think you need one, and because if it's at least conceived here, in this Jewish place, it will be almost right."

For the thousandth time he felt himself drowning in his love for her. "It will be all right wherever it's conceived, Barbara."

"I know. But here it will be perfect."

40

The reporters were lying in wait as the Alessandros emerged from the customs hall at JFK.

"Mr. Alessandro, is it true you're planning a racing comeback?"

Andreas smiled good-humoredly. "Just a rumor."

"But you were at the Nürburgring in Germany this week."

"Can't I watch a race?"

"And last week you were seen driving at Watkins Glen."

"I often drive, but that does not, unfortunately, mean I can race." Andreas took Roberta from Alexandra's arms and swung her in the air. "This, ladies and gentlemen, is all the comeback I need."

"Is Bobbi going to be a gourmet or an artist?"

"She's going to be a beauty, just like her mother."

Focus turned on Alexandra and flashbulbs exploded, making Roberta rub her eyes. "Ali, are you going to stay at being a wife and mother now that Bobbi's going on three years?"

She laughed. "She's only just two, so I think she may need me for a while yet. But I've never stopped being an artist. I'm very lucky—wife, mother, and painter go hand in hand."

They turned back to Andreas. "Mr. Alessandro, we have a sports car outside. Could we have a few shots of Bobbi behind the wheel?"

Andreas's eyes became chilly. "Certainly not. This child is not in a circus." He passed Roberta back to Alexandra. "Let's go."

"The car's a gift from our magazine, sir," one of the photographers pressed him, "if you'll give us some exclusive shots—"

"We hardly need your gifts!" Andreas snapped, and began to push past them. "Now let us through."

"We're all very tired from our flight," Alexandra explained more gently, "so I'm sure you'll excuse us, ladies and gentlemen."

"Just one more shot—" There was the sound of smashing glass as Andreas knocked the camera from the man's hands. "There was no call for that, Alessandro! That's an expensive camera!"

"Next time it'll be your face!"

The small sea of journalists parted to allow them to pass. Alexandra turned back apologetically. "Send us the bill for the damage, please."

"Damned right I will!"

In the cab she turned to him. "There was no need to get so angry, darling."

"What do they think Bobbi is? An animal in a zoo?"

"They think she's a celebrity. It's a little ridiculous, I know, but you've always made headlines, so now it's her turn."

"Daddy?" Roberta turned her green eyes enquiringly on her father, then on her mother. "Why Daddy get mad?"

"Daddy was quite right, sweetheart." Alexandra ruffled her black hair. "Anyway, you're tired, aren't you?"

"Not tired."

Three minutes later she was sound asleep, her little head in her mother's lap. Gently, Andreas stroked her plump hands, keeping his voice to a croon, grunting softly with displeasure when the driver took a corner sharply in case he wakened her. She was the hub of his universe now, there was no denying it—without his Bobbi he'd be a cold, empty shell. His Roberta, who had spoken clearly before she was eighteen months old, who hardly shed a tear when she fell and scraped her knees. She was his life, his pride and joy, his daughter.

Later that evening she woke up crying. Andreas was in the nursery even before Alexandra, feeling her forehead.

"She's hot. I think she has a fever."

"Let me." Alexandra laid her hand first on her cheek, then on her chest inside her nightgown. "She is warm."

"I'll call Dr. Caldwell." Jack Caldwell was the top pediatrician in New York City, and Andreas had refused to rest until he'd made space for Roberta on his already overloaded patient list.

"Not yet, Andreas, it's very late. I'll give her a little aspirin first and try to cool her down."

"Bobbi, angel?" Andreas spoke softly to the child. "Do you feel bad?"

"Head hurts."

"How about your tummy?" Alexandra asked.

"Not tummy. Head hurts, Mummy." Her mouth crumpled.

Alexandra brought her an aspirin dissolved in water. "Let me just take your temperature before you have this, baby." Obediently Roberta kept the thermometer under her tongue until her mother withdrew it, glanced at it, and gave her the aspirin to drink.

"How high?" Andreas asked tersely.

"A hundred and two."

"Call Caldwell."

"Andreas, children often get this kind of fever, even with a cold. We really should wait awhile and see if the aspirin does the trick."

Within a half hour Roberta's fever was down to normal and she was sound asleep. Alexandra suggested that they, too, could retire for the night.

"You go," Andreas said tensely. "I'm going to stay with her in case she wakes again."

"Darling, I'm sure she'll sleep right through. We can leave our door open in case—"

"I'm staying," he said stubbornly. "I can catch a nap in the armchair."

She knew there was no shifting him. "Hot toddy, maybe?"

"Not a thing."

"Want me to stay too?"

"No, you're tired from the journey. I'll call you if there's a problem."

Alexandra smiled. "Good night, Daddy."

The dull, sickening sound of Roberta's small head smacking against the side of her cot awoke Andreas just after four o'clock. With a bound he was out of the armchair and staring anxiously down at her.

"Bobbi, angel, what is it?" Cold fear filled his bones. She was burning hot again, her eyes were half open but terrifyingly glazed, and her small body was twitching spasmodically.

Andreas ran to the door and yelled for Alexandra. She was with him in less than thirty seconds, her eyes wide with fright. "What's wrong with her?" She rushed to the cot. "Oh, my God, it's a convulsion! Get Caldwell!"

"I told you we should—"

"Never mind, Andreas, just call him now!" Carefully she folded back the covers from her daughter's blazing body and touched her cheek. "Okay, baby, Mummy's right here, you'll be fine," she crooned, but Bobbi seemed only half conscious, still thrashing and twitching.

Andreas was back at her side. "No better?"

"How long has she been like this?"

"I don't know—I was dozing . . . ."

"Go fetch a basin of tepid water. Not cold in case it shocks her —and bring a washcloth."

"Caldwell's on his way."

"Good. Now go fetch the water," she hissed, fighting to keep her own panic under control. She'd read somewhere that convulsions were commonplace in young children, and that the most important thing was to get the fever down gently.

For what seemed like an eternity but was in fact no more than ten minutes, they worked on Roberta, trying not to alarm her, praying for Caldwell to come. The convulsion was over, and the fever at a manageable level by the time he arrived.

"She seems fine now," he reassured them outside the nursery a little later. "I'd give her a little more aspirin and change her into a fresh light nightgown to make her more comfortable, and I reckon she'll sleep till morning. I'll come by again tomorrow."

"But what if it happens again?" Andreas demanded.

"It's unlikely, though not impossible."

"Isn't it dangerous?" Andreas wanted to shake the doctor for his calmness.

"More alarming than dangerous, as long as it's brought under control."

"But why did it happen?" Alexandra asked. "Her fever was right down earlier, then shot up again."

"That will have been the cause, depending on just how high the temperature was—"

"But what caused the fever? What's wrong with her?" Andreas demanded, almost beside himself with impatience.

Caldwell shrugged. "It may be a touch of the flu, or it could be the start of any one of the children's standard illnesses. If a rash develops, that'll be some clue." He checked his bag and closed it with a click. "Or this might be some kind of virus, which would explain the fluctuating fever."

"What should we do, Doctor?" Alexandra asked.

"One of you should maybe stay with her, just in case. And not so many covers. The nursery's quite warm enough; just a single sheet will do. Those blankets may be what tipped the scales, in fact." He had another thought. "Either of you have a history of convulsions?"

"No," Andreas said quickly.

Alexandra shot him a glance. "I haven't, but—"

"Neither of us has," Andreas said sharply.

"It's just that there's often a high familial incidence, but apparently," he said, smiling, "that isn't the case here."

As soon as Caldwell had left, Alexandra said, "Do you think we ought to ask John Manetti?"

"What?"

"Ask Manetti," she repeated. "Just to check."

"Check what?" he asked, darkening to a scowl.

"You heard what the doctor said, darling. About familial incidence."

"We told him no."

"Yes, but we can't know for sure."

"Of course we can."

"Only fifty percent." She looked at him in perplexity. "Andreas, this isn't the time to start raking old wounds."

"Then don't."

"But it's only a precaution, for Bobbi's sake. I'm sure they screen the donors carefully, but maybe we should check that her father had no—"

"I am her father."

"Well, of course you are," she said swiftly. "You know perfectly well I meant her biological father."

His tone was ominous. "I am her only father."

"No one would ever dispute that, darling."

"Don't patronize me," he snapped.

"I'm not!"

"Before you gave birth to Bobbi," he said clearly, "I had problems relating to her, I can't deny that. Once she was born, I realized just how wrong I had been. There are ties between us that no one, no one on earth, will ever break."

"Of course not."

"Good. So I don't want ever again to hear John Manetti's name mentioned, even whispered, in my presence. What you choose to tell your friends is your own business, as long as it doesn't hurt our daughter."

"Andreas, I would never—"

He turned his back on her. "I'm going to sit with her now. I'll call you if there's any change." He walked rigidly up the staircase.

Alexandra sat on the bottom stair. She shut her eyes and tried to breathe normally. No need to panic because Andreas was behaving irrationally. Wasn't this what she'd prayed for? Andreas believing himself to be Bobbi's real father. *She'll be fine by morning,* she told herself. *In a few hours her fever will be completely gone, and she'll be right as rain.*

Her eyes opened.

I wonder if Dan Stone has a history of convulsions.

It was a twenty-four-hour virus. Next day Bobbi's fever disappeared and her headache with it. Though she didn't feel like eating, she managed a little weak chicken broth that Alexandra brought her.

"Nice." She lay back in the bed, tiny against the large white pillow. She closed her eyes. "Go to sleep."

Alexandra bent and kissed her. "Good girl," she said tenderly. "More soup later."

Outside in the hall, she looked down into the half-empty cup, and remembered the night three years before in Saint-Paul when Dan had fed her chicken soup.

A few days later, Andreas sat down at Daniel's table in the King Cole Room. "You look great."

"You look tired. How's Bobbi doing?"

"Much better. Into everything, and won't consider her afternoon nap."

"That's fine. Tell Ali I'm very glad."

"Thanks." Andreas leaned back in the chair. "What are you drinking?"

"Chivas. Same for you?"

"Uh huh."

The waiter brought a fresh bottle to the table and poured.

"So how was Israel?"

"Exciting. Emotional. Filled with pride." He laughed. "Barbara says it's even more Jewish than New York."

"You know," Andreas said, "I've been doing some thinking, and I realize that you and Ali hardly know each other. It's crazy."

Daniel took a shot of whiskey, playing for time. "I thought you wanted it that way."

Andreas hesitated. "Maybe I did." He shrugged. "But now you have Barbara, and we have Roberta—things are changing."

"We're getting older."

"Not you. Not with Barbara." He sat forward. "So how about it? Will you come to dinner?"

"When?"

"I don't know. Soon. I'll talk to Ali." He thumped the edge of the table softly, like a boy satisfied with a new plan.

"Fanny and I have to take a trip soon. Might be a long one."

"Where?"

"Europe, to publicize the new guide. Interviews, book-signing sessions, lecturing." Daniel winced. "Imagine that, they have me lecturing now."

"They don't often get such multilingual writers. Will you go to Germany?"

Daniel shook his head. "They'd like me to, but I won't. Fanny can go—she has friends in Berlin. I find it hard enough in Switzerland, but there at least I have happy memories as well as bad."

"My father would be glad if you'd visit him."

"I'll call him as soon as I know the dates." Daniel glanced at his watch. "I should leave. Barbara has dinner waiting for me."

Andreas drained his glass. "And I'm overdue at the restaurant. Talk to you in a day or so."

Daniel walked into an apartment ablaze with candles. Barbara was waiting for him wearing a turquoise silk robe she'd bought in the Yemenite quarter of Tel Aviv.

"What's this? A power failure or a seduction?" He kissed her. "I'd prefer the latter."

She spun away from him. "Later. Take your clothes off anyway."

He followed her into the kitchen. "What's cooking?"

"Nothing."

"Okay," he said easily. "Want to go out?"

"No." She poked her head into the refrigerator. "Go into the bedroom. I'll bring dinner in." She glanced around. "I thought I told you to take off your clothes."

He grinned. "Yes, ma'am."

When he came out of the shower and padded barefoot into the bedroom, she was sitting on the quilt. She smiled at him. "I love your body. Don't get fat, will you."

"I won't if you won't."

Dinner was on a silver tray at the foot of the bed; a big pot of beluga, a dish of toast, half a lemon, an ice bucket with a bottle of Bollinger, and two glasses.

"Don't tell me," Daniel said, joining her on the bed, "you've found a sugar daddy."

"I already have one." Her eyes gleamed. "I have two pieces of news, both good. Which do you want first?"

He touched her cheek. Young flesh, warm and firm and alive. "This is the best news," he said softly.

"There's more." She got off the bed and with a swift, graceful motion, struck a balletic pose. "Can you guess?"

"You got the part."

"Yes!" She ran forward, flung her arms around his neck and hugged him.

"When did you hear?"

"I went for the third recall today. I didn't tell you in case you worried."

"And?"

"And I got it! *Hair!* Imagine me, Barbara Zabrisky, in *Hair!* The most successful show in years! Can you believe it, Danny?"

He stared at her. "Yes, I can. You're very talented. I've always known it was just a matter of time."

Her eyes were moist. "You want the second piece of news now?"

"Is it as good?"

"Better. Much better."

He knew before she spoke. He saw the change in her, the sheen. It was like what happened when they made love, yet different somehow, more intense.

"You're pregnant."

She nodded, slightly, swiftly, her hair silvering in the candle-light, and he was reminded again of the young, tender fawn in the Swiss forest. "We're having our sabra, Danny. Just like I said."

"You're sure?"

"Sure as eggs is eggs."

"Come here." He found her lips and clung to them. Tears seeped from her lashes and mixed with his own. "The part," he said suddenly, sad for her. "You can't take it, can you?"

"Yes, I can—for a while at least," she smiled. "It's not that big a part, and in *Hair* even if I start to show it won't matter. The doctor says I'm strong and healthy."

"You did ask him?"

"About the part? Of course I did. You think I'd risk our baby?"

"My God," he said. "My God, I'm so happy! I never knew it was possible to feel so happy." He hugged her tightly, then more gently, mindful of her fragility. "Barbara, we have to get married."

She smiled. "We don't have to, you know."

"Maybe not, but I want to." His mind raced. "When Fanny and I get back from Europe." Anxiously he looked at her. "Can you wait that long?"

"In such a hurry to make an honest woman of me all of a sudden?" she breathed against his neck.

His heart thumped against turquoise silk. "Is this allowed? Is it okay for the baby?"

She laughed. "Of course it is, silly. Really, I'm tough as old boots, the doc said so."

Daniel removed the tray carefully and placed it on the floor. He looked around.

"Better blow out the candles. Don't want the place burning down." He thought of the caviar on the rug. "Where's Cat?"

"At Mrs. Levy's, getting fat."

"Like you."

41

London, August 3, 1968

My darling Barbara,

Just a few hours, my own beloved, and almost on the other side of the world. In 1946, sailing out of Marseilles, it took us a whole week to reach New York. Times, thank God, have changed.

London, too. When I was here last, staying in my "safe haven," the 1950s were trailing inconsequentially away; the city was dignified, but bored as hell. No more. The people are the pacesetters of Europe all over again—and let's face it, is there a young New Yorker or Californian alive who doesn't wish *their* great land had hatched the Beatles or the miniskirt?

Fanny is in Paris with Céline. She made me promise not to fret about you, told me that you're tough and bright. I pray she is right, and that you will forgive me for being so far away from Broadway your first night. You should have let me rip up my contracts when I tried.

Later this afternoon will find me behind a table in the book section at Harrods department store, smiling and signing copies of the guide. If no one buys, I'll never know; the publishers supply fake customers, I hear, for those disasters. I've heard of ghost writers, but never ghost readers! Tomorrow morning I'm a guest at a literary luncheon organized by Foyles, the most famous bookstore in town. When I make speeches in London, I am doubly aware I still have an accent.

Through it all I shall dream of our little sabra, and of you.

Paris, August 8

Last night Fanny and Céline made dinner for me at their love nest on Avenue Kléber. The occasion was formal (I wore my tuxedo, the one that brought us together), and surprisingly uncomfortable. I fear they'd had a fight before I arrived, but I'll probably never find out. Fanny's private life is, as always, a state secret.

I don't like Paris; it depresses me, always has done since my first time in '54. Maybe it would be different with you. We could be tourists, strolling hand in hand in the Tuileries, making love in the Latin Quarter, dancing the night away in Montmartre. Oh, yes, my love, with you it would be different. Next time.

Tomorrow I hope to have two spare hours, and I shall brave the stern *vendeuses* in Faubourg St.-Honoré in search of something pretty for you to wear—something cool, with space enough for two.

Lyon, August 11

This is the part of the tour I anticipated like a little kid before Christmas. Officially I'm here, as you know, to dine at Paul Bocuse for *Paris-Match*, but the main reason for my joy is that soon I shall see my wonderful friends the le Ducs again. For the first time I curse *Hair* for preventing you from meeting Jean and Gaby. Thank God they are apparently in good health, but they're old now, very old, so we must fly you over the ocean before too long.

I'm a little apprehensive about my reunion with the great lady, Madame Edouard. In '54, she was so remarkable and gracious; she pointed me in the right direction, and taught me much of what I know. I still recall her words to me in her salon at our first meeting: "If food is your life, write about it." A daunting idea. Well, I've tried, but I still find myself hoping she's never had time to read a Stone guide. Does she despise my efforts, I wonder, or is she more tolerant than that? Only time will tell.

Fanny's in a curious mood, like a skittish cat—more puma than pussy, of course. She sends you warm love. (How is Cat?)

Rome, August 16

City of popes, pasta, *palazzi, and piazze.* I feel insulted to be so near and yet so far, but one night is all I'm permitted. We arrived at seven this evening, checked into the Hassler, and tomorrow morning I shall have mere glimpses of the miracles from our car window as the PR woman from the publishers whisks me to another bookstore, this time on the Via del Corso. Then it's directly to the airport and on to Milan, where I'm to speak to about a hundred Italian housewives (with an interpreter) in a hall at the Biblioteca Ambrosiana.

I told Fanny I want to visit Monza, where Andreas so nearly lost his life. There won't be any racing tomorrow and I've never been to a race circuit before, but I hold a mental picture—an image of a contemporary coliseum, full, even when deserted, of ghostly drivers. Fanny says I'm morbid and foolish. She is still behaving strangely. The day after tomorrow, when I go on to Vienna, she will abandon me again for two days in Berlin.

Tonight, though, I sleep in Rome, close to so much beauty, but thousands of miles away from my own *bellezza*.

Vienna, August 19

Little time for letter writing here, my love; the Austrians drive a hard bargain. They run *The Gourmets* over here, dubbed, of course, and so I'm being shepherded between Austrian Radio, the television station, two bookstores, and, hopefully, as many restaurants and cafés as the schedule will allow. I'd like to have visited the Fine Arts Museum and heard a few snatches, at least, of Strauss, but the *Herr* whose mission it is to steer me through the streets of Vienna is bullheaded, broad-shouldered, and a Teuton!

You sounded tired when we spoke. Is it the show, or being woken in the middle of your night? I feel like a beast disturbing your sleep, but what choice do I have? If I call you between signing sessions and dinner, you're rehearsing or in class; if I wait until later, you're onstage. Take care not to overdo things, sweetheart. Consider our little one if you won't think of yourself.

Fanny's meeting me in Zurich. She sounds happier. I have a feeling she wants to tell me something.

Zurich, August 22

When I was here in '42, Barbara my love, I was a fugitive on the run; if a kind lady glanced twice at me, I had to slink into the shadows and vanish. I was half starved, filthy, and alone. And yet today I walked along the Bahnhofstrasse under the linden trees, past the banks and jewelers, a man of thirty-seven years in reality, who has somehow never been able to undo the lie told of necessity so long ago, and who is therefore still, on paper, four years older—a man of property, a gentleman in a neat, dark suit with a handmade white shirt and silk tie—a papa-to-be. It happened to me, yet I find it hard to believe; *now* always seems to be the reality, doesn't it.

Fanny is in love. We have infected her. She has terminated her friendships of God knows how many years with both Céline and Robin. Her name, apparently, is Lee Schindler; she's a French-born divorcee who married a German furniture manufacturer, then realized she liked girls better. Right now she's still living in Berlin, but Fanny says she will come to New York soon. What are the words of that song in your show? "When peace will guide the planets, and love will steer the stars . . ." If Fanny Harper is so much in love that she's willing to disrupt that well-ordered private life of hers, perhaps the age of Aquarius really is dawning!

Tomorrow night Roberto Alessandro is coming up to the Dolder for dinner, and if there's time to spare next morning, he may take me on a tour of the old Pfister–Alessandro farmland near Lucerne. More needle stabbings into my muffled head of memories, to be shaken and sifted and raked over. You remember my fawn . . . I wonder, will you be waiting for me in the forest again?

Fawn or no, I shall be home in a few days. The poet Emily Dickinson wrote: "Where Thou art—That—is Home." I've lived in more places than most, Barbara, but I'm inclined to agree with her.

Your Danny

42

One week before the wedding, in the middle of the night, Barbara woke from a nightmare, screaming.

"It's all right." Daniel tried to calm her. "It's just a bad dream."

"Danny," she gasped. "I thought they were coming for the baby."

"Who was coming for the baby?"

"The people next door."

Daniel smiled. "The people next door are almost eighty years old, sweetheart. I'm sure they don't want our baby."

She was coming out of the dream now and her eyes were losing their glazed, terrified look. "It was the movie," she said weakly, but relieved.

"What movie?"

"One of the guys in the show took me to see Polanski's new movie *Rosemary's Baby*, between shows today."

"For God's sake!" he exploded. "Didn't he know that you're pregnant?"

"No," she said. "Don't be mad, please."

"I can't help it. You must have known what it was about," he said, perplexed. "The publicity's been everywhere. It was crazy to see it."

"I know, Danny. I'm sorry."

"I'm not sure you should carry on with this show, Barbara."

There was a short silence."

"I really want to." She paused. "Do you mind very much?"

He sighed. "Not if it's so important to you, which I can see it is."

"It is."

"You're too easily led," he went on anxiously. "Too sweet-natured. It's not safe to trust everyone, baby, you must learn that."

She cuddled closer. "New York frightens me sometimes."

"There's nothing to be scared of, as long as you're sensible."

"I'm not used to being on my guard all the time."

"Los Angeles isn't that different, surely."

"I was never afraid there."

He held her tightly. "You are happy, aren't you, sweetheart?" Her vulnerability alarmed him; he cursed himself for staying away so long.

"Of course, Danny," she whispered, and kissed him. "It's just that ugly movie that's upset me. Don't worry."

Daniel stroked her hair off her forehead and turned out the light. "Put it right out of your mind, and think about us instead, the three of us."

They were married on the eighteenth day of September at a synagogue on Park Avenue. Leon Gottesman gave the bride away, and Andreas was Daniel's best man. The minister blessed the couple and spoke of the strength and joy that was to be gleaned from the successful uniting of two souls in love. Too often, he said, intermarriage was condemned, but if two separate, different entities could be placed into the crucible of life and melted down, the blending could be even more fruitful than a more conventional marriage. Dan Stone and Barbara Zabrisky had harmony and an aptness for marriage on their side—they were a true, snug fit.

After the service, they partied for five hours at Alessandro's, and then Daniel sat in the front row at the theater and watched *Hair* for the tenth time.

Later, in bed, they held on to each other and stared into one another's eyes.

"Is this what the rabbi meant by a snug fit?" Barbara asked mischievously.

"Forget sex," Daniel scolded. "How right does this feel to you?"

"It feels as if it's you I have in my belly," she whispered seriously. "Like from this moment on, I'm going to carry you inside myself forever."

He put the palm of his right hand on her stomach. "I wonder what it'll look like."

"Like you, I hope. Without the beard or the scar."

"It might look like someone in our families. What did your parents look like?"

"I don't really know. I only have four photographs, and they were taken from a distance."

"I'll take a bet, though, that if the sabra did turn out to look like one of them, you'd recognize them."

She drew closer, so that their heartbeats blended and became almost one. "I don't care what it looks like, Danny, as long as the three of us stay together."

He kissed her mouth. "I'm going to concentrate on every part of you now, Mrs. Stone. I adore your dimples, and your little breasts, and your long, hard legs, and your tight, round belly."

Her eyes glistened. "And I adore you, Mr. Silberstein."

Two weeks after the wedding, Andreas called Daniel at the office and invited them to dinner.

"Long overdue, don't you think?"

Daniel smiled. "But welcome."

"We've asked Fanny, too, and she's bringing her friend. I gather she's flying in at the end of this week."

"That's right. Fanny's nervous as hell."

"Hard to picture."

"But true. You know Robin kept the Murray Hill house, and now Fanny's rushing around like a cat on hot bricks, getting things straight in her new place at the Pierre ready for Lee's arrival."

A few minutes after Lee Schindler had settled back on Fanny's new gleaming leather chesterfield, champagne glass in hand, she surveyed the room and winced slightly.

"What's wrong, Lee?" asked Fanny.

She tapped the stem of her glass with a slender red fingernail. "It's just the furniture."

"What's the matter with it?"

"Nothing, if you like leather."

"I thought you loved leather."

"No, *chérie*, it's suede that I like."

Fanny was fleetingly thrown. "Do you dislike it very much?"

Lee was reluctant to offend. "Of course, it's not so bad as that. It's just—well, you told me I must feel at home, and it's hard if I find my surroundings hostile. The smell and touch of leather always makes me slightly ill."

Fanny was by her side instantly. "Tomorrow morning, first thing, we'll go shopping. You pick out whatever you like."

"But will they take this back?"

"Of course." Fanny smiled. "As long as we're careful not to mark it." She looked at the clock on the sideboard. "I must call Dan. He's dying to meet you."

"But not tonight, Fannee." Lee extended the last syllable like a caress. "It's getting quite late, and I'm very tired."

"Oh, my dear, of course. Just because I never suffer from jet lag, I expect everyone else to be the same."

"Not all of us are as strong as Fanny Harper." Lee slipped an arm around Fanny's waist. "Do you think your maid is finished with the unpacking yet?"

"I'll go check." Fanny rose, then bent and quickly hugged the other woman. "I'm so happy to have you here, darling, I can't tell you."

Lee's lips curved. *"Moi aussi.* Now go and get rid of the maid and come back to me quickly."

It was only fifteen minutes before Fanny returned, but Lee was pulsating with impatience.

"I'm sorry," Fanny said, smiling easily, "but Jenna likes to get things absolutely straight, so I gave her a hand."

Lee's elegant nose tilted disdainfully. "I find some of these black girls intolerably slow. How long has she been with you?"

"Long enough," Fanny answered firmly. "I'm very fond of Jenna. She's a good, intelligent, loyal woman."

Lee laughed. "Anyone would think I was suggesting you fire her." She patted the settee. "I'm just in a hurry for us to be alone, Fannee."

"Just one more minute, darling. I did promise Dan I'd call."

"Merde!" Lee slapped down her glass on the coffee table so that some of the champagne brimmed over onto the polished wood. "Surely he can wait until tomorrow?"

Fanny looked surprised. "It won't take a moment. Dan's very dear to be so thrilled about meeting you. The least I can do is telephone."

Lee pouted. "If you must. As long as you don't expect me to be thrilled when I meet him. Dan Stone may be a big celebrity in New York, but in Berlin no one has heard of him."

"That's Dan's choice, I'm afraid."

"Why? Does he have something against Berlin?"

"Just Germany in general," Fanny said dryly. "He lost his family to the Nazis."

"Ah, yes, you mentioned that. I can't recall whether you said he is a Jew or a gypsy."

Fanny bristled. "You left out homosexual. Maybe you remember that Hitler wasn't too fond of us as a group either. And yes, Dan is a Jew. Does it matter?"

Lee shrugged. "Not to me, *chérie.*"

Fanny relented. "I'm sorry. I'm overreacting. Too much excitement maybe."

"Probably." Lee took a cigarette out of the silver box on the table and lit it. "So go and telephone your friend."

"Thank you, darling. I really won't be long, I promise."

Lee shrugged again, still irritated. "Take your time." Carelessly she flicked the cigarette, and a little red-hot ash fell accidentally onto the leather settee. She made no effort to brush it away, and sat quietly, watching the tiny black hole appear.

43

Alexandra was nervous. She knew that everything in the kitchen was perfect. She knew that she looked just right in the Givenchy velvet and crepe. She knew that the dinner guests ought, in theory, to be a marvelous blend. And yet . . .

Six friends. Three pairs, tight, private, and loving; love and tensions overspilling and permeating. Bright, open aspects turned smilingly toward each other, secret faces turned darkly inward. Friends. Old, new, unpredictable.

Alexandra was nervous.

"What's wrong with you tonight, Danny?" Barbara said, staring at him. "Don't you feel good?"

Daniel smiled. "I'm terrific. Why do you ask?"

"Because that's the sixth time you've tied the same tie, and it was fine the first time. It's not like you to worry about the way you look."

"All men are vain."

She shook her head. "Not you. You're anxious about something."

Daniel took one more look in the mirror and fingered his old scar. "You're imagining things, sweetheart. It's your condition." He turned around. "Ready?"

"I've been ready for twenty minutes."

"Do come on, Lee. We're dreadfully late."

"Please stop fussing, *chérie*. If your idiot maid had not ruined my dress, I would have been on time."

"Jenna isn't accustomed to being asked to press Dior silk at twenty minutes' notice. And she hasn't ruined it. It looks wonderful."

Lee turned from the glass, mollified. "Really? You mean it, Fannee?"

Fanny put an arm about her shoulders, mindful of the soft chignon put together by Lee's hairdresser in a two-hour session that afternoon. "Sometimes, darling, you act like a beautiful but rather spoiled child." She smiled tolerantly. "Yes, it does look wonderful."

"And you, Fannee, are stupendously chic as always." Two small frown lines marred her otherwise perfect brow. "But *chérie,* I cannot promise to adore your Stone. You mustn't be sad or angry with me if I do not."

"You'll love him," Fanny said. "I guarantee it. You always say how much you admire my taste."

"In most things, yes—and in most people."

"In this too." Briefly, Fanny's easiness wavered. "Lee, please try to understand how much I care about Dan. He's much more than a business partner, he's my dearest friend."

Lee tilted her chin. "You love him."

"Yes, I do." Fanny's sharp hazel eyes looked into those of her lover. "But in a very different way from my love for you."

"You don't always like me, though, do you?"

"Not every minute," Fanny answered truthfully. She stroked Lee's gleaming brown hair. "But I haven't felt this intensely about anyone since I was very, very young," she said huskily. "I care for you very much, you know."

Lee's eyes were bright. "And I, too, Fannee. You must know that you have changed my whole life." Quickly she patted Fanny's hand, removing it gently from her hair. "And now, my love, we must stop this, otherwise we shall both weep and destroy our faces."

Fanny picked up her purse. "Shall I tell the desk we're on our way down?"

"I want to wait until the car is outside."

Fanny grinned. "Of course, your highness." She picked up the telephone.

"One small thing, *chérie.*"

"What?"

"Don't make me jealous."

"Don't be silly, Lee. You know there's no one else."

"There's Dan Stone."

Andreas opened the door. "Welcome, both."

Fanny kissed him. "You look brutishly handsome tonight, darling. Black velvet becomes you."

"And this lovely creature, I take it, is Lee?"

"Yes, indeed."

"I'm happy to meet you, Mr. Alessandro." Lee smiled. "It's always fine to meet a legend in the flesh."

Alexandra appeared behind Andreas. "Fanny, how lovely to see you again." She kissed her warmly and turned to Lee. "Madame Schindler, it's very good to meet you. We've been hearing so much about you."

"Please, I beg you not to call me that," Lee said with a grimace. "Schindler is far behind me in Berlin, and that is where I choose to leave him."

Alexandra laughed. "I'll call you Lee, then, and I'm Ali to all my friends."

"And to your admirers."

"You know my wife's work?" Andreas led the way into the living room.

"Don't all art lovers?"

"After that, you deserve a drink," Alexandra said quickly. "Please sit down. My husband will pour while I fetch the others. They're out on the terrace, staring at the park."

"What can I get you, Fanny?" Andreas queried as Alexandra disappeared. "There's champagne and almost anything else."

"Champagne sounds good."

"And Lee?"

"Absolument."

"Lee drinks champagne the way other people drink coffee."

"But champagne is much healthier." Lee glanced up as Alexandra came back into the room, the others behind her.

"Fanny?" Andreas said. "Will you make the introductions?"

"Certainly." She rose and hugged Barbara. "Hello, gorgeous." She drew the girl toward Lee. "This is Barbara Stone."

Lee smiled. "The child bride."

Barbara offered her hand with charming shyness. "I'm so happy to meet you. We've both been longing to for ages, especially Danny."

The sheer weight of the sudden silence in the room seemed to crack the air like ice. Confused, Barbara lowered her hand, unshaken, and looked to Daniel for explanation. "Danny?"

He was staring. He looked like a man at his first haunting, his eyes disbelieving and shocked.

"Dan," Fanny said sharply. "What's the matter?"

His eyes still locked hard on Lee, he said, his voice strained, "Fanny? Is this—Lee?"

Fanny's mouth hardened with impatience. "Of course it is." She took Lee's arm protectively. "This, Lee darling, acting very strangely, is my very dear friend Dan Stone."

Lee seemed about to speak, then changed her mind. A mask fell over her face. She raised her right hand, held her chin high, and curved her lips mechanically.

"Mr. Stone," she said steadily. "How do you do?"

Daniel took the hand, shook it swiftly, and dropped it as if he'd been stung by a wasp concealed in her palm. *For Fanny,* he urged himself on. *You have to, for Fanny.*

"Glad to know you," his voice rasped, and then, catching Fanny's dismay, he forced a semblance of a smile, though the bile was rising in his throat.

Lee Schindler stood perfectly still in her dress of royal blue silk. Slender legs, arms, and neck, like a frosted cornflower. Features still sharp and perfect, lips thin and tightly drawn. Eyes still vixen and brown.

Lee Schindler was Natalie Bresson.

"Danny, are you sick?"

Daniel lay in bed, eyes closed, rigid.

"Danny, I know you're not sleeping."

Under cover of his eyelids, Daniel's mind seethed and lurched and despaired.

Barbara threw back the quilt angrily, sat on her haunches, and said, "I figure there has to be a logical explanation for why you did your best to ruin everyone's evening, especially Fanny's, so I'm just waiting to hear it."

Daniel said nothing.

"Okay, fine!" She threw the words at him. "Don't talk to me. Why should you, I'm only your wife!" She flung herself onto her side and dragged the quilt back up to cover herself.

Daniel shuddered once and opened his eyes. "I'm sorry."

She huddled in the quilt, punishing him with her back. "Sorry's pretty lame after that."

"I know."

"Sorry doesn't buy friends."

He winced.

"Was it Ali?" she asked suddenly.

Daniel felt almost winded. Where the hell had that come from, and why? "Ali," he said cautiously. "Why Ali?"

"I'm not sure," Barbara said slowly, still muffled by the quilt. "I guess I've felt for quite a while that there was something between you." Quickly she added, "I don't mean an affair—at least not now."

"My God, I should hope not!"

"Was it?"

"Was it what?"

She emerged from the quilt, her cheeks flushed in the light of the bedside lamp. "Was Ali the reason you acted like a weirdo all evening, or was it something else?"

"Of course not."

"Of course not what?"

"Of course it wasn't anything to do with Ali—and I don't know where you might have got that idea."

She smiled suddenly. "So what was it?"

He sighed. "Come here." He held out his arms. "Come on—get back over here and I'll tell you."

She wriggled quickly into his arms, laying her head on his chest. "Tell me." She felt him shiver. "Danny, for heaven's sake, what happened tonight?"

"I recognized Lee Schindler." There—the words were out. But he felt no relief.

"Really? You already knew her?"

"Yes."

She raised her head. "How? Where?"

"You forgot 'when.' "

"Okay. So when?"

He took a sharp breath. "I first met Lee Schindler in 1945."

She rested her head back on his chest. "The year I was born."

He smiled. "I know, baby. Don't remind me."

"Why not?"

"It makes me remember my age, that's all."

She tweaked a dark chest hair. "You're really a dope sometimes, Danny. Anyone would think you were an old man. You're not even middle-aged yet."

"Thanks for the 'yet.' "

"You're welcome." She grew impatient again. "So what about Lee Schindler? You say you met her in 1945."

"That's right." He paused. "Only in those days her name wasn't Lee Schindler."

"What was it?"

"Natalie Bresson."

She thought for a moment. "Her maiden name, right? And Lee's just a contraction of Natalie."

"Don't you remember that name?" He spoke slowly, deliberately. "Think, Barbara. You've heard me use that name before."

"I have?"

The room was silent. Suddenly, Barbara raised her head again and swiveled around to face him.

"My God, Danny. Her?"

"The very same."

"The Nazi?"

His mouth quirked. "Not exactly, but woven of that cloth, yes."

"Oh, shit," she breathed. "Poor Fanny."

"Yes."

"That's some coincidence."

He said nothing.

"You do believe it *is* a coincidence?"

"Of course. Fate."

"Wow."

Again he fell silent.

"You're not thinking of saying anything to Fanny, are you, Danny?"

He swallowed.

"Danny, you mustn't," she said urgently. "It would be wrong, terribly wrong."

He shut his eyes. "You think not telling her is right?"

She moved a few inches farther away. "I don't know. Perhaps not." She touched his hand. "Fanny's in love, Danny. You've said yourself she's been a different person since they met."

"Different, yes," he said ironically. "Tenser, less self-confident, moodier than I've ever known her."

"And happier. You said that too."

Slowly he nodded. "I know it. Don't think I've forgotten."

"I don't," she said sympathetically. "This is horrible for you."

Daniel narrowed his eyes. "She hasn't changed, you know. She knew me at once, and the loathing was there immediately."

"You can't know that."

He smiled wanly. "I'm talking about hatred."

Barbara shook her head, and there was genuine confusion in her bright eyes. "I've never understood that word, Danny. I just know you mustn't tell Fanny. She loves you, and you love her. Don't be the one to steal her happiness."

"Not even if Natalie's dangerous?"

"You just *think* she's dangerous." She looked earnestly at him. "Look, Danny, she was just a girl in 1945, and you were only a kid yourself—a sensitive, desperate kid. Hitler's been dead a long time." She smiled. "You've said yourself that there's something irrational about your refusal to go back to Germany with Fanny."

He shook his head. "But I've never really believed that, not in my heart. You've seen Yad va-Shem, Barbara." He shrugged and fell silent.

Barbara wrinkled her forehead. "You really think she might hurt Fanny?"

"I don't honestly know. If she's still the same creature she was—and believe me, when I saw her on the street in London just a few years back, she looked at me as if she longed to see me drop dead in front of her right there and then—if she's still the same person, then yes, I do believe she might hurt Fanny, even if it's one way of striking at me."

"But that's crazy!"

He nodded. "You're right."

"Maybe she really loves Fanny," Barbara suggested hopefully. Daniel's mouth twisted.

"Do vermin love?" he said.

In Fanny's apartment, Natalie Bresson Schindler knelt on the bed and massaged aromatic oil into the older woman's back. First she kneaded and rubbed gently, then she let her hands slide under Fanny, so that they glided over her flattened breasts, down over her abdomen, and into her pubic hair.

Fanny moaned softly.

"Like it?" Natalie purred.

"God, what a question!"

Natalie parted Fanny's thighs with one hand, firm as a man, and squeezed three fingers of the other hand tightly together to simulate a hard penis. "I don't care much for your Stone," she said with malice.

Fanny shivered. "I don't want to discuss Dan now." She groaned as Natalie's fingers probed deeper. "Christ! Let me turn over."

"No!" Natalie straddled her, knees either side, gripping tightly. "You led me to expect charm, at least. I was disappointed." She played with Fanny's clitoris, teasing and rubbing.

Fanny quivered in distress at the blend of delight and pain. "I really don't know why he acted that way tonight," she gasped.

"Perhaps he's sickening for something," Natalie suggested helpfully, straightening her knees and lying full-length on top of Fanny. "Jews usually do have a capacity for charm." She brushed Fanny's skin with her hard nipples.

Fanny tried to raise herself on her elbows. "Don't start a fight, please, Lee darling. Let me turn over so I can hold you."

"I just wish you wouldn't devote so much time to such a man."

"Lee, please . . ." Fanny tried to laugh. "You're heavier than you look, you know . . . I can hardly breathe."

Natalie held her powerfully. "I should have known. After all, a murderer . . ."

"What are you ranting about now?" Fanny began to struggle angrily.

Natalie moistened her lips with her tongue and dug her long red fingernails into Fanny's soft inner thighs. "He killed the Bernardi woman, didn't he?" She laughed. "Fannee, *chérie*, you told me yourself."

"Shit, Lee! You're hurting me!"

Natalie released her suddenly.

"My God, Lee," Fanny hissed, gulping air and shifting with relief. "I wish I'd never told you anything about Dan."

"Then why did you?"

"It's called sharing, dammit." There were furious tears in Fanny's eyes. "I wanted you to know him, to understand him, because he's important to me. Anyway," she lashed out, "you kept asking me, and you got so wounded when I held back that I gave in." She flushed suddenly, a rare deep color high in her pale cheeks. "If Dan ever found out I'd betrayed his trust, that would be the end of our friendship. And if you *ever* say one single word of anything I've told you to a living soul, I'll—"

"You'll what?" Natalie rolled abruptly onto her back and laced her fingers behind her head. "Don't you want me now, Fannee?"

"Not if you're going to behave like a prize cunt."

Natalie grinned. "How else should a prize cunt behave?"

Fanny was tight-lipped. "I warn you, Lee—if you ever say anything about—"

Natalie's eyes were icy slits. "And I said what will you do about it?" She frowned. "Besides, Fanny, you did tell me that Stone killed that woman."

"You know damn well I said the poor bitch died while they were together. That's hardly the same thing, is it?"

Natalie tossed her hair and shrugged. "I don't see why. He fucked her to death, didn't he?"

Next morning, while Barbara lay on her exercise mat and did modified sit-ups and muscle-strengthening stretches, Daniel stood in the doorway of the bedroom holding a cup of coffee.

"I've fed Cat," he said, "so don't let him fool you into a second breakfast."

"I won't." Barbara sat up gently and patted her stomach. "A couple more months at most," she said. "Then I guess it's 'good-bye *Hair.*'"

"You feel okay?" he asked anxiously.

"I feel terrific," she smiled. "But the sabra's starting to take up more space."

"Will you mind? Giving it up, I mean."

"Are you kidding?" She shook her head. "Danny, I've been so lucky having this break, being in the show at all." She got easily to her feet. "But there are some things, believe it or not, that are even more important to me than my career." She kissed him on the neck. "You smell so good. Sure you have to go out?"

"If I said no, would you have time to spare for me?"

She wrinkled her nose. "Well, Mike's expecting me early this morning. We had notes after the show on Saturday and—"

Daniel stopped her with a kiss on the mouth. "I'll see you later."

"Danny?"

"Yes, sweetheart."

She hesitated for a moment. "You aren't going to tell Fanny, are you? About Natalie."

Slowly, Daniel shook his head. "I don't see how I can. I mean, you may be right, and her feelings for Fanny may be real."

Barbara squeezed his hand. "Try to believe it, Danny. You'll feel better."

He forced a smile. "I'll have to explain last night some other way. And we'll both have to stick to calling her Lee, don't forget." He pulled a wry face. "That is, if we have to see anything of her. Something tells me, though, that Lee Schindler's not going to be pressuring for too many return games after last night's fiasco."

At Fanny's breakfast table, Natalie was aiming for a truce, even to the point of thanking Jenna almost civilly for the fresh-squeezed juice, eggs, toast, and coffee laid before her.

"Perhaps that girl isn't so bad," she said to Fanny after Jenna had left the room.

"I'm thrilled you think so," Fanny said frostily.

Natalie sipped her juice. "I apologized last night for what I said. Can't you forgive me, *chérie?*" She reached tentatively for the older woman's hand, but Fanny drew away.

"Frankly, Lee, I don't know. I don't so much think it's what you said—I've heard enough bitching from you in the past, Lord knows—but it's the way you said it. You can be very malicious sometimes." Fanny's eyes were guarded. "And I've told you before, too, that I don't go for sadistic love play. It may make some people happy, but it certainly doesn't go hand in hand with caring."

Natalie hung her head. "I know," she said contritely. "Please believe me, Fannee, I am truly sorry." She laid her hands in her lap. "To be honest, *chérie* . . ." She sighed. "I was jealous of Stone."

"For Christ's sake, Lee, Dan and I aren't lovers."

"There are different forms of love, as you've told me."

Fanny relented. "Sometimes, Lee, I'm not sure whether you're being childish, catty, or just a plain horse's ass."

Natalie chuckled. "That's better." She got up quickly and put her arms about Fanny's neck. "That's much better—much more like my wonderful Fannee."

Fanny pursed her mouth. "You're a total mystery to me, you know."

"I know." Natalie looked kittenishly down at Fanny. "Kiss and make up?"

"Only if you swear to make a real effort with Dan."

Natalie sat down again. "Listen to me," she said tersely. "No bullshit, okay?" Fanny nodded. "I am certain that your Stone disliked me as much as I did him. No, don't protest, you know it's the truth." She shrugged. "Maybe it's better if we just avoid each other. At least for a time. After all, it's you I came to New York to live with, not Stone."

Fanny leaned back in her chair, disappointment clear in her eyes; but she took the blow squarely on the chin. "I can't very well argue with that, can I," she said wearily.

Natalie smiled. "No." She picked up the coffeepot. "And now, since the bullshit is past, perhaps I can make some decent coffee."

In spite of herself, Fanny laughed. "Lee, I think you're irredeemable."

"Probably." Natalie beamed. *"Enfin*—where shall we go today? I feel we should spend money."

"You go right ahead, but it'll have to be without me, I'm afraid."

"I meant together."

"I know you did, dear, and I wish I could, but it's just not possible."

Natalie put down the coffeepot on the counter with dangerous gentleness. "Why not?"

"Business. Obviously."

Natalie switched off the percolator; the liquid was tossed into the sink, followed by the grounds. "Not to me."

"It's obvious that I wouldn't have any other reason for being unable to come with you," she said patiently.

Natalie's eyes glinted. "And if I say that it's very important— really important to me, to our relationship even—that we spend today together?"

Fanny sighed again. "I could meet you later on. This afternoon, perhaps. Would that do?"

Natalie turned. "Would that do?" she flared. "Am I now a child to be humored? You want to appease me with an hour this afternoon? Tell me what is so crucial that you must do this morning? Don't you have enough success? Enough money in enough banks? How can business be so damned important?"

Fanny raised an eyebrow. "Are you through?"

"No!" Natalie screamed in fury. "Tell me what is so fucking important!"

Fanny rose with dignity. "I have a meeting in just under an hour," she said quietly.

"With whom, may I ask?"

"With Dan." She left the room.

Natalie's livid trembling took a moment to cease, and her face grew whiter. "*Je me rappelle de vous*, Silberstein," she whispered harshly. "I remember you." Then she turned and spat into the sink.

44

Three days after the Alessandros' dinner party, Daniel got out of a cab close to his apartment building and noticed a young man hanging around on the corner of 11th Street and Fifth Avenue. There was something vaguely familiar about him, Daniel thought, watching him for a moment, but he couldn't quite put his finger on what it was. He was no more than eighteen or nineteen years old and he seemed out of place in the area, shabbily dressed in unfashionably tight and badly stained denim jeans, his hair greasy and unkempt. He shifted constantly and uneasily from one foot to the other and hugged himself as if suffering from the cold, though the mid-October weather was, in fact, uncommonly mild.

Daniel greeted his doorman and glanced back again at the corner. The stranger seemed to be staring right back at him, but Daniel was too far off to gauge the expression in his eyes.

"There was a guy outside earlier, hanging around," he said to Barbara later that night after she had come home from the theater. "He looked kind of familiar. Did you see anyone you recognized when you came in?"

She finished towel-drying her hair and picked up the hair dryer. "No, but I didn't look."

Daniel bent, ruffled her wet curls, and kissed the back of her neck. "I'm going to start fetching you after the show," he said.

"You do anyway most nights."

"So now I'll do it every night."

She frowned. "Why, Danny? Is something wrong?"

He ruffled her hair again and sat on the edge of the bed. "Of course not. I just don't like the types who seem to be out on the streets late at night. You shouldn't be on your own."

"I always take cabs, you know that."

He smiled. "I know. But sometimes you have to wait around and it makes me nervous."

Barbara laid down the dryer. "You're so sweet sometimes, Danny." She got up, came over, and sat down beside him. "It isn't necessary, you know. You get tired at the end of the day. I can't see any reason why you should have to wait around for me."

"How about that you're my wife and you're carrying my child? That reason enough for you?"

She laughed. "I carry your child in a cab just as well as in your car."

"Do me a favor," he said seriously. "Humor me."

She stroked his cheek. "Okay."

"And dry your hair—you'll catch a cold."

The next night, as arranged, he met Barbara outside the stage door. A group of kids surrounded them as soon as Barbara and another cast member emerged, asking for autographs.

Daniel touched Barbara's arm. "That's him," he said quietly. "Over there by the wall." He pointed casually to the boy who waited patiently on the fringe of the small crowd. "You know him?"

Barbara signed another autograph. "Sure," she said. "That's Luis. He often waits for me after the show."

"He does, does he?"

She looked at him in amusement. "He's harmless, Danny. He's a sweet kid." She lowered her voice. "I think he has a crush on me." She grinned at the group still gathered around them. "Who's next?"

Daniel took another look. The boy was fingering a crucifix around his neck and his eyes were fixed unwaveringly on Barbara. "I don't like the way he's staring at you," he said into her ear.

Barbara tugged him back toward the stage door. Her face was sweetly serious. "Danny, I know you mean well, but these people are my fans—well, perhaps not exactly *my* fans, more the fans of the show itself. Some of them just take it more seriously than others. Luis Rodrigo's one of those. He waits out here just to see me every day, rain or shine, and he leaves me things."

"What kind of things?" Daniel asked sharply.

"Small gifts—candy bars, flowers, or sometimes just notes."

"What do the notes say?"

She looked at him curiously. "You're taking this too seriously. This kind of thing happens to everyone."

"Let's just say it's an aspect of your life I never took into consideration before."

"Okay," she said carefully, "but don't be jealous. Notes like that don't mean anything to me."

"What do they say?" he repeated.

"Just that he cares for me," she said shyly. "That he holds me in
—" She smiled. "How did he put it? 'In high esteem.'" The
dimples sprang into her cheeks. "Luis seems to find me pretty."

"The notes may not mean anything to you," Daniel said dryly,
"but they seem to mean a good deal to Rodrigo." He took her
arm firmly. "Come on, we're getting out of here."

She extricated herself gently. "Not until I've signed all their
books or programs."

"You've done enough."

"No, I haven't. You have to understand, Danny. They've all
waited out here for us, and it's downright impolite to ignore them
now."

"Okay," he said. "I'll wait in the car."

She kissed him on the cheek. "I won't be long."

He unlocked his door and slid into the driver's seat. Through
the rearview mirror he watched as Barbara chatted to the fans and
then had a special word with Rodrigo. The spotlight over the stage
door was bright, and Daniel saw an expression of sheer delight
spread over the boy's sallow face. Then Barbara moved away, and
Daniel noticed that Rodrigo's hand went straight to his crucifix
and grasped it tightly.

"Is he a devout Catholic?" he asked Barbara as she got into the
car beside him.

"Why do you ask?" she said, surprised.

Daniel started the engine. "I just wondered."

"He is, as a matter of fact." She smiled. "He just told me he
prays for me every night."

He raised an eyebrow. "What else did he say to you?"

"Not much."

"Tell me."

Her cheeks colored. "He said he's sure the baby will be as
beautiful as me."

He took his eyes off the road. "You told him you're pregnant?"

"No—not exactly," she said, flustered. "I—he overheard me
talking to a friend one time when we left the theater, that's all.
Honestly, Danny, I can't see why you're making so much fuss.
He's just a nice, muddled boy with a few problems, that's all."

Daniel's eyes narrowed. "What kind of problems?"

Barbara's hands gripped her purse more tightly. "I'm not saying
one more word about him. He has no more to do with me than
any of the other people you just saw out there, and you're not
interrogating me about any of them."

"None of them have been hanging around our home."

"Danny, please!" She was clearly upset.

"I'm sorry, baby." He reached for her hand and held it. "I just get overanxious, I don't know why."

"It's only since you found out about Lee. You've been nervous and upset from that moment on."

He sighed. "I know it."

"Did you see Fanny at the office today? How does she seem?"

He shrugged. "She's okay. Seems happy enough—a little tense, but I'm not surprised. Life with that woman could never be a bed of roses, even if they're having the best of relationships."

Barbara drew his hand to her lips and kissed it, then placed it back on the steering wheel. "I still feel you're doing the right thing not telling Fanny the truth."

"I wish I could be sure of that."

"You can always change your mind. If Fanny has problems with her in the future—if she seems unhappy—you can still step in then before it's too late. That would be the right time." She leaned back, suddenly weary. It usually got her that way after a show; at first she was so buoyed up by adrenaline, she didn't notice. "Let's hope that time never comes."

Daniel flashed his headlights at a junction. "Let's hope."

The following Saturday afternoon Daniel dropped Barbara at the theater in time for her matinee and then drove home to work on some papers for the Los Angeles office. Coming out of the underground garage into Sixth Avenue, intending to walk to the drugstore on University Place, he saw Luis Rodrigo standing on the far side of the street in conversation with two men.

Daniel stopped in his tracks. Both men were much older than Luis; both wore dark, well-tailored overcoats, one was balding, the other wore a homburg. They seemed to be speaking intensely to Rodrigo, who was shaking his head and gesticulating with his hands, clearly upset and angry.

Daniel thought of crossing over to challenge the boy, but how could he justify it? Hanging around stage doors was not an indictable offense, nor was talking with friends on street corners. Daniel watched them. Friends? Doubtful. Rodrigo had the same restless stance as he'd had the first time Daniel had spotted him near the apartment. The man in the homburg put his hand in his pocket, and Daniel saw a flicker of white as something changed hands. Drugs, he thought.

Upstairs in the apartment he surveyed their security precautions. Two stout locks and a bolt on the front door, and a security chain.

Daniel buzzed the doorman. "Joe?"

"Hi, Mr. Stone."

"Joe, how careful are you and the other boys about security?"

"Why?" Joe sounded anxious. "Something happen up there?"

"No, nothing like that. I'm just checking precautions. You can't be too careful, you know."

"Sure can't, Mr. Stone." Joe was relieved. "We're all on the ball down here, don't worry. No one gets past us unless they're welcome."

"What happens if you have to leave the door?"

"Never do."

"You must have to sometimes."

The doorman laughed. "You mean if I gotta take a leak—pardon my French, sir. The doors get locked till I'm back at my post. I promise, you got nothing to worry about." He paused. "Okay?"

The telephone in the apartment rang. Daniel thanked the doorman and went to answer it.

"Dan, it's Fanny."

"I just got in. How're things?"

"Peachy. I was just calling to remind you about tonight."

"Tonight? Dinner at Lutèce, I haven't forgotten." Cat came into the room and sprang nimbly onto Daniel's knee, purring loudly. He stroked him.

"Fine. By the way, it's going to be a late one. I know you like to get Barbara after the show, but you'll never make it tonight."

"Maybe I could leave early."

"Of course you can't." Fanny sounded tired. "You're not the only one who's put out. Lee's been moody for two days because we can't have Saturday evening together." She laughed wryly. "Guess that's what I've been missing out on all these years, huh? Lovers' tiffs."

Daniel felt the tension creeping into his spine. "Things not so hot, Fanny?"

"Oh, no, they're fine." She blew him a kiss down the line. "See you around ten."

Daniel jabbed his finger on the hook and dialed the number of the theater. Barbara was unreachable, so he left word for her to take a cab home after the evening show. "This is her husband," he said. "I'll try to get back to her between shows."

Cat stood up and balanced balletically on his left knee, swaying from side to side.

"Okay, show-off." Daniel smiled. "I see you. Is this a new act?"

Cat miaowed purposefully.

"You hungry again?" Daniel remembered his aborted trip to the drugstore. "I meant to pick up some more cans, but I got diverted. Sorry, pal—" He stood and Cat spilled gracefully onto the rug. "We'll just have to find something for you in the icebox. I seem to think we had a good helping of lox left over from brunch. Suit you?"

He called Barbara at the apartment just after midnight from the restaurant.

"Hi, beautiful. You home safe?"

"No, I'm down in the subway on my way to Queens, getting mugged."

"Very funny. How was the show, comedian?"

"Pretty good. Great crowd. Danny?"

"Yes, sweetheart."

"I think I felt the baby move tonight."

"Really? Isn't it too soon?"

"I don't know. It happened during 'Aquarius.' "

"How did it feel?"

"Beautiful. Danny?"

"Yes?"

"Will you be home soon?"

"I wish I could be, but I reckon I may be stuck here at least another hour, maybe a little more. I'm sorry. I'd much rather be with you."

"Poor old man. Stuck in Lutèce." She smiled. "Anyway, you don't have to worry about your wife," she added brightly. "I have fine company. There's the sabra, and I've a handsome black athlete right here beside me."

"Cat snuck into bed again, huh?"

"Of course."

"Don't let him steal the blankets." Daniel heard his dime giving out. "Sleep well, sweetheart," he said. "I love you."

Her voice was sweet and low, like soft rain. "I love you too, Danny."

It was gone two o'clock when he walked into the lobby, brushing the rain spots from his coat. The night porter greeted him sleepily from his corner. "Good evening, Mr. Stone?"

"Not bad. Good to be home, though—it's coming down hard out there."

The elevator doors slid open.

"Good night, Mr. Stone."

Upstairs, the floor was deserted. The scrawny French poodle that inhabited the apartment closest to the elevators growled at Daniel as he passed his front door. Daniel felt in his coat pocket for the door keys, and fitted the first one into its lock, but it wouldn't turn. Daniel made a disapproving sound. She'd forgotten to double lock again. He inserted the second key, turned it, and heard the tumbler lift. The door opened and he stepped inside the dark hall.

Closing the door softly, he took off his coat and laid the keys gently on the table so their jangling wouldn't waken Barbara.

Pausing, he crouched low. "Cat?" he whispered. "Don't trip me up, fella."

No sign of him. A sliver of light came from beneath the bedroom door. Maybe he was in there, he thought. Or getting an early breakfast at Mrs. Levy's.

For a long time—or it seemed that way—he thought he was hallucinating. Barbara was sleeping on the floor, covered with a red blanket.

We don't have a red blanket.

Then his reflexes gave a massive shudder and he saw the stuff seeping slowly, like claret, into the pile of the rug.

It was everywhere around her. The bed was drenched in it, and the headboard; the silk shade of his bedside lamp was splattered—even the ceiling.

Blood. A bodyful. Barbara's.

He began to pray.

She lay, spread-eagled, on her back, her nightgown up around her neck. Her wrists were lashed to the legs of the bed, and her ankles joined to the wrists with the same binding.

Her head lolled a little to the left, and her golden hair, frosted with blood, covered her right eye. The other eye was closed.

Daniel looked down.

She'd been cut.

Not stabbed. Not slashed. Cut. In two straight lines—one from the base of her throat, down between her little breasts, right past her navel and down through her womb—the second cut horizontal, all the way across her body, just below the breasts.

Two lines. A cross.

Daniel knelt.
No pulse. No breath.
He rested his hand on her wet, bloody belly.
No sabra.

He heard the sound from the corner and turned his head.
Cat lay sprawled just below the drapes. His fur gleamed crimson. He opened his yellow eyes and watched Daniel.
Help me.

Daniel crawled to where Cat lay. He heard another unfamiliar sound, like crazy castanets, and couldn't understand that the sound was his teeth chattering.
He touched the animal.
Warm. Quivering.
The knife had caught him in his side but not too deep.
Daniel heard another sound.
Purring.

And then another.
Screaming.

45

At twenty-five minutes before seven that morning, a prebreakfast jogger in Central Park discovered the body of a young Hispanic man lying in a clump of bushes near the rear of the Metropolitan Museum of Art. The jugular vein on the left side of his throat had been sliced through, and the blood-drenched knife lay at his side next to a Bible.

At nine-fifteen, right after the call from the New York Police Department to the offices of Harper and Stone, Kate, with shaking fingers and ashen face, telephoned first Fanny at the Pierre, and then Andreas at his apartment.

Three hours later, at the midtown coroner's office, the body in the park was formally identified as that of Luis Albert Rodrigo. His older sister, Marietta Rodrigo, was hysterical with grief, and when two detectives from the 90th Street Precinct told her that they had reason to believe her brother had committed suicide after murdering a woman in the West Village, Marietta flew at them like a madwoman, clawing at their eyes and screaming that Luis was the gentlest, most God-fearing boy on their block, and that they would be punished in the next world for their wicked lies.

"We're sorry, Miss Rodrigo," the older detective said, "but it all fits."

"What fits?"

"You said your brother was religious?"

"Deeply."

"A Bible was found at his side."

She shook her head in confusion. "And that makes him a murderer? Are you crazy or something?"

"No, ma'am," the younger man said quietly.

The other detective took a small photograph from an inside pocket and laid it on the table in front of her. "Do you know this woman?"

She stared at it quickly and shook her head. "No." She breathed in sharply. "Is it—?"

"That's right, ma'am. She's the woman we think your brother murdered."

Marietta fought for control. She stared again at the photograph, signed in the bottom right-hand corner. "Barbara Zabrisky?"

"Yes, ma'am. Her stage name. Her married name was Stone."

"An actress?" She almost spat the word.

The younger man spoke again. "A recently married, twenty-one-year-old, four-months-pregnant woman."

Defiantly, Marietta raised her chin. "But why do you accuse my brother?"

"Her husband claims that Luis was hanging around Mrs. Stone."

"He's a liar!"

"Mr. Stone is in the hospital right now, ma'am, doped to the eyeballs because he just found his pregnant wife carved up on their bedroom floor," the younger detective said harshly.

The other man spoke more gently. "We don't think he's lying, Miss Rodrigo. This photograph was in your brother's pocket when he was found."

Her eyes were round as marbles with horror. "And because a boy carried a photograph of an actress—a boy who lies dead in this building—a boy who cannot defend his good name—" Fiercely she scrubbed at her eyes. "You accuse him of murder!" Wildly she tried to gather her thoughts. "What does the Bible have to do with your fantasy?"

The two men looked at each other. "Why not?" The older man shrugged. He took a notebook from his back pocket and flipped through a few pages. "No fantasy, Miss Rodrigo. There were some lines in the Bible, ma'am, which seem to have been specially marked."

She clenched her fists. "And?"

"They were in the New Testament. To be exact, in Romans. Chapter Six." He held the notebook up closer to his face and read clumsily: " 'For he that is dead is freed from sin.' And there's another one. We've all heard this one before: 'For the wages of sin is death; but the gift of God is eternal life through Jesus Christ our Lord.' " He lowered the notebook.

"Well?" Marietta's voice was shaky. "I told you that Luis was God-fearing." Her eyes flooded with fresh tears. "Maybe you're right. Perhaps he did kill himself. I don't know, maybe he believed he was a sinner. We are all sinners. How does that make him a murderer?"

"We don't think your brother was referring to himself when he marked those lines, Miss Rodrigo. We think they related to the victim."

"I don't understand."

"Three reasons. He marked another line." He raised the book again. " 'So then if, while her husband liveth, she be married to another man, she shall be called an adulteress.' "

"This woman was an adulteress?" she asked softly.

"We don't know. The second reason, ma'am, is the way he marked all those lines."

"How?"

"In blood."

"Whose?" she whispered.

"We won't know that until the reports are filed."

"But you think it's hers." It was a statement, not a question. Her eyes dulled with shock.

"We'll see."

"You said three reasons."

"Yes." He paused. "The woman who died was marked too."

"What do you mean?"

"She was cut with a knife. Whoever killed her cut a cross into her."

Marietta swayed and shut her eyes. Quickly the younger man got a cup of water from the cooler in the corner of the room, and put it into her hand. "Take a sip." She obeyed, and a minute later opened her eyes.

"I have to ask you a couple more questions. I'm sorry. Are you okay?"

She nodded weakly.

"Did you know your brother was on drugs?"

"Yes," she said, so softly they had to strain to hear her.

"We think he was an addict. Is that true?"

Marietta seemed to slump back in her chair. "I begged him to stop," she said. "He kept bad friends. He was too trusting."

The detective made a note. "Did he have a job?"

"Yes," she said, and began to weep again. "He was out of work for a long, long time . . . he fought so hard to find work . . . any kind of work."

"But he found a job?"

"Just a week ago," she sobbed. "He was so happy, so proud!"

"Where was that, Miss Rodrigo?"

"At a liquor store. On 91st near Broadway."

"What kind of job? Do you know?"

"Of course I know. Luis told me everything."

"Not quite," the second man murmured.

"He was a delivery boy," she flashed. "You know, running all over the city, collecting orders, taking boxes to customers." She jerked her chin proudly. "He would have made good, I know, if —" She broke off.

"Do you know the name of the store?"

"Sure. Bernardi's. They got stores all over."

He made another note. The name signified nothing to him.

To Daniel, it would signify everything.

On the fifth floor of St. Vincent's Hospital, Andreas, gray-faced with shock and fatigue, spoke with an intern about Daniel. It was just after five in the afternoon, and Fanny had just gone home to get some rest.

"You should do the same, Mr. Alessandro," the young man said. "He's very heavily sedated. He'll stay that way till morning."

"What if he wakes during the night? I don't want him to be alone."

"If he comes to, sir, the nurse will give him another shot right away. Mr. Stone was in real bad shape when they brought him in."

"Are you surprised?"

"No, sir." The intern shook his head. "Tell the truth, I've seen a lot of patients in shock, but never—" He stopped. "They tell you about the cat?"

"No. What?"

"Seems when the neighbors heard the commotion, they came in and found Mr. Stone holding this little black cat all covered in blood."

"Christ."

"Apparently he wouldn't let it go. Hung on to the poor beast all the way over here, like they were welded together. They gave him a shot in the emergency room, after he'd spoken to the police, and took it away."

"Is it dead?"

"No." The intern smiled. "Matter of fact, I heard they patched it up right there in Emergency, and seems it's hanging in." He shook his head. "Damnedest thing."

In her apartment at the Pierre, Fanny looked in weary disbelief at the last of Lee's empty wardrobes, and sat down heavily on the bed.

"Why?" she said out loud. "For God's sake, Lee, why?"

Wretchedly she wandered into the kitchen, and saw the note, written in Lee's clear hand, propped on the breakfast bar.

Hands trembling, Fanny picked it up.

> I'm sorry, Fanny, truly sorry, but I have to go, and quickly.
> Ask the Jew. He will explain.
> Think cruel thoughts if you must—but know that I love you.
>   Natalie

Fanny ceased to breathe.

She stared at the note.

Ask the Jew.

And at the signature.

And as the words, like ugly ragged cuckoos, came home to roost, the truth began to scorch itself into her heart and mind, leaving deep, searing scars.

They were calling her flight, but Natalie pushed another dime into the slot. A copy of the *New York Post* was under her arm; sweat trickled down her back, staining her silk blouse.

"I said I want to speak to Joe Bernardi," she said, lips close to the mouthpiece.

"Who's calling him?"

"Just put me through."

"Not without your name, ma'am."

"Tell him it's about Silberstein."

"Who?"

She repeated the name. The seconds ticked by.

"Yes."

"Bernardi?"

"This is a colleague. What do you want?" The voice was nasal Bronx and rough.

"I want to speak to Bernardi."

"He's busy, you'll have to talk to me."

Natalie ground her teeth. She turned to face the wall and lowered her voice to a hiss. "I want to know what the hell happened."

"Happened?"

"You know what I mean, bastard. I'm talking about murder."

"Murder?"

"Salaud! Let me speak to Bernardi!"

"I told you, he's busy."

"Listen, *imbécile,"* she spat into the phone, sweat breaking out on her forehead. "I gave Bernardi certain information so that he could make Silberstein pay for his past. I never even dreamed of murder! I never thought he would slaughter the man's wife!" She heard a strange click and guessed that others, perhaps Bernardi himself, were listening in. "This boy, Rodrigo." She clutched at the newspaper. "They say he was crazy. What did you do to make him crazy enough to kill in such a horrible way? Or perhaps it wasn't Rodrigo who killed her at all!" She stopped, aware she'd said too much. It was like screaming into a ravine and getting nothing back, not even an echo. "Are you there?"

"I'm here." The voice was uglier than before. "And I got two suggestions."

"Which are?"

"Mr. Bernardi doesn't like anonymous calls, and false accusations make him very angry, so either you wise up and keep your big mouth shut, or—"

"You tell him to go straight to hell!" she shrilled.

The pause was short. "He'll see you there, but he prefers the scenic route, so you better not hold your breath. You want the second suggestion?"

"I want nothing from a dago pig!"

"Start saying your prayers every night."

The receiver was slippery in her hand as she replaced it on the hook.

If Joe Bernardi ever found her, she was finished.

Natalie picked up her brand-new crocodile-skin traveling bag, the last gift from Fanny. They'd chosen it together in Mark Cross just a few days earlier.

By now, Natalie thought bitterly, Silberstein would have told Fanny everything, and she would hate her until the day she died.

Sharp, acrid tears filled her eyes.

As if from a great distance, she heard the final call for her Paris flight. It had taken too many precious hours already to find a seat on any plane to Europe, and she was damned if she was going to risk missing it now. A curious mixture of irony, hatred, and sorrow filled her, together with an absolute awareness.

She was damned if she went. And damned if she stayed.

At four in the morning of the night after Barbara's murder, the blackest time of all, Daniel woke in his hospital room, and was alone.

For a brief, blissful moment, the drugs reprieved him. The door opened, and he saw a glint of fair hair, like angel down.

"Barbara?" His soul soared like a skyrocket from his heavy body.

And then he saw the uniform.

"All right, Mr. Stone?"

Daniel closed his eyes, and Barbara lay again on the rug, and he saw the gaping wounds, and heard his own screams, and smelled the blood . . .

He opened his eyes, and the hypodermic was suspended in mid-air. He reached out and grasped her wrist.

"Help me," he whispered.

"Of course, Mr. Stone." She patted his hand. "Let me give you this shot."

He tightened his grip. "I want to die," he said clearly. "Help me, please. Kill me."

The nurse's face was young and sweet as she bent over him. Daniel's arm fell limply back to the sheets.

"You have to live, Mr. Stone," he thought he heard her say gently, condemning him, and the needle slipped into his arm, and put him to sleep.

They brought him, with Cat, back to Central Park West, and put them both to bed in the guest room, and fed them with sedatives and chicken soup and love, until some of the shaking began to ease. On the fifth day, they left Bobbi and Cat with a neighbor, and flew to Minneapolis, from where they drove with Barbara's coffin to Northfield, in convoy with Fanny, Leon and Sarah, and Roland and Kate. There Barbara and their sabra were laid to rest with her parents in their family plot. The friends stood helplessly by, fearful of what Daniel might do when the moment came to toss soil onto the polished lid. Daniel did nothing; just threw down damp earth, and came away.

He sat after the funeral for four days on a chair with a hard, straight back, and lay for four nights trying not to close his eyes, Cat beside him. He did not speak, did not weep. Bobbi, knowing little but understanding enough, stood patiently next to the hard chair for an hour at a time, clasping his cold hands with her own warm, soft ones, while her mother stood in the doorway, half hidden by shadow, watching them, and her father paced, like a mad silver-haired creature, silently raging.

On the eleventh day he wanted to go home to the apartment, so Andreas and Alexandra drove him there and spent the night, in case he harmed himself. When Andreas checked on him in the morning, he found Daniel sitting on the rug, where the bloodstains had been laundered out, glassy-eyed, Cat in his arms.

"He has to let it out!" he cried to Alexandra.

"You have to give him time," she answered. "Maybe we should leave him alone now."

"I can't!"

"You must."

When Daniel began at last to communicate again, he spoke only of his own guilts. He was consumed by them: childhood guilts, adolescent guilts, manhood guilts. He sat in his library and, as always when in pain, drew on quotations; he found Sophocles and Aeschylus and Corneille all in agreement with him—Bernardi could not be condemned for avenging his wife's death. If Daniel had not run in 1954, as he had run so often before, he tortured himself, the Sicilian could have punished him instead of Barbara. His personal sins tormented him . . . his mother and sister, who had stayed in Germany and died, while he had left and lived . . . his father, too, whom he had abandoned for his own sake . . . And finally, his wife and child.

Daniel's crimes, real and imagined, writhed and seared like venomous snakes in his belly.

"I have to do something!" Andreas said to Alexandra.

"But there's nothing to be done. The police can't be told the truth about Bernardi or Natalie, we all agreed to that from the first. It would only bring Dan more grief."

"I have to do something," he repeated insistently.

"What can you do except be a friend to Dan?"

"When he speaks about Natalie, he dismisses her as if she were nothing but a catalyst!"

"Maybe that's all she was."

"No!"

"What, then?"

"She is a monster."

Andreas hired a private investigator to locate Natalie, not quite knowing what he would do when he found her. It took nearly two months to track her down to an eight-room apartment on Avenue de Neuilly, close to the Bois de Boulogne in Paris. For five days after he received the investigator's report, Andreas waited, questioning his own motives and searching his conscience. There was little doubt in his mind that if he passed the information to Daniel, it would cause him additional suffering. But if he did nothing at all, Natalie Bresson would go unpunished. That was intolerable.

On the sixth day, Andreas walked to a phone booth on Lexington Avenue, and made an anonymous telephone call to Joe Bernardi.

Five days before Christmas, Natalie, living under her mother's maiden name, Jourdan, arrived home to find three armed and hooded men waiting for her.

They offered her a choice. Either she would swallow a bottle of barbiturates in front of them, or she would take a dive from the parapet of her balcony.

Natalie begged, she pleaded, she wailed, cajoled, and bribed, her eyes rolled in their sockets, but they were relentless. They pushed the bottle of tablets toward her mouth, and she shrieked and chose the balcony.

The leader patted the top of the parapet invitingly. "Up, madame." She struggled and sobbed against the leather glove that silenced her. "Quicker is easier than slowly," he said.

They took hold of her legs, careful not to bruise, and lifted her until she half lay, half sat on the parapet. The glove released her face, and the still-living beast of her own survival instinct rose up again inside her, and Natalie opened her mouth and screamed like the queen of hell—but the hands were at her back, pushing, and then she was rolling and flying and diving and plummeting down through the icy night air, and the dark concrete was coming closer, closer . . .

On a visit to Zurich the day before Christmas Eve, Andreas read the item in the *Herald Tribune* describing the abortive suicide attempt of a noted society beauty in Paris, who now faced the remainder of her life in a state of near total paralysis, unable even to speak.

On his return to New York that night, Andreas showed the cutting to Alexandra.

"Poor woman!" Her eyes were horrified. "It's a life sentence."

Andreas was silent.

"Whatever you do," she added swiftly, "don't show this to

Fanny." She shook her head. "Poor Natalie. What terrible guilt she must have suffered to come to this."

"You pity her?"

She looked surprised. "Of course. Whatever she did, no one deserves to be condemned to something like that." She stared again at the cutting, and shivered. "I wonder why she chose to jump. God knows there are easier ways."

Andreas said nothing more. He hoped his wife would never learn that he had called Bernardi. He wondered about his own feelings. Guilty? A little, certainly, for he was sure Bernardi must have played a role in Natalie's bizarre fate. But pity? Paralysis was surely a living death. . . . And then he thought about Daniel, and about Barbara and the child, and he realized, with a slight chill, that he could not feel any pity at all.

Early on Christmas morning Andreas went to Daniel's apartment on 11th Street, and without a word laid before him three clippings, from the *Herald Tribune*, *Le Monde*, and *France-Soir*.

Daniel read the words in silence, nodded once at Andreas, and left the room. In the bathroom, he vomited until he was empty, and then he walked into the hall and picked up the cat. He carried him into the bedroom and sat down, the animal on his knee. He bent his head, buried his face in Cat's soft black fur, and began, at last, to weep.

46

. . . Do you begin to understand, Bobbi, how it was? How hard it became?

After the killing, Dan was brave, remarkable even. It was agonizing to watch him dragging himself through that first year, rebuilding his life as a single, lonely man. He told me once that he sometimes felt Barbara had been unreal, a dream. His time with her stood out from the rest of his life with such warmth and vibrance that he felt as if he could carve it out in a ring, like cutting a perfect round shape out of flat dough with a cookie cutter, and lock it away for safekeeping in a drawer of his mind, leaving the rest flat and unchanged.

Barbara's death put a strain on us all. Fanny's guilt almost crippled her. She had loved three people, and all three were destroyed because of the trust she had placed in one of them. I don't think she ever really hated Natalie, condemned as she was to a living death. People say we're allowed one mistake. People can be wrong.

And what could I do for Dan? After the first few weeks I couldn't go to him, hold him, comfort him as I admit I longed to —I could do nothing to replace the wife and child he'd lost. Day after day I stared into your eyes, my own darling daughter, and studied your gestures, your facial expressions, your movements, and wondered.

Andreas, as you must know, is a superstitious man—it stems from the racing days. He had only just begun to relax, to enjoy life again. After you were born, while you were still an infant, completely dependent on us, the center of our universe was securely planted in our home—and when Dan found Barbara and settled down too, at last Andreas seemed able to share the people who mattered most to him. I think we formed an enchanted circle in his mind, and when that was so brutally snapped, I believe your father's visions of security went with it. You grew, and abandoned our cozy triumvirate for kindergarten and friends your own age. I got back into the studio and back into the public eye. The artistic existence was not as unworldly and rhapsodic in Manhattan as it is in this creative bolt-hole in France. In New York City it meant dealers and gallery owners, as of course it does for me even in Honfleur; but it also meant business managers, lawyers, and tax advisers! It all became so much more complicated than simply shutting myself into my studio for a few hours each day while you were in school. In short, your mother was too busy to see what was happening.

What was happening was that Andreas thought I no longer needed him. He poured it out one day when it was too late—I was beautiful, he said, accomplished, able to fend for myself, even to bear a child independent of him. He was so wrong, Bobbi! I needed him more than I had ever done. He began to treat me as many Italian men treat their wives; loving me as the mother of his child instead of as a lover and friend. I couldn't blame him for going to other, younger women; they didn't serve as a constant reminder of what he still mistakenly thought of as his ineffectiveness.

So what did I do? I threw myself more completely into my work, and only consolidated the independent image Andreas had of me. You were the mainstay of my life, the bedrock. You kept me going as our marriage went downhill. I remember that finally my work began to suffer, too, and I turned increasingly to sculpting because I found it good therapy—as my happiness soured, the sculptures became uglier, but the critics loved them. Professionally, I just couldn't seem to fail. . . .

Part Five

Part Five

47

On a baking, sour-smelling afternoon in August 1970, Alexandra left the apartment to collect Bobbi from a friend's home. Generally on a Wednesday they went directly to Bobbi's dance class on the other side of the city, where Alexandra would watch or wait outside with the other parents, but today her friend's mother told Alexandra that Bobbi had been feeling under par all afternoon and ought perhaps to go right home.

Alexandra knew there was a stranger in the apartment even before the front door closed behind them, even before she smelled the unfamiliar perfume. Too late, she called out to Bobbi, but the little girl had already tossed aside her ballet shoes and was rushing up the spiral staircase in search of her father.

Alexandra dropped her purse on the floor and ran after her. The door to the bedroom was open before she made it to the landing, and the deafening, appalled silence that clanged through the apartment was as loud as the bells of St. Patrick's on Christmas Eve.

They sat rigid and naked, covered only to the waist by the sheets. The girl was fair-haired and tiny, with pert flushed breasts, flaming cheeks, and little runnels of sweat glistening on her skin. Andreas was ashen, his eyes riveted in horror on Bobbi.

Acting on instinct, Alexandra grabbed Bobbi's arm and dragged her down the corridor, pushing her into her bedroom. "Stay here, darling."

Bobbi began to cry.

"I'm sorry, baby, but you have to stay in here. I'll be back in no time."

She locked the door and dropped the key into the pocket of her skirt.

In the bedroom, they were scrambling to get dressed, wild-eyed and silent. Alexandra picked up the girl's shoes and stockings and held them in the air.

"You get out right now," she said in a dangerously quiet voice.

"My shoes—" The blonde held out her hand.

"Go get them." Alexandra stalked to the open window and threw them out.

"You're crazy!" Andreas yelled. "You could kill someone!"

She ignored him. "Didn't I tell you to get out?" she said to the girl.

She was out of the bedroom and at the front door in a flash. "He didn't tell me he had a kid!" she shrilled up the stairs. The door slam vibrated through the whole apartment.

Down the hallway Alexandra could hear Bobbi sobbing, but she turned on Andreas, aware of the trembling starting in her limbs. "I've put up with a lot, Andreas," she said shakily. "I've put up with the knowledge that for the past six months you've slept with any ten women rather than touch me; that you've spent almost all your free time with Dan and Fanny instead of me; that you keep all your plans, all the good and the bad things that happen in your life, a secret from me. . . ." Her eyes burned with tears she refused to shed. "But this was it. The end."

His jaw was set. "I had no idea you and Bobbi were going to come back."

"Obviously."

He moved toward the door. "Let me go talk to her."

"Don't you dare go anywhere near her!" Alexandra blocked his exit. "I've locked Bobbi in, and she's going to stay safely out of your way until you leave."

"Get out of my way!" Pushing her aside, he ran toward Bobbi's room and tried the handle. Behind the locked door, the child's sobs changed to panicked wails. "It's okay, sweetheart," he called through the door. "Don't cry, Bobbi, it's okay." He turned. Alexandra was behind him. "Give me the key!" he demanded.

"Absolutely not. You're in no condition to see her."

"Give it to me!"

"No!"

Enraged, he rushed down the stairs and into her studio. Like an animal on the rampage, he set about tearing the room apart, ripping at canvases with his hands and hurling sculptures to the floor. Plaster, clay, and terra-cotta showered everywhere, dust clouded the air. Wood splintered as he snapped frames, glass jars filled with palette knives, brushes, pencils, and charcoal smashed onto the block flooring. He was about to seize a wrapped canvas from the far corner of the studio when Alexandra's voice, clear and sharp with fear and anger, stopped him.

"If you even touch that painting, Andreas, I swear, as God is my witness, you'll never see me or Bobbi again!"

She saw the hand clenched into a fist too late, ducked too late—the blow sent her reeling against the wall, knocking her down.

When she could see again, her vision still blurry, she saw his face, aghast, staring down at her.

"Don't worry," she muttered through clenched teeth, "I'm all right. You haven't killed me."

"I didn't mean . . ." he floundered. "Ali, I—"

She rose shakily, with what dignity she could muster.

"Good-bye, Andreas."

Later, when Bobbi was calmer and Alexandra had kissed away her tears, she gave her a light supper and took her gently into the den.

"Just wait here a second, sweetheart, while I fetch something from the studio."

"Don't lock the door, Mommy!"

Her heart tore. "Never again, I promise."

She returned a moment later with the wrapped canvas she'd stopped Andreas from destroying earlier. "I want you to help me hang this, okay?" Her fingers trembled as she ripped off the brown paper.

"What is it, Mommy?" The little girl touched it delicately, respectfully, as her mother had taught her.

"It's the most important painting I've ever done, at least it is to me." Alexandra straightened and surveyed the wall. "I think we'll put it up there, over the fireplace."

Bobbi chewed at her lip, contemplating the abstract work, gazing at the shadowy figures and the small glowing shape in the center of the canvas. "Don't understand it, Mommy."

"No, baby," Alexandra said softly. "But one day, I'll explain it to you."

Bobbi turned her gaze on her. "Why was that lady in your bed with Daddy?"

It was like staring into a mirror; those cool gray-green irises, their perfect innocence confounding.

"They were—playing."

"Why did you and Daddy get mad?"

Alexandra reached out and rumpled the tender curls. "Let's get that painting up on the wall."

Her daughter's bottom lip quivered. "When's Daddy coming home?"

For four days and nights Alexandra waited for him. *I'm the proverbial wife who watches and waits,* she thought, *and would forgive anything for the sake of her child.* On the outside, she carried on as usual for Bobbi. "Of course Daddy's coming home, sweetheart. He's gone away on business for a few days, that's all. Hurry up and eat your breakfast." *Let him at least telephone,* she prayed. And then: *Let him come back.*

Downtown on 11th Street, Daniel was confused by Andreas's misery.

"Why don't you call her? You love her—you made a mistake; a bad one, but not unique, not irreversible. Pick up the phone."

Andreas's face was bleak as he scratched the fur behind Cat's ears. "It's no good, Dan. Not anymore."

"Two people who care about each other? Since when is that anything but good?"

Andreas smiled. "You sound like your friend Sarah. That's the kind of thing she'd say."

"And she'd be right!" Exasperated, he stared at his friend. "What is this, Andreas? Some kind of self-destruction? It's crazy."

Andreas shrugged. "Maybe I am."

"You're not crazy, you're just pretending." Daniel whacked him on the shoulder. "Do us all a favor and go home."

"There's no point." Andreas shook his head obdurately. "It's over, Dan."

On the fifth night, he called.

"I'm sorry," he said, his voice flat.

"Oh," she replied. "I've been worried sick."

"I've been at Dan's."

"I guessed you would be. It didn't stop me worrying."

"No."

Her trembling began again. "Andreas?"

"Yes."

"Come home."

"I can't."

"Why not?"

He waited a second. "I want you to get a divorce, Ali."

"What?"

"You heard me."

"No. Andreas, no!"

"It's for the best. Believe me."

Alexandra's free hand screwed into a tight fist and balled into her side. "I don't believe you." She wanted to scream at him, but Bobbi was sleeping two rooms away. "I don't think you've thought about it, not rationally."

"I've done nothing but think about it." The dullness never left his voice.

"Come home. Let's at least talk things over." Desperation burst up through her chest and out into the words. "Twelve years! We have a child! We *love* each other!"

"I know," he said.

For the first time she sensed a cracking. "Then please, please come home."

The crack sealed over. "I want you to file for divorce right away, Ali."

"No," she said. "Absolutely, categorically not. I refuse to set fire to everything in life I care about."

"Then I will."

His words whistled the air like an axe delivering a coup de grace.

"Why?" she asked, growing numb.

The pot boiled over and agony scalded his voice. "Didn't you see me wreck it all five nights ago? Didn't you hear me?"

She dredged up some pride.

"I heard you."

It all happened so fast. Afterward, they both wondered if somehow it had happened without their participation. They were the principal protagonists in the affair, and yet the chorus took over. The moment lawyers were appointed, the marriage never had a hope in hell. Alexandra went to her first meeting praying that a last straw might be extended from the awful mess; instead, the straw was quickly ignited by her counsel's solid-gold cigarette lighter, and dumped on the ashes.

"Everything," he said. "I presume we go for everything?"

"No," she said, already bewildered. "I don't want everything."

"Of course you don't," he said smoothly, "but you must nevertheless think of the future and of your child." He consulted the notes on his desk. "Roberta."

"My husband wouldn't want anything but the best for our daughter."

He smiled. "I'm sure he wouldn't, Mrs. Alessandro. But he has an excellent lawyer, hasn't he?"

"I don't know."

"I do. It's my business to know."

"And I know my husband."

"Who has employed a top-rate attorney to look after his interests."

She disliked him intensely. "He's got a good lawyer because he doesn't want the . . . divorce"—she still had to fight to say the word—"to drag on."

The man laughed mirthlessly. "Mr. Alessandro's counsel will protect his client against us in every way, believe me. I understand your reluctance to come to terms with the harsh facts, but there they are." He tapped a manicured fingernail on his alligator-trimmed blotter. "Now, I think we should get down to business, Mrs. Alessandro. This meeting has already cost your husband the price of lunch at Alessandro's."

While Alexandra changed lawyers twice before she finally found someone who understood her moral scruples, Andreas was otherwise engaged, trying to find the finest custody specialist in the city. The pain of losing Ali was bad enough. The concept of being without Bobbi was worse than death. Suddenly, driven by the same self-destructive demon that had caused him to wreck a marriage he still yearned for, Andreas developed an irrational notion that Alexandra might, if pushed by counsel, use his infertility as a factor against his fitness to be Bobbi's father.

"Don't fight this too hard, Mr. Alessandro," his lawyer advised over and over. "I warn you, you have no chance of winning. Far better to go for generous visitation rights."

"No!" Andreas exploded. "I've told you before—I will not become a Sunday father! I will not have my baby strung like a yo-yo between us! I will not resort to buying her love with weekend treats! *I will not give her up!*"

His lawyer shook his head gravely. "I'm afraid you may have to."

Andreas pounded his fists on the table. "Are you or are you not the best custody lawyer in the city?"

The man shrugged. "On a lucky day, maybe I am." Then he sighed. "You're quite welcome to try elsewhere if you prefer, Mr. Alessandro. I do have an excellent success record. I'm not that keen to foul it up."

On the seventeenth day of May 1971, while Roberta was in school, the judge awarded Alexandra sole custody. To Andreas she offered good wishes, assurances that his fitness as an excellent father were not in dispute, and a visitation package that included alternate Sundays, one weekend each month, and a two-week vacation, either to be taken in one piece or to be divided into two, as convenient to Roberta's mother and himself.

Andreas threw it in the judge's face, was given two warnings, and then fined for contempt of court. Three hours later he came to Central Park West, packed up the rest of his belongings, and, in front of Bobbi, thanked Alexandra for destroying his life.

The child sobbed inconsolably for the rest of the day, the longest of her young life. Bobbi never threw tantrums, rarely resorted to tears in order to win something she badly wanted. On this occasion, buried in every choking sob was another plea to her daddy to hear her and come back. But next morning her father was still gone.

"When are we going to see him?" she asked at breakfast, pushing a slice of French toast from one side of her plate to the other. There were deep smudges under her red eyes.

Alexandra felt as bereft as the child. "Soon," she promised, still certain she spoke the truth.

Sunday came and went. The last weekend of May limped slowly closer, and then vanished, barren as the one that had preceded it. Alexandra invented excuses and reasons for Bobbi as her own mind became darker and less comprehending.

She telephoned Daniel.

"He isn't here, Ali."

"Where is he?"

"In Europe."

"With his father?"

"I doubt it. Roberto would be the last person to understand this."

"Do you understand, Dan?"

"Of course not."

"It's breaking Bobbi's heart."

"It's broken his already."

She decided, finally, on half-truths. After school one day, she took Bobbi to Central Park to feed the squirrels.

"I think you're very grown-up for your age," she began. "So I want to try and explain why your daddy hasn't come to see you."

Bobbi turned wide, scared eyes on her.

"You know the way you cried the day he went away?"

The child nodded.

"It hurt a lot, didn't it, sweetheart?"

"Yes."

"If Daddy came to see you right now, and then left again, you'd cry again, wouldn't you?"

"Yes."

"But that doesn't stop you wanting to see him, does it?"

"Of course not, Mommy."

"That makes you quite brave, Bobbi. Knowing something will hurt, but still knowing it's worth it." She forced herself to continue. "Do you know what a hero is?"

Bobbi nodded. "Someone brave. Like Superman or President Kennedy."

Alexandra smiled. "That's right."

"What do they have to do with Daddy?"

"Your father used to be quite a hero. Before you were born—a long time before."

"You mean when he was a racing driver?"

"That's right," she said again. "So you know he is a brave man, don't you?"

"Yes, Mommy."

"Right now, though," Alexandra said slowly, "Daddy isn't himself."

"You mean he's sick?"

"Kind of. A little." She saw the frown on Bobbi's forehead deepen. "Nothing to worry about, darling, truly. It's just that he's scared."

"Of what?"

Alexandra paused. "Of crying every time he has to leave you."

"Daddy doesn't cry. He never cries."

"He would then. Because leaving you would hurt him just like it would you."

Bobbi's eyes filled with tears. "But why does he have to leave me, then? Why doesn't he just stay like before?"

Alexandra's lips quivered, and she caught at them quickly with her teeth to stop herself from weeping too. "Because we don't live together now."

"Because of the divorce?"

The word sounded shocking, tumbling so easily from her mouth, but even among Bobbi's peers at school, twenty-five percent were already victims of split marriages, and the children batted words like *divorce* and *custody* and *alimony* back and forth effortlessly, never quite relating them to the pain they themselves suffered in consequence.

"Yes, Bobbi," she answered. "Because we're divorced."

The child's hands knitted together tightly in her lap, the knuckles whitening. "Will Daddy always be scared?"

Oh, God, I wish I knew!

"Of course not," Alexandra lied, her heart breaking.

As 1971 passed by, Andreas remained remote, and Alexandra and Bobbi were forced to learn to cope with their loneliness. Where once Alexandra had hardly found enough time for her own work, now, with Bobbi at school most of the day except during vacations, there was little else to occupy her but her studio. Her friends were kind and thoughtful. Theo Salko and Rudy, especially, never let a week pass by without checking to see all was well with them, and numerous acquaintances arranged well-intentioned but uncomfortable dinner parties, inevitably seating Alexandra beside some eligible, unattached man.

She didn't want another man; of that, at least, she was certain. She had not yet stopped loving her husband, and the thought of love seemed to equate too much with anguish than anything else. She was aware that this would pass, that the nights spent in the lonely chill of the big bed would, in time, become less sleepless and interminable; that the choking sensation in her throat that attacked her each time she saw Andreas's portrait in the hall, or heard his name mentioned, would eventually diminish. But for now, if she couldn't have Andreas, she wanted no one else. She was not prepared to sham for the mere sake of companionship.

She became troubled by her lack of a close woman friend. She thrived on the company of other women, but her life had been so overflowing in the past—she'd had her husband, her child, and more than enough career to take up any slack. What time had there been for the warmth of female conversations over coffee, or for the simple pleasure of joint shopping expeditions with a friend? Until now, she realized with a slight jolt, she'd enjoyed her own company, been too self-absorbed.

So, as at other times of crisis in her life, Alexandra threw all her stamina into work. Another solo exhibition was planned for the summer of 1972, and she was seeking fresh themes upon which to base it. With too many memories crowding into her studio at home, she rented space on the West Side; a vast, airy penthouse where the increased floor space and towering ceiling allowed her to throw up ladders and work on a triptych and, when that was complete, a series of giant abstracts based on New York City life.

She worked too fast and too hard, often at the expense of quality and durability, but she was coping and would continue to cope.

Her husband had condemned her for her independence, determination and strength. So be it.

Andreas, too, had become a workaholic. The restaurants no longer enough to fill the empty minutes, he opened a chain of informal "cafés" serving lobster and steak dinners. He guaranteed freshness, top quality, and perfection in cooking, bought a helicopter, learned to pilot it himself, and flew from one Café Alessandro to the next to ensure his promise to the public was kept. By the fall of 1972 the "Alessandro Flight," as it became known, was a regular Saturday night spectacle when Andreas touched down under floodlights at Great Neck, Easthampton, Montauk, and Westport to greet his guests, check quality control, and take off again for the next destination. During the week he flew in scheduled airliners from Manhattan to Washington to Zurich to Paris; once a month he visited Roberto, but on those occasions questions about Ali or Bobbi were strictly taboo.

He became accustomed to loneliness, and forgot that happiness existed.

Rudesheim said he was a misery junkie, a spoiled kid in the throes of a permanent tantrum. Daniel was more sympathetic and tried to cajole him into analysis.

Andreas got up every morning and lived and breathed and worked and screwed around.

He got by.

48

In the spring of 1973, desperate to cure Bobbi's wistfulness, Alexandra took her to Europe. It was an instant love affair. No sooner did the seven-year-old step off the Pan American clipper at Heathrow Airport and hear the cockney tones of the baggage handlers, followed by the mellow, almost Shakespearean consonants of the officials at passport control, than Bobbi threw back her head and laughed uncontrollably with sheer pleasure. And miraculously they, in spite of their emblazonment of decades of stuffiness, laughed with her, enchanted by the tall woman-child with her accent as American as baseball, her skin tones as flawless and peachy as a nineteenth-century Shropshire maiden's, her hair as thick and glossy black as a Latin's, and her eyes as glowing and rare as . . . only now they turned their attention to her mother, and saw the same eyes, cool gray and warming to polished malachite as she smiled back at them; eyes that had regularly graced the covers of scores of magazines over the last ten years.

The passports were stamped with a flourish and Bobbi was treated to her first salute before they tripped off to the joys of the Connaught Hotel and a week of culture, tradition, and daily horseback riding in Hyde Park, where Bobbi took to the English saddle like a duck to the Serpentine, overtaking the dignified regulars on Rotten Row at a canter, shrieking with merriment, hair flying from beneath the hard hat her mother insisted she wear.

The love affair continued in Paris, where Bobbi practiced her school-learned and horribly basic French without mercy, rolling her r's like Fernandel, and finding apparently unbounded pleasure in frowned-upon but such well-worn words and phrases as *"Merde!" "Nom d'un chien!"* and *"Salaud!"* She flung them inappropriately, beaming ravishingly at her mother while they shopped under the watchful but benevolent eyes of the black-clad *vendeuses* in the Rue du Faubourg St.-Honoré and lunched gloriously at Tour d'Argent, Lasserre, and the Ritz-Vendôme.

It was in Normandy, however, that mere flirtation turned into something far more intense. They made Deauville their base, sharing a huge, airy suite at the Royal, a graceful white hotel. It was still naked of the chic polo and gambling set who would later in the year pour out of Rolls-Royces and Bentleys into the Royal and Normandy hotels and great mansions of the area, and stroll exotically along the Promenade des Planches, which in May stretched emptily beside the beach and the gray Baie de la Seine.

Every morning Alexandra and Bobbi took turns in the vast marble bathroom and then breakfasted at the open French doors on *oeufs au plat*, fresh baked *petits pains*, croissants, and brioches, with jelly of *groseilles* and *myrtilles*, before climbing into the rented Renault that stood ready before the front door of the hotel. Then Alexandra would drive with blissful calm through the Normandy countryside, inland from Trouville past Pont-l'Evêque to Lisieux and back to the coast to Honfleur. She introduced her young daughter to the greenest, lushest grass, to the fattest, most contented cows who daily provided the creamiest, tastiest cheeses to the human inhabitants of the region, perhaps among the most fortunate, tranquil, and secure in all the world.

"This is great, Mommy," Bobbi marveled, letting her hand trail out of the car window so that the breeze stroked her skin, while her mother drove at a remarkable ten miles an hour, safe in the knowledge that there was almost no other traffic on the road to be irritated by such luxurious languor.

An inner peace was beginning to invade Alexandra, a feeling that for the first time in years she was doing something that was right, utterly right both for herself and for Bobbi.

"Are you as sorry as I am that we're leaving?" she asked.

"I wish we didn't ever have to go, Mommy."

Alexandra raised an eyebrow. "Really?"

"This is the most beautiful place I've ever been. Don't you think so?"

"I certainly do. I've always loved this part of the world."

Bobbi turned appealing eyes on her. "Can we stay here? Instead of going to Switzerland?"

"No, sweetheart, of course not. We can't possibly disappoint your grandfather. He's longing to see you, you know."

Bobbi pulled a face. "But I don't really know him."

"Roberto Alessandro is one of the finest people I've ever known," Alexandra said firmly, curtailing any possible argument. "I promise you're going to love him just as much as I do, Bobbi. And yes, we do have to go."

"Can we come back here after?"

Alexandra kept her eyes on the road, amused by the child's tenacity. "Now that's a different question altogether."

Bobbi bounced eagerly on the seat. "Can we, can we?"

"Well, not right away, no. You have school, in case you'd forgotten."

Her daughter grimaced. "School's dumb."

"Which is what you'll be if you don't get back there soon, miss." She relented. "But we might come back here again sometime."

"Soon?"

"That depends."

"On what?"

Alexandra smiled to herself. "On all kinds of things." She inclined her head to glance directly at Bobbi. "If you had a choice— hypothetically, I mean—"

"What's hypothet—?" Bobbi faltered.

"Just imagining," Alexandra explained. "Imagine you could choose where you'd live over here, where would it be?"

"Really live, Mommy? Not just stay."

"Really live." She checked the rearview mirror. "Deauville?"

"Honfleur." She sounded decisive.

"Why?"

Bobbi wrinkled her nose in concentration. "It's neat."

"Try to explain, darling. What did you like especially?"

"The harbor. The lady who sold the butter before sunup." She sighed enviously. "The way no one had to wear good clothes all the time."

Again Alexandra smiled. Getting her daughter to change out of dungarees into city dresses or skirts was always a battle royal. What seven-year-old wouldn't swap sophistication for comfort? "Don't you think you might get bored? Life in a small town is often the same day in, day out."

"But it's like that at home too, Mommy. School, homework, waiting for you to get finished in the studio."

"But you have your friends. You'd miss them if you left New York, wouldn't you?"

The child thought for a moment. "We could be pen pals. And there are kids in Honfleur too, aren't there?"

Alexandra pulled over to the right and stopped the car. A sign hung from a tree, pointing the way down a narrow side road. CALVADOS À VENDRE. "I'd like to buy some calvados to take home. Okay, sweetheart?"

"Can I come?" Bobbi opened her door.

"Sure."

They left the car, not needing to lock the doors as they'd have to back in New York, and strolled down the leafy lane toward the old Normandy farmhouse where an old lady in black, her face leathery and lined, waited, a beige dog with bright eyes at her feet.

Alexandra greeted her and asked in French if she might buy some calvados.

The woman turned and pushed open the door. *"Vous voulez en déguster?"*

"Ce n'est pas nécessaire, merci, madame," Alexandra replied, and translated for Bobbi. "The lady asked if we want to taste some."

"Sure we do, Mommy!" Bobbi whispered.

"You're too young."

"All the kids here drink."

"That's wine, and with meals, not hanging around distilleries in the middle of the day."

"Oh, please, Mom, just a little bit."

Alexandra laughed and ruffled her hair. "Okay, but just a small taste." She followed the old lady inside. *"Oui, madame, nous voulons déguster, s'il vous plaît."*

They took the glasses of golden liquid out into the warm sunshine, and Bobbi sipped a little and pretended to like it, and fondled the dog. Alexandra looked around at the white blossoms that seemed to stretch forever along the horizon, that would in a few weeks cloak the grassy fields in soft, scented snow to make a space for the apples that would follow. She glanced at Bobbi, sitting comfortably in her blue dungarees, knees bent, leaning against a wall of the farmhouse, and something deep inside her twanged satisfyingly, like the well-tuned string of an old violin.

"It felt right," she said to Roberto a few days later. They were sitting in the dining room of his Zurich apartment after dinner. Bobbi was already asleep in her room, and the maid had just served coffee and cognac to them at the table. "And I know it must sound crazy to you, but I decided right there and then that we should move."

At the age of sixty-one, Roberto's hair was still plentiful and completely white. He looked, Alexandra thought, like a biblical sage who shopped for clothes on Savile Row and went to a barber on Fifth Avenue. She wondered, as she had often done, why he had not married again. Anna had been gone for more than fifteen years, and there must have been countless women clamoring for his hand. *What a strong woman she must have been,* Alexandra thought, *to have kept such a hold over him, even from the grave.*

Roberto frowned. "It's not just a house move you're talking about, Alexandra, *cara.* To move thousands of miles is much more complicated."

"I've done it before, Papa," she reminded him. "Twice over, three times if I count when my mother left my father and went to England before the war."

"Then you realize the implications." He patted her hand. "Of course, for me it would be a boon. To have you both so much closer."

"What worries me most," Alexandra said quickly, "is that I might be abusing Bobbi's trust. She really does believe I know best."

"She has sound instincts." He looked at her fondly. "Like her mother."

"She's become my best friend, you know, Papa. She's such a wonderful companion—it's been as good as having someone of my own age along, better maybe." She took a sip of coffee. "Even if we don't move to Europe, we'll have to move out of the apartment soon, you know. Bobbi's fine, truly she is, but in New York she's wistful so much of the time. The city, and especially the apartment, are too filled with memories for her to be completely happy." She looked at Roberto, her eyes bright with sudden unshed tears. "I want her to be happy, Papa."

"Of course you do." Roberto's face darkened. "If I live to be a hundred years old I will never understand Andreas. How a son of mine can—"

"Don't, Papa, please." She stopped him gently. "You don't know. There are reasons."

He shook his head. "No reasons. For divorce, maybe—I have imagination, I can comprehend how some things happen." His face was full of pain. "But Roberta is his child—his beautiful daughter, his own flesh and blood."

Alexandra took a moment. She'd never shared the truth with anyone, had vowed she would never do that to Andreas. But this was his father, who would never hurt his son, who still loved him more than anyone.

"No," she said quietly.

It took several seconds for her meaning to sink in. Roberto became pale under his tan and his mouth quivered. "What . . . ?"

"She is not his flesh and blood, Papa." She took a breath. "She is his daughter, as surely as if she was made out of his seed, but she was not."

"Oh, my God." It was not an exclamation. It came flatly from his lips, and yet it was filled with anguish. He stared at Alexandra, and for a brief second she saw such wildness in his dark eyes that she was afraid.

"Tell me." It was a command.

Afterward, they both wept. In grief and in consolation, taking comfort from each other.

"If Andreas knew I had told you, I think he might kill me."

Roberto took a large white handkerchief from his trouser pocket and wiped his eyes. "The child knows nothing?"

"Of course not. Andreas is her father."

He shook his great shaggy head. "How he must have suffered." He looked at Alexandra. "And you, too, *mia cara.*"

"Not as much as he did. And still does, I'm afraid."

"Until he learns to share pain, he will have no choice." He stood up. "Come," he said in his deepest voice. "Let's go to her."

Bobbi, in repose, still had the angel aura about her that all children share. Her lips, untouched by makeup or men's kisses, were slightly parted and a natural soft pink, her lashes, black and incredibly long, fluttered faintly as she dreamed, and her skin was flushed.

Roberto bent and tenderly planted a kiss on her hairline, careful not to wake her. Then he drew Alexandra out of the room.

"If Anna had come to me with such an idea," he said when they were back in the dining room, "I don't know how I would have reacted."

"I think you might have agreed, Papa, in time." She smiled. "You loved her so much, you would have done anything for her."

"Perhaps." He shook his head. "But it would have been hard." His eyes grew hazy. "I could imagine her having come to me pregnant by another man—inconceivable, in Anna's case, of course. But infidelity might have been easier to bear. Less contrived, less mechanical and scientific."

A wave rippled through Alexandra. *Would he still feel that way if he knew about Dan, I wonder.*

"But that's exactly what it was intended to prevent," she said calmly. "Thoughts of infidelity, suspicions. It was a deliberate act, carefully thought out by both of us, because we wanted a child." She recognized her own hypocrisy. "Or rather because *I* wanted a child."

"He wanted her too, Alexandra," Roberto reassured her. "You have said yourself that this terrible hostility is the result of his great love for Bobbi, because he cannot bear being parted from her."

"But he brought that on himself!" she cried, her calmness dissolving. "The divorce was his idea—he insisted on it."

"I know, *cara,* I know." He nodded suddenly. "I think perhaps you are right, about moving to Honfleur. It can do nothing but good."

"I won't do it, won't think of it, unless Andreas agrees," she said hastily.

"Do you think he will?"

"So far he's agreed to everything I've suggested. It's as if he doesn't care, though we both know that isn't true. When I contacted him for permission to bring Bobbi on this vacation, he answered through his lawyer." She shrugged helplessly. "Since he never sees her anyway, I can't imagine he'll object to this either."

Roberto looked thoughtful. "It might shock him," he said slowly, "bring him to his senses."

Alexandra sighed. "I don't know. I begin to think nothing will ever do that."

"Life is long." Roberto put his arms around her. "I'm grateful you felt you could share this with me at last."

"I wish Andreas had told you himself years ago. You could have helped him in ways I couldn't hope to." She rested her cheek against his strong shoulder.

"A suggestion," he said suddenly.

"What?"

"I think we should open the bottle you brought me from Calvados. It would be fitting."

She smiled. "After wine and cognac?"

"After news like that, anyone is entitled to get a little drunk." He went to the walnut cocktail cabinet in the corner and took out the bottle. "Sit down," he said, uncorking it and pouring it into two snifters.

"What shall we drink to?" she asked.

"To Honfleur," he said, handing her a glass and pulling his chair closer to hers. "To new beginnings, to new hopes, and to old friendships."

"I love you, Papa," Alexandra said softly. She reached out and stroked his cheek, stubbly with nighttime. "As I love your son."

"I know."

She raised her glass. "To our future," she said. "To our child."

The calvados glinted golden in their glasses.
"To Bobbi," they said together.

It took Alexandra just seven days into Bobbi's long summer vacation to find their house, and then it was by purest accident.

"L'Alouette" stood all alone at the top of a small incline above the road that ran between Honfleur and Deauville. In July 1973, when Alexandra first set eyes on it, the house was chaotic, hence the shock and open disapproval of the representative of the *agent immobilier* in Trouville, whose brief had been to show this famous and wealthy American woman only the most meritorious available mansions in the vicinity. L'Alouette was crumbling white plaster, partially rotting beams, and unruly thatch, and that was just the outside! The interior was a nightmare of ancient wiring, rickety plumbing, and birds' nests. But when Alexandra glanced out of her window one evening, on her way back to the hotel in Deauville, the house had been set aflame by the sunset. The plaster was flushed pink, the ivy that twined hectically through the thatch was aglow, and the wild roses that had grown unchallenged in the garden and up the broken trellises surrounding the front and side doors, as fresh as a bridal bouquet.

Alexandra could hardly bear to tear her eyes away from it. She longed to paint it there and then.

"But Madame Alessandro," the real estate agent protested on the telephone, "there is a house just become available in Deauville, formerly the home of the mayor and in pristine—"

"I want to buy L'Alouette," Alexandra insisted. "It's absolutely empty, there's no sign of anyone living there, so it must be for sale."

"But it's a terrible house! No one has lived there for more than two years!"

"It's a wonderful house," she said stubbornly. "I'm quite aware of the difficulties, but there's nothing that can't be put right given time and money. Now can you help me, or do I have to go elsewhere?"

There was a heartfelt sigh from the other end of the line. *"Bien sûr,* Madame Alessandro. If that is what you want."

"It is."

It was the following spring before L'Alouette began to approach habitability. Alexandra wrote to Andreas through her lawyer, telling him she'd decided to sell the apartment on Central Park West.

She sat back and waited for the now customary formal reply, and was surprised to learn that Andreas sought a meeting.

On the fifth of June, they met on neutral territory, at a table in the Oak Room at the Plaza Hotel. They were not surprised by the painfulness of the encounter. They spoke like courteous strangers, exchanged papers; their fingers touched lightly, accidentally, and were hurriedly withdrawn.

At last, they spoke of Bobbi.

"I've wanted to thank you, for a long time," Andreas said awkwardly, "for the photographs and school reports."

"It seems only fair."

"More than fair."

Silence came between them again. Alexandra longed to leave; she'd known it would be like this, unbearable, excruciating. She forced herself on, playing with her salad, every mouthful like straw.

"Is she well?" the question came at last.

"Very well." Alexandra smiled slightly. "She's beautiful, and healthy, thank God." She lowered her eyes. "And looking forward to France."

"I'm sure." He flushed suddenly, darkly. "I'd like to see her, Ali."

She laid down her fork. Her heart pounded in confusion. "It's been more than three years, Andreas."

"I know."

"I don't know that it would be fair."

For a moment anguish showed clearly in his eyes, then the shutters came down again. "I see."

"Do you?"

"Of course. She's become used to not having me around. It would be too hurtful if I just appeared for a brief visit." He took a quick swallow of wine.

Alexandra felt helpless with pity, and angry with herself for it. "Why now, Andreas?" she asked quietly. "Why not before? She needed you so badly."

He flushed again, and bent his head, staring at the plate in front of him. "I've been seeing an analyst."

Alexandra said nothing, waited for him to go on.

"I called John Manetti a few months ago and asked him to recommend someone." He shrugged. "He did."

She was filled with astonishment, aware what that must have

cost him. To go to Manetti, of all people—the man he'd always considered primarily responsible for his pain.

"I've learned quite a lot about myself," he continued slowly. "About my feelings after the crash, about the artificial insemination . . ." His mouth quirked. "About my blind acceptance after Bobbi was born, about my hostility—" He stopped, unable to go on.

"It's all right," she said, waves of compassion sweeping her. "Don't."

The waiter appeared to pour more wine.

Andreas moistened his lips. "Could I write to her, do you think?" he asked, uncharacteristically humble.

"To Bobbi? Why, yes, I think that's a fine idea."

A flash of hope and yearning appeared in his face. "You think she'd write back?"

"I don't honestly know. I guess it would depend on your letters."

"Does she hate me very much?"

"I don't think she hates you at all, Andreas. I've never seen a single sign of malice or resentment in her. But she is deeply hurt."

He took hold of his glass, his fingers wound so tightly around the stem that Alexandra was afraid it might split in two. "Is it too late?"

Her heart melted. "I hope not," she said. "She's only eight years old." She remembered Roberto's words. "Life is long."

They had both reckoned without Bobbi's still-developing but already strong streak of female obstinacy and loyalty to her mother. When the first letters began to appear in the pigeonhole at the front desk of the Royal in Deauville, where they were staying until L'Alouette was ready for them to move into, she was panic-stricken and too frightened to read them herself.

"What does he want, Mommy?"

"He wants to get to know you again."

"But why now? Just when we're starting over."

Alexandra's heart went out to her. "He's feeling stronger, Bobbi, just as we hoped he would. He's brave enough to face seeing you without holding on to you."

But as the letters continued to arrive, now dropping onto the mat at L'Alouette, Bobbi began to sense a cowardice in the tentative notes which only seemed to heighten her own feelings of rejection.

"He doesn't know anything about me, Mommy. He writes that he wants to see me when I'm ready."

"He doesn't want to rush you, sweetheart."

Bobbi crumpled the latest letter into a ball and hurled it savagely into the wicker basket in the corner of her bedroom.

"I'll never be ready to see him," she said with childish finality.

Once Bobbi had gone out into the garden to play with Flic—the German shepherd puppy the Trouville police force had rejected because of her abject refusal to growl, bare her teeth, or bring back anything she was commanded to retrieve—Alexandra went back into her daughter's room and took the crumpled letter from the basket.

She sat down at Bobbi's desk and straightened it out. It was handwritten in Andreas's uneven, sloping style, and Alexandra smiled, knowing how much he hated letter-writing at the best of times, and generally used a typewriter when he was forced to attend to personal correspondence. She glanced quickly through the contents. Bobbi was right, it was stiff, unfamiliar, overpolite, even to the signature:

> Your father,
> Andreas Alessandro

No wonder Bobbi was scared by the letters, scared and scornful. Andreas had a long way to go if he hoped for a reunion with their strong-willed daughter.

She went over to the window and looked down into the back garden, just beginning to be tamed by Victor, their new gardener and handyman. Bobbi and Flic were rolling in the long grass at the rear, treacherously close to the recently planted bed of larkspur. Alexandra raised her hand, about to rap on the glass with her knuckles, but stopped. The fooling around was over, and child and dog were at peace. Bobbi, in dungarees as usual, lay on her back, oblivious to the fact that at least a dozen or more insects of different varieties were probably seeking out a home in her soft, sweet-smelling hair, and Flic, looking ridiculously handsome, lay beside her young mistress, front paws crossed, head erect.

Alexandra remembered Andreas's tales of Rolf, the German shepherd who'd been his boyhood companion and protector in Switzerland. *That's one thing they have in common,* she thought, and made a mental note to write to Andreas herself, suggesting that he might perhaps dig out some old snapshots of himself and Rolf to send to Bobbi.

I'll never be ready to see him, Bobbi had said.

Alexandra slipped the crumpled letter into the bottom drawer of her daughter's desk.

Never is a long time, she thought.

49

On a dark, smoke-scented afternoon in November 1980, Bobbi Alessandro, just home from school, flung herself down on her bed, rolled over onto her stomach, looked for just a moment at the blank sheet of notepaper in front of her, and began to write:

Dear Father,
I've decided I would like to spend Christmas with you, if the invitation still holds. I shall, of course, have to be back in Honfleur for New Year; Mother and I always wish each other *Bonne Année* here at L'Alouette with our close friends.
If I've left it too late, please don't worry. I'll understand.

Roberta

She read it through quickly, folded the paper over and slid it into an envelope, addressing it and dropping it into her briefcase to post next morning on the way to school. Then she sat down at her desk to concentrate on her homework. *Thank God for English verbs!* she thought fervently. At least that was one area she'd never had to waste precious time grinding over.

"Mom?" she began later as they sat down to dinner at the long pine table in the kitchen, where they ate most of their weekday meals. When visitors were expected, they sat in splendor in the thirty-foot-long, twenty-foot-wide dining room that Alexandra had refurbished with matching damask walls and drapes falling in long, graceful lines to the floor, concealing all the windows except the magnificent stained-glass centerpiece, tastefully illuminated by concealed spotlights.

"Yes, Bobbi?" Alexandra plunged the silver ladle into the huge porcelain tureen, and withdrew it again steaming with freshly made *potage de légumes*.

Bobbi laid her napkin neatly in her lap. Was there a gentle way to drop a bombshell? she wondered, but dropped it anyway.

"I've written to Father."

Alexandra's eyebrows arched, but she continued what she was doing. In long, smooth, practiced movements, she poured soup into their two bowls and thanked providence that this was Claudine's night off.

"That's good news," she said mildly. "Any special reason?"

Bobbi chewed her lip. "Yes."

There was a pause.

"Do I get to hear what it is, or am I supposed to guess?"

"I wrote and said I accept his invitation."

"Which invitation might that be?"

"Christmas."

Alexandra replaced the cover on the tureen and picked up her spoon. Gladly she noted that her hand barely quivered. "That's a sudden decision, isn't it?"

"No." Bobbi dipped her own spoon deep into the soup and brought it up again, letting the hot, thick liquid slide off the silver edge and drip back onto the surface.

"Don't play with it," Alexandra said mechanically.

"Sorry." Bobbi put down her spoon. "It wasn't sudden, Mom. A lot of thought went into it."

"I'm sure it did. I think I meant it seems sudden to me." Alexandra's appetite had vanished. She wasn't sure whether she wanted to laugh or cry.

"I'm still not really certain, even though I've written the letter." Bobbi's eyes, scared and huge, appealed to her mother for help.

"Maybe—" Alexandra fumbled for wisdom. "Maybe Christmas is the wrong time for this." *Oh, Lord, that sounds selfish. Who am I kidding? It is selfish.*

"I thought it might be the best time, Mom."

"I mean, perhaps it might be a little—heavy?"

Bobbi nodded slowly. "In a way, that's why I chose it. He's been writing to me for so long, so many years, and he's asked me so many times."

"And you've always refused." Alexandra chose her words with caution. "I'm just trying to work out why you've picked this time to change your mind."

Bobbi stared down into her soup. "I thought maybe he deserved a break."

"And you decided Christmas was appropriate. Good will to all men, even your father." *Isn't this what you've prayed for for such a long time, Alexandra? What you always hoped would happen? So why do you feel like someone kicked away your crutches?* She picked up her

spoon again and began to dig away at the cooling soup, drinking it
down without tasting it.

"Don't be mad, Mom."

"I'm not."

"You sound it."

One of the logs in the fireplace shifted with a thud, sending out
sparks, and Flic, dreaming by the hearth, whined in her sleep.

"Just do me one favor," Alexandra said.

"Sure, Mom."

"Don't be afraid to change your mind again. If, that is," she
added hastily, "your father doesn't change his first."

"I said in my letter I'd understand if he did." Bobbi's tone was
defensive.

"I doubt very much that he will, honey," Alexandra said gently,
"but there's no sense in our pretending he hasn't disappointed you
before."

"Not for years, Mom."

"You haven't seen him for years."

Bobbi's eyes were still afraid. "I don't even really remember
him. The clippings you kept for me, the photos—they're just paper. All I know for sure is that one minute he was the greatest
father in America; I remember this strong, handsome guy who was
some kind of hero and wanted to give me the world. And the
next, he was gone."

Alexandra reached over the table for her daughter's hand and
held it tightly. "Do you think you can forgive him, darling? Are
you beginning to feel you understand what he did?"

Bobbi shook her head and her hair, captured in a thick, lustrous
ponytail, swung and caught the firelight. "I'll never understand,"
she said, "but maybe, just maybe, I'll be able to forgive him some
day." Quickly she squeezed her mother's hand in return, then let
go.

Silence fell again, and the only sounds in the kitchen were the
logs crackling and the electric fan spinning around in the oven.

"One more thing," Alexandra said carefully. "Don't romanti-
cize your father, don't fall into that trap."

"I'm not that dumb, Mom," Bobbi protested.

"No, you're not, far from it. But you are a teenager, and you do
read a lot of romantic fiction—"

"I read classics!"

"Most of them romantic. And you see a lot of movies. And your
father is an attractive, exciting, extremely successful man."

"So?" Bobbi asked aggravatingly.

"So," Alexandra responded calmly, "he's also a human being, and he makes mistakes."

"You always say everyone makes mistakes."

"Sure they do. I'm just pointing out that if you do go at Christmas—and believe me, I hope you do—"

"Mother," Bobbi warned.

Alexandra raised her hands in self-defense. "Okay, okay. Just don't go expecting too much."

Bobbi relaxed. "I won't, Mom, I promise. Don't worry so much."

"Easier said."

Over by the fireplace, Flic's ears pricked, and slowly she picked herself up, stretched, and padded over to the oven.

Alexandra got up too. "The chicken must be done."

Years of being spoiled by the three generous females at L'Alouette had taught the German shepherd to assess with uncanny precision the very second that anything baking, roasting, or broiling was at its best and ready for serving. Claudine adamantly refused to use the timer on the new electric oven Alexandra had ordered from Paris; Flic was a much better judge than any mere American gadget!

"I'm not hungry, Mom."

"Oh, yes, you are. We let the soup get cold—if Claudine comes home and sees we haven't touched anything, there'll be hell to pay." She opened the oven door, donned her asbestos-lined gloves, and took out the roasting tray. Flic's tail thumped approval.

"Mom?"

"Mmm?"

"I think I might need some clothes if I'm going to New York, don't you?"

Alexandra sliced off a piece of chicken breast, blew on it, and dropped it for Flic. "If we start Friday night," she said casually, "we could shop most of Saturday in Paris."

"Oh, Mom!" Bobbi had recently begun to see the merits of having more than just torn denims and sloppy shirts in her wardrobe. "Could we really?"

"Certainly. Provided you eat some dinner."

Bobbi leaned back in her chair, grinning. "Well, hurry up and carve, will you? I'm starved!"

Mother and daughter were at Roissy Airport early on Christmas Eve, fighting back tears and failing dismally. Bobbi, at nearly fifteen, was trapped right in the middle of the no-man's-land that stretched through the teenage years between childhood and womanhood, and to Alexandra she had never appeared more vulnerable and scared.

"You take care, you hear me?" she said fiercely, hugging her.

"You too, Mommy." Bobbi wiped her running nose with the back of her hand. "And don't worry about me, I'll be fine."

"Are you sure about this?" Alexandra bent and peered into her daughter's face, trying to penetrate the quivering mask of control. "I mean, really sure? And don't fly off the handle, I'm not suggesting you don't go—I'm just reminding you that arrangements can be changed."

Bobbi became suddenly calm. For just a moment, their roles seemed to shift. "I'm sure, Mom. Even if it doesn't work out, even if we really are strangers. I don't want to go another day without giving him a chance."

Alexandra smiled. "Send me a postcard."

"I'll be home before it gets here."

"I won't throw you out."

Bobbi touched the protective padding on the painting her mother had given her as a peace token for Andreas. "Is he expecting this?"

"No, of course not."

"Does *he* understand it?"

"Its content, perhaps; its essence, I doubt."

"Then why are you sending it to him?"

Alexandra's eyes softened. "Because I want him to have it."

Bobbi sighed heavily. "Mothers! Who can understand them?" She picked up the soft red suede tote bag she'd chosen in Paris, which toned perfectly with the buttons and braid on her new gray winter coat. "Do I look okay?"

"You look beautiful." *I wonder what Andreas is expecting—a New York teenager? I send him photographs, but will he be ready for this Franco-American stylist?* She gave Bobbi a gentle nudge. "You'd better hurry, darling."

Bobbi's upturned face was suddenly wistful. "Oh, Mom, wouldn't it be great if—"

"*If* has no roots, sweetheart. It's comforting in its place, but it's a waste of time, believe me."

"Okay, boss." Bobbi grinned. "I get the picture." She heaved the bag up on her shoulder and searched for her passport and ticket. "I'll spare a thought for you this evening, tucking into oysters and turkey without me. Don't forget to save some for Flic."

"Has she ever gone without?" Alexandra hugged her again and let her go quickly. "God bless you, Bobbi. And make sure you get back this side of New Year—one holiday without you is quite enough for me."

Tears welled up again in Bobbi's eyes. "Just try keeping me away."

She was back two days earlier than planned, and this time when Alexandra met her at Roissy, she was shocked at the contrast. Bobbi's face was pinched and strained, and she seemed actually to have lost weight in the four days she'd been away. When Alexandra tried to extract the reason for her obvious distress, Bobbi clammed up completely.

"I want to go home," was all she would say.

But later, when her bedroom door was closed for the night, with only Flic for company, Alexandra heard the weeping begin.

She went downstairs to her study, shut the door, and called Andreas.

"What the hell happened?" she demanded.

"You should know."

"What does that mean?"

"You're the one who made her go back."

"What are you talking about, Andreas?"

"You know damned well. When I came yesterday after a business appointment I couldn't break, Bobbi told me how upset and lonely you'd sounded on the phone."

"I don't know what you're talking about," she repeated. "I never—" And then she stopped as light dawned. It was clear he was speaking the truth, in which case Bobbi had evidently felt she needed an excuse to escape. Maybe it was better Andreas should blame her, rather than find out the truth.

"Do you deny calling her?" Andreas accused.

"No," she said. "I'm sorry." She paused. "How was it? Seeing her after so long." *Tell the truth,* she pleaded silently. *Say it was heaven and hell all mixed up—that four days wasn't long enough to cement over all those cracks. That way maybe I can see to it you get another chance; that way maybe we can talk about our child together, as we should.*

"It would have been fine," he said stiffly, "if we'd had the time you promised."

She sighed softly. "I'm sorry," she said again, and put down the phone.

Next morning after breakfast they went for a walk in the woods that backed onto the garden. Bobbi was back in shabby jeans and army surplus jacket, and Flic darted about her skittishly, never running far, overjoyed at having her mistress back but wary that she might disappear again at any moment. Bobbi carried an armful of sticks. Flic had never adopted the accepted habit of retrieving a stick thrown for her—she loved to run for it, adored clamping it between her jaws and then teasing Bobbi by refusing to drop it at her feet on command; but after a while she invariably became distracted by something else—a bird, a squirrel, or just a falling leaf—and then the stick would fall by the wayside and be lost.

"It's no good," Alexandra said as Bobbi hurled the fourth stick of the morning and Flic hurtled off to find it. "Flic's a sophisticate. She only pretends to like those games because you do. She's much happier directing Claudine in the kitchen."

"I missed her," Bobbi said, striding long-legged beside her mother, kicking leaves and earth with her boots.

Alexandra shot her a sideways glance. "Was that why you told your father I wanted you home early?"

Bobbi kept her chin tucked down, staring at the ground. "No."

"Why then?" She stopped and called after Bobbi's retreating back. "Would you mind telling me what went on?"

Bobbi stopped too, but said nothing.

"I don't exactly mind carrying the can," Alexandra said reasonably, "but I'd be happier if I knew the reason for it."

Bobbi turned to face her. Flic, sensing tension, dropped her stick and came to sit beside her, panting. "It didn't work out."

"I gathered that much. In what way?"

Bobbi made a face. "Every way, I guess."

"You didn't give it long, did you. I told you not to expect too much."

"I know. And I tried hard not to," she said earnestly. "But he did."

"I see."

"Do you really, Mom?"

"I begin to."

Bobbi squatted and put an arm around the dog, hugging her close. "I could tell right away that six days wasn't going to be enough for him."

"Did you expect them to be enough?"

"No, of course not. I hoped they wouldn't be. But I thought he'd take things slowly, let them build naturally, and then maybe ask me back again."

"But that's not the way it was."

Bobbi's face darkened. "Right from the first evening it was all or nothing. I was really tired after the flight and everything—and I was excited about seeing him and being back in New York, but I just wanted to stay home with him and get an early night so I'd be in good shape next day."

"But he had other plans?"

"He had a whole party set up at the restaurant—all his friends, decorations, the works."

"Poor baby," Alexandra sympathized. She sat down on a log. "Didn't you tell him you were tired?"

"Sure I did, but he was counting minutes. I honestly don't think he minded because of the arrangements, but if I'd gone to bed early that evening we would have lost a couple of hours of our time together."

"Couldn't you understand how he felt?"

"Of course I could, and a part of me was happy he felt that strongly. But another part just got grouchy and mean, thinking he should have felt that way years ago—and the rest of me thought it was just too much of a strain to cope with."

"So you went to dinner?"

Bobbi nodded. "And if I hadn't felt so beat it would probably have been great. I remembered some of the people there—Dan Stone and Uncle Rudy, and Dan's partner Fanny Harper, and Jerry the doorman's still there. It was nice seeing them again, and they all seemed real happy I was there, but . . ."

"And after that night?"

"Plans the whole time. Even when we had time alone together I felt he'd planned that too. 'Three hours for understanding.'" Her expression was bitter. "As if a few hours could make up for almost ten years."

"What I don't quite understand," Alexandra said slowly, "is why you sliced two whole days off the time. Wasn't that a little cruel, knowing how much every moment meant to him?"

Flic licked Bobbi's face and lay down. Bobbi shook her head. "I didn't mean to be cruel. I just didn't know what else to do. He wanted me to stay on over the New Year."

"But he knew you were due back here."

Bobbi nodded miserably. "I know. I kept trying to explain, but he said he wanted to arrange something extra special, and that you'd had me on New Year's Eve for the last ten years, so now it was his turn."

"So you tried to get out, without hurting him."

"I'm sorry he blames you, Mom. I couldn't think of any other way out. I was wrong."

"No, you were absolutely right. Anyway, he'll get over that." She reached out and scratched the top of Flic's head. "What was probably a mistake was choosing Christmas, and restricting your stay to six days. Next time I think we should—"

"There won't be a next time," Bobbi said sharply.

Alexandra looked at her. "Sure there will, Bobbi. Give yourself some time to work this out and—"

"I mean it, Mom." She straightened up, and Flic got up too, instantly alert. "He chose this route, and I guess we've all been on it too long now to change again."

"It's always possible to change course if you love someone enough," Alexandra said gently.

"Maybe it is." Bobbi's face was set. "But trying hurts too much."

In New York, in the library of Andreas's town house on Sutton Place, Daniel was trying to get his friend to see sense.

"It wasn't Ali's fault, Andreas, it was your own. You didn't take into account that Bobbi's her own person."

"Of course I did."

"No you didn't. You assumed you were going to have a nice pliable houseguest, someone who'd fall in with all your plans, who'd sigh with joy because you gave her a Van Cleef and Arpels heart on a chain, who'd even love you to order. You forgot you had to get to know her again first."

"That's shit."

"No, it isn't. Where was your subtlety, Andreas? You must have known she'd keep her soul under wraps, at least to begin with. She showed a lot of spunk coming over here all alone after so many years. You should have taken it slowly, shown some sensitivity."

Andreas scowled at him. "She left early because her mother decided to tug on her heartstrings, not because of something I did."

"You don't believe that any more than I do. In the first place, it isn't Ali's style to act that way. She isn't that selfish."

"What do you know about Ali?" Andreas stormed. "You hardly knew her when we were married, and you haven't seen her in years."

Daniel bit back his retort. "You want to hear what I think?" he went on steadily. "I think you blew it. And I think you know it."

For another moment Andreas held his eyes angrily, and then he seemed to sag defeatedly. "I planned it all so carefully," he said wearily.

"That was half the trouble, don't you see?" Daniel's expression was gentle. "You're going to be fifty in a few years, Andreas, and you still don't understand one basic rule of life."

"Which is?"

"You can't plan love."

The flames in the fireplace crackled. Daniel glanced up at the unfamiliar painting that hung over the mantelpiece.

"Did Bobbi bring that with her?" It was a perfect, snug fit in the oak paneling.

Andreas nodded.

"It's wonderfully interesting." Daniel peered at the date under the signature. "But not recent—1966."

Andreas smiled vaguely. "It was always a favorite of hers. She said it was special when she painted it, but she wouldn't hang it, kept it wrapped up. Bobbi told me they hung it in the den at the apartment after I left."

"And now she's sent it to you." Daniel's eyes were unreadable. "Does it have a title?"

"It's called 'Life Drawing.' "

Side by side the two men stood, warmed by the leaping flames, and stared up at the painting.

50

In the spring of 1981, Daniel bought a house in East-hampton on Long Island. In terms of size, it was fairly standard for the district, having nine bedrooms, four bathrooms upstairs plus another two downstairs, four reception rooms, two studies, a vast kitchen area and a separate guest-house with all amenities. In addition there was a large paved terrace, part-covered, a round, heated pool, a tennis court and a summerhouse complete with three barbecues, six changing cubicles and two showers. The gardens, however, were the high spot. Divided into three sections, there was a rose garden, of rampaging, divine colors and scents; a gently sloping landscaped English garden leading to the beach; and finally, almost totally concealed by weeping willows, there was an exquisite water-lily garden, in the style of the artist Monet at his home in Giverny, where clusters of blossoms and lily pads floated on a dark, silent pool.

The roof of the main house was a delicious rosy pink, and its Belgian former owners had called the house "Le Chapeau Rose," or "the pink hat."

It was Daniel's haven, and it was also the inspiration for his newest and happiest venture with Fanny and Andreas as partners; a school of *grande cuisine*. One quarter of the building was cut off from the private areas and transformed into the school, and Daniel taught two-month-long courses each year, employing first-rate tutors for the rest and persuading great chefs and restaurateurs from all over the country and Europe to lecture at monthly seminars. Le Chapeau Rose brought Daniel peace and greater pleasure than any business venture he'd ever embarked on. The school brought him old and new friends; Madame Edouard, now nearly eighty, came from France to visit, and stayed longer than planned as the house and gardens spun their magic about her. And there were, of course, the students—young and old, capricious and intense—to prevent Daniel from settling too comfortably into sleek, euphoric clover. Cat was transported, fretfully, from Manhattan, but quickly anchored himself arthritically but serenely to his new heaven on earth. Before the first six months were past, school courses were sold out for two years in advance, Chapeau Rose diplomas had become respected certificates of achievement, and a revival of Daniel's NBC series *The Gourmets,* which had lapsed seven years earlier, began filming on location at the house.

In February 1982, Fanny had a heart attack on her way to the office, and found herself one hour later in intensive care at Mount Sinai Hospital. More than alarmed, she was irritated. When Daniel arrived, ashen-faced, she snapped at him. "Don't you start hovering over me like the rest of them! I feel like a newborn infant—every few minutes someone comes and ogles at me, makes reassuring noises and goes away again."

Daniel smiled. "Thank God, you still sound like Fanny Harper."

"Who would you have me sound like?" she said, weakly acidic. She indicated the monitoring equipment near her bed. "They may have me trussed up like a turkey, but I still have my mind, thank the Lord."

Daniel took her hand. "Will you please do something for me?"

"Depends what it is."

"Do whatever they tell you. I want you back."

"You'll have me back." She closed her eyes.

"Are you in pain?" Daniel asked anxiously.

"Not anymore. It felt like a bus was riding on my chest at first, but they give me so much dope, I keep falling asleep."

"Good," he said softly, and bent to kiss her. "You get some rest. I'll see you later."

"Don't keep coming by, Dan," she murmured. "I plan on being back at the office in no time."

"Sure you do."

Her eyes snapped open. "And don't you dare patronize me," she said clearly. "I'm not your ancient maiden aunt."

She was in the hospital for two weeks, and then home in her Park Avenue apartment for another four. Daniel wanted her to come to Le Chapeau Rose to convalesce, but she refused. Neither of them had mentioned Natalie for years—shortly after Barbara's death Fanny had moved out of the Pierre, trying to leave memories behind; even Joe Bernardi had died of cancer eight months back. The past was dead and gone, but the guilt would never leave Fanny, and would always stop her accepting kindness from Daniel, no matter how earnestly he tried to give it.

She came back to Harper and Stone in mid-May, a full month earlier than the doctors recommended. She was only sixty-nine years old, she said, glaring at Daniel when he tried arguing with her, and she had no intention of being treated like an old woman a second longer.

"If you're trying to kill me," she said defiantly, "you're going the right way about it."

He gave in. "I'm just begging you to be sensible. At least take it slowly."

He should have known better. Fanny Harper had never been capable of moderation. One week after returning to work she suffered a second, massive attack in the office. Daniel sat beside her in the ambulance and held her hand on the way to Mount Sinai, but she never regained consciousness and was pronounced dead on arrival.

At the funeral, as they lowered her coffin into the earth, Daniel turned his head away from the image of Fanny going down into the ground and raised his eyes to the sky. Halfway there, his gaze came to a halt.

About twenty yards from the mourners, two men in chauffeur's livery got out of the front of a black limousine with darkened windows. One of them opened the trunk and took out a folded wheelchair, which he proceeded to unfold and wheel to the side of the car, while the second man opened a rear door, reached inside, bending almost double, and lifted out a woman in his arms. Slowly and carefully he lowered her into the chair, laid her hands neatly in her lap, and stood well back.

Daniel stared.

She was like a spider, frail and thin and dressed entirely in black. A lace veil covered most of her face, long suede gloves were drawn up over her hands and wrists, and her legs, deprived of elegance and clad in thick black stockings, were planted in flat shoes on the steel foot rest. She was immobile from the neck down.

He knew her immediately.

Nudged gently by Andreas, standing beside him, Daniel turned back to the open grave, stooped, and picked up a handful of damp, sweet-smelling earth. Slowly he straightened up and opened his fist, stretching his fingers wide, and the earth fell with a dull rattle onto the gleaming lid of Fanny's coffin. And then he turned again, and walked, calmly and deliberately, toward Natalie Bresson Schindler, stopping just a few feet from her chair.

Not many people would have recognized her. The small portion of flesh that was visible was wasted and grayish. She sat, rigid and upright, propped like a wax doll against the padded chairback.

Daniel felt Andreas's hand on his shoulder, and shook it off. "I'm all right," he said.

He watched the living corpse, and something approaching pity rose in him. He could see her eyes through the veil, no longer vixen-like, no longer filled with malice, drooping badly at the corners. She never even gave him a glance. She stared past him, past Andreas, to Fanny's grave, and two slow, large tears slid down her sallow cheeks and fell onto her paralyzed hands.

Part Six

51

It was a pity, Bobbi thought, staring into the mirror on the back of her bedroom door, that she had no special talent. Or at least not the kind of talent that seemed to be expected of her by her teachers and her mother. Well, perhaps that wasn't quite fair; her mother had never pushed her in any direction she was unwilling to go.

Madame Maurier, the art teacher at her school in Trouville, had realized the lack in her from the first, and her disappointment had been intense. For a teacher in a provincial school to be granted the development of the child of a famous and gifted artist was a thrill that had occupied Madame Maurier from the second she learned that the Alessandros had come to live in the neighborhood. Each morning, as she traveled by bus from her home in Pont-Audemer to Trouville, Madame Maurier had fantasized about unraveling the latent talents of young Roberta when she joined them for her first term. But oh, the soreness of the disillusionment that had awaited her! Roberta Alessandro had seemed a graceful enough, feminine child, with the kind of capable, long-fingered hands suited to an artistic life. But she brought those hands to school most days covered in scrapes and scratches from climbing trees and pummeling boys in the playground. Presented with a stick of charcoal, the girl had invariably clutched at it so fiercely that it snapped and smudged the blank sheet of paper before her, as well as her hands and face.

Bobbi unarguably had a good brain, so when Madame Maurier had given up hope, the other *institutrices* had taken up the battle to find the natural endowment that a child of such a mother must surely have been born with. After all, Mademoiselle Delys, the headmistress, reasoned, it was well known that Ali Alessandro had in her time been far more than a creative artist—she'd also been a hugely successful businesswoman. None of the teachers ever considered Bobbi's father. A racing driver, with his absurd mania for speed and danger, could have little to offer a daughter.

By 1982, Mademoiselle Delys and her colleagues had long

since given up the quest. Bobbi was an adequate all-rounder; she would never disgrace the school, nor would she ever glorify its name. At least, they sighed in the staff room over their morning *café au lait,* she no longer scrambled up and down trees like an animal, and at sixteen she had finally come to realize that boys were not for fighting with.

Bobbi studied herself again in the mirror. The boys of the region did not, it was true, seem in the slightest perturbed by her lack of intellectualism or creative genius. They recognized good horse sense and speed of thought, and—Bobbi smiled, pulling her thick glossy hair into yet another style, and wondering if perhaps, in spite of her clear and naturally glowing complexion, she ought to start using foundation cream on her cheeks—they did appear to find her attractive. Especially—she blushed just thinking about him, and watched her gray eyes sparkling into vivid green—Lucien Joffrey, whose father owned a stud farm near Deauville, and who had for the last seven weeks been paying her considerable attention.

Bobbi noticed the time and leapt into frenzied action. Lucien was calling for her in less than an hour, and she hadn't even had a bath yet. She dashed into the bathroom, turned the taps on full, and poured a generous capful of scented oil into the water. Steamy perfume filled the room, and for a moment Bobbi leaned against the marble wall, caught off balance by a sudden attack of something that must be—had to be—desire. Until recently—until Lucien, Bobbi realized—she'd been sexually dormant for a girl of her age. But the handsome eighteen-year-old with his aristocratic bearing and seductive mouth had changed all that forever. When Lucien had kissed her for the first time, Bobbi had drawn away, startled and slightly alarmed, but he had placed one hand behind her head and tugged her gently but firmly back again, and then it was as if he had located a hidden switch deep inside her and flicked it skillfully on, igniting a flame that burned brightly every time she even thought about him.

A bubbling sound from the bath reminded her it was about to overflow, and quickly she turned off the taps, took off the man's cotton shirt she used instead of a peignoir, pinned up her hair, and stepped into the warm water, rubbing a bar of Chanel soap against the natural sponge and then scrubbing her arms, legs, and breasts, and more cautiously at her neck, careful not to wet her hair, which she'd shampooed only that morning. When she soaped her pubic hair and between her legs, there again was that electric charge of desire. Swiftly she sank into the water, using all her willpower to resist the urge to linger and explore. She must not be late—she deplored people who deliberately kept others waiting, and besides, Lucien had once told her that he liked the fact she didn't play that kind of foolish game.

Drying herself with a big turkish towel, she mourned the fact that she couldn't wear something soft and feminine this evening, but Lucien was taking her to the go-Kart track near Le Havre, and it would be plain ridiculous to wear anything other than jeans. There was nothing to stop her from wearing something striking with them, though, and quickly her mind sorted through her wardrobe—the emerald silk blouse her mother had bought her in Deauville? No, it might match her eyes, but it would look awful with blue denim. She settled on scarlet silk and matching belt, and she could wear her new sneakers—they had a bright scarlet flash along the sides.

She arrived back home late that night in a state of high excitement. There was oil on her jeans, the scarlet silk blouse was ripped all down the right sleeve, and her hair was in disarray, but her cheeks were flushed and her eyes sparkled brilliantly.

Alexandra was sitting in her bedroom, listening for the sound of the front door before even considering sleep. Bobbi was at the dangerous age in so many ways, she realized, and though she tried to give her her head as much as she could, it was impossible not to worry.

There was a soft rap at the door.

"Come in."

She saw the tousled hair first, as her daughter's head poked around the door, and smiled inwardly.

"Mom, you're still awake."

"As you see. Come in."

The rest of Bobbi appeared hesitantly, and Alexandra sprang out of the armchair in alarm. "What happened? Did you have an accident?"

"No, Mom, no accident." Bobbi's smile was so happy, so wide, that Alexandra knew suddenly that only one thing could have put it there. Quickly she searched her mind for the correct attitude; for the last year she'd prepared herself for this moment, but now she felt utterly confused and unready. Clearly, Lucien had not disappointed or upset Bobbi, that was something to be grateful for —and Bobbi had come straight to confide in her, that was another thing.

"So what happened?" she inquired lamely, still wondering how a courtship conducted by gentlemanly Lucien Joffrey could possibly have culminated in that torn blouse and all that dirt. Bobbi looked as if she'd been rolling around in mud.

Bobbi sighed contentedly and sank into the second armchair on the other side of the fireplace. There were few rooms in L'Alouette without open fireplaces, and the one in Alexandra's bedroom formed the focal point for everything else in the room. The door opened a little farther, and Flic trotted in, tail wagging, and settled down beside her.

"Mother," she said, and sighed again. "It was wonderful."

"What was?" Alexandra wasn't going to let her off the hook that easily. Open, innocent sensuality was one thing, and she was glad Bobbi wasn't going to hide away guiltily from her, but still . . .

"Lucien."

"I gathered that," she answered dryly.

Bobbi smiled again, dreamily. "We went to Le Havre, to the go-Kart track."

"Really?" Not a place she'd have chosen for a seduction.

"Lucien belongs to a club there."

"I see," Alexandra offered, and waited for more.

"Did you ever drive a go-Kart, Mom?"

"Can't say I did."

"It's the most terrific thing I've ever done."

Alexandra frowned. "You drove? I thought Lucien was the member."

"He showed me how." Bobbi shrugged. "He said I took to it really quickly—not many girls enjoy the speed, he said."

"Did he indeed?" She paused. "And then?"

"Then what?"

"Then what did you do?"

"Nothing. We spent the whole evening there, and then we came home."

Alexandra was utterly perplexed. "So would you mind telling me why you look as if you've been horseback-riding in a hurricane?"

"It's just machine oil, Mom."

"Not the sleeve."

Bobbi fingered her blouse ruefully. "No, I'm sorry about that. It happened when I was getting out of the kart, it just got caught."

"It sounds dangerous."

"No, Mom, not at all. At least, not the kind of speeds I was driving."

Alexandra sat forward, her eyes narrowing. "If I'm not mistaken, go-Karts are those little machines with no protective bodywork, where the driver sits very close to the ground."

Bobbi grinned. "You got it."

"Then I'm not keen on your going again."

Her daughter's face fell. "Mom, it's only the professionals and the really experienced club members who drive them fast. People like me just move them around, like the electric cars at the fair."

"How fast *did* you drive? Do you know?"

Bobbi shook her head. "Not faster than, say, twenty miles an hour."

Alexandra's lips were set. "People get killed on the roads at speeds like that, it's a proven fact."

"Mom, people get killed crossing the road."

"Don't dodge the issue, Bobbi."

"I'm not!" she protested. "You're not being fair. I had the best time of my life tonight."

"And I hope you will again, and with Lucien. But not at the go-Kart track. Is that clear?"

"No, it isn't."

"Bobbi, don't make me play the heavy mother, please. I don't often make rules, do I?"

"I don't see why you have to start with this," Bobbi said sullenly.

"Because it's dangerous, and it scares me."

Bobbi's eyes glittered. "I know why you're making a fuss. It's because of my father, isn't it?"

Alexandra's eyes widened. "What?"

"It's because it reminds you of his racing." Bobbi stood up, challenging her.

"It's because you are only sixteen years old, and because it's a dangerous sport!"

"Are you sure?"

"Of course I'm sure," she shot back, reeling at the unfairness of her daughter's accusation. "Anyway, where does your father suddenly figure in this? You haven't mentioned him in months, and now because it suits your point of view—"

"He doesn't figure in anything!" Bobbi's eyes began to fill with aggrieved tears. "Though it might just have occurred to both of us that for the first time in my life, I might have actually found something we have in common!"

Alexandra got up and tried to put her arms around her, but

Bobbi drew away angrily. "Darling, please, you're obviously tired. Calm down."

"I'm perfectly calm, thank you, and I'm going to bed." Bobbi stalked toward the door, and Flic went with her, ears folded back, uncomfortable with their raised voices.

"That's a good idea," Alexandra said stiffly. "And in the morning we can discuss this further."

"There's nothing to discuss." The door slammed shut behind her.

Slowly, Alexandra returned to the armchair and sank down in it. Her mind was in turmoil. This was a development that had never entered her head. She looked down at her hands and saw they were trembling. She closed her eyes, and a mental image of Bobbi behind the wheel of one of those fragile little karts passed before them. She shuddered. Damn Lucien! Damn his rich, sporting parents who encouraged such an idiotic pastime!

She stood again wearily and untied the belt of her peignoir. There was nothing to be done tonight except to go to bed and get some sleep. By morning, she hoped, things might seem brighter. Their quarrels never lasted long, and neither of them ever bore grudges. Bobbi was a sensible girl; she would soon realize it was only concern on her part.

Alexandra yawned, and turned off the overhead light.

It'll pass, she thought philosophically. *I hope.*

It did not pass. Three weeks later an envelope arrived in their mailbox, addressed to Bobbi, with the embossed stamp of the Go-Kart Racing Club on the back. Alexandra bit back anxiety, aware that motherly intervention at this stage would just turn a light fancy into a full-blown passion. She persuaded herself it was nothing but a teenage fad. Most of Bobbi's friends went go-Kart driving; there was nothing about it any more dangerous than riding pillion on that damned motorcycle of Lucien's. Lord knew she was scared half to death each time her daughter donned her vivid blue crash helmet and waved good-bye at the gate.

"Honestly, Mom," Bobbi said, laughing, one Sunday morning after Alexandra had suggested Lucien might take his perfectly fine BMW car for a change, instead of the bike. "This is 1982! Kids aren't wrapped up for safekeeping anymore. You surely don't want me to spend all my time at home in my room, do you?"

"I'm not suggesting you stay home, merely that your boyfriend sticks to riding his motorcycle when you're not with him."

"But Lucien's a terrific rider—I'm safer with him on the bike than with some boys in cars."

"Then you'll be safer still in *his* car, won't you."

Bobbi pulled a face. "Why do you have to make such a fuss about everything, Mom?"

Alexandra felt exasperated. "You're being childish, Bobbi. Haven't I been perfectly reasonable about the club? I let you join, didn't I?"

"True," Bobbi conceded. "And you don't mind it that much, do you?"

"So long as you stick to the rules."

"I will." Bobbi's face changed, her expression half nervous, half flippant. *This is it,* she decided. *If I don't tell her now, I never will.* She looked down at her feet. "I'm glad you're happier about the club, Mom," she began.

Alerted by the change in her tone, Alexandra took a hard look at her daughter. "Why's that?"

Bobbi couldn't meet her eyes. "Because there's another branch of the club I've been thinking about joining."

"What kind of branch?"

Bobbi's chin came up defiantly. "Motocross."

For the first time since her daughter's birth, Alexandra was filled with such intense anger against her that she was unable to speak.

"Mom?" Bobbi ventured nervously.

She found her voice. "I trust this is a joke."

"No joke."

Alexandra stared incredulously at her. "Is this another of Lucien's ideas?"

"Lucien does belong to the club team, yes," Bobbi said with a calm that astonished even her, "but it's not his idea that I should take it up."

"It's your own idea?"

"Absolutely."

Alexandra took a breath. "The answer is no."

Bobbi's cheeks flushed. "I'm pretty keen, Mom."

"You're a schoolgirl, Bobbi. In case you've forgotten, you have work to do. Between Lucien and the club, your time has been overstretched as it is."

"That's not the reason you're saying no," Bobbi said, becoming excited. "And I don't need to stay at school, come to that."

"You most certainly do."

"I can leave at sixteen, and I *am* sixteen."

"Sometimes you act more like thirteen!"

"Thank you!" Bobbi's eyes flashed with insult.

"You're welcome."

"I don't have to stay at school, you know," she repeated.

"You're staying until baccalaureat." It was a statement.

"What the hell for? I'm not going to university."

"Don't swear."

"Oh, *merde!*"

"Bobbi!"

"When we first came to France and I swore, you thought it was funny."

"Because you were a child and didn't know what you were saying." Alexandra tried to take the fight back under control before things went too far. "Darling, do you think I like having to be so heavy-handed? Do you think it's easy being mother and father?"

"You don't need to bother as far as I'm concerned," Bobbi snapped back. "In case you've forgotten, I do have a father—a man who writes to me every single month, and who might just be very happy to think his daughter has inherited his love of speed!"

Alexandra was silenced. *Oh, shit!* she thought. *Now we really have problems.*

Before Bobbi's next date with Lucien, she took from the back of her dresser drawer the Van Cleef and Arpels heart on a chain that Andreas had given her on her visit to New York, and hung it around her neck.

Alexandra said nothing. She had no choice, she realized, but to watch and wait.

It didn't take long. Come July, with no school, Bobbi had extra time on her hands. Go-Kart driving was no longer enough for her, she insisted; she wanted more. Alexandra read the sheet of rules issued by the Fédération Internationale Motocycliste, laid down a dozen more extra ground rules of her own, and gave way.

Bobbi was ecstatic. "Oh, thank you, Mom!" she exulted, flinging her arms around Alexandra and hugging her. "I swear I'll be so careful—you come and watch if you don't believe me—and this really is it. I won't ask for anything else!"

Alexandra's heart sank like a stone. *I don't have to be a gambler to lay odds that means she will.* Her mouth was dry with panic. *How long?*

"You have to strike while the iron's hot," Lucien said, flashing Bobbi a glance, then returning his attention to the road.

"But it isn't."

He smiled. *"Mais c'est chaud, n'est-ce pas?* In French we use the same word for hot and warm."

"I'm not sure it's even tepid," Bobbi answered wryly.

Lucien pulled over to the side of the road and stopped the car. He fixed her with a hard stare. "Do you want to drive or not?"

"Now? Not really."

"Not now, *idiote.* Do you want to race cars?"

Bobbi sighed. "You know I do, Lucien. But it's not that simple."

"Sure it is. If you want to be just a secretary or a housewife—"

"There are other options, you know."

Lucien shrugged. *"Oui, naturellement.* If you stay at the lycée until *baccalauréat,* then go to university and study some more. Very sensible. I'm all for it."

"But I'm not."

He shrugged again. *"Enfin."*

"I guess I do have to talk to Mom," Bobbi said reluctantly. "I just hate upsetting her. She's been through it all before with my father."

"It isn't your fault, *chérie,* that your papa's blood runs in your veins." He slid closer, as far as the gear shift allowed. In the last few weeks they'd dispensed with the motorcycle—the car offered comforts and conveniences that a bike, even one made for two, never could. *"Ma petite,"* he murmured, and put his right arm around her shoulders. She'd grown even softer and more beautiful during the summer, he realized with pleasure. This was a wonderful time to know a girl, when she was grown but still growing, when her body's tempting curves were accentuated subtly with each passing month. He found her mouth and kissed her, gently first, then more fiercely.

"Lucien," Bobbi tried to say, wriggling away.

He couldn't stand to leave her lips, their softness, their moistness. His free hand found the top button of her blouse and unfastened it, and then the second, and the third, and then he felt her breasts, so young, so perfect—thank God, he thought fervently, Bobbi never wore a brassiere . . .

"Lucien!" Bobbi protested, more urgently.

"Quoi?" Surprised, he stopped. "What's wrong, aren't you enjoying it?"

In spite of herself, Bobbi burst out laughing.

Lucien frowned. "What's funny, might I ask? I'm not in the mood for teasing."

Bobbi gasped with mirth. "I'm not. It's just your face—and—"

"And what?" he said crossly.

Eyes round, she gazed past him. "And the gendarme who's been standing beside the car for the last four minutes."

"*Merde!*" Lucien shot away from her. "Fasten your blouse, Bobbi!"

"Why?" she asked innocently. "I thought this was the land of romance."

His lips were tight. "It is, dammit. But this is a no-parking zone." He wound down his window and peered out at the policeman. "*Bonsoir, monsieur,*" he began. "Is there a problem?"

Later, as they parted at the front door, they could hear Flic on the inside, whining impatiently.

"Come in," Bobbi said. "My mother's still awake—she'll be glad to see you."

He shook his head. "Not tonight."

"Why not? It's still early."

He looked down at her fondly. "Because, mademoiselle, you're going to talk to her, aren't you?"

"Am I?"

He tilted her chin and looked encouragingly into her eyes. "You are." He kissed her forehead. "And just remember, blame it on the genes. It's not your fault she married a racing driver."

Bobbi sighed. "I guess you're right." She made up her mind. "You are right."

"That's my girl."

Bobbi tossed her hair. "My mother prides herself on her logic." She grinned. "Even she can't possibly argue with that, can she. After all, I am what they made me."

Three days later, gripped by foreboding, Alexandra tried calling Andreas in New York, leaving messages at his home, at Alessandro's, and at all the lobster cafés. Finally, twelve hours later, he called her back.

"What's wrong? Is it Bobbi?"

"Yes," she said, relieved to hear his voice. "But not the way you think, don't worry."

After she'd finished telling him, there was silence.

"You have to help me," she said.

"How can I?"

"Talk her out of it."

"How?" he repeated. "I haven't seen or spoken to her in almost two years."

She gripped the receiver more tightly. "Andreas, for God's sake, we have to stop her from making a terrible mistake. She's our daughter! The whole idea's insane, ludicrous."

"Why is it ludicrous? Because she's a girl? It's 1982, Ali. If a woman wants to race cars, no one thinks she's crazy anymore."

"I'll tell you why," Alexandra burst out. "Because she thinks that racing's in her blood, that's why!"

There was another brief silence. Andreas said, softly, "That's what I used to tell my mother."

"Maybe so," she said relentlessly, "but at least in your case it was true." She grew gentler. "I'm sorry, Andreas, you know I'd never bring this up unless I had to—but Bobbi's talking herself into something for all the wrong reasons. I think she's looking for a way to identify with you at last."

"And that's wrong?"

"No, of course not. I'd be so happy if you two could work out a way to be father and daughter again. But this isn't the way. It's wrong, and it's dangerous."

"What makes you think she'd listen to me, Ali? You're so close, such good friends—surely it would be better coming from you?"

"I've tried, believe me," she said wearily. "It's the standard teenage scenario, isn't it—mother suddenly becomes the enemy because she doesn't agree with daughter. Only usually the fights are about boyfriends or alcohol or maybe drugs. I think I could handle that. But this is beyond me. Frankly, I'm lost."

"So what do you want from me? You want me to tell her she'd make a lousy driver?"

"No!" Alexandra cried. "I don't want it to get that far! I don't want her on a racetrack, ever!"

"Why not?" Andreas countered. "In case she's good?"

"That has nothing to do with it! For pity's sake, don't you see? If Bobbi starts driving, her perceptions of her own potential will be false from the start. She'll push herself farther than another girl would, simply because her father was a champion and she'll think she must have that same talent somewhere inside herself." She paused. "I don't want to have to tell Bobbi the truth, Andreas. Not ever."

The line crackled, reminding her of the vast ocean between them, and her last words echoed in her ear.

"All right," Andreas said suddenly, surprising her. "If I invite her back to New York, do you think she'll come?"

"I can't be sure, but I think she may."

"Would you rather I come to France?"

"No," she said slowly. "Better to get her away from Lucien for a while."

"Who's Lucien? The boyfriend?"

"Yes. He's a perfectly charming young man, but his influence gets a little too vigorous at times."

Andreas hesitated. "You're sure, Ali? You'd have no objections to her spending time here?"

"It's the only way as I see it," she answered simply. "And it might resolve two problems in one fell swoop. You could become friends again."

"It could also turn her against me forever," he said quietly.

"Not if you're careful. I believe Bobbi would rejoice to know you love her enough to be interested."

Again the line hissed and crackled.

"I'll write to her," he said.

"Can't you call? The mail's so slow."

"Ali, Bobbi's not stupid," he said with authority. "If I call her out of the blue, she's bound to be suspicious that you've put me up to it. No, I'll write today—that way she'll have the letter in just a few days."

Her relief was so great, she wanted to cry. "Thank you, Andreas," she said fervently, "from the bottom of my heart. I truly am sorry to lay this on you, but I don't know where else to turn."

"I'm glad you remembered I'm still her father."

"I've never forgotten that, not for an instant." Anxiety gnawed at her again. "You will write today, won't you? Don't put it off."

"Just for once, Ali," he said, not without irony, "I'm afraid you're going to have to trust me."

Mademoiselle Delys, taken into Alexandra's confidence, agreed with the decision to send Bobbi to her father for a time. If Monsieur Alessandro could be prevailed upon to see that the young lady studied regularly from books the school could provide, her missing half a term might not be too disastrous.

"Less so, anyway," she smiled, "than embarking upon such a dangerous and unsuitable career."

"I doubt that she'll be away that long," Alexandra assured her. "She may be gone only two or three weeks."

"All the better." Mademoiselle Delys patted Alexandra's hand gently. "It will be hard for you, I know, to be without her."

"It would be easier," Alexandra agreed, "if I could be sure I was doing the right thing."

The headmistress shrugged expressively. "We can never be sure, madame. Much depends on the child herself. Roberta is a little complex—loving and thoughtful in many ways, but headstrong and obstinate also."

Alexandra smiled. "You understand your children well, mademoiselle."

"C'est nécessaire, madame."

Bobbi left Paris from Roissy Airport on the twenty-second of September. She had enough luggage for a month's stay. Lucien accompanied them to the airport. Alexandra turned diplomatically away as the young couple embraced, but when Bobbi ran into her arms, her lower lip quivered like a scared girl's.

"I'll be back before you know it, Mom," she whispered vehemently into Alexandra's ear.

"But this time," her mother said, holding her at arm's length for a moment and looking into her eyes, "give him a real chance. He's only human, Bobbi, and he loves you very much."

Tears spilled from Bobbi's eyes. "I love you, Mother. Thank you for making me try again."

They hugged again, tightly. "I just want what's best for you," Alexandra said chokingly. "You know that, don't you, darling?"

Lucien approached, looking awkward. "Last call, madame."

Bobbi scrambled out of her mother's arms and wiped the tears away with the back of her hand.

"Safe journey, darling," Alexandra managed bravely.

"I'll call when I get there, okay?" Bobbi picked up her bags and forced a wavering smile. "And I swear I'll write you both every day."

"Don't make promises you won't keep," Lucien said.

Bobbi made a face. "Well, maybe every other day."

True to her word, she called Alexandra less than an hour after her arrival, sounding tired but excited. Her first letter to Alexandra, written on Andreas's embossed stationery, arrived four days later.

Darling Mother,
     Things between us are better than I'd dared hope. After the last

time I was worried our relationship was really wrecked, but I guess if the caring is there, anything is possible.

I knew it was going to be okay as early as JFK. That other time he was all over me, stifling me yet stiff and anxious at the same time. This time was so different. He approached me very cautiously, and instead of hugging me or anything, he just shook my hand. One second later there we both were, making fools of ourselves, holding each other and really crying! He got a bit uptight again after that—I guess we both did—but we knew it was just defense, something to stop us going over the top too soon. After all, it's only natural that all the ice that's built up over the years should take a while to thaw out completely.

We're going out to Long Island this weekend to stay at Dan Stone's place. It's supposed to be the prettiest place, and we're all going to take things easy. Then next week, Father says he may take me to Washington when he visits the restaurant there.

Have fun, Mom, and don't even *think* about worrying about me —I'm in good hands.

I love you very much. I don't suppose you'd consider a trip yourself?

Bobbi

For three weeks the letters came thick and fast, and when Alexandra telephoned Bobbi on October 20 to find out when she was planning on returning, she was hardly surprised or dismayed when Bobbi said she'd like an extra week or two. She sounded so happy that Alexandra couldn't see any reason to refuse her. But another three weeks after that, she could have kicked herself for failing to see the warning signs.

Dear Mother,

I won't beat about the bush. I want to stay here for a while. Perhaps for as long as a year.

First, I want you to know that Father has been trying real hard to change my mind about driving. All his reasons sound logical enough, but they just don't seem to add up to anything if I compare them to this gut feeling I have inside me. You must know what it's like, Mother—to need something so badly it's like a burn. If someone asked you to give up painting, you couldn't stop, could you? Your father was an artist, and he passed it on to you. It's the same for me.

Father wanted to call you, but I asked him to wait until I'd written. I didn't want you to think we'd been plotting.

The main reason I want to stay is that I know my father is the person who can help me most. I know he won't let me stay unless you agree—and I know he wants me to promise that if he and Uncle Rudy decide I have no talent, I'll quit. I can't imagine quitting. I hope you *will* agree.

I can imagine how you must feel, reading this. I miss you terribly, Mom, please believe me, and I miss L'Alouette and Claudine and Flic too. Lucien's written, and says he may come and visit for a while. Nothing would make me happier if you could be here with us too. But I do know how hard that might be for you.

How's my darling Flic? Give her a great hug for me, please, Mom, and tell her lies about when I'm coming home.

Can you begin to understand?

Bobbi

The big looping handwriting swam before Alexandra's eyes, and she put the letter down on her desk. Nothing in her life—not her father's death, nor Andreas's accident, nor their divorce—nothing had hurt as deeply as this. It was madness. It was a betrayal. It was too devastatingly unfair to be real!

She stared back at the letter.

I can imagine how you must feel . . .

Never! Not in a thousand years.

He wanted to call you.

Damn him to hell! What on earth had possessed her to trust him? She must have been out of her mind.

She was still burning with rage and anguish when Andreas telephoned late that night.

"You got her letter." It was a statement.

"I got it."

"And you don't understand, do you?"

"No." She was aware her voice had never sounded so bitter.

"I don't blame you."

"How noble."

"But you're forgetting something."

"What's that?"

"I've been there, Ali. Out in the cold. I was there for more than ten years."

"So this is your revenge."

"Of course not."

"What then?"

"It's really very simple, Ali. I don't want to lose her again."

"So now it's my turn?"

"You know that isn't what I want."

"Do I?"

Silence gaped between them.

"Ali," he said suddenly, tentatively. "Why don't you come over here too? Come and join us."

Her laugh was brittle. "You want us to be one big happy family again, is that it, Andreas? You're crazier than I thought!"

"Maybe I am."

It was unendurable. "I trusted you!" she cried in despair. "You were going to talk her out of this lunacy! Instead you've used the time to steal her from me!"

He sounded stiff. "I'm sorry if it seems that way to you. It isn't like that at all."

"It seems exactly like that."

"It isn't easy to explain . . ."

"I bet it isn't."

"Will you give me a chance, for Christ's sake!" he shouted suddenly.

"That's just what I did give you, and I've lived to regret it."

"I couldn't talk her out of it! You must know better than anyone what a stubborn streak she has, you've lived with her long enough!"

Alexandra collapsed into defeated silence.

"It wasn't easy, you know, trying to smash her ambition," he went on, desperate for her to understand. "It hurt like hell, don't you see? It was my first chance to share something with her—it brought her back to me again, gave me another chance—"

"*I* gave you that, not the driving."

"You think I don't know that?" Now Andreas was choked with emotion. "I know it was never your fault—none of it. Not our breakup, not the way I abandoned Bobbi. I was crazy, and I've suffered for it."

"And don't you understand that we're *all* going to suffer if you let her continue with this, Andreas?" she yelled passionately. "I've gone through it all before when you were racing—the sheer terror, day after day! Do you truly want to experience that yourself when it's Bobbi in the car instead of you? When she's just passed the stands and disappeared around a bend and you hear a voice shouting that there's been a crash, but you can't tell if it's Bobbi or not!"

"Ali, calm down! Bobbi's a million miles away from racing.

She's riding bikes and she's driven a sports car—just a regular sports car around a circuit upstate—"

"But it won't stop there."

"Well, that's where I come in, isn't it. I won't let her do anything crazy. Bobbi's going to have to prove herself, to work damned hard before I let her touch anything more powerful."

"Sports cars are dangerous enough!"

"Driving on a private circuit is much safer than driving on the open road, Ali," Andreas pointed out, "and as soon as she gets her license, she'll be legally entitled to do that. At least this way, if nothing else she'll be a better driver than most of the kids in the state."

He lapsed into silence. Alexandra fought to calm herself. "Is she any good?" she asked at last, tentatively.

"Frankly, I'm not sure. There's too much energy and enthusiasm so far, without enough skill. You have been right about her wanting this for the wrong reasons."

Thank heaven for small mercies, she thought. *At least he seems to be thinking rationally.*

"I swear to you, Ali, if that does prove to be the case I won't let her continue. I'm going to send her to Dick Moran—with your permission. He runs a professional driver's school. I want to see what he thinks of her. She'll have a chance to prove herself under safe conditions, and we'll both watch her like hawks."

"She mentioned something about Rudy—"

"He's been around a lot lately. He agrees she has to be studied. He thinks she may not be suited emotionally."

"What if this Moran thinks she's good?"

"Then she'll probably apply for her SCCA license."

"What's that?"

"Sports Car Club of America. You can't participate in any event without their license."

"And then she could?" Alexandra asked, already frozen with fear at the prospect.

"Well, legally she could, but then I'd pack her back to Moran for a more comprehensive course. Ali, I promise you that if we think it's not for her we'll talk her out of it, no matter how cruel we have to be."

He sounded so sincere that Alexandra almost found herself believing him. She wanted to believe him.

"What about school?" she asked. "I mean regular school."

Hope sprang into his voice. "Anything you say, Ali. I'll make inquiries and consult you every step of the way."

"I'll want complete details of a range of schools. And the best."

"Whatever you say."

"Okay."

He hardly dared ask. "You agree?"

"Do I have a choice? If I drag Bobbi back by the hair, we all end up losing."

"I don't have to tell you how grateful I am, Ali, do I? And Bobbi will be, too, when I tell her."

"*I'll* tell her," Alexandra said sharply. "I'm going to make sure she realizes she's not getting any soft option."

Andreas hesitated. "Would you consider coming over yourself? For a visit?"

"I'm very busy."

"We'd both be glad—Bobbi would be overjoyed."

Something stirred deep inside her. *Does he mean that, I wonder, or is he just plain grateful?* "I don't think it would be a good idea. And I've only agreed in principle, not in practice, don't forget," she reminded him. "I'll want the information about schooling, I'll want to know about the setup at your home, about—"

"Understood," he said quickly. "You have much more courage than I ever had, Ali," he added softly. "I admire you for it."

"Just look after our child, Andreas," she said harshly, "that's all I ask. If you let anything happen to her, if I think you're putting her in any way at risk at any time, I'll be—"

"Ali," he interrupted. "You're giving me another chance. If I blow it now, I know I won't deserve another. Ever."

52

The day after she'd attended Dick Moran's for the first time, Bobbi was enrolled in Spence Upper School for the remainder of the autumn term and the two subsequent terms. She knew she would have to wear school uniform, but for the other hours in the day she bought two pairs of jeans, soaked them in water and bleach until they were tight and faded enough to pass muster, and then did her best to catch up with the current Top 40. After all, it was going to be tough enough fitting in with a clique of girls who'd been together for at least five years, without being seen to be ignorant of something as vital as American rock music! She wasn't worried about work. In the first place, her lycée in Trouville had high standards; in the second place, once she had her SCCA license, Bobbi had no intention of staying on at Spence or any other school!

Alexandra was still worried sick. Neither her ex-husband nor her stubborn daughter could be entirely trusted to make a sensible judgment over the next few months. Andreas might be perfectly sincere right now, but given that he'd never really got over having to stop racing himself, and more importantly, given the possibility that if Bobbi flunked out she might choose to come back to Honfleur, who was to say that he might not delude both himself and Bobbi?

She needed a surrogate, Alexandra decided, another pair of eyes and ears closer to events. She needed a spy. There was only one possible candidate for the job, one person she could trust; or at least she knew she'd be able to trust him once he knew the truth. Telling him was the hard part.

They both entered the lobby of the Ritz in Paris on the dot of noon on Thanksgiving. Alexandra thought he looked rather younger than a man in his early fifties ought to look, but then Dan Stone had the kind of face that aged easily—it was craggy rather than puckered—and he also had an enviably full head of graying hair and a slim waist, considering his occupation. Daniel thought Alexandra even more beautiful than before, if that was possible. His most forceful memory of her had been of her tall, slender figure in her foolish summer dress, limping gallantly away from his car into the Colombe d'Or in Saint-Paul. Today she looked vibrantly healthy, her hair was as dark and rich as ever (whether with or without the aid of tinting mattered little to him), and those extraordinary eyes, though undeniably anxious, sparkled with life. He swallowed before speaking.

"You look wonderful, Ali." He kissed her cheek.

"You don't look so dusty yourself." She smiled, and kissed him back, French style, on both cheeks. She was aware she cut an elegant figure even by Ritz standards, wearing matching tawny suede hat, suit, and shoes, but her stomach was knotted tight and she longed, unusually, for a cocktail to give her the courage she needed.

"Life isn't bad," Daniel was saying. "Not as I'd have planned it, that's for sure, but things could be a lot worse." He nodded in the direction of the lounge. "Shall we have a cocktail in there, or would you prefer something at the table?"

"Oh, the table, don't you think?" She smiled into his eyes and took his hand.

"So . . ." Daniel took a sip from his martini and gave her a hard look. "Now that we've ordered, what do we do next? Catch up, like the old acquaintances that we are? Or do you plow straight on and tell me what's on your mind?"

"It was very kind of you to come, Dan," Alexandra said slowly.

"I told you a long time ago that any time you needed me I'd be there." He smiled. "And it's obviously hard for you to come to New York right now."

"That's true, but I'm still very grateful." She took a long swallow of her own martini, followed by a sharp breath, and made up her mind. "Which does lead me to what *is* on my mind."

When he had heard it all, Daniel closed his eyes and sat very still.

Alexandra held her breath. "Dan?" she ventured after a while. "Are you all right?"

His eyes were still shut, but his lips moved. "I'm okay. Don't worry."

Oh, God! she thought in distress, *I was wrong to tell him. But how could I ask him to watch over her without telling him the truth?*

The silence continued. Little curls of steam rose from the Rosenthal soup cups that had been placed before them, and then they vanished and a thin skin began to form over the *crème de faisan.*

He spoke at last, hoarsely, and opened his eyes.

"I hardly know her."

"I know."

"I'd be a liar if I said it hadn't crossed my mind when she was born, but"—he gazed at her helplessly—"I dismissed it. The odds against it were immense." He smiled painfully. "And besides, to think otherwise seemed an even worse sin against Andreas than the one I had already committed."

"I know," she said again.

"What does your instinct tell you, Ali?" he asked. "You must have been tortured, not knowing. Was there never any clue, any—?" He stopped, unable to go on.

"I wish I could give you a straight answer, Dan, but I can't," she said simply. "The day she was born I thanked God that she had *my* hair, *my* eyes and coloring. I made up my mind there and then that Andreas was her father—her one and only father—and that I would do everything in my power to forget what happened between us." She looked steadily at him. "I'm sorry, Dan, so terribly sorry. That must sound very hard. I can only assure you that it was far from easy."

Slowly, Daniel reached for her hand and touched it gently. "I do understand. It was the only thing to do, the only way to behave. For her sake as much as his."

"And my own. I acted out of selfishness as much as anything. I wanted Bobbi so desperately—but I wanted Andreas too."

"You loved him," he said simply.

"Yes."

He leaned back in his chair, looking drained. "It explains so many things. About Andreas, about your breakup—even, way back, about what you were going through when you came to Saint-Paul." He shook his head. "Andreas never said a word about that side of his injuries or about the insemination."

"Would you have expected him to, knowing him as you do? He told no one, not even his father."

They sat in silence for several moments. A waiter hovered nearby, uncertain whether or not to remove their soup cups.

"It's been more than ten years since the divorce," Daniel said finally. "You haven't remarried, neither has he."

"My life is full," she said, a little defensively. "There have been men—"

"I'm sure there have," he smiled, "but none of them important, apparently."

"True. But, you know, that's partly because I've elected to live in Normandy. Things are quieter there, the people thrive on serenity and peace."

"That's absurd, Ali. With Deauville on your doorstep? The wealthiest, liveliest people in the world thronging there year after year! If you'd chosen to emerge from your artistic cocoon, you'd have been snapped up a dozen times over."

She laughed. "Thank you."

"You still love him, don't you?"

The question startled her. "It's been more than a decade, Dan, you said so yourself." She shrugged lightly. "I'm fond of him, of course—I'll always care for him—but everything else has been dead between us for a long, long time."

He took her hand again. "If I really believed that, Ali," he said thoughtfully, deliberately, "if I thought that it was all over for you and Andreas, you should know that I—"

"Don't, Dan, please," she said, pulling away.

He flushed darkly. "I'm sorry."

"And don't be sorry! Please! I didn't mean—" She stopped, dismayed.

"I know you didn't. It's all right. I shouldn't have said that." He smiled ruefully. "Anyway, we've strayed from the important subject, haven't we. Bobbi. She's the one who matters now."

"I hope I haven't caused you too much distress, Dan, dear," she said anxiously. "You have every right to be bitterly angry with me."

"What in God's name for?"

"For dropping this bombshell on you, of course. And for keeping it from you all these years."

Daniel signaled a waiter to remove the soup, and assured him that the chef was not at fault. He turned back to Alexandra. "I can't pretend it isn't a shock," he said, "and yet in a way—I told you it entered my head when she was born, and maybe—" He sighed. "Maybe I didn't put it away as successfully as I'd thought."

"We mustn't forget," she felt compelled to remind him, "there's a fifty percent chance it may not be true."

"Possibly more, I'd say. Somehow, though, I don't feel that the statistics are very important, do you?"

She shook her head.

"Let's look at the facts, such as they are. One truth emerges. I have, suddenly, on Thanksgiving Day, 1982, a possible daughter of sixteen years. A miracle. A dream child." His face grew somber. "I had a child like that before, Ali, a will-o'-the-wisp baby— but she was never to be. This one exists. She lives and breathes and laughs and cries, and causes her mother pain and joy." His eyes were bright with tears. "You think I should be angry with you, Ali? For bringing me the very possibility of Bobbi?"

For a moment she was unable to speak. Then it was her turn to reach for his hand and clasp it warmly. "One thing is certain," she said huskily, "it brings me gladness in many ways to think that Bobbi could be your daughter." She battled to find the right words, the honest words. "That was the worst part for Andreas, not being able to have his own child—"

"Andreas is Bobbi's father," Daniel said abruptly, cutting her short. "Nothing can change that. Nothing must ever be allowed to change that for either of them, Ali."

"I hope it won't, Dan," she agreed softly. "And that's really why I came to you for help."

"You want me to keep an eye on her."

"I want you to guard her, Dan."

"Difficult, if she's not to know why I care." He looked troubled. "And deceitful, too."

"Dan, dear . . ." She leaned closer. "Surely now that you have an explanation for Andreas's actions over the years, for his irrational moods—"

"But he's better now, Ali. He's realized his mistakes, knows what he lost."

"I don't want him to lose Bobbi again, believe me. I'm just concerned—no, terrified—that one day he may lose his clearheadedness for one dangerous moment, that impulse and emotion may take over." She bit her lip. "Bobbi could be injured, Dan. Physically hurt. Even killed."

"I do understand that, Ali, but—"

"All I'm asking is that you keep me informed of what's going on. Bobbi's always been an honest child, but lately she's been afraid to confide in me in case I disapprove—and of course she's probably been right. And now, when I'm thousands of miles away, I'm terribly afraid of losing any remaining control I may have had."

"Maybe you should consider coming to New York? For a while, at least?"

"I don't think that would be right. It's too much like stating openly that I don't trust either of them. I do want their relationship to have a real chance, Dan. I owe Andreas that."

He considered another long moment, then nodded. "All right. I'll keep an eye on things for you. I'll even send you reports, if you like, on her progress. On her driving, that is. Their private life is taboo."

"Absolutely," she agreed. "It's a caring, rational adult I'm after, Dan, not a private detective."

He laughed, lightening the atmosphere.

"I can't begin to tell you what a relief this is for me," she said.

"I think I can guess."

"Can you, Dan?"

"I think so."

She looked down. "I'm not at all hungry, you know. What will they think of us?"

"Probably dismiss us as ignorant Americans."

She chuckled. "They probably think we've been having a lover's tiff," she said, and flushed.

Daniel smiled at her. "Probably."

Alexandra shivered.

"Cold?"

She shook her head. "Not at all. I was just wishing that this was next Thanksgiving, that Bobbi was safely back home, and that all this was over."

"I understand," he said gently.

Her eyes widened with anxiety. "Promise you'll look after her, Dan!"

Daniel's expression was distant. "She's my dream child, Ali, I told you. What else can I do?"

The warning arrived in Daniel's seventh report, at the end of the following June. Alexandra was on the telephone even before she'd finished reading.

"Why, Dan? Why on earth didn't you tell me this was coming?"

"If I'd known, believe me you'd have been the first to find out. As it is, they've been keeping their plan under wraps from almost everyone, including young Lucien."

"How long has Lucien been there? Bobbi said he was thinking of visiting her, but she never told me he'd arrived."

"He's been here over two months, Ali, and I gather he's very upset about this."

"I'm sure he is."

"It was Rudy who let the cat out of the bag."

"Thank God for Rudy," she said fervently. "Is Andreas completely mad?"

"The general consensus," Daniel said reluctantly, "would seem to point that way. But I can tell you he seems convinced they can do it."

Alexandra drummed her free hand in a frustrated fist on her desk. "You really think I should come?"

"I can't think of another solution."

She paused. "I need a couple of days, Dan. If anything new develops, you'll keep me posted?"

"Of course."

A few minutes later, Alexandra looked down again at Daniel's letter.

> . . . The latest. I've just learned that Andreas is planning a comeback. That in itself is bad enough, but it's not the reason for this report.
>
> Bobbi and Lucien Joffrey, who is now living in New York, were apparently hoping to race as partners in the fall in a long road race. I gather, however, that Andreas has other ideas. He's ousted Lucien, and intends to make his first reappearance as his daughter's co-driver/navigator in her own debut race. I'm convinced he feels he can help her, but indications all round are that it could be risky.
>
> We have about two months to stop this. I think you must come.

She closed her eyes. When she opened them again, they were cloudy with tears, but her mouth was set. She had no choice, she realized despairingly. There was no other way left, God help them all.

She waited until late evening to begin. The window and the chintz drapes in her study had been left open, and soft, mild air and the night sounds of the Normandy countryside seeped comfortably into the room. Honfleur was already dark and quiet; its families slept in peace and honest weariness, gathering strength for the morning's work. Upstairs in her bedroom, Claudine dreamed and snored, and in the study, Flic, grown lately rheumatic in her back legs and white around her muzzle, moved slowly away from the dying log fire and lay down to sleep close to Alexandra's feet.

Where do I begin? Alexandra wondered. *Where do I begin? And when?*

She picked up the pen and laid a fresh sheet of paper on the blotter.

My dearest daughter,
  I do not know where to begin.

If this were a canvas, or a lump of clay, she knew her fingers and eyes would lead her, but this . . .

Despair has brought me to this. It is to be part chronicle, part confession, part appeal.

Down by her feet, Flic stirred and stretched, and outside in the garden a breeze fondled the leaves and branches of the lilac trees. She began a second paragraph.

For many artists, the art is enough, the paintings and sculptures are their whole life, they need nothing more. For your mother, for many years, that was not true. I needed love more than art.

Alexandra's fingers quickened.

Andreas, alerted by cable, met her at JFK at lunchtime three days later. He looked much older, but remarkable, she thought in spite of her tightly controlled rage.

"Something agrees with you," she said, her heart pounding uncomfortably.

"The sun," he said, smiling warmly. "You're a sight for sore eyes yourself."

"Thank you." She looked around for a porter.

"Don't bother," he said, picking up her bags easily. "My muscles need the training." He strode for the exit. "I'm parked out front." He went ahead of her through the automatic doors and unlocked the trunk of a brand-new, gleaming midnight-blue Mercedes sports car.

"What happened to the Porsche?" Alexandra asked. "Bobbi wrote ecstatically about it."

"I loaned it to her for a few days." He slammed the lid of the trunk and opened the passenger door for her. "Don't worry," he said, reading her mind. "She's a good driver."

"Where is she?"

Andreas glanced at her as he slid into the driver's seat. "You told me not to bring her."

"I know that. Is she at your place?"

"She's at Lime Rock Park in Connecticut. Practicing."

"Is Lucien with her?" she asked lightly.

"No." He seemed uneasy.

"I see."

"Your cable was a little short on explanation," he said carefully, "so I told her you wouldn't be here for another three or four days. She'll be back in the city Friday."

"Fine."

"Or we could call her if you like. Surprise her. She'd be back like a shot if she knew you were here."

"No, Friday will be soon enough." She watched the highway opening up before them. It was hard to believe she'd been away for so long. "We have some talking to do before then."

"I figured we might." He changed into top gear and edged into the fast lane. "I wish you'd given me a little more warning, Ali. I have to leave town tomorrow morning myself. It was too late to reschedule."

She cursed inwardly. "When will you be back?"

"Thursday evening."

"Could we talk this evening?"

"Sure we could, but I've invited Dan and Rudy to the restaurant for dinner. They're both longing to see you." He glanced at her again. "Is that all right with you? Only another old friend of yours was planning on joining us—I told Theodor Salko you were flying in."

"That was kind," she said, genuinely pleased but wondering if he'd just made these elaborate arrangements in order to avoid an early confrontation. Did he realize she knew about his comeback plans? Would he be so ill at ease if he didn't? Maybe he would.

"We could still cancel if you prefer."

"Of course not."

"How long are you staying? I hope it's longer than a flying visit."

"I have an open ticket," she answered noncommittally, and saw his quick smile with a pang of something close to pleasure. *Really, I'm too absurd!* she thought angrily. *Ridiculous! I haven't seen him for nine years, and I'm only here because of his betrayal. How can I still feel this—this girlish wrenching when I lay eyes on him?*

"Where are you staying?" he asked.

"The Pierre."

He raised an eyebrow. "Why there?"

"Why not? Is there something wrong with it?"

"Of course not. But you always liked the Plaza." He trailed off awkwardly.

"I can always move."

"Of course."

Dinner that evening was part purgatory, part pleasure. Andreas seated Alexandra between himself and Theo Salko, who, she noticed sadly, was showing his age badly, but who still clearly understood the power of a compliment. Rudy, at sixty-nine, appeared to have withstood with remarkable equilibrium nearly fifty years in his wheelchair, as well as bereavements, sundry illnesses and the passage of time. He still bellowed with laughter or anger like a roaring bull, still had the ability to wither Andreas with a single glance. And then there was Daniel, suffering the guilt of treachery, sitting quietly, taking pleasure from the gathering but dreading the days to follow.

Halfway through the evening Andreas confounded both Daniel and Alexandra by suggesting she should check out of the Pierre and move instead into Le Chapeau Rose.

"You said you might change hotels, and this would make more sense," he urged cheerfully, apparently far more relaxed than he'd been earlier in the day. "I'm going to be out of the city, and Bobbi won't be back till Friday. You have to go to the island anyway, Ali —no one in their right mind would want to miss Dan's house, it's Elysium on earth. What do you say, Dan?"

Daniel looked calm. "It's a fine idea," he said. "But Ali may have other plans."

"She hasn't," Andreas answered quickly. "She told me. Shopping can be done just as well next week as this, can't it, Ali?"

Alexandra was completely thrown. She was irritated by Andreas's cavalier attitude, and she felt that staying at Dan's house was anything but a good idea, but she couldn't very well refuse the invitation without seeming oddly churlish to everyone present.

"All right," she said, "if Dan's sure he won't be put out."

"Certainly not. There's plenty of space," Daniel said pleasantly. "I'd be delighted, though I'm afraid you'll have to share the gardens with twenty students. There's a course in progress right now, and though they never get into the main part of the house, I think it's only fair to let them have free rein outside. It's part of the attraction, after all."

"I should think it is." She smiled at him. "It sounds wonderful."

Dinner stretched into five courses, and by the end of the evening Alexandra was buzzing with jet lag, fatigue, and sheer dread at what she still had to do before the night was over. As she thought of the letter in her purse, she felt sick with self-disgust.

"Andreas, you'll drive me to my hotel, won't you?"

"With pleasure."

He means it, she realized, her guilt magnifying.

Sitting in the Mercedes in front of the Pierre, Alexandra waved away the doorman who had come swiftly forward to open her door.

"I guess you're too tired for a nightcap?" Andreas said.

"Much too tired." Her stomach writhed, but she forced herself to continue. "Besides," she said quietly, "after you hear what I'm about to say, I doubt somehow that you'll feel like drinking with me."

The fear that darted instantly into his eyes was a knife in her heart. *But it's all his fault,* she told herself insistently. *If he'd only kept his promise to keep Bobbi safe from harm, none of this would have to happen. I could say good night and go to Le Chapeau Rose tomorrow, and in a few days Bobbi and he would be here, and we could pretend to be a family again for a while, and she could come home to Honfleur again and—*

She tried to still the pounding in her chest, and stared straight ahead through the windshield, unable to face him.

"I know," she said.

"What?"

"About your plans."

"What plans?" he asked, but she felt him stiffening.

"The plans you've been making to race again, with our daughter as your co-driver."

"I see."

She turned to look at him. He was impassive. "It's true, isn't it?"

"Yes."

She looked away again. "I can't let it happen."

He didn't speak.

"I can't let it happen because I'm sure it's a terrible and dangerous idea for both of you. I have no right to prevent you from doing whatever you want, personally; I never had and I never did. But I have every right as Bobbi's mother to make sure she knows exactly what she's up against."

"What does that mean, Ali?" His voice was harsh.

She drove herself on relentlessly, opening her purse and withdrawing the thick envelope. "I've written her a letter." She took a deep breath. "More than a letter. A full account. A chronicle."

"I see."

"Do you? I doubt it." She looked at him again. He was ashen. "It tells her everything."

"I see," he repeated.

"I don't have to give it to her," she said clearly. "It depends on you. On what you decide to do."

"Blackmail? That isn't really your style, is it?"

"No, it isn't."

"Then why?"

"Need you ask that?" She was trembling. "Desperation, Andreas."

His jaw was set rock hard. "And you think you're right to do this?"

"Right!" she cried suddenly. "Nothing about this is right! Was it right of you to lie to me?"

"I never lied to you."

"The hell you didn't!" Her voice shook. "You promised that if she wasn't good enough you'd stop her."

"Who says she isn't?"

"Just about everyone!" She was past caring now, past worrying about hurting him. Only Bobbi mattered now, keeping her safe. "I know that Rudy thinks she has very little talent, that even Lucien wanted to co-drive with her chiefly to protect her from the mistakes he worries she'll make. And I know that most people think the idea of any kind of comeback for you is downright insane! That you're—"

"I should have known," he interrupted bitterly. "Why did I kid myself, even for a second, that you would really trust me? I should have guessed you'd spy on me."

"Call it what you like," she said. "But I think if you give it a little thought, you may find you call it love."

"Love!"

"Yes."

"You call destroying everything Bobbi and I have finally built up 'love'?"

"No, I don't. I call it tragic. I'd give the world not to. But if you leave me no other choice, Andreas, that is what I'm going to have to do." She returned the envelope to her purse and grasped the door handle. "I'll wait till you're both back in the city. I want you to have some time to think hard about it."

"How generous."

"Please try," she pleaded, feeling her strength sapping, and quickly opened the door. "For all our sakes try." She got out. "If you want to talk to me, you know where to find me."

She walked swiftly around the car, past the doorman, past the marbled pillars, and into the hotel. She didn't look back, but she heard the screech of tires and smelled their burning as the Mercedes took off at high speed down Fifth Avenue and vanished into the night.

53

For Daniel, the four days and nights that Alexandra spent with him at Le Chapeau Rose were sweetest torture. She felt his pain, understood his regret. It was strange, she reflected—and remarkable, too—how some emotions seemed never to die while others faded into obscurity and could hardly be recalled. She knew now that a part of Daniel had always been in love with her, and that she had chosen not to see that all those years ago in Saint-Paul because of her own love for Andreas. It didn't diminish Daniel's feelings for poor, sweet Barbara, who would have given him nothing but joy had she lived, who would have given him a child of his own. If Barbara had not died, Daniel's love for Alexandra would have dwindled to affection, to a warm memory and nothing more —but now, so many years later, that love was alive again, leaping and searing, causing him pain and wonder. Pain, because he knew as well as she did that she still cared for Andreas, and wonder, because he had believed his own capacity for that kind of emotion had died along with Barbara and their baby.

We seem joined together, the three of us, Alexandra realized, *inextricably entwined.* She had only come to understand that fully as she had written down the facts for Bobbi. *Divorce means nothing; time means nothing; just as all those years apart meant nothing to Daniel and Andreas.*

Daniel watched Alexandra sketching on the lawn of the water lily garden, sunning herself by the pool, sipping wine opposite him at dinner—sometimes merry, often troubled and preoccupied, always desirable. She and the house were made for each other, he felt. He found himself spinning fantasies around her: Ali as his wife, his lover, his companion into old age. He knew that with the slightest crumb of encouragement from her, his remaining resolve would dissolve, and he would take her in his arms and beg her to stay.

But encouragement never came.

Breakfast, taken in the sunniest room of the house with the doors
flung open to the rose garden, was almost at an end on the fifth
morning at Le Chapeau Rose when the maid summoned Alexandra to the telephone.

It was Andreas.

"I'm back," he said. "And Bobbi will be here tomorrow morning."

Alexandra felt the air still around her face. "Have you reached a
decision?"

"I have."

She waited.

"I won't bow to blackmail, emotional or otherwise."

The pain struck at her almost as intensely as if a limb had suddenly been severed. She could not speak. She'd been so certain—
so absolutely sure that he would see sense, give way.

He spoke again. "You might like to know that my father flew
into New York last night."

Roberto. Alexandra closed her eyes. *Now I have to cause him more
pain too.*

"Bobbi will be at my house by ten o'clock in the morning. I'll
be out, and so will my father. You can see her then."

Her voice was hoarse. "It . . . will take some time," she said,
"for her to read—"

"That's all right," he answered. "You can leave word for me at
the Park Avenue office. I shan't come home before."

The telephone went dead in her hand.

I can't! she thought desperately. *I can't just let this happen! I have
to give him one more chance.*

She waited in a cab outside the house in Sutton Place until she saw
the dark blue Mercedes slip into the underground garage. She was
standing at the front door, shivering, when he appeared, keys in
hand.

"I have to talk to you."

"There's nothing more to say." He put the first key in a lock
and turned it, and then another. The door opened.

"Andreas, please. I have to."

He paused. "All right."

"Is Roberto here?"

"No, he's dining with friends."

They stepped into the hall. It was small but handsome, she
noted, with sleek lines and plenty of oak.

"Come into the library. You look cold, and it's always warm in there."

Her painting hung over the dead fireplace, as Bobbi had described. Alexandra shivered again. *The five figures.* Had Andreas ever completely understood it, she wondered.

"A drink?"

"No. Thank you."

He stood, back to the grate. "So what is it you want?"

"I'm not sure."

"I will have a drink." He opened a cabinet between two bookshelves and poured a large Scotch.

"I guess—" she began.

"Yes?" He faced her. He looked, she thought, unyielding.

"I guess I hoped I might still be able to change your mind."

"No," he said.

She gestured helplessly. "But isn't it a terrible price to pay, for something so—"

"Trivial? Unimportant?"

"No! Not trivial at all, Andreas, not to you, I know! But compared to the possibility of losing her . . ."

"Your price tag, Alexandra, not mine." He took a large swallow of Scotch. "It's simple. You gave with one hand, and now you're taking back with the other. It's your prerogative. You're her mother."

"It isn't like that at all."

"No?" He advanced on her, and she realized that just then he truly hated her. "You're doing exactly what my mother did, you know. You're dismissing Bobbi's needs as less important than your own. You're assuming she has no talent when you've never even seen her behind a wheel."

"I'm not doing what Anna did!" Alexandra protested. "It's not the same at all. Bobbi's a young woman, not a boy with some great need to prove his masculinity to the world! And racing *was* in your blood. It isn't in hers!"

His face was grim. "You think I want to race again to prove my masculinity? You've been listening to gossip, Ali. From people who are still jealous of my success, even now. I'm not a popular hero any more—I'm no Niki Lauda coming back after a nightmare! It's been too long. I'm a has-been—you think I don't know that? But what you don't know, Alexandra, is that I can still drive!"

"Then drive without Bobbi."

"I can't."

"You mean you won't!" Alexandra tried to check her own anger, to take the sting out of her words. "What you still refuse to understand, Andreas, is that what the two of you share is so much more important than genetics! You've always been Bobbi's father. Why can't you be satisfied with love? Why do you need to prove more?"

"Because there is more," he answered. "Because Bobbi, entirely of her own accord, developed a passion for speed, for control over machines, just as I did when I was a boy—just as my father did. Only she was so far away from me, from my influence." His eyes glittered. "I can't explain that away, and neither can you, but it sure beats hell out of biology."

"Andreas—"

"No more, Alexandra. She needs it, and she wants it. And I, for one, am not going to take it from her." He turned on his heel and slammed his glass onto the table with a resounding crack. "She'll be here in the morning by ten, as I told you."

"Yes," she said quietly, defeated.

His mouth tightened. "Do your worst."

The cab pulled over at the corner of Second Avenue and 57th Street next morning. Alexandra paid the driver and got out to walk the rest of the way. She needed more time.

It was a perfect late-June day. Mild air that stroked the cheeks like silk, tidy city trees with leaves full of juicy sap that would, within a week or two, grow prematurely brown under the stress of summer heat and pollution; small Manhattan birds dreaming of upstate meadows packed with worms, fluting sweet songs from their slender throats.

Alexandra tried to stroll, to delay, but her feet carried her forward mechanically, closer to Sutton Place, her heels clicking crisply against the concrete sidewalk. Her head pounded in time with her heart. *Oh, dear Lord, if I am wrong, stop me now, strike me down before it's too late.*

Her feet walked briskly on, and she was not struck down.

The door opened even before she reached for the bell, and there was Bobbi, standing with outstretched arms and tears sparkling in her eyes.

"Mother."

Alexandra stood motionless, captivated by her daughter. She was taller, stronger, her face and arms tanned dark, and the gray-green eyes were crisper and more indomitable than she remembered.

"You look—superb."

Bobbi smiled almost shyly. "Aren't you coming in?"

They both laughed then, and Alexandra stepped over the threshold and they fell into each other's arms, holding on tight and weeping.

"I've missed you so much," Bobbi whispered, and pressed her soft, cool cheek against her mother's. "I'm so glad you're here."

"Oh, darling, I've missed you too—you'll never know how much . . ."

Minutes passed, and still they stayed locked together, Alexandra holding on because all too soon it would be over, this easy, pure joy between them. *Will she ever forgive me? Will she be able, ever again, to trust me?*

Bobbi pulled away first, wiping her eyes. "Come on," she said, starting for the library.

"No, darling, not in there."

Bobbi looked surprised.

"Isn't there a sitting room?"

"Sure. It's just that the library's my favorite room. I spend a lot of time there."

"Later, darling. Okay?"

Bobbi smiled. "Of course. Come on." She led the way into another room, freshly decorated in apple greens and rusts, a pleasant room overlooking a small backyard, made for peaceful conversation or a good book and an after-dinner cognac.

"Like it?" Bobbi asked.

"The house seems very nice."

"Father said you were here last night. Did he show you around?"

"No, not really."

"Would you like to see the rest?" Bobbi was eager.

"No, darling, thank you. Maybe later."

"Ah, yes," Bobbi said, planting herself in an armchair and curling her legs under her. "The mystery."

"What?"

"Father said you were going to talk to me about something this morning, but he wouldn't say what." She grinned, eyes dancing. "Now you're not going to kick up a great big fuss about my driving, are you, Mom? You know I shan't pay any attention, however much I love you, don't you?"

Alexandra's lips smiled. Her eyes did not. "I do know that."

"Well, then?" She sat up straight. "Are you getting married again?"

"No, of course not."

"So what is it?" The laughter went out of her face. "This is serious, isn't it?" She looked suddenly afraid. "You're not sick, are you?"

Alexandra shook her head slowly. "No, Bobbi, I'm not sick." She could hardly bring herself to look into her daughter's eyes.

"Mother, what is it? You're frightening me."

Still she hesitated.

"Mother!"

Alexandra sighed. "All right."

"What's wrong, Mother? Tell me quickly, please, before I burst."

"I wish it were that easy, Bobbi, I really do." She opened her purse and took out the envelope.

"What's that?"

Alexandra swallowed, but the lump in her throat refused to shift. "It's a letter," she said faintly. "From me to you. I never wanted you to see it, but I know now that there was never really any other way."

Bobbi looked puzzled, anxious. "What does it say?"

Her mother smiled wearily. "You can see it's thick. It's a long letter, many pages." She stood up shakily and handed it to her.

"You want me to read it now?"

Alexandra nodded. "I'll go for a walk. Is there a park near here?"

"Yes, at 60th Street." Bobbi's expression was still frightened. "What is it you want me to do, Mother?"

"I want you to read it. It'll take you a long time. And then, if you can, I would like you to come and tell me how you feel about it."

"Okay." Bobbi's voice was small.

"And Bobbi?"

"Yes."

"I'm sorry."

Alexandra held her head high until she was out of sight, knowing that Bobbi watched her for a long time, and then she felt herself droop, like a crushed flower, feeling all the weight she had carried for so many years suddenly descending on her, devastating, threatening.

In the park she found a bench and sat down. She wondered idly how long it would be before Bobbi came. If she did come. Mothers passed back and forth in front of her, pushing babies, leading dogs. Some smiled at her, others glanced at her curiously.

Alexandra sat and stared into the distance.

Almost two hours later, Bobbi, seated in the library, was nearing the end. Several waves of weeping had come and gone, leaving a wreckage of mascara and shock on her face. Now she was numb.

Her eyes ached and burned, but she went on.

She turned the last page.

> . . . And so, Bobbi, we are in the present. Tomorrow morning I shall leave Honfleur, my safe haven, and I shall come to you with this journal, this record of our lives.
>
> I never wanted you to know, and perhaps that was wrong. As I have already said, I lacked the essential courage. I am only letting you read this now because the mistake you may be about to make terrifies me so deeply. I cannot, will not, allow my only daughter to risk her life because of lies.
>
> Look again at the painting. It speaks the truth. So help me God, Bobbi—Andreas is your father, as certainly as if his seed had been planted in my body. Take from him what inheritance you must, my darling child, but take it with open, clear eyes and a wise heart.
>
> And if you can, forgive us all.
>
> Your mother, Alexandra

Something deep inside Bobbi moved. She was aware of it, as one might be aware of a physical pain—primitive, stretching, clawing. It flamed and scorched and writhed for a moment—and then, with uncanny calm, it grew less, and was finally still.

Bobbi folded the pages very carefully and replaced them in the envelope. Then she stood, walked over to the fireplace, and looked up at the painting.

"Life Drawing." She remembered how she had asked her mother what it meant, how fascinated she had been by its glows and shadows.

It speaks the truth.

"Yes," she said softly, and reaching up, she touched it gently, laying her fingers lightly on each of the five figures in turn, coming to rest in the center.

Why don't I mind? she wondered in confusion. *Why do I feel so— peaceful?*

The answer came so forcefully that for a moment the whole painting before her seemed illuminated, seemed to pulsate with life.

Because now, at last, I understand.

She found her mother in the park, still sitting.

"Mother?"

Alexandra turned her face slowly. Her eyes were misty and far away. Bobbi touched her hand. It was ice cold.

"Come home with me."

Her mother's eyes cleared. She seemed to force herself to speak, to gather strength. "Do you want me there? Are you sure?"

Bobbi sat beside her on the bench. Their bodies touched lightly. She sighed softly. "I never knew," she said, "how brave you were."

Alexandra turned her head and stared at her in wonder. "Brave? Never."

"Oh, yes. Very brave." Bobbi's mouth curved gently. "Come home, please."

Alexandra hesitated. "And—Andreas?"

"We can telephone him when we get back."

They strolled together out of the park and back along Sutton Place toward the house. They were silent for most of the way—until just before they reached the front door, Alexandra spoke.

"He doesn't know. About Daniel."

"I know. Does he need to?"

Alexandra shook her head. "Not unless you want him to. It's your decision."

"Then—no."

Inside, they went, inevitably, to the library.

"I asked Father once, after I brought him the painting, if he knew what it meant."

"Did he?"

"I don't think so. He just knows it's important and I've often seen him staring at it. Like me, I guess he always found it compelling."

"But now you understand it."

"Yes."

Alexandra paused. "What about Dan? How do you feel about him?"

"About Dan?" Bobbi smiled. "I'm very fond of him. He's always been very kind to me. And caring."

"He's a good man. He's had a hard life."

"I know," Bobbi said. "In spite of all that success, he seems sad. And I guess I'll never know for sure—but I don't feel that he's my father."

"You could do worse."

"I realize that, Mother. But somehow I think, now that I know the truth—well, don't you feel I might have some sense of recognition? If he were." She looked searchingly at Alexandra.

"I can't answer that. Dan asked me if I'd had any flashes of intuition about it, but I couldn't honestly say I had. You've never once reminded me of him—maybe you're too much like me. And then again, I spent so long making sure I thought of you as Andreas's child . . ." She looked compassionately at Bobbi. "This must be so difficult for you, so frustrating."

"Not so very much," Bobbi answered thoughtfully. "It would be different, I guess, if our lives had always gone squeaky clean till this minute—if you'd told me suddenly, out of a clear blue sky, that I was adopted or something." She smiled. "But I spent so many years wondering why I'd been rejected by my father, that the truth seems actually easier to accept than some of the stuff my imagination dredged up. At least I know how much I was wanted."

Alexandra fell silent for a while. At last she said, "And Dan. Don't you mind? About us?"

Bobbi's reply was both contemplative and realistic. "I think a love affair with him was pretty reasonable under the circumstances."

Her mother stared into the grate. "I don't know if I could be so understanding in your place."

"Sure you could. You told me your own father was a terrible seducer, and you loved him anyway." She watched Alexandra smile. "And I can hardly accuse you of promiscuity, can I?"

"That's true enough." Alexandra thought of all the long, contented, quiet evenings at L'Alouette, with Bobbi and Claudine and Flic for company; of all the invitations she had refused, of the few she'd accepted.

"Who knows," Bobby said, becoming more serious, "maybe I *was* conceived in France. But whether it was there, or in the doctor's office in New York, I still have only one father—one real father."

"Maybe it's time you called him. He and your grandfather must be climbing the walls."

"I will."

Alexandra drew her close, kissing her hair. "And when they get here, I think Roberto and I'll just disappear for a while. Okay?"

"Thanks, Mom."

"De rien."

Bobbi looked at her. "Don't start crying now."

Alexandra shook her head and wiped her eyes. "I was just thinking how damned lucky your father and I were, getting you for a daughter."

Bobbi grinned. "I'm some kid, huh?"

"You sure are."

Andreas came up the path, gray-faced, white-lipped, his father a few paces behind him. He walked slowly, almost painfully. Every one of his almost fifty years seemed to squirm and then stiffen in his limbs. He felt the scars deep in his legs.

Her voice was so grave.

The front door was opening. He had a swift glimpse of black hair rippling, of young skin gleaming.

If I lose her now, shall I bear it?

Her arms were open. Her mouth trembled. Her eyes brimmed over with tears and silvered through gray to jade.

Her voice was low.

"Hello, Father."

Andreas ran. The years receded and were shut tightly back into a box in his mind. The pain in his legs was gone.

Roberto smiled.

Later, the four of them sat together. They sat away from the painting, in the polite, easy room of greens and rusts, and they were all immeasurably glad.

Bobbi's gaze traveled from her mother to her father. The shimmer did really exist, she decided, like a nimbus. It was more than just a whiff of rhapsody on her part.

Well, I'll be—

She arched an eyebrow, and curled her lips.

Alexandra looked down at her hands, folded calmly in her lap.

Still one more ugliness.

She made ready.

It will hurt him, but it will not destroy him.

"Bobbi," she began.

"Yes."

"Now that you know," she said. "Now that you understand."

"Yes."

"It must have—" She stopped, scrambling for the right words. "You must also see why I've been so very much against your driving."

"Of course."

Out of the corner of her eye, Alexandra saw Andreas stiffen and her heart went out to him. "I don't want any snap decisions, believe me," she said carefully, "but at least now we should be able to sit down and discuss this like reasonable adults."

"There's no need," Bobbi said.

"But there—"

"I do understand."

Thank God. Alexandra stole another pitying glance at Andreas, who sat impassively.

"There's really nothing to discuss," Bobbi said.

Alexandra's eyes were warm. "I'm so glad."

Bobbi caught Andreas's eye. "I—I don't think *you* understand, Mother."

"What do you—?" Alexandra stopped.

"I mean," Bobbi said, answering slowly, deliberately, "there's nothing to discuss because it doesn't make any difference. Yes, I do see why you were worried, I honestly do. But you were wrong."

"Bobbi, I'm just asking you to—"

"I know exactly what you're asking me to do, but there's no point." Bobbi's expression was gentle. "Maybe racing isn't in my blood—"

"It isn't." Alexandra's eyes were widening.

"Or at least it wasn't there at birth." Bobbi got up, came over, and crouched at her mother's chair. "But somehow, Mom, it has crept into me, it's gotten *into* my blood. And all the letters and all the facts in the world can't change that." She took hold of Alexandra's hand, but it was jerked away. "Maybe it's your turn to face facts, Mother," she said, pained. "You're here now, so why don't you take a look? See what I can do." She tried to smile. "I'm not going to act foolishly, you know. Father made me swear that I'll quit if I don't shape up, make the grade, and I'll stand by that. It's not as if it's something I can do forever in any—"

"Forever!" Alexandra's anguished cry startled them all. "Bobbi, if your bones are crushed to pulp, or your face is scarred to the bone, or you're stone-dead on a slab, the only *forever* you may know will be in the grave!"

Bobbi's voice was quiet, dignified. "I know that. I do have enough sense to be scared."

"All drivers are scared." Andreas had spoken for the first time. "All good drivers."

Roberto sat in the corner by the French doors. He looked and felt, as never before, like an old man. Silently he sat, lost in thought, trapped in memories, and sometimes he shook his head.

Alexandra stared from Andreas to Bobbi. "You've already talked this over, haven't you? We left you alone—I left you for a few moments of honest caring—and you lost no time, did you?"

"Ali, darling—"

"Don't you dare call me that!"

Andreas looked at her helplessly, pityingly, now that the tables had again been turned. "Papa," he said, looking at Roberto, "can't you say something?"

Roberto stared at his son from out of a haze, and shook his head. *"Un cerchio,"* he murmured.

"Papa?"

Roberto sagged. *"Sono colpevole."*

"No, Papa! That's not true!"

"What did Grandpa say?" Bobbi asked softly, but no one answered her.

Alexandra rose and went to Roberto, concerned. Gently she stroked his shaggy head. "It's not your fault, Papa. None of it. You mustn't blame yourself."

He held her hand against his cheek. *"Mia cara."* His eyes were wet with tears. "Can't you try to understand them?"

"No, Papa, it's impossible."

He sighed. "I know." Slowly, painfully, he stood from the low armchair and walked out of the room, closing the door quietly behind him.

"Perhaps you should spend a little time with him," Alexandra said to Andreas in a cold voice.

"Ali, for goodness'—"

"There's nothing you can say to me, so don't try."

"Mother, can't you just—"

"No," she said flatly. "I'm leaving now."

"Where are you going?" Bobbi asked in dismay.

"Ali, please! Stay here," Andreas begged. "Let's talk, let's be together!"

"What for? You've heard what our daughter has to say. Do you disagree with her? Of course not, how could you? It's everything you ever dreamed of, isn't it!" She strode to the door and wrenched it open.

"Mom, please at least tell us where you're going!" There was a note of real fear in Bobbi's voice. "You're not going back to France, are you?"

Alexandra twisted around, and the unhappiness inside her was so agonizing that she thought she might crumble and give way, but she did not.

"Does it really matter?"

She pulled the front door to with a solid bang, and closed her eyes.

One door shuts, she thought wryly. *Another one slams.*

54

"Do you mind?"

"What?"

"That I've come back."

"Need you really ask?"

"No."

Daniel and Alexandra sat in the water lily garden at Le Chapeau Rose, on hard white chairs made comfortable with wild-silk cushions. It was six o'clock, and the sun still hung in the sky, warming them through.

"Have you ever been to Giverny?" Alexandra asked dreamily, gazing into the water.

"No."

"I should like to have met Claude Monet," she mused. "He spent his childhood in Normandy, you know."

Daniel smiled at her. "What else would you like to have done? Or what do you still want to do?"

She shrugged. "Not so much. Everything." She sighed. "To find a little more peace, maybe. Monet's kind."

"How's your work recently?"

"Well enough. Honfleur's been good for me, I think." She yawned and stretched. "Since I've lived there, I've really grown to dislike portrait painting. Nature is so much less self-conscious than we are. She takes it all in her stride. When it's time to beat the drum, she belts it out; when it's time to wilt, she goes gracefully."

"Have you ever painted Bobbi?"

"Often. Especially when she was younger."

Daniel stirred the grass with a bare foot. "I remember your first painting—I think it was the first—of Andreas. He showed it to me. The one that hung in the hallway at your apartment."

Alexandra smiled. "Silverstone, England. It brought us together."

"It was dramatic and rather tantalizing. I remember how you caught the car almost as a living, breathing thing—it seemed a part of Andreas."

"That's how I saw them, as extensions of each other."

Daniel hesitated only briefly. "But that's not how you see Bobbi."

She raised her eyes, faintly wounded. "Not you too, Dan."

He shook his head. "No, Ali, not like that. I just wondered if you'd tried seeing her that way."

"It isn't the same."

"I guess not." He stopped pushing, and they fell silent for a while until he spoke again. "Why were you so upset when you got back from the city?"

"I'd sooner not talk about it, Dan," she said, her face pained. "Do you mind?"

"Of course not."

There was a sudden distant murmur of voices, moving quickly closer. A man and a woman laughed; her sound softer and lower, carrying on the breeze and blending with the quiet bubbling of the mysterious fish that swam beneath the dark water in the pool; his more raucous laughter flying higher on the wind, going out to the ocean with the crying of the gulls.

"School's out," Daniel said. "I'll have to go see them off in a while."

"Please don't wait around on my account. I'm fine."

"It's okay, they'll want a dip in the pool first, they usually do. One of the perks of the school."

They heard a soft mewing, and from under the wall of weeping willows came a small black cat, gliding smoothly toward Daniel and jumping onto his lap.

"Who's this?" Alexandra asked, surprised.

Daniel smiled. "This is Claude. He's one of Cat's sons."

"How come I never saw him last week?"

He tickled the small animal under the chin and it began to purr loudly. "This is a big place, and when school's in progress Claude ensconces himself where the goodies are. He's as smart as his dad."

"How long ago did Cat die?"

"Nearly two years ago—very old, very arthritic. But I think he made the most of his twilight years."

"How come you called Junior here Claude?"

"After Monet. Cat and I both assumed he was long past his prime when we came here—until he took a look at this garden. After that, this was where he brought his ladies."

"*Voilà.*" Alexandra grinned.

Daniel watched her for a moment. "This is a very romantic place, you know."

She said nothing.

In the dead of night, when Le Chapeau Rose and much of Easthampton slept, Alexandra rose from her bed in the guest room and padded over to the window.

All the floodlighting was turned off, but the moon was full and the stars were loading the sky with almost frosty brilliance. She shut her eyes; suddenly the pain and longing were too intense to bear. How had she allowed this to happen? How could she, who always prided herself on her common sense and tolerance, have gotten so close to what they all yearned for, and then have sent it crashing down again into the void?

She turned abruptly away from the loveliness of the night and from herself, and walked quickly out of the room, along the corridor, and into the section of the house where Daniel had his suite of rooms.

She hardly hesitated. She raised her right arm, tapped lightly but clearly on the door, and opened it. It was a large room and almost completely dark, but she knew instantly that he, too, was awake, and that he had been waiting for her to come.

He lay on his side, resting on one elbow, his hair tousled, his face in repose, but his dark eyes open and watching her. Alexandra knelt beside the bed, leaned toward him, and kissed him gently on the lips. His soul leaping, Daniel brought up his free arm and curled it around her shoulders.

"You're freezing," he whispered. "Come to bed." He rolled over to the center to make space for her, and she clambered swiftly in and covered herself with the quilt, her heart beating furiously.

"Do you mind?" she murmured in confusion.

"Mind!" The painfulness of his laugh was like a muffled gunshot in the dark. It was what he had prayed for, what he had thought would surely never happen again.

She came into his arms like voluptuous scented silk, like an unanticipated warm wave, knocking him suddenly off his feet. He buried his face in her heavy hair and inhaled her skin.

"Ali, dearest, I'm so glad . . ."

She had haunted him for eighteen years, this glorious woman. The memory had slept, had almost been forgotten, but she had always remained there, firmly tucked away at the back of his mind. If anything, he marveled, she'd grown more beautiful; the loveliness was rounded now, more complete. He was touched by the slight sorrow in her eyes, longed to see it replaced with contentment, felt deep down that given time, he might replace those tender, remote smiles with real, joyful laughter.

Carefully, longingly, he began to stroke her back, to kiss her neck, rejoicing when she quivered in response.

"Dan," she whispered.

"Yes, my love, what is it?" He felt her cheek rubbing against his.

And then Alexandra moved her face and the moonlight struck her eyes, and he saw the glint of tears. His fingers fell away from her body. A deep, mournful sigh escaped his lips.

No. Not mine.

"I can't," she whispered in distress.

"I know."

"I'm so sorry."

His mouth drew painfully tight for a moment, and his eyes closed, and then he said, "You have nothing to be sorry for." He laughed slightly, no more than a small exhalation, and added, "I feel like an honest thief."

"Oh, God," she railed at herself suddenly, "I'm so very sorry, Dan. It's unforgivable of me." She began to get out of bed, but Daniel drew her back.

"No, don't go, Ali."

"I must."

"No, it's all right. I understand, I swear it." He leaned past her. She heard a click and the room was bathed in soft light. "See? It's okay—truly." His smile was wan and wry. "I can't deny I'd have liked us to go on—" She started to speak, but he laid a finger on her lips. "No, don't start apologizing again." Unexpectedly, he got quickly out of bed on the other side, but in another moment he was back, holding a robe. "Why don't you put this on; I think you'll be more comfortable. And then I think we should talk."

She looked morose.

"I believe that's the real reason you came in here tonight. I just misread you, that's all."

For the first time, Alexandra let herself relax.

"That's better," he said. "So now we'll just sit up in bed like old friends, and you can start by telling me exactly what went on in New York."

Later, he lay back against the pillows and shut his eyes. "You want to hear what I think?"

She nodded. "Sure."

"Really?"

"Yes."

He opened his eyes. "Just three things. But you may not like them."

She punched him lightly. "Spit 'em out, Stone."

He shrugged. "Okay. One: I think Andreas is an asshole. Two: I think—correction, I *know*—you still love him, whatever he is." He swept on. "And three: Do you really need reminding that Anna Alessandro lost her only son because of her goddamned stubbornness?"

Alexandra's face was grim, but she said nothing.

"But," he continued, "Anna was nowhere near the woman you are, Ali. She was a narrow-minded, inelastic, isolated human being who couldn't see farther than the forests that surrounded her family's precious land. You can. You just have to prove it."

There was a long, long pause.

"Tell me what to do, Dan."

"You know what to do." He tried manfully to smile. "We'll get some rest, then first thing in the morning I'll drive you back to the city."

"What do I tell them?" she beseeched him. "The way I left . . ."

"You'll know what to tell them when the moment comes."

"But I'm right!" she burst painfully. "She could be killed."

"People die," he answered simply.

"You know," she murmured distantly, "I've done some thinking lately."

"I'll bet you have, poor darling."

"Maybe it's a terrible mistake to alter perspectives on people. Either way. To get close to someone you've always admired or, when you're already close and loving, to go farther away and to observe."

"All relationships shift emphasis sometimes."

"But they can be destroyed! It was that way with Andreas and Anna. It has been for Andreas and me. I was so desperately afraid it was going to be for Bobbi and me too!" She took Daniel's hand, clutching it tightly. "And I suspect, Dan, darling, that if you got really close up to me and saw me for what I am, it might just be a dreadful disappointment."

Daniel smiled. "I doubt it."

She still held his hand. "May I stay here for the rest of the night? To sleep. I don't want to be alone."

He looked at her, a long look, trying to take in every small detail of her dear face; the fine pallor, despite the slight sun flush of the afternoon, the tiny featherlike lines at the corner of her eyes and running between her nose and lips, lines that came from years of tugging from repose to laughter; the narrow, elegant nose, too long for perfection yet such a perfect fine plunge down to that sensuous mouth. And lastly the eyes. He could not look into those eyes for more than a moment without betraying himself utterly.

Gently he disengaged his hand, and turned out the light.

It came in a dream. She was in the water lily garden with Claude the cat, and Monet himself, white-bearded and formidable in an oppressive dark suit, was standing at a great canvas, instructing her with awesome wrath, "No, no! The car must float on the water! We must *believe* it!"

She plunged her brush back into the dark green oils and touched the canvas lightly, delicately—but the car rocked and began to submerge, and then she realized that Bobbi was inside the car . . .

"Do you understand nothing?" Monet raged. "It must float!" And suddenly he became Roberto, and the fury disintegrated and with it the beard, dropping like snow into the lily pool, and together they watched the car sinking deeper into the dark water, and their eyes were round with horror, and tears streamed from Roberto's.

And she heard the surf, rolling and pounding on the beach and she thought a storm must be building out on the Atlantic, but it was curious because the sky over the garden was such a perfect blue . . . And the sound of the waves came closer, cracking crisp as a thousand layers of tissue paper, then roaring louder—

Alexandra woke with a jolt and lay for a moment, assembling the shattered jigsaw of her dream with her strange surroundings. Beside her, Daniel slept shallowly, murmuring slightly.

There was the sound. Surf pounding on the beach. They were close to the ocean . . . you just walked out through the English garden, out through the little gate, and there was the scrub that led to the grayness . . .

Someone was cooking. Her nostrils flared, inhaling an unfamiliar spiciness, like charcoal on a barbecue, burning meat left too long and spitting smoke into the air.

Alexandra's eyes closed and flickered—and then realization hit her with a massive surge of terror.

"Daniel!" He stirred and moaned slightly. She shook him roughly. "Daniel! The house is on fire!"

He came fully awake, eyes wide, pupils dilated. He knew even before she had reached the door, her hand on the brass—

"No! Ali, don't!"

Too late, the door was open and a torrent of choking, acrid smoke poured into the bedroom, gushing through the air, filling their noses and mouths and throats, stinging and burning their eyes.

Daniel slammed the door out of her hand, grabbed her by the shoulders, and dragged her to the French doors. He yanked at the handle, but the doors were locked. He turned, tore a sheet from the bed, wound it roughly around his right hand.

"Get back! Cover your eyes!" He smashed his fist through the glass—once, twice, three and four times, clearing enough space to climb through. Shards of glass clung to his arm, and blood seeped through the sheet from his hand, but he didn't notice.

"Onto the balcony!" he ordered.

"You too!"

"Get out there! I'll join you in a minute."

He snatched up the telephone and punched the emergency number. "Can you hear the smoke alarms?" he asked.

She tried to listen, but the crackling roaring sound that had woken her still filled her ears. "No—yes—I'm not sure, Dan!" She moved closer to the door. "Yes, I hear a siren."

"Good. They'll be on their way anyhow." He spoke tersely to the operator, gave brief information, then slammed down the receiver. "I told you to get onto the balcony, Ali." With force, he propelled her out through the hole in the glass. "Now, for once in your life, do as you're told and stay put! I'm going to check the staff—"

"No, Dan, you can't!" she said shrilly. "It's crazy!"

"This is my home, Ali!" For the first time he seemed to tower over her in a curious sort of rage. "They're my people, my friends!"

"But the fire!"

"It's just smoke out there so far, or we'd never have got the door closed again." He ripped another sheet into two, dashed into the bathroom, and brought both halves back soaking wet.

"Here." He gave her half. "Save it—if the fire gets into the room, protect yourself with it. If the smoke really starts getting into your lungs, breathe through it! If you just stay outside you'll be fine. The fire department will be here soon—they'll get you down."

She was gripped with terrible fear. "Dan, stay with me, please!"

"I may take another way out of the house, so don't panic if I don't come back." He kissed her quickly on the mouth and was gone before she could plead with him again, out through the door into the ugly yellow-black smoke that filled the hallway.

Downstairs, Daniel reached the front door, ripped open the bolts, and tore it open. He thought of going back for Ali, but she was safe on the balcony and there was no time. He covered his face again with the wet sheet and ran through the back hallway into the staff quarters.

"Sam!" he bellowed up the stairs. "Is everyone out?!" And then, looking out through the swiftly blackening windows, he saw the two young housemaids and Sam, the gardener, outside on the path, staring around in a daze. With his still-wrapped right hand, Daniel smashed the glass.

"Everyone okay?" he yelled.

Sam looked heartily relieved to see him. "All present and correct, sir!" he shouted back. "Get yourself out here!"

"Is Claude with you?"

One of the maids shook her head and looked around.

"No, Mr. Stone!" Sam bawled anxiously. "But he's probably out here somewhere, it's still too dark to see. Get yourself out!" he repeated. "It's in the school and it's startin' to get a hold!" His head turned automatically as the sound of bells and sirens boomed through the night air, and the first of five fire trucks stormed toward Le Chapeau Rose.

"Thank God! Sam!"

"Yes, sir."

"Tell them to get Mrs. Alessandro down first! She's on the balcony outside my room. Before anything else, you understand me?"

"Sure thing, sir!" Sam turned and ran. The two maids on the path stared in growing alarm at Daniel and clutched each other.

"Aren't you coming out?" one of them called. "Best leave it all to the fire department!"

"I'll be there in a minute! I'm going to find the cat!" Daniel turned and ran back into the house.

Alexandra stood on the balcony, trembling violently from fear, cold, and anguish. With sudden overwhelming relief she heard the blessed wail of the trucks, and leaning over the parapet she distinguished through the murky light Sam's heavy shape coming into view, followed by another man.

"Here!" she screamed. "Up here!"

The second man skidded to a halt, his shoes spitting up gravel from the path. He looked up. Alexandra stared incredulously and gasped.

"Andreas!"

His face was gray with terror. "Ali! Thank God! Stay where you are, darling! Don't move!"

She couldn't believe it. Heart thudding, she took the sheet and rubbed her eyes.

"Are you okay?" he yelled anxiously. "Don't move!"

"Andreas, what are you doing here?" Tears began to pour down her cheeks at the sight of him, and then the smoke penetrated her lungs and she started to choke and cough.

"Where's a ladder?" Andreas roared at Sam.

"The men are on their way around, sir. The lady's fine if she stays put, sir. The fire's on the other side of the house in the school."

"Never mind that, man! Fetch me a ladder!"

"Yes, sir!" Sam ran for the outbuildings.

"Andreas!" Alexandra called out, renewed fear growing. "Have you seen Dan? Is he out?"

"I haven't seen him, but I think everyone's out! And you will be too in just a moment, darling!"

"He was checking to see if the staff were out! Please go and look for him!" she begged, almost hysterical.

Andreas stamped his feet in frustration. "Where's that fucking ladder?"

From around the other side of the house, with no regard for the lawns, appeared the fire truck, driving over the grass.

"Over here!" Andreas yelled, waving his arms to attract attention.

Three men leapt down and ran to him, just as Sam came back into view, dragging a ladder, his face scarlet with exertion. The firemen ignored him, assessing the situation. Two ran back to the truck while the third man addressed Andreas.

"Is she the only one left inside?"

"I'm not sure. The staff are out. But I haven't seen the owner."

"Mr. Stone was still inside when I last saw him," Sam blurted. "He was looking for Claude."

"Who's Claude? A child?" the fireman asked.
"The damned cat."

In a few minutes Alexandra was safe in Andreas's arms, while one of the firemen attempted to wrap a rug around her shoulders.

"I don't know what you're doing here," she sobbed against his shoulder, "but I've never been as happy to see anyone in my whole life!"

"Ali, darling, don't cry," he comforted her, and then drew back a little to examine her face. "Are you really sure you're all right?"

"I'm fine," she said, still weeping. "Dan pushed me right out on the balcony—he broke the glass with his hands and made me get out—" Abruptly she twisted around, alarmed again, her face chalky white. "Where is he? Where's Dan?"

Andreas looked at her strangely. "They're looking for him," he said.

Daniel opened the heavy door that separated the main house from the school, and recoiled as the intense heat struck him. The flames leapt ceiling-high just one room away, in one of the kitchen areas, and the extra air as he opened the door fanned them even closer.

"Claude!" he called out. "Claude!"

He strained his ears, but it was impossible to hear anything over the noise of the fire. It was no use—if the poor creature was in there, he was probably already overcome by the smoke. He began to cough violently and turned away, eyes streaming.

The sound was so faint, he thought at first he'd imagined it. But there it was again. Daniel clamped his eyes shut so he could get his bearings, fathom which direction it came from. From the right!

"Claude!" he shouted again.

The answering wail was a long, drawn-out, and piteous mewing. Daniel pulled the sheet, almost dry by now, up against his nose and mouth and began to grope in the direction of the sound, staying close to the wall.

It came again, clearer this time but getting weaker. He called the cat's name again, choking on the fumes. And then he saw the little animal, wedged in tightly between an oak dresser and the scullery door. Its eyes were swollen almost completely shut, and Daniel thought he could smell singed fur as he stooped to pick him up in his arms, dropping the useless sheet to the floor.

"Hello, puss," he whispered into the fur, absurdly glad to have found him. "I guess you still have credit for another eight lives."

Keeping one hand firmly but gently clamped over the cat's small nose and mouth to protect him from inhaling any more smoke, Daniel staggered back into the main hallway and out of the front door into the cool night air.

Behind them, in the school kitchen, the ceiling gave way and the windows exploded, showering molten glass and roasting splinters of wood everywhere.

They gathered in the summerhouse while the fire department assumed control, shocked but safe. The younger maid busied herself in the small galley kitchen, making hot drinks, glad for something to occupy herself with.

In a corner, close to a radiator, Alexandra huddled, still wearing nothing but Daniel's robe and the fireman's rug. Every few minutes she shivered involuntarily and then sipped from a mug of hot, sweetened tea that Andreas had given her. He stayed nearby, watching Daniel, caring for her, saying little.

After a time the firemen appeared, tired but satisfied, and once the chief and Daniel had spoken for a few minutes, they drank tea and returned to work. Daniel came over to Andreas and Alexandra. He was still holding Claude.

"Is the house okay?" Alexandra asked.

He nodded. "It will be. The fire's out, and they'll be damping it all down for quite a while yet, but the chief reckons the structure's safe enough."

"The roof is damaged," she said regretfully.

"Some of it's a little more black than pink right now, but it's nothing that can't be fixed. We were lucky."

"Yes," she agreed fervently.

"Yes." Andreas's voice was strangely harsh. They looked at him, startled.

Daniel drew up a chair and sat down carefully, not wanting to wake the little cat who slept soundly in his arms. "What were you doing out here in the middle of the night, Andreas?"

"I came to talk to Alexandra."

"In the middle of the night?"

He nodded. "That's right."

Daniel smiled. "You got more than you bargained for."

"I did."

An edgy, strained silence eddied between them. Over by the door, shifting about in the spooky predawn light, Sam and the maids stared out at the house.

"Andreas," Alexandra said quietly, "maybe we should go someplace and talk."

"No," he said. "I want to talk to Dan." He looked at his friend. "Are you fit enough?"

Daniel shrugged. "Sure. Why not?" He raised his arms gently. "Would you mind, Ali?"

"Of course not. Poor Claude," she said softly, taking him and laying him on her knee, arranging the robe around him. "He's had a nasty shock."

"Yes, but he's tough."

Alexandra smiled. "Like his dad."

The men went outside. The round swimming pool gleamed golden, reflecting the dawn, and the morning chorus of birds and surf rolled about them, mixing with the light breeze that came off the ocean and ruffled the leaves and branches on the trees.

They walked through the English garden, through the gate and down to the beach. Daniel, wearing only a robe, was chilled to the bone, and the sand scraped inside the sneakers he'd found in the summerhouse. But he didn't complain.

Several feet from the ocean, Andreas stopped and faced him.

"What was she doing in your bedroom, Dan?"

In spite of himself, Daniel flushed. "We were talking."

"I see." Andreas's jaw clenched.

"I don't think you do."

"Oh, yes. Ali's not my wife anymore. Not for a long, long time. It's only—" His eyes swiveled away from Daniel's over the rosy water. "I thought you were my best friend." He started moving again, going away down the beach, digging into wet sand with every stride.

Daniel stared exhausted down at his own feet. Then he raised his head. "Andreas!"

Andreas continued walking.

"Andreas, stop right there!"

Andreas stopped, but didn't turn.

"Okay, my friend," Daniel shouted sharply, his voice carrying on the wind, "I have a few things that need saying. If you can bring yourself to listen."

Andreas turned around. "I'm listening," he said sourly.

"Good." Daniel approached him slowly and stopped three feet away.

"Well?"

Daniel steeled himself. "First—your proposed comeback."

Andreas's eyes glinted. "What do you know about that? Did she tell you?"

"I told her."

"You did what?"

"I found out about it some time ago, and I wrote to Ali because I thought she should know."

"It was none of your damned business, Dan!"

"Perhaps not. But since Bobbi's involved I thought it was Ali's. I'm not going to fight you over that." Daniel stood his ground. "But I am going to finish my piece."

"You had no right—"

"I had every right! You know why? Because I care. From all I hear, you're in no fit shape to compete in any kind of race. You've never been since Monza, and now you're nearly fifty years old— you're over the hill."

"I'm warning you, Dan, you better stop now!" Andreas was scowling belligerently, his fists clenching and unclenching by his sides.

"I know why you want Bobbi as a co-driver; because no one else will drive with you and you know you can't make solo. You're a has-been! You can get your mechanics to make a thousand adjustments to your cars but they still won't compensate for your stiff old bones and muscles!" Daniel was aware he was shooting off his mouth uncontrollably. The long, terrifying night had just got to him, but it was too late to stop now. "Bobbi's not really good enough a driver either, is she? You know that too—and if you think you're going to boost her like some kind of fair wind, forget it, because all you'll be to her is a handicap!"

"You son of a bitch bastard!" Andreas roared.

Daniel's face darkened. "It's high time someone had the guts to tell you the truth," he stormed back. "You're too old! Just as you're too old to expect Ali to tolerate any more selfishness!" He felt like a boxer in for the kill, jabbing cruel truths home while his opponent hung helpless on the ropes. "And I'll tell you why Ali was in my room. She *was* there to talk to me, but I would have given everything—my business, the school, this house, everything I own—to have her in my bed with me!"

With a bellow of anguish, Andreas threw himself at Daniel, knocking him down onto the sand and hurling himself down on top of him. Wildly, insanely, the devil at his tail and the roar of the Atlantic filling his head, he began to punch and kick, striking out, feeling the good shocking contact between flesh and bone, sweating and discharging the pure rage that erupted inside him. At first Daniel just lay there, exhausted by his own torrent of words, taking it. But then to protect himself he started to fight back, scratching, blocking with his arms, throwing fists, ramming elbows and knees—anything to stop this. . . . And then suddenly his mind seemed to remove itself from the beach, and they were back forty years in the apple orchard in Küssnacht. They were boys again, and he was Daniel Silberstein, a wild-eyed refugee, thin as a half-starved whippet, and Rolf was standing on the sidelines barking furiously. And in spite of the blood that ran down both sides of his face, in spite of the pain in his ribs and down his legs, Dan Stone stopped fighting and began to laugh.

Andreas stopped too.

"Are you—" He gasped for breath. "Are you crazy?"

Daniel nodded madly, laughing so hard that the tears trickled down his cheeks. "Yes!"

"Why?"

And then Daniel touched the newly opened scar tissue under his left eye, from which fresh blood now seeped in the same old curve. And Andreas understood.

He sat back on his haunches, and he trembled from his head to his feet and stared at his hands.

"Andreas," Daniel ventured, still breathless.

He nodded, wordless.

"I meant what I said. Every word. I would have given everything to have her." He watched his friend's black, pained eyes. "But we didn't, because she wouldn't."

"It's all right, Dan."

"No." Daniel shook his head slowly, with an effort, still flat on his back in the cold sand. "It's not all right. She loves you, Andreas. Not me."

"Dan, I don't know what—"

"I swear it." He touched the scar again. "In the love, blood, and friendship of forty years."

Andreas was silenced. Daniel moved a little, and groaned. "Help me up, old friend."

Tears suddenly in his eyes, Andreas leaned forward, wincing at his own pain, and gave Daniel his hand. "Christ," he said, with an attempt at humor, "we're both old men."

"Too old for this, anyway."

"Too old for many things." Painfully, wearily, they climbed to their feet and embraced quickly, gladly. Then, arms still clasped about each other's shoulders, they started to limp back in the direction of Le Chapeau Rose. The sun moved up in the sky, and overhead the gulls whirled and mewed.

They both noticed Alexandra at the same moment, running toward them.

"Andreas," Daniel said, "give me something to clean my face. Quick. Yours too."

But it seemed that she didn't even see the blood or the bruises and shame that covered them, or notice that their arms and eyes spoke of friendship. Her own face was ashen, her eyes wide with fear and grief.

She went directly to Andreas and took his face in her two hands.

"Your father," she said clearly but shakily, trying not to cry. "Papa has had a heart attack. Bobbi telephoned. He's been taken to New York Hospital."

55

Roberto was lingering in a half-life and was aware of it. Whenever he dragged his eyelids open, which took great effort, he saw the wires running from his chest, and uniforms, and calm eyes, and sometimes he saw Andreas standing at the end of his bed, and at other times he saw Alexandra sitting quietly in a corner, smiling at him, and once, when he was harried out of his gray sleep by a painful pricking in his hand, he saw Roberta, her face young and afraid, speaking to a man in a dark suit. When he closed his eyes again and lapsed back into that nameless, crepuscular sleep, he saw his mother, hard at work in the back room of their house in Naples, and heard his father's voice, complaining. *You always spoiled the boy, Marina. He should have stayed here with his own.* And then, suddenly, like a miracle, there was Anna, his Anna, young again and pretty as a picture, sitting up in their marriage bed, waiting for him in her white batiste nightgown. *It will be a boy,* she was saying, aglow with confidence, *a son to grow strong and help you and my father.*

"Papa?"

Roberto slept on, smiling at Anna.

"Papa, it's Andreas. Can you hear me?"

Unwillingly, the eyelids fluttered and drew back; the eyes, grown dim, focused slowly, then cleared in recognition.

"Andi," he murmured.

Andreas reached for his father's hand, careful of the intravenous tube attached to him. "How do you feel now, Papa?"

"No pain," he said groggily.

"That's good, Papa."

Roberto's shaggy white head stirred against the square hospital pillows, grown limp with laundering. "I thought I saw Alexandra and Roberta."

"You did. We're all here, Papa. Daniel too."

His father smiled faintly. *"Bene."*

"Go back to sleep now. Rest is what you need most. We'll all be here when you wake."

The sick eyes turned their gaze on Andreas. "I saw Anna," he said dreamily.

Andreas swallowed. "Did you, Papa?"

"She was so young." He closed his eyes, and his voice faded to a murmur and was silent.

Outside the room, a doctor, a young man with sad eyes and full lips, advised them to stay. "It's a risky time," he said, and Daniel, standing nearby, was taken back to his early childhood and the woman who had supervised the *Trauer Abteilung* in his father's store, the department selling mourning attire, and who, he recalled, had been employed mainly for the sorrowful luster of her eyes.

"Is my father going to die?" Andreas asked the doctor, his voice and face composed.

"It's likely." The young man patted his arm. "If you need anything, a private room, perhaps, it can be arranged."

"Are you okay, Bobbi?" Alexandra asked her daughter a little later, when the two of them sat alone in a small, sparsely furnished room.

"No," Bobbi answered quietly.

"No, of course not," Alexandra said dully. "It was a foolish question." How could she be, when the last twenty-four hours had wreaked nothing but chaos and confusion in her life?

"It isn't—" Bobbi began, and paused. "It isn't just because Grandpa may be dying. It's because he seemed so—so sad, and"— unhappy tears sprang into her eyes—"and guilty."

"Bobbi, darling." Alexandra got up from her hard chair and went to her daughter. "There's nothing you can—"

"I know why he felt guilty," Bobbi went on jerkily. "It was because he heard us all fighting about my driving, and he thinks it —it all goes back to him, because he loved racing so much when he was young."

Alexandra looked at her sharply. "Don't you start thinking his heart attack has anything to do with you."

"No, I'm not—truly, Mom. I know it might have happened anyway. But I don't want him to feel the way he does."

"I think perhaps he just said that, about feeling guilty, in the heat of the moment, Bobbi."

"No, Mom, you're wrong. In the last few months Father told

me a lot of stuff about the problems he had with his mother because she was against driving, and the trouble it caused in Grandpa's marriage because he wanted to back my father up. I guess he feels now that it's happening all over again, and that somehow it's his fault."

"Which is so very wrong," Alexandra said slowly.

"Of course it is." Bobbi's mouth struggled between tears and a wan smile. "I mean, we're not even related, are we. Not by blood, anyway."

"Don't let's start that over again, please, darling," her mother said. "Blood ties seem, after all, to be of very little significance, don't they? It's other things that bind us together."

"Maybe I could tell Grandpa I'm going to give it up."

Alexandra smiled. "But that would be a lie, wouldn't it?"

Bobbi reddened. "Maybe. I don't know."

"Sure you do. I don't think you should tell someone a lie when they're—"

"No," Bobbi came back quickly. "You're right."

The door opened, and Andreas came in with Daniel.

"He's getting weaker," Andreas said. "They told me we should be with him now if we want to."

Roberto was conscious, but his face seemed to have drawn in upon itself so that most of the bones were visible under the fine skin, and the voice, which had once been so rich and sonorous, was little more than a whisper.

"You've been fighting," he said to Andreas, as if he had only just noticed the bruising on his face.

Andreas smiled. "Yes, Papa. With Daniel."

"But you're friends again?"

"Yes, Papa."

Roberto's eyes sharpened just a little. "Where is he? I want to see him."

"He's just outside." Andreas nodded to Alexandra, who went out briefly, returning with Daniel.

"Let me see your face, Daniel," Roberto whispered. And as Daniel came closer he smiled with great warmth, and tried feebly to reach out with his hand. "Like the first time," he said.

"Just the same," Daniel agreed huskily.

"Andi—"

Andreas leaned over him, and Daniel withdrew again, out of place. "Yes, Papa."

"Un cerchio grande," he said with a marveling expression. "Life is a circle, Andi, a great circle."

Andreas nodded, not able to trust his voice. All the battened-down emotions of so many years seemed suddenly to be welling up inside him with his tears, and he longed with all his heart to scoop up his father from the pillows and hold him tightly in his arms before it was too late, but the wires and tubes were like a damnable, unassailable wall between them.

"You should not drive anymore, Andi," the old man murmured. "It makes your mother sad."

Andreas looked up at Alexandra, then back at his father. "I won't, Papa."

"You promise me?"

"I swear it." The tears began to fall, and he glanced again at Alexandra, and saw that her face, too, was soaked.

"Take me back to Anna," Roberto whispered.

"Of course, Papa."

"Bene," Roberto said, and shut his eyes.

"You meant it," Alexandra said a little later, real wonder in her voice, as they sat again in the small room. "You're really giving it up."

"Yes." Andreas looked steadily at her.

"Then, thank you." Simple words, but he understood their meaning. The rest he drew from her eyes.

In the corner, Bobbi shifted uncomfortably, her long legs beginning to cramp up from hours of waiting around, her head aching from lack of sleep.

"Maybe you should go home, sweetheart," Andreas said gently. "Get a little rest."

"No, Father."

"There's nothing you can do here."

"I'm going to stay," she said clearly. "I'm fine."

"Why don't you at least ask if you can lie down somewhere, like Dan?"

"Dan's house burned down tonight and he swallowed a gallon of smoke," Bobbi pointed out.

"It didn't burn down, thank God, only part of it," Alexandra said, for the record.

Bobbi looked searchingly at Andreas. "We're not entering that race together, are we."

"No, Bobbi, we're not. I'm sorry to let you down." He paused.

"And I think a race of that length might be too much for a beginner."

She didn't blink. "Grandpa was glad."

"I know."

"But you'd already made up your mind before he said anything, hadn't you?"

"Yes, I had."

Bobbi had a wealth of questions burning on her lips, but she knew she could never ask them. Just one. "Do you want me to go on?"

Silence descended on the room.

"I would like to ask your mother that question," Andreas answered at last, and his eyes rested calmly on Alexandra.

"But Father, I—"

A look from Andreas stopped her. "Ali?"

Outside in the corridor a babble of voices was raised—an overwrought family group perhaps, learning of birth or death, recovery or relapse—and was swiftly hushed. *Respect*, Alexandra thought, *for the dying. Consideration for the soon-to-be-bereaved. For us,* she realized, *for our small family, all together again here in this little sad room.* Her mind wandered back to another time in this same hospital, another room, and the fear and the afterglow of her daughter's entry into the world . . . and still another time, in another hospital, far away and long ago, a building with gleaming white walls and linoleum floors, through which she had glided alone for hours in an endless agony of suspense, waiting for word . . .

"Ali?" he prodded her gently.

"Mother?"

She raised her head, and saw them waiting, and understood that in the final analysis it seemed they trusted her. It was the most she could ask for.

Family, she reflected. *Family equals pain. And perhaps sometimes it is necessary.*

"What do you say, Ali?"

Andreas has courage, after all. Have I the strength to match it?

"I say . . ." She wavered only a little. "I say that Bobbi must choose her own route." She looked into the eyes of her child, and continued softly, "As we all must."

And suddenly, pain and joy flowed side by side.

Roberto died in his sleep one hour later.

When they emerged at last into the street, it was three in the

afternoon. The noise and brightness of Manhattan traffic seemed
to slap them shockingly. They were all haggard and exhausted.

Andreas took Daniel to one side. "Will you come home with
us?"

"I think not, old friend."

"You can't go back to Le Chapeau Rose. You're in no shape to
drive, and the house—"

"I've had some rest, and the house," he said gently, "is exactly
where I need to be."

"If you're thinking you'd be in the way, forget it. We'd be glad
of your company."

"No. For a few hours, at least, you have to be alone. With your
family."

"You're part of that family, Dan."

Daniel shook his head. "I'm not your family. I'm your friend.
And glad of it."

Andreas sighed. "I'll walk you to your car." He turned to Alexandra and Bobbi. "You two mind waiting a few minutes?"

"Of course not," Alexandra replied. "We'll sit inside."

Slowly, companionably, hardly speaking, the two men strolled
around the block to where Daniel had parked his car on a meter
early that morning.

"If you need anything, help in arranging flights, or calling
friends, whatever, I'll be there," Daniel said, feeling in his pockets
for his keys.

"I know. Thank you."

"You've always been there for me."

"Not always."

Down on Franklin D. Roosevelt Drive, cars whipped alongside
the glittering East River, like brightly colored beads strung on an
automatic, unceasing giant abacus. Daniel looked up at the sky. It
was a perfect, cloudless blue. "He picked a good day," he said.

"Yes."

They paused.

"After the funeral," Daniel said softly, "I won't be coming back
here for a while."

"Where will you go?"

He shrugged. "I'll stay in Europe, I guess."

"Dan—" Andreas was troubled. "There's no reason to go away
so far as I'm—"

Daniel stopped him, smiling gently. "I know that. But my publishers have been onto me for a while now to start on my autobiog-

raphy. I guess this is as good a time as any to give it a try." He slid the car key into the lock.

"Mightn't that be painful? I mean, I can see how it would make a hell of a memoir for the reader, but do you really want to put yourself through it?"

Daniel opened the door. "I'm not sure. Part of me's afraid to touch those old scars. But I've done so much running in my life. Now may just be the moment to do some facing up."

Andreas looked into his face. "Speaking of scars, how's the eye?" Carefully, he touched the old wound with his fingers. "Some gift, huh?"

Daniel grasped quickly at his hand, his eyes sparkling with tears. "I know what you have given me," he said, turning one of his favorite quotations on its head, "but I do not know what you have received."

Their arms went around each other, and they stood for a full minute, clasped like brothers.

"More than I can ever say," Andreas whispered.

And turning, he walked away.

Late that night, when Bobbi was sleeping upstairs, they lit a fire in the library and sat together before it, on the rug.

Alexandra looked down at the big man's shirt and pullover she was wearing, and smiled. "I'll have to fetch my clothes from Le Chapeau Rose."

"I'm sure Dan will send them over tomorrow."

She looked at him. "Do you mind my staying here until we leave for the funeral?"

"What do you think?"

"I think Bobbi will like it."

"She isn't the only one."

Alexandra stared into the fire, and shivered involuntarily.

"What's wrong?"

"I'm not sure . . . the flames, I think. Made me remember last night."

"Want me to put it out?"

She shook her head. "No, that would be silly. I love fires."

"You're just exhausted."

"Not as much as you. You should go to bed."

"I'd rather not."

"All right," she said, understanding.

"You know what I would like to do?" He smiled wearily at her.

"I'd like to lie down here, with my head in your lap, and go to sleep that way."

"Be my guest."

"It wouldn't be fair. I'd probably sleep all night, and you'd be stuck."

She chuckled softly, and they fell silent again, each aware of the other's thoughts but not yet ready to speak them aloud.

"Alexandra," he said after a while, "what about the future?"

"I don't know. What about it?"

"How do you feel? About me?"

She noticed a pulse beating in his temple, and longed to stroke it with her fingers. *Speak the truth.* "I love you dearly," she said, her mouth dry.

His eyes closed for a moment, and she watched his white-gold lashes flickering.

"I never really stopped," she added quietly.

He opened his eyes and looked directly at her. "So what shall we do?"

"What do you feel we should do, Andreas?"

His gaze was unwavering. "It's never ended for either of us, has it? What we had, what we shared, the caring."

"I think that's true."

"Would you consider—" He stopped, still staring at her. "People do marry a second time."

She smiled, with all the warmth in her soul. "But not us, Andreas. Or not now, at least."

"When, then? When we're sixty? Seventy?"

She lifted her hands uncertainly. "Maybe never. Maybe soon. But not now."

"Papa would be happy."

"Papa would be glad for the enmity to stop, Andreas. It hurt him badly."

Andreas's expression was somber. "I don't feel as if he's gone, not at all. It's strange."

"Not strange at all, my darling. I don't feel it either, but I don't expect we ever will. I remember when I was a girl and my father died. I never really understood that I wasn't going to see him again, even though I'd seen him in death." She smiled. "It helps a little, I think. It's a comfort."

"Maybe."

The quiet returned again for a while, until she sat up abruptly and said, "You've never seen L'Alouette."

"No."

"I don't believe you could really know me anymore unless you saw my home."

"I know you, Ali—"

"That's not quite true. You can't understand my life, as an individual, as an artist, as a European. You've been an American for so long, Andreas—"

"I've always traveled."

"That isn't the same. You were always on the move, all your life. Racing drivers don't really have homes, at least until they retire, and even when you stopped racing you kept on, never able to stand still."

"It's the way I am, Ali."

"But not the way *I* am. Oh, I loved the travel when we were young, who wouldn't have? It was thrilling, and a way to be with you. But it was only when I found my beautiful house that I discovered I do have a stillness inside me. I need that, Andreas. I don't ever want to give it up."

"I won't ask you to."

"Yes, you will. I think you will. I don't think you'll be able to help yourself, given time. We are different."

"But we love each other."

"Yes," she said, her eyes growing moist.

"How do we resolve that? How can we reconcile those differences?" His face was afraid.

"By accepting them." She took his hands. "I'm not suggesting we should exist separately, Andreas, in two lonely compartments."

"What, then?"

"Spend time together. Get to know each other again. If you will, come to Honfleur . . . I hope Bobbi's going to live there again, for a time, at least. See how I function, how I've existed for the last dozen years without you. And let me come into your life too."

"You know I want that."

"Don't you see how dangerous it would be for us to just up and get married again? We've both—no, all three of us—we've had to keep so many complex emotions so tightly under control for so long. They need time, they need release."

Her words seemed to linger in the atmosphere, mingling with the spitting, humming flames.

"One step at a time," Andreas said quietly.

"*C'est ça.* That's it exactly."

He leaned his head back against the settee and shut his eyes. "My God," he said, "I am suddenly so tired."

"You have to get some sleep, darling. You'll need all your strength tomorrow, and Bobbi's going to need you too."

"And you."

She nodded. "I'll be here."

He started to struggle to his feet, then stopped. "After the funeral. What then?"

She smiled warmly at him. "Maybe I'll stay awhile. Before I go back to Honfleur, for a time at least."

Andreas took a sharp breath. "Bobbi will be ready for her first race soon." He watched her, testing her reaction. "More suitable, and safer than the rally. A sports car meeting out on Long Island in less than four weeks."

Alexandra looked up at the painting.

Sometimes, she thought again, *pain is necessary.*

She turned her face up to his, and her heart was clear in her eyes.

"I wouldn't miss it," she said.

56

They sat on the edge of hard wood benches, at the end of a row, barely touching each other. Andreas, with Rudesheim on his right in a wheelchair, shut his eyes and tuned in to the sounds. Alexandra, on his other side, closed her eyes too, and wished herself a million miles away.

Just a small meeting, Andreas was thinking, *and yet the sounds are so much like Monza, or the Nürburgring, only quieter. It's a couple of thousand people instead of a hundred thousand or more, and the voices are mostly American, but still I can shut my eyes and hear the old, old sounds . . . steel crashing, grinding, clanging, engines turning over, revving up, throbbing, breathing fire . . .*

I remember the first time. I thought then it was like a monstrous orchestra tuning up for the greatest concert on earth. It's still the same.

I remember the first time, Alexandra, too, was thinking. *Silverstone 1958. I thought I would die of the noise, of the fear . . . that I would never hear anything else again. I remember closing my eyes like this, and all I could see, all I could imagine, was Andreas in his little red machine, hurtling through the air, steel crumpling like eggshell, flames soaring. Did I think I knew pain that day? Did I believe I felt pain when I agreed to this insanity?*

I knew nothing of pain until this moment.

"There! Do you see her?" His voice, loud in her ear, dragged her back.

She opened her eyes. "Where?" The brightness dazzled her. "Where is she? Is she all right?"

"Down there! Standing with Lucien! Near the crowd in the blue overalls!" He stretched out his arm, pointing.

She followed his finger and saw her.

"Oh, God," she said, "she looks so small."

"She looks," Andreas said, almost bursting with pride, "like a goddamned spacewoman. All that stuff she's wearing, Ali, and that big helmet she has under her arm—that keeps her safe. If I'd had that—"

"Please!" she begged. "Please don't talk."

He stopped, understanding, yet longing to go on talking, to yell. *The difference between us.* He looked sidelong at her. Fear, such terrible fear. How could he ask her to accept this?

"Ali?"

"Please, Andreas, no more."

"Just this one thing." Gently he lifted her chin, tilting it so that she faced him. "I swear to you, as God is my witness, that I'm going to watch her like a hawk from this second on. If there is the smallest sign of weakness at any point, I'll find a way to stop her. I swear it, Ali."

The fear in her eyes didn't budge. "And if there isn't?"

His gaze never wavered. "You told Bobbi. It's her route. Her choice."

They looked down again at the circuit. The drivers were all in their cars, helmets strapped, faces covered, gloves on wheels.

The starting judge held up the flag.

Next to Andreas, Rudesheim took out a stopwatch and shot a swift look at them both. He sat forward. His voice was hushed but clear.

"Five. Four. Three. Two. One."

The engines gunned into life. Two thousand voices screamed.

"Ali!" Andreas said sharply in her ear. "Look away from it. Look at me." He held out his hand, and Alexandra took it.

Their fingers clenched into one.